THE SUCCESSION

D0370720

BOOKS BY GEORGE GARRETT

Fiction
King of the Mountain
The Finished Man
In the Briar Patch
Which Ones Are the Enemy?
Cold Ground Was My Bed Last Night
Do, Lord, Remember Me
A Wreath for Garibaldi
Death of the Fox
The Magic Striptease
The Succession
An Evening Performance
Poison Pen
Entered from the Sun

Poetry
The Reverend Ghost
The Sleeping Gypsy
Abraham's Knife
For a Bitter Season
Welcome to the Medicine Show
Luck's Shining Child
The Collected Poems of George Garrett

Plays
Sir Slob and the Princess
Enchanted Ground

Biography
James Jones

Criticism
Understanding Mary Lee Settle

THE SUCCESSION

A NOVEL OF ELIZABETH AND JAMES

GEORGE GARRETT

A HARVEST/HBJ BOOK
HARCOURT BRACE JOVANOVICH, PUBLISHERS
SAN DIEGO   NEW YORK   LONDON

Copyright © 1983 by George Garrett

All rights reserved. No part of this publication may be reproduced or
transmitted in any form or by any means, electronic or mechanical,
including photocopy, recording, or any information storage and retrieval
system, without permission in writing from the publisher.

Requests for permission to make copies of any part of the work
should be mailed to:
Permissions Department, Harcourt Brace Jovanovich, Publishers,
8th Floor, Orlando, Florida 32887.

First published by arrangement with Doubleday and Company, Inc.

Versions of some parts of this book have appeared in the following
publications: *The Agni Review, The Bellingham Review, The Bennington
Review, Black Warrior Review, Carolina Lifestyle, Chelsea, Crescent
Review, The Georgia Review, Hard Scuffle, Jeopardy, Lowlands Review,
New Mexico Humanities Review, New Virginia Review, The Sewanee
Review, Sounding Brass, South Carolina Review, Texas Review, The
Virginia Quarterly Review, Willow Springs Magazine.*

Library of Congress Cataloging-in-Publication Data
Garrett, George P., 1929–
The succession : a novel of Elizabeth and James/George Garrett.
— 1st Harvest/HBJ ed.
p.   cm.
ISBN 0-15-686303-0
1. Elizabeth I, Queen of England, 1533–1603 — Fiction.   2. James I,
King of England, 1566–1625 — Fiction.   3. Great Britain — Kings and
rulers — Succession — Fiction.   I. Title.
[PS3557.A72S9   1991]
813'.54 — dc20   91-22756

Printed in the United States of America
First Harvest/HBJ edition 1991
A B C D E

For Susan
without whom there would be nothing

For my children—William, George, and Alice
who shared in all the sacrifices and hard times
without asking to and without complaining

For Sam Vaughan and Betty Heller
whose interest and support was so much more
than merely professional

And for certain close kin and a few close
friends who kept the faith

NOTE

As the Elizabethans seem to have known as well as anyone, our best plans are always changing and so very often turn out in the end to be almost entirely different than they were supposed or intended to be at the beginning. Adventurous voyagers, they knew that every long voyage is not fated to failure, but rather that original destinations have a way of fading and being replaced by others.

Take this story, for instance.

It began easily enough and it should have been a tidy and limited task, if not an easy one. It began with the letters—first with the actual letters of Queen Elizabeth (weighty in syntax, knotty in thought, generally obscure in their gnarled tangle of motives) to James VI of Scotland, her godson and cousin and, as it might come to pass, perhaps her heir. His letters, almost always answers and reactions, tend to be more open and obvious to us even though (it seems) he aimed to be sly, canny, clever, forceful, and persuasive. The gist of that story was to be, purely and simply, a narrative accounting of the two of them, Queen and King, exchanging letters over the years, each seeking to come to know and understand the other with a kind of urgent and thorough intimacy that even lovers seldom achieve.

Some of those letters are still here. But what happened to that story and to me was that in trying to contemplate two splendid characters, I was forced to summon up many others to help me, ghosts from that time, some of them "real" (Sir Robert Cecil, Sir Robert Carey, the Earl of Essex) and some of them "imaginary" —a messenger, a priest, a player, some Scots reivers, etc. And very soon it was clear that if they were to bear witness, they must be allowed to tell their own tales also. They jostled each other for places in the story. And so, finally, here they are in a story which has changed its shape and form many times before it settled into this one, a story which surely took its own sweet time to become a book.

As in my one other venture into the imaginary past, *Death of the Fox*, I have done my best to be faithful to the facts even while striving to preserve the freedom of fiction, which means that there may be distortions and there will be mistakes, but I hope there are no lies.

These people, real and imaginary alike and equally, were generous guests and good company, but altogether unhurried. For what does expense of time mean to a ghost? I am grateful to them for all of it and hope they will prove good company for you.

GEORGE GARRETT

The high, the lowe: the riche, the poore: the mayster, and the
   slave:
The mayd, the wife: the man, the chyld: the simple and the
   brave:
The young, the old: the good, the bad: the warriour strong and
   stout:
The wyse, the foole: the countrie cloyne: the lerned and the
   lout:
And every other living wight shall in this mirrour see
His whole estate, thoughtes, woordes and deedes expresly
   shewed to bee.

ARTHUR GOLDING—*The XV Bookes of P. Ovidius Naso,*
entytuled Metamorphosis (1567)

Care not then for the morrow: for the morrow shall care for itself. The day hath enough with his own grief.

Matthew 6:34

THE SUCCESSION

QUEEN

MARCH 1603

To be a King and wear a crown is a thing more glorious to them that see it than it is pleasant to them that bear it.

Queen ELIZABETH—Speech to Parliament, November 30, 1601

With youth is dead the hope of love's return,
Who looks not back to hear our after cries,
Whence he is not, he laughs at those who mourn;
Whence he is gone, he scorns the mind that dies.

Sir WALTER RALEGH—"The Ocean's Love to Cynthia"

Now there is no one for her to listen to. No one left for her to hear. To whom should she give her attention? Should she now turn away from the snarls and skeins of memory, from the long shadows of inner sorrows, to study the idle matters and soft laughter of her young Maids of Honor? Daughters they are, only frivolous children. No, let us at least be truthful. They are by now granddaughters. Granddaughters of kinfolk and of old friends (even some of old enemies) long gone from the fading light. And of them all—ah, how they glowed and glittered once, then, upon their time!—many have gone to darkness and perhaps some few to enjoy eternal light.

Let light perpetual shine upon them.

These close around her, except for a very few servants of her own age who have somehow endured the journey with her, are only young. And say what you will, there is nothing much to be gained from the young.

Never mind. Let her Maids of Honor be wholly busy in their idleness.

Now, as for these others, Gentlewomen of the Privy Chamber, they are, most of them, near enough to her own age. She can, if she should choose to—and at times she has done so, too—exchange with them the inevitable news of the body's decay. Like a state of siege. Siege of Antwerp. Siege of Calais. . . .

Siege of Jerusalem and the Fall of Rome.

She can sit at sewing and embroidery and compare wrinkles and wounds. Can share tales of woe, new versions of ancient stories, rumors, and gossip. But finally all of these pleasures, at least when fitted out in the masks and costumes of common speech, have become only echoes of each other. Time is a birch-rod schoolmaster, and she knows the tunes and melodies, all the conjugations and declensions, by heart. Worldly wisdom has her soon nodding and yawning. All of their songs, the songs of this world, begin to sound like lullabies.

Yet she does not sleep very much. Not well or deeply these days. Truth is, she does not dare, no matter how weary her limbs, how heavy and gritty her eyes, to lapse into a sleep that is deep and long. For fear that she will begin to dream again and, even worse, to remember those dreams later. Oh, my God, the things that she has seen in dreams! Best not to think about it. Best not to speak of it, not to anyone.

If there were someone to speak to. Even if there were anyone alive whom she could trust to listen wisely and well.

Perhaps, here in Richmond Palace, this palace of her grandfather with all its wealth of little listening nooks, she should keep very still and listen to the secrets and squabbles of servants. High and low. Some high and mighty in robes and fine clothes, with seals and silver badges and their wands and staffs of office. All gracefully solemn, tactful and discreet. With only the eyes of their flat, guarded faces left alive in spite of all craft to the contrary. Eyes brimming with the undeniable shine of hungers and fears and, always, down to the last faint rattling gasp of breath, down to the final stuttering heartbeat, shining with insatiable ambition.

Their tongues are not to be trusted. Not now or then or ever after, world without end. Tongues which rest heavy and meaty in the mouth. Swimming fatly in the broth of sweet lies and the savory tastes of flattery. Tongues as fat and still as fish in a creel. And yet those same heavy, lazy tongues are quick enough, when called upon, with their flourishes of wit.

When it is she who is breathing her last, when it is she who must cough and gasp and choke into silence, when it is her heart that staggers and comes to a halt, then no doubt they will prove to be quick and lively, too. "The Queen is dead!" they will cry out. "Long live the . . . !"

Not yet. This Queen is not dead yet.

Does she hate them? She might if she could find any reason to envy them.

Maybe she should listen to her more humble servants. Hear what they are saying in the woodyard or the stables or the kennels, brewhouse and bakehouse, scullery, spicery, and shambles. Anywhere in this hopelessly unwieldy and extravagant Court where there is real work to be done, work that must be done and then begun and done again, winter or summer, rain and shine, war or peace, Queen and no Queen. Thinking, not without warmth, of those who must continually fork and shovel the huge, stinking dung heap above which a cloud of buzzing flies flaunt their brief dream of the sun.

Imagine that.

Imagine that, would you?

Imagine King or Queen, here or anywhere else in Christendom, with a secret hiding place. Some cabinet with a peephole created to spy out not the subtle plotting and devious mischief of the nobility and officers but, instead, the deeds and words of common servants. Imagine that this same imaginary Queen, disguised and concealed, is truly thirsting for at least that much of the truth of this world. Eager to swallow it all down whole, though it may prove to be as bitter as the dregs of spoiled wine.

There was a King of Scotland once, not along ago, who, it is said, used to wander among his people in disguises. To learn what they were thinking and saying and doing. Fat good it did him! No doubt he learned something. But whatever it was he carried it with him into an early grave. And like most other monarchs, wiser and less so, he managed to leave his kingdom somewhat worse than he had found it.

But who are these common servants of hers?

They are grandchildren also. And even assuming their tongues could be trusted, which, God knows, they never can be, their grasping hands and clever sticky fingers are far more dependable. Can be depended on. As can, likewise, their not so simple, deeply mischievous hearts. God's death on the wooden Cross! Once they (meaning their grandparents) stole discreetly and with some of the nip and foist, agile dexterity of, say, your clever London cutpurse. But in this decayed generation, they will steal anything at all, given half a chance—a jewel, a gold button, a pair of gloves. A horseshoe nail or a loaf of bread. They will pluck the down and the feathers from a living swan. Only her faithful bodyguards will be able to keep them from picking clean her royal corpse, as it chills and stiffens.

Her guards. By gateways and doors and entries stand her silent, scarlet-clad guards. Emblem of her family's rose set proudly in gold thread on their backs. What sort of emblem, what colors will they wear when she is gone? She should be thankful. They have guarded her body and her life well. And for a long time. Chances are that she shall not die violently. And yet not all of these tall young men taken together, with their bright, scoured, shining poleaxes and gilt halberds, can contrive a security which will keep the dark, patient, invisible Prince from arriving at his leisure.

Oh, he will be here, soon or late, and when it pleases him.

Lately she has taken to sleeping not in a bed but on a soft mattress and cushions set on the floor. It is fortunate that there is no one left to ask why. How would she answer? Because I fear that the Black and Invisible Prince, Death himself, lies coldly waiting for me there! When the curtains are drawn, he will take me to him. I fear I shall die in darkness and silence.

But if that is true, if you fear darkness and cold and silence, why is it that when you dream you dream of fire? Of yourself as a thin flame of pain in the wind? Of wind as a music of howls?

Well, then, awake and with a sigh raised up from weariness like a bucket from an old well, she can turn and busy herself with the endless affairs of state. To papers and letters and accountings. To reports of the doings, the comings and goings, of Princes, of Emperors and Sultans and Czars and Popes. But all of these, glittering their hours, are children or grandchildren, too. And all of the news of this world is stale. It is as if there were a precedent for everything that may happen under the sun. And as if she, like some old judge richer in pedantry than wisdom, knows every precedent for every case since the action of Cain and Abel. Tedious lists and catalogues and summaries. News and rumors of the usual plots and seditions, factions and conspiracies, marriages and infidelities, births and deaths. Troublesome accountings of her diminishing treasure. Schemes for taxes and loans. For exchanges of lands and the sale of offices.

And all of these are things that, strangely, once upon a time, indeed a time as near as this Christmas past, she was once famished to listen to. Ravenous to know.

—Five wounds of our sweet Lord and Savior, Jesus Christ! I'll savor no more of that diet. I have lost all appetite for it. Let drums beat and trumpets sound. Let each of the impeccably prepared dishes for my dinner and supper be, one at a time, ceremoniously bowed into place on my table, prayed over and tasted and tested. Yet I'll touch none of it. What pleasure is left when the taste of meat and bread is the same? Let my cup overflow with ale as subtle as woodsmoke. Let them bring a jeweled chalice with wine so sweet that my gums wince and my teeth ache and my tongue shivers like a fish in a net. And still I shall not swallow a drop of it. For the plain truth, the hard truth that no voice can tell me, except for that inner voice which is like the voice of an insolent stranger speaking in whispers close to my ear, the truth is that the time of my life has come upon me when wine and water are also one and the same. Neither to be changed back to what it was again, as once by and through our Lord's first miracle at the wedding party at Cana. Is it a miracle to have done the opposite—to have turned wine into stale water? No, my only miracle, it seems to me, is to have lived so long and to have become so old. . . .

Her mind has tricked her again. She fingers a scar on the third finger of her left hand. Thinks of weddings bitterly. She who has had none. She who has known many suitors. Some who may have truly loved her. Who knows for sure? Some whom she may have loved—she cannot remember. Her only wedding band was her Coronation ring. Married to this kingdom, to her people. Several generations of them. Until this year. When the ring, which had never once been removed since her Coronation, caused a soreness, then a festering. Had to be filed away like a prisoner's irons.

Bitter riddle to grin at—what Virgin Queen was bride and wife to a multitude?

Best not to think on these things. Best to give attention to other things.

Well, she could certainly pay attention to the Privy Council. And she can, if only to relieve the tedium, call upon the counsel of her Secretary. Sir Robert Cecil, sometimes her Elf and sometimes her Pigmy. All aquiver with energy like a trout in a pool. Not yet to be easily hooked and netted by anyone. A long way away from poaching or frying. Cool creature composed of so many hidden fires.

Well, she understands that. Even admires it in others though she despises it in herself. Oh, once did hate her player's role as Queen. On account of all the things that must be hidden. But now—and here's something to make her laugh out loud—she has lived so long that what she had once hidden is now hidden from her. Gone and forgotten. Even if she found something as, say, you might suddenly discover the right lock for one of a baffling string of rusty keys, she could not remember what she had hidden it for in the first place.

Foolish thoughts play in her mind like firelight and shadow in a dim room.

Better return to what she knows. To Cecil. Little and broken-bodied, crippled or not, he is as lithe and strong and persistent with ambition as any salmon at the falls. Quick as a deer or a hare running before the hounds. Cunning as a fox. Once, not long ago, it was all a time of swaggering swordsmen. But they are old or gone also. And now the time of clever foxes is afoot.

Think of his little body as a peddler's pack. Consider that beneath the layers of rags and bones and odd, old buttons, lies something hidden, something pure and priceless. Like a single perfect jewel.

Faithful in outward and visible service and in the strict performance of his duties, he lives, like a fortunate heir, upon the ample income which derives from his dead father's experience in the ways of the world. Yet his inherited portion of Burghley's worldly wisdom has proved to be, thus far, something less than she had expected and even permitted herself to hope for. Possibly less, too, than Robert Cecil may have wished.

Perhaps he has not yet encountered the circumstances to test and to prove himself fully.

Meantime, whatever else, she cannot fault him for his capacities for hard labor, for the expense of spirit in her daily service. Much as the old monks and nuns in this country (before her father scattered them, as a hawk will scatter a flock of hens) were said to pray without ceasing, so he labors ceaselessly for her. As to his thoughts and plans and schemes? She will hear him out on any subject whatsoever. But without truly listening to him. Certainly without truly believing him. For she knows that his heart and mind are chiefly elsewhere. Are uneasy in attendance in Scotland. For a fact. Heart and mind secretly in service of that man he takes to be most likely to be the King when she is gone.

She, according to long custom and habit, sees and hears everything and says nothing. And what should she say to him, now or later, if chance arrived? It would be like talking to a ghost. In that sense, at least, he can be taken to be no more or less a ghost than his dead and buried father. No, perhaps more ghost than Burghley. For alive he has always been more distant than the memories she holds of the father. That's one of the tricks of time. Cannot blame him for that. And in truth she, too, has lived to become a kind of a ghost. Her heart and mind are elsewhere. As if she were exiled to a strange place, a far country she cannot yet name or imagine.

Ghost to ghost, then. That's how it is and will be. There is nothing more substantial here than shadows whispering together like insects at twilight.

It is as if in this rain and cold, coming after an unseasonably warm December and the hope of an early spring, this sudden arrival of north winds richly laden with cargoes of cold and wet, bad weather which has cloaked and hooded the whole kingdom, prolonging winter by weeks, delaying the promise of first daffodils, as if she has been isolated by the weather. Left alone by servants, friends, kinfolk. To wander private in a gallery. An imaginary gallery much like this one, the long, many-windowed gallery directly overlooking the walled garden with its shiny, rain-swept rows of fruit trees, here at Richmond Palace. Much like this gallery here and yet somehow different.

Herself, then, alone and walking there. Just as she does here.

Herself walking. Back and forth, up and down, to and fro. Walking quick and brisk and never mind the pain. To stir her blood.

Rain spatters against glass. The trees huddle against it, then vanish in a silver mist of rain. The fires are sputtering and smoking, dying in fireplaces. She could easily amend that. Could call out in a commanding voice. Someone would surely come. Come running to heap up dry wood and feed the flames. If she cared to call. All the candles of this gallery have been left to burn too long. They are melting down to nubs and fat ends. By only hinting at it she could change all that. Observing, for instance, that in this light she cannot clearly distinguish the faces of the portraits hanging on the walls. At the least hint from her there would be immediately new candles, tall, sweet-scented candles molded and shaped with the finest beeswax, set in every sconce and lamp and candlestick and candelabra. New bright small tongues of flame, all singing together the psalms of fire and light.

If she wished to. If she cared to. If only she cared.

But it is a curious comfort to be here alone in this gallery with its dying fires and smoky candle ends. If someone else could see her now, if someone could for one moment share this her vision (which, you understand, she can see more clearly than anything before her eyes), that someone would see only a woman, thin and bent a little, stiff from more than weather, more than the cold and damp. An old woman walking up and down. To and fro.

True enough. The picture is not false. But there is more than meets the eye. She is not ever truly alone even for an instant. She is moving amid a moving crowd of ghosts. Some of whom are known and named. Named and more or less remembered. Others are like figures from a dream. They are perfect strangers. Messengers or perhaps even ambassadors coming from that still unknown, unnamed kingdom toward which her heart and mind are voyaging. Which kingdom, God forgive and God be willing, she will be permitted to enter into and freely to pass. Not as a Queen, not as the Queen of England, but only as a pilgrim returning home at last from a journey so long and arduous that home itself seems altogether foreign now.

Not having been forgotten but having been slowly and subtly transformed beyond all remembering.

MESSENGER

1566

I cannot speak and look like a saint,
Use wiles for wit, or make deceit a pleasure,
And call craft counsel, for profit still to paint.

Sir Thomas Wyatt—"Satires"

Here comes the man, slope-shouldered and loose-limbed, rocking easy to the rhythm of his shaggy-haired Scots horse. Reins rest lightly in his hands as he lets the little horse have her head, picking the way at a walk. Moving south. Finding and following the trails along the eastern edges of the Lammermuir Hills. Slim paths cutting through rough grass, patches of heather and of broom, and of low, clumped bracken. Here and there muddied by quick brooks and freshets running down and away toward the sea to the east. He moves among the wide spaces of these low hills, treeless all around him except for, startling and lonesome with an abrupt extravagance of young leaves, the stunted shape of an oak or alder. Or sometimes isolated birches or hawthorns. Horse and rider gilded by afternoon sunlight, bathed in the whimsical cavorting shadows of clouds blowing across from the northeast. A faint scent, which may be heather, spices the air.

The horseman is bearded. His blue eyes are shaded by the broad brim, pulled low, of a featherless hat. Clothing is plain, too, clean and plain, made of coarse wool and leather, and all of it in various shades of that color which Scots call sad brown. He is not armed. No harness and sword. He has not a jewel or ring in sight, no buckle or row of buttons to catch sunlight. For the horse he has neither stirrups nor saddle. Sits instead, according to the custom here, on a large flat pillion, like a folded blanket stuffed with hair. And also the horse is only half shod. Shoes for forefeet only. His feet are not booted and spurred, either, but instead are covered by a loose wrapping of deerskin, held in place by knotted rawhide laces. To dangle free at grasstop.

Horse and rider might as well have been formed out of this raw earth and summer grass, out of bracken and heather.

And so he can be anyone, of no importance at all, going on some ordinary errand. Taking his time under a wide and windy, cloud-teased sky. Sky where gulls wheel and float in high gusts of shattered whiteness. And where sometimes there will be the raucous reedy cawing and the heavy-winged, ragged-feathered flying and swift swooping down of flocks of crows and rooks. And sooner or later, in this particular piece of country just above the Borders, his horse will have to start and shy away from the sudden flight of flushed grouse.

So he might be anyone going somewhere nearby, nowhere urgent, and not in any haste. Which is how he means to have it. Which is how he intends to be taken. If he should happen to be observed by anyone. If he should smile to himself, his beard will hide it. And if his eyes are as patiently alert as the eyes of a crouched cat, well, the shadow of his hat brim will conceal that, too. In truth he might as well be half asleep.

Ask him his name and he'll answer you with any of a dozen different ones which lie at the tip of his tongue.

Demand to know his purpose and destination. And he will play you a false tune and be completely plausible.

He carries no pack or saddlebag, only a cloth roll tied with rawhide and slung across his back. And cheerfully enough, if it ever comes to that, he will untie his cloth and make a show for you of his possessions—flat tin cooking pan, black from the making of many oatcakes; bag of oatmeal mixed with dried kale; wooden spoon with a whistle carved at the end; a rusty table knife sharp and dangerous enough for bread and butter. He has a worn leather bag for a purse, containing only a few coins, mostly old and French and none of them of much value. He carries no papers. For papers, with writing or printing on them, could awaken curiosity here where so many cannot read and write, and so many must make a mark for signature when they have to, being unable to take up a pen and put down their own proper names.

This rider will not arouse much interest. Will not create any prickling of suspicion. Not even when (soon) he is into the Border country where the habit is—a habit of life and death—to watch over the comings and the goings of strangers almost as closely as (Scripture informs us) God Almighty Himself will brood over the falling of a sparrow.

Which is also as he intends it to be.

For the aim of his craft is not so much to be ignored as to be taken for granted at first sight and then easily forgotten.

"Not the best qualities for a man of some learning and ambition—a gentleman of our Queen's Court, for example," he would tell you. "Yet it is altogether necessary and worthwhile for such a one as myself. Who has become—oh, never mind the reasons—a creature of the shadows. You may call me Jack Scarecrow if you wish. Or anything else that pleases you and seems to suit me. And you can be sure that I'll be happiest if you shrug your shoulders and go along without wasting as much as a second thought on me."

Only last night he was alone in a crowd of strangers, among the lesser servants of lords and gentry from all over the kingdom. Most of the men who matter, together with many of their clan and kin, bands of companions and servants, had been gathering in Edinburgh for many days. And a good many of these men were assembled within the Castle. It seemed that everyone was there, or anyway represented. Except for servants and close kinfolk of the most recent conspirators against Queen Mary. Those being chiefly of Douglas blood. Who had banded together in this past March and had murdered her sly little secretary, David Rizzio, in the royal presence. These are now in exile. Most said to be settled in Newcastle. Waiting for a change of alliances or a new order of events which will allow them to return. Which, in spite of all that has happened, is not what anyone would call an unreasonable wish. For, look now, are not the Earls of Moray and Argyll, both of them not long ago put to the horn as outlaws, as traitors to Queen and country, freely lodging in this same Castle and (it seems) restored into favor? Likewise her very own husband, Henry Stuart, Lord Darnley (in England) and styled King Henry here. Whose knife was found placed in Seignor Davie's back to prove beyond any doubting his part in the plot. Darnley is lodging in the Castle also; though he seems to be spending his nights outside of the walls, enjoying adventures in the city. And so, except for the chiefest conspirators, Morton and Lindsay and the Douglases, all the lords of Scotland have come to Edinburgh.

Oh yes, excepting, too, the outraged and insulted family of the Hamiltons. These are furiously absent. Since, in what is taken as a satiric gesture, the Queen freed their chief, the young Earl of Arran, from imprisonment in the Castle at the time that she moved herself and the Court up there from Holyroodhouse. Poor Arran was set free, pardoned for his offenses, and sent away, home to his family. But his freedom cannot be worth much, since he seems to have lost the last traces of his already sparse wits during his confinement. Witless, he can now be called harmless, also. A sad condition for the head and hope of a great Scots family with, saving only the Queen herself (and her offspring, if any), one of the strongest claims to the throne of Scotland. But for Fortune he might have been King. Once they wished to marry him off to Elizabeth of England. Later to this Mary, Queen of Scots, when she returned from France. Now the Earl is wed to sorrow and madness.

"Ah, well," this horseman will tell you with a sigh. "I ask you to try to conceive of any single occasion, even the length of a short day during all the long, bloody chronicle of Scotland, then or now or as it will be ever after, world without end, try to imagine the time when there will not be at least one large covey of exiles over the border in England. Waiting and watching. Biding time like Highland wolves. Do you think there can ever be a time when at least one among the noble families, believing itself to have been ill treated, unjustly deprived and insulted, is not busily planning some elaborate mischief and likely a bloody revenge? No, rather consider it to be truly remarkable that at this one time, in these days of early summer, a large part of the proud and barbarous gentry of proud and barbarous Scotland has somehow managed to swallow some of their damnable pride and, out of a common hope for the future, has been able to put aside their interminable business of quarrels and feuds with each other and the crown. Call it a kind of a miracle. Then forget that it has happened. For even before this season has turned, I'll wager all I can hope to possess, that they will have all changed hands and sides and partners again, like country dancers at a fair. Will be having at each other as fierce as ever before with their swords and battle-axes. . . .

"Don't misunderstand me," he'll add. "My time in Scotland has been well spent. And I do hope to live long enough to miss my friends in Scotland. And, as I sit and grow old and cranky by the fire of an English alehouse, I shall think of them creaking with savage agues in their misty climate. If nothing else, Scotland has taught me that somewhere in the world there is weather that is worse for man and beast than England's."

By glare of the horn lanterns, smoky flickering of torchlights, and by the dull glow of the fires made of peat and charcoal, he spent the night in the crowd of Scots. Under moon and stars in the open space of the Castle Close. And because the windows of her chambers within the Palace face out over the walls of the Citadel, looking east over Edinburgh, he was not able to see the light of the candles burning for the Queen there. But he could see what he wanted to, what he had planned to. Could keep an eye on the long, narrow, pointed, glassless windows of the Queen's kitchen. What he was waiting for would come from there.

If it came at all.

Meantime these Scots were keeping their closest watch on the sky. Looking for any falling or shooting stars or strange-shaped clouds or mysterious colors. Any natural things which might rightly be taken as portents.

He did not leave the Close to try to enter the Hall. Where at least there would be plenty of rush light and even a wood fire burning for the comfort of the more important servants and even some of the gentry. Those who, for one reason and another, had not been able to find chambers in the Castle or in the houses and inns of the city. There he would surely find some of Highland lords, snoring on the stone floor, wrapped in their huge plaid blankets. In the Hall he might have passed the night with the solace of cold roast meat and salt fish and barley bread, all laid out on the wide trestle tables together with bowls and stoops for strong Scots ale and, ah!, stronger by a bowshot, the distilled malt spirits which the Scots call usky and *usque baugh*. Scots will drink that smoky, fiery, living water until it renders them too thick-tongued and light-headed to give it any name at all. There would have been music playing some of the time. And some of the men there would have been whiling away hours with cards and dice. Ripe for plucking by a man like himself, someone with the practiced craft for the skillful handling of both. But once ensconced within the Hall, no matter how comfortable and even profitable it might be, he would have been out of sight of those kitchen windows. And besides it was always possible—likely enough to be something to try to avoid—that even behind his new-grown hedge of beard and clad in this shapeless and ordinary clothing, he might still be recognized by someone. Not something to be much feared. No trouble, he imagined, that he could not escape from by quick talking. But, nonetheless, there was no use taking chances on being interfered with. Outside in the Close he could be one more among many common men, most of them strangers to each other.

There were the redshank, barefoot wild Scots from the mist-haunted mountains and the high blue lochs of the north, wearing their coarse, loose, saffron-dyed shirts and all wrapped about in plaid cloaks. Talking to each other in their own ancient tongue and not speaking much to anyone else. There were the servants of the rich town gentry and the Lowlands lords. Some few of them embarrassed in brand-new livery with silver badges. (No Scotsman seems to be easy in livery.) Most of them, though, wearing customary sober gray or sky-blue clothing and flat soft caps. And not to forget those other, in fact saving them like the sweet wine for the last, those swaggering creatures clad in leather and brass and iron. With their hard, wind- and sun-ripened faces. Against which the color of their eyes shone like knife blades in firelight. Men of the Border Marches. Trusting no man very much and least of all each other.

Among these strangers he could lean and slouch against the outside wall of the Hall, yawn and spit, deal in the merchandise of everyday gossip, or wander over to wait a turn to use the common privies.

Finally first streaks of dawn in the sky. Night fading, rinsed to gray, stars winking away, vanishing as if ceremoniously snuffed out. He crouched then, hunkered down with others over the coals of a fire and cooked his oatcake. Like any Scotsman born and bred. Mouth full of that satisfying ashy, nutty taste, he listened to them beginning to talk about the prospects of feasting. Coming soon enough. God willing. God's will be done, there will be plenty of belly cheer for everyone. For—and hadn't they seen it?—sheep and oxen and young small calves, too, had been brought up into the Castle or set to pasture close by the loch below the north walls. And someone has seen, in the space of the Castle, flocks of chickens and ducks, cages and bags of seafowl and moorfowl. There are grouse and partridge and wild swans waiting to be plucked and cleaned and cooked. There are huge casks of fresh-caught fish. Herring and haddock from the sea, salmon and trout and eels from the rivers. Mussels by the bushel carted here from Musselburgh. Not even to mention such things as pasties of venison and the strong flesh of wild boar. All these things and many others too that a common Scotsman must wait a long time for a special occasion to taste. Plenty of eggs and fruit and cheese. Sweet jellies from every sort of fruit and berry and flower. Rich, implausible French puddings. And all the ale they can hold between pissings.

Perhaps even this very night, tonight if it be God's will, the bonfires will be burning in the city; and then we'll go down into the streets and wynds, our ale-soused, wine-soaked brains turning everything arsy-versy while we dance and dance to the noise of ringing bells and the sounds of the music of horns and drums and the sweet sad crying of the pipes played by wild Scots from the mountains. The cannons of this Castle, even ancient and celebrated Mons Megs, will thunder salutes from the battlements. There will be fireworks bursting into the shapes of stars and flowers far above the high roofs of the city. And the women! There will be the sturdy women of Edinburgh to dance with in the streets. With some luck, there may be some to hug and to hold even closer than that.

No priest of the old faith and, no, not even the most outspoken preacher of the Kirk, will dare to look upon our joy with a stern face.

Hunched over dying coals, cooking and eating plain oatcakes and washing these down with no more than sourish well water, these strangers were united in hope and expectation. They waited for news to come from the Queen's chambers.

By full daylight, with the dawn's fog burning and blowing away, there was still no word. Restless, the men talked in low voices. Four days earlier, on Saturday, there had been the beginnings of a celebration. A sudden time of bells and cannons and cheers. All founded on the strength of false rumors. Now they were gathered in tense clumps in the Close. Watching quietly as one or another of the nobility, so conspicuous in court finery, threaded a way through the crowd, entering or leaving the palace and the Hall.

He noted their coming and going. Who they were. By name and rank. What they were wearing. What pieces of their talk could be overheard. Stored these things in memory. Because it is his craft to do so. And he does it well enough even though he doubts the value of most of these signs.

"We must assume," he tells you like a schoolmaster, "that powerful and influential men, so long as their greatness and influence last, for safety's sake must take for granted that all other men—that fine gentleman next to you at table, that shabby, bowlegged boy, seen only for an instant, he who came running to take the reins and walk your horse cool after the hunt, any and all of these and here in Scotland, yes, even your own brother unless he has been proved beyond doubt—all are interested witnesses whose testimony will come to the attention of your enemies.

"Because, after all, it is precisely your enemies who have the greatest interest in your condition.

"Clothing as costume, then, and face no less than a mask, their gestures, their laughter and tears as false (or as true) as any player's on a public stage, these have learned that hypocrisy is a lesser illness of the soul than despair."

Or so it seems to the man who calls himself, for the time being, Jack Scarecrow. Child of his times, he finds the truth of Holy Scripture as he reads the story of the world. Who seeks to save his life shall lose it. Who is first now shall be last later. All who have power and influence here and now shall in the end possess no more of either than any beggar lying in a ditch.

"Any man who has lived long enough to be wise in the ways of the world," he tells you, "will say that disappointment is the best schoolmaster. And if that is true"—here comes a hard laugh and a wink as if to deny the shame of any self-pity—"then surely I must be among the learned doctors of this age, being so well versed in the grammar and syntax, in the cases and declensions of disappointment. Come, let us drink to disappointment and be done with it."

Toward the middle of morning, with the sun high enough above the walls for a man to begin to think of dinnertime, and the sky a clear blue, almost cloudless, the young woman he had been waiting for appeared at one of the windows of the Queen's kitchen. A serving girl, and not of the Queen but of Mistress Margaret Asteane, the Queen's midwife. The young woman leaned out of the window to empty a cooking pot, splashing water to raise a small ghost of steam from the cobbles. Then she paused for a moment, red-haired, her young skin the color of fresh cream, as she dabbed at her face with a blue-and-white kerchief. Her face revealed nothing but weariness. She leaned from the window breathing the morning air, tasting and testing the new day's weather. And as she did so, sunlight glinted on a gold chain around her neck. A small fine gold chain with a little medallion or locket, like a lady's, but worn by an ordinary serving girl. That blue-and-white kerchief was also a lady's thing. But in and around Court, even in frugal Scotland, a young and pretty servant might easily come to own such things. Once it had been his handkerchief and his gold chain. He won the chain at cards, though he told her it had belonged to his mother, bless her memory. Gave it to the creamy, red-haired servant girl, together with a few other tokens of affection—several yards of good cloth, a silver bracelet, an old ring, a little money, some sweet kisses and sweeter promises—to earn her trust and goodwill. And to pay for the signal she had just given him.

Well, she kept her word, her part of the bargain. Next she was yawning. Glancing, still blankly, at the figures in the Close. And so was able to catch his eyes without any sign of recognition. Looked at him. Looked away. Turned away from the window to go back to her chores.

He had touched the brim of his hat, adjusting it, the sign that he had seen and understood her signal. And he was already walking away when she vanished from view.

Nothing had changed there in the Close. No stir of any kind.

There was nothing to support the truth of her signal. And yet everything for him was now changed. He was lit like a lantern from within.

Just then he saw Lord Darnley, a head taller than any man in the Close. Elegant in perfectly fitted satins, taffeta and velvets, all in his favorite shades of peach and flower colors. Strolling toward the palace doorway in the company of some of his men and with his father, Matthew Stuart, Earl of Lennox. Followed some armed men of the Lennox Stuarts. And saw next, though not for the first time in the last few days, in black (like a preacher of the Kirk?) James Stewart, Earl of Moray, bastard half brother of Mary the Queen. Saw the young Lord Seton, clad in scarlet and gold, including even his flat hat and feather, his shoes, the hilt of his sword and scabbard, and carrying the scarlet-and-gold wand of the Master of the Household.

All of these separately moving toward the palace. As if without any but casual purpose.

Saw also, quietly coming out from the palace, a woman in the plain cloak and hood of a serving girl. But something about the way she carried herself said *lady* to him. And even at this distance he could recognize her as one of the Queen's Four Marys, her lifelong attendants and companions.

He went briskly across the Close toward the old Fore Well, a small leather bucket dangling in his hand. Waited his turn with others. Drew a bucketful of well water. Then walked away, following the crenellated shadow lines of the wall. Above, on the wall, gunners were standing waiting for word to fire their cannons in salute whenever the news came. With each step he expected to hear a trumpet or some hoarse shouting from the Close and the ringing of bells. But nothing yet. Maybe his red-haired woman was wrong. Or had chosen to wrong him. Well, he'd know soon enough. Walking on, steady and purposeful, with his bucket of water. Passing the small castle yard and gardens. Some shepherds there with a flock of sheep. Waiting to become mutton.

Now passing by the ancient chapel of St. Margaret. And still no voices and no bells ringing.

Pausing a moment, lowering the bucket to the ground, at the top of the narrow, twisting flight of stairs which leads down from next to the Constable's Tower. Able to see from there the sunlit, wind-blown water of Leith and, far across, the wide, white-capped spaces of the Forth. A deep breath of the sea air. And now down the steps to the outer ward of the fortress. Thinking that a man with a bucket of water—especially here in dry Edinburgh with its precious few fountains and wells—would be up to no mischief for sure. Came down the steps and then down and along the rough, narrow cobbled way past the Inner Barrier and through the Outer Bridge Gate. Nodding a straight-faced greeting to the cluster of armed men there. Noting that there were two or three who were wearing the badge—horse's head and neck, bridled, and the motto *Kiep Trest*—of James Hepburn, the Earl of Bothwell. And that surprised him somewhat. For the story was that the Earl's request for lodgings at the Castle had been denied. He was said to have left the city with some show of anger. To tend to his Warden's duties on the Border. Surprising that some of his men, armed and openly wearing his badge, would still be here and in trusted positions, too.

Nodding at those guards and shuffling out the gate and over the open drawbridge.

Large crowds gathered in the Lawnmarket outside the gate and moat. Chiefly townspeople in their best clothing. But some country folk also. Trying to make their best appearance by wearing shoes. Even if there's no other sign to mark them as plain Scots farmers and village folk newly come to the city, their boots will offer irrefutable evidence. Boots so stiff and clean, shiny and unscratched, that they look brand-new from the shoemaker's. And this because they will have carried these shoes for many miles, finally putting them on just outside the walls of the city. Oh, never your English ostentation and extravagance of wearing their stocking and shoes for a whole day!

Thinking: *They have come a long way. Well, this time they will not be disappointed.*

Now passing the stalls, Luckenbooths, at the edge of Lawnmarket. Walking then out onto the wide pride of Edinburgh—the magnificent High Street. All along that roadway, said to be the widest city street in Christendom and why not believe it?, elegantly paved with evenly dressed, square-cut stones, and lined on both sides with flagstone gutters, the whole street running for a full Scots mile and a bit, gradually downward from Castle Hill to and through turreted Netherbow Gate of the Flodden Walls. And on through the suburb of Canongate to Holyroodhouse and then the open country.

Seeing down the length of that street the piles of firewood (so precious in this almost timberless land). Heaped for the bonfires. Fire loose among the wynds would spread quickly and destroy much. He glances at his hand holding the waterbucket. And in that instant can picture other hands, strong hands poised to grasp bell ropes and ready to batter wild music from every bell in Edinburgh and all across Scotland.

Easing a way through crowds at the west end of High Street. Seeing how the wooden balconies, the galleries, and the outside stairways, mounting the tall gray granite, many-storied houses on both sides of the street, have been decorated. Hung with carpets and painted cloths and flags. And running away from the street between the rows of houses and leading into hidden courtyards and closes, the steep, narrow wynds have been hung with decorations, too, brightened, tented over with rainbows of color.

Streets cleaner now than he can remember. More than he believed possible. All piles of rubbish, middens, mounds of manure, having been hauled away somewhere in the night. Edinburgh seeming almost new made.

Well, so it is, in a sense; for it is only twenty years or so since an English army sacked and burned a large part of it.

Now passing the Tolbooths, the new and the old. Prisoners kept in the latter will be hoping for an amnesty today. Or tomorrow. Next the stern face of the Kirk of St. Giles. Hugely sprawled beneath its tall square central tower and crowned steeple. Here will come trooping, when the time comes, the nobility and the gentry, Catholic and those of the Kirk together, side by side, for once. To say the prayers and to sing the psalms, joining with the important people of the city. And never mind, for now, for this one time, that all of the Catholic altars (more than forty of them) are overturned and all gone. Trying not to notice that all the images of holy saints have been set free from their niches to rest now in new peace at the deep bottom of the North Loch. Oh, there may well be, most likely will be, a day of reckoning for all of that. But not yet. Not upon this happy holiday-to-be.

Moving on next near the tall shaft and shadow of the Mercat Cross. Where the fountain's gently playing and the stocks and pillory are empty. Here the public proclamation of the news will be made by a royal herald. Tonight the fountain will run with wine.

Then turning away, leaving the street soon after, just beyond Fishmarket Close. To follow a wynd between overhanging houses. Going down steeply as if toward Grassmarket. But not there. Stopping short at a small stable heavy with the odors of hay and horses and horseshit. Black flies singing in warm air. Buzzing from the long shafts of light and into motley shadows and back again. Sounding like a musician's bow drawn back and forth across untuned strings.

There he paid for the keeping of his horse and added the leather bucket as a gift.

"If fires catch in thatch, you'll thank me for it."

"Ah, then, you think there will truly be bonfires tonight?"

"God alone knows for sure," he said. "But it seems to me likely to happen. And if it does, you can credit me with the gift of prophecy."

"You know, that's a sad piece of horseflesh that you own," the Scot told him. "You would do just as well to walk to wherever you are going."

"No doubt about it, sir. But she's a quiet and gentle horse. And she is all mine for better or worse, like a man's wife, for as long as she may live. Which, when I think on it, will probably be longer than I shall."

"Well, no need to fear losing her," the Scot said, laughing. "No man, not even a Gypsy, would think of trying to steal her from you."

He laughed too. Waved a farewell as he took her reins and walked away, leading her up the wynd toward broad bright High Street again.

Turned down past the Butter Tron. Where the city's market goods are weighed and measured according to the laws. Heading down for the city walls and Canongate and Holyrood's tower. Able to see already, above battlemented Flodden Wall, the wide, steep-climbing green of Holyrood's park. And that high, curious, anvil-shaped hill that they call Arthur's Seat rising in the near distance.

Truth is he was well pleased with his horse. For though she may look somewhat sleepy and old, she's sturdy and strong. Not much for show in towns or stables. But she's a good reiver's horse. Can endure miles and miles of the roughest country that would break the spirit of a prouder mount. And she can be away and running, be gone like a fresh breeze, if that's your purpose. He has won good money running her against the better-looking horses of men who trusted pride too much and depended more on their eyes than on their judgment.

Tells himself that once he is clear of the city and suburb, out under the wide sky on the open road, he will hunch down and tuck in close, gripping his knees to her body. Give her a swift kick and then hold tight for a while as she runs hard and fast and free. All for the joy of it. For, sadly, he must soon leave her behind. She would do him no good in England. But in Scotland (as he will be telling Englishmen later) she was the best companion he had found.

Beyond the gate, he dismounted to walk his horse a way in the Burgh of Canongate. Passing the fruit-and-vegetable markets and then the line of booths of the meat market. Where tonight, for a change, each booth would surely be festooned with many lights instead of the single fixed lantern that the law requires.

Canongate . . . With both sides of the wide street faced with the tall town houses of Scots lords. Most of these new built. And many of them extravagantly fronted with imported timber. All with enormous brass-studded doors of imported hardwood.

At the Canongate Cross he again mounted his horse and rode on at an easy walk to the place where the Burgh gives way, by ancient custom, to the lawful sanctuary of the Abbey and Palace of Holyrood.

Then the road turned away, to the south and east. And almost at once gave way to open fields.

He could not have been even a mile down the road, going at a gallop at last, dust rolling behind her flying hooves, when the Castle's cannon cracked and boomed. So sudden and loud that his horse shied and nearly threw him. He pulled her in, eased her to a walk again. Then he could hear the sound of bells. First from the Castle, then in the city.

By and by the formal announcements will be made.

Now through the long afternoon the sound of the jawing and ringing bells, like a slow, steady, rising tide, will spread all across the Lowlands. And come late twilight (or the gray half-dark of this time of year) and bonfires and beacons will be carrying the word to all of Scotland and swifter than bells of men. Men . . . Soon, if not already close behind him, messengers from Edinburgh will be riding to all points of the kingdom. Though with so much of the kingdom already assembled in the city, who is left to be informed?

No matter. Still, he guesses reasonably, here and now in the country of the Merse and moving on toward the Border, he is well ahead of the noise, the news. It's not foolish to hope so.

From Edinburgh he followed the old road east toward the coast. Crossed the bridge across the swollen Esk (for there has been much rain here ever since spring) at the fishing village of Musselburgh, its whitewashed houses with their red and orange tile roofs bunched close to the mouth of the river.

Passing nearby, in sight, a place called Pinkie where in '47 the Earl of Hertford routed the Scots. And there his master, Cecil, serving then as secretary to the Earl, learned his first lesson of war. Standing too near the mouth of a cannon to observe the action, Cecil would have been blown into chunks when the cannon was suddenly fired, if a captain had not lunged forward and knocked him sprawling. Saved Cecil's life, though it cost the captain his right arm to the shoulder.

Past Pinkie and into red-soiled farming country. Past Seaton and Haddington. Crossing the Tyne at the ford close by Hailes Castle. Next to East Linton where he found the tower of the old Trinitarian Friary had been newly transformed into a dovecote by the reformers. Going on to the rocky little harbor of Dunbar.

Traveling south along the rocky coast for a time. Seeing an army of choppy whitecaps mustered by northeast wind. Huge waves shattered against rocks below the road. And sky was all of a sudden ablaze with wings, alive with seabirds—gulls and terns, black and long-necked (like haughty ladies) cormorants, and clouds of the swift, small, darting, fork-tailed sea swallows. Such a swarm of crying and calling in the blown sea air!

After fording Pease Brook, just south of Cockburnspath, he has turned away from the sea and from the North Road to follow these trails over Eye Water and through the eastern edges of the Lammermuirs and finally into Border country, the Scots East March, with its wide skies and long views all around and easy-rolling spaces. The countryside looks almost empty at this time of year. Herds of cattle have been driven off to graze the high grass in their shealing places to remain there until sometime in August. To be kept there, as safe as they can be, protected against raids by the English reivers.

Sometimes he passes within sight of a cluster of huts made all of earth and thatch. Huts which, if they can be easily toppled and destroyed, can be just as quickly rebuilt. Here and there stand pele towers, each a tall square sentry of stone. He is deep into the country of these towers and of ancient, small, crumbling castles. And of fortified churches. Not many miles to the west of him are the ruins of the largest abbeys that were ever in Scotland —Kelso, Jedburgh, Dryburgh, and Melrose. All four tumbled by the English invaders. And then picked clean as an Easter goose by Scots reformers.

He left the high road so as not to have to cross into England at the garrison town of Berwick. It would be easier, of course, to keep to the road. To enter England by Scots Gate. And to go on through the narrow streets that twist among tall houses and buildings of gray stone with red tile roofs. Then going across the wide Tweed, south of the fortress town. Clattering over that old, long, shaky, loose-timbered bridge. . . .

Better by far than any roundabout way. Except that the Lord Warden of the East Marches and present Governor of Berwick— Francis Russell, Earl of Bedford—knowing nothing at all of him and not knowing him to be Sir William Cecil's man—will be, at the very least, suspicious. If Bedford does not know him to be Cecil's man, it must be because he is not intended to. Both Bedford and Cecil are members of the Council, are friends and allies, indeed are close neighbors in Westminster. And yet, as the world knows, it is all too often a necessary exercise of practical wisdom for friends and allies to keep a few secrets from each other. If nothing else, it does not allow good friendship to be tested. It is sometimes far more dangerous, Cecil has allowed, to trust a friend with a secret than an enemy. The enemy can never wholly credit the truth of it whereas your friend has no good reason to doubt you.

Thus Bedford could find good reasons to delay him in Berwick. After all, no matter whose servant the horseman may claim to be, he has neither appropriate letters nor any other lawful document, such as a passport, to prove it. Now, if he should fail to come forth with an adequate explanation of himself and of his movements, he might find himself detained in Berwick indefinitely. At the leisure and convenience of the Governor. If, on the other hand, to establish himself, he should blurt out his news, why then the Earl would have to consider—fool if he doesn't!— that perhaps his own messenger going directly to the Queen and bypassing Mr. Secretary Cecil, would do some good for himself. At the price, at the worst, of a slight irritation to Cecil. Who, in any case, need not ever learn that his own man could have brought the news first.

If rumor is to be credited, Bedford is already weary of this service so far from home. So far removed by time and distance from Court. Too far from the possibility of rewards. Every day he grows a little less rich, exiled up here at the ragged edges of Scotland. Therefore, though he may be loyal without question, he is also unquestionably unhappy to be so loyally wasting both time and substance while others prosper by doing nothing much beyond keeping close to the throne. Like lazy old men dozing in the chimney corner.

So this horseman aims to leave Scotland not at Berwick, but at some eight miles west of it and a little more than three miles east of Tillmouth and the ford at Coldstream. Plans to cross over into England at a bend in the Tweed, an old reiver's ford, under the high red sandstone walls of Norham Castle. A good place to cross the river. Though he must be careful, for the Tweed flows deceptively calm and smooth there. River polished silver and gold in the slanting light. With always a swan or two. Each riding proud upon its own drowned and ghostly reflection, carried along by a current of sunlight and clear water.

He will go over at the place named Ubbanford, skirting round the tangled brush of the small island at midstream. Looking directly up at the high square keep of the Castle. Then climbing the low, timbered hill in the shadow of the walls on the cliff. Riding down the straight lone street of Norham village. Going clear to the far end of it—the triangular market green at the southeastern side. Across that market and past the market cross. To the alehouse set near to the yard of St. Cuthbert's Church. There to dismount and stretch weary legs. And with the promise of a halfpenny to send a boy running back down the street to Little Bulwark, as they choose to call the repaired tower and gatehouse to the Castle. Where word can be passed to old Mr. Richard Norton, Captain of the Castle, that a strange Englishman, dressed and mounted and looking for all the world like a common Scot, and giving the curious name of Jonathan Beanstalk, is now seated at an outdoor trestle table, set behind the alehouse in the garden, washing dust from his tongue and throat with English ale. And he says that if the Captain wishes to see him . . .

While he is waiting for the Captain, he will, indeed, take some refreshment. The first, except for stream water where he knelt in soft mud to drink side by side with his horse, since he cooked and ate his oatcake at dawn. Some ale, some bread and cheese. And if old promises are both remembered and kept, he will soon be leaving his Scots mare and taking in exchange a fresh English horse, nearly twice her size and shod on all feet. He will discard this pillion for a true English saddle. And now he will have knee-high boots and spurs and saddlebags, too. These bags will have some letters to be dropped off along the way. And there had best be some documents, forged credentials. Perhaps even certain tools or instruments of a trade—identifying him as a musician or a dentist or maybe the agent of a London printer or bookseller, all of which roles he has had to play before. More likely, though, he guesses, since Norham and the whole thin strip of country running from here eastward to the Farne Islands remains still, as in ancient times, part of the Palatinate of Durham, he will be given something or other identifying him as a lesser retainer of Bishop Pilkington of Durham. He will at least be given some few documents marked with a wax seal and some bits of ribbon.

Which things, though they might not deceive the youngest apprentice in London, will look powerfully authentic to the average
North-country man.

And he will soon change into clean, plain English clothing.
But will keep his hat. For he likes it and it fits him well. Though
he must give it a brushing and maybe find a way to dress it up
with a piece of ribbon and a feather or two.

Who in all England would ever want to wear a hat without a
feather?

He will carry no sword or pistols. But will have with him a
good, strong, short-bladed knife, one of the kind that the Scots
call a whinny. No reason to arm himself with a sword and pistols
here in the Border country. For even if these rogues (from both
sides, of both Kingdoms) will steal each other's cattle and sheep
and crops, will chop down trees, burn fields and houses (after
helping themselves to pots and pans and anything useful), will
even, without much regret, commit rape or murder in the course
of a feud or for the sake of revenge, still they will not so demean
themselves as to rob a traveling stranger or do him any kind of
harm or mischief, so long as he does no harm to them.

If all goes as planned, if promises are remembered and kept,
he'll remain in the village long enough to drink a cup of ale or
two and to share his news with Captain Norton. What Norton
will make of this news, how he will take it, he cannot guess. Certainly the Captain will be very pleased to send someone—the
same pennywise village lad?—rowing over the Tweed in a cobble
to tell the Scots of the village of Ladykirk. Norton will be happy
to have them learn their own best news from the English side of
the river.

And the Captain will be pleased to pass the word on at
Norham too

But as to whatever it might possibly mean to him . . .

Although this Captain Norton is a loyal and trusted servant to
the Percys of Northumberland and, like them, can be rightly understood to favor the old forms of religion and perhaps even to
question the clear legitimacy of our Queen, he is nevertheless not
without his own share of the wisdom of the world. Not without
knowledge of the supple ways which are so widely practiced.
This is a newfangled time, one in which even an honored virtue,

like the servant's loyalty to the master, if too blindly followed, if too rigidly adhered to, if practiced without an occasional cynical wink or skeptical shrug, can prove to be as brittle as a dead tree in the wind. Bend or break, man, bend or break. That's the essence of the new covenant. Or, as Sir William Cecil is wont to put it, "the practick art of wisdom is the best."

Captain Norton, an old soldier of an old Border family, kin to many and allied to many more, an old soldier with the scars to prove it, has lived too long to fret too much over any future which lies much further ahead of him than tomorrow's sunrise.

It may be that refusal to accept either the wounds or the blessings of the unimaginable future before it arrives and, thus, ceases to be a future anymore, is what these two men, messenger and soldier, have in common.

This much Captain Norton will be sure of—that the Percys will want to know the news from Edinburgh Castle as early as can be. The Captain will ask the messenger to deliver a brief memorandum from himself. So to pass on the news at Alnwick Castle.

The messenger will agree to that. For there is no purpose in doing injury to Norton and thus to the Percys. Why not do them a little service just as Captain Norton is willing to do some little favors for him and thus for Sir William Cecil? It may be that the news has already come to Alnwick. By some other means. For the Percys have been spying on the Scots, warring with them and dealing with them, one way and the other, not for years, but for centuries. They may know already. Yet he doubts it. . . .

The messenger is relaxed and satisfied for the time being. Savoring the ironic truth that it is oftentimes wiser to deal with enemies (as, with candor, he must count the whole tribe of the Percys and their kin and their servants and dependants to be—at least the enemies of Cecil and his friends and all the reforming faction, if not yet, in truth, enemies to the Queen) than with friends.

Wise in ways of the politic world, here he is riding miles across country, risking that he may lose the slight advantage of time and, in the end, arrive in Westminster too late for Cecil to have the news first, and doing all this to avoid any possible encounter with Cecil's friend—the Earl of Bedford.

It may be wise, too, to delay his journey briefly (may it be very briefly indeed!) to be sure that Cecil's enemy, the Percy Earl of Northumberland, receives the news of Scotland before Bedford does.

No worthy enemy desires to dissipate the strength of his malice on petty slights and inconsequential offenses. Among such enemies as the Percys the messenger feels wonderfully protected. Like a herald in battle. Safe and more or less invulnerable like sulky Achilles among Trojans.

Moreover the messenger believes that he knows his own master well enough so as not to fear that there is any risk taken in the performance of some little service for Cecil's enemies. He believes that Cecil will, as he must, assume this to be the case, anyway. By reason and by common sense (and without passing any judgment) Cecil must assume that the loyalty of any of his servants has its limits. Must therefore especially allow that a confidential agent, like this one, is at least likely to be tempted to double his services.

That Sir William Cecil knows that he needs to protect himself, as well as can be, against what he assumes to be possible, lifts a great burden of responsibility off the shoulders of the messenger and makes Cecil, finally, a trustworthy master to serve.

Just so, it is also what makes Cecil, in the eyes of the Queen, a worthy servant to herself. Surely that Lady knows better than most Princes (counting all of the living and many of the illustrious dead) having herself been a child of Fortune all of her life and so having been wonderfully tossed and turned, that bonds of need are far more to be depended on than many bonds of loyalty and devotion. True loyalty is much more rare than anyone might imagine. All the more so since expressions of devotion are so commonplace and so easily gained. Loyalty seems to be so common because it is so seldom put to the test. But the test of loyalty is the only true definition of it.

Just so, up to a point, the messenger and Captain Norton can trust each other. The messenger can be at ease knowing that the Captain has already accepted some modest favors from Cecil. For some simple services rendered. Not enough reward, even in aggregate, to corrupt a man, not even a poor man. And never asking him to do anything that might be misconstrued as disloyal to the Percys. Why force the Captain to test his own loyalty? It might turn out to be true and deep. No, the Captain has so far been asked for ordinary things, demanding from him only a measure of discretion, perhaps a little silence, and, on this occasion, for example, to provide some hospitality to a man in need. Which —a loaned horse, a saddle, a change of clothing, some money—he might have offered anyway. Simply as one Englishman to another. Might do so, even though the other gent, like this one, had arrived in Norham all dripping wet from fording the Tweed, well and credibly disguised, in clothing and manners, as a common Scot, and without a passport or any other paper to prove his name. Of course, the messenger knows the Captain. But if he did not, he might not be any more reluctant to cross here, provided he had enough money (hidden) with him to lend veracity to his assertions. With money any assertion, within reason, might be acceptable. And plausible rhymes and reasons in this part of the world are different. Far from the lights of the Court, things here often cast vague shadows. Chances are Captain Norton would offer such an imaginary Englishman (provided he could clearly demonstrate qualities of gentle birth, no matter what his disguise) some honest hospitality. There's more inducement, however, in the prospect of earning credit with the Queen's Secretary. No harm at all in that so long as all parties are fully aware that the power and influence and, hence, the glory of the Secretary (or, indeed, anyone else in high office and standing close to the sun) can vanish quicker than the wink of an eye.

Even the sun can vanish from sight. One sun sets and another sun rises.

Meantime consider Captain Norton as he stands with the messenger (who will be dressed and ready to ride by then) in the little garden behind the alehouse almost in the shadow of squat old St. Cuthbert's Church in Norham village. Sun beginning its summer glide toward twilight, bleeding a faint and wavering reflection of Norham Castle onto the steely-smooth flowing of the Tweed. See Captain Norton as a white-haired, white-bearded fellow. A man made out of well-seasoned barrel staves. His leathery skin guarded by leather boots and a studded leather jerkin. Watery pale eyes. Which he squints often even to look at what's nearby. But which can also be, after all, as steel-smooth as that river. He studies the messenger. Studies and follows the lazy falling away of a leaf from the short gray alder that shades them. A single leaf—waxy green on one side, dusty gray on the bottom, ribbed and shaped like the fat bowl of a lute, floating in motley shade, lighting on the chipped gravel of the footpath, resting briefly between the toes of the four boots of the two of them, then, touched by the merest sigh of breeze, lifting all at once like a book page to tumble away. Sipping his ale from a wooden cup and over the slick rim of it studying the messenger who is laughing as he tells some tavern jest he has heard in Edinburgh.

Consider the Captain. Who must be thinking how far London lies from all this, village and castle. Though a proud North-country man, born and bred, he will have seen the city of London and the glories of Westminster in his time. And must now be fearing, and with some justice, that he will never again see that brightest flower (as they say) among the world's cities. Especially if sharp winters, like these last few, repeat themselves. Especially if wet summers continue. Some say the weather of the world is steadily changing for the worse. That may be true. But Captain Norton has to allow that, with every year's aging, it is he who is changing. His blood growing thinner and weaker, he can feel it. His joints more painfully racked by damp and chill.

The messenger shares the tavern jest and drinks his ale. He'll soon be mounted and riding away. If he had time, he would linger to listen to the Captain's hard-knuckled tales of raids and ambushes, kidnappings and hangings, along these Borders. He would not be weary hearing again of the old battlefields. Would listen with outward attention even though he might smile inwardly. That inner smiling offered in payment for the old man's innocence. For (to this messenger) the old have their own forms of innocence and ignorance and, thus, are as worthy of pity as are the very young. Born into, schooled and raised up in simpler times, when all the world's changes seemed understandable and when the motives of men were naked and clear as the point of a sword in the sun, the Captain has lived too long to understand fully the sly forces of this new age. Study it as he will, he will never be able fully to imagine the dangers even to his own well-being. Cannot, for instance, comprehend these things. That Sir

William Cecil, and thus his man, this messenger, acting on behalf of the master, would never wish him so much as one day of bad fortune or ill health. But that on another day, whenever that day might fall, when this Captain might have become an embarrassment, an annoyance, an encumbrance, even a lesser irritation like a pebble in a boot, no more than that really, why then, upon that selfsame day this same Captain will learn how it is that a man can be disposed of like a goose in the marketplace. Will discover how a man, together with all previous acts of service and demonstrable professions of loyalty, can be sold off like a bag of dry beans or a bushel of barley or a stack of hay. Can be dispensed with and without a second thought. No, not even the first thought, really, let alone any twitches of regret to commemorate the occasion.

"For that," the messenger would surely say if he were near enough to explain it, "is the bitter truth at the heart of the statecraft of our age. This truth being that there is no one—no servant, no ally, kith or kin—who cannot sooner or later be sold off like a sheep . . . or merely the wool sheared off his back . . . or the pasture he grazes on be traded away like any other piece of goods, whenever that should seem worthwhile to whoever it is who has the power to act upon his own wishes or fears." Now there are some who in good faith will argue that just such stratagems, such a marketplace of flesh, are better by far than bloody sword and buckler, the pickax shambles of a battlefield. Where hundreds and thousands of more or less honest and well-meaning men without names to remember, will have to die. Lucky ones will die there on the field. Unlucky will learn how to assume crippled shapes, will wed themselves to pain and to pity and fear of others for life.

"And all of this will be done, sir or madame, for things of less value to anyone (even including the Captains who pocket the pay of the dead) than the clouds of dust they raise in the air. Plenty will argue, and with persuasion, that this is now a better and wiser world than that old one in which a man was expected to offer up life and limb, to risk all of his future for the sake of loyalty and friendship.

"But then," the messenger continues, "our old Captain Norton knows next to nothing about the kinds of plots and stratagems employed by the great ones of our new age. He can only act as he knows how. According to a book of rules he learned long ago. God willing, this Captain will die quietly enough. Will die in his own warm bed. Will die at peace and still in his happy state of ignorance. Will die peaceful and not perplexed. Will die never so much as dreaming of a time and place of a newfound, new-made world in which such a one as I, if so commanded, would here and now, even as we are both laughing at an old jest and as his watery eyes follow the falling of an alder leaf, slip some inches of a steel blade between his ribs. Would do so, and would never ask why. And would never lose a wink of sleep over the matter.

"Ah, things I could tell the Captain, mysteries I have for daily companions that would wrinkle his brow and puzzle his brain, I do believe."

Nevertheless, the messenger wishes there were some signs of truth, some forms of that life left in that now nearly imaginary place where the Captain lives out his days. Old England is gone for good and forever. But the Captain does not know that. So here he stands, every inch the old Captain who guards an ancient fording place from the walls and the enormous keep of Norham Castle. Where the chronicles tell us that Kings (once upon a time) held Court. Which Castle has withstood the fury of full-scale siege. Norham Castle which could be reduced and leveled to rubble, in almost no time at all, by a sufficient concentration of artillery.

Surely the Captain cannot imagine his castle (and with it his life, his history, his beliefs) lying in ruins on all sides of him.

What does the Captain know of the world? Only the oldest, most familiar ironies. How things are not always as simple in fact as they seem in theory. For instance, he will have told the messenger that when he rides off toward the coast and the high road, he need not be on the lookout for the quickset hedges with which Archbishop Young and the Council of the North, away and safe within the white walls of the city of York, have recently ordered that all the farms and pastures along the Borders should be enclosed. This, as the Council sees it, will serve to discourage the Scots reivers and witriders and will deprive them of ease of movement across the countryside. Well, sir, it might, indeed, *slow* the movement of the Scots horsemen somewhat. *Deprive* is too strong a word. Doubtful that weighty chains on hands and feet would actually *deprive* your Border reiver of movement. And as to *discouraging* them, those whom death by gunshot or knife blade, or by prompt hanging from the nearest tree limb or doorway, has never deterred, ain't likely, are they?, to fall into a mood of melancholy at the prospect of encountering a few thorny hedges where there used to be open fields. Truth is (and your typical roughneck Borderer will be among the first to perceive this) the Council's hedges will be more advantage than anything else. For one thing, the hedges will pen up the English cattle and save the reivers time and trouble to round them up. And then when they've taken all the cattle and are headed for home in Scotland, why, the hedges will frustrate any English pursuit. And also—though, of course, this can never be openly considered at sessions of the Council—the chief argument that the English Borderers will have against the hedges is that they will tend to hinder the *English* moss-troopers in their goings and comings from Scotland. And so this latest command, which must have seemed wise and thoughtful to someone in York, is being wisely and thoughtfully (and always loyally) ignored.

They will both have a chuckle at that. And at that moment the messenger will feel older by far, in bones and sinew, in blood and brainpan, than the proud (though ever so slightly bent at the shoulders) stiff-jointed, hoarse-voiced Captain. How he envies the Captain his scars! He envies the plain truth that the pain of the Captain's wounds has long since been forgotten and been replaced by harmless pride in them. His own scars, as the messenger conceives of them, are both deep and disguised. Their pain, he sometimes allows himself to imagine, is continual. And they can be (he sometimes believes) numbed only by death. Which death, even as he seeks not to imagine it, averts his face from any picture of it, almost certainly will be sudden and violent. He does not fear death, but fears imagining it. What he fears most is the death of old age, slow decay of body and mind, of memory and hope, more than any sudden death he has ever seen or can imagine. But even as he fears the cumulative losses of time, whose final reckoning is death, still he envies the Captain his impeccable simplicity.

Here Captain Norton could help him somewhat. And with things more valuable than horse and saddle, some clothing and a purse.

If and when they both had the leisure and inclination to be more openhearted, not so much to tell truth as to exchange truths . . . Certainly it's true the Captain could never fully comprehend all the forms of subtle double dealing which are the anatomical bare bones of Jack Scarecrow's craft. Of course the Captain would have had to begin somewhat gruffly. By telling the young man, who is not young except to the Captain's old eyes, to spit out childish pity for himself and be done with it. Saying, there's no place for that kind of indulgence between good and true men. Saying, it must have been Adam and Eve who first felt pity for themselves after they had eaten of the apple in the garden. Well, sir, we are all their children. But we need not waste our precious strength in the cultivation of shameful petty vices. . . . What the Captain does know—more so even than the messenger can—is the many and varied forms and shapes of death. He has seen and knows them well. And he knows that sudden death is nothing to be wished for, even as a bargain against the sorrows and infirmities of age. Never. The Captain will always wish for more life, even though that life may be daily more painful and disappointing. He will continue to desire to live for as long as his heart is beating and he still can breathe.

It is precisely because the Captain loves the gift of his life and has never discarded the last of his hopes, that he has not feared death for as long as he can remember.

The Captain will also perceive—though he will have better manners than to say it—that men who earn their bread by affectation and disguises, by use of false names and forged documents, men whose profession it is to perform services for other men who are powerful and ambitious and influential in the world, need not waste their precious time fearing (or wishing) for sudden endings. Chances are the messenger will die that way.

The Captain does not need to know very much about the new statecraft or the ways of the changing world to understand that the odds are good that this messenger's days will be short and that the end of them will be sudden. He knows how it is written in the Psalms, how *Bloody and deceitful men shall not live out half their days.*

Here is where the Captain might speak to the subject of innocence. Still misconceiving the messenger to be literally young, he would say this: that only the young will spend their time fearing or wishing for what is bound to come to pass anyway. Only the young or the foolish can believe that they choose their fortune.

Tell me, does the ox choose to wear his yoke?

But none of these things will be said between the two men.

They will drink to each other's good health.

And then the Captain, having, as promised, delivered the messenger a purse of money, will allow the messenger to pay for the ale that the two of them drink.

They raise wooden cups to their lips. Their eyes meet briefly as they salute each other and drink to health and good fortune.

Neither seriously expects ever to see the other one alive again.

Then the messenger will mount up and ride away.

He's off again following old trails through a grassland which is threaded by many little streams. And he will be watching for any of the patches of green or purple which signal a dangerous boggy place.

Off to the south lie the low Cheviot Hills. Place of bracken and ling, heather and furze for brushwood, and of few trees. Home for red and roe deer and for herds of gray wild goats. And up there, alone in all of England, there are wild, white, long-haired, long-horned cattle.

Soon he'll be hearing the loud, slow, trilling song of the curlew. And will begin to see more cattle than sheep being driven to the evening safety of barmkin and Bastel House.

Riding as hard as the trails allow, hurrying to rejoin the North Road near to the sea.

Four miles and a bit from Norham and he can look north and east, across fertile farmland, to see a landmark—the three-storied, fortified parson's tower of the old Church of St. Anne at the village of Anncroft. There's an inn there he'll remember, the *Lamb*, where a man who is in no hurry to be anywhere can rest and eat well.

From there at that point turning southward so as soon to pass by the fortified manor they call Haggerston Castle. Noting, for the sake of his master's curiosity, its present state of repair. Cecil will want to know; for Haggerston is a center for those who are strong in the Catholic faith here on both sides of the Border. And the Mass is still said by a priest in full vestments in the chapel of Our Lady and St. Cuthbert. He will pass south, well below the manor house, between it and the Kyloe Hills. Those hills rising up nearly five hundred feet, craggy and well covered with brushwood. There he can see St. Nicholas Church (fortified, too, like nearly every manor and church and farmhouse in this country) standing at the highest point of the hills. Still, as for years beyond remembering, a guide for sailors.

Again there are gulls crying and sailing the air. Then soon a scent of sea and next the sound, the low murmuring of distant surf. Across sloping fields leading down toward dunes he'll see the flashing of sunlight on waves. Waves breaking like scoured, burnished metal. And soon after to see the rocks of the Holy Island of Lindisfarne. Close by, really, just out beyond Goswick Sands and Fenham Flats. If he could be there at this time of year he would find the air frantic and shrill with clouds of seabirds, with gulls and terns, petrels and cormorants, guillemots and razorbills. And always the eider ducks which, the legend tells, St. Cuthbert first tamed there on the island. Could see, too, the gray seals splashing and barking in the island's surf. And the rock face brightened with wild flowers and flowering herbs.

Riding on, he will see the light and shadow playing across the red sandstone buildings of the old monastery. The tall central tower of the Priory church and the outer courts and walk of the Prior's Hall. All of it now, under the terms of the reformed and monkless faith, being called what it's used for—the Queen Majesty's Storehouse. Close by those walls and gathered close around the marketplace, with its market cross and the parish church, are the thatch-roofed, whitewashed huts of the few fishermen and farmers (both together acting as pirates whenever occasion allows) who live on the island. At the south end, hunched upon the high, conical crag there, so as to guard the entrance to the harbor, stands the small round fort called Lindisfarne Castle. Said to be, and looking so, in good repair and garrisoned.

Once, not many years ago, the Earl of Bothwell was taken and kept captive there for a time. Pity he's not still captive there. Or in some stronger place. To this day . . .

He will rejoin the North Road at the village of Beal, a clot of huts made of sticks and turf, belonging to beekeepers. Meeting the road to the accompanying music of summer bees and the wild calling of seabirds, he will turn and spur south. Will be riding at a gallop whenever he can, though mostly at amble or hard trot, depending on the state of the road and how the horse he is riding has been trained and ridden before. Will ride as long as he safely dares to by daylight and moonlight, glad that the days are longest now and that the moon is close to full. Grateful that, here in the north at least, there is usually light enough to play at cards or dice all the night long without even a candle at this time of year.

He will trade spent horses for fresh ones at the innyards in villages and towns every dozen miles or so. Leaving the horse behind for a stableboy from the last inn to come and collect. Allowing a boy from this inn to fall in with him, soon far behind him (as the messenger will be soon gone, fled like a sunbeam) to eat his dust on the next leg of the journey.

At each of these places stopping only long enough to change horses, he will peel himself, sore and stiff-jointed from the saddle, swinging down to stand on earth again with the whole length of his legs feeling as if strung with loose-knotted ropes of pain. Will gulp down a cup of ale or beer. Or will have to kneel to drink at a horse trough with his hands. To eat he'll have bits and pieces of dried fruit and salt fish he's brought from Norham.

Always paying out coins for a good post-horse and for the stableboy, too, to follow and bring the horse back home. Always paying something a little too much, a penny or two more here and there, than the lawful rates. For he has neither the livery nor license of a royal post rider. And because there is no time, either, to be lost in haggling. So paying whatever he has to and then mounting up, all in a few breathless moments. Testing first of all the feel of saddle and stirrups and reins. Being very careful, gentle and easy; for a fall now or anytime could be the end of his journey. Seeking to learn something, all that he can, of the spirit and habits of each new horse before using switch and spurs.

And sometimes—heaven knows where—snatching at a brief, groaning, dream-flickering sleep, when he has to and there's no choice, in the soft prickly straw of a stable.

Sometimes he'll be slowed to a walk by a flash of rain and a muddy stretch of road. Forced to pick and thread his way through groups of other riders. Strings of donkeys and pack-horses and shepherds (for this is the month for it) prodding flocks of sheep to the places of shearing and washing. And from there broggers laden with the new wool. Herds of cattle and pigs and sometimes chickens or ducks or even a lazy noisy cloud of geese being driven along to the next market town. And here in the north, where the workhorses and even the oxen for pulling and hauling are fewer than elsewhere, there will be gangs of the packmen that they call badgers, moving on foot and burdened like beasts. And at the last, when he is finally nearing London, he can expect to encounter more of all of these things as well as having to contend with a traffic of heavy, two-wheeled carts crowding and rutting the roadway. Some of these so large and so loaded down with goods of every kind (and passengers) that they need six or more stout horses to pull them.

Yet, for all of this and more often than not he will follow only the flowing space of an empty, open road. . . .

Begins here with windy sea nearly to the east. Though soon enough out of sight except from high places. Still, for a good while, feeling of sea breeze and a taste of cold salt in the air. Westward the wide moors climbing bleakly away toward hills and low mountains, though broken by dales, like ribbons of rich green, along the banks of the rivers uncoiling toward the coast. Any trees will catch his eye here in the north where wood is now often so scant that the poor must burn turf and furze and ling, sometimes only cow dung, for their warmth and cooking. Even the sea coal that is dug here is shipped off to be sold in the south. Or, if kept, it must be saved for the forge, brewhouse, and bakehouse.

From that place where he is riding between sea and moors, the road begins to work gradually inland. Running between moors to the east now and the western shapes of mountains. Next entering the country of fenland, marsh, and wold. The road itself, as if in flattering imitation, beginning to wind and unwind like the slow rivers among reedy, marshy places. Space of willows and poplars, of wide stands of reeds and bullrushes. Home for the heron and the kingfisher who looks, in his flight all flash and dart, as if he were made from scraps of rainbow. And then at last arriving in a place of rich farmland and of rolling green sheep pasture. With standing forests, coppice with standards, of huge ancient oaks, and of ash and elm, the earth beneath these like a woven turkey carpet of wild flowers. Or tall, straight, smoke-colored beech trees, whose high canopies of luminous leaves convert the sunlight to cathedral tones. With calm, lazy streams, sweet to drink and best for malting. There the road will sometimes be marked by hedges of sloe and hawthorn, or buckthorn or of blackberry. Whitely flowering now. And whiteness, too, from privet and birdcherry and the guelder rose. And whitest of all, or so it seems, the new blooming among the gloss of the holly leaves. There, too, the road will be shaded, for stretches, by lines of trees. And he will go riding in a rush among the flashing shadows of sunstruck leaves. Air will be sweeter and warmer there. Sky will be blue and clear and the sun bright. It will be like coming suddenly, as if stumbling by chance, into a summer garden. Bold with blossoming pinks of every name and kind. Sprinkled with proud congregations of gold-crowned marigolds. Burning alive, and away, with a wild extravagance of red and white roses. Ah, then the summer air of England will be to him like the taste of a distilled cordial. A cordial compounded of the perfume of many flowers, then sweetened with the aroma of the thickly flowering honeysuckle.

Wild oakwood strawberries will be swelling and ripening, sweet and fat among ground leaves. Apples will be tight little fists of green. Cherry and fig trees will be heavy with full fruit.

By then he will have come a far way, farther than the hours spent and more than the sum of measured miles, from the bare rough spaces of the north, that stony country of walls and cold castles and stark pele towers and bastel houses. That rough country where all things, even the folk who live there, look to have been whittled out of reluctant hardwood or else chipped and carved from stone. By then, burned by sun and rinsed by the sudden showers, he will have become a curious creature made of dust and mud and covered with both as if painted and daubed from the ends of his beard and his eyebrows to his boots. His feet will be swollen and cramped as if nailed to his bootsoles. Body, sore and saddle-weary, will be tightstrung with an intricate net of aches and pains. In that haze of pure weariness, swaying and clinging high on the horse (which will by now be no ordinary post-horse but will have become a powerful composite mythical beast made out of all the horses he has ridden in a lifetime), following the lunging road, he will begin to feel the light and shadow blending within him. Will sense himself changing, becoming something other, more than weary flesh and bones. It will be as if he were poured water. As if he were water flowing from spring or well into one of these quiet, easy rivers, and that river slowly moving on, settling gently, falling into a dream of the dark shores of everlasting sleep. . . .

So also will common sounds all around him begin to blend and in a free counterpoint set upon and above the steady drumming of the hooves. Hooves pounding the road, ringing on the stone streets of the towns, making a brief echoing *basso* on the bridges. Breeze will rise and fall as if the earth itself, breathing deeply, were sprawled asleep in the sun.

Birdsongs falling around him like raindrops.

True, his whole day could be clocked and measured by birds. From the mist of dew-heavy dawn, announced, even before cock has shivered and stirred to bugle the sun, by the long, clear, liquid exaltation of a rising lark. Through noon and the noontime calling of a solitary cuckoo, hidden in the fringe of the woods just beyond a sunny field of grain, past twilight, and the time of the hunting owl, and on into the rich, late, starlit, spilled music of the furtive nightingale.

Always the birdsongs. And rushing and rustling of many wings. Crowing of cocks and the cluck-cluck-clucking of the hens. Cooing and whistling soft chorus from each village's tall dovecote.

And there, silent and perfect, like a formal solemn dancing to music just beyond hearing, the hungering fury of a wide-winged hawk (perhaps it is some hunter's trained bird) soaring along the smooth tides of the wind.

Sometimes the belling of a pack of hounds. Dogs running to the sharp, polished notes of a hunting horn.

Rattling sigh of windmills. Slow creak and flash of waterwheels turning.

And always, near and far, birds and the sound of bells tolling and ringing to each other in the towns and villages. Bells in every tone of voice, from cockcrow day bell at first light until evening curfew and, even after that, to the solemn tolling of midnight. Bells sending out their signals and telling their stories in ancient sequences of voices and numbers. With every shire, often each single village, keeping its own customs, having its own language of bells. To announce birth and death. To call to prayer and communion, baptism and burial, and the marriage feast.

Only the priest bells have fallen silent (again) in England now. And yet sometimes still in the north country they, too, will ring as they always have, as they did long ago.

Barking of the chained dogs in the villages. In towns the crying out of street vendors. From open windows floating the clear voices of children singing or reciting lessons together.

And work being done—song of the wood saw, the hammer and chisel of the stonemason, clatters of the cart maker (for now is the season for mending of carts) and the sound of the blacksmith, somewhere not far away, pounding clean slow tunes on his anvil.

All of these sounds together and so many others, becoming as if parts of one music, single and continuous. Seeming to be remembered. As if each were an echo even at the first moment of hearing it. Happening to him, then, like the wedding of light and shadow within. Someway akin to the dreams and wishes of water as the rills and becks and streams flow together to turn into rivers, and then these rivers meet and join together, mingling as if in marriage, in a lust to seek the sea and to vanish there.

Surely, too, there will be voices singing the English psalms, heard from the church. Perhaps male voices singing above the soft sound of lute or cithern, coming from the lit open windows of a tavern at evening. Fiddle, whistle, and tin drum from the alehouse and marketplace. Proud and elegiac lament of the

Northumbrian pipes. The shrill mysterious whistling of the Lincolnshire fenman. Who will be cutting reeds for thatch and rushes for the strewing of floors. Who will be walking on stilts to herd their geese. Or will ease along through the reeds in the little marsh boats they named skerries, calling the cows to come home. And well before the restless clamor of London rises up to drown out everything else and finally even the memory of it, he'll hear and rejoice in the wordless song (like an echo of the busywork of summer bees) of a man with a scythe in a Hertfordshire meadow, sharpening and sharpening the edge of his blade while all around him a cloud of yellow butterflies is flashing. Like the resurrection of the ghosts of April's daffodils. . . .

SECRETARY

1603

Wisdom for a man's self is, in many branches thereof, a depraved thing. It is the wisdom of rats, that will be sure to leave a house somewhat before it fall.

FRANCIS BACON—"Of Wisdom for a Man's Self"

I am the rose of the field and the lily of the valleys. Like a lily among thorns, so is my love among the daughters. . . .

Words in his mind. Best not to think on them. The text, from Solomon's most excellent song, the mere least fleeting thought of it will distract him. In a moment, if he allowed that, these words would breed others like them and clothe themselves like dancers in his memory. And he will be (again) sorely wounded, struck dumb with loss and sorrow. Liable (since he is alone, no one to see) to weep.

Which must not be. No, he must now keep mind and eye, even heart and soul, fixed upon the question.

✶ ✶ ✶ ✶ ✶

There is only this one overwhelming question.

Who is it who shall (lawfully) succeed the Queen?

It is (paradox, if you please) a question that must be answered, but one that may not be asked. At least aloud.

Who next will wear the crown?

Simple enough question. It's the hidden answer that is knotted with complexity. It is doubtful and no doubt dangerous.

There are eight or nine serious claimants to her crown, and all but two of them are here in England. Where, at least, they can be closely watched.

But this is no new question. The Succession has been a deadly serious matter since long before he was born, yet another continual burden for his father during the more than forty years of service to the Queen. Was first treated by her first Parliament in the first year of her reign. And was first silenced then and there by the Queen. Yet, forbidden or not, the question has vexed this kingdom ever since. Even the beginning of her reign cannot be claimed as the beginning. Surely it must have begun before she was born. When everyone had been so desperately certain that a son would be born to King Henry and his new wife—Anne Boleyn. So certain that everything, from the proclamations to the cradle for the infant, had been prepared for a prince.

A late Sunday afternoon in September of '33. Lazy end of the summer at Greenwich. And the King is called to the chambers of his Queen to view . . . a daughter.

"Well," the King said, with as much gallantry as he could manage, "she shall have brothers."

And from that moment the whole scheme of the Succession became a matter for weighty speculation. Became a matter of more urgent concern upon that later day in early November, the sixth day of November in the year of 1558, to be precise. . . .

He believes in the value, almost magical, of simple accuracy. Precision wherever possible. Not, mind you, that he is such a pedant of what can be measured or numbered that he's unwilling to speculate beyond known limits. No, he's more than willing to gamble whenever he feels he has to. Which is much more often than those who believe they know him best may imagine. Indeed gambling, on large and small things, has become, gradually, an obsessive vice with him. But now, in this matter of Succession he must hazard hugely. Must make the greatest wager of his life. In a real sense it is a wager with his life.

This is Sir Robert Cecil. Principal Secretary to the Queen and Council, Chancellor of the Duchy of Lancaster, and Master of the Court of Requests. Second son to the late William Cecil, Lord Burghley, Lord Treasurer of England.

He is forty years old but looks older. He is a tiny man, not much larger than the Queen's dwarf. He is frail and, due to some childhood accident or sickness, somewhat misshapen. He walks with some difficulty. He has sad eyes and the fine nose and features of his father. His hair has been gray for some years now, ever since (they say) the death of his young wife in '96.

Set me as a seal on thine heart and as a signet upon thine arm: for love is strong as death. . . .

Elizabeth Brooke, the daughter of Lord Cobham. She whom he deeply loved. More wonderful (and never mind the laughter of the rude world nor the scorn of even her own kinfolk), she who loved him and greatly pleased him. For a few years, in the mystical number of seven like unto Joseph's best years in Egypt, they were contented together. She gave him children—William, son and heir, and the two daughters Catherine and Frances. Left him with three small children to love and to cherish when she died. Left him lonely in a world without sweetness. A bitter place, then, where the salt has lost its savor.

My sister my spouse is as a garden enclosed, as a spring shut up, and a fountain sealed up. . . .

He is said by enemies to be ruthless and untrustworthy. He is described as a reckless gambler and as an inveterate and insatiable lecher.

He is thought by friends (few) to be too much subject to melancholy.

He is known by all who profess to know him as an indefatigable worker in behalf of the state and for the Queen.

Perhaps wisely, he has never courted popularity. (Just as well, they'll tell you, for the Queen does not favor popular servants.) He is, in truth, extremely unpopular these days. Taken by the many who do not know much—but who are not discouraged from this misapprehension by some who know better—to be a bad servant and a greedy Councilor. Nothing at all like his wise father who, safely dead, is now loved and honored more and more. And in a time of war when swordsmen are precious, what's the use of a little clerk, only a scribe of other men's deeds? Yet he is believed to be exceptionally influential with the Queen. Outside of her nearest kinfolk, there is no one nearer. She values his advice too much. Especially since the fall of Essex. It was (as they believe) exactly against Cecil's wicked counsel that Essex was forced to rise up in righteous rebellion. Since which sad time much has been said and even more whispered against Cecil. Some of which has found its way into scurrilous print. Even into popular song. There are tavern ballads, cruel satirical things to mock him and his wicked friends:

Little Cecil trips up & down
He rules both Court & Crown

He owns, by inheritance from his frugal father, one of the most magnificent palaces made in all of this age of prodigious building—the house called Theobalds. His elder half brother, Thomas, and Lord Burghley, inherited the seat at Stamford Baron together with the lands and estates. And rightfully took possession of old Burghley House on the Strand. But Robert Cecil has nevertheless newly built a mansion of brick and timber on the other side of the Strand, the river side, just west of Russell House and close by Ivy Bridge. It is called Cecil House and is enviably grand. He has leveled and cobbled the Strand around it to make it smoother for coaches (which are all the fashion now) in their busy comings and goings. And recently he has been honored by the Queen. Who, since she could not attend the warming of the house in November, on account of cold and foul weather, came instead to dine there on the sixth of this December past. Came with many of her ladies and gentlemen. Came with her drums and eight trumpeters. There were gifts for her and for her people. Plays and dialogues. And she insisted on inspecting the house. Calling for a staff to use to mount the stairs. Remarking with admiration at the collection of new and ancient weapons in the Hall. Leaving in the fading light of late afternoon, she was cheered by a huge crowd in the street.

Yet even with the income and the privileges arising from his many offices and perquisites and monopolies, he still lacks ready money. Worse, he lacks both means and prospects for increasing either income or assets. Land is the only true wealth, and he has precious little. Unless he shall find himself raised to new offices or shall receive grants and gifts or whatever. . . . The acquisition of the forfeited properties of traitors is always a possibility. But first there must be treasons hatched and discovered. Then a traitor, or, better, several, must be tried and convicted. And next the Queen (or whoever it is who shall come to succeed her) must desire to reward Sir Robert Cecil with some of the prizes.

Prizes. . . . He is also a partner of the Captain of the Guard, his seafaring friend, Sir Walter Ralegh, in some secret matters of privateering. Where the risks are very great, but, with a flash of good fortune, the rewards may be enormous. Fortunes have been made from shareholds in a single cargo. Always a gamble, however, and one of the most anxious kind. For he must give his money into the hands of strangers over whom he has neither command nor control. And these, these independent, largely indifferent strangers, are themselves utterly at the mercy of winds, tides, and weather. Assuming that they do take a valuable prize and bring it safely into port, then they are apt to steal the best part of it without anyone being wiser. He is, after all and on behalf of the Queen, still searching for some of the fortune in gold and jewels which vanished from the great carrack *Madre de Díos*, taken in '92.

Meantime he can continue to borrow from rich merchants, the goldsmiths of London. At the highest rates of interest.

At present Sir Robert Cecil is heavily in debt.

If his hair had not already turned to gray, it would surely do so now.

Now, if the Queen should die and if her Successor, as is to be expected, should remove Cecil from offices and appointments to be replaced by one of his (or her) own men, someone among the many whom the new monarch must reward, then in short order, Cecil will be a ruined man. And even if he should somehow stave off bankruptcy, he will not long be able to continue to maintain his style of living.

Any new monarch is bound to have a multitude of servants or suitors to reward and enemies whose loyalty must be purchased. Any new monarch in England is going to be more than a little disappointed. For, on account of the long and expensive wars in Ireland, the Netherlands, in France, and everywhere against Spain, the Queen's treasury is much more depleted than is well known. She has been forced to sell off crown lands, offices, even (lately) her jewels and plate.

Her close advisers will have to explain this, indeed answer for it, to the Successor.

Cecil must therefore gamble everything upon the Succession. Must not only support the rightful Successor, but also must seem to select him. And must do so in such a way that it will be clear to the Successor that he is beholden to Cecil for it. Yet not so greatly obliged as to feel threatened by obligation.

There is, in all honesty, more to the gamble than that. Truth is, the whole kingdom is now at hazard. It is possible that the death of the Queen could be (*may very well be*) followed by a civil war to settle the Succession. Like the long bloody Wars of the Roses. Which, though they ended more than a century ago, are much on everyone's minds these days. Whose ruins, in spite of so much change, are still plainly evident in many places. And there is the near and new example of France. When the last Valois, King Henry III, was murdered in '89, it took six full years of bloody wars and the deaths of many thousands before the rightful heir, Henry of Navarre, could overcome the other claimants. It likewise was required that the King, whom the English had so long supported, must change his religion and return to the Catholic Church before he could be crowned as Henry IV.

Which has given much comfort and some inspiration to Papists everywhere. Especially here in England.

How shall the matter of religion be settled next? No one knows how many secret Papists, or indeed ordinary Englishmen who are simply weary of confusion and disputation and who long for a return to old and settled ways, there may be. The Successor to this Queen may be the first to know their true number. Perhaps upon a field of battle.

It is Cecil's duty and employment, then, as leader of the Privy Council to work for a peaceful, lawful Succession.

As for peace, the world knows that the war with Spain must somehow be settled. Even now in Ireland there are as many dangers from Spain as from the rebels. There looks to be no end of it. Except that precisely because that is so, and known to all sides, an end must now be reached. Not possible, however (or so it seems), while the old Queen reigns. And with the kingdom so long at war and crawling with a whole generation of bitter veteran soldiers, it seems likely that the Succession will be attended by . . . well, at least commotion, if not rebellion. That must be anticipated, must be prepared for.

Lawful?

Ah, well now. Many vexing questions of Law concern the rights of each claimant. Case can be made for and against any of them. As ever. Was not even the Lady Jane Grey a lawful Queen? In the sense that Edward VI named her as heir and Successor. She endured nine days before becoming a prisoner of Mary Tudor, who was fortunate to have force, as well as sound arguments, on her side.

And Elizabeth?

Speak this more softly than any whisper, and say it only to the face looking out of your glass.

Though she was truly named by Queen Mary (with certain provisions which were not acknowledged or honored for long), there was a strong case against her from the beginning. Did not Mary Queen of Scots, then in fact the Queen of France also, have a good claim? Didn't she quarter the arms of England with her own and style herself as Queen of England also? (Thus the War of the Insignia.) She had (say it) a lawful claim and lacked only power to make her arguments fully credible. When Elizabeth's first Parliament assembled in January of '59, it was necessary at once to pass a statute establishing Elizabeth as "rightly, lineally, and lawfully descended from the blood royal." It was also necessary to declare as void any act of earlier Parliaments which might seem to contradict this.

The Succession, after almost a half century, is even more obscure and doubtful now. Cases of Law seem likely to be made, commotions and civil broil to occur. This even if the Queen, following the examples of her sister and her brother, should openly name her Successor.

Which seems not likely. For the most she has said (sticking to it from first to now) is this: "So long as I live I shall be Queen of England. And when I am dead, they shall succeed that have the most right."

So long as she shall live. Well, sir, never mind that all through this past summer, and especially during Christmastide, the Queen has seemed to be almost restored in health. Rejuvenated. Surely stronger and healthier than in at least a dozen years. Never mind that. Never mind that her physicians have privately allowed that she has the vitality to live at least another ten years provided she is not troubled by any sudden illness. The time must come soon. No, can come soon. At any time. Any sort of indisposition, a sudden chill, an attack of indigestion, even (at her age) the impact of some surprising piece of bad news, anything could carry her away.

It is easy enough for him to think about. Easy to consider. Beyond that, though, he can do next to nothing. Whatever is done now must be done in the safety of shadows.

We must also and always be very, very careful what we say about the question. And to whom we say it.

Thus the Succession has been a matter of gravest concern ever since it was, in fact, settled upon her by Mary on that mentioned sixth day of November in '58. In that first week of November Queen Mary, who had been ill since midsummer, showed some signs of improvement. Fever left her. Pains eased. It seemed possible (briefly, briefly) that she might get well. It was then that Council came to her and persuaded her that, for the sake of domestic tranquillity and good order, she should name Elizabeth as heir.

Reluctantly, she did so.

Fortnight later, on the morning of the seventeenth, after a relapse and after (they tell) waking from fever dreams, strange visions of many happy children playing and singing for her pleasure, the sadly childless Queen was dead.

Long live the Queen!

No one imagining that this young woman, the new Queen, would then reign longer than anyone in all her family.

Lords of the Council rode out into Hertfordshire to carry the news to Old Hatfield Palace, where Elizabeth had lived much of her youth. Where they came upon the Lady Elizabeth, slender and handsome, walking together with some of her servants among the fallen oak leaves of the park. All of them so modestly, soberly dressed.

Hailed her as their new Queen. And as they doffed their hats and knelt, as her servants and ladies also knelt, she herself kneeled down to thank Almighty God. Tossed aside for posterity her fine embroidered gloves and clasped long-fingered, delicate hands together in an attitude of prayer. Cried out clearly a verse from the one hundred and eighteenth psalm—"*A domino factum est et mirabile in oculis nostris.*"

("This is the Lord's doing, and it is marvellous in our eyes. . . .")

Robert Cecil can smile now, a half century after, at this outrageous, memorable piece of theater. The Queen was ever a player. From her childhood. Is every bit as much the player now as she was then.

When the Lords looked to that psalm for other signs of her intentions, there were verses there to make them (at the least, these being Mary's Councilors) uneasy:

"They kept me in on every side, they kept me in, I say, on every side; but in the Name of the Lord will I destroy them.

"They came about me like bees, and are extinct even as the fire among the thorns; for in the Name of the Lord I will destroy them."

His father used to tell this story with a sober reverence. Sir Robert Cecil, no less impressed but of a newer, harder generation, grins at the shrewdness of it. Shrewdness together with a skilled player's sense of the mood and expectations of an audience. These have not deserted her, these qualities which, in her youth, must have saved her from much woe by denying access to her hidden thoughts, her inmost feelings.

And because it has now become so pertinent he cannot fail to recall another story often told him by his father. How when Sir James Melville, the Scotsman sent here to bring news of the birth of James, son of Mary, Queen of Scots, came to Greenwich Palace on a late June evening of '66 he was ushered into the Presence Chamber by Sir William Cecil. Everyone was dancing there. The Queen stopped the dance to greet him and asked him what news. Melville told her. She reacted as if shaken. Sat down in a chair. Faced the silence and stillness in the room. Then said in a loud clear voice—"The Queen of Scots is mother of a fair son. And I—I am of barren stock!" A moment later she signaled for the music to begin again. Took Melville, smiling, by the hand and led him to begin the dancing. Melville had no idea what to make of it. Could not determine which part of her mood, if either, were true. Neither could Robert Cecil's father. Who had carefully and privately told her the news—and to no discernible reaction of emotion at all—a full day before that.

In the fall of that same year, the Parliament pressed her hard, against her wishes, to marry or at least to name a Successor. So she summoned a delegation to hear her and left little doubt in their minds. There was nothing obscure about her style or sentences:

"Was I not born in the realm? Were my parents born in any foreign country? Is there any cause why I should alienate myself from being careful over this country? Is not my kingdom here?

Whom have I oppressed? Whom have I enriched to other's harm? What turmoil have I made in this Commonwealth that I should be suspected to have no regard to the same? How have I governed since my reign? I will be tried by envy itself. I need not to use many words, for my deeds to try me . . . !"

She would marry and have children ("otherwise I would never marry") "as soon as I can conveniently." As for the Succession:

"A strange thing that the foot should direct the head in so weighty a cause. Which cause has been so diligently weighed by us, for it touches us more than them. I am sure there was not one of them that ever was a second person, as I have been, and have tasted of the practices against my sister—who I would to God were alive again. . . . There were occasions at that time when I stood in danger of my life, my sister was so incensed against me."

She told them that she had consulted many learned men of the Law, who could not agree or answer the question. Clearly there was no agreement in Parliament. To name her Successor would only be the cause of great trouble. To permit the Parliament to debate the matter would be even more perplexing. "There be so many competitors," she said. "Some are kinfolk, some servants, and some tenants. Some would speak for their master and some for their mistress and every man for his friend.

"As for my own part, I care not for death. For all men are mortal. And though I be a woman, yet I have as good a courage, answerable to my place, as ever my father had. I am your anointed Queen. I will never by violence be constrained to do anything. I thank God I am endowed with such qualities that if I were turned out of the realm in my petticoat, I were able to live in any place in Christendom."

* * * * *

When she was saying these words to a kneeling delegation from Parliament (his father kneeling before her with them), Robert Cecil was still in the nursery, only three years old. Was he happy then, that child, content with love and care and his toys, who could not know yet that he would always be frail and crippled and small? For are not all little children frail and crippled and small measured against a world of loud tall giants and the huge things made for only them to use and enjoy?

Learned and knew well, then, how to endure, to prosper, to thrive and bloom amid that tall world of others. Armored and nurtured by love and care, he learned, though never imagining that these were the same skills he would have to live by for as long as he might live. Child never imagines for himself anything other than one day growing up to be like all of these tall and sturdy others. Himself being bound, by some natural law of changing and becoming, to be like his loud, proud, swaggering, much older half brother, Thomas, whose boots are hooves on the stairways (*was he ever small?*), whose laughter sounds as if someone were playing it through a brass horn. Child, though eager for transformation, urgently, anxiously eager to change, ceasing to be a small, sly gnarled self, unlike even other children (as all children are unlike each other), to become at last not lonely, but only another, one more among all these others. Praying—for he knew, like any child, what prayer was even before he was properly taught by heart to whom to pray and how—to leave himself behind. To lose childhood like a cast-away cloak. To shed childhood like a skin. In order to be . . . well, something else. Something altogether different. Yet, even as he wished and prayed, he was also profoundly afraid of that difference. Not merely afraid for not being able to imagine how it might feel. But, more frightening, not knowing how to endure within his next new shape and form. Not knowing how well he might perform in his next life, prisoned (like Thomas) in loud, proud, strutting, laughing manhood.

Paradox being that his fear like his opposing wish was mostly wasted. He would never be able to cast aside the frail deformed child of himself as others would and did. But rather (thus rarely gifted) he would be permitted to keep the child, alive, with him always. His weakness becoming a strength. For these fortunate, tall and sturdy others have dismissed the child that they were, having (they truly believe) no more need for him now. Therefore Cecil becomes a match for any of them. No, more than that. Truth is, none of them is any match for him. For, though seeming weak and hindered, in body at least (which is much, much!), he has at his service all the power, cunning, secrecy, and innocent ruthlessness of a child.

So, at the moment he chooses to remember, he was three years

old. May be that autumn they were at the house in Wimbledon.
Though with his father so busy with the Parliament and all the
other affairs of the state, it seems to him they would all have
been kept away at Stamford. Blustery and chilly November
weather in either place. Fine to be indoors. With a warm fire.
With toys—his soldiers; his ship; an old wooden doll, dressed as a
crusader knight in crude armor, that he loved. With his thoughts
for his closest, most trusted company.

Not that he could not have imagined himself as he is here and
now, close to a half century later—well, forty years almost, to be
exact; though it often seems to him a century and a half, no less.
It had been no trick to picture himself at the heart of the business of government just as his father was. Though not looking
like his father. Of course not. Nor really much like Thomas either. No, if he saw himself grown, it would be as a large, full-
sized version of his wooden knight. Mere child in nursery, how
could he imagine anything like that? Like every child in nursery
since Cain and Abel, he did so easily. That child would not be
surprised at what he is now. That was what the child expected.
Paradox being that the child would be astounded only to discover that almost a half a century later a grown man would want
to look back, as if over his shoulder, and seek to rediscover himself. Look back to see a little boy playing with toy ship and toy
soldiers (his wooden knight as huge as the Cyclops alongside
these other creatures) close by a fire, a slant of November sunlight from the window lighting his own pale, pinched face. . . .

The child looks up from play to see a small deformed man, at
first a stranger, staring at him wistfully, his hazel eyes light-
riddled, his high-arched eyebrows forever questioning or . . .
supercilious. It might make the child sad to know how the man
loves and fears him, hopes for him, wishes him well. If so, the
child, at three years old, is already much too sly to show it.
Instead he makes a face. He sneers at the grown man he will
become and turns back to his game. . . .

* * * * *

And if the child is to be left there, content in the immemorial
nursery, then what of the man?

Where will the man be now while he ponders on these things?

He will be where he must be while the Queen reigns. He will be wherever the Queen may be, where the Court is in attendance.

Her diminished Court.

So few of the renowned elders remain. Most of those celebrated courtiers and councilors have gone from the light. Most (he thinks) have gone into the silent dark and, as Scripture promises, left not even the shadow of memory behind.

"All these were honorable men in their generations and were well reported of in their times." (*So it is written.*) "There are some of them that have left a name behind them so that their praise shall be spoken of. There are also some which have no memorial and are perished as though they had never been. And are become as though they never had been born, and likewise their children after them. . . ."

Of their children, the young and bright and brave there are few, always fewer. Too many, and among them many of the finest, proved to be disloyal. Essex dead. His motley band broken and scattered. And of the others, all but a few, they are away at the wars or rapt in their private adventures. These latter not looking for what may not be found at Court anymore. And so it is, you see, that, like it or not, Court and Council belong to Cecil. True, he has enemies aplenty even here. But he has no more worthy rivals. So he rules while she lives.

Though he was always threatened while Essex lived, still he was freer then. With no deadly rival he is collared and leashed to the Queen more tightly than ever before. Because of her age and frailty he can never allow himself to be too far from her. If he were not on hand and she should fail; if she were to die while he was elsewhere; it does not bear contemplation. . . . In the old days (oh, not so long ago) anyone with ambition feared to be absent from Court. Never mind banishment, which was and is a kind of death. Any errand or mission could lose a man both place and reputation. Nevertheless his father could be about his business efficiently in his Westminster offices while Queen and Court were as near as Greenwich, say, or Richmond or Nonsuch or Windsor Castle or Hampton Court. It was not necessary for Burghley to follow her in the summer Progress.

Robert Cecil lacks that liberty. And he can imagine how, in

spite of all precaution, he might arrive at Court to find the gates locked against him. By others. Which others? Ah, in the absence of known enemies he cannot imagine who they might be. Might be anyone.

And he can picture himself at home in Cecil House being suddenly waked by loud knocking and louder shouting. Dragged away by torchlight to the curses and jeers of strangers. When you are made to be a clerk only, forever, never a swordsman, then your only weapon is knowledge. You can never afford the luxury of indifferent ignorance. You must work without ceasing so as not to be ignorant of anything that can be known.

To know you must be near.

And he needs to be close to the Queen for more simple, practical reasons. Now she is often preoccupied, even forgetful, and he must be able to catch and to hold her attention to the business of the kingdom. Whenever she is able to render her full attention. With the Queen (he remembers his father, too, slipping into the shadows of a failing memory) there are times which are better than others. He must be there at her best times. Likewise he must be there whenever she may feel the need of his presence. Which is more often these days than ever before.

And he can be safe, truly safe from her scrutiny, only when it is late at night and she is sound asleep.

He must be always wide awake.

Not so long ago, on an autumn afternoon in the park here at Richmond, they were riding together in her coach. Gilt wheels rolling across a carpet of red and gold leaves. Oh, she is still a brisk walker in the early mornings, warm or cold, gallery in rain and garden in sunshine. But often in the afternoons she will call for her coach to sit and enjoy the view and the weather. And to talk and to listen. Sometimes to do a little business if there's any.

He had papers with him that afternoon. And for a while they were busy. But the air was warm with the rich ruins of autumn in it. So soon she nodded. Dozed a little while the coach rolled on. Abruptly came a hard, clear sound. Harsh bugling of a royal post rider's horn. And she jerked awake. Blinked and smiled and called for the coach to stop and for the rider to approach. Rider dismounted and knelt.

"Where do you come from?" she asked.

"Scotland, ma'am," the rider said.

Cecil, heart sinking or rising, like a child's toy on a string, quickly stepped out of the coach.

"Yes, Elf, by all means," she told him. "I want to see the latest news from there."

Knew she would say that. As if on an impulse to please her, he had almost leaped out of the coach to approach the rider kneeling at his decent, respectful distance. One of the guards, who walk near the coach, could have easily brought the leather dispatch box to her. So, Cecil moved first. The guard stepping back, making way for him. Less courtly than it might seem. For Cecil had every reason to fear that in that box from Scotland would be at least one letter for him. One which she should not (then or ever) see. A letter from the King of Scotland to the Queen's Secretary dealing with . . . unauthorized matters.

Opened the case and, oh my God in heaven!, there it was. Royal seal and all, addressed to him.

"What news from Scotland?" she called. "Bring me the box."

Bent over the open box, his legs weaker than ever, his stomach a-churning as if he had swallowed a dose of physic, he was suddenly struck by pure (oh, thank God!) inspiration. Her fastidious sense of smell. . . .

"Oh, Madame," he said, turning to her, holding his nose. "'Tis a very foul-smelling packet. It must be the leather of the case. Allow me to sort and air out these letters before you handle them. It appears there is nothing urgent here."

Not the least flicker of suspicion as she nods agreement. Distaste, perhaps, that a royal dispatch case, one of hers with her royal arms embossed upon it, would stink. Nothing more.

Well (with an inward sigh), something to tell his children one day. Perhaps something to tell James of Scotland, too. How once upon an autumn afternoon the Queen almost intercepted one of their private letters. How by a wild inspiration he was able to prevent that from happening. Yes, something to tell King James. If and when they ever meet.

He has come here to be with Queen and Court at Richmond. To which she has returned early this year from Christmastide at Westminster, acting upon the impulse of extraordinary weather. For in early January there came a kind of springtime. False or true, it seemed bright enough to believe in. Of a sudden the air turned warm as fresh milk in a pail. Ragged clouds of December ran away across the sky in full retreat. Driven by trumpets of the sun. Sprouts began to crack and crumble the earth. Already there were the first few gold-helmeted scouts for coming swarms of dandelions and coltsfoot. Primroses waving gently like lazy yellow gloves. Pink and white anemones turning with the turning breeze. Kingcup close by the riverbank, flaunting its burnished gold.

No one could recall a January season like it.

Already it seemed safe to think forward. Toward such soon flourishings as the crowds of bluebells bent and hooded like monks at prayer. Daffodils, each of them a chalice made to hold sunlight. Time to imagine the subtle perfume (soon, soon) of the violet. Time to dream the almond trees in blooming pink, the peach with its careless extravagance of white and pink and crimson.

Where they had been picked to the bone, the trees began to grow graceful again, ever so lightly glossed with new buds.

But near to the end of January that dream of an earliest springtime disappeared. Change back to winter came suddenly. On the twenty-first day of the month. Precisely the day when Queen and Court left Whitehall for Richmond. Her Maids of Honor, in a little group close by her, were dressed all in white. And the Queen was clad lightly as for a summer's day. And so came all the Court (Cecil himself also) following the Queen's example, affecting their best springtime clothing. Gentlemen Pensioners and Yeoman of the Guard marched, their ceremonial gilt halberds glittering. One and all moving toward the river to the rhythm of drums and to the fanfares of trumpets. Bells ringing in Westminster and over the river at Lambeth, too.

She boarded the painted royal barge at Whitehall stairs. Twenty oars dipped and flashed wet as the oarsmen pulled to midstream. Soon behind came the bobbing fleet of smaller barges, of tilt boats and wherries and hoys carrying the Court. Crowds of people lined the banks. And most of the boats of London and Southwark had come upriver to watch this.

Queen and her Maids stood openly for all to see. More bells from both banks. Hats off and cheers from boats all around.

Somewhere—perhaps from an anchored ship—someone fired a small cannon in salute.

Standing directly next to the Queen was the old Lord Admiral. Hat in hand, beard and white hair blowing, he grumbled disapproval of summer clothing in January. She laughed at that, but he was proved tediously correct when, in a quarter of an hour, the weather turned. Wind sprang up out of the northeast. River roughened into smart chops and slaps. And the false spring ended then and there as cold rain began to fall. Soon the sky rained everything but potatoes on them. Even under the canopy of the barge the Queen and the Maids and Lord Admiral were soaking wet. And all the others, those on the many boats and barges in the needling rain, were limply shivering. The Queen refused to gratify Lord Admiral Howard by displaying any sign of discomfort. But the crowds on the riverbanks and on the river prudently vanished. Spires and rooftops dwindled in the haze of the rain. Veiled by it, many of the Court dropped back. Turned away, planning to follow later. By land if the foul weather lingered. Wagering that though she could not help observing how the rain had shrunk the size of the Court, she would not notice particular absences.

The others—who could not make that choice or did not dare to —gritting teeth into a semblance of smiling, followed her, blinded by rain, rolling on the wind-whipped water. All of them thinking that soon enough they would have deep coughs and runny noses, most likely the flux also, to prove their loyalty.

Not so the Queen. She has had some chills, but she is well, if somewhat weary. And now that she is safe in Richmond, her warmest palace, all the things that can be done for her comfort and well-being are being done.

There are those who believe she will live forever. Or at least long enough to bury most of this Court.

Picture it then. Sir Robert Cecil in a small chamber there, off a quiet, inner courtyard. A small obscure chamber, no more than a kind of closet or storeroom. Fitted out with nothing much more than a chest for papers, a plain, rough working table, a clerk's stool. A place which, if entered and examined during his absence, would arouse next to no interest. Let alone any suspicion.

Here very late at night, while Queen and Court sleep and

dream, while only a few of her guards and gentlemen remain awake at the Gatehouse, in the Guardroom and the presence Chamber, while most are sleeping and cold wind is prowling outside, he is poring over his papers and collecting his thoughts. Like his father (bless his memory and pray for his soul) he works for painful long hours and sleeps only a little while. For though he has the quickest wit and though he has learned (by burning and freezing through seasons of kisses and curses) so much of the world that he is now called wise, even by those who may envy and hate him, still he could never prosper, would never have thrived for long, faced as he always has been by rivals and enemies who are in fortunate possession of so many advantages, if it were not for his habit of ceaseless hard labor while they, and most of the rest of the world, are happily sleeping and dreaming.

As they sleep here in Richmond tonight. The worthy and honorable alone beneath warm blankets and curtained against drafts and chill. Lesser gentry, two to a bed, in smaller, plainer chambers. Guards and servants in corners, at doorways, on the floors of chambers on their truckle beds and pallets. As even now an old, incurious servant of his own snores just outside the closed door of this chamber on a pallet bed.

Let them all sleep and dream well.

Let the tall and the handsome, the favored and the fair, let the strong and the brave, let the proud, with their ancient and noble blood to sustain them, and the clever, those who possess the special power to move others (especially the Queen) to delight, to laughter and tears, who have the ability to play upon the feelings of others and thus are able to gain their desired ends gracefully, idly, with what seems to be at no more cost than a lighthearted jest, a merry tale, a snatch of poetry or a piece of song, let them, wrapped warm in good fortune and contentment and satisfaction, dream safely like any child who has said prayers and to whom a lullaby has been sung.

Someone might imagine that, awake, alone with his aches and pains, shadowed by all his losses (*O my well beloved, flee away and be like unto the roe or the young hart upon the mountains of spices*), his only inner warmth the bitter ashes of his thoughts, one could believe he wishes his enemies, those who have trespassed against him, no kind of comfort. That instead he hopes the thorns and nettles of memory will keep them from sleeping easily. And that when at last pure weariness overmasters them, they will soon start awake in a cold sweat, hearing their own strange voices cry out forgotten names.

Not so. He wishes no such thing.

True that fear and envy and malice have long been his closest companions. True that now ambition, almost boundless, has come to be his chief household god. (All the more so since she who was most like a goddess has been taken from him.) In all of this they fail to take account of his pride. Pride which must be ruthlessly concealed. Lest, that which he fears most, the worst pain he can now conceive of, he be taken to be simply ridiculous. No, he will never be able to swagger and strut like a crow in the gutter. But in secret, and especially while they safely sleep and dream, he will dance a country dance on their graves. Rejoicing in fury. Because his hatred is so deep, he wishes his enemies to have more comfort and satisfaction, more security than they do now. Wishes that they may enjoy a contented awareness of their blessings.

He thinks of it this way: that they are swine, one and all. But that some of these pigs, the fattest and least blemished, are selected by the swineherd to be covered with cloth. For what purpose? So that they may lord it over their naked fellows? No, instead for one purpose only—so that their skins may bring the best price and be used to make more expensive things. That sow's ear will never make a silk purse, but this smooth pigskin may someday become a great man's purse.

Thus he makes no effort to discourage any comforting illusions about themselves.

Nor does he seek to correct misapprehensions concerning himself.

If he prays for them, it will be in the words (he has by heart) of the eighteenth psalm:

"They shall cry, but there shall be none to help them; yea, even unto the Lord shall they cry, but he shall not hear them.

"I will beat them as small as the dust before the wind: I will cast them out as the clay in the streets."

Poised over his papers, he rubs his eyes and smiles to himself.

His honored father always told him to seek for consolation and wisdom in Holy Scripture.

"So I do, father. So I do. But now, sir, please speak and tell me where it is written how a little crippled man can promise and deliver a king's crown."

PRIEST

1587

The harvest is great, but the laborers are few, Pray ye therefore the Lord of the harvest, to send forth laborers into the harvest. Go your ways: behold I send you forth as lambs among wolves. Bear no wallet, neither scrip, nor shoes, and salute no man by the way.

Luke 10:2–4

My tale was heard, and yet it was not told;
    My fruit is fall'n, and yet my leaves are green;
My youth is spent, and yet I am not old;
    I saw the world, and yet I was not seen:
        My thread is cut, and yet it is not spun;
        And now I live, and now my life is done.

CHIDIOCK TICHBORNE—"Elegy"

Sir—

I heartily commend myself unto you.

Herewith, respectfully submitted, are such papers of the priest as we have been able to discover. In our opinion some of these writings appear to be of not much more purpose than mere notes and aids made to himself for the sake of memory or private recollection. Others, it seems, are parts of prayers and meditations such as the Papists are wont to employ and to depend upon for their salvation. Among the papers included in this packet are some which seem to represent fragments and, in some cases, even full and fair copies of memoranda and letters written to his family and kin, friends and acquaintances, perhaps also to traitors and conspirators, such as Jesuits and seminary priests etc. etc. Not all of those to whom these letters have been written have, as yet, been identified. However, I hasten to assure Your Lordship that we are even now continuing to study out these questions. It is our aim, and more than simply a hope, that we shall soon be able to furnish you with more reliable and more useful information.

It will also be clear to you, as clearly it is a matter of concern to us, that we cannot be certain yet as to which, if any, among the aforesaid writings enclosed, may in fact have been finished and sent out by him. Nor which of these may have been delivered to others. Insofar as we are able to do so, we present this evidence in the order that we presume the pages to have been composed by him. But we must admit what will be obvious to Your Lordship—that this is more a matter of guesswork than firm conclusion.

Lastly, sir, we have not been able to determine to what extent there may be any codes or ciphers cleverly concealed or interpolated in the text. In a few cases there are false names of places and people, as well as numbers signifying one person or another. We shall make an effort to determine who these people may be. But the discovery of all but the most elementary of such things is beyond both our training and experience. However, we are certain in the belief that if any codes, ciphers, or other secrets are contained herein, these will not escape the vigilance of Your Lordship's skilled servants. We are certain that Mr. Thomas Phelippes and Mr. Anthony Gregory, and other among your trusty servants, will be able to unravel all threads and to untie all troublesome knots.

We are, sir, deeply aware of the perils of these times and of the particular urgency of this matter. And we shall not shirk from difficulties or slacken our efforts or fail to do our several duties to you, sir, and on behalf of Her Majesty the Queen. Indeed, it is precisely on account of our understanding of the present peril that we have hastened to place these papers so promptly in your hands. . . .

I will praise Thee upon the harp, O God, my God. Why art thou cast down, O my soul? And why are thou disquieted within me?

↑   ↑   ↑   ↑   ↑

O blessed Virgin Mary, Mother of God, most gentle Queen and Mother, look down in mercy upon England, thy Dowry, and upon us all who greatly hope and trust in thee. By thee it was that Jesus, our Savior and our hope, was given unto the world. And he has given thee to us that we may hope still more. Plead for us thy children, whom thou didst receive and accept at the foot of the Cross, O sorrowful Mother. Intercede for our separated brethren, that with us in the One True Fold they may be united to the Chief Shepherd, the Vicar of thy Son. . . .

↑   ↑   ↑   ↑   ↑

Bloody. Blood of others, not my own. Who would have imagined it—so much blood?

Their cries and prayers. In pride and anguish they cried out prayers. I prayed for them also. But with my lips sealed. Teeth tight. Prayed in silence.

No altar there. No priest and holy victim. Not by bread and wine. By flesh and blood. O horrid ceremony, awful sacrifice! Cries and prayers. Hanging (briefly too briefly!) in thin air. To dance so briefly on the thin air. Then, cut swiftly down, down they fall. Stunned, but awake and alive. Cries and prayers! Bloody knife and bloody ax. Bloody hands of butcher. Bloody apron, gouts and clots. Clotted blood to elbows. Men turned to meat. No miracle that. The true miracle—and wondrous testimony and witness to our beleaguered faith—how first Ballard, the priest, and then the others did kneel to kiss the hands. Which after Ballard, each in his turn kissing, were horrid bloody hands. Smeared and dripping after his butcher work with the first crying and praying carcass. Each did kneel to kiss those hands before climbing the ladder.

Deliver, O Lord, the soul of Thy servant, as Thou deliverest Job from all his afflictions.

Myself? Mouth full of vomit. Tears swallowed too. Vomit gags and spews out. But not alone. Not even noticed there. Half this crowd sick and heaving. Many weeping unashamed.

Joseph, patron of the dying, I earnestly recommend the soul of this thy servant in the sufferings of his last agony that he may by thy protection be delivered from the snares of the devil and from the eternal death and may merit to attain everlasting joy.

Half the crowd weeping. Some shouting in rage and shame. "These be men, not beasts!" a gentleman near me shouted. In the beginning, when they were brought here, dragged on hurdles at horses' tails, they were cursed and jeered and spat upon. My brothers. Whose deaths have too soon silenced and sickened.

Lord Jesus.

Salvum me fac.

Save me, O Lord, for there is now no saint. And the Truths are decayed among the children of men.

✦ ✦ ✦ ✦ ✦

Idle as I am now, not by choice but by necessity, I am deeply weary. In my lassitude (or is it only sloth? I hope and pray it is not), yawning on the ragged shores of sleep, yet in comfort and safety, I feel fear most. Feel it in flesh and bones, in joints and bowels first, then as a pain and throbbing as if a blacksmith had set up his shop in my skull. Feel it possess my body even before I can rightly name it.

Would it not have been better, wiser for me, if I had never allowed myself to witness those deaths at Tyburn? Indeed, and not to witness other things as well. Too many in a few short years.

How can I perform my ministry if I am crippled with fear and doubt? Fear for myself. Doubt of myself.

Yet how could I forsake them, these my brothers, in their hour of need? (Lord, will I be forsaken if that hour should ever come to me?) If I had done so, if to spare myself the risk of being seen in the crowd there . . . perhaps even taken then and there as thieves are sometimes found at the hanging of other thieves . . . I saw hard-faced, hard-eyed men, servants of great men no doubt, and no doubt the men of Burghley and Walsingham and Whitgift, too, among them, studying the crowd. If I had kept to safety and, to spare myself danger, had forsaken my brothers, then I would surely hate myself even more than I do now.

I hate myself out of shame for the fear. Out of shame and sorrow for my little faith.

The fear is always there within me. Needs only idleness or weariness to be awakened. To take charge of myself. And now, ever after that day, I cannot efface the pictures in my mind. Crawling and writhing in their blood and offal. Screaming their broken prayers.

O God, dear God, how deeply I wish that I might somehow whitewash the walls of my mind. Might smash and destroy all the images I have kept secret there. As once these poor deluded heretics did destroy the wall paintings and cloths, the colored glass and the wooden and stone carvings of our churches. In madness they did empty them of all beauty. Oh, I would embrace madness if I believed it could empty my head and free me from fear.

Lord, You know that I pray without ceasing. And yet You know, You from whom no secret may be hidden, how I cannot dispel the fear that cripples me. Cannot rid myself of the knowledge of it or my shame of it.

What good, what use, is a coward priest?

*   *   *   *   *

Father—

Though my long silence might seem to give the lie to me, I want you to know that I have set out to write to you many times. And at no time have I been able to finish a letter to you.

It should not be so difficult for a son, even a sort of prodigal son, to write to his own father.

Surely, with time you have come to see that. . . .

Surely, now that time has passed, your wounded feelings are healed and your disappointment in me is somewhat mitigated. . . .

Oh, Father, I can understand how disappointed you must have been when your eldest son, against all your advice and wishes. . . .

Father—

Over years I have written enough letters to you to fill a book. Written many. Sent none.

For, no matter how it may seem to you, I am, as I have always been, ever conscious of my love and duty toward you. And it pains me to know that I have caused you pain.

I understand how disappointed you must have been to discover that I would not follow in your footsteps. How you must have . . . !

Disappointed? That I did not choose to spend my life in the country, drinking and wenching and spending my best hours hunting large and small beasts?

Just because the father is an old fool does not mean that the son must follow after.

Father—

The other day I was mounting my horse in a country innyard when, with a great halloo and clatter, here came some randy, raunchy, mud-bespattered hunters (together with their mangy pack of dogs) drunk not as lords, but as any louts at a Whitsun ale, shouting and cursing each other and everything else. And one fellow, a great tub of guts like a boar before slaughter, fell from saddle and flat on his back among the pack of hounds. And, Father, for one strange moment, I thought it was you. You yourself, sir, sprawled out there with the dogs crawling all over you and licking your face.

And I thought, how lucky I am to be far away from home. . . .

✒ ✒ ✒ ✒ ✒

And touching our Society, be it known to you that we have made a league—all the Jesuits in the world, whose succession and multitude must overreach all the practices of England—cheerfully to carry the cross you lay upon us, and never to despair of your recovery while we have a man left to enjoy your Tyburn, or to be racked with your torments, or consumed with your prisons. The expense is reckoned. The enterprise is begun. It is of God, it cannot be withstood. So the faith was planted. So it must be restored.

—EDMUND CAMPION

✒ ✒ ✒ ✒ ✒

Shepherd—

According to your instructions, which were conveyed to me by Player and Mariner when we met together in Southwark at the tavern called *Bear at the Bridgefoot*, I have now made my way north again to the castle. A quiet journey it has been, though not an easy one this time of year with hard frost on the fields and roads, and often frozen ruts (more and more wagons are being used on these roads and will be the death of them unless something is done to slow that heavy traffic) and the cold winds and rains, sometimes ice, day and night. Still I cannot make serious complaint, for I had the benefit of an adequate road all the way to Huntingdon. My difficulty began when I left the highway to cross country on muddy trails. A quiet journey it has been for me, though, going only short distances each day. Stopping at known and safe houses, to enjoy some warmth and comfort and goodwill, and to hear confessions and to say the Mass. To baptise some and, once, to bury.

I am sorry to say that in most places the last priest to have passed through was myself.

Anyway, I arrived here. Not followed, I believe. This time, however, it has not been possible for me to be easily admitted within the gates and walls of the castle. Even with the benefit of my elegantly prepared, signed and sealed papers (for which I thank you kindly and, also, compliment your draftsmen who have much improved on their skills and soon someday may even begin to match the forgeries of Walsingham's servants), I could see that it would be exceedingly dangerous for me to attempt to enter without being detected. There are half an hundred soldiers here and, as well, it appears that many of the great men of England are arriving or are here already.

There are others of ours, however, who have been more fortunate. I saw "XIII" and am certain that he is now safely inside. He managed to make his way, to work his way, literally, inside the walls as a jakesman. One of a group of the same pressed into service to clean and maintain the castle privies for the large crowd. Likewise (I also saw him once, though we had no opportunity to speak) "XIX" is already there. Has been able to continue as a common servant ever since the Queen was still at Tutbury. My guess is that he is still not fully trusted by her French servants—and why should they trust anyone? But I have reason to believe he is not doubted by anyone among her keepers. Which is more to the point.

Since I arrived, the castle has been locked tight and closely guarded. None, as far as I can tell, but the great men and officers are free to come and go. Nevertheless, we do have those two men, that I am sure of, inside. And I am here at the inn.

It's a pity, but poor "XIII" must keep on with his dirty work until such time as his whole group is released and permitted to depart. When I think of "XIII," how fastidious he was at seminary, an example for us all, with his supply of sweet soaps and his distilled herbal waters. With his clean-brushed clothes and gown, his scented handkerchiefs and perfumed pomanders. How he hated to be out among the crowds at the marketplace or on feast days! Because he could not bear the odors of unclean breath and unwashed bodies. I conclude that his new role as a pioneer for privies is much more than a virtuous offering up. It is in the nature of an undeniable sacrifice.

I have remained here at the inn. Which is becoming crowded now with lesser officers of government and with servants of the men arriving at the castle. It seems I am in no danger of losing my chamber or even of being asked to share my bed with a stranger. Because, in spite of the comings and goings of these important persons, I am taken to be of more practical value hereabouts. Once again—what choice did I have, since I was here in the selfsame capacity as recently as October last?—I am here in my disguise as a drawer of bad teeth.

And, yes, good Shepherd, you are certainly entitled, if you wish to, to muster up some laughter at my expense. Even amid the tears of the things of this world, some traces of laughter are ever present. There were no tears in the Garden, but surely laughter was there, if only among the rustling of the leaves. Is laughter, then, honest laughter and not the laughter of pride or malice or cruel derision, is laughter yet one more precious gift of the Holy Ghost, the Comforter?

Anyway, you may laugh at the news that once again I have been called on to perform dental services. And to pull teeth of various and sundry folk of various and sundry ages in these parts. You will remember my telling you, I reckon, how busy I was when I was last here in the fall. Which was because no dentist had traveled these parts for a good while. Well, sir, I am sorry to tell you that none—excepting one poor old man with the palsy, one whom no one will come near—has been here since then. In the meantime my repute as a gentle and skillful master of the craft has spread for many miles around.

Now, I know that you will find that hard to believe, Shepherd, but the truth is that I am much improved, since that time when we were traveling together in the West Country. It was, after all, the first time I had ever played the dentist, and I never believed then that I would be called upon to try to demonstrate my craft. But I had not anticipated—truly had not so much, in those silly green salad days, even *imagined* such a creature in the world— that we should encounter anyone like that stout old captain from Calais. Called himself a knight, he did. And he may have truly been so, though I think he was more likely a knight of the cup than of the crown.

Do you recall it?

How we made the mistake, it being a dusty, sunny July afternoon and both of us parched with thirst and weariness, of stopping at an alehouse. Little crossroads village of limewashed cobhouses with thatched roofs. And the alehouse, sign of the Saracen (looking more like a Welshman than anything else), was cool and shadowy and inviting after the blaze and glitter of the roadway. And, after all, we would only pause there a few minutes to refresh ourselves with a cup or two while the horses rested. So into the heady, yeasty odor of the place, blinking, waiting to accustom ourselves to the light and to see what we would see. And there, lo and behold, was our captain, stout as an old English warhorse, grizzled and frosted by time, but armed with a sword and dagger and, for all the world, ready to march off to war to recapture Calais for England. At a moment's notice. Meantime, however, drunk. Very drunk.

Remember? As we entered the low door, he rose from his stool, like a courtier, to bow and greet the strangers. Slipped and fell on his arse, with a rattle and clatter of sword and dagger, knocked over his stool and spilled his cup.

—Ha! He cries, drawing himself to his feet, dusting himself off and adjusting his harness. Trying to stand with some dignity, and, in truth, standing straight enough, if swaying a little like a hop pole in a wind.

—Ha! He cries. —A couple of doctors. I can tell. Doctors of medicine, no doubt.

—Sir, I assure you, we are not.

—Don't contradict me! I am drunk, but am no fool. Do you agree? Do you?

—Now, Captain, you mind your manners and do not trouble these travelers, the alewife began.

—Hush, woman! He says. I repeat. I am drunk, but no fool. And I ask you do you agree?

Eyes set in a fierce squint. Right hand clasping the rusty hilt of his sword.

—Oh, good sir, you said, it's clear that you are a little cup-shotten. Not drunk. I would never say drunk.

—Foolish?

—Perish the thought, sir. I would prove myself to be a perfect fool to call you one. Now, wouldn't I?

—Lucy! He shouts, as if across a wide field, to the alewife. Who's not more than a yard away from him. Just far enough to step aside if he falls again. —Lucy, pour these two doctors of the road each with a cup of your very best. And add it to my reckoning, you hear?

—Sir, we thank you, but we cannot. . . .

—Never, never, *never* decline a drink when it's offered to you in friendship, love, and charity. Decline a drink and you insult the giver. Next thing he may be inclined to slit your gizzard with six inches of cold steel. May *have* to do so for the sake of honor.

—Well, here's to your health and welfare, Captain. And we thank you.

—To be sure, I am drunk. Not fully cognizant, coherent, you understand. And such a long way from my true home in old Calais. Which they surrendered, nay, they *gave it away,* the cowards, to the Froggies. Damn 'em! . . . You two aren't a couple of Frenchmen, are you?

—Oh no, sir! We are both Englishmen born and bred.

—Are you now? Hear that, Lucy? A couple of true-born Englishmen. Let's drink to that. Bottoms up, boys!

—We thank you, Captain. And now we must be going. For we have a good stretch of road ahead of us.

—Why, then you'll need another drink in preparation. *Preparatio,* as the old Papist priests used to tell us.

Ah, Shepherd, my blood went cold at the thought that the old fellow might be, in truth, sober as a judge. Might be playing a role as much as we were.

—I confess to almighty God, to blessed Mary ever Virgin, to blessed Michael the Archangel . . . I forget the others, John the Baptist is one, Peter and Paul also, he continued. —To all the saints I confess and to you, Father. That I have sinned exceedingly in thought, word, and deed. Through my fault, through my fault, through my most grievous fault . . . !

—Hush now, Captain, says Lucy, or these gentlemen may take you for a Papist.

He shrugged off her hand. Steadied himself by leaning back
against the wall. Being sly now.

—Do you take me for a Papist, gentlemen? For if you do, you
do *mis-con-strue.* . . .

Squint eyes again. A long pause. The alewife watching it all.
And then three men, the village blacksmith and two other
fellows, entering.

—Why, no, sir, Captain, we take you for an Englishman just
like ourselves.

—Besides, you added, Shepherd. —Besides, if you were a true
Papist, it would have all been spoken in Latin.

—Never truer words, the captain says. Suddenly teary, wiping
at his eyes with a dirty sleeve. —They have taken away our
Latin, too, together with everything else.

Whoops of laughter from the blacksmith and his friends. And
the alewife scurrying to pour them beer. The captain finding his
stool, taking it very slowly. As if he were mounting a strange,
skittish horse. Speaking to us *sotto voce.* So as not to endure any
more laughter and ridicule from his countrymen.

—Well, it's true and no purpose in denying it. I am somewhat
drunk this afternoon. But, as I live and breathe, gentlemen, I
must remind you of the truth of the proverb. To wit: there are
more old drunkards than there are old physicians.

—Ha! Called out the blacksmith. Pay no mind to that old fool.
He was never in Calais or even near it. He has never been farther
from here than Exeter and that's the truth.

And then, my Shepherd, in all good faith and goodwill, you
placed me in hazard.

—We are not, either of us, physicians, you told that old man.
—But my young friend here is a fine drawer of teeth from
London town.

—Ah! Says the man. —Thank God you are here at last! You can
pull my bad teeth for me. It's the ache and pain of them, you
see? The only reason I drink in daylight is to ease the pain. Pull
out the bad ones and ease the pain. Make me a sober and
industrious gentleman again.

—It will take more than pulling some teeth to accomplish that
trick, the blacksmith said. —It will take a very Papist miracle.

And now began the trouble. As I sought to explain that it was perhaps not wise to try to extract his bad teeth then and there in the village alehouse. And the others, together with a fair-sized crowd of newcomers, all gathering around to enjoy the fun of it.

—Sir, you shall pull my teeth and pull them out now! He said.

And then, at last, out comes the sword from its scabbard. Not even the least fleck of rust on the blade of it. One edge like a honed razor and a point bright and sharp as a new steel needle.

So there was nothing left for me to do but unpack the shiny new tools which I had never yet used or even planned to use. Someone held a candle close by his wide-open mouth. And I was thinking, Shepherd, that if I fainted—which has always been a possibility ever since, as a lad, I did indeed faint when the dentist yanked a tooth from my mother—not even you could save me from being known as a false dentist and, thus, a man in a disguise and up to no good. I was short of breath and queasy and the sweat formed huge drops on my brow and ran down my face. I could not see clearly. But nonetheless bent close and clamped down upon a tooth and pulled and pulled and, there!, at last jerked it free!

—God's wounds, young man! You have pulled out my best tooth! You have taken the one truly good, sound tooth that's left in my head!

He on his feet and not at all unsteady now. With the shiny point of his sword an inch from the point of my chin. And such a quiet came into that alehouse that I could hear mice moving in the thatch of the roof.

Then you, Shepherd, coming to my rescue.

—Why, sir, you said. —'Tis all the latest practice in London, the newest learning.

—What is? What is? Damn it all! To take a man's good tooth and leave the bad, is that it?

—Exactly, sir, you are telling him. And, as you do so, the others gather close by to hear better. —It has been proved beyond any question or doubt that the cause of much trouble among teeth is the power and dominion of one great, fat, solid tooth over the others. This tooth—though sometimes there may be more than one, depending on the age, general constitution, and good or ill fortune of the patient—this fat and lordly tooth does set himself up like a hardhearted, arrogant, rack-rent landlord. He does take away the health of the mouth at the expense of the others, his poor tenants, leaving those scranny, shabby fellows nothing but decay and discoloration and grief. He, this great, rich, fat and lordly tooth does grow huge and white like a spoiled ram grazing on common land that has been enclosed and taken away from the people!

—And is there no cure, sir, for such an injustice? Says the blacksmith, as serious as can be.

—Well, you have just seen it done, you add. —My young companion here, with one look into the captain's mouth, saw the problem and the remedy. He has removed the oppressor tooth and now, in time, the others will surely heal and thrive again as before.

The point of the sword goes slack. The captain, thoughtful, manages a slightly bloody smile.

—By taking the one you have saved me the others? he says.

—You could say so, I allow. —God willing, of course.

—Then, by God, sir, we shall all drink hearty and deep in praise of these newfangled arts of healing, he says, sliding back onto his stool.

—Lucy, bring out the best double-double beer for everyone here.

And we drank until our heads were turning. And I practiced my craft on the other people there, beginning with the blacksmith and ending with poor Mistress Lucy. Pulled many a hale and hearty tooth and was (Lord, forgive me) paid for it, too, before we rode away from that village. As soon as we were out of sight we galloped hard and long into the failing afternoon light, our heads clearing but our guts awash with several kinds of strong drink, seeking to put as many miles between us and that place as we could before night.

Never to return there. Not to that corner of Devon again. Where by now half of the smiles must be ragged and ruined, and the chief diet of the place must be soft bread and milk.

Ah well, Shepherd, I sometimes wonder how it was for the next dentist, a real one, who arrived there.

Having freely surrendered their best teeth, they would surely not be happy to hear that they had been gulled by a pair of

errant false knaves from the city. I prefer to imagine him as
something of a knave himself. Who, seeing the way that things
had gone there and sensing the strength of their feelings, simply
shrugged away conscience and continued with our kind of
toothcraft. Pulling the good and leaving the bad.

Perhaps, with his good example, the word has spread more
widely. And by now half the good teeth of Devon are gone.

Forgive me as I indulge myself in such foolery. I must be
giddy, light-headed (if heavyhearted) from this sharp weather
and a cough and a touch of fever.

I turn back to that time, truly not so many years ago, though it
might as well be taken out of some chronicle of olden times, so
much has passed, so much is greatly changed for all of us. So
much has changed that I cannot easily recognize myself in my
own story. Or is it, good Shepherd, that after profound changes,
we do not recognize the face, the form, the stranger that we
meet in the looking glass? That we can only believe in what was
there, but has now vanished, like frosty ghosts of breath on these
winter days, like smoke blown away by the wind? Never mind.
It's for certain that when I am idle and anxious, and when I can
choose, I find myself turning back to that time when we were
newly returned to England together and our ministry was new to
us here. More hopeful than fearful then. Remembering, wistfully,
as if it were as far behind us as childhood, how we could still
laugh at the world and even at ourselves. Perhaps because we
could love both better than we can now. Though it may prove to
have been extremely foolish to allow ourselves to love either one.

Shepherd, you and I, we have come a far piece since then. A
long way in a short time, at least as the world measures time.
And have gone our different and difficult ways. Yet as I picture it
(always whenever I remember) I see the two of us setting off
down the lane in that Devon village, scurrying a gaggle of geese
and troubling a flock of sheep as we gallop into the fading light.

Sometimes, out of weariness, I think that we have been riding
from light into darkness ever since. Our purses carrying precious
little laughter and even less hope. . . .

It's a gray, raw wind that is prowling among the low fields.
The River Nene is ruffled by it, as it flows past village and castle,
soon to wander among the ice-crusted reeds to the east. From my

high window I can see flags on the towers of the castle being whipped by the wind. Can see the old lantern of (what is still left of) the ancient Church of St. Mary and All Saints. Most curious that lantern, being of eight sides and set atop a square tower. Which once served to light travelers in the Forest of Rockingham. In the days before the Dissolution.

Outside it may be windy and cold. But here in my chamber, tight and snug as a sea chest, I am warm enough. Good fire burning. Time on my hands as I wait for any news. Pen and ink and paper. And just now a pitcher of wine and some walnuts brought to me by the innkeeper himself. Who, it seems, may soon return to ask me to take a look at an aching tooth in the mouth of some guest here. Which tooth must be aching in the mouth of someone of importance. I infer the distinction. Believing, nay *knowing* that our innkeeper, not a bad soul though powerfully lazy, would surely have sent someone else to climb to my chamber, anyone other than himself, unless it concerned a person of considerable importance.

Meantime, thinking on this urgent matter at hand, I cannot convince myself that they truly intend to take the life of the Queen of Scots. To kill a Queen! What a great folly that would be! These men, our mortal enemies, who will cheerfully have you and me divided into four parts for their pleasure (if they catch us, if they can), may well be rooted in the wicked pride and invincible ignorance of their heresies. And yet they are not fools in this world. Far from it. They are wise as serpents. Shrewd as goats in the knowledge of the world. Considering all, I cannot believe that they intend to allow the execution of the Queen. No matter how much they may hate her and fear her. (And, oh, how they must hate her after all these years!) For they have nothing to gain from her death now. On the contrary it will be likely to bring great grief to them and to England. I can imagine only troubles, tumults and commotions and confusion. Most likely war will follow.

And even if these men have lost their minds, surely the Queen has not. Will never permit it.

The innkeeper, a confirmed and sturdy heretic if there ever was one, is more emphatic in what he says than I am in my thinking.

—Oh, they will never kill the Queen of Scots, he says. —They could not do that, you can be sure. For though she may have been a great whore in her youth, and even if she is now, and no doubt about it, a scheming and conniving Papist, heart and soul, still, in freedom or captivity, she is an anointed Queen. And she may not be touched or judged by anyone in this world. Not withouten a great shame and a greater peril.

He says, and I think the same, that all these goings on here appear to be a show. Some sort of play or pageant.

But played for whom and for what purpose? It is a mystery to us.

There is the rumor that she will be spared, will be given her life and allowed to live not as a Queen but as a nun, secure in the Tower of London.

Or, another rumor, that the whole affair is to test her son, the young King James the Sixth of Scotland, or to win some promise or concession from him.

Someone has mentioned this rumor to the innkeeper.

—Well, he said, —if harm comes to his mother, I reckon that her son will be obliged to avenge her. Or else be called a coward ever after. Now, I do not claim to have much experience in these matters of state—though, in truth, many important men have stayed here in my inn and on occasion, when they perceived my quality and obvious loyalty, they have even discussed matters with me, not reluctant to ask my advice. But I have been acquainted with enough Scotsmen to conclude that any of them would prefer to die a dozen painful deaths than to live long and be known as a coward.

Thus, at present, all things remain cloudy.

As soon as I . . .

There! The innkeeper has called me to come and to see to the toothache of this guest. This letter to be continued later. Soonest possible. . . .

❦ ❦ ❦ ❦ ❦

Thou hast given to her her heart's desire; and hast not withol-den from her the will of her lips. For Thou hast presented her with blessings of sweetness. Thou hast set on her head a crown of precious stones . . .

The Queen of Scots is dead.

Taken from us this morning by the headsman's ax.

Who can believe it?

Today dawned fair and bright, a warm south wind with an odor of spring, a promise in it. Hard ground melting to mud. And by this afternoon I stood with the innkeeper (who seems to know all that can be known) and watched smoke rising from above the walls from the castle courtyard.

—What can that be? I asked him. —What are they burning?

—It will be the heading block and the bloody wood of the scaffold. It will be the clothing that she wore.

—Why burn that?

—They fear the Papists will take her for a martyr, he said. —They fear that the Papists will make relics of these things.

—What do you think?

He eyed me closely, blank of expression beyond his curiosity about myself. Behind him the column of smoke was blown apart by a gust of wind.

—I think they are right to be afraid, he said. —But I do not think that burning the bloody clothes and the bloody lumber and burying her secretly will do much good for them. Or for us. I think, I fear there will be much more blood and fire from this.

—There may be blood and fire all over England before this is settled.

—Let us pray not so, he said. Then: —And let us speak no more of these things of which we know nothing.

One month ago who would have imagined they would dare to do such a thing?

Poison perhaps. Or a pillow that leaves no mark. We had feared for the Queen's murder. The more so since her most trusted servants were kept from her. Feared that her keeper, the Puritan Sir Aymas Paulet, deep in his heresies, would think nothing ill of killing a Catholic Queen. He thought nothing at all of insulting and humiliating her. More likely he was afraid to do anything. Knowing the character of the Court and Council. Knowing he would suffer for it. If only to ease their consciences and to spare them suspicion.

We had feared her death by secret murder at any time. Especially since she stood, however unlawfully, convicted and condemned. But we . . . I at least, in my ignorance of affairs and the logic of these heretics, never imagined that they would execute her under the guise of Law. Never believed They could be so brazen, heedless, ruthless, fearless of consequences.

I pray that she died well and in the faith. Nothing is known yet of all that. We hope that sooner or later the truth will be told. How can they keep the truth a secret for long?

Meantime, though, the castle is locked tight and closely guarded. Even the two Earls, of Kent and of Shrewsbury, have not left. Only one horseman, he all alone, rode out and south in the late afternoon. And the gates were locked behind him.

No announcement made in the village. Yet everyone seems to know. The innkeeper says (and I believe him) that all the ports, and the Borders as well, will be closed to coming or going. He said that already the regular post riders have been discontinued. Not to discourage the spreading of the news. For surely the news of the death of the Queen of Scots will be celebrated by the ignorant. And by the wicked. The wicked who, nevertheless, must seek to encourage the ignorant in the cultivation of their invincible ignorance. Perhaps they believe that the news and the ringing of bells in celebration and the singing and dancing and rejoicing of foolish and empty-headed crowds will strike fear and astonishment in the hearts of the truly faithful.

No, I cannot believe that they plan to hinder the news, but instead they hope to hold back the whole truth of it until their own falsehoods have been carefully planted.

No one except a few of that Queen's trusted servants. . . .

As near as a year ago, I would have written, *our Queen*. Whoever she is now, I cannot believe she is truly ours. God forgive me. Perhaps, so surrounded by wicked, ruthless, and ambitious men, she can no longer discern what's true and what's false. Perhaps all these plots and conspiracies against her have frightened her or hardened her heart. Who knows?

No one except a few of the Queen's well-trusted servants will be allowed to leave the castle. Perhaps tonight. All others, and most especially the servants of the Queen of Scots, will be kept there. Thus forced to keep silence. For a time. Not forever, that silence. Truth will come to light. Truth will speak and be heard.

Truth will (sooner or later) speak and be heard to the ends of the earth.

I say to you, that if these shall hold their peace, the stones will cry out.

Qui seminant in lacrimis in exsultatione metent. . . .

My hands tremble when I think on it.

To lie down, blindfolded as in some child's game. Chin and head placed carefully, exactly, on a smooth wood of the block. To pray and then a sudden startling blow. A moment of horrid pain and bursts of light. The spurt of blood.

I have seen the lips of the dead still moving in prayer.

Early this evening a man from London, the guest from whom I took a tooth last night, returned to the inn. With his young servant. That youth looking sickly. He hurried off to their chamber, carrying their heavy cases. The master, Mr. Bull he's called or calls himself, came to join the innkeeper and myself close by the fire. He asked for sweet wine and three cups.

—I am very grateful to you, sir, he told me. —When I woke this morning, the aches and pains of my head and jaw had all gone. You have fine and gentle hands, skilled hands, sir.

He gestured with his own powerful hands. Setting his cup down, held them a moment close to the flicker of flame in the fireplace. I looked at them. Huge and separate from him. Swimming (it seemed) in a stream of flame and shadow.

Something, a coldness, swept over me. I gulped my wine for its warmth.

—Well, sirs, Mr. Bull said, the lad and I must leave at first light. I bid you both a good night.

—Is your business done so soon? I asked.

He looked at me strangely, at first almost as if in anger, then smiled, the hard lines on his face easing.

—Oh, yes, he said. —All over and done with. You and I have this advantage in our work. Done well or ill, it is quickly over.

Before I could say anything more I felt the innkeeper gripping my elbow. I said nothing. Nodded as Mr. Bull took his leave and mounted the stairway toward his chamber.

After he was gone, the innkeeper released my arm, turned from me, and looked into the fire. Looked and then tossed his wine into the flames. Where it flared and sizzled on the coals. I noticed that he had not sipped a drop of that wine before he threw it away.

He continued to stare at the fire.

—Don't you know? he asked softly.

—Know, sir? Know what?

—Don't you know who that man is?

—Who—Mr. Bull?

Turning then to look at me with weary eyes.

—Mr. Bull is the headsman sent up from London.

(*Kiss the bloody hands!*)

—Today he has cut off the head of the Queen of Scots, he continued. —It is no doubt her money which pays for the wine.

A moment of horrid pain and bursting light. Then the spurting of blood.

Blood forever (I hope and pray) washing clean all the stains of her past life. Whatever the sins of her youth, so long ago, may have been (and who can say or will? all her enemies have vilified her name) she is now free of them. I pray that she died strong in the faith. For the faith. And so died rejoicing.

As for them, her captors for all these years. Now her murderers. Now the world will surely come to them. And will avenge this murdered Queen. Will come here to England to restore our ancient religion, to avenge our broken and martyred priests.

To pay for all that blood and suffering shall now rivers of blood flow in England.

Fire and blood.

I would rejoice in the prospect of that justice, if I could.

Cannot. Do not.

My God, Lord God, I have seen much fire and blood and suffering already. Like Mr. Bull's apprentice, I am sickened by it. By the memory of it.

Timor mortis conturbat me.

Turn away from.

Not to see it. Not to bear it anymore.

Will pray for the soul of the dead Queen.

Will pray for the soul (*as she did, must have, it is the custom*) of Mr. Bull.

Will pray for strength and courage for myself.

After the innkeeper left me standing there—another traveler

had arrived in need of a chamber—I walked outside. The wind had turned around. Blew cold now. Only a few lights and torches from the castle.

I walked toward the river. Thinking that the sound of it, the sense of its moving on, unhurried and indifferent, would calm my mind.

There was still mud from the day's thaw. Soon my shoes were heavy with it.

Looked up into a clear cold sky. So many stars. So many bright stars. . . .

To whom, Lord, shall I turn in my weakness?

Who or what can spare me from the long sorrows of my own doubts?

* * * * *

Her beauty.

I have seen pictures of her and have listened to others who saw her. An old priest who knew her young in France. "XIII" & "XIX" who knew her at the last. Tall & fair & full of beauty. In youth an animal grace. In age a spiritual radiance.

Shepherd used to tease me on account of this. May be why he sent me off to Fotheringhay in February.

Shepherd used to say: —Oh yes, she has great beauty—for a Queen.

When I complained against that wit he said: —We must be truthful. And the truth is that if you put the Queen of Scots or our Queen Elizabeth into a crowd of milkmaids at evening, you would never notice either one of them.

It is said that when the executioner—could it truly have been Mr. Bull from the inn?—seized her hair to hold up her severed head for the crowd in the Hall, when he reached to raise the bloody head, his fingers snarled in the hair, the head fell away. Her auburn hair, at the end, was a wig. It's said that her natural hair was gray and cut short.

He held up high a fine auburn wig. Her bloody head rolled away like a ball over the edge of the scaffold.

* * * * *

Herewith an accounting of the last meeting I had with Mariner.

We met again, by accident and no more than to exchange the briefest of greetings, in the crowds along Cheapside on the occasion of the funeral procession to St. Paul's made in honor of Sir Philip Sidney.

That would be the sixteenth day of this same month.

Myself only just returned from Fotheringhay. Still stunned by it. Still shabby and threadbare, road-weary. Every inch a nondescript country traveler newly arrived in the City. Mariner, always surprising (to me at least) wore elegant mourning colors. Was clad as an officer of horse with a fine, feathered, jaunty hat; short cloak and a small, starched, snowy ruff that could not have offended even the most extreme Puritan; heavy belts, sword and dagger, knee-high boots and spurs. He could have been a faithful servant, even a dear friend of the dead knight. Tall and handsome as he is, he stood out clearly in the crowd.

—My best disguise, he has always said, is to be most easily visible and thus most easily ignored. Not forgotten, mind you. Indeed, I am as easily remembered as I am noticed. But for that same reason there is no sense of threat about me. I swagger when I should skulk and am as safe as I would be in the perfect priesthole. No one would take me for a priest. A bishop, perhaps, or even a cardinal. But never a common priest. . . .

In Cheapside, in that huge crowd, our eyes met for an instant. And he, with companions equally debonair, tipped me the slightest of nods. Then we heard the sounds of fifes and muffled drums coming and the crowd surged like a breaking wave to see.

Next day, by means of a small bribe and the sincerity of my sober Protestant clothing and their Geneva Bible clutched under my arm, I was able to spend the morning with some of the close prisoners at Newgate. Who, because they wait to stand trial on felonies and such, are so often left to themselves. I know that there are far more of the faithful being held at the Marshalsea over in Southwark, for instance. But there's no shortage of priests coming and going there. If you count them all, Jesuits and seminary priests alike, you will find more priests than prisoners there on certain days. Not so many at Newgate. And sinners or no, felons or not, they, too, have great need of our ministry. I do not, however, take much pride in my work there. Once I may have. Thinking it was a danger and that each time I entered might be the time I would not leave, but would find myself in irons and sleeping on straw also. It's a sorrowful place, but not so dangerous. At least not as long as there's some money to purchase the shrugs of the keepers.

I took some food and drink and a purse of money to be distributed among the prisoners. Never enough, of course, to do any of them much good beyond denying them the right to dispense with all hope. But, then, our Lord fed the multitude with the scraps of a few loaves and fishes. I prayed with the faithful, Papist with Papist and (I must confess) almost a very Protestant when I found myself alone with one of those.

I was finished by late morning, with dinnertime approaching. So I set out walking to our bookseller's in Paul's Yard. To learn if any messages had been left there for me. And thinking that a short walk in the fresh air would clear my head of the damp and stink of the Newgate. But most of all because when I emerged from that tomb of a prison I walked directly into a cold, brisk day with a hint of springtime in the brightness of it.

At the bookseller's, biding my time because he was busy with customers on such a day, I discovered that Mariner had left word that he was likely to be found, and at just about this hour, over in Paul's Walk in the Cathedral. Among the many idle men looking for employment.

—Well, he said, when I found him, if you hadn't arrived when you did, I was ready to rent myself out as a witness.

He was still affecting a proud horse officer's style, though much more colorfully now that the funeral was over; and he was wearing an amazing ruff, like a huge white platter on which to carry his head, close to the limits the law allows, if not excessive of them.

—I hope you have not given all your money away to felons and criminals, he said. —I hope you have kept a little to serve the poor.

—You look prosperous enough.

—Well, the truth is that I'm poor as old Adam's cat. Not for long, mind you. But I find myself somewhat light in the purse today. Plainly and purely empty, if the truth must be told. . . .

We had joined other strollers, taking a slow turn, up and back the long, shadowy nave.

—Have you been robbed, then?

—You might say so, he said, though I doubt it. More likely you would say I've been somewhat foolish.

—Was it cards or dice?

—A little of both and a long night of it. There was a time, not long past midnight, when I had what some men—not you or I, but some more gullible and less ambitious souls—would call a fortune. A little after midnight, and I could have bought myself a ship, rigged and victualed her, hired the crew, and sailed to the Spice Islands. I could have built myself a house, all windows and brick chimneys, in the country.

—And?

—By the time the sun was considering rising, I was so disfurnished that I knew I would be lucky to end my days among the itchy debtors at the Fleet.

—I would have found you there, sooner or later.

—I know you better than that. You waste no prayers on common debtors. To gain your attention I would have to go out and perform some horrid and felonious act.

—May I suggest . . . ?

—What?

—That you discuss your criminal vocation as my guest at dinner.

—I know just the place. Not a long walk from here and with several altogether adequate taverns between here and there.

Then of a sudden he clapped me on the back and embraced me. Laughing out loud so that heads turned to look.

—And what do you suppose they think we are when they see us together like this—you in your tedious Puritan habits and I, I like a braggadocio captain of horse?

—I imagine, I said, that any sane man would conclude one or the other of us is dissembling.

—Exactly! Exactly so! He was coughing with spent laughter now. —But not a one of them is such a cynic as to believe that we both are. Come now, let us find a tavern and drink to each other's dissembling health.

He led me to the *Dagger Tavern* on Friday Street. Where the owner has a license for food as well as drink. We ate a cold pie, said to be partridge but tasting strongly and toughly of chicken. And drank our share of their Gascon wine.

—It's common enough, but never spoiled here at the *Dagger*, he told me. —So you don't have to drink it down with closed eyes and tense jaws. It comforts the spirit marvelously.

Soon the wine loosened his tongue, and troubles showed in and around his eyes and in the drumming of his fingers on the table. He kept his voice low and did not look directly at me.

—Listen to me, he said. —Your name, your rightful name, is there on a list of Mr. Secretary Walsingham.

—Well, I should hope so, I said, feeling the wine more than his seriousness. —Here I have been all up and down the countryside and in and out of London for years now, trying to do the Lord's business—the Pope's business, Mr. Secretary would say . . .

—I myself have seen it there.

—And if by this time Sir Francis Walsingham, with all of his shadowy intelligencers, if he has not . . .

—Seen it written, bold and clear.

— . . . then God help England and God save the Queen, for our spies are not worth their wages, and nothing stands between us and all our enemies but some deal of rough water.

He shook his head unsmiling. And then it dawned on me what he was saying.

—You saw my name?

—Of traitors to be hunted down and taken.

—All of them priests?

—I did not recognize all of the names.

—Where?

—At Walsingham's house.

—Then you have been there.

—Yes.

—When?

—This same week. Before the funeral.

—Why?

—To get a passport to leave the country. Why else? he said. Then: —I have played this part too long. I've lost the heart for it. Most days I'm half drunk before noon. Listen, we are losing ground each day. They have killed the best of us. And we shall all be taken before long.

—And so out of desperation you went to Walsingham. Daniel entering into the lions' den.

—Not quite so, he smiled wanly. —I went for a passport. With roads and ports guarded, now that the Queen of Scots is dead, I would be in much greater danger without one.

—Anthony Babington went to get a passport.

(*Kiss the bloody hands!*)

—Tell me nothing about Babington. He was a fool. He died badly and he caused the death of the Queen of Scots. And he's likely to cause the death of us, too.

—It was a great misfortune. He was too innocent, too inexperienced for it . . .

—Listen, he interrupted, leaning across the table so close to me that his nose was only an inch from mine, and whispering softly. —I'll tell you what I think. That Babington was, all along, a secret servant of Walsingham's. And so was John Ballard, the priest. That the other plotters were simply fools to fill up the crust of the pie. That the true aim of the plot was to catch the Queen of Scots.

—But Babington, Ballard as well, they were sentenced to death and died with the others.

—By all means. A tighter grin now. —They both knew overmuch. There was neither means nor purpose in sparing them. Though, of course, they would both have been led to believe they could expect mercy on the scaffold. Until they were swinging at the end of the rope, nay, until the executioner's knife had entered their astonished bodies to scoop out their bowels, they must have maintained some confidence that they would walk away alive. And, all in due time, be rewarded for their troubles.

—But they were tortured. Or so it's said.

—Indeed so. Well racked. Half crippled by it. How else could their confessions be credible? And how better to remind them of the wisdom of playing out their parts to the appointed end? They betrayed the others and were, in turn, themselves betrayed. That's the long and the short of it, man.

(*Parce mihi Domine Jesu.*)

—That is all much too wicked for me to believe.

—Believe it, he said. —It is the way the world goes in this late day and age.

He eased back, stretched on his stool, and drank wine from his cup. He seemed, for the moment, relieved. As if the thought of this world's huge crop of subtle malice and implacable cruelty were in some way a comfort to him.

—Were you given a passport?

—I was coming to that, he said. —Although the place seemed to be in a state of confusion, crowded with the suitors and with messengers coming and going (I was soon to surmise that the day's usual business was hugely increased by the arrangements that had to be made for the funeral), the clerks were most hospitable to me. Too much so. I was attended to while others had to wait. And while I was modestly pleased that my fancy of myself as a gentleman, sir, seemed to be confirmed by their deference, I was also more than a little suspicious. Meantime I was passed along from one to another. Each discussed the matter with me and then concluded that it must be dealt with by someone of more authority in the household. At least an hour, perhaps more, had passed, and I began to conclude that these delays were diversions. That something more than my request for a passport was on their minds. With that realization something like an invisible cold wind turned my flesh to goose bumps and stiffened the hairs on the back of my head.

—I pleaded an urgent appointment, begging my leave to depart and to return another time.

—Certainly you are free to leave whenever you choose. How can it be otherwise? The clerk told me. —However, I believe you might wish to speak to Mr. Secretary first.

—I had to clench my fists to keep my fingers from trembling.

—He then led me away, by means of a flight of private stairs, concealed behind a hanging cloth. Up to another chamber. Pleasant, well lit with candles, with a fire in the fireplace. Some chests, a fine broad trestle table, a few joint stools and one magnificent chair of carved oak wood with cushions. Probably made for a bishop long ago.

—The clerk excused himself and left me, pulling the door shut behind him. I heard no turning of key in lock.

—I went to the windows and looked down over a forlorn garden in the courtyard. Muddy, partly frozen ground and some neat squares of hunched, bare-branched old fruit trees. A few fat snowflakes swirling in the gray air. I watched wind tease the trees and blow something or other—ah, it was a lone glove, a man's leather glove, lost or dropped—across the court.

—So you are the one they call 'Mariner'?

—I whirled. And there he stood, Mr. Secretary, Sir Francis Walsingham, staring at me, sizing me up. Plain gown and a little skullcap set on short hair. Small, dark, bright-eyed man. But tallow-faced also, with a slight purse to his lips. As if his stomach ailed him.

—Well, sir, I am delighted that you have come here to see me of your own free will. And not a day too soon, either.

—I could, of course, have pissed myself out of pure surprise and fright, then and there. But I managed to bow politely.

—Tell me, if you can, if you know, what is this place, this house . . . ?

—It is your house, sir. And it is called the Papey. Everyone in London knows that.

—Which is why I am not asking you that question. I mean, what was it called before?

—Before what, sir?

—Before our King, great Harry may he rest in peace, had the royal wisdom to dissolve and to suppress all monasteries and convents and chantries and the like, together with their wicked, superstitious, utterly foolish practices!

—He said it with feeling enough. No question but he hates us, but with a certain polish of irony. If you know what I mean. Not as if he wished to deny the validity of his judgment. But as if he had said these things, these selfsame things, too often. As if he were willing to mock even the depths of his own hatred.

—True or false, that inference was a comfort. And frightened half witless or not, I could see nothing to gain by advertising my fear and trembling. So I made myself keep my chin and head up and looked down on him.

—This place was the Brotherhood of St. Charity and St. John the Evangelist. It was a place set aside for the care for poor priests and priests who were crippled and lame. But you are wrong, sir, if I may say so.

—Wrong? Wrong? How's that? What do you mean?

—The clerk had returned to stand near behind him and was openmouthed and bug-eyed at my audacity.

—In this sense, sir. That it was not suppressed in the time of King Henry the Eighth. The Brotherhood remained securely here until the reign of King Edward.

—So it did. So it did. And I stand corrected by you.

—He moved past me then, myself stepping aside, so as to ease himself onto the cushions of the chair.

—Yet it is appropriate, don't you think?

—How so, sir?

—Because of the laws of this kingdom, because of my bounden duty as the principal Secretary of the Council and our Queen, here in the Papey is where many a fat priest, many as young and hale and hearty as yourself, has come to commence the schooling which will soon leave him poor and is likely to leave him crippled and lame as well.

—And, sir, upon graduation from the school, to be miraculously divided so as to be able to be in four separate places at one time.

He laughed out loud.

—Death of wolves is the safety of sheep, he said.

—So it is said, though in all my life I have yet to see or even hear of one wolf in England.

—Peter, he ordered, bring out the list.

The clerk bent to open a chest. Fumbled among papers. I continued to look Sir Francis in the eyes, fearing to look away lest he strike at me like a snake. Hoping that he might possibly misconstrue my attitude for some kind of courage. But it was as if he could read my mind like an old tale he had by heart.

—You have a proud bearing and an engaging manner, he said.
—Even a certain honesty. But I'll not confuse them with courage. Not that I value courage above other virtues. For there are many kinds of courage. You know, as well as I do, how we have ways, both old and new, to test a man's courage. And I am able to tell you that we have never yet met the man whose courage is without limits.

—Sir, I said, I am sure that you have seldom, if ever, encountered one like myself, a man with so little desire to be tested at all.

—Tell me, he said. —Have you ever heard of our Mr. Topcliffe?

—Yes, sir.

—What have you heard?

—That he has skill. That he relishes the exercise of it on the bodies of Papists. That he is a sort of master organist at the Tower of London in playing upon the Duke of Exeter's Daughter, as the rack is vulgarly called. That he plays upon that organ and brings forth a whole choir of cries and groans from a single body.

—And have you been told that he now has permission of Law to practice his craft in the privacy of his own house?

—No, sir. I had not heard that.

—And that he has lately invented an engine (God knows what it may be) compared to which the rack is but a child's toy?

—No, sir.

By then the clerk had spread papers on the table and placed a candlestick close by. We moved there to look at them.

—A long list of names. Many names. Mine there among them. And yours. Some of them, dead already, had the mark of the gallows crudely drawn next to the name. . . .

—Tell me why you wish to have a passport, he said. —Have you given up your faith?

—I hope not, sir. Hope that I haven't lost my faith. But I begin to be certain that I have lost my vocation.

—Is it something to be ashamed of?

—Only a fool can be proud of his own weaknesses.

—And you do not imagine that you are a fool?

—Alas, sir, I could easily be led to that conclusion.

—Where will you go when you leave England?

—To Italy where I have friends and some kin now living. Perhaps to Rome, maybe to Padua. . . .

—A wonderful place, Padua, he said. —I lived and studied there during the reign of our Queen Mary. How delightful Italy would be, if it were not for Papists and Italians.

He returned to his chair, sighed as he settled on the cushions, and motioned for me to put on my hat again and to pull up a joint stool close by so that he could talk without strain. He told the clerk to wait beyond the door until he was called. Clerk seemed reluctant to leave. Walsingham spoke more sharply to him. He bowed and left us.

—He is concerned for my safety because you are armed with sword and dagger.

—I had forgotten, I said, truly.

—I am not concerned, he said. —Should I be?

—No, sir.

—Then permit me to speak freely with you. Pay close attention, please, and listen to what I have to say, for I have only a short time to spend with you.

He added that, ideally, we should have more time to discuss these knotty things. But that he was busy beyond his capacity to bear it. And that the recent execution of the Queen of Scots had now added to his burdens. And now, also and alas, the time had arrived for the great funeral ceremonies for the Shepherd Knight. His celebrated, handsome, learned, pious, courageous, much-admired and much-loved son-in-law. Who had managed, this veritable model and pattern of perfection, by neglecting or forgetting to put on leg armor in battle, to acquire a wound serious enough to cause the death of him. Whose body had been sent off in November from Flushing to the Tower of London, by more than a thousand marching soldiers and many cannon salutes and volleys. Landed from a ship specially equipped for mourning with black sails, amid great pomp and ceremony, and conveyed from there to the Minories, just outside Aldgate. From which place this same body was now to be taken to St. Paul's for a state funeral the likes of which has not been seen here except for royalty. Perhaps aptly, for he had left behind him enough debts to make a King wince. Debts which, in the absence of a King's revenues or ransom, Mr. Secretary Walsingham must now find a way to settle.

He paused, still studying me for whatever he might find.

—The poor man's body has been resting, in relative peace and in more or less arrested decay, over in the Minories ever since the fifth day of November. And here we are in the midst of February. Why do you imagine we have decided to bury him, and with such honor, flourish, fanfare, and, alas, such expense to me, just now?

I waited a moment to see if his question were only rhetorical.

—To begin, sir, it is a diversion from the news of the death of the Queen of Scots. It will distract the citizens of London. And not merely the citizens of London. For with the Hilary Term only just ended, you will attract many who are still here on business, who will carry the word of this event to all corners of the kingdom. A week earlier would have been too early. A week from now would be too late.

Impassive, nothing of his face or expression alive except the eyes, he nodded for me to continue.

—Next, sir, it will prove to be a bringing together of many different kinds of people. For Sir Philip Sidney was equally popular, and so will be equally mourned, among all sorts of Englishmen. Even, if I may say so, among such as Papists and Puritans.

—And even among the courts and councils of foreign countries, he added.

—True, but more to the point, this ceremony, which will be reported by their agents and ambassadors here, will indicate a stronger sense of unity among Englishmen than strangers may have conceived. And it will make the same sort of reassurance here at home. Easing the minds of those who fear that rebellion is near. Warning others, if there be any, who may hope for it, or may even be scheming for it. And, finally, we have need of a hero, sir, someone living or dead, but preferably and safely dead (for there's many a hero who has too soon outlived all admiration), someone who can stand for the best and bravest that we all aspire to. A King or a Prince could be that hero for us. But though our Virgin Queen is greatly loved by her people, she cannot be asked to represent the example of noble warrior also.

—I think she might relish that role, he said. —Say a little more concerning the Queen.

—Nay, sir, I have already talked too much and too impertinently.

—What do you fear, man? By the Law and by precedent you are a traitor, as much so as if you had been tried and found guilty, simply by being a Papist priest in England. By Law you are as good as dead even as you sit here. May not the dead say whatever they please?

—No doubt, sir. So then I say this: It does not, shall not, please me, dead or alive, to speak or to think ill of our Queen Elizabeth.

—Ah, it is a pity you are such a confirmed Papist, Walsingham said. —You might have learned the arts of diplomacy. Are you dry?

—Sir?

—I usually drink a cup of wine at this time of day. You have answered all my questions and must be dry. I invite you to join me. I recommend it.

—I am grateful, an it please you.

While we sipped our wine, the best Canary I have ever tasted, he presented a sort of case and made me a kind of proposition. In this fashion: that he, privately, would not wish to shirk from the lawful disposal, by hanging and drawing and quartering, of every traitorous Papist priest and Jesuit in England. And indeed, also, any of those in France or the Lowlands that his men might find and seize and bring home to judgment. Their torments, my torment included, would be entirely just. But that he, as the Queen's loyal servant, must always follow public policy without regard to private wishes. That it is the policy of the Queen to act mercifully whenever that is possible.

That now, step by step, we are moving toward war. Certainly with Spain and all its empire. Perhaps also with the whole Catholic League. That war is now inevitable. That the Queen must be able to depend upon the love and loyalty of all her subjects, including her Catholic subjects.

But that she does not wish her loyal Catholic subjects to be vexed by their divided loyalties. Nor does she wish that her other subjects should have any reason to imagine that the Catholics are disloyal.

That the key to this matter is with the priests.

That it is known and understood, and is even recognized by the Law which defines them as traitors, that they are creatures of divided loyalty. At the least. At the worst many may honor the papal bulls of excommunication and the divers Papist inducements to disobey the Queen. Indeed to overthrow, even to murder her.

That the plots and conspiracies of the times—Ridolfi's, Parry's,

Babington's etc., and who knows how many others?—prove the danger. But, still and all, these have been few. That therefore there must be very few priests who are truly disloyal.

That among priests who have been discovered and taken, even under torture and torment, almost all have sincerely professed their loyalty to the Queen.

That it is, therefore, the firm belief of the Queen, together with many of her Privy Council, that most of the native-born, English priests are as true and loyal subjects as any other in this realm. And that they are likely to remain so until a war of religion will force them into acts of treason.

That it is the stratagem of foreign powers, which are the enemies of the Queen and of England, to bring war to this country. Which will then force the priests into the commission of acts of treason. Which, in turn, will force the government to kill them, one and all. Which, in turn, is likely to result in much tumult. And in a great slaughter of the innocent, regardless of who may be victorious. All of which will serve the purposes of our foreign enemies and may lead to foreign domination of this land.

That it is the same domination, even more than the restoration of the Papist religion, which is the primary purpose of our enemies.

That, therefore, it should be understood that the foreign powers which permit young Englishmen to come and to study at the seminaries there, and then encourage them to return to England to do missionary work in the face of the ever-present danger of martyrdom, are eager for English priests, as many as possible (if not each and every one of them), to die.

That, whether I chose to believe this or not, and no matter either way, the difficult task of his agents in gaining information concerning the English priests, in following their comings and goings, in hunting down the most dangerous of them, has been made much easier by the aid and comfort offered and given to him by the servants of enemies—by high and trusted servants of the Valois of France and of the family Guise, of the King of Spain, of the Emperor and even of the Pope.

That most of the time he could cheerfully dispense with the expense of maintaining his own network of agents in this matter and could depend on the knowledge and services of our enemies.

That it is almost impossible for a young English priest to begin packing a chest to come home without Walsingham knowing it before he has finished with his packing.

That, once they are home in England, there are precious few, if any, of the priests who are not continually observed and their whereabouts precisely known.

That if I wished it, he could show me a log and a journal of my comings and goings, almost day by day, for the past two or three years.

That he was not alone. For in these days of danger, many of the Court and Council had discerned that knowledge, in and of itself, can be as worthwhile as gifts or good service to gain favor of the Queen.

That Archbishop Whitgift, with the Church of England at his service and no lack of money, had already developed a large network of intelligencers. And that I should consider myself fortunate not to be, even at this moment, answering for myself in Lambeth Palace.

And that there is scarcely an upstart ambitious courtier these days, to say nothing of great men and high officers, who is not willing to pay well for knowledge.

That all this could well be taken as a clownish sort of comedy, a sort of Punch and Judy puppet show, with spies tripping and falling over each other and spying upon each other and repeating the same gossip and rumor as true secrets etc. etc. etc.

And that yet there were even some benefits from this ridiculous condition. For instance, that the real business of gathering knowledge could go on undetected amid this confusion. Just so the smoke and noise of a battle can be advantageous to those who know how to make use of them.

That not all these newcomers were as wise in experience, as discretionary and understanding as they might be. On the contrary many, well-born and educated men, were ignorant fools, playing at a game beyond their understanding and, in turn, poorly served by cozeners and ignorant, arrogant, spleenative, knotheaded scroyles!

That one undeniable benefit of the war soon to come would be when the hotbloods of the Court were all busy at it, by land and sea, and their ne'er-do-well, scarecrow servants had been pressed into service and sent off to rot in Ireland or run from the Spanish *tercios* on the Continent.

But that men could as easily die from folly as malice. And that, therefore, he must admit to some pity for the Papists.

That Papists may be some sort of holy fools, but are fools nonetheless.

That, perhaps something of a fool himself, he was eager to take advantage of my fortuitous arrival. To offer a proposition. To propose that I should seek out as many priests from his list as I could find. That I should inform them that if they wish to leave the country now and to return to the Continent, it can be arranged. That even if they do not trust the Secretary to make such arrangements (and who can blame them for feeling doubt, considering the present state of the Law and the public record of the Secretary?), they should be strongly urged to depart from this realm with all good speed.

That this need not be conceived as banishment or exile. For it has ever been the hope of the Queen that, once the safety of this kingdom and of her throne are secure, once there is no manifest threat against her, from without or within the kingdom, then steps may be taken to assure a greater toleration in religion. And then the native-born Papist clergy may well be welcomed home to minister to their flock.

That I would not be asked to do more than to act as a messenger in the matter. Acting on the Secretary's behalf.

That I was not being asked to betray my brothers or to reveal any other information.

That in reward for this service (a favor and duty to my fellow priests as much as to myself), I shall be given a passport. And in the meantime will be given some money to defray such costs as I may incur. . . .

Mariner seemed brightly giddy as he told me these things. Almost blithe. I felt a knot in my guts, a heaviness of heart. He smiled and shrugged.

—It was that money which I lost at gambling last night.

—I can give you a little money, I said. —Not much, but. . . .

—Thanks be to God, he said. —I can get more at the Papey, but not so soon.

—But you must run for your life, I told him. —Before they have you stretched out on the rack . . . or worse.

—You have it arsie-versie, he said. —I am here to warn you. You must leave England now.

—Surely you did not believe him?

—He was very persuasive.

I said nothing. What could I say?

—If only you had been there with me, he continued quickly. As if to fill in my silence. As if my silence threatened him. —You would have been persuaded, too. Oh, I know, you will say that the Devil himself is the greatest persuader. But Walsingham was very candid with me. He did not pretend to be anything other than . . . *Why are you doing that? Why won't you listen to me?*

I discovered that I was shaking my head.

—Forgive me. —I had no other choice, he said, tears in his eyes. —My name was on that list. I was caught like a rat in a trap.

—Our names have always been there and will remain there until the faith and Holy Church are restored in England. Or until some clerk of his draws the sign of the gallows next to our names in the margin.

—It does not have to be so.

—You have been a fool, I told him. —A poor, deluded fool. He did not need the rack or the thumbscrew. All he needed was to talk to you. Now good men will die on account of your folly. Count on it.

—What are you saying to me? Why are you saying these things?

—You have sold your brothers in Christ for a passport and a signature, I said, then laughed. —I'll not wager a halfpenny that you'll ever see that passport.

—I am trying to help you.

—You are his beagle hound. His stalking-horse. Someone will have followed us here from Paul's Church. Someone is waiting for me now out in the street. Or maybe even here, in this tavern. Someone is waiting even now. To apprehend me. Or maybe merely to follow me to wherever I may lead. You have betrayed me.

—No. Never! he said. He was drunk now. Drunk and weepy. I knew I must leave. Must run out of the back to escape, if I could, in the busy streets.

—I would never, ever betray you or any of my brothers, he said, too loudly. —I am, God knows, a bad priest. I have always been a bad priest. But you must believe that I would never do such a thing.

—But you have done so, I said. —And now you know exactly how Judas Iscariot felt.

I stood up quickly, turned and walked out of the back door. Then quick across the garden and up and over the low wall and onto a footpath. Which led first in to Maiden Lane, then to Distaff Lane and then south to Knightrider Street. I went east and entered Trinity Church. Where I waited for a half hour, feigning prayer, to be sure that I was not followed.

Knowing that now I must find a place to hide. A new disguise to wear.

Remembering that I had left my expensive Protestant Geneva Bible at the *Dagger*. Well, let him sell it.

After a while I walked down to Thames Street, then east all the way to Fish Street. And thence across London Bridge among the crowds.

Large noisy crowds. There must have been a bearbaiting or some such show at Bankside. Something bringing out penny stinkards as honey calls up flies. Thus my face (and myself) became one more face among them. Another bland sheep in the bland flock. Moving with each step toward safety. Which was to be found (as in a maze) among the back alleys and footways of Southwark. Behind and beyond the precincts of old Winchester House. . . .

There indeed found some safety. Like a running fox gone to ground. Waiting and praying. Wondering what I must do next.

Sent out word, carefully, in code. Sent word to Shepherd. No reply from him.

After a fortnight I had heard no word from anyone. Concluded that I could not remain in that place much longer. No, what joins me with my enemies in this enterprise is the need for knowledge. The hunted beast must know what is happening among the hounds and hunters. Or else that beast shall surely die. May die anyway and sure enough. But best not to die in blind ignorance.

And these good and faithful souls who had taken me in from danger must not now be exposed to the even greater risk of keeping me there too long. Others in danger, perhaps graver than mine, would have need of them later on.

I determined to try to seek out Player. No doubt his company was somewhere in the City now, with Ash Wednesday so soon to be upon us, performing plays in the innyards before Lent put an end to that.

So, made new and strange with black hair and a black beard and dressed out and equipped as a kind of raggedy, threadbare captain home from the Continent and the wars there (not for the first time; this disguise seems to suit me, and the best of it is that, with sword at side and dagger on the hip and face set in a permanent scowl, there are few who even wish to talk to me), I went back into London looking for him. Looked at the *Bull* in Bishopsgate, the *Bell* in Gracechurch and the *Cross Keys* upon Gracious Street. Before, at last, I found these actors where I should have tried first—at the old *Boar's Head* in Aldgate. That large inn, with a yard suitable for the presentation of plays and shows, and with several stories of gallery all around. I paid to stand in the yard and watch them prance and rant and declaim the speeches from some old play. Most of the actors were moving like dreamers, like sleepwalkers, like ghosts, through the actions of their dreary tale of woe. The audience was yawning. Player appeared, first as a wicked Saracen lord. Who was jeered at by the audience and soon after killed to cheers and applause. Then reappeared as an arrogant and ignorant Bishop, Italian I suppose, of Holy Mother Church. Again he managed to wake up the audience and rouse them to some hooting and the throwing of oranges and such. Tall and deep-voiced, Player seems to have a gift for the actor's craft.

I was pleased that I was a complete stranger to him in my disguise. At least until I spoke to him. A good sign. I sent a lad from the inn, with a cup of wine and my greetings, to find him in the tiring room. After a while he emerged. Still wearing his costume of Bishop's robes. And once he knew me, we took a turn together around the yard. Which was almost empty. A trample of raw mud, scattered with orange peels and nutshells to prove there had been a crowd there.

—We must be exceedingly careful, he said. —I do not think we are being watched. But we could be.

—I'll hire a chamber in the inn, I said. We can have supper there and talk.

—No, he said. —This company is leaving London. I must help them pack to go.

—Will you go too?

He touched my arm.

—Shepherd has been taken. Did you know that?

—God's blessed wounds! Where is he now?

The two of us, false Bishop and scowling captain, by fear and subterfuge, long ago well trained and schooled, would have looked to anyone else in the world, at six feet's distance or more, to be no more than two easy, idle fellows. Both of us nodding and civil. Even smiling now, though our words were like nails. Like little knives.

—He has been taken to Topcliffe's house.

—And what will happen now?

—He will die. Or they will try him and kill him. But not until he has been made to tell too much.

—Not Shepherd. He is strong in the faith.

—Don't talk like a fool. They can make any man's tongue wag as free as a flag in the breeze. Shepherd will keep silence as long as he can. Longer than most can. But in the end he will tell them everything they want to know.

Up on the scaffold, some young apprentice players were dismantling the last shabby scenery. And others were packing chests and such things into a high-wheeled cart.

—I must hurry, Player said. —Must pack up my costumes and get dressed.

We stopped, looking into each other's eyes.

—Was it Mariner who betrayed him?

—We can never know that.

—Why? Where is Mariner now?

—Hadn't you heard about that, either? Mariner was pulled out of the river. Drowned. Whether by accident or his own doing or at the hands of someone else is not to be known.

I listened, nodding. As if he were telling me his thoughts about the weather, nothing more. But my head was pounding.

—You must leave the City at once, he said. There is no hope for us now.

In the gradually dying afternoon, as if winter light had passed through a depth of water, I could see that his eyes were wet. I thought that if he should let go and begin to weep, then so would I. How could I help it? And wouldn't that be something to behold? A false captain and a false Bishop weeping at the misfortune of their friends while they stood together in the muddy yard of the old *Boar's Head.*

—I pray that we shall meet again, I said. —But let it not be at another of these plays.

Suddenly he laughed at that. Too loud, but at least saving us both (for the moment) from any tears.

—Well, he says. —We are not England's best company of players. But we are somewhat more honored in the farther towns and villages. Where they have not been spoiled by City spectacles.

He took my hands in his.

—God be with you, he said. —When you pray for Shepherd, try to bring yourself to pray for the troubled soul of Mariner, too.

And I do so. I do pray for his troubled, restless, guilty soul.

In other days he was blithe enough, and more wise and learned than he would ever had admitted.

It is true that he was a bad priest for our bad times. But in a better world he might have been a good one.

Grant, O God, that while we lament the departure of this Thy servant, we may always remember that we are most certainly to follow him. And give us grace to prepare for that last hour by a good life. . . .

⚹ ⚹ ⚹ ⚹ ⚹

In condemning us you condemn all your own ancestors—all the ancient priests, bishops, and kings—all that was once the glory of England, the island of saints and the most devoted child of the

See of Peter. For what have we been taught, however you may qualify it with the odious name of treason, that they did not uniformly teach? To be condemned with these old lights—not of England only, but of the world—by their degenerate descendants is both boldness and glory to us. God lives. Posterity will live. Their judgment is not so liable to corruption as those who are now going to sentence us to death.

These words, by Edmund Campion, taken from the speech he made upon being condemned in '81.

✦ ✦ ✦ ✦ ✦

Mother—

I commend myself most heartily to you.

I have not written to you, or to any family or kinfolk, for a long time now. And I am sorry for the silence which must have troubled you. And which may have led you to imagine that I have lost all my sense of love and duty.

Oh, I know (and I remember it with some shame) how I wrote to you from Rheims in my zealous days at the seminary. I remember then preaching you a little sermon on paper upon the text of Chapter 10 of the Gospel According to St. Matthew. Where Jesus Christ is sending forth the Twelve Apostles. Where he says: "He that loveth father or mother more than me, is not worthy of me; and he that loveth son or daughter more than me is not worthy of me." Jesus Christ spoke Truth, but it is a hard saying and more knotty than a young man, whose zeal has not yet been tested, can imagine.

I mean to say this. You have my love, and my duty to you, as always before—even more so now, as I have become older and more experienced, if not much wiser. Indeed I do love and honor my family, one and all.

And yet I love God and His Holy Church so much the more.

You can understand that the chief reason for my silence and seeming indifference has been my desire not to impose any danger upon you. Not to test your love and charity with the peril I carry everywhere with me in these days.

It was sad enough to learn, while I was still studying at Rheims, that Council had ordered our return to England and had forbidden all support of us and all dealings with us by loyal

Englishmen. As I understand, it was necessary (these things, I can hope & trust, not being always rigorously enforced) for Father to give my name to the Bishop of your diocese. And that you were, as still you are, prohibited from making any contribution toward my support.

I have also seen that by that same proclamation (a copy of which you can be sure we sadly studied at the English College, word for word as if it were a text worthy of exegesis) you were given four months "to procure the return of said children." I regret that I was unable to help you to comply with this requirement.

By one means and another, I have always been able to gain some news of the doings at home. So I knew that nothing more than some embarrassment resulted from my absence. I suppose it might have been different if Father still held any office at Court. Or if he were ambitious for advancement there. But since he is not, and since he has not, to the best of my knowledge, been injured by my actions, I decline to feel any weight of shame for that.

Indeed I have done nothing that I am ashamed of in that sense. There is nothing for him to be ashamed of except that I have performed my duties as a priest. For it seems clear to us Catholics, who are as true and loyal English as any other, that these many things, all these traps and snares of Law, have been devised not against treasons and conspiracies or against the stratagems of foreign powers, but wholly against our faith and against Holy Mother Church. It should serve to give us strength, few in number as we are and poor as we may be, to know that our oppressors are so fearful of the Truth that they will go to such lengths against us.

Why should I break a long silence to write to you now?

Because this may prove to be my last chance to write to you while I am in England. I expect to be leaving soon to return to the Continent. How and where and by what means I plan to make my departure, I cannot tell you. For your own sakes as much as mine.

I am writing to you during a brief time of safety. I have every reason to believe that the letter will reach you safely. But even if it should not, even if, by mischance, it should fall into the wrong

hands, it can cause you no harm. It will do them very little good
either. The bearer of the letter is completely dependable.
Because, by the time he brings it to you, he will not know where
it originated or, precisely, from whom, there is very little for him
to reveal even if he should wish to do so.

Mother, not so long ago, only this past autumn, I came along
the road within sight of the house. I could see and smell the
sweet white woodsmoke rising from the chimney clusters. I saw,
too, the gold of late afternoon sunlight on the windows and on
the high gilt weather vanes (Father's greyhounds) turning as the
gusty wind kept shifting and turning.

I pulled up and dismounted by the edge of the road. To drink
from my water bottle and to wipe some dust from my face.

From not far away I could hear the clear sound of axes
chopping and the rasp of a crosscut saw. I looked to see a group
of men cutting down a large dead tree—that tall old elm. The one
where, as I remember, my brother and I so often climbed.
Pretending it was a tower from which we could spy on our
enemies. I stood there listening to the slow, steady sound of the
saw, and by then I could even see the glint of axes. And then
from the distance I heard the sound of dogs barking. Hounds out
there running in a pack.

I knew—could see him, clear as a figure on a new painted
cloth, perfectly in my mind's eye if not in flesh and blood—that it
had to be Father. Round and sturdy as a barrel, red-faced with
joy and fury. Father and probably my brother and a group of
their companions riding out to hunt in the winey autumn
weather. All of them tricked out in their best hunting costumes.
Father, as usual, clad as if in autumn leaves—all reds and russets,
yellow and gold. My brother favoring shades of green and never
mind the season of the year. Galloping off across the fields in
breathless pursuit of some running beast or other.

Ah, if hunting and the art of venery were the only true
religion, Father would be named a saint!

For that moment standing by the edge of the road, listening to
familiar sounds, I allowed myself to wish (as deeply as anyone
can wish for what will never be) that I, too, might be there with
them. Riding hard, hallooing in the wind. Wrapped, as if in a
heavy blanket or a warm, full cloak, in the rich warm odors of

horses and dogs, of my own sweat and leather. Drumming of
hooves and heartbeats. Wind teasing and tugging at clothing.
Wind trying to lift off my hat by the brim. And joy, joy pure and
simple, leaping within me; my heart leaping like a trout in a
brook.

My own heart becoming as quick and agile as any hunted
beast.

(Ah, Mother, I fear that figure of speech comes closer to truth
than I would prefer.)

The truth is, though I never found a reason to say it, that I
loved hunting and hawking almost as much as Father. Loved
those long days on horseback under the wide sky. With no more
thoughts or troubles in my head than the sky has. I could picture
it. All of us riding together. Father proud of me again, as once he
was. And all of us together, innocent as the very beasts we ride,
the beasts we are hunting. . . .

But that cannot be. It is not the Devil that whispers the
sweetest lies in our ears. It is the world and the flesh, wedded in
contentment. A kind of drunkenness. World and flesh as no more
and no less than a lighthearted April daydream on the edge of a
deep sleep. Often on the coldest nights in Rheims when the fire
was ash and my candle was so nearly gone that there was more
light from the moon to read by, I could warm myself with the
image of ourselves on horseback on a fine day. Riding as if to
find the horizon and then to leap over it.

But that ancient elm tree groaned and sighed and fell to earth.
I had to go on past our house, our lands, your lives, my
memories. . . . Soon passing through the village. Past the church
and the common and the cluster of houses there. Past the old
dovecote and the long tithing barn from the abbey days. Past the
clean, sweet, thick odors of the brewhouse and the bakehouse.
Keeping my hat pulled low, slumping in the saddle lest I should
(somehow) be recognized. A foolish thought after years, for I
was well disguised. Just beyond the far side of the village I had
to hold up and wait for a young swineherd. A new face to me.
(Though he could easily enough be old Walter's son, who was
close to my age, and who would be grown up and grown tall
now.) Bringing the pigs back to their pens from the forest.
Where they had been feeding themselves fat with acorns and

such. And he with his little beanbag. Teasing and leading them
home with beans.

You might not believe this, Mother. (Though Father might. It
would likely confirm his bleakest expectations.) You might not
believe that I, too, have herded swine. It became a necessary
disguise for a time. Well stained with walnut juice and dressed in
raggedy hand-me-down country clothes, I was accepted as a
swineherd born and bred. Latest generation of a long line of the
same, Father will be pleased to know. (Well, Father, there's a
certain kind of truth in that emblem, wouldn't you agree?) Even
the pigs were tricked by my appearance. Or perhaps it meant not
the slightest difference to them. They would as lief be led about
and cared for by a Catholic priest as anyone else, so long as he
knows where acorns and beechnuts can be found. And just so
long as he is generous with his beanbag. Sometimes I thought
perhaps I had missed my true vocation in the world. Until I
thought that maybe it is much the same kind of vocation. Of
course, few of the faithful would accept the pig as an
emblem for themselves. Precisians of Holy Scripture, they prefer
to think of themselves as sheep. But, Father, you would say—as,
indeed you used to say out loud whenever it came time for
singing or saying of the Psalms, or when a reading from Scripture
concerned the emblem of Jesus Christ as our good
Shepherd—that you would rather be almost any kind of beast in
this world except a . . . (I can hear you say it now):

"Except a damned dirty little woolly helpless ignorant
emptyheaded bleating animal whose only value lies in the wool
that grows to cover its nakedness and the meat that covers its
bones. Fit to eat grass where once beans and corn and other
good things did grow. Eating grass and growing shaggy wool to
be sold to some double-dealing Dutchman or a pox-ridden
Frenchman, a Froggie Frenchman with a soft palm like a
fish belly and a face like a lady's pet ferret and the easy
insinuating manner of a snake in the grass!

"By God, sir! by the six bloody wounds of Christ!" You'd
thunder, wonderfully joining your blasphemy with your habit of
. . . well, *inaccuracy:* "I would rather be any other beast in
Creation—a fox or a hare, if I had the choice—than a blank-faced,
snarl-wool, turd-dropping sheep!"

I tend to agree with Father in that matter. If it were up to ourselves and a matter of comfort and content, I do believe I would choose to be a pig. True, they die badly, in blood and great squealing (*as do many good men in this wicked age*) but they live well. Like Lords and Princes.

But we are sheep and can thank our Shepherd for it.

End of sermon.

You see, I might have been one of your loudmouthed and long-winded Puritans, as puffed up as the best of them. If I hadn't been taken into Holy Church as a common soldier, I expect, given half a chance, I could have climbed into the pulpit and put large congregations to sleep.

Anyway, I passed the village and the common and the parish church. I had a strong wish to stop long enough to enter into the church. To see what has been done to it. Or left undone. People tell me that because of the Queen's disapproval and perhaps even by a change of heart among some, they have ceased to deface so much that was well made and beautiful to look upon. I do not know what to make of this, however. It could well be a devious means of seeking to win the hearts of many of those who have been much offended by the destruction of beautiful religious things in the name of religion.

True, it is much, much worse in France, what with the coming and going of armies of heretics and mercenaries. And sometimes gangs of savage bandits, deserters from one army and another, loyal to no cause or faith, come out of the forests where they live to loot and pillage and destroy. There are ruins everywhere. Fields given over to weeds and nettles. Forests given over to bandits and wolves. Forlorn empty churches. Schools without pupils. And we hear that it is even worse than that in Flanders and The Netherlands.

I pray for all of you, each day and each night, to be converted and to return to the True Faith. That would give me the greatest joy. But even as I pray for your salvation, I pray also that it may come to pass in peace. For I have seen blood and fire. Have seen women crawling in their own blood and the blood of their children. No more! I pray that the conversion of England may be accomplished without that. We have spilled enough blood.

When you pray, pray for peace also.

To return, I had a strong desire to see the church where we had so often worshiped together when I was a boy. So many of the words and phrases from *The Book of Common Prayer* still echo in my mind. But I could not stop. I had to push on smartly if I hoped to arrive safely where I must before night fall.

Soon out on the open road again. Crossing the brook and then climbing the hill. From the top of which I could twist around and look back once more to our house, sitting proudly in its place. From there looking as small as a toy. Feathers of white smoke rising from the chimneys. Dancing, swaying, then blown away by brisk wind. Late light splashing, like surf breaking on the shingle, against the windows. Again I heard the belling of the hounds, returning. Nearby in a stand of timber, I listened to the sudden uproar of a congregation of crows. Who had decided, for some obscure reason, that the moment had come to scold us all for our long chronicle of follies and sorrows.

I wanted then to weep.

Not out of foolish pity for myself. But for the sake of all of us. Yet not daring even to do that.

Wishing that, instead of going on, I might have left the high road and turned down the long, winding leaf-strewn lane, to our old gatehouse. There to dismount and stretch my legs, to hand over my horse to Gabriel, to give old Gabriel the horse to walk and cool and to feed and look after. Though I fear that he would not approve of my riding such a swaybacked, sleepy-headed, lazy nag as I have to be content with these days.

Is he still alive, old Gabriel? How can he be? He was already mostly deaf, half blind, half lame, and stiff with age and infirmity.

He was the last one I saw when I rode out of the gate that early morning, mist still rising from the fields and the brook, headed for London—and for Lincoln's Inn, as all of you thought. He knew better. He stood by the lane, just beyond the gatehouse. Took off his battered straw hat in respect and to wish me Godspeed and farewell. But I was too young and too proud and hardhearted—and too timorous, also, fearful that I might change my mind and turn back—to do so much as acknowledge him. Rode past him, close enough to have leaned over and touched him, my young, proud, ignorant head in the air.

Thinking that I would never see that old man or the house or the fields and forest again. Thinking, then, so be it. Telling myself that I was right glad of it. That it was well and good to put off everything old, to begin my life anew.

And so it is—as many things go despite our best wishes—that I stiffly ignored that old man.

He who had first taught me (even before the horsemaster) how to ride, how to mount and to sit up proud in the saddle. He who had patiently taught me the art of angling in the ponds and the creek and the craft of snaring and catching birds. (And both angling and snaring have served me well and have filled my belly at times when nothing else would do me good.) Taught me, too, how to use an old English walking staff: how to defend myself; how to break a pate or some lewd and naughty bones if it should come to that. And that's a skill which has saved my life on the wild roads of France.

But alas for it, I passed Gabriel by with my face set and blank. Rode past him without looking and without looking back.

And he has haunted my memory ever since then.

Sometimes nothing seems so indelibly clear as the recollection of that old man raising his battered, sweat-stained, wide-brimmed straw hat to reveal a patch of thin white hair and a head and face as wrinkled and tanned as his jerkin and his boots. Leaning his weight on a stout walking stick so as to spare his lame leg. Waving one broad, calloused palm. One of his eyes—left or right? cloudy and white, the other one always blue-bright and weepy as if lashed by a twig. Lifting his hat to wish me well.

In those days I had no love and charity for anyone except myself.

Mother, if he is still alive in this world, give him a greeting from me. And something or other in my behalf. Does he still have his weakness, and the taste for it, for fine jumbles and gingerbread all washed down with Spanish Bastard wine? Give him something in my name and for my sake; tell him that I pray for his soul.

I could imagine that if I came riding up to the gatehouse, disguise or no disguise, he would have known me. So would the old dogs who are always dozing there, believing that they are the bold protectors of our house. They would slowly uncurl themselves and stretch, ears up and sniffing, as I came riding up the lane. Then they'd begin to bark. Would come barking toward me, but, then, scenting me, they would whimper and wag their tails and lick my hands.

For a few moments I wanted to turn off the road. To come home, perhaps for good, after all this time. To stand with my back to the fire in the Hall. With a cup of wine in my hands. Seeing how waves of firelight fall like a lazy surf across the cool, polished silver. And then to tell all of you the story of my journeys, my adventures and misadventures. As I pictured it, Father would by now (somehow) have come to understand and could bring himself to forgive me for the choices I have made, for the vocation I am following.

It may be that I shall find the time to write Father before I leave England. But where will I begin? How will I tell him what is in my heart and do so in such a way that it will not seem altogether ridiculous?

Sometimes, from studying myself as I might a stranger, I feel it is fear of the ridiculous that separates us more from love and charity with each other than our sum total of sins and wickedness.

Much as I longed to come home to the love and fellowship of our family—and, Lord save us, I have even come at last to miss the grim, enigmatic faces of our ancestors, distinguished and nondescript alike, those portraits which I used to torment by making faces at them, like a clown, when no one was there to see me do it—I dared not test Father's powers of forgiveness. Never his strongest virtue. I remember him saying of some quarrel or other that was about to be patched up or amended:

—Now what? Now what? I can preserve a grudge as well as any man alive, but damned if I know that I can bear so much goodwill and fellowship!

I dared not, even, to do my duty as a shepherd of souls, to seek to bring you all back into the fold of Holy Church. I have learned to console myself, without impertinence I hope, that even Jesus Christ had difficulty with His kinfolk. So much so that He speaks of it, in the sixth chapter of St. Mark: "A prophet is not without honor, but in his own country and in his own house and among his own kindred."

And I did not dare to endanger you, or myself, by my presence. Terrible things have happened in this kingdom. I hope you have been spared all but the unquenchable rumors of these things. Father's choice, so many years ago, to renounce the life at Court, to shrug away that kind of ambition, settling for a life in the country as an honest custodian of his estates, may prove to have been a blessing for all of us. It must have been a disappointment to you. For with your natural grace and wit and beauty, you could have found a place and have been an adornment at any Court. Father, however, even when he was as young and slender and handsome (as his portrait shows he was), could never have made much of a courtier, could never have learned to smile and smile and keep silent and swallow his pride and his temper. Sooner or later he would have spoken his mind.

He's better off at home, where he can always speak his mind to horses and can harangue the hounds. Especially his greyhounds. Who cannot speak back at him.

But terrible things are happening, and I thank God that you are spared these things. I try not to think of them excepting in my prayers. I cannot speak of them. If only I were able not to dream of them! Sometimes in the middle of the night I wake up aroused by my own cries. I wake trembling as if with chills and fever, crawling with cold sweat. I wake with no sense of where I am or when, in my life, it may be. I might be a child again, startled awake by lightning and thunder. Sometimes I wake now and find myself waiting for you to come again, pale in the light of the candle you are carrying. Sweetness of herbs and some kind of perfume (I imagine that you have been helping late in the stillroom to make distilled waters) mingles with your own familiar aura. Which I remember as being much like new-baked manchet bread. Sweetness of you moving toward me. Then the light of a candle coming closer. Then a tall shape bending over me, your smooth palm cool on my forehead. Then finally the sound of you, sound of your voice, half humming, half singing a country lullaby as I close my eyes again and let sleep like a slow river bear me away, carrying me wherever it will.

Even the memory can soothe me to sleep.

Mother, I know that you would have been more contented if I had married well as you and father had planned—to young Alice, joining a piece of her family's fortune to ours, and fathering grandchildren, sons to bear our name. And truth is if I had not been called out of the secular world to serve God, I can think of no life that could have pleased me more. Were I free to marry, I can think of no one whom I should prefer over Alice to be my wife. It was never that I preferred another or loved anyone more. If anything, I loved her too much, too well. Which is why, Mother, I felt I must not write to her or pretend (even to myself) that our parting could be anything but final.

Perhaps I will be able to write to her one day and offer apology for my life, for any wounds I inflicted on her. They will have healed by now and I hope that life goes well for her. I have heard that she is well married. Is that true? I wonder even as I wish her well.

As for the family and our name . . . well, my brother is at home with you and must be almost a man by now. God willing, he can marry and father children to carry on the name.

Edward, my brother, if you should happen to read this, I understand, very well, your anger against me. It speaks well for you. For most all of the younger sons of England are, by laws and customs of inheritance, forced to hate and to envy the firstborn. Wishing that the eldest might do anything but live long and well. You are an amazing exception. Your anger against me, as I understand it, is because I have left. Because, by my own choice and out of my priestly vows of poverty, chastity, and obedience, I have relinquished inheritance and placed it upon your shoulders. Because of your sicknesses as a child, which have left you somewhat frail and with one leg that does not serve you as well as it ought to, you are naturally bitter against me—I, who have always had good health with never more than the slightest of infirmities.

It is true that I could run and dance and swim, could fence with a sword and fight with a quarterstaff. But you were the better horseman. I could not match you at playing a lute. It took all the skill and patience that I had to tune it. Oh, all of this is foolish and childish! Except that it is over these childish things that brothers have always quarreled since Cain and Abel.

I understand how I may have hurt you. And for that I ask your forgiveness. Though I would not, Edward, change anything that I have done. Except—if an occasion for revision were offered to me—to try to do better than I have been able.

I am often fearful. You may find that hard to believe. For in my arrogance I laughed at you and your fears—of thunder, of ghosts and spirits. Laughed at you because it pleased me and eased my own fears.

It is, in your view, my fault that you have not been permitted to follow after me. To study at St. John's in Oxford or at Lincoln's Inn. You feel that you have been deprived of your chance for education and advancement. You feel that it is because of me that you are being punished in my place. There may even be some truth in that. But it is mostly based upon Father's misconception of how things came to pass. Father blames St. John's and the whole climate of Oxford for my conversion. Surely, Edward, even as you understand how Father might see things in this way, you are old enough in the world to know that this is not how deep changes come upon a man. A man does not learn things which utterly change his life by changing residence from one place to another. Or by studying with a new tutor. It is true that all of Oxford, and St. John's especially, at least while I was there, was a theater of religious disputation. Ideas were in the very air we breathed. And that was, indeed, a change. It is true that, by the time I came to study there, there were good Catholics who had come and gone before us and who had gone into exile for their faith. Some of these have been martyrs since then. Others have done mighty works for the glory of God. Surely the spirit of these men was there to inspire a young man already troubled by spiritual confusion. And, God willing, that spirit will continue to breathe and shine there, to inspire other young men toward the truth for as long as there may be colleges gathered together in a university at Oxford. But it would be a grievous error to assign my conversion to that time at Oxford. Seeds were planted there, true. But the field had been long since cleared and plowed, made ready for the broadcasting of seed.

I have no intention to rehearse the story of my conversion. It would have to be the story of my whole life. If Father needs someone to blame for it let him go to his looking glass. I was far too young to know anything except that the service of worship at the parish church changed. And I had that story at second hand, from the muttering of my elders. Father did not mutter, at least. No whispered discontent for him.

Do you remember Father Martin? Probably not. You were too young, too sick in your childhood. Though the old man did come to pray over you. Father Martin had been a true priest in the old days. And he remained our parish priest. He took the oath and changed with the times. And without much strain or inner strife. He had seen it all, all the changes. Had turned with them as a weather vane turns obediently to the wind. I shall not judge him. It has taken me years of hard experience to come to the simple awareness that old Father Martin was a good man. What kind of a priest he was, I cannot fairly judge. Measured against the saints and martyrs, he was a poor example. But we had no saints and martyrs to know of without him. He was our only priest. His failures are with his own conscience. I know that he performed every kind of service that the law required. I know how he buried the plate and the vestments and the Missal and the crucifix. Then dug them up again when the time was right. And I'll wager they are safely in some place in the churchyard now. Hidden, forgotten, now that he has gone, but waiting for the restoration of the Faith.

When that day does come to pass—and it will, Edward, no question of it, how I should like to be the priest who comes to say the first Mass in our church again!

Where was I? Ah, yes. Our father and old Father Martin . . .

Of all people in the world, Father chose Father Martin to blame for the topsy-turvy of religion in our age.

—Damn it, sir! he'd cry, tossing *The Book of Common Prayer* over his shoulder as if it were a bone or a piece of meat intended for one of the dogs. —Damn it, but my mind is not trained up to remember by heart too many things. All I want to do is to say prayers in the morning and the evening and to come to church as the law requires. I am not one of your zealous men. I seldom have quarrels concerning theological matters. You will have to grant me the truth of that.

—Oh, indeed, sir, Father Martin would say, speaking softly in the hopes, perhaps, of lowering the tone of Father's voice to match his. —Oh, yes, indeed. I would never think of you as a disputatious fellow in theological matters.

—Never, Father would allow. —All that I ask is that you churchmen put your heads together and reach some sort of agreement. For myself, it is of no matter. Candles or no candles. Crosses or no cross. Kneeling or sitting or lying flat on my arse. Singing or not singing—though I confess I do enjoy the occasion to exercise my voice in your church.

—And a fine voice it is, sir, a rich and resonant bass . . .

—Never mind. Never mind that. It's high time you churchmen agreed on the correct order of worship. So that those of us with other things to do and important things on our minds, can memorize the service once and for all and then forget about it. I hardly know how to pray anymore withouten one of your books in my hand. And my eyes are not so keen for reading as they once were.

—Don't trouble yourself unduly, Father Martin would tell him. —God will hear your prayers and listen to them in any form. So long as you speak truly, from the heart.

Edward, you can believe that those foolish arguments between Father and Father Martin were (now that I can look back and can see the path I have come by) the beginning of my spiritual education.

—Father, I am tempted to tell him, I am doing what you wanted. As a priest I am working and praying for the day when all good churchmen shall join together. And when the faithful, even the ignorant faithful like yourself, will not have to trouble themselves always in learning new words and ways.

I doubt that he would be much amused.

My first instruction came from Father Martin. Now that he's gone, I can say that. (If he were still alive, Father would cudgel him black and blue for making me a priest.) I was not formally instructed by him, of course. I asked questions and he answered them. And once on a spring day we happened to be out riding

together. Hawking, I imagine. Father Martin dearly loved to
hunt with his hawk. Like a gentleman. It was one of his little
vanities.

Well, our riding took us into the neighborhood of the old
abbey. And when we were there and as thirsty as can be, Father
Martin drew us some water from the well. We drank it from the
old cup still chained there. The one thing left among those ruins.
No one would steal it or take it away, he explained to me,
because that old well was thought to have healing powers.

—No one, he told me, not even a pagan has courage enough to
scorn healing water.

We drank the water and he took me through the ruins,
showing me how and where things had been there before the
Dissolution. It was very quiet, except for the birds in the new
leaves, so quiet I could picture it as he described it. And I loved
what I saw.

Of course half the stones in our house, all of the new part, and
of the barns also, came directly from that abbey.

Once I complained to Father about that.

—The monks are gone and forgotten, boy, he said. —And I
didn't run them away. It was the King did that. And it was the
King, thanks be, gave me the right to use that stone. A stone is a
stone, lad, and cares not at all what wall it lies in and calls home.
Do you hear the stones complaining?

So who were my teachers? Who turned me toward my
vocation? Not so much fellows at Oxford or wits of the Inns of
Court. Not even Father Allen and the masters of the English
College, though it was they who accepted me and taught me
what I had to know. No, it was Father and Father Martin. And it
was old Gabriel, too. When we fished the brook or the ponds or
tramped the fields to catch birds. We would talk. I would ask
questions about the old time. And he would tell me how he
remembered it. His father had worked for the monks. And
Gabriel (it was they who gave him that name, he said) had a
child's memory of them in their robes and of the wonder of the
hours and offices there. He could not read or write, but he could
recite and sing the offices beautifully, though I doubt he knew
the meaning of every word. Except that every word was

love—*caritas*. He knew that much. And that much, finally, my brother, is all.

If Father truly fears book learning will separate you from him, and from what he takes to be your proper duty in this world (namely & to wit, to follow in his particular footprints) then he is foolish to think so.

Or, on second thought, perhaps not.

His true folly may lie in imagining that he can—by keeping you safely at home and occupied with the quotidian details of country life, secure in pristine ignorance of the large and wicked world elsewhere, safely isolate from what he must certainly believe is the disease & infection of learning in these times—that he can save you from your appointment with the Truth. I say *Truth*, not only because I am (by the Grace of God) persuaded of it, but also because I think that Father believes that also.

Strange, is it not? Strange that Father does not imagine that you might learn to be a firm and unquestioning believer in the Queen's adulterate (and heretical) Church of England. Or that you might not, by study and thought and persuasion, arrive at some sort of Puritanical Protestant (what Father means by "Germanical") way. No, he fears that any exposure to learning will teach you, as it has taught your brother, to become a Catholic. You see, he fears that because in his heart he knows what the Truth is. He can imagine no other. And likewise it is because he expects so much of learning, values it so highly—as do many ill-educated men—that he is certain that learning will surely lead any reasonable man directly to the Cross of Truth.

He fears to let you go forth into the wide world and to increase your knowledge of it by visiting the cities and celebrated places of the Continent. He need not fear that. I have seen Paris and Rome and even, briefly, some parts of high and windy Spain. And in those places I have rejoiced in the freedom to worship, and to serve, as a Christian, in the ancient unbroken tradition. Where Faith seems still to be unthreatened.

I know that when the Faith is gravely threatened anywhere, as on all this island, in Scotland as well as in England, then the Faith is threatened everywhere. And it cannot be said that all things are secure in France. The sense of danger is always there, amid the tribulation of these days. Yet in the centers of the

Faith, like the city of Paris, that threat can seem very far away. And there is an ineffable joy being able to kneel freely among other penitents and pilgrims in the holy places of Rome. Pleasure and pride, to see that ancient city again abustle with new life. With the restoration of many ruined and decayed things and with the building of many new wonders. There is contentment to be where the power and glory are all Catholic, where the Truth need not be secret or fugitive.

Yet . . .

None of these things contributed to my conversion. I came to these places as a reconciled Catholic, as a seminarian and then as a priest. Also as an Englishman. Who had somehow come to find his true vocation. Who had come on his knees to the Truth, and in so doing found his place in the world. Who had done this in a place, England, where most of the power and all of the worldly glory has been given over into the hands of Caesar.

I confess that, measured against the complacency of believers in foreign places, where their belief is seldom questioned or tested, even measured against the solace of their tradition of meet and right worship, I felt an impulse to swagger. I was possessed of a rough pride at being an Englishman. It was as if we, the young English priests, had come through an ordeal of fire. The fiery furnace. (Or so it seemed to us then—whose greatest trials and ordeals still lay ahead for us, over the horizon of our imaginations.) And in a sense the foreigners encouraged us in that pride. It seemed that they felt somehow humbled by our history. Some of them envied us for it. Others seemed uneasy, as if, in heart of hearts, they wondered if they could have held to the Faith, or to have come to it, in our (almost) unimaginable situation.

And we? We were not truly humble enough (yet) to understand that a proper pride in being English Catholics did not allow us to be proud of ourselves.

Never mind all that.

What I mean is that I now believe that had I visited those places and *not* experienced them as a Catholic and a priest, I might have been more sorely tested. I think that if I had seen the Church in Rome, doing its own day-to-day business in the world much like any other Court in Caesar's world, if I had found myself among the throngs for whom so much of holy worship seemed more like a market fair or a Whitsun ale than the mystical sacrifice and celebration of the crucifixion and resurrection of Jesus Christ, if I had seen this first, before my conversion or my ordination, I doubt very much that either one would have easily followed. There was much to be offended by. And, indeed, some of my brothers from the English College were deeply offended.

All of this is a way of saying I cannot imagine that time spent either at the university or on a journey to the Continent could lead you to the same sort of conversion that I came to. And which I, indeed, devoutly hope and pray for you, too.

I believe that you can find the Truth there at home. (Even though Father Martin is long since dead and gone.) There is much that can lead you to walk in the way of Truth.

Take, for example, the portraits of our ancestors. Which Father has placed in the gallery, as if we were among the great families of England. Ask him about them. Who they were. What they believed. He cannot deny you that. Indeed, it would not occur to him; for he is proud of most of them. (Not all. There is a handsome young man there, a cousin of Father's, who is portrayed as a soldier. Who found himself dancing in thin air at the end of a rope after the failure of the Pilgrimage of Grace.) But when Father waxes eloquent upon the subject of his progenitors, you will discover many good Christians among them.

There were even some of our people among the monks at the abbey. Did you know that? I saw for myself some of the old records, which had been removed to safety in France. Our name is often there.

On the next occasion that he entertains friends from London, or when he keeps the customs of hospitality during the twelve days of Christmas, next time he unlocks that Italian close cupboard, to show off his various coins and precious stones and other rich or odd things, take notice of some things you will have seen often without thinking about them much. The silver pilgrims' badges of our grandfather. Like his father before him, he was one for going on pilgrimages. At least in England. His dream was to make a pilgrimage to the Holy Land. His little vanity was in these badges. Most often the pilgrims' badges were made of lead or tin or pewter. When he brought these home, he had them copied in silver. Father is proud of them (they have value) and proud of his father also.

Ask him if he thinks his father was a fool to be a pilgrim.

Ask him what his father and grandfather believed.

Ask him what may be the meaning of the largest badge, the one with an angel and the Blessed Virgin, representing the Annunciation. No, do not ask him. I will tell you. It is the badge for the Shrine of Our Lady at Walsingham. Our grandfather went among the gentlemen who accompanied the young King Henry VIII there. And like the King, he left his horse at the River Stiffkey, so as to go the last miles on foot. Left shoes, then, at the Slipper Chapel. To walk barefoot to the priory at Walsingham. Where he kissed the holy relic of the finger bone of St. Peter. Then went to bathe in the icy healing waters of that shrine. Which—*you ask Father if this is not so*—was believed by many, and our grandfather among them, to work the most wonderful cures for the ailments of the stomach and the head. And it was also attested that, if you followed the instructions very nicely, the well could cause the granting of wishes within a year.

I have been to holy Walsingham. Never mind how or when it was. Say my duties have taken me, at one time and another, to Norwich and to King's Lynn. (Bishop's Lynn it was, before the King took it for himself and with the Dissolution drove out the Whitefriars and the Greyfriars and the Blackfriars and the Austin Friars.) I allowed my feet to follow my heart to the place. Now the relics and holy images and the statue of Mary the Virgin are gone. And the place is much spoiled and overthrown. But many people, I discovered, do still go there for the sake of those cold, healing waters. Now that the waters have also been reformed, it is no longer accepted that they can cure headache or stomach pain. But no one, even unto this day, seems prepared to deny the power of the waters to make wishes come true.

So I have drunk the water of Walsingham. And once, too, I have been on the old way, by Watling Street, from London to Canterbury, to the cathedral and the ruined shrine of the blessed martyr St. Thomas Becket. This was even before I was converted or knew that I was preparing myself for that. Went there, partly on horseback and partly by walking, with some friends from Lincoln's Inn. Something to do—anything other than studying the dreary Law—in the fine days of early April. It was more for the sake of a poem than belief that we all went there. We followed the path that Chaucer's pilgrims followed. The monks and the relics, some wondrous and some, no doubt, purely superstitious, they might never have been there. But that huge cathedral stands as if patiently waiting for its ghost and its property of holiness to return. And the Water of St. Thomas, which miraculously healed so many for so many years, will one day perform its offices again.

Ask Father to tell you about the silver badge of a Bishop on horseback with the little figure of a groom leading his horse. That will be St. Thomas Becket. And the proof that our grandfather went upon that pilgrimage, too.

And then ask Father . . .

No. Perhaps you should not ask him any of these things. It can only wound him.

Sometimes I believe that Father (*and therefore, I must suppose, all of us also*) was born into the wrong age. Pilgrimages do not interest him three chips' worth. But if there could be a *battle* at the end of it! He would gladly have gone out with the Crusaders to fight the Saracens.

As for me?

Since I am so quick to pass judgment on others, how do I judge myself? More harshly than you might believe. Perhaps I should have been a monk. A brother in one of the orders sworn to silence, prayer, and contemplation. Then you would be spared this letter.

You would be spared everything except my prayers.

Mother—

This began as a letter to you. It was early when I began to write and now is late. My pen is dull, my ink is almost dry. The candle was new and now is dying.

I must soon finish and seal it. Must try to sleep a little before dawn. I have much to do on the morrow, far to go.

The more I think about it, it may be best not to show this

letter to Father. Or to speak of it to him. If that discretion is possible. I shall try to write to him, as I have often tried to do before. I want to send him my love and my honor. And yet I must do so without shame for the calling that I now follow.

I understand his disappointment in me. Since he despises the life at Court—the flattery, the lies and hypocrisy, the double dealing and inequities which accompany ambition there . . .

I have heard him speak (shout) on the subject often enough.

—God's wounds! he'll say. —I would rather be a common apron man, woodcock, or a cross-eyed Abraham man fresh out of Bethlehem's hospital, would be anything under the sun other than a silk-and-satin, diddering and doddering, bat-fowling, rabbit-sucking, bleating-cheat, one of your arse-kissing rascals they call courtiers these days. Let me die of the pox or the Neapolitan scurf before I pucker my sweet lips again to kiss the stinking foot and the hairy arse of any great man of Court and Council!

Who can blame him?

Yet I believe that part of his disappointment with me comes from the notion that I should be the one to go to Court and succeed where he had failed. At first I wondered why, if he truly hated the life of the courtier so much, he would wish that upon his son. It baffled me. No longer. I understand his thinking, and now, with safe years separating me forever from that possibility, I can even agree with him. I conceive that I began with as good a chance to make something of myself at Court as anyone else. I confess that I possessed some natural skills for it. Perhaps, with a touch of good fortune, I could have found some favor there.

Father may have allowed himself to count on that. For there he was, living off his lands and, all in all, living well enough. At the least maintaining his patrimony. But he could see others, his inferiors in many ways, grandly rising. Coming into land and estates. Building new extraordinary pleasure palaces. New names, newer than ours, moving upward in the world, some even into the nobility. Whilst Father stood fast. Holding and keeping his own, but without hope of any new wealth. And living at the mercy of drought or too much rain, winter cold and summer heat.

He hoped I would change that.

Well, Father, I am sorry. I have gone to serve the Court of the one true King. Whatever treasure I am able to lay up for you will not be of this world and cannot help you here. My advice, as a priest and as a loving friend (whoever heard of a son giving advice to the Father?) is to try to spare yourself the fever of these our times. With envy and ambition, which seem to be everywhere in England today, come the deepest dissatisfactions. For there are never enough riches and honors to satisfy the hunger for them. Try to rejoice in the gifts you have been given. They are enough to live well and to do all such good works, out of love and charity, that it is God's will you should walk in. My love and honor to all of you. You have my prayers. Pray for me also. For I need your loving prayers. Written in haste now, but ever with love—

* * * * *

If we suffer, we shall also reign with Him. If we deny Him, He will also deny us.

My heart is troubled within me: and the fear of death is fallen upon me. Fear and trembling are come upon me and darkness hath covered me. And I said: Who will give me wings like a dove, and I will fly and be at rest?

She hath not hearkened to the voice, neither hath she received discipline: she hath not trusted in the Lord, she drew not near to her God.

Her princes are in the midst of her as roaring lions: her judges are evening wolves: they left nothing for the morning.

Her prophets are senseless men without faith: her priests have polluted the sanctuary, they have acted unjustly against the law.

* * * * *

Father A—

Greetings to you and to my brothers of the English College. I commend myself unto you all. I am joined in these greetings, and in hearty prayers for your welfare and for the success of your good works, by others who are here with me now. All known to you. But not to be named here. Even in cipher. For this letter, if it should reach you at all, must go a long journey, by land and by

sea. These things are not as easy as they once were, even a year
or two ago.

It is strange to think of that—how much time will pass
between this writing and your reading of it. Here it is high
summer, the last, long, soft days of August. Harvest has begun.
From high windows and best of all from the little banquet
towers and the leads of the roof, we can see the fields beyond the
park. Where the harvesting of the corn goes on, the reaping and
binding and stacking afield. Soon they will begin the carting to
the barns. Where the corn has not yet been cut and stacked there
are still bright poppies growing.

You will remember it well.

Indeed, sir, you have been to stay here in this same house,
when last you were in England. Much has changed since then.
Even in the house where there are new priest holes and hiding
places for us. Where we must be careful who it is that sees us.
But where, also, much is the same and ever will be. Like the
harvesting in those fields. Like the high chapel where we gather
to say the Mass. Always remembering that you have done this
here before us. Soon will we come together to celebrate the feast
of the Apostle St. Bartholomew—*But I, as a fruitful olive-tree in
the house of the Lord, have hoped in the mercy of my God. And
I will wait on Thy name. For it is good in the sight of Thy saints.
Gloria. . . .*

Ever mindful that half a world away you and our brothers will
likewise have donned your violet vestments to celebrate the vigil.

We shall soon, all but the old priest (you will remember him)
who is always here, have moved on. If we are in any way
threatened before that time, this letter will be burned. If not, it
will surely be early autumn, at the least, before an appropriate
courier is found to start this letter on its pilgrimage to you.
Which, with goodspeed and good fortune, may reach you in
Rome sometime before Christmastide.

Ah, I delight to remember the Christmas season there. Those
churches lit as must be the halls and chambers of heaven. Priests
and Bishops and Cardinals in their finest vestments for the feast
days. Crowds of the faithful gathering. Outside—sometimes
inside the churches, as I recall, to the dismay of pious
strangers—the pipers will have come down from the Abruzzi

(where it will be the time of snow and hungry wolves), to play their ancient wailing tunes. Jugglers and dancers and all kinds of tricksters will be in the squares. I remember seeing a rope dancer cavorting dangerously and joyfully to celebrate the birth of Jesus Christ, dancing on a rope hung from rooftop to rooftop high above the piazza. Odors of roasting nuts in the chill crisp air and vendors cooking pungent Italian foods over little fires and charcoal stoves. Sharp spicy taste of them! And all washed down with the good clean wines of Frascati and the hill towns. . . .

You see how little I have changed from my student days. Still in need of rigor and discipline. And in a sense so are we all, here. For I am speaking in this letter as much for the other priests as for myself.

We are much the same. Yet much changed. As this house, this kingdom—which, in many ways, you would not recognize.

It is true that we are briefly idle, more or less at leisure and in peace. But we are, I think, like soldiers resting after battle, *between* battles, like sailors after a storm.

It is our hope, Father, that you will share our news with our brothers in the College and also, if means can be found, with our brothers and teachers in Rheims. It is our hope that whatever I report may serve to strengthen and confirm their resolve when the time comes for them to join those who are here in England.

I pray, let the words of my mouth and the meditation of my heart be always acceptable. Be also an encouragement for these others, known and unknown to me, who may read these words.

I pray, may my actions also, in felicity and adversity alike, be worthy of my vocation as a soldier and servant of Holy Mother Church.

Pray for me, Father, that I may ever be steadfast.

Since the murder of the Queen of Scots and the close watching, not only of the ports, but now also of every kind of coming and going within the kingdom, we are hard put to reach each other with words of comfort. Or even with ordinary warnings. These latter seem to be all the more urgent now that the statutes are all being ruthlessly enforced against us and all true believers. Of this last, especially the fines and penalties being assessed against Catholic families, you should understand that these are a great burden to them.

Our group seems mostly to be in disarray.

Mariner is dead. Shepherd has been taken. If he is still alive, then he is being held secretly in some place. For we have no word of him. The best that we can hope for Shepherd, I fear, is that his life will be spared. That in due time he will be banished. And now there is a rumor that Player, too, has been taken.

That could constitute grave danger. For on account of his constant travels with the company, Player knows many houses, throughout the shires, where priests have been safe and where Mass is said. This information appears to be of more concern to the Council's pursuivants than even the taking of priests.

There are swarms of spies, intelligencers, and informers everywhere working against us. Those whom we can trust are few and far between.

I am impertinent to add, Father, that it seems to us that there must be some spies and informers planted among you in the colleges and among the exiles on the Continent. Too many among the newly arrived priests, seminarists and Jesuits equally, seem to be easily taken. Taken whenever it suits the authorities. Some are seized almost at once upon landing. Others are taken later, but with such results that it would seem they had been watched and followed from the moment they arrived in England.

The few of us left in our group do not know where to turn. Or to whom. In some way deeper than reason or common sense we do not, finally, trust each other.

You see how confused we have become.

I have come here from Peterborough, where, together with a faithful brother, I witnessed the funeral rites for the Queen of Scots. These things happened on the last day of July and the first day of August. All this time, since the dead of winter in February, her body had been kept, unburied, in the castle at Fotheringhay.

Before Shepherd was taken he sent me there to observe and to report . . . *why play with words so primly?* Shepherd sent me there to be a spy. To spy out anything I could.

This summer I have been close by that place, in a different role and disguise. To seek to find either or both of two priests we had known. By happenstance, both had been within the castle at the time of the Queen's execution. Neither was a witness to that event. But both were able to gather sufficient information from others who were witnesses to all or part.

Since the Queen's servants, French and Scots alike, are still being held there (despite promises made to the Queen before her death) and are unable to depart for their homes and countries or, as yet, to carry on communication with her other servants in Paris or in the Courts of France and of Spain, and of Brussels and of Austria, it seems possible to us that no one abroad may yet know the whole truth of what occurred.

To maintain this ignorance seems to be the policy of Queen Elizabeth's government. Of course this cannot be continued indefinitely. Sooner or later the truth will cry out. But until that truth is known, the heretics stand to gain time and also to sow confusion through rumors.

As soon as it may be accomplished you will hear an account of the death of the martyr Queen. This from a priest who, as I say, was within the walls of the castle at the time. And there is some reason to expect that sometime soon they will begin to permit the Queen's servants to pass out of England.

You are to understand, Father, that as Dowager Queen of France she asked, and it was promised to her, that her body might be sent for burial in France.

You are to understand, also, that for whatever reason (probably fear of crowds) her body was brought to the Cathedral late and by torchlight on the night before the funeral took place. Between one and two o'clock of the morning, attended by Garter King at Arms, other Heralds, some horsemen, and some of her own servants, her body was brought from Fotheringhay Castle to the Cathedral. And placed in its appointed vault. This vault is set within the sanctuary, directly across from the vault and monument for Queen Catherine, the first (and only lawful) Queen of King Henry VIII.

There was, at ten o'clock on the following morning, the morning of Tuesday, August first, a large procession from the Hall of the Bishop's Palace to the Cathedral. For the Queen of England came the Countess of Bedford, as Chief Mourner. There were two Earls—Rutland and Lincoln; and there were two Bishops present—the Bishop of Peterborough and the Bishop of Lincoln. The Lord Chamberlain and the Lord Steward were there, together with many lesser ladies and gentlemen. Helm and crest, the target and the coat of arms were borne by Heralds. In honor of the Queen's charity there were one hundred poor women in black gowns.

All this pomp and ceremony was sufficient to attract some thousands of people (ourselves among them). For nothing of its like had been seen there since the burial of Queen Catherine. Yet still it was a shabby and forlorn occasion for an anointed Queen. In London there would have been laughter at the poverty of ceremony.

The funeral procession and the rites for Sir Philip Sidney were in every way more majestic and important.

It was, then, a shame; though the plain folk of Peterborough had no cause to think so.

Likewise it was a shame for this Catholic Queen, who died strong in faith, to be subjected to Protestant obsequies. Outrageous that the Dean of the Cathedral should be so prominently there, when it was he who harassed her, on account of her faith, at the very time of her death. He preached a sermon on some verses of the thirty-ninth psalm. And he gave her short shrift in his prayers.

You are to understand, Father, that though she was buried meanly and with heretical ceremony, that though she was not allowed to have the service of a priest of her faith at the time of her death, she died as much in the faith and for the faith as any of our martyrs here.

It may be that you have received report of her death from other sources. It may also be true—and we pray that it will be so—that, by the time this letter is safe in your hands, her servants will have been set free. And that the whole truth shall be known to the world. But after standing amid the crowds at Peterborough to witness that sad and inadequate ceremony and after coming together in the calm of this house, we have been speaking of these things. And that is the purpose of this letter. To inform you, Father, of what we have decided. In the absence of any clear instruction we must seek to make decisions for ourselves. Not with impertinence. Not out of any intention to be disobedient. But because, considering the state of things, we have no other course.

Father, it has been agreed that at least one of us should attempt to depart from England, as soon as it may be possible, to bring an accounting of the death (and now the funeral) of the Queen of Scots. It has been agreed that I shall be the one to do this.

Since the ports remain under the closest watch, we have concluded that I should soon try to cross into Scotland. Where there is more safety (at least in some places) for a priest. Where, we have heard, the Society of Jesus is bringing priests now to do work there and to enter into England from that direction.

It is also our supposition that the young King of Scotland may not have heard, even now, any full accounting of the death of his mother. That we should find a means to bring this report to him. And it is the thinking of all of us that this may be a most propitious time to seek to restore the King to the Faith. Surely he can be stirred by the example of his mother's suffering.

Beyond the matter of the Queen of Scots, however, it is also our belief, Father, that someone must carry out report of the present state of the Faith in England. That someone must speak up for the faithful here. If we may say so, humbly, it seems to us that much is being misunderstood and misapprehended by our superiors on the Continent. So many things are different now from when others, such as yourself, Father, and Father P—, were last in England. We wonder if you can well imagine it. The statutes against us and against practice of religion are being mercilessly enforced. Our people are suffering. It is well to counsel them to stand firm and to bear all things. But they are vexed and troubled. And I fear that many, even among the best, cannot be expected to endure. Especially since it is so simple, merely by attending the required services of the Church of England, to ease their pain and misfortune.

Most of our people have no vocation as martyrs. While they can live for and by their faith, even under duress, they will do so. But only a very few are willing to suffer death for it.

I know well what the correct answer to this is. That the many, the weak and the lukewarm, we do not need in the battle. If they slip and slide, so be it. We shall regain them all when we have again restored the Church. That the blood and sweat and anguish of even a very few blessed martyrs can do more for the faith and for the restoration of the Church than all other things taken together.

We have no desire for discord. We have need of instruction, Father. But for the sake of giving good counsel and instruction all of you, our superiors, need to know the true condition of England.

There is much talk, openly by the heretics and secretly by the Catholics, of the Enterprise Against England. It is said that the Queen of Scots has bestowed her rights and claims lawfully upon the King of Spain. And that he shall be coming here, in power, to claim his kingdom. Much is rumored and little is known. I have no doubts that England could be taken by blood and fire. From what little I have seen I conclude, as do my fellows, that the musters of men from the shires would be no good match for the Spanish *tercios*. But we also agree that it would be a mistake to depend upon our English Catholics to rise up against the Queen. This is what the heretics are saying. And it is to their advantage to say it. Perhaps even to believe it. It is our thought, sir, that the time for a rebellion by our people has passed. The will for it has been dissipated by the earlier rebellion and by all the plots and conspiracies which, whether true or false (and many of us believe them to have been either false or provoked), have failed again and again. With each failure the troubles for the faithful have been intensified.

We have no way to know for certain, Father, but we agree that most of our people will obey the Queen. They will not rise up against her if England is attacked. Whatever her Councilors and other agents have done in her name, she still retains the love of most of our people. They feel, and not without some reason, that she is closer to them than to the Protestants and Puritans who are around her. They pray for her. It may be that they are simply bedazzled by appearance; for it is clearly the Queen's policy to delight the people with shows and spectacles.

To whom are these great shows addressed? Not to the more precise heretics, for whom such things are, at heart, offensive. Rather they are for the chief part of her people. Including our own faithful who have been deprived of so much of the splendor of their lives. The Queen has come to be loved and admired by the people, as much by our own people as by any. And nothing, not the murder of the Queen of Scots nor the martyrdom of our good priests, seems to have diminished that love.

There is yet another reason I aim to leave England soon. I have spoken of this to no one, Father. Saving to myself in meditation. And always in my prayers.

I asked you to pray that I may be steadfast and unflinching. For I am deeply afraid, Father. I fear I may be tested and . . . no, surely I know that I *will* be tested to the quick. Sooner or later. My greatest fear, and it has been growing in me, is that when I am put to the test I shall fail. I find myself afraid—often so much so as to be deeply ashamed—that in spite of all prayer and hoping I may prove to be no more than a broken reed. May prove to be a cracked vessel unfit to carry the sweet wine of Verity.

And, oh, I know, sir, how that fear, *my fear,* is testimony to more than a weakness of my flesh. That fear questions my very faith. Strikes at the roots of my faith. I believe with all of my being. And yet, I confess, my spirit is weak.

I do not trust myself.

I can hear you even now. As if you were in this high chamber with me. Patiently trying to teach me, as you have often done before. As I picture it, hearing your soft voice, seeing and indeed feeling the unquenchable brightness of your gaze, you are reminding me, first of all, of the story of St. Peter. Strongest of all the Disciples. The Rock upon whom all else is founded. How even he, Peter, slept in the garden while Jesus prayed in sweat and agony. How Peter said to Him, "Lord, I am ready to go with Thee, both into prison and to death." Nevertheless denied the Lord three times before the cock crowed. How Peter wept, but with his faith unshaken.

And then you remind me of the example of our Lord and Savior Jesus Christ, in that same garden of Gethsemane, sweating and praying. Jesus Himself profoundly perplexed and troubled: "Father, if Thou wilt, remove this chalice from me. But yet not My will, but Thine be done."

You would send me, as you have so often sent us all, to study the lives and deaths of the saints and martyrs. You would send me, as was done in the house in Rheims, to study bloody pictures of martyrdom to prepare myself and my flesh against it. Nay, by study and prayer and meditation to *desire* it, Father. To wish devoutly for that crown and blessing. And so we did, Father.

And yet we knew so little! Our strength was false because it was based upon ignorance.

Pray for me, Father. How I wish I were worthy of your love and kindness.

Pray that, even as I go about my priestly chores—hearing confessions, administering the sacraments, saying the Mass—my faith will be restored. Will be deepened and strengthened. Pray that my restless spirit may find that peace beyond all understanding.

Strange. Strange that after so many months of trouble and danger, now that I am in safety and embraced by loving care, I should be harvesting a crop of fears.

Surely, Father, there is some other service I can perform, something else I might do in the Church for the glory of God. Might I not find a place teaching at the seminary in Rheims or in Rome or in any of the other colleges that will soon be preparing priests for England? Is it not possible that I could assist our brother, Gregory Martin, in the task of translating the Old Testament into English? He will speak for me and such ability as I possess for that task. For he was also a scholar at St. John's.

Once I imagined that my true vocation would be as a brother in one of the ancient monastic orders. Believed that silence, prayer, contemplation, and hard labor expended on the most humble tasks were what I was best suited for. I dreamed back days in England before the Church was so beleaguered. Often my journeys have taken me past one or the other of our abbeys, which now stand so ruined and crumbling. I can picture them as they were. And I can picture myself among the brothers.

Surely, Father, when we recover England, we shall restore the abbeys to their former glory. Then we shall have need of English monks to serve there.

Father, I am so weary. I am so afraid. As much of myself and my weakness as of any terror. Please, Father, consider my weakness. . . .

We have heard the rumor that you may soon be named a Prince of the Church. Our first English Cardinal since the time of Queen Mary. We rejoice in that news. Believing that it is an undoubted sign of the favor of the Holy Father and of the Church. For what you have already done. And for what you are planning and doing. If the rumor is true, as we hope and pray, we salute you.

But how can you pretend to imagine, far off in the safety of Rome, the lives and the fates of your poor flock here in England? This is not weakness, Father. Weak or strong, the sorrows of our people would break your heart. You and others send us advice and instruction which cannot apply and which cause great anguish among the faithful. You send books and pamphlets which do not lift our hearts and which outrage the heretics and confirm them in their worst expectations of us. It is easy, and utterly foolish, for some pious exile, safe in Brussels or Paris or Valladolid, to encourage the murder of Queen Elizabeth. But here the faithful shudder at the thought of it. And here the heretics torture and kill the faithful. And feel that they are justified. Our own people, desperate for our priestly services, are suspicious of us. Are we spies or priests? Do we come for love or for murder?

Forgive me, Father, I . . .

(Better not to finish this. Better not to send this. Better burn it. Better begin again, afresh. When there is time.)

(*Kiss the bloody hands. Are there not princes of the Church whose soft white hands are as bloody as any butcher's?*)

(*Forgive me for even thinking it.*)

✶ ✶ ✶ ✶ ✶

They that sow in tears shall reap in joy. Going, they went and wept and cast their seeds. But coming, they shall come with joyfulness, carrying their sheaves.

✶ ✶ ✶ ✶ ✶

Cleanse my heart and my lips, almighty God, who didst cleanse the lips of the prophet Isaias with a burning coal.

✶ ✶ ✶ ✶ ✶

I have loved, O Lord, the beauty of Thy house, and the place where Thy glory dwelleth.

Take not away my soul, O God, with the wicked, nor my life
with men of blood.

✶ ✶ ✶ ✶ ✶

My charge is of free cost to preach the Gospel, to minister the
Sacraments, to instruct the simple, to reform sinners, to confute
errors—in brief, to cry alarm spiritual against foul vice and proud
ignorance, wherewith many of my dear countrymen are abused.

EDMUND CAMPION

. . . and all of these papers and letters, my lord, were taken
from the priest when he was flushed from his hiding place in a
haystack. He was cold and wet, to be sure, so weary and hungry,
that I do believe he was glad to be taken. When our dogs found
him out, he came forth of his own will, half covered with hay
like some kind of a harvest player, laughing aloud in a womanly
fashion, saying that he wondered what on earth had kept us from
catching him sooner.

We laughed with him at that, my lord, though it was no
laughing matter that in a few more miles, a day's walk give or
take, he would have been in Scotland. Whether that would mean
safety for him or no, I leave to your judgment, sir.

We have no more information to add to what is contained in
the papers. For unfortunately, the fellow died before we were
able to ascertain anything of significance from him. Perhaps your
excellent servants can unravel such things as his proper family
name, place of birth and home, from the evidence of his notes
and letters.

We deeply regret that we have failed you in this matter.
However, it is our best judgment that this priest was of no
special importance to the Papists and could not have been of
much value to us, either, even if he had wisely chosen to be more
cooperative. Since he was not, he was subjected to considerable
rigor. And it may be he was not nearly as strong and healthy as
he appeared to be. At any rate, according to the jailer here and
to our own physician, he died in his sleep sometime during the
night after our first session of interrogation.

Our man, though not nearly as experienced as your servants in
the Tower, or by any means as ingenious as Mr. Topcliffe, is

nevertheless (in our view) honest and capable. He has expressed his disappointment at failing ourselves and you, sir. I have reassured him that we place no blame on him for his bad fortune and that, since you have the priest's various papers in hand, no great harm has been done.

It has been agreed by the physician and the jailer that it shall be given out (to the shame of the Papists) that the priest, in fear of torture or of death by execution, has hanged himself in his prison cell.

Perhaps, sir, the clues contained in his papers will lead you to catch bigger fish. I hope so.

Speaking of which, I am pleased to send you by this same courier some excellent smoked salmon, Tweed salmon prepared in the Scots fashion. May they bring you pleasure and good appetite.

Written & sent in haste.

I look forward to meeting with you in London during Hilary Term, when I shall have a case at Law in Westminster.

Your obedient servant—

COURTIER

1626
(1575)

With an old song made by an old aged pate
Of an old gentleman that had an old wealthy estate,
Who kept an old house, and an old bountiful rate,
With an old porter to relieve poor people at his gate;
    Like an old Courtier of the Queen's
    And the Queen's old Courtier.

                  "The Old Courtier of the Queen's"

. . . Young man, when you live to be as old as I am, when you arrive at my present state of age and decay, you will find that memory is more than a deceiver. Memory's a hard schoolmaster who rules by the rod. Muscles sag and turn to fat. Sinews go rotten like old points and laces. Joints are needled with aches and pains. Eyesight fades, and hearing is often garbled. There's little distinction between sweet odors and foul. Most things begin to taste the same—which is to say tasteless. Your guts go into windy rebellion, and no amount of fasting or purging will rule them for long. And as for the other appetites . . . well, I regret to report that lust is as hot a fever as ever. But the body lacks the means to satisfy it. Cupid's arrows are limp in the quiver, if you take my meaning.

. . . Now, all this decrepitude is hard to bear, but could be endured with at least some grace if the mind's decay were not also part of it.

Even as the old man goes on talking, the summer morning air is fresh and clear. And, as if in blithe indifference to his catalogue of woes, birds are making invisible fireworks with their songs.

Hop, hop, hop. Pause and freeze. Go still as stone. Except for the high-lifted alert head. Cocked head twists and turns. Eyes watching everything. Then again moving. Hop, hop, hop, then stop. . . .

A robin moves across a patch of grass. Plump brown robin wearing a proud splash of orange on his breast. And now across the garden path comes, arrogant, untroubled, a swaggering black swordsman, one fat glossy crow. Waddling without fear while doves, out of sight, make a soft flute music. Bees are tuning strings among the flowers. Somewhere a woodpecker begins to hammer. Lunatic drummer. The thrush joins in. Sings his call four times over from nearby.

Now into the space of silence left by the thrush, from sunlit field and forest beyond the garden's wall, comes the sound of a cuckoo.

The listener, taking these birdsongs to heart, cannot imagine he will ever be old. He is a young man with many things on his mind. Yet he would give much (much more than he owns, for he owns very little) if he could turn himself into one of these birds and fly over the wall and away. To where? To anywhere else. Leaving the old man to talk to the empty air.

. . . I am often troubled into amazement by the many things I ought to remember but cannot. And just so I am sometimes startled by a rising of memories. They come unsought and unwilled, without warning, rising up like the ghosts of All Hallows Eve, wrapped in rot like Lazarus. As if to scare the few remaining wits out of me.

As the young man vaguely listens, he dearly hopes the truth of his thoughts is not printed on his face.

. . . Called to give evidence at Judgment Day, I would prove to be a poor witness in my own behalf.

. . . Well, no matter. No matter. Oblivion will swallow up all things equally. Oblivion is marvelous indifferent to everything else but the promptings of its own insatiable appetite.

This old gentleman is Robert Carey, Baron of Leppington and newly made (the seventh of February of this selfsame year) Earl of Monmouth by the new King Charles I. Before all that, in the reign of Queen Elizabeth, he was Sir Robert Carey, knighted by his friend and commander, the Earl of Essex, at Dieppe in 1591. He was cousin to Queen Elizabeth. Cousin also (though less said the better) to Lady Jane Grey and Mary Queen of Scots. His father, Lord Hunsdon, was a celebrated soldier and Lord Chamberlain for the Queen. Likewise his elder brother, George, was Lord Chamberlain. Robert Carey served the Queen in divers affairs, at home and abroad, for half the years of her reign. He is well remembered for looking to serve himself, at the time of the Queen's death, by being the first man to bring the news of it to King James in Scotland.

Carey has paused to lean on his walking staff and laugh at his own words.

Politely, the young man laughs with him. In a moment or two they will continue their walk, the Earl talking and he listening, moving a respectful half step behind the Earl's left elbow, hat in hand, no more emphatic a presence than a suave attentive shadow.

This young man, only just come down from his college at Oxford, has been sent here by his master and kinsman, Sir Ferdinando Gorges. To serve a time, perhaps no more than this summer season, as a kind of clerk for the Earl. To assist him in the preparation of his memoirs.

"Carey's my old and dear friend," Sir Ferdinando has told him, "truly one of the last fantastics left over from the age of the Queen. But he's not a fool, lad. Never forget that. He's no kind of a fool."

"Well, he will surely need all the aid I can give him," the young man has written, not to Sir Ferdinando, but to old friends at Oriel. "For though he is fluent enough, indeed long-winded in conversation, the Earl's a miser when it comes to written words. He uses a pen like a carving knife, as if he had to whittle every word. He professes to believe it is unseemly for a nobleman, especially one who has lived a life of active service and adventure, to affect any other style but the plainest. He takes the *Gallic Wars* of Caesar as his model, which may be the most difficult Latin the Earl encountered in his brief schooldays.

"Much of what he tells me is very strange. He might be a Red Indian from the New World, clad in feathers, telling tales of other savages. I find myself imagining that time of Queen Elizabeth (where his memories always return to roost like pigeons in a dovecote) as another country, a place on the far edge of some ragged map. Inhabited by people as different from us as Blackamoors or Chinamen. At times I listen with amazement. And other times I smile and nod and pray for the hours to pass."

This young man knows little of the old Queen's times. His

heart is set on the future. The dead neither taunt nor challenge him. He envies no man in the past. Nor does he envy this gentleman who stands already in twilight shadows, most of whose friends are dead and buried, and whose finest days are buried with them. Whatever the Earl pleases to say will be good enough for him. If the Earl wants to believe that England was peopled by fallen angels in the times of Queen Elizabeth, then let that be his pleasure. But, as far as this young man can care, angels or devils, they have all turned to dust.

To seem to pay polite attention is no real sacrifice. He can listen and nod and wear the blank face of a puppet at the fairgrounds.

. . . It has proved a blessing that my mind is not yet as weary as the crumbling castle of flesh it must inhabit. (The Earl continues, *killing the calf*, as stage players call this talking in monologues) . . . For I always sought to avoid intellectual hard labor. In my youth my mind could be safely described as safely sleeping. My mind slept and snored like a full dog by the fire.

Ferdinando spoke the truth. The Earl's not such a fool. And he can surely read this young man's mind; for he has not forgotten how it was to be young. He lived through that long restless season when bold dreams and self-pity wrestle for possession of the soul.

Clearing his throat and spitting in the grass, he begins to walk again. A pair of gardeners, clipping at a hedge shaped like a bear on hind legs, raise straw hats as he and the clerk move past them. The Earl notes, with satisfaction, that the two fellows have wreathed their hatbands with wild flowers.

The Earl and his family and kinfolk, his servants and retainers, have come here to Kenilworth Castle in the heart of Warwickshire to pass the summer months. For pleasure, to be sure, but chiefly to avoid the Plague. A summer ago and many thousands died of it in the City, one out of every five alive there. Death bells rang day and night. Cartloads of corpses were carried to enormous common graves. Surely it was the worst time for Plague since the summer of 1603.

So with the coming of warm weather this year, the Earl packed up his goods and gathered his people and set off, by easy stages, for Kenilworth. Vowing not to return to Westminster until the Plague Bill lists fewer than thirty deaths in a single week.

Meantime no wonder he looks to the past for comfort. They have come to the proper place to indulge him, a place where England's history casts huge shadows. The Castle was already more than five hundred years old when Queen Elizabeth gave it to the keeping of the Earl of Leicester. Who spent a fortune repairing and refurbishing and building anew also. He fully restored the high red sandstone outer walls and towers which enclose seven acres—Swan Tower, facing the hundred-acre lake to the west; Lun's Tower; the Water Tower on the deep moat at the east; and, at the southern end and angle of the curtain wall, Mortimer's Tower. To which he added a walled Tiltyard stretching a hundred and fifty yards and ending at the Gallery Tower; place where his wealth of portraits could be hung and curtained with veils of fine silk; place where the Queen could comfortably watch games and tournaments within the Tiltyard. For the inner court he restored and richly furnished the Lancaster Buildings (where once the legendary John of Gaunt had lived), at the western edge overlooking the lake. Added three-story glass windows to the walls of the hall on the north side. Likewise repaired and furnished King Henry VIII's Lodgings on the eastern side of the inner court. And then to close out that court (which had never yet been fully enclosed) and to balance the hulk of the ancient Keep, called Caesar's Tower, he built a many-windowed, three-storied tower at the southeast angle and named it Leicester's Building.

Just beyond the outer walk, between Tiltyard and moat, he planted an orchard—apple and cherry, pear and almond trees. Made a new garden with terraces and arbors, with hedges cut into many shapes and especially the shape of his crest, the bear with a ragged staff. Set a two-story banquet house against the north wall. Dug cunning caves to hold flocks of singing birds and rare birds of brilliant plumage, strange creatures whose cries, until then, had been heard only in New Spain, in the Indies and the Islands, in far China and Japan. Covered the ground of the garden with a carpet of wild strawberries and with every worthy kind of herb and flower. Centered it all around a white marble fountain, elegantly, intricately carved, spilling into pools where there were fish as colorful and rare as the wondrous jokes of God. Fountain whose splashing mist cast continual little rainbows and cooled the garden on summer days.

. . . The whole thing was cut and carved by his Italian servants, the Earl explained . . . Who could not have been brewing Leicester's poisons and love potions all the time, could they? If only for the sake of good appearance, they had to busy themselves with other common Italian enterprises—singing and dancing and playing on musical instruments, tumbling and juggling, gardening and cutting stones.

To south and west, beyond Castle walls, Leicester repaired the dams and refilled the lake. And he created seven hundred acres of park as a place for red deer and several kinds of game.

. . . The kingdom could have been governed several years for what he paid to repair this place. And that's not to take into account the expenses required whenever the Queen came here on a Progress. As she did a number of occasions, each time expecting to be entertained more lavishly than the last. Until she came to stay here for the better part of a month, in July of 1575, and set the Earl so deep into debt that nothing, not even possession of the mint, could have restored him.

Given the decay of fifty years (the young man thinks) *and it is hard to believe* (harder to prove) *his memories. Yet . . .*

"It is a fine place to be this summer," he has already written his friends at Oriel (which is near enough so that they might come to celebrate Midsummer with him). "I have never seen the like of the flowering here. The Earl claims that it was even more so in the summer of '75, though chances are his memories are better than truth was. He says that the Queen's Court, though they were all decked out in gardens of silk and satin and velvet, set aglitter with a spray of jewels, of silver and gold, were outfaced by the wild flowers in the fields.

"In wisdom the Queen chose to keep herself and her ladies in white by daylight. For candlelight and moonlight they changed into their most extravagant clothing, which seemed to have been plundered from the very essence of the morning meadows.

"Or so the Earl insists.

"The garden is still as rich as can be with red and white roses. And with iris and the gillyflower so favored by butterflies. (Favored by the Earl of Monmouth, too, who soaks petals of it in his ale for the sake of a scent like cloves.) With violets forever faithfully blue. With heartsease, which they call *pansy* here and honestly believe will cure the French Pox.

"And out beyond the walls, amid the growing grain, are the blues of the cornflower, the purple patches of corn cockles. And the poppies which, given a ghost of a breeze, begin to dance beneath their wide-brimmed scarlet hats, like a college of drunken cardinals.

"Meadow and pasture are carpeted with red clover, loud with bees. And the wasteland and fallow look as yellow as green with clusters of dandelions and buttercups, with ragwort and bright torches of toadflax. With blithe little golden bells of cowslip. With drifts and tides of dog daisies, each one a huge, unwinking, yellow eye. . . .

"Who cares what happened more than fifty years ago when there is such pleasure for the eyes here and now?"

He does not guess, though his friends might, that it is the Earl's tales of times gone by that have served to make the present time so precious to him.

No matter. Nothing will stop the Earl from telling how he remembers it was. It is the wonder of this summer in Warwickshire that sets him free to journey to the past.

. . . And why not? He has asked the unprotesting clerk. . . . This is a place where time and the clock in Caesar's Tower stopped long ago.

. . . Do you know how that came to be? That clock was fixed forever at the moment the gates were opened for the Queen in '75. All the clocks in the Castle and indeed the watches of everyone here were commanded to be stopped at that same instant and not permitted to tick time again until after the Queen had departed. The clock in the Tower has never moved or struck a bell since.

. . . I was in my fifteenth year then, believing nothing of the world beyond what I could see with my own eyes. And wishing for nothing so much as to be able to sit a horse as proud and handsomely as Leicester.

. . . And Leicester, what was he hoping for?

. . . I have come to believe it was his intention to give to the Queen (and, thus, to give to England) something so rare to remember that whatever came after it would be altered by it. Something unforgettable. Something that must be remembered.

. . . By that time there was nothing he was fishing for. Master of Horse, Knight of the Garter, he had received his title to nobility and gained his place in the Privy Council. He was then High Steward of the University at Cambridge, Chancellor at Oxford, and he had lands and parks and monopolies. He had next to nothing to aspire to. Except, perhaps, the Queen's hand in marriage and the throne.

. . . It has been said that those summer pleasures here were his last courtship of the Queen. I doubt it. By then his first wife was mysteriously dead, and he had a bastard by Lady Sheffield. Poor thing, she believed she was lawfully married to him.

. . . Why, even while Queen and Court were here, he was secretly courting my own cousin, Leltice, Lady Essex.

. . . Anyway the Queen was not foolish enough to be flattered by his extravagance. She knew his assets and income to the penny. And why not—when every penny of both had come from her.

. . . If not flattery, then honor. Which is something she would accept, even as she understood that he was bound to share it, understanding that he hoped it would cause the two of them to be coupled in memory, if never in fact.

. . . Leicester was determined that the doings here should be widely known. He was not willing to wait while rumor and gossip ran a natural course. No. He arranged for the writing of letters, by various hands, describing the entertainments in great detail. And he saw to it that his poet of the time (Mr. George Gascoigne it was, who wrote many of the speeches and, indeed, spoke some of them himself) should make a book all about it. Which was published within a few months, well before the next Progress. I remember having a copy of it. Perhaps it is still among my books at Blackfriars.

. . . My guess is that the Queen was amused by his motives. Who knows?

. . . She could not fail to be pleased that he sought to link all his future with hers. Let others, he seemed to be saying, win victories and make discoveries, he would be pleased to offer her merely the grandest entertainment of the age. And thus (at least in that sense) to remember her would be to remember him.

. . . Now in those days my father was not yet named Lord Chamberlain. The Earl of Sussex was still alive and held that office. Father was Master of Hawks and Governor of Berwick, nothing more. But he was cousin to the Queen, and he had done good service against the Northern Earls in the rebellion of '69. He had won a victory, against formidable odds, against the traitor Crookback Dacre of Naworth Castle, at the ford of the River Gelt just below the market town of Brampton. A battle you have never heard of, lad, in a place you are likely never to see. No matter. He had done well for the Queen, and she knew it, said so, rejoiced in it.

. . . And so my brothers and sisters and I were children of a hero. Father came for three weeks to Kenilworth. My mother was one of the Queen's Ladies of Honor for the whole summer until the Progress ended at Reading in August. That year she brought nearly all the Court and Council with her, and she all but emptied her palaces of servants. And more. There were trumpets and drums and flutes, every sort of musician; porters and footmen and messengers and coachmen and sergeants at arms; Walter the Jester and the Queen's Bear Ward; brought with her four different sets of singing boys—the children of St. Paul, of Westminster, of Windsor, and of the Chapel. And more, so many more.

. . . I can remember counting seven Bishops in attendance on her of a Sunday.

. . . There were many hundreds of carts and wagons, miles of them, and thousands of horses to pull them. More than a thousand horseback riders. Fifty horses for her messengers alone.

. . . Imagine, my lad, how much hay and oats it took to feed them, how much water they would drink up and piss away in a day! Oh, there could not have been much horseflesh left in all of

London and Middlesex. It must have been a summer when everyone walked to go anywhere. Must have been a happy time for tanners and shoemakers.

. . . But I thought none of these things then. All I did was open my mouth in awe. When I first saw it from a treetop—that procession winding slowly through green Warwickshire like a huge, many-colored dragon—it's a wonder I did not fall down out of the tree.

. . . They came here, as Caesar's clock will tell you, at eight of the evening, a Saturday evening. Twilight with the torches already burning. For it would be full dark before they had made entry into the Castle. There were crowds there watching who had come from the towns around, some from as far as Stratford and even Banbury. They came patiently every day to go where they were allowed to and to see everything they could.

. . Well, when the Queen was in the park, perhaps a bowshot from the gate to the Tiltyard, a tall and beautiful woman, clad in white silk, came forth from an arbor by the roadway. To greet her with a poem of welcome. Next, as the Queen and her procession approached the gate to pass in, six gigantic mechanical trumpeters (each with a living trumpeter concealed inside) suddenly rose up on the battlements and blew a fanfare.

. . Next thing came an astonishing surprise. What you must bear in mind, my lad, is that the Queen did dearly love to be surprised. And she did not wish to tolerate anything for long, excepting the most solemn occasions, without some laughter.

. . This I can claim to be witness to. For there I was, with two of my brothers, Edward and Thomas, and with my two younger sisters—Philadelphia and Mary. As I recall it, Edward Hoby (who was later to marry my sister Mary) and some others were with us. Was Philip Sidney there, too? I cannot remember. Oh, he was certainly there at Kenilworth and enviably grand, in our view, since he had only just come home from some years of traveling on the Continent. Leicester was his uncle and was sponsoring him for a place at Court. I doubt that he was with us. More likely part of the procession.

. . . Anyway, we were watching from the windows of the Gallery. Able to see and hear everything, though my ears were still ringing from the noise of trumpets.

. . . The procession had moved the length of the Tiltyard to-ward Mortimer's Gate. Which gate was still closed tight, so we all knew something would happen before it was opened. Here came the Queen and her maids of honor, dressed in white and silver and gold, each mounted on a specially chosen horse; and walking beside each, holding the reins, was a nobleman. Walking next to the Queen, in peacock finery, here was the Master of Horse and host—the Earl of Leicester. He was still a wildly hand-some man in those days, sturdy, yet graceful as a dancer. His hair and beard, those elegantly drooping mustaches, were only lightly touched by white.

. . . Suddenly there came rushing out onto the sward, a burly hulk of a man carrying a chain of keys and hefting a huge club. He was clad in rags and patches (of finest silk, to be sure) as Hercules, the Porter of this Gate. Later I learned it was a fellow from Oxford named Badger, but at the time I was prepared to believe he was Hercules or anyone else he claimed to be.

. . . He came out angry as a hornet. Having just been awak-ened by the trumpets and annoyed by the coming of all these strangers. As far as he was concerned, the whole to-do was an outrageous garboil. He swore at them that none should pass through the gate.

. . . Then, seeing the Queen, he changed his manner com-pletely. Took her for a goddess and ran toward her. Fell to his knees and offered up keys and his club. He humbly bade her and all of her company welcome to the Castle.

. . . The Queen laughed and the gate was opened. It was at that moment that the clocks were stopped in her honor. There could be no more past or future until her departure. The clock in Caesar's Tower chimed and then ceased forever. And all the can-nons in the Castle fired salute.

. . . They entered the gate to discover a pool, flowing out of the moat and the lake, had been newly dug there; and a high, arched, timber bridge had been built for the Queen to go over. But before she crossed over, a floating island, ablaze with torches, appeared. And standing on it were King Arthur's Lady of the Lake and some of her nymphs. Who then, by a cunning trick, stepped off the island and seemed to walk on the water to greet the Queen. The Lady delivered a speech, offering her lake as a gift and promising to join the Queen's Court to serve her.

"Why, good lady," the Queen said, frowning, speaking as if in anger. "We thought this lake was always ours. Do you presume it is yours now to offer? Well . . . !"

. . . Then suddenly smiling: "We shall talk more of this hereafter."

. . . People laughed and applauded. And then Leicester's musicians—who must, for the occasion, have been swelled by half the musicians in England—came forth to play the Queen across the bridge. At the other end of the bridge a Poet, dressed in a strange blue gown, came forward to welcome her to the inner court. And Leicester helped her from her horse.

. . . And just then, the moment her feet touched the earth, all the cannons boomed again; and the sky was lit like noonday by a storm of fireworks. When that faded, behold!, every chamber of the Castle was lit up at once by thousands and thousands of candles. The musicians began playing, and the Earl led Her Majesty inside.

. . . I remember that those of us in the Gallery were served a strong cordial in Venetian glasses. We drank to the Queen's health. And that cordial might as well have been Circe's magic cup. For we fell directly into a kind of dream from which there would be no waking for eighteen days.

He tells the young clerk of feasts and banquets at which hundreds of Leicester's servants, all in brand new livery, presented more than a thousand different dishes. Hunting and bearbaiting, tilts and chivalric tournaments. Dancing and music and masques for the garden and in the Hall. Plays performed by Mr. Brubage and the newly licensed Earl of Leicester's men. A very old play done by yokels from Coventry, for laughter. Pageants on the lake, in the park and garden. Tumbling and juggling and ropewalking by the Earl's Italians.

. . . Every night there were new wonders with fireworks, the likes of which I have never seen since. His Italian artist could turn midnight into clear day for as long as he pleased. He could make any shape you can imagine out of fire in the sky. The fellow swore he could transport live cats and dogs back and forth across the lake in fiery chariots. Ah, I would have given much to see that happen! But the Queen would not permit it. We had to be content with lesser marvels such as rockets which arched up and bloomed in many colors in the sky, then fell away into the lake and seemed to die there. But suddenly rose out of the water again in flames, like so many phoenixes. And again and again. . . .

He tells how the Earl had something prepared against every eventuality and every kind of weather. Which was well he had; for there were some days so hot that no one would stir outside until the cool of evening.

. . . I do believe Leicester was prepared for everything except the end of the world and Judgment Day. If it had snowed in July there were plenty of furs and firewood handy. There were so many boats in the lake we could have ridden out a second Deluge.

. . . And he had more hidden surprises than a peddler's pack. I remember a most elaborate pageant set on the lake. Where there came, as if swimming toward the Queen, a wonderfully shaped Dolphin. It was big as a sailing ship and contained, hidden in the bowels, a band of musicians playing. Riding upon this Dolphin's back was Orion, who began to sing a song composed in honor of the Queen. But then, as the Dolphin drew close to her, his voice began to crack and change. His tongue began to thicken. As if he had been drinking to gain courage for this moment. His tone was hoarse as an old crow's. And next thing, he could not remember the words to sing.

. . . Everyone was shocked and silent. Deeply embarrassed (or secretly amused) for Leicester. Feeling pity for the foolish actor, whoever he was, standing there, clumsy and dejected, on a mechanical Dolphin. When he pulled off the mask that had covered his face and head.

"Oh, ma'am!" he cried out in a loud voice. "What am I doing? For I am truly none of this Orion. I am no one else but plain and honest Harry Goldingham!"

. . . Harry Goldingham—a name I hope to remember till my dying day. For when I lose it, *all* my memory will be gone. The Queen laughed and clapped her hands.

"Please sing some more for me, plain and honest Harry Goldingham."

. . . And so, as that Dolphin moved away, the musicians began to play again. This Harry Goldingham began to recover his wits and his voice and words to go with the melody. And then to sing even more beautifully than before, as if inspired by her presence. Until the sight of them was lost and the last sounds had faded away over the water.

Clock or no, it is nearly noon now. The young man sees servants, bearing plates and linen, cups and glasses, moving toward the Banquet House to prepare the tables for dinner. The old Earl has a hearty appetite these days. Perhaps it comes from all this walking and talking.

We shall eat well and drink deep, the clerk thinks. And then, thanks be to God, the old man will have his sleep.

Fearing that his face may somehow reveal his thoughts, and lightly ashamed of thinking them, the young man makes himself ask the Earl what became of Leicester.

. . . It is strange how things turn and change. Strange the distance between beginnings and endings, the Earl allows. One of the few blessings of my old age is to have lived long enough to see how Fortune makes sport of our best hopes and wishes.

. . . Leicester, though he did not live long enough, after all, to be truly old (at least in years), grew fat and old before his time. He was soon so richly endowed with aches and pains that he could sit a horse only with difficulty. And when his proudest moment finally came, when he was the Queen's General at Tilbury Camp in '88, when he commanded the English army waiting for the landing of the Spaniards from the Armada, when the Queen herself came to Tilbury to see the soldiers march and to speak to them, why by then (you see?) Leicester was too old and too fat and too sick to gain anything from it but shame and embarrassment.

. . . Think of it. All his life the Queen had indulged him. Tolerated his faults. Relished his diversions. Forgiven his failures. She had spoiled him for the sake of some great service he could do for her. And here was the time to prove he was worthy of her best judgment of him.

. . . But his accomplishment that summer was to parade the army for the Queen. The war was elsewhere, on the water, and lesser men (myself included) won honor there. The finest horse-man of our age had trouble sitting on his horse. He paraded the army, then sent it home. Packed himself off by coach toward Buckstones. Hoping and praying that those hot blue waters would cure him. Would restore him, if not to the glory of his youth, then at least to the dignity he imagined he had earned. He planned to go first to Buckstones and then to come back here to Kenilworth. But he died along the way without reaching ei-ther place.

. . . I was sick to death myself and knew nothing of Leices-ter's fate until later. But when I heard the news, I had to con-sider it was providential for England. I served with him in the Netherlands and I believe he was the worst commander I ever served. If the Spaniards had landed in '88, I have no doubt they would have chased him all the way to Scotland.

. . . It is odd, young man, the way Fortune—I speak not of Providence, for that subtle design is beyond my understanding and I take it by faith alone and without any questions—will con-trive to dispose of the occurrences of a man's life. Strange how reputation will take up a man's public life and dismiss the greater part of it as being without meaning. Choosing instead to call attention to a single action, a gesture, one particular event, great or small, as the most characteristic one of his life. An em-blem for all of the rest of it. Time has made great men into fools and vice versa.

. . . So—Fortune is nothing if not ironic, lad—his death in dis-appointment may have spared him from something worse.

. . . But, I must confess, how wonderful he seemed to me that summer of '75 here. He was the perfect model of the perfect courtier. To be admired, to be imitated in all things.

. . . He was in every way different from my father. For all my pride in him, my father was a source of embarrassment to me. He was so downright and plainspoken. He cursed and swore like a sailor, talked more like some swag-bellied captain than a gentle-man of the Court. Do you know what they said of him—that his Latin and his powers of dissimulation were both alike; that is, he had none of either.

. . . Lord, how I cringed for him when no cringing was called for. Father was one of the few men the Queen fully trusted. She might be in or out of love with Robert Dudley, Earl of Leicester. But (wisely) she trusted him no farther than she could fling him.

. . . I was bewitched that summer. A spell was cast on me. But, look you, in the end enchantment served me well enough. For I was ruined for the life of a courtier. No Court could match my memories or expectations. Which (you see?) was just as well considering that the largest part of my life in those days was spent in service far from the Court. No matter how disappointed I was, I can see now I was spared a deeper disillusionment. For the Court is mostly what you young and Puritanical fellows (don't deny it!) think of it—a gathering of the most idle and worthless fellows in the kingdom. A place without true honor or justice. Indeed a place where truth is either ashamed or hidden.

. . . As it was, lad, I preserved the best memory of it. I kept my illusions until I was too old and it was too late to matter whether they were true or false. I call that a blessing. When I was here in my fifteenth year I was more sure of many things than I have ever been again. Now my certainties are few and far between, but I trust them like old friends.

. . . And one of my old friends, my stomach, tells me it is dinnertime. He never lies. Let us go in and say our grace and drink a toast to the ghosts of Kenilworth.

Messenger

1566

I saw the little boy in thought how oft that he
Did wish of God to scape the rod, a tall young
man to be.
The young man, eke, that feels his bones with
pains opprest,
How he would be a rich old man, to live and lie
at rest.
The rich old man, that sees his end draw on so sore,
How he would be a boy again, to live so much the more.

HENRY HOWARD, Earl of Surrey—"Youth and Age"

Will be riding southward along the North Road first from Beal to Belford, a place of no more than a market square and a row of mean houses made mostly of sticks and loam and roofed with heather and sod. Into open country, lonesome Cheviots to the west, sea and a spray of islands to east. Splashing through light streams, like Warrenbrook and Priestdean Burn, till at last he comes downhill to cross the arched stone bridge over the clear, swift-running River Aln. Across which, wrapped in a formidable mile of twenty-foot walls and guarded by four towered gate-houses, stands Alnwick. That town in turn defended by the walls and sixteen towers of Alnwick. Home for the Percys and space enough to hold three thousand horsemen. Everywhere painted and sewn on cloth, cut and worked in wood and stone, is the stiff-tailed lion of the Percys.

Will be leaving the letter (from Captain Norton) at the gate of the Castle. Changing horses at an inn near cobbled Grass-market. Passing out of town walls at Hotspur Gate to climb again for a clear wide view of sea and Cheviots. . . .

Well, what's to be known of this fellow, servant to Sir William Cecil, who favors disguise and has already, laughing, called himself Jack Scarecrow and Jonathan Beanstalk?

He may seem to be a man who casts no shadow.

He will not at first speak of his past or, if he can help it, offer any easy clues to it. Yet if he's disguised in the present and reluctant (so far) to reveal the past, he is not afraid to share a picture of the future. Which at least proves something—that though he must act out a part in the present, a shadow among shadows, still he cannot suppress a vision of the future.

Sees himself older, grayer of beard, yet still in posession of health. . . .

"After all, if I am to allow myself the indulgence to imagine my future, then why not imagine myself as having the well-being to enjoy it?"

Owner of a house and some land in a sunny shire, far from cold and wet of the north. With perhaps a modest pension and the income of the lands to live on. Perhaps also there should be a warm and soft-bodied woman, a widow. . . .

"Let her be soft-spoken, also, if you please. For there's nothing like a shrill and nagging woman to put a man, even a Protestant, into an early purgatory."

Someone, yes, soft-spoken then, who will share his bed and help him to manage house and servants and business matters. Let this widow bring something of her own to the marriage— some land, some income. Yet not so much of either that she would feel wholly secure without him.

"May she be plump and clean, as sweet and yeasty as new-baked. wheat bread. Not given to much teasing and not at all to whining and quarreling. May she bring no troubles to my life, if you get my meaning."

We can infer that, for all his sad or scornful worldly wisdom, he does not choose to imagine life without a woman to share it. Something has made him wary of excess. Made him prefer calm and contentment. He favors simple comforts over passionate seasons of fire and ice. Well, for a reasonable man to arrive at that choice (and he is nothing if he's not reasonable), he will have to have known the chills and fevers of love well enough to wish to avoid them ever after.

Ah then, he has surely been a lover in his time. Suffered the storms of desire and satisfaction. Surely he has loved and lost.

"So be it. Some pieces of land, a modest income, the company of a good woman, albeit one without many angles or hard edges to her. The two of us together in a house not far from some pleasant village. A village where time and trouble stopped long ago. Where there has not been dust or clamor since at least the Wars of the Roses. A place where I do not know a living soul now, or out of the past. A place where I have neither kith nor kin. . . ."

Early summer is the time to imagine it. Fresh new leaves. Herbs and flowers blooming wild and in his gardens. He can see himself at table in a shady place behind the village tavern. Drinking with a few companions. Talking idly of timber and pasture, wheat and beans, sheep and cows, sun and rain. A lazy game of cards, a child's game, more luck than thinking involved. Played for the prize of a halfpenny or two. Leafy shadows play across faces and the rough wooden table as he shuffles the deck and deals out the cards.

You pick up your hand, sort it and begin to play, sipping strong beer, hearing leaf-rustle of squirrels and the whistling of summer birds. Half listening to the voices at the table, your own among them. Caring now at last no more than a long sigh and a lazy shrug for all the lost fruits of bygone ambitions. Here you can feel safe to talk about your past. Here, for sure, these village tavern companions—another yeoman landowner, say; a schoolmaster; the parish minister; an old soldier; the cheerful, ruddy Justice of the Peace, himself the spendthrift elder son of the late and sometimes lamented owner of the manor house—are willing, indeed eager to listen to you. Here at last would seem to be the place to tell your story.

"Depending, for instance, on how well memory serves. For even in the best memories shapes do often change and sometimes even vanish forever."

Well, then. Depending also on whether (after a lifetime devoted to the arts of equivocation, the craft of amphiology) lying has not become as easy and thoughtless as your habit of stroking the ends of your short beard while you study your cards. Or the way you pull at your left earlobe just before you let a burst of laughter go free.

"Depending, as well, on whether these newfound companions of a summer afternoon find true recollection to be as interesting as the things that fancy can create. Depending on whether, on a lazy afternoon while enjoying the pleasures of good beer, nuts, and cheese and a game of cards under whispering leaves, anything out of the past, over and done with, seems worth the effort of summoning back."

And all of this depending on the somewhat dubious prospect that a man with deception as his craft and danger as close as a shadow will live to find himself sitting there.

"Which is to say if you choose to wait for, let us say, another quarter century of time, hoping at the end to hear a true story, still you may not learn anything worth knowing."

Ah, except we already know that the only future this gambler and adventurer imagines for himself is to be without serious hazard, without even a wish for more adventure.

Crossing Cawledge Brook and Hampeth Brook and passing through the hamlet of Newton on the Moor on high ground. Then from Newton to Felton by the side of the salmon-rich Coquet. Five miles of moor, then pastures and the road twisting down into the windy vale of the Wansbeck. Where stands the walled town of Morpeth, astride both sides of the river, held together by a narrow stone bridge of three arches. Past market bell-and-clock tower, Castle and parish church. Up Kirkhill with the first good stand of wood, light-leaved birch and ash, since Edinburgh. Then all of a sudden in wide fields again and ambushed by acres of yellow broom and of flowering gorse as rich as ripe oranges.

And next will ride the dozen miles to Newcastle. Old fortress town, still strongly defended; yet newly prosperous from the buying and selling of sea coal. With many tall houses of timber and stone, and with all of the streets (even the least paths and wynds they call *chares* here) handsomely paved with cut stones. And with a cluster of most excellent inns near to the marketplace —*Swan* and *Unicorn*, the *Fighting Cocks* and the *Golden Lion*, each extravagantly announced by an enormous painted sign. One of these being the right place for him to pause for an hour. To seek a table within and drink a stoup or two of near-black Northumbrian beer. And to gather as much news as he can for his master. For there are few well-kept secrets in Newcastle.

Especially to learn what he can concerning the Scots exiles. Will learn that old Lord Ruthven has been dead as a nail for a month; that only George Douglas and Patrick Lord Lindsay are often seen these days. What of the exiled Lord Chancellor of Scotland—James Douglas, Earl of Morton? He has vanished from view for more than a week. Most likely gone back to the Borders to work some mischief.

Telling next to nothing of himself—"I have been at Norham Castle for more than a fortnight, sick with a fever." Yawning and strolling unhurried to mount a new horse in the yard.

Soon over Blackgate Bridge with its ten high arches over the Tyne and entering the Palatinate of Durham, Tyne to Tees, where the Bishop rules. Soon riding hell-for-leather across bare Framwellgate Moor. Toward the three-towered Cathedral of Christ and the Blessed Virgin and the Bishop's Castle, both atop a steep wooded hill overlooking a wide meander of the muddy River Wear.

Will not pause there if he can help it.

"For the simple reason," he abruptly allows, "that in another place and at another time I knew them both."

By which he means James Pilkington, now Bishop of Durham and, as well, his new Dean of the Cathedral, the learned William Whittingham.

"To be sure. Knew them both (though separately then) not so long ago, in the days of exile in the reign of Mary I. We knew each other as only exiles and fugitives can. And either of them, disguise or not, might recognize me at sight and not as some fellow of the road named Scarecrow or Beanstalk. . . ."

No, not to pause there, but hurrying on to cross the Wear on Framwellgate Bridge. Going into the valley of the Skerne toward Darlington—best market town in Durham for cattle and for wool. There crossing over the Tees. . . .

"It is not that I would fear discovery," says he, interrupting. "I have never done any serious disservice to either one—at least nothing they would be likely to know of. And even if they should have cause to mistrust me, I am Sir William Cecil's man, and he has been a patron to them both. But—you should understand this well enough and without knowing too much—there would be questions. There would be, if only for the sake of friendship and good manners, a delay I cannot afford.

"But you will be wondering how it is that I came to be an exile on the Continent. How I came to know the likes of Pilkington and Whittingham. Wishing to know—no use protesting otherwise; it clearly cannot be denied—how and why I came to my present condition as . . . well, shall we say, a private servant of a public man. And what's the harm in telling? It was some time ago and I can tell the story without retelling any secrets."

Tells how it was in the last years of the reign of King Edward VI and how he came down to London, from his college at Cambridge, at the request of Sir William Cecil. Who was both master and patron since childhood and more of a guardian than either. Came first to stay a brief while in Cecil's house on Canon Row in Westminster.

"London, ah London . . . , it was there I had my real education, much of it a great waste of time. But some of it useful to me every day since then."

Came first to stay for a time at Cecil's house on Canon Row. One of those which had belonged to the canons of St. Stephen's Chapel nearby, and was well placed for Cecil's purposes. Close to Westminster Hall and Old Palace Yard. Near to the landing at Old Palace Bridge from which tilt boat or wherry could carry you quickly anywhere along both banks of the Thames, from here to the Bridge and even beyond. And on that same short paved street lives his father, Richard Cecil. Old and ill now, though still a gentleman of the Court. From the garden behind Cecil's house, small but shaded by old trees, you could lob a stone through a high curtain of leaves and wait and then hear the splash in the unseen river. At least at high tide.

"The sound that I came to know best," he says, "was the sound of the bells of the stone clock tower in Old Palace Yard. Which day and night tolled every hour and could be heard all over Westminster. Some said that on a calm day you could hear those bells across London, as far as the Tower. I doubt it. What I believe is that anyone who heard those bells as close as we did on Canon Row, carried the echoes, banging and clanging in his head, wherever he went."

Cecil always believed there were many practical things any educated man should know something about. His house was full of books and maps and charts and all kinds of tools and mechanical devices. "This world is a shop of instruments," he used to say, "whereof the wise man is the master." Cecil believed an educated man should be well versed in the history and geography of the nations and the genealogies of their kings and ruling families.

He gathered portraits and drawings and busts of these, celebrated or notorious rulers from the past. And those of the present
time, also, to be studied for the outward signs of their strength or
weakness of character. Astronomy and medicine, surveying and
the making of maps, building and farming and gardening and
the keeping of accounts, the making and the maintenance of
weapons and warships, mining and smelting and minting, details
of all of these things fascinated Cecil. He expected his friends
and servants to share his interests.

"Clocks . . . Sir William Cecil's houses are full of clocks. Every
kind, old and new. And it is an urgent matter for everyone that
they be kept in working order and on time. If wasting time out-
rages him (and it surely does), he's greatly annoyed at the
thought of the loss or gain of time in a faulty clock. And yet, you
see, when you have so many clocks handy, some of them inevita-
bly will be fast or slow. You can only pray that their bells and
chimes will come close enough together to create a certain harmony."

It was a happy time for him in Cecil's household. Brief as it
was. He was more like kinfolk than a retainer. And, fresh from
school as he was, he often talked of the classics with Mildred
Cecil. That tall, thin, elegant, handsome woman who was as
much a scholar, and especially in the study of Greek, as any man
at the universities.

"But none of this was for long. They had other plans for me.
There was only time to smooth off some of the rough edges.
Time for some modest tailoring and barbering and some general
instruction on the manners and dangers of life in the City. And
then off I was sent, accompanied by a servant of my very own.
Stephen was his name—there, you see, it has come back to me at
last! Stephen! What a wonder is man's memory. I remember him
as a clumsy, cheerful, goodhearted country boy. Came from somewhere close by Stamford. He was being sent by Cecil to begin to
learn his trade just as I was."

He was sent to live within the brick walls of Gray's Inn and to
study the Law. As Cecil had done. Sent off wearing his new
doublet and hose, all sober and correct, as befitted his station, his
master's taste, and the sumptuary rules of the Inn.

"But please understand that my garments like my life were

. . . *paradoxical*. Being, in fact, well cut and well tailored and of the latest fashion and the best cloth. Being brightened by some subtle pinking and slashing, by an excellent silk lining, and by a set of gold buttons. I may have looked like any other student, but I felt every inch a gentleman and scholar."

And there at Gray's Inn he found he must pore over the old statutes and perfect his Law French and read the new books. He had to attend the regular moots and boltings and readings. Was required to worship with the others in chapel. In the evening he studied by candlelight while Stephen sponged his gown and brushed his clothes and polished his shoes close by the hearth. And he learned to bear with patience the forty strokes of the bell of Gray's Inn, tolling curfew at nine o'clock.

Out beyond the Inn were open fields. But in the opposite direction, beyond the gates, there was busy Holborn, lined with a hundred inns and taverns and cookshops for travelers and leading directly to Newgate and the City.

"Ah, there were too many wonders, too many wondrous things between Gray's Inn and Paul's Church, were marvelous distractions to snare the fancy of the most dedicated scholar. I'll wager a saint could have been diverted from the straight and narrow. Jerusalem or Babylon, a place sharing something of both. I was still young and careless enough to piss in a chimney if I felt like it.

"There was a time when I believed I could find my way any place in London or Westminster with my eyes tight shut disguised as a blind beggar. Able to do so simply by the sounds and scents of things. I was eager to hazard a wager. But nobody at the Inn would try his luck against me. " 'Tis too easy," they said. "If you listen you can tell one parish bell from another and you'll hear the people talking. And you'll hear the sounds of the crafts. Like the screeching and the turning of candlesticks in Lothbury. Like the skull-ringing sound of the bell founders of Aldgate Ward."

"Too easy?" I answered. "Why you can blindfold me and then stuff my ears with beeswax and I can still sniff my way like a hound, all the way around the city and then back home again, without once being lost."

I swore I could be packed into a cask and hauled away in a cart. Dumped out any place they pleased. And by the power and wisdom of my nose alone, I could determine for certain what ward I was in. Perhaps even the very street I was standing on.

"All of which was an exaggeration, but, still, this whimsy had a kernel of truth at its center.

"It is not such a trick as you might imagine. For instance, if it's waves of odors of hay and manure and the warm scents of many country animals—cows and horses and sheep and swine, why, then, sir, you are likely to be in or very near to the Smithfield market. It you smell the business of the butcher and the poulterer mingled, chances are it's the St. Nicholas Shambles next to Newgate. But if it's butchers and fishmongers blended together, then you're near to the Market—where Cornhill meets Three Needle Street and Lombard. Though I suppose the Exchange will make an end to that. Now, say that it's butchers working close by the smoke of many cookshops, and I say you have to be in East Cheap. If it's an odor of fish and the smoke of the cookshops married, you must be in Thames Street, close by Stockfishmongers' Row and near to the Ropery. If it's plenty of poultry, to be sure, but mixed with the dry fatty stink of the skinners tanning their furs, well you are on Poultry, but coming close to Peltry. And if it's the smell of fish and nothing else, then you are either somewhere on Bridge Street or else at the old Billingsgate. Then if it's the musty odors of all kinds of grain, you must be where Lombard Street comes to touch Bridge Street. Fresh fruits and vegetables (these all raised in the city and so likely to be freshest) mixing with the odors of bakehouse and brewhouse, and you'll find yourself just south of Paul's Churchyard in Carter Lane. If it's garlic, you're on Thames Street again, just west of Knightrider.

"And now try to imagine you are suddenly breathing a little paradise of spices—mace and cinnamon, almonds and anise, ginger and clove and nutmeg and so forth and so on. Essence of all these happily confused with black English peppermint, rosemary, wild thyme, sweet violet, chamomile, lemon-scented sweet flag, sweet cicely, and sweet woodruff as licorice as any anise seed. Why, sir, this very cathedral for delight of the nostrils can be no place other than Bucklersbury. Where grocers and apothecaries gather up so much of the world's sweetness and health. Now, I know there are fastidious souls who complain against what they call the stink of London. The kind who will not go out on an errand in the streets unless they have armed themselves with perfumed cachets and fresh nosegays and pomanders. Let them keep their opinions. But I could wish them, anyway, a day or two in Paris or Antwerp or Padua or, my God, stinking and shining Venice, and then they would come home here and drink the air of London as if it were wine.

"Which I took it to be. Oh, in those days I must have been bewitched. And why not? Why not enchanted, when every morning I woke to breathe the bluesweet delicate perfume of lavender which grew thick in the fields of Holborn. And just so, when I fell asleep at the end of a midsummer's day I'd be breathing in a cloudy invisible sweetness rising from the acres of roses, whose harvest is counted not in bushels but by cartloads, blooming in the gardens of Ely Palace. Sinking into sleep, I pictured myself falling into dreams as if I were slowly drowning in a moonlit sea.

"Waking to the bells at daylight, I blinked and breathed and wished only to dream again."

And here, in memory which is no kind of dream, he staggers into his chambers at Gray's Inn late on a summer night. It will have to be in July of 1553. He will have been somewhere he should not have been. He will have done (again) what he ought not to have done.

"So I fell onto the bed, half drunk, muttering to myself, weary to the marrow of my bones. Cursing my servant for being absent when I needed him. Swearing I would beat him black and blue for stealing away. Then I woke to the sound of a soft, steady scratching on my door. Someone, no more than a whisper, calling my name. Staggered to unbolt the door. Barefoot, bleary-eyed and wool-tongued. Blinked and squinted into lantern light and the face of one of Sir William Cecil's household servants.

"I was to pack a small bundle light enough to carry on foot or on horseback. Dress for travel. Not to forget the sword that I had been keeping hidden here against the rules of the Inn. (*Now, how did they know about that?*) Otherwise to leave everything in this chamber just as is. To speak to no one. Must be at Cecil's house on Canon Row by first light. Did I understand?

"I replied that I did so and I would comply."

Just before dawn, the air still heavy with the perfumes of the gardens of Ely Palace, he slipped away from the Inn and walked to Westminster. Where gentlemen were on horseback riding in every which direction. Servants, most of them without livery or badges, dogtrotting, carrying chests and small coffers and such. Here and there carts, loaded high with household things, rumbled along the Strand. By riverside, at the water gates, there were crowds calling for boatmen.

At Cecil's house candles, lamps, and lanterns were burning. It could have been Christmas Eve. Except for the men under arms and the burning of papers.

He was sent into the garden. One of the kitchen servants, recognizing him, gave him a bowl of ale. In the garden it was quiet. He drank his ale. Which was, thank the Lord, strong enough to subdue the headache from last night's drinking. He stood watching two young men, workmen serving the gardener, as they were watering and tending plants. They worked, careful and calm, as if this garden had nothing to do with the smoke and the confusion in the house. They worked slow and steady as if their tasks alone truly mattered. As if they had a hundred years of growing and blooming to keep in mind.

Perhaps they were right: whoever shall own this house, whoever shall have come to rule in England, no matter. They serve nature and this garden. And the only end of their time will be the end of the world.

His name was called. He was taken to Sir William Cecil. Who had come into the garden himself. Dressed simply and soberly and booted for riding, too.

"Walk with me while we talk," Cecil told him. "Rather walk with me while *I* talk; for I would prefer that you should not speak until I have finished what I have to say. Because time is short, we must dispense with the amenities."

They were moving along gravel paths bordered by flowers and herbs. Sun was up now and a few birds singing. Light sparkled where the gardeners had sprinkled fresh water.

Cecil spoke quietly and, for the moment, seemed to be unhurried. Told him that he ought to consider himself fortunate. As Cecil might now consider himself fortunate to have this young man in his service.

"You may call this a variant upon the parable of the prodigal son. Except that here it's not a question of the son's repentance or the return to his rightful home, where he is received in joy and the fatted calf is slaughtered in his honor and so forth and so on," he continued with a faint, tight smile. "In this our version the father now has need of someone with some experience in riotous living and the ways of harlots. The father has need to call upon the services of someone who has gone down upon all fours to feed on swill with the swine."

"Sir, I . . ."

"Please do not interrupt me. There's not time left for protestations and excuses. I am sure that your expensive education has not been utterly wasted on you. Am certain you could make some argument for yourself. I concede that much. I shall not listen to you at this time, but I am willing to allow the truth of the proverb that *a horse thinks one thing and he that saddles him another.*"

Cecil continued. Quickly, quietly, calmly. Scholar of inns and alehouses and taverns, master of all games of chance, the young man had come a good way toward becoming a learned doctor of idleness. Now, then, in ordinary times, Cecil most likely would have had him pressed into service as a soldier and sent off to boggy Ireland. Where, if he happened to live—and that, young man, was a wager with long odds against him—he might yet save his immortal soul even as his mortal flesh acquired its chronicle of printed wounds and scars, and his bones and joints stiffened and ached from the wet humors of that godforsaken land. Better that than remaining in England. Where he would likeliest be disposed of by some cuckold. To be found in a ditch or floating in the river. For all the world the victim of some brawl between himself and other ruffians. No one the wiser or wishing to be so.

But he must go farther than Ireland to safety. Would that Cecil could be going with him! For all things have changed, swinging to and fro like a bell, in the past few days.

With the surprising death of the young King Edward, the Duke of Northumberland has seized the throne for his Protestant daughter-in-law—the Lady Jane Grey. But now his plan looks doomed to failure. All of Norfolk and Suffolk have risen for the rights of the Princess Mary. The fleet at Yarmouth has mutinied and gone over to her side, furnishing their cannon shot. Mary has more then twenty thousand men under her banner at Framlingham Castle, and more are flocking to her. And she can depend upon the support of the Emperor Charles V. If it comes to that.

Meanwhile the Duke has marched out of London with an army to battle against Mary's forces. His numbers are dwindling from desertions.

"He has reached Cambridge and is waiting there for reinforcements," Cecil says. "But there will be none."

Council has turned against the Duke. For certain Mary will be lawfully proclaimed as Queen, by Council and the Heralds, no later than tomorrow—which is Wednesday, the nineteenth. What happens next, God knows. It may be settled in blood and can go either way. The Duke is a soldier, no question; and though sorely pressed, he may yet rally his forces and save himself. With aid from the King of France, with whom he is dealing, he may yet impose Queen Jane upon the throne.

Each and every one of Council is seeking to save his own skin if that proves possible. . . .

"If the Duke succeeds, then, for having betrayed him, I am a dead man," Cecil says. "And the best my kin and my people can hope for is a license to beg. If, on the other hand, the Princess Mary comes to wear the crown, I have small hope for favor."

She cannot love Mr. Secretary much. Indeed she has, and very recently, spoken in anger against him. As Secretary, acting for the King and chiefly for the Duke, it was his unpleasant duty to deal with her. Especially concerning her intransigent adherence to the Papist religion.

Cecil shrugs. He has some hope. Some of his in-laws are close to Princess Mary. Even now his wife's sister, an old friend to Mary, is going to her to make a plea in his behalf. And he has some plans. Among which is this: that he is willing to wager a considerable sum of money that this young man will continue to serve him. Betting that his hunger for adventure will inspire him even more than fear. Adventure and, too, desire for a new beginning in his life. All that the young man will hazard is that Cecil will be alive to serve in the future.

"And consider, that may not be the risk that it seems. My fate will be clear soon enough. Better to be safe in another country with a sum of money in hand than alone and friendless in England."

The only true risk is Cecil's.

"As a gambler you should understand this," Cecil tells him. "The only worthwhile wager I can make, never mind the odds, is that I shall live. And why not? If I lose, I shall neither know it or care. True, I shall have squandered a sum of money on you. But in heaven or hell (or even purgatory if the Papist faith proves true, after all), I will not need anything more than prayers."

And so it came to pass.

"Came to pass that with sleepy head full of cobwebs, my tongue heavy and rough as a turkey carpet, eyes burning, guts grumbling and my poor, overexercised groin as limply sad as a wilted daffodil, with my soul so heavy with guilt that it could only shrug like some hopeless felon awaiting his turn at Tyburn gallows, and with my heart full of sorrow . . . so it was that with my few possessions, together with the largest sum of money I had ever seen, let alone carried with me, stuffed into a pair of saddlebags, and aching feet stuffed into a pair of high riding boots, I went out onto King's Bridge Landing and called Oars! Oars! until a waterman, a man silvery of head and beard, sunburned brown as a roasted nut and as wrinkled as a ripe fig, but with eyes of unaging, new-minted blue (how is it that we can sometimes remember perfectly one stranger's face out of thousands of faces when we so often find ourselves unable to recall even the shape of the lips or the color of the eyes of a lover?) came alongside in a small, narrow hoy. And from there carried me across and upstream to Lambeth Stairs. Close by the brick gatehouse and towers of the Archbishop's Palace. Where I would find horses belonging to Sir William Cecil.

"Tide was rising, nearing full. The day was windless and the water calm. Looking back, I could see, as one might see a painted cloth in a theater—and, as well, in the clear water, a twin to this picture—the roofs of Westminster, the spires of the Abbey, the long high roof of the Hall, the steep slope of Star Chamber, gates and buildings of Whitehall, the peak of Charing Cross, and all the way downriver along the north bank to the high embattled turrets of Durham House and then the huge gray looming of the Savoy.

"Shifting myself slightly, I could see across the wide open space of Lambeth Marsh. And then see it all, everything on both sides, as far down as London Bridge and Southwark and the top of the Tower beyond all that.

"And my vision was as watery as the reflection in the river. For I felt I should never live to see any of this again. So it was, or seemed so, farewell to London, farewell to love. . . ."

—Well, sir, the Waterman said to me, rowing easy with the tide. —It has been a busy morning on this river, I'm here to tell you.

—Do you know why?

—Not I, oh no, sir. Whenever the gentry are all of a sudden stirred up like a nest of hornets or an anthill that has been trod upon, and they are going up and down and back and forth across the river, wearing the grimmest faces and whispering to each other, why, sir, I play the part of a garden snail. I pull in horns and I curl up safe and snug in my castle. I cannot wonder or worry about it. Perhaps they have had private news of the end of this world, that the Judgment Day is upon us. In which case no amount of worrying and wondering will do me any good. Nor even praying. For it would be a mockery of God's mercy to begin to pray first at the ending of things. And if it is not to be Judgment Day, then whatever else it may be is nothing much to me. Now, understand, sir, I am a trueborn loyal Englishman. But still the truth is that Kings and Queens, Courts and Councils, great men and common fools may come and go. And come and go they do, in truth, as God wills. Providentially, don't you know? But whether they are coming or going, this world will remain the same for me. I shall be rowing the river in sunshine and rain, windy or calm, just as today. And there will be people who will be wanting my service.

—I take it then that you do not fear we are standing next to Judgment Day.

—Not yet, sir. It seems we must still wait awhile.

—Well, then, in the meantime, as we all wait together, who do you suppose will rule England?

—As I understand it, we shall have a Queen. It seems uncertain, though, which Queen it shall be. And whether this lady will rule as well as to reign over us remains to be seen. Whoever she

is, I'll raise my cap when she passes by and cry out God bless
her. Then I'll tend to my business of rowing the boat. And here
we are now, sir, at Lambeth. I wish you safe journey wherever
you are going.

"And I paid this wise man and set off for the Archbishop's stables."

Finally by the time—between five and six o'clock of the afternoon of Wednesday the nineteenth July—that the chief members
of the Council, together with Heralds and trumpeters rode out
from the gate of the Earl of Pembroke's residence at Baynard's
Castle, then up the Ludgate Hill to meet with the Lord Mayor
and the Aldermen at Paul's Churchyard, and from there to go on,
all together, to the Cross at Cheapside to proclaim the Princess
Mary to be "by the Grace of God, Queen of England, France and
Ireland, defender of the faith, and in the earth supreme head of
the Church of England and Ireland," by that solemn moment he
was drinking some wine with the master of a French bark
anchored fore and aft and floating gently in surprising calm
water beneath the Castle and cliffs of Dover. Waiting for wind,
for the least stirring of any kind of breeze at all, to set sails and
to cross over to the shores of France. Later he would hear how
London rejoiced. How bonfires flamed in the streets and fields all
night long. How the conduits were flowing with wine. How waits
and minstrels made music. And how crowds of people danced in
the streets. How the bells of London rang without ceasing for
two days and nights. How from the Tower and from anchored
ships, and from all other fortified places, cannon cracked
and thundered salutes. How rich merchants and gentlemen, and
even some from the nobility, came forth from their houses to
throw gold and silver coins to delight the crowds. How not even
the oldest could recollect seeing, or hearing told of, anything to
equal that celebration.

Early next morning, sea sparkling with sun and choppy from
wind, and with Dover's cliffs rising and falling and tilting and
dwindling away behind him, he cursed the ocean and the wind
and the inventor of sailing ships as he leaned perilously over the
side to puke himself empty and weak from knees to toes. He
would not have cared a shopkeeper's brass token to learn that, at
that very moment, the hated Dudley, Duke of Northumberland,

having learned the news from London and having learned, too, that no French aid would reach him in time, could find neither herald nor trumpeter left among his diminishing forces. So he, was forced to go forth from his inn in Cambridge and out into the open on Market Hill. There to tear down with his own hands the printed proclamations announcing the accession of Queen Jane. And then and there to proclaim the true, lawful, and un-doubted accession of Queen Mary. His white truncheon was steady enough in his gloved hands. But he had to hold the paper close to his eyes and squint to read this variation on the tradi-tional words:

". . . And we do signify unto you that according to our said right and title we do take upon us and be in the just and lawful possession of the same; not doubting but that all our true and faithful subjects will so accept us, take us, and obey us as their natural liege sovereign lady and Queen, according to the duties of their allegiance; assuring all our good and faithful subjects that in their so doing they shall find us their benign and gracious sovereign lady, as others our most noble progenitors have here-tofore been. . . ."

He was already standing on shore again (. . . *and we praise Thy holy Name that Thou hast been pleased to conduct in safety, through the perils of the great deep, this Thy servant . . .*) at the time that Northumberland and his sons, the youngest weeping like a girl, rode bareheaded and under guard through jeering crowds from Bishopgate to the Tower.

Ashore at Boulogne and at that moment willing to hear the French language or any other barbarous tongue, for the rest of his days if he could be sure that never-ever would he have to set foot on any ship again. Not even a ship at anchor! Not in drydock!

And by the time, a month later, Northumberland was be-headed by a crippled executioner (after attending a Mass and there confessing that he had erred and strayed from Truth for these past fifteen years); this young man was living in Strasbourg on the west bank of the Rhine. Strasbourg was then a Free Impe-rial City, committed to the faith of Martin Luther, and safe, for the time being, behind its walls and tall, thin, rectangular watch-towers. A place of sturdy, half-timbered houses with orange tile roofs, built facing on cobbled squares. And all of it dominated by the extraordinary spire (almost five hundred feet above one of the western towers) of the red stone cathedral.

A place where other Englishmen, some from his own Cambridge college, settled in. More were coming, and none but the oldest and saddest of them would permit themselves to imagine this exile would be for long. None could have conceived that soon even the faintest hope of change for the better would be a kind of wound. None of them at first, again except for the saddest and wisest and the weariest of the ways of the world, would have been able to imagine that the time was coming when hopes soaring or hopes dashed would be equally hard to bear. That soon the easiest thing to believe in and, thus, to endure, would be the old exiles' fable that all hope is lost and gone.

But then it was sunny summertime in the Rhineland. Soon harvest time and the pressing of the new wine in those wonderful vineyards. He was young and healthy and had money in his purse, and most of the others still had coins to jingle also. There was an English Church where the reformed English liturgy was performed as it had been in the days of Edward VI.

It is here, then, with his arrival in Strasbourg, that he began, so gradually, to ease himself into the shadows. Performing little services for Cecil. Cecil (he learned) lost his posts and offices, yet saved his life and everything else—even his good repute. For the new Queen commended him in public as "a good and honest man." In England Cecil was keeping his own counsel. And all that he expected from his servant in Strasbourg, as from any other servants he employed among the exiles on the Continent, was news. The opinions, arguments, judgments, and wishes of others were news, but not those of his hirelings. Since he was freed from wrestling with such distinctions, the young man was able to take the world as it came to him, well or ill, true or false.

And so he began to ease himself into the shadows, listening to and watching others.

By November with last leaves gone and the bare branches and the roof tiles and the stones of streets and squares glistening with rain, with the skies gray and the river misty and metallic, and the coins in their purses almost spent as they huddled close to the little German tile stoves, the exiles were in a gloom at the prospect of the English Queen taking a husband. By Christmas it seemed certain that her husband would be the Emperor's son—Philip of Spain. And almost at once there was talk of a rising before Easter in England.

Inexperienced as he was, he reasoned there could not be much hope for a rising, the success of which would, after all, depend as much upon secrecy as upon efficient execution, if someone as insignificant and, yes, indifferent as himself, only trying to keep his hands and feet warm in a little chamber in Strasbourg, could learn all about it.

Came then the first cold and dreary Christmastide in this city of strangers. When the exiles seemed joined together at least in memories and longing for home.

Here they had to conserve their candle ends. Here the chief music of the season (it seemed to them) was cold wind howling off the river, creaking of shutters and signs, rattling the window-panes. Talk was abundant, but nothing else.

Soon after Twelfth Night a London merchant, ruddy hulk of a man, fat and round and proud as a friar, the friend of a friend of a friend of Sir William Cecil, arrived with some letters and news and a little money. Together with instructions that he was to move on and to join the exiles at Frankfurt. This merchant took pity on him and invited him to dinner at a tavern which served the needs of those who could afford to pay the reckoning. One of those places where he had long since learned to hold his nose as he passed by so as not to smell and to be tempted by the witch-craft of well-cooked food. So as not to drool and beg like a hungry dog.

"From then on, and for the next five years . . ."

But it could have been longer. Might as well have been for the rest of his life. For who among them, even the most prescient and hopeful, would have dared to imagine that after all, after the failure of risings and rebellions, plots and conspiracies against the Queen and Philip, of "Philip & Mary, by the grace of God King and Queen of England, France, Naples, Jerusalem, and Ireland; Defenders of the Faith; Princes of Spain and Sicily; Archdukes of Austria; Dukes of Milan, Burgundy and Brabant; Counts of Hapsburg, Flanders, and Tyrol," against the French, against the Pope, and ever and always against each other, who would have dreamed that after these failures and after the savage persecutions of faithful reformers who remained in England, after all that, Queen Mary would sicken in the summer of '58 and be dead by the middle of November? That the Princess Elizabeth would be the Queen? That Sir William Cecil would be her first-sworn Councilor?

And that not long after that the young man would be coming home to England again?

He did not imagine it. Or even wish for it much. From Strasbourg he stepped into the shadows, took mystery about him like a cloak. Like a vestment. For he recalls dinner with the fat London merchant as his confirmation. Call it an ordination. As if the merchant, acting as bishop, had laid hands on him. Inducted him into a life of feast or famine. A life of movement. From Strasbourg he would go to Frankfurt and Emden and Basel, Aarau, Zurich and Geneva, the cities of the reformers. To study the exiled English and to send back report on their comings and goings, their doings, their endless disputations. How tedious to him these arguments came to be. But he must listen. Listening, whether intently or behind glazed eyes and a jaw rigid with suppressing an overwhelming urge to yawn, he learned more than he had to. Learned early that the nature of these most zealous precisians of reformed religion, these "sacramentaries," as the Papists named them, was much harder and more ruthless in practice than their theoretical paradigms had seemed in Cambridge where ideas were tossed back and forth like feathered shuttlecocks.

The merchant had asked him about the most zealous and radical of the reformers. And, because he was inexperienced and because the wine had gone to his head, he answered him. Though no harm was done. The merchant proved to be just what he seemed—a man of moderation in all causes but the care and comfort of himself.

"What can they hope to achieve?" the merchant said. "They are few in number. They are weak in power. And their doctrine— even if it were true—is too harsh and unbending for the rest of us."

"They are like a hand," he told the merchant. "No more than four fingers and a thumb, and each one alone is frail and brittle.

Yet clenched, taken together and gripped as one, they become a fist. Which fist can break a man's bones. Can kill a man!"

The merchant laughed at that.

"Then we must take care," he said. "Must make sure they use their fists on our enemies, or on each other, and not ourselves."

And before the five years was done he would have been to more dangerous places, places requiring care, more refined duplicity—Paris, perhaps, and the commercial city of Antwerp; maybe over the Alps and down into Italy, to Padua, to Venice, even to Rome. . . .

Ask him directly about this, and he'll tell you nothing much.

"It is for certain, just as true now as it was then, that you can find Englishmen everywhere on earth and wherever you least suspect them. I cannot imagine where I could go to flee from the English if that were my purpose. Italy, did you say? Well, any Englishman who has been in Italy brings home three things to prove it—a naughty conscience, an empty purse, and a weak stomach. You can judge for yourself."

What you can judge for yourself is a man who has known some deep disappointments, a gambling man who is bound to have lost much—many friends certainly and likely someone he truly loved. In those five years, whether spent in the shadows or in the light, wouldn't a young man have fallen in love? A man who has been close enough to death, in danger and probably in sickness, too (smallpox and perhaps the sweating sickness which has taken many as suddenly as upon a battlefield), to have almost overcome both the fear of it and the fascination of it, if not (sometimes) a kind of secret lust for it.

As for himself, because of the nature of his craft and because of danger and illness, disappointment and loss, he may not clearly remember those years on the Continent. Looking back now, a memory within a memory, he recalls a fat London merchant in Strasbourg, the look of him and not his name. Who brought him money and letters and news. And, better than all of that, who invited him to dinner. He can recall that dinner to this day: a fat goose and a roasted conny; a few roast larks on toasted bread; some eels in sauce; a pasty of vension; and then hot apples and pears cooked in a sauce of candy and distilled spirits.

All washed down with a cool Rhine wine. They must have spoken of everything, he and his red-faced unwitting bishop.

"*Looked like a bishop,* he did. A London Protestant, to be sure, but not so much so that he allowed faith to interfere with business affairs or to endanger his prosperity. Truly a man of the world.

"He must be dead by now, poor man. My Bishop Worldly Wise. Laid hands on me and bought me a dinner I shall always remember. He must have said something, too. Something at once disillusioning and inspiring. Something to encourage me to dispense with the last of my illusions. Something intended to urge me to persevere. We talked for hours, there at table, as I recollect. But I cannot for the life of me remember our conversation. I do not know what secrets of the world he may have imparted to me.

"I remember one thing only. And not what occasioned it. I must have been complaining (something we exiles did well and copiously) about promises unfulfilled. I remember a shrug and his spoon, as full as a ditcher's shovel, pausing in midair, halfway to his wide and wonderful open mouth. 'Promises,' he snorted! 'There are more promises broken each day than piecrusts.' And the spoon completed its journey. I would not have been surprised to see him eat that spoon, too, handle and all. All he gave me, all that he uttered, was a shopworn proverb. A milkmaid could have done as much. And yet looking into that round, red, pig-eyed, sweating, chewing face, and thinking on that literally—a man for whom promises were no more than piecrusts, it came over me that, ordained or not, I should never be a bishop of this world. Only a common laborer in the vineyard. And that was a great relief to me. I could have kissed the fellow for the joy of knowing I would never live to be like him."

The merchant had drained off the wine in his cup and then, raising his voice, called for the reckoning. They walked out of the warm tavern and into a windy square. The thin afternoon light was already beginning to fade toward night. They paused to exchange pleasantries, to bid farewell, and to go their separate ways. The stout sturdy London merchant to continue his journey eastward to the cities of the Empire. And he, wrapped up in a patched and shabby cloak, hurrying home to his chamber which was, too often, as cold as the cobbled streets. Hurrying to huddle next to a charcoal stove and later to lie, in a narrow pallet bed, shivering beneath blankets and his cloak.

Staring into darkness.

Trying, even then, not to fall asleep. . . .

REIVERS

1602

What camelion, what euripe, what rain-bow, what moone doth change so oft as man? Hee seemeth not the same person in one and the same day. What pleaseth him in the morning is in the evening distasteful unto him. . . . Hee is pressed with care for what is present, with griefe for what is past, with feare for what is to come, nay, for what will never come; and as in the eye one teare draweth another after it, so maketh he one sorrow follow upon a former, and everie day lay up stuffe of griefe for the next.

WILLIAM DRUMMOND—"A Cypresse Grove"

"My hands are tied, but my tongue is free,
    And whae will dare this deed avow?
Or answer by the Border law?
    Or answer to the bauld Buccleuch?"

"Ballad of Kinmont Willie"

"Well then, let us hear the tale of Kinmont Willie."

"Not yet."

"We drew straws fairly. You must wait until the time comes."

"Someone fetch a jug."

"Can you drink and listen at the same time?"

"Yes, by God, and cut out your liver with my free hand, too."

"You have already been at the jug."

"Enough. Enough. Let Sly begin his tale."

And so he does.

Here is how one fellow, no wiser or better than you or I, learned a wonderful thing—a spell that could change him from man to bird and back again. How his magic pleased him for a time, but how a time came when he wished with all his heart he had not ever come to know the powers of the dark.

Once upon a time, yet not so very long ago, there lived a red-haired man, no more than an overgrown boy from over there, that way, near to Kelso. . . .

"Pass that jug."

"You'll need a long drink to believe this tale."

"Speak for yourself. For I know it to be the certain truth that there once was an old woman from the village of St. Monance by the seaside in Fife, a widow woman who did not need a man to be content. She could turn herself into a gull by day and catch and eat her fill of fish. Became a bat at night to go and do whatever she pleased. Well, they would lock her in prison, but could not keep her there. The witch could fly out the window or up the chimney. She had to be caught in a snare like any other wild bird. They kept her in a basket until they burned her, basket and all."

"And what form did she take for her roasting—a fat chicken perhaps?"

"Most likely a duck."

"Ah now, I could eat a duck, a whole roast duck by myself here and now, all crisp and covered with a sweet wine sauce."

"Who are you to be talking of ducks and wine sauce? You are lucky to fill your belly with burnt oatcakes."

"Be quiet and pass me the jug."

Who knows if Sly believes the tales he tells? They will listen to him, anyway. While they are all waiting here together. Passing time.

So Sly continues, staring into the thick smoke and rich, leaf-burning odor of the peat fire they are gathered close around. A deep hoarse voice, as if made of the smoke of the peat. His rag-gedy beard, flecked with gray. Eyes reddened by the fire's glow. His hoarse voice continues softly while the cool jug of usky passes among them. Those murky distilled spirits of malt have a taste, too, as if well smoked by peat. Cool going down, and sud-denly warm at the pit of the stomach. A good long swallow will bring tears to the eyes and pinwheels behind them. After a pull or two, and time for the usky to settle in and warm the innards, they will all be ready and willing to believe this tale and any other tale that is told. At least for time it takes to tell it. Which is all that matters, after all. . . .

This fellow did not come from Kelso but from close by. Not a townsman. Came from the country, barnyard mud on the soles of his boots. From out beyond Smailholm Tower. A farm lad, noth-ing more, stout and lusty, strong as an ox, with maybe the wit of an ox and maybe the wisdom of a sheep in the field. And never to be, on his own, as quick and as wise in the ways of the world as a goat.

He would come to Kelso on market day and always for any fair. Lead his father's packhorse there to the cobbled market square. Bringing this and that and the other thing from the farm,

which was, at the most, no more than a plowgate of leased land.
Trading one thing for another. Buying one thing or another that
might be needed. And then perhaps, if trading had gone well
enough, and buying and selling had left him with a penny or two
to rub together in his purse, why, then, he could buy himself
something to eat and drink down a stoup of wine. He would
wander through the market looking at the goods, especially
savoring the fine things he could not afford. Not now or ever,
even if he lived a hundred years or so. Because the only profit his
life was certain to yield up was a weary body and a bent, sore
back, and himself too old and frail to work anymore, too cold-
blooded and ague-pinched to dare to stray far from the kitchen
fire. Another old man condemned in his last years to the company and goodwill of women. And with nothing more than memories to content him.

"Thanks be to God I gave up plowing earth to live the life of a
reiver!"
"I say it is better to die young with boots on and teeth in your
head."
"How can you say such a thing? You have lost most of your
teeth already and you had to steal the very boots you are wearing from some dead Englishman."
"Wrong! I have seldom if ever stolen anything off the dead. I
took them from him just before he was hanged. Fellow agreed
that they would be of no more use to him and they fit me fine."
"Hush, both of you, and pass me the jug."

Well, then.
Handsome he was and lusty and strong as an oak tree. Blithe
as a cock on the walk he was.
Now on a particular afternoon he was feeling free as a cloud as
he wandered about the market square. He had an hour to waste
on pleasure before packing his horse and pointing toward home.
He had eaten some fresh fruit and some good goat cheese. He
had a wash of wine in his belly and the taste of it still on the tip
of his tongue, and the spirit of the wine was rising like smoke to
his head. So he hadn't an ache or a pain or even a sorrow to give

him grief. He would have danced if they had allowed any dancing in the town of Kelso. He looked like a man about to break
into a jig, no matter what the others might say, in the next step
or two.

It happened that on that same day at the market there was a
little band of Frenchmen. Some men and women with a gaily-
painted, high-wheeled horse cart. Who had come there to perform tricks and entertainments for the people. One could swallow fire from a torch. Another could walk on a rope tied across
the square from one rooftop to another. And all of them could
tumble and leap about. And you can be sure they had the
lightest, nimblest, most educated fingers for many miles around.
They were learned doctors of the art of taking and keeping
valuable things, belonging to other folks, that caught their eyes
and attention. You can believe they could empty a purse as quick
as you can gut a trout. By daylight they would perform tricks
and shows. And steal a little when they had half a chance. Come
night and the Frenchmen would find a way to arrange, for a
price, for a man to have some private pleasure with one or another of their pretty Frenchwomen in the quiet of their cart.

"Is that how you were conceived, Sly—in the arse of a horse
cart?"

"Well, the cart might be dark as a dug grave, but it would
never be a quiet place if I climbed in. These Froggie women
would be making more noises than a Highland pipe. Seeking to
persuade me never to stop."

"No doubt the cart would begin to roll. And roll all the way to
Jedburgh."

"Was it the French Pox, Sly, that made you as ugly as you
are?"

"Who was your father? Tell us the truth now."

I will tell you nothing at all. I'll not even tell you the rest of
this tale if you are not prepared to listen for a while.

"Go on with it."

Is that all?

"Pray continue to tell your tale, Sly, an it please you."

That's better. That does sound better and ever so much more polite.

"Well?"

Now our young lad from the farm near Smailholm had never seen anything like these Frenchmen before, who were not, in truth, any more French than you or I are, being Gypsies every one. He knew no better. There he stood wishing he could step forward and join in while they danced in a ring to the sound of a fife and drum.

Now. If he had never seen anyone who looked in the least like them, well, *they* had seen a thousand Scots louts who looked so much like him as to be his brothers. They knew how he felt, standing there scratching at his crotch and staring at them. They knew that they seemed like fallen angels to him.

But there was one who saw him somewhat differently. A tall Gypsy woman with sturdy limbs and with long hair the blue-black color of the feathers on a raven's back. First she was dancing, then she stood aside and played on a little drum with bells whilst the others did their steps and turns. She noticed him because, you see, she was especially looking for just such a lad to be her passport to better things. For this woman was weary to her bones with Gypsy life, weary of her companions and of traveling and of always being in fear of the Law. Weary of the beatings and abuse she had at the hands of Gypsy men. Tired to death of lying down on her back and opening her legs to strange Scotsmen without names or faces. And never permitted to keep a penny of what she earned that way, either. And she was every day growing older and felt her years, too, though she was still a pretty young woman only just turning. Just before going to seed.

Above all she could feel life in her belly. Soon that belly of hers would swell enough so that she could not hide it or deny it. Then what?

And she noticed what was different about this lad, namely his flaming red hair. There was something about red hair that was a pure pleasure to her.

Why?

Well, maybe because she was tired to death of her black-haired, black-bearded men.

And last, but not least, this woman was a kind of a witch herself. She knew some magic and she could cast some spells when she had to. Though she feared to. Fearing to lose her soul to the Devil. And fearing even more to find her body tied to a stake and set on fire.

It took no witchcraft for her to catch a simple farm boy. She fixed her eyes on him until he felt them and looked at her. She wet her lips with the tip of her tongue and raised one arm to smooth back her blue-black, shining hair. And he nearly swooned then and there. Was as much her prisoner as if she had clapped him, wrists and ankles, in irons.

That night she led him by hand not into the common cart—which was anyway already as busy with bodies as a filled salmon creel—but into the musty quiet of a stable. Gave him a few minutes of pleasure in the soft hay . . . and whispered warmly that she loved him.

And he believed her.

Now then. Of all things in this tale that may be the most difficult to believe. It is easier to believe a man could turn himself into a bird and back again than to accept that anyone, even such a dimwitted farm boy, could take such a declaration of love without any serious doubt. Can we say and agree, you and I, that we would never trust any such woman, daylight or night time?

"I cannot even trust my wife. And we have been married for a dozen years."

Exactly so. And if you will not trust your own good wife, how soon will you believe a stranger?

But there is the mystery of it. For there is scarcely a man alive who would not believe the words of a pretty woman, especially a stranger to him, who swore she loved him with all her heart. No. He would gladly trust her with his purse, his body, and his soul. Which has been the ruin of many a man, and good and wise men as well as fools.

I have wondered how this could be. And I believe it is because of this. As much as a man may love or hate himself (and usually it is a blending of both together in us all), there's no man who doesn't imagine that he is worthy of the love and admiration of women. What he imagines to be becomes a wish. And when that wish seems to be granted it becomes nothing wonderful, but only common justice.

Seethe and sighing of the fire.

Sly clears his throat and spits into it. His face, in red shadows with smoke rising around his large head like the mist of morning, is as hard and blunt, as time-worn, as the faces of old knights and lords carved from slabs of stone to decorate tombs. His face belongs there. Some say his father must have been a nobleman. Perhaps he is descended from one of Scotland's philandering Kings. Who knows? He will say nothing about it. Other than in jest or easy insult, no man, not any among these, will ever ask him.

If his grizzled and silvered, weathered face could turn to stone (just as in the kind of story he so loves to tell), it would look handsomely well. But not with the body he has been left with. Limp and shriveled legs. Like a child's. Without two sticks of stout ash to hold his weight he must slither along like a seal on land. Wriggle and writhe. Enemies, one time and another, or else wild and ignorant fools who knew no better, have kicked his walking sticks out from under him to watch him wiggle in dust or mud. Sly weeping with rage while they roared with that deep laughter which men reserve for those things which disgust or frighten them most.

These companions know him better. They know how, though no more than half a man on earth, on a horse he has been in better days a better man than many alive and many in story and legend. Fearless, ruthless, proud. How he has paid back in full (and with interest) every insult rendered. How even now, with his huge right hand and his arm as big around as the upper legs of any ordinary man (his left arm's no more than a piece of loose rope, his left hand a crumpled claw), he's as cunning with a whinny as you can imagine. Could strike even now like a snake and cut you from breastbone to balls, spilling the eels of your guts into the fire to cook there, before you could pull and bare your own knife blade.

It is toward the middle of a moonlit winter's night. Perfect for the reiver's trade. And their lord and master has gone forth and is over the border and well into England by now. With fifty and more horsemen with him. Raiding for cattle and to settle an old score or two. Which will be brought back to this same tower and barmkin before dawn.

These men, close around a smoky fire in the tall round tower, have been left behind. To guard that tower and the women there (women who are gathered together by the fireplace on the topmost floor of the tower) and to protect their master's horses and cattle, kept in the high-fenced circular yard. Out there in the moonlit cold the youngest lads stand guard. Ready to blow on a ram's horn at the first sign of danger (for on such a night as this you can be sure the English have come over to take cattle and horses somewhere on this side) or when the master comes galloping home with his band.

Once in a while one of these men will rise up, wrap himself in a blanket, and walk outside to see that all is well and that no lad is sleeping out there. Coming back after a while to call for the jug and to take a place close by the fire.

Inside, except for the fire and the moonlight falling through the deep thin slits of windows, there is no other light. They will not waste torch or candle. What is there to see in this large, round, rudely bare chamber except each other? Leftovers, left behind for one reason and another, they are men of the Borders and proud of it. Loyal to the death to their master and kinfolk. Proud to be Scots, but equally proud that no King or country can command their undivided loyalty for long.

Reiving is what their lives are about, young and old. And they cannot imagine it to be otherwise.

Sly tells his tales because he would prefer to believe that ghosts and marvelous changes are as possible here and now as in the stories of ancient ages.

He tells them how the red-haired youth was so ambushed by the raven-haired Gypsy woman that he took her for his own truelove. Stole her away from the Gypsies that same night and carried her back to the farm near Smailholm to be his wife.

His father and mother were fearful of her. But he was their

one and only spoiled son and they dared not to offend him too much. Besides which, curiously, and one directly after the other, father and mother soon took sick, with a wasting malady, and died. He buried them and moved himself and his woman, as she wished, into their good bed.

His two ugly sisters waited on them both, hand and foot. . . .

Now the Gypsy woman was more or less content for the time being. For she had found herself a father for her unborn child. (He was no wiser that it was not his own.) She had a warm bed, best in the house, to lie in, plenty to eat, and two women to serve her.

But she did not know much of the laws of Scotland. How the young man could lawfully inherit the lease to the farm which his father had held, but only by payment of a heavy tax to his lord and by giving up the best beast of his poor herd.

So soon they were truly poor, and that caused her much discontent. And because she was great with child she decided she must try to teach her man enough magic to change their fortunes for the better.

By now, as trained as any dog could ever be, he would do whatever she told him to and be happy doing it, too.

So she taught him a magic potion and a spell that would turn him into a bird and back again. It was her thought that he could fly to the houses of rich merchants and lords and the like and discover their most secret hiding places for precious things. Especially jewels which he could easily carry away in his form as a bird.

At first he was fearful and careful, but soon he learned to fly so well that he loved it better than being on earth. He loved to soar and sail with the breeze. He loved to go great distances and to see the earth spread out below him like a picture. He would follow the wind half the way across Scotland, and sometimes deep into England, to steal a fine bracelet or a string of pearls or what-have-you. And fly home proudly with it clenched in his beak.

She soon had a chest full of jewels. But she was worried, for he had no more wisdom as a bird than he had as a man. She had to warn him again and again: to be wary, to beware of hunting hawks, to keep far away from fowlers with their snares and nets and fowling pieces, to watch all around himself, as any bird does, for stalking cats.

By now the child, a son, had been born. And though it looked nothing like him, she swore it was the living image of her dear father in the city of Paris, and that was enough to satisfy his suspicions. For he was eager to believe whatever she told him was true.

"Ah, they'll all deceive you if you give them even half a chance. Especially the pretty ones."

"Why then, I believe you were wise to marry the woman you did, for she'll never have the first chance to deceive you."

"What about the sisters?"

Ah, yes, the sisters. Fat and freckled and as pretty in the face as a matching pair of bulldogs.

Well, now that she could afford to have all the servants she wanted, the sisters were not of much value to her. So it might have been their unfortunate fate to die of the same mysterious disease as the parents. Except that the Gypsy woman thought it would be more delightful to find husbands for them.

She found for each of them a vain and handsome, swaggering fellow, men with money in their purses and rings on their fingers, good horses in stable, land of their own.

Happens that both of them were men she herself had known in her Gypsy days. Were men she remembered, begrudged, envied. Hated. So she plotted to teach them a lesson, and she cast a powerful spell upon them, a charm that worked like a German clock. The spell was that in their eyes, and their eyes only, these two ugly sisters would be creatures of extraordinary beauty. So much so they would not stand on ceremony or the demand for a dowry and such like, but would consider their wondrous soft bodies and fair faces to be reward enough. Would consider themselves to be the luckiest of men if they could win the hearts of such beauties.

Nothing would do but a wedding and a wedding party. With half of the county invited to come and share the joy of it.

Now the spell was broken and the plain and undeniable truth was suddenly revealed (just as in Scripture it tells of the scales falling away from the eyes) at the finest, brightest moment of pleasure—in the wedding bed.

"What happened then?"

Just as you would imagine. Much weeping and wailing and gnashing of teeth. From the husbands at least in private. The women were much better off. No spell had been cast on them. They knew who they were in a looking glass, and they had gained what they wanted. For the husbands, there was nothing to do but pretend that what they had believed to be true was true. Better to do that, in the view of a vain man, than to admit you were a fool.

So then, each conny of a husband continued to treat his wife with all love and courtesy as if she were a princess, a living daughter of the goddess of love. And all the while burning inside with secret shame.

But take heed how the world works spells of its own. For many a wise man has told how we are more what others believe us to be than what our eyes tell us when we look directly into a shiny steel glass or a clear pool of water on a windless day.

"Meaning what, Sly?"

Meaning that the tricked lads felt like fools and were taken to be such forever after, no matter what they did or said. That whenever one of them would dare to peek at a looking glass, he would see himself with a long-eared, long-jawed head like a braying ass.

That the sisters rejoiced in their good fortune and were content.

That even though nothing, except perhaps another witch's spell, could serve to make them beautiful, still they gradually began to look a little better to their neighbors as time passed by.

And a little can be much when you begin with next to nothing.

They understand it is the malt spirits that are making him show pity for himself. Not too much usky but too little. Because as he is talking, he falls behind in the drinking. Drinks enough to feel sad, but not so much as to feel no pain. Soon he begins to feel sorry for himself, and then his stories begin to be sadder than they ought to be and are soon as richly adorned with wise say-ings as a preacher's mantelpiece.

Now Sly has every right to feel sorry for himself. And don't we all (each differently), don't we all, sometime and another?

Nevertheless it's an unworthy feeling, as every man knows. And the certain ruin of many a story. Let him keep his sorrows for his prayers. They will do likewise.

So they pass him the jug and make him drink deep before they will listen to another word. And soon the spirits of malt have done their work by lifting his own. And he has forgotten (for a time) half the sorrows of a poor man in a wicked world and is back to his cheerful tale of the farm boy who could fly like a bird.

Telling how the boy grew up and became a man. In the shape of a man he had learned little or nothing and was too ignorant to imagine how much of the world he knew nothing about.

In flesh he was a simpleton, a huge child.

But in feathers he became a scholar of the book of this world. To fly high above it was to read it. To see others who had no thought that anyone could see them was to learn more than any book, except for Holy Scripture, can teach you.

Is there any need to say (Sly is telling it) how easy it was for him to learn the secrets of women? Perched on a twig, hidden in the leaves, he could know them better than their husbands. And when he chose to he could fly in and out a high window as a bird, but be only a man, and a lusty one, in the bedsheets.

But we must not forget, as he did, that he was married to a witch.

"So am I!" cries one.

"So are we all," says another.

He tells how she gradually became suspicious as he began to spend more and more time in the shape of a bird. Reminding them that one difference between a true witch and any of their wives is that it is easier for a witch to confirm or assuage her sus-picions.

Which she did.

Casting a spell to turn herself into a bird. So as to follow him where he went one night. He flew straight and swift to a house in the town of Sterling. Flew into the garden and took his perch on a tree near a lighted window. And sang and sang like a nightingale.

His wife, in the shape of an owl, settled to watch everything from a place nearby.

After a moment or two, the window opened wide. And there a beautiful young woman, all blond and fair and ripe as an apple, appeared. She peered out, looked left and looked right and all around her to be sure that no one was watching. Only a ghostly, white-faced barn owl slowly blinking. Owls did not frighten her. She smiled and motioned as if to a friend. The nightingale ceased its waterfalling song and flew into the chamber window.

Now, Sly has them laughing at a scene they can well imagine when he tells them how the man flew (somewhat weak-winged) home, arriving at dawn. To find the woman waiting for him. Her questions. His lies. Her sudden anger. Not at what he had done— for she did not wish to reveal that she was now spying on him. But raged that he had come home empty-handed, without jewel or trinket or coin to show for himself.

He promised to try to do better, then fell into a contented sleep, deeply snoring.

She need not be a witch to guess the truth. Need not use witchcraft to wake him, either, but poured the chilly contents of the chamber pot all over his handsome head. And up he rose, snorting and cursing.

What happened next you can easily guess. They quarreled, loud and bitter, like any husband and wife. She threatened to denounce him to the Kirk as an adulterer.

"Oh how you would look, dressed in sackcloth with a fool's hat on your head, perched on a high stool by the pulpit!"

"You would look no better strapped in the ducking stool."

"You would not dare!"

"I would and, by God, I will! No. More than that. I'll denounce you as a witch, as the witch that you are."

She laughed and squinted her eyes.

"Well," she said, "they would burn me for it."

"Most likely."

"Pray to remember, lover mine, that they would burn you, too, if it came to that."

He had, as is the habit of angry and thoughtless youth, spoken too much.

"Ah, I was teasing," he said.

"And so was I."

Like many another wife she thought to save her man by moving away and changing the ways of their life.

It is what a Gypsy would do, is it not?

Moved then to a town by the seaside. And with all their ill-gotten loot it was easy to set him up as a merchant there with a ship or two of his own and a house by the harbor. Wearing fine clothes and pretending to have been a merchant always from where he pretended to come from. Who would trouble to doubt them when they gave freely to the Kirk and were generous to the poor? Why, they seemed to be sent from God.

And from his shop he sent out salt fish and wool and animal skins to the world. Bringing back timber and wine, wax, spices.

And he would lend out money at easy interest to other merchants and to any impecunious lord.

Soon he was so busy with weighing his goods and counting his money that he had no time (and no need either) for flying away in the shape of a bird. Besides which he had promised his wife never to fly out in search of love again.

"What kind of a promise was that to make? I would never promise a woman to be faithful."

"Which is easy to say when you have no woman to lie to or lie with."

"And who in the world would want your fidelity, anyway?"

But (Sly continues, raising his voice to silence them before it came to blows or even bad feelings), promises or no, he was soon as restless as a torch flame in a breeze. For that's how it is, the mystery of it, that what is forbidden is far more desired than what is allowed.

"Ever since Adam and Eve, amen."

And what's more than that, though all women are much the same . . .

"All cats are gray in the dark, alas."

. . . you will never meet the man who cares to believe the truth of that. When it comes to women, he is always ready to believe that whatever he cannot possess, or has not yet possessed, is bound to be better than anything he has known before.

"Aye, we men are born and doomed to disappointment."

"Ah, but the dulciness of it! Let me be often disappointed till the day I die."

Besides his house was filling up with runny-nosed squalling children. And his Gypsy woman, content to fart through silk and satin like a lady, had let herself become as round and happy as a sow in a pigpen and cared not a fig.

So he would find himself thinking of the blond young woman in the castle. A trueborn lady she was, white as fresh milk and smoother than silk. Yet as lithe and supple as a young doe. Flying was a fine thing, a breathless, heart-pounding joy. But lying with his young blond lady had been even better.

He devised a plan. He went aboard his ship to make a voyage to Flanders and do some trading there. This was his thought. That soon as the ship was safe out of sight he would turn into a seagull and fly away. It would be thought that he must have fallen overboard and drowned. And it would be more than a month before the ship returned and his wife received the sad news. By which time he would have vanished forever with his lady love.

All went well, better than he had hoped. For after he left the ship, in the form of a gull, a storm blew up and that ship went down to the bottom of the sea with all hands on board.

What he did not know and had no way to know was that his wife had made friendship with another witch in that seaside town. And that the old witch had cast the spell which made the storm which sank the boat.

For, you see, the Gypsy wife was weary of him, too, and eager to be a widow.

"I do believe for once Sly is going to tell us a tale where there is a happy ending. Where all will receive what they deserve."

"God save us from our just deserts."

Meantime a single seagull flew across Scotland to light near a castle window and to see what he could see. What he saw was his lady, fair as spring flowers and clad in a shift as fine and thin as a spider's web. Brushing her long golden hair . . .

It will never be known how Sly might have told them what happened next.

For what in fact happened next in the silence thick with their breathing was a loud rude blast of the ram's horn outside. Shouts from out there. And then a cursing and a clatter as all who were able to scrambled for swords and steel bonnets and clambered and tumbled down the ladder to the vaulted ground floor of the tower. Where already the best horses and cattle were being herded. Rushed down the rickety ladder and out into the moonlit yard.

Sly, poised on his wooden staves, listened as the shouts died out and then became laughter.

"It's Hob and Willie of the Park and some of the Armstrongs, I do believe," says Blind Jock, who has not moved from his place near the fire. To whom a voice is as clear and distinct as a face is to you or to me.

Sure enough, they have come riding twenty miles to meet with the master when he returns. To talk plans of a ride in the West March. Soon before the moon is gone.

They come climbing up the ladder. With much laughing at the fright they gave by coming up so quietly and taking the lads in the yard by surprise.

"Good lads, though, good lads," says Hob. "That boy put the horn to his lips and blew like Gabriel as quick as he saw us."

They have brought more with them to drink. And though from the breath and loud fury of them it can't have been long since they last drank, they claim to suffer from a powerful thirst.

It's a good half hour, maybe more, before they have settled down and someone then remembers Sly's tale and bids him to bring it to a close.

It is too late now for more than the skimpiest ending. And with a dozen new listeners there can be no going back. So he ends it as briskly as he can.

How the lady of the castle had been married to a jealous lord, old enough to be her father.

How to give her freedom the young man cast the one spell he

knew and turned her into a cooing dove. And off they flew together, as a pair of doves.

How the old witch in the seaside town knew this. For she had
a magic glass in which she could see everything in all of
Scotland. Except for the Highlands, which are too misty and
damp and where no decent person, not even a witch, would want
to see what happens.

How she quarreled with the Gypsy woman and told her. The
Gypsy could not, would not, believe her. So the witch made her
look in the glass for herself. And there she saw them. Not as a
pair of birds, but in their undeniable human forms. The Gypsy
swore revenge on them both and turned herself into a hawk and
flew away to find that pair of naughty turtledoves.

How on a balmy day the two of them were flying high above
the fields and forests, careless and happy as children. And, as in a
child's game, the lady flew ahead alone to make him pursue her.

So never saw the shadow of the hawk that fell upon her from
above and broke her neck and ripped her with its talons. When
she struck the earth, at the moment of her death, the spell was
broken, too. And there she lay in some pasture, terribly mangled.
Bloody as a butchered pig.

He saw it happen and fled for his life. Flying to find some safe
place to light and change into a man again before the hawk tore
him to pieces, too.

Down came the hawk and ripped his back wide open before
he struggled free and touched the earth and turned to a man
again.

He in a field of barley, a naked man with a wounded back,
weeping sadly.

And this story I know to be true because I have seen the man.
He lived like a hermit in a wild place. An angry old man to
throw stones at and run away from. When he died they took off
his clothes to see. And there, I swear to you, were the terrible
marks of the hawk on his back.

"Whatever became of the Gypsy woman?"

There is no one who knows.

Perhaps the old witch might have known. But she came to
grief in another matter, concerning a wax image of a high and
mighty lord. And she was well racked and burned for it.

Some say the Gypsy woman was caught while she was returning home, against the wind, lost in the joy of her revenge. They
say she was taken by a falconer. Before she knew what had happened he sealed her eyelids and put a hood over her head. Put
jesses and vervels on her legs. And took her to train as a haggard.
Well. Nothing to do then but learn the sport quickly if she ever
wanted to eat and to sleep again. Must let herself be manned before she could go free.

"And?"

I have heard she found herself to be the hawk on the fist of a
man she could truly love. And was happy to be so and never took
on human form again.

"Aye, who would want to be an old woman, or an old man either, if you could choose to be a hawk?"

"What I'd like to know is who was the man."

The Earl of Bothwell.

Now then. That makes for a hush in this chamber.

It is finally Hob who speaks first.

"Are you talking of Patrick the Fair Earl?"

Sly savors this moment. True, the unexpected arrival of Hob
and Willie and the others spoiled the shape of his story, but not
the ending of it.

He spits in the fire. Red-faced, fierce to behold again, from the
heat and glow of it. His broken body concealed in shadows. His
hard face wreathed in thick smoke. As if he might be no more
than one terrible, smoking, cooking head.

"Not Patrick Hepburn," he says slowly, thoughtfully, as if in
the act of remembering. "For he was killed at Flodden, as I recall. No, I mean to say it was the next one—James, the Fourth
Earl. . . ."

As quick as the quiet had come now rises up a rush of noise.
Laughing and coughing, their voices all talking loudly and all at
once. Sly could not have contrived a more just fate for the Gypsy
woman who dabbled in witchcraft and became a hunting falcon.
Could not have discovered a better ending for his broken tale.
The sound of their loud voices is cheers and applause to him.

He lowers his head into shadow to smile to himself and not to
be seen.

Not one of them here who does not have the strongest kind of feelings concerning James Hepburn, Earl of Bothwell. Bothwell never allowed the world to take him with a yawn, to dispose of him with a shrug. To this day to talk about him can lead to quarrels. To fists and knives.

Love him or hate him (and there are some here who rode with him; others who were always against him), they love the flock of stories, true or false no matter, that circle him like gulls around a fishing boat.

And how did he feel about them—the men of the Borders? Men whom he'd as lief hang from a tree or a door as wish a good morning. What was it he said about them when he was first made Lieutenant of the Border? Ask Blind Jock. He has it by heart. The others relish the truth of it.

"They are like Job," he said. "Not in patience and piety, but in sudden plenty and poverty."

Drink to that. To plenty. To English beef in our bellies and English wood to blaze in our fires. Here's to English money in the chest and the Devil take the rest.

Noble or no—and there's no denying his title and blood; wasn't Patrick his father once even a suitor for the English Virgin Queen?—he was in a deep sense more like one among them than most of the lords of Scotland. Even their own masters, the lords of the Borders. Old George Buchanan named him "an ape in purple." And that will do fine. Does not displease them, these men who will die without ever wearing anything grander than fustian and white leather. And if he held high offices in this land—Warden of the Marches, Sheriff of Edinburgh, Privy Councilor, Lord High Admiral of Scotland, Duke of Orkney and Shetland, and almost . . . once upon a very brief time for him . . . the King of the Scots, he ended his days (in this world of sorrow and tears) in a Danish prison, a ragged lunatic, chained to a post. And not much beyond forty years of age when he died there.

Even those who still hate his guts and would gladly have spilled them and draped them to decorate bracken and feed the ravens will admit it is unworthy to envy the good fortune of any man who came to such an unhappy end.

He owned a dozen castles and houses and had the keeping of as many others. And yet on a raid or in the shieling hills, he would wrap himself in a horse blanket and sleep beneath stars like any reiver.

Was he married (some say all at the same time, for he hated to divorce any woman he loved) to three proud women—a Danish lady and Lady Jean Gordon and last of all the tall fair Queen of the Scots herself? Well, true, but he was nevertheless never too proud to take any woman, milkmaid or turnspit, who was handy, into his embrace. And some fine ladies, too. It's believed he was long the lover of Janet Beaton, the Wizard Lady of Branxholm.

"Is not the wild hare the crest of the Hepburns?"

"And if there was no woman handy," Hob says, "why he was not so proud and chaste that he would not take his pleasure wherever he could find it."

Meaning that his man, Dandy Pringle, swore an oath that Bothwell did bugger and sodomize all of his servants over in France—not only Dandy but Nicholas Hubert that they called French Paris and Gabriel Sempill and Walter Murray and two or three others.

"Dandy Pringle was a lying dog and so was his father Sandy."

"I'll not disagree and would never waste my time speaking well of anyone by the name of Pringle. But you know what the Froggy Frenchmen are famous for."

"And wherever the Earl of Bothwell went he always followed the customs of the place—riding and singing and dancing and fighting."

"And even French buggery!"

"It was a Frenchman, that Esmé Stuart, came over to teach our King that French art."

"They can hang you for thinking that."

"Have to catch me first."

"Every time they caught Bothwell he escaped."

"All but the last time."

Now begins a round of tales, no more than quick jests really. A dissonant chorus of reivers to tell them. Disreputable choir to sing Bothwell's praises and recite his follies. Bits and pieces of the man's lost life. True or not, no matter.

They relish the contradictions of him.

That he was often crude and filthy of speech, blasphemous and irreverent, yet that he was well schooled and could write the French language fluently in a fine, skilled Italian hand.

That he, like his father before him, was a Protestant from beginning to end. And when the Queen of Scots married him, pious Catholic that she may have been, his will prevailed; and they were wed as Protestants in Holyrood Palace. Protestant and yet . . . he hated and fought against the Lords of the Congregation. Indeed he fought against all rebels for the crown. Hated the Protestant lords and kept friendship and company with the lords of the old Faith. With Athol and Errol and with Huntly, the Cock o' the North. And married Huntly's sister, too.

Like any Scots lord worthy of title and name, he fought his own countrymen, in wars and rebellions, feuds and ambushes and raids, without pity or mercy. But like only a precious few he was always loyal to the crown. Which was why he was given the color blue, for loyalty, to wear at the christening of James VI. And like very few he was faithful in hatred for the English, only serving the English once in his life, and that as a trick to gain his freedom from them. How he otherwise gave them fits. Aches and pains, long days in the saddle and sleepless nights.

How (somebody knows) on All Hallows Eve of '59 he managed to capture the money being secretly sent from England to pay for the rebellion of the Lords of the Congregation. Much gnashing of teeth in Scotland and England alike when that happened.

They like to hear the stories of his betrayal of his enemies. How he tricked the young Earl of Arran and drove him mad. How he blew up the house at Kirk o' the Field with Henry Stewart, Lord Darnley (who called himself King Henry) in it. Stood trial for the crime and was acquitted of it. And within three months was himself the husband of Darnley's widow—the Queen of Scots.

They love to hear stories of his escapes.

How he managed freedom from high and rocky Edinburgh Castle, together with his man—James Porterfield. By rope and by bedsheet in the windy night. Porterfield fell and broke his leg. So

Bothwell carried him safely to a house before he himself fled the city.

How he escaped from Borthwick Castle by broad daylight. When he and Queen Mary found themselves surrounded there. A sudden rush from the Postern Gate. And a wild shouting gallop, pistol in hand, directly through a crowd of his enemies. Had taught his new wife, the Queen, some tricks also. For she followed behind him a day or so later, escaping disguised as a man.

Escaped from Holyrood Palace that night in March of '66 when a crowd of the Lords came to murder the Italian, Rizzio, and to seize the Queen. They would have killed Bothwell, too. But he jumped from a window and into the little walled garden where the lions were kept. Sprinted across it, climbed the far wall, and ran to freedom.

Who else but Bothwell would have run without so much as a second thought through a garden full of lions?

How, unable to free himself from the Tower of London, he gained his freedom by promises and smiling words. Promised to serve the English. Took their money, too. And then took his liberty and soon enough betrayed them.

Now comes a favorite of them all. It falls to Red Tom to repeat this one.

How one time Bothwell was trapped and almost taken in a midnight raid. Happened in the town of Haddington. He had to flee from his lady's chamber. Or perhaps it was no lady at all, but once again was Bessie Crawford, the daughter of Willie Crawford the Blacksmith. With whom, in many places thereabouts, he so often did the ancient dance of love. Once, they say, toiling and wrestling, riding with round and buxom Bessie as you would handle an unbroken horse, up in the tower of St. Mary's Church, just beyond Haddington. When someone or other began to ring all the bells in that tower as if to celebrate the occasion.

Earl and Bessie both were deaf for two or three days.

Well then . . . Middle of a moonlit night. Noise. Hooves and whinnying. Shouts. Torchlight and loud knuckling on the doors. Which was warning enough for the Earl of Bothwell. Even dreaming in his lady's arms. He leaves that bed as if fired out of it by a gunpowder charge. Bootless, hatless, half naked, and with no time to pause and look for his sword, he bids the lady farewell and is out the window and tumbling down in Goul Lane. Running for his life to try to reach the River Tyne. Down the lane breathing hard and sees the flat gray of the river, like a blade in the light, and slows to a walk. Which is lucky for him. Because then, walking, he sees something else give a wink in the light, closer to him than the river. And that's a real blade in moonlight.

And he's whirled and gone racing back up the lane with shouts behind him.

Ran into a house he knew. And borrowed the clothes and bonnet of a turnspit girl there.

Not dreaming his enemies would remain there, looking for him, for several days. While he must remain dressed as a woman and acting that part. They searched and could not find a sign of him. Except his horse in a stable and his boots and spurs, hat and gloves. Which had been tossed out the window behind him into the dirt of Goul Lane.

Soon they gave up and left, fearing he had escaped and would soon return with his men. And ever after that he paid the kitchen girl a pension for the use of her clothes that saved his liberty and probably his life.

Hard to say, as Red Tom tells it, which part pleases them most. Bothwell leaping barefoot out through the open window, feet and legs churning as if he were already running. As if he had at least a faint hope that he might run away in the empty air. Or Bothwell, in petticoat, apron and bonnet, turning a roast on the spit, red-faced and sweating. While some rough and ready fellow pats his little rump and whispers promises into his ear. Hoping to take this sturdy turnspit girl into the hay of the stable after dinner.

Now Blind Jock coughs and clears his throat to tell one.

"Pour Jock a bowl."

Someone pours out spirits from the jug. Brings it to him where he sits, with his back to the fire, facing them as if he still had light in his eyes to see them.

How it was in the autumn of '66. That being the same year, mind you, that our King James was born, in June, at Edinburgh Castle.

The Earl of Bothwell had come down to the Borders to Liddesdale and settled himself at Hermitage Castle. Not raiding the English, but instead riding against the Elliots. Who had already ravaged and pillaged their foes, the Scotts, well enough to spare him the trouble of dealing with them. He had a mind to bring peace and quiet to that part of the Border. In the only way he knew—by sword and by fire. By the hanging rope.

How Hermitage Castle was a right place for Bothwell to call home. Being (as some of you know) a rude, ancient castle, sitting there, miles from village or hamlet in the wide treeless land close by Hermitage Water.

Many of them will have seen Hermitage Castle. So stark and lonely in its wild place. Will have been within its walls and have walked in its little courtyard. Will know it as well as Jock. But not the long shadows which time has cast upon it.

"Hermitage is a grim place," says one, as if to himself, while Jock takes a sip or two from his bowl.

As well it ought to be. Grim and sad, indeed. A forlorn place which has passed through the hands of many a family—the Soulis, the Dacres of England, Douglas and Hepburn . . .

"And even now, tonight, in the keeping of the Scotts of Buccleuch."

Yes, the Scotts at last have the keeping of it. But Hermitage has never yet brought to any man any good luck.

Now. Is there a man here among you who can tell me how that murderous wizard, William Lord Soulis, came to his just deserts?

(He waits for no answer. For, even if they know, they know better than to say so.)

Lord Soulis had caused the death of many a man. And he was as greatly feared by his servants and vassals as he was by his enemies. Perhaps even more so. For his enemies were free of him unless they fell into his hands. While his servants and vassals were always handy for his cruelty and mischief.

But there finally came another and greater wizard, called Thomas of Ercildoune. Who bound him tight with three magic ropes of sand. And they took Lord Soulis away to the hilltop place called Nine Stane Rig. Where there is a circle of stones from a time beyond all men's remembering. There they wrapped him snug in a cope of soft lead and set him in a brass cauldron full of water. They built a fire beneath it and slowly boiled the man to death. They danced around the cauldron to the music of his shrieks.

And still on a windy winter's night, when the moon is no more than a slice in the sky, you can hear the groans of his ghost as he boils forever in hell.

So there, in September and early October of '66, was the Earl of Bothwell filling the castle dungeon with Elliots. And it seemed most likely he would make an end to that family once and for all.

Here hoots and catcalls from the Elliots and their cousins who are here. The sense of which is that it would take all the Hepburns in the world, together with their friends and kin—the Ormistons, the Blackadders . . .

"And the Pringles. Do not forget his friends the Pringles!"

. . . to catch and hold one sturdy Elliot.

Well, now. Nevertheless it was a bad time for them that autumn. Until one day when he happened to meet the one they called Little Jock Elliot of the Park. In single combat on horseback.

Bothwell and a band of his men came upon Little Jock and took him by surprise. Jock was all alone and riding along slow and easy, in no hurry to be anywhere else, when they found him. He had been spending some days and nights, merry as a mouse in malt, with a woman in the neighborhood. And someone must have betrayed him.

Now it looked to Little Jock that he was shortly to die in the saddle (if he had had a saddle, which he did not) or at the end of a rope. Oh, he could run for a time, to be sure, but with all of that band, and the least one of them better mounted than he was, there was no way he could escape for long.

So instead of riding away as soon as he saw them, he pulled up short and sat there. And they pulled up too and looked at the shabby little scarecrow across the distance.

Then he called out to them in a loud voice daring Bothwell to come forth and try to take him. Man to man.

This caused much laughter. Nothing could suit Bothwell better. Little Jock would have not a whit more chance to live in single combat with him, and it would be quicker by far than having to chase him down and then finding a tree to hang him from. Besides it would be pure pleasure for the Earl to kill Little Jock then and there for the edification and entertainment of his men.

Bothwell yelled back that it suited him right well. Then he rode out alone across the field to fight Little Jock.

Now then.

Let us here remember what Bothwell, in all his fury and murderous skill as a fighting man, chose to forget. Forgetting the simple truth that Little Jock of the Park had not managed to live long enough to be there that day by being a loon. And only a fool would have undertaken to dare the Earl of Bothwell to single combat and expected to live to eat supper and sit by the fire.

Which is why so few men ever chose to take up a challenge given by Bothwell. Never mind the shame.

And which is also why the Earl was so free with challenges. Knowing that because of his skill and reputation the chances were that no man (excepting always a fool) would ever accept his challenge.

So here was Little Jock of the Park, looking forlorn and all alone, and weak and spent too, from days and nights of doing the oldest dance in creation with a healthy and willing wench.

(*Hoots and hollers in the smoky chamber!*)

And caught on a little nag that he had borrowed and was none too sure of. And caught without any weapons other than his whinny and short sword. Thinking to himself, no *knowing* it for how else could it be, that it is no accident that Bothwell and his scruffy men have happened to find him. Knowing himself to have been betrayed, then. And sadder, if no wiser, on account of it. For who else could his betrayer be but the wench he had been with? Thinking sadly that, if he lives beyond this afternoon, never again will he hold her, hot and slick and heaving like a salmon in a net between his legs.

(*Hoots and hollers and cheers!*)

Thinking he will have to kill her for it. For we cannot have wenches feeling safe to betray us, can we? If he is not killed dead himself in the next quarter of an hour. Thinking all this even as he is calling out his challenge to the Earl of Bothwell.

Who comes forth now, proud and laughing and well mounted, sitting firm on a fine Morocco saddle. It would take a lance or a

cannonball to unseat him. Whereas poor little Jock of the Park
has no more than a piece of wool between his bony arse and his
borrowed horse.

And, you know, maybe it was a lust to own that saddle which
gave to Little Jock the inspiration to dare the Earl to combat.
For Jock was born a thief and was destined not to cease the habit
of thievery until they shoveled earth to cover over his bones. For
there is a certain kind of Border man who would find a way and
a means to pick the purse of the hangman at his own hanging.
Not for the earnings but the joy of it. Because it is his skill. Because it is his nature.

(*Amen to that! And pass the jug around!*)

Jock was thinking that if he acquired possession of that good
horse and that fine saddle, with only a bit of a start ahead he had
a fair chance to outrun them all.

Here comes the Earl of Bothwell for him.

And so he begins to ride forward himself, as if to meet and to
clash with the Earl. Then, as he comes closer, suddenly he turns
about and rides off hard as if to make a run for it. Which you can
believe, causes much laughter from the Earl's men. Who take
Jock to be a fool and a coward to boot. Laughing and yelling, for
they know the Earl will run him down like a greyhound catching
a hare. They sit where they are to watch it happen.

Now Jock gives the Earl a bit of a run. Because he knows the
ground better and knows he can thread his way among soft
boggy places. Which can spill a man and break his bones for
him. He weaves in and out of the wet places. Forcing Bothwell
to go more carefully as he follows behind.

Bothwell calling after him to turn back and fight.

Little Jock of the Park throwing insult over his shoulder and
urging the Earl to come closer, close enough to kiss his arse.

Thinking that if the Earl gives way to rage, he might perchance
be careless enough to fall.

Then, as sudden as he had turned coward and run away, Jock
whirls back like a born hero. Found a piece of ground to his liking and turns back to take the Earl by surprise. Comes straight
and hard for the Earl with sword drawn now and grinning like a
dog with a bone.

And so discovers himself to be looking directly into a grin as large as his own.

For the Earl has prepared a little surprise for Little Jock. Something Jock had not thought of. Not until he is looking at it.

Which surprising thing is a heavy, short-barreled dag—a pistol lock, all primed and loaded and stuffed with steel shot the size of beans.

Jock of the Park is riding straight toward a tight grin and the muzzle end of a pistol that looms as large to him as the mouth of a cannon.

He has no time to curse his luck. Only time enough to feel his scrotum shriveling and his asshole clenching like a fist as he hears a roaring noise all over and around him, smells and tastes gunpowder, and feels himself sitting not on a horse any longer but out in the air and tumbling amid a rush and rash of wounds stinging him like a hive of angry bees. A breathless rumbling in the air, stinging and blood-slick, and then all the breath of his body kicked out of him as he hits the earth and rolls to lie there face down. As still as any corpse you have ever seen.

The Earl circles around him looking. Seeing no sign of life or breath. Seeing the body of Little Jock still as a rock. Seeing a pool of blood all around him in the grass.

Then swings down from his horse and, drawn sword in hand moves to look at the face of the man he has killed. Kicks at him with the point of his boot.

Suddenly to find his boot and his leg snatched out from under him . . .

(*Cheers!*)

The Earl himself falling backward and his sword flying free from his grip as the back of his head hits the earth and bounces. And before he can get to his feet again, Little Jock of the Park has taken that same sword and wounded him well in three different places. Has left him lying as still and as bloody as he had been. Not looking back, but hearing the shout from Bothwell's men on the hill behind him as he vaults up to sit himself on that fine Morocco saddle and to ride away on the Earl's horse as if he were blown by a gale wind.

He is gone from sight before they can reach the Earl and try to staunch his wounds and save his life. There's nothing much left of him but groans. So they bandage his cuts as best they can and hurry him back to Hermitage Castle.

Where, I am pleased to report to you, there was yet another unseemly surprise waiting for them.

For while they were gone out to ambush and chase Little Jock of the Park, the other Elliots, the ones they had imprisoned in the castle, had broken free. Overpowered the guards and took over the castle. So when Bothwell's band returned, the gate was locked, and there on the walls and at the windows were the Elliots yelling and hooting derision. Would not open the gate without an unconditional promise of freedom. Which they were given then and there. And all the Elliots rode out and away, sitting on some of the Earl's best horses, before the Earl and his men could enter in.

Fire glowing. Quiet for a moment in the room. Outside one of the lads whistles to another. Horse snorts. Dog barks, then is quiet.

Blind Jock, his hands folded in his lap, waiting. For someone to speak.

"It was at that time, Jock, was it not, when the Queen of Scots rode clear across the country from Jedburgh to Hermitage and back in one day?"

"For what?"

"To see for herself if the Earl was like to die."

"Did she care?"

Blind Jock tells them.

How she had come down here (so they said) for a Justice Ayres in Jedburgh. Though many believed that she came down to be away from her husband, Darnley, and from all the troubles and broils of the Court. Her newborn son, not yet even christened, was safe in Stirling Castle.

And so she was here in Border country, living in that pele tower (every one of you well have seen it over in Limmerfield in the town of Jedburgh), the one belonging to the Laird of Cessford, the one with the stairs built with a backward twist on account of the lefthandedness of the Kerrs of Cessford. You know the one. A stout and sturdy place it is.

"Would God we had it here and were in it tonight."

And how coming from Hermitage, not far from Hawick, the Queen took a great tumble off her horse in the bog.

"I have seen where. And it is a cousin of my mother who has the house where she came to clean off the mud and to mend her dress before riding on."

Aye. And how there is a curious truth at the heart of these things. To begin, that Bothwell should have died from his wounds. But was healed and whole in no time at all.

"Perhaps it was witchcraft that healed him."

Well, perhaps.

How anyway he was healed and almost as good as new. Except for three scars, one good one on his head, that he took delight in showing off whenever he could.

How it was the Queen who came closest to dying. From fever and ague. How she returned from her ride to Hermitage Castle and took sick. And how for a time they truly despaired of her life.

"But she lived to keep her appointment with an English headsman."

"Damn them for killing our Queen, devil or no!"

How Bothwell recovered and lived to kill her husband. And soon after to marry the Queen himself. And then to live in order to die like a dumb beast chained in the stinking dark. Far from country and home. How you could pity the man if there wasn't a rough and ready justice to it all.

"And Little Jock of the Park. What became of him?"

Ah, well. He died in his own warm bed, of course. Many years and smiles later. Dying as easy as anyone could wish and pray for.

"It's the truth. For I myself have seen the man, not more than ten years ago. A little fellow, tan and wrinkled all over as if he had been dipped and stained in walnut juice. Had a terrible temper, too, in his old age."

How it is not to be debated that when a face and body have been well hit, riddled with shot at close range, it will do nothing to improve a man's good looks. But keep in mind that Little Jock could bear the changes more easily than most men. For Jock was never, even on his best day, what anyone would want to call handsome.

"Ugly is what he was."

"Ugliest little man I ever saw!"

Exactly. How the shot then only added to his natural ugliness. How it made him even more careless and fearless. And, thus, even more to be feared.

How he rode away on the Earl's horse to find the house of a cousin. To hide there till he healed.

How he sold Bothwell's horse to an Englishman. But kept that Morocco saddle to his dying day. Thinking he would have to be killed to give it up.

"And the woman that betrayed him, what became of her?"

Well, now. How he could not know that for sure, now could he? He had guessed it was the woman who did it. For who else could it be? But how, as he lay in his cousin's house, sweating and itching and slowly healing in the couple of dozen places the shot had torn his flesh, he thought often of her smooth, warm, sweet, soft, unblemished flesh and what pleasure it had given him.

How he began to speculate that she had not been the one who betrayed him.

And how, even if she was, she would be powerfully surprised when (soon as I'm hale enough to mount a horse and go there) he came, a ghost risen from the dead, walking into her house without so much as knocking. Thinking if he could mount a horse and ride there, he could mount that wild and milk-skinned woman and ride her, too.

Thinking that justice is justice and no denying that. But thinking, too, that mercy is mighty rare and powerful. And certainly proper in the case of a pleasing woman in a world where pleasures are few and far between.

How he planned then, itching and burning and healing through that winter, to go to her house more often than before. How he did so. With this difference. That he never again rode alone. But always with at least a dozen of his best men. Believing that with a dozen like him no man, not even the Earl of Bothwell, would dare to come after him.

Believing then, in those days, that if he had a hundred others like himself he could take the whole island from the English.

Here would be the likeliest place to turn to Red Tom and his tale of Kinmont Willie and the doings at Carlisle Castle. And indeed it must be what Blind Jock has planned. For he has lowered his voice to no more than a whisper. As if to bring his part of the telling of stories to a close. But it is not to be. Not yet. For one of the others, a youngster only with all his future before him, proud of that and yawning at the past, speaks up.

What the lad says out loud is this: "Well, too bad this Little Jock of the Park did not live to see and enjoy it. For the whole island shall be ours. And we shall live to ride and raid as far as London, and even beyond that, when it pleases us."

"How will that be, lad?" asks another.

"Well now," says the boy. "If our King becomes their King too, when their Queen dies (as she must die soon), and if he is taken to be their King, then we shall at last be free to ride wherever we please there. I have heard, from a man who has seen it for himself, that south of Humber lie the fattest, greenest farms, with cattle twice as large and fat as any that we have ever seen in these parts. And they have not even towers and walls to protect them, they are so soft and ignorant there."

"Ah, lad," says Blind Jock, raising his voice again. "It will never be that way. You are young and I wish you nothing but well. But it will not be that way. I promise you it will not."

Stung and thoughtless, the young man snaps an unmannerly answer. Perhaps it is malt spirits speaking through him.

"Old man," he cries out, more loudly than he meant to. "Blind old man, you have a long memory of things that have long since passed. But that has not made you a prophet with the power to see what is still to come. I mean to say when it comes to that, to telling the future, though I may be young and ignorant, I have as much right as any. And better than some who are slow and dim-witted. And better than you because I still have my own two eyes to see for myself."

The others are struck dumb by it. Silent. Waiting to see what Jock, who has a terrible temper, will say or do. And he is silent for a moment, too, clenching his fists into hammers. Breathing heavy through his nose. Smoke from the fire wreathing his white head.

Even the lad is silent. As if he is astonished at what he has heard himself saying.

He is even more astonished, and relieved, when Blind Jock laughs softly. More to himself than at the lad's expense.

It is true, lad, Blind Jock says. I am no prophet. I am, it is also the truth, an old man who is mired in and besotted by the past. Loving it too much, maybe. Living there more than I ought to. And it may well be true, also, that my blindness is the cause of that.

For I could not see your face just now as you spoke out loud. And I wished that I could have. I have never seen your face. But I knew your father and mother and your grandfather before that. And so I have a picture of you in my mind that is likely to be as true as what you yourself see when you look at your face in a steel glass.

"Sir, I am sorry that I spoke so rude and thoughtlessly."

"And well you ought to be, you silly loon."

"Lucky for you that you didn't earn yourself a whipping for speaking to your betters like that."

"No man here is going to whip me, by God!"

"I say we should put him out in the yard with the little bairns to guard and keep cows."

"Touch me and I'll introduce you to the sharpest knife in this room."

Be quiet! Jock roars out. Be quiet all of you and listen to me for a moment or two.

We shall not let our fellowship this evening end in shouting and fighting amongst each other. Though that is how too many things, time out of mind, have ended here on the Marches. It has been the death of many of us. And it takes no prophet to see that it is likely to be the end of us.

Takes no prophet, either, to see that the end is coming. The end for us and all of our kind.

(Now they are all very quiet. Full of wonder at this thing they cannot imagine.)

I know that every one of you believes that better days will come to us if our King comes to wear the English crown. And, in truth, I think it is altogether likely that it will be so—our King James that will be the King of England and of Scotland, too. God willing. And I believe it may come to pass soon enough for me to hear the news of it. And hear the bells of Scotland ringing to announce it.

But the bells will not gladden my heart. For they will mark the end of us.

What will become of us all, the men of the Borders, when there are no Borders between the two countries? Have you thought of that? Do you think this James Stuart loves us so much he will leave us alone to pursue our merry ways?

Ah no.

He cannot do that and still hope to govern the English. Even if the King ever loved us at all—which he has not and does not, he would have to offer us up to the Law. And believe me Law is coming.

But more.

For the truth is he loves us very little. Indeed, I think he hates us all. And what I see, my friends, is fire and sword, the scourging and purging of us from the face of the land. What I see in my blindness and out of my hoard of memories is the end of it for us.

"Enough of this gloom and grief, Jock. If you continue in this fashion, we shall have to crawl into our coffins and sleep like the monks used to in the old days. I say, we need a little laughter, some merry tale out of times gone by, to prove that there's more to the history of the Scots than blood and tears."

Well then. What would you like to hear?

"Tell us once again," Sly says, "the story of the good man of Ballangeigh."

Why not?

You will remember how this King, James the Fifth, loved to wander alone disguised in common clothes and looking much like any other man you might meet on the road or in the market-place. This way he could tell for himself the true, unfeigned temper of his people and the times. Let others depend on the craft of their paid spies and informers. He was his own spy, depending on his own wits and craft.

Now there was another good reason for the King to wander about in disguise. And it may well have been the true reason for which all others were no more than excuses. This King James the Fifth was, as everyone knows or ought to, a great lover of women. Especially fair and sturdy country girls. And in his wanderings he left more bastards behind than anyone, even the King, knew of or counted.

To be sure he was generous to his lovers. Left them richer in return for their favors. Which, if you think on it, was not without a certain advantage to many another Scotsman with a wandering eye. For when any shabby fellow is likely to be the King himself in disguise, no woman could well afford to be too proud to share herself with a stranger.

It was a fine time for fornication in Scotland if not for much of anything else.

Well now.

The King had found a young woman who caught his fancy, and she lived in the village of Cramond. Which sits there close by the mouth of the River Almond and is no more than a good walk from Edinburgh. King was living at Holyrood then and could slip out and away and be back safe in the morning. With no one any the wiser.

One time, he lingered in pleasure longer than he meant to, allowed the sun to catch him in her bed. When sunlight lit her chamber, up he jumped and dressed himself quick as he could. Kissed her farewell and hurried away to take the road back to the city. Slipped out of the village unseen and unknown—as far as he knew. But as he was crossing the bridge across the Almond, four sturdy fellows came at him, two from each side. They were armed with blades and cudgels. And he had no choice, if he wanted to live, but to draw his own sword and fight them as best he could.

Well, the King was a swordsman, and these four rough fellows, hairy as Highland cows, were not nearly so skilled as he was. Besides which that little bridge is narrow and only one at a time can cross. So at no time could more than two of them, one from each side, get at him. He could hold them off of him, then, for a time. Until he wearied of it, and then they would surely stew his ears.

Now then. If we can leave the King there on the bridge, holding his own for the time being, defending himself with his sword, first this way then that, we ought to ask ourselves—who on earth were these loony fellows who set upon the King?

It is true that they could not know this plain-dressed fellow to be the King. Could scarcely have guessed it from looking at him, plain and wrinkled and rumpled and bed-weary (ah the best weariness under the sun). . . .

(*Amen to that!*)

Could not at sight have known this fellow to be the anointed King of the Scots.

Or did they?

It must have crossed the King's mind, even as it does yours and mine, that perhaps someone had betrayed him. That here was a plan to kill a King and to lay the blame for it on robbers and the folly of the King's habit of wandering about alone and in disguises.

Even as he blocked and cut and thrust with his blade, the King must surely have been thinking of who it might be who would want him floating in the River Almond.

Maybe it was what it seemed to be, a common robbery on the road. But even so that could hardly lift his spirits (or yours and mine either if it had been you or me and not him). For the simple reason he would likely be dead and gone from this world as soon the one way as the other. Maybe sooner if these were robbers; for, except for his sword, he had nothing of value with him. Nothing worth robbing and killing for. Which condition is sure to enrage your city-bred robbers. Who are, as we all know, a cowardly bloody lot. And in a just world would be whipped and hanged for their doings to teach them better manners.

So then. Assassins they may have been. Robbers they might have been. Or something of both at the same time.

But, you'll be thinking, just as the King did, they might not have been either one. What if that lusty, fair-skinned woman had a brother or two to look to the preservation of her reputation? Might be she had kinfolk who thought to teach him a lesson. But once you allow for that chance—and how can you not allow it, for it does seem as likely as murder or robbery, both of which could be better and easier done in the night. Once you allow that possibility, there are others that run behind it like a pack of barking dogs behind a bitch in heat. Suppose it is not father or brothers or kinfolk, but instead a jealous lover? Who is the world's worst kind of felon since there is nothing he will stop short of to ease the pain of his jealousy. Or just suppose (as the King surely did) that there could be a husband about whom the woman had somehow neglected to tell him. Now that would add a whiff of righteous anger to their actions. And all the world knows that crimes done in the name of righteousness are likely to be the worst ones of all.

Which sobering thought would lead him (as it does you and me), as sure as a moth to the comfort of a candle flame, to the next thought—that all of this might well be the doing of the woman. Betrayal on her part. Either alone or in collusion. No matter. Either way he would prove to be a fool. And a dead fool, instead of a living King, at any moment.

Now the King was so busy fighting, and thinking these heavy thoughts which might be his last ones, and they, these four scurvy fellows, were busy, too, and thinking whatever thoughts, if any, cloud the dull minds of such ill-bred city scum, that none of them saw the farmer who had come out early to cut the field on the other side of the river.

This farmer was a man (here's a good name to remember and honor) called John Howison. Who was tenant of the farm of Braehead there. Now. Being a plain and honest man, this John Howison was not troubling himself to wonder who these people might be or what could have possessed them to do what they were doing to each other. No. What he saw was five strangers fighting on the bridge. Four of them rough and ready rogues and the other a man something like himself when he put on his best clothes for the city. A man who might have been a tenant farmer, too, except that he had his shoes on. Which was a very suspicious thing.

But none of these things troubled good John Howison so much as the odds. Four against one is not a fair fight. So he picked up his scythe and let out a great holler. Came running across the field toward the road and the bridge.

All five on the bridge paused to look. And they saw a man as big as a bear, running as swift as a dog, coming toward them. Bellowing like a bull. And what caught their eyes and attention the most of all was that scythe blade, sharp as a razor and naked as a needle in morning light.

One look and the four rough fellows dropped their weapons and departed, two by way of the river and two like frightened deer, gone down the road and leaving no more behind than puffs of dust to prove they had been there.

And you can believe that there stood a grateful King on the bridge.

John Howison, not dreaming who this might be and much too courteous to ask, led him off to his house, over across the field. Where his wife could tend to the man's clothes. Where he could wash himself and bandage the nicks and cuts he had earned. Where he and John Howison could sit to the table for bread and beer. Before he set out for home.

They drank and talked a little of this and that. And finally the King found a chance to ask him what thing in this world he would want to have if wishes could come true. An easy question for Howison. His land, he told the King. Above all things he would most wish to own this fine little Braehead Farm. Which he rented. And for which he paid a stiff fee, too.

"Well," says the King, "tell me who owns the farm. Who is your landlord?"

"This land is owned by the King of the Scots. So there's never a chance that I, or any other man, could come to own it."

"I wouldn't say that," the King replied. "I've heard that the King is a decent and a reasonable man. I think he might be willing to talk to you about it."

"To me?" John Howison poured them both another bowl of beer. "What would I ever say to the King? Why would he wish to give up his good land?"

"That I cannot say," the King said. "But the King owns patches of land all across Scotland, Highlands and Low. And he would hardly miss the loss of this one little place. And as for the rent . . . well, the King is not a rich man, yet he could continue to live and to thrive without the rent that you sweat to put into his purse. I'm thinking that the King of the Scots might take some pride in a farmer who chased away four felonious rogues from the King's own highway. And set thereby an excellent example for all the people."

And so on. And so on.

A bowl or two more of beer. And then the King, allowing that he had a friend or two at Court, told the farmer that he would tell them how his life had been saved at the Cramond Bridge. And perhaps something good might come of that.

Kind and stouthearted as he was, John Howison was no fool. He knew it would rain ripe pears from the sky above before he would hear again about this matter. But he was grateful for the thought of it and did not laugh in the stranger's face. So it was agreed that if something should happen that the farmer might be rewarded for his courage and kindness, why, he would send word for John Howison to come and present himself at the Palace of Holyrood.

"Fine," say the farmer. "You send me the word and I shall surely come there."

The King then told him that he was known as the Goodman of Ballangeigh. And he bade John Howison farewell, with many thanks for saving his life, and started off walking to Holyrood. Reeling a bit on the way. For he was not used to drinking so much strong beer so early in the morning. And, anyway, his legs were still weak-kneed from the fight on the bridge and sleepless night in the bed. A little bit drunk, then, and more than a little weary, the King smiled to himself at the surprise he was already planning for John Howison.

Made his plans and let a little time go by. So that nothing would arouse the farmer's suspicions. Then sent word, by a messenger disguised as a traveler, that Howison should come to the Palace on Thursday next and present himself to the Porter of the gate and ask for the Goodman of Ballangeigh.

So John Howison washed his face and head. Trimmed his beard. Sponged and brushed his best clothes. Put on a clean straw hat. Slung his shoes over his shoulder (aiming to put them on at the gate of the Palace) and set off walking on that Thursday morning.

At the gate he hesitated and thought of turning back. For here, coming and going, were many people, dressed like a gang of proud angels who had fallen to earth from the sky. Men on horses as fine as any he had ever seen in his life. And servants (even prouder than their masters) in livery colors or sky blue.

With bright brass buttons and shiny shoes. Who brushed past him as if he were no more than a shaggy dog standing in the road. And the Porter was a haughty, fierce-looking fellow. Who could, with one scornful look, make you ashamed to be on this earth if you were no more than a common tenant farmer from Cramond.

Howison thought seriously of turning back and heading for home. But maybe he would never have another chance in his whole life to see this place and the people in it. And he had promised his wife to remember everything so he could tell it to her. She would be much disappointed if he came back without any sights or wonders to report. Besides the Goodman of Ballangeigh might be disappointed not to see him. . . .

"You there, fellow!" the Porter called out. "Why are you standing there like a sparrow on a cow turd? What is it you want?"

Howison whipped his straw hat off of his head, gulped, and mumbled his business.

"What? What? Speak up so I can hear you, man!"

Some idlers laughed and that stung him just enough to overcome shyness and shame.

"Ah well," the Porter said, somewhat more kindly, "why didn't you say so? Wait while we send word you are here."

Perhaps, the farmer thought, the Goodman had given this Porter a coin to help him to remember. He waited quietly while the Porter sent a lad—one of those who had only just now laughed at him—running off to find the Goodman.

King was in the Presence on his throne, doing kingly business, when the message reached him. Jumped up out of his throne and rushed out through the astonished Court to his chambers. To change into his disguise as the Goodman of Ballangeigh. Dressed and hurried out to meet the farmer at the gate and bring him inside.

The King had strictly instructed the behavior of everyone so that no one would act in such a way as to spoil his plans. He met the farmer at the gate. Shook his hand and clapped him on the back. And together they entered the Palace. Took him first to the Buttery. Where they shared some refreshment and washed down the dust of the road with some of the King's best malt spirits.

Then the King took him around and about the Palace showing him many wonderful things.

Finally a bell rang and people began to scurry about.

"What's that?" said the farmer. "Is it time to leave?"

"Oh no," the King told him. "It's the bell to tell that the King is to be in the Hall and that all who have business with him can come there."

"Oh."

"Would you like to go and see the King?"

Howison hesitated.

"Perhaps I ought not to," he said. "I'm not rightly dressed for it."

And at that moment he discovered, to his everlasting shame, that he had not remembered to put his shoes on.

"Nonsense," the King told him. "Look at me. I am dressed much the same as you, sir. King's not such a fool he can't tell there's more to a man than the clothes on his back."

"You have the better hat by far," Howison said.

"Then take it," the King said. "We shall trade, and I will wear straw."

"Better not. They are likely to laugh at you."

"Oh," said the King, half to himself. "I shall be very surprised if anyone laughs at me."

The bell rang again.

"Come, we must hurry if you want to see the King."

"Let me put on my shoes," the farmer said.

"No time! No time!" the King said, leading him firmly along by his arm. "Shoes or no, it will not matter in the least."

Just at the entrance to the Hall John Howison stopped him again.

"Please, sir," he said. "How will I know which one is the King?"

"Easy," the King told him. "As easy as can be. All of the others will take off their hats."

So in they went to the Hall. Which was crowded with more than a thousand of the greatest lords and ladies of Scotland. The whole Court was assembled there. In silks and satins and jewels and all. Drums beat and the trumpets played. And a path cleared wide for the two men as they walked forward, one barefoot and both as plain as a man can be. A thousand hats were doffed as they walked by together.

"Now, John Howison, my friend," the King said, no longer able to contain himself. "Do you know which one is the King?"

Howison thought about it for a moment.

"Well, sir," he says. "I cannot be sure. But I think it must be either you or me. For all the others have taken off their hats."

And the King's laughter filled the Hall. He embraced John Howison there before his Court. Gave possession of the land of Braehead Farm ever after, to him and his descendants. Provided that whenever a King of Scotland comes past on the road, the owner must bring him a towel and a basin of sweet well water to wash his hands and face of the dust. And though it is not a part of the proviso, the King allowed that if that King of Scotland happened to be himself, then a bowl or two of the farmer's beer would be appreciated.

Now as laughter fades it has finally come to be Red Tom's turn. What most have been waiting for. Not on account of his gifts as a storyteller. Like any man of the Borders he is able to tell a story when and if his turn comes around. But he is not much like Sly or Blind Jock, either. He is a reiver first and always. And he would not choose to be here this night if he had that choice; if his wound were healed well enough so that he could bear the pain and the itch of it, tonight he would be far from here. With the Master and the others. Miles over into England.

He has no contempt for these others—the old, the blind, the halt and lame, the too young. But, like most men who still have their health and strength, he is somewhat uneasy in the company of those who do not. Feeling that somehow their misfortune might be passed on to him like the pox. Feeling embarrassed at the question he must ask himself about the cripples—the terrible doubt that he could bear for as long as one day the life they have to lead always. As for the old and feeble, well, Red Tom hopes to live to be old; yet (mercifully) he cannot picture himself with all of his strength and vigor gone. And now in his prime of life he has not the least envy of the fumbling and ignorant young.

Not fearing sudden death by the sword or the hanging rope, Red Tom does fear that he would not have the courage to be Sly. Would never be able to be so calm with the burden of remembering and wisdom as Blind Jock is.

Times when he thinks he would as lief be a woman or an Englishman as to change places with any of these.

Something about them makes him feel shy and ashamed. If he were not who he is, a brave man who, whatever his self-doubts may be, has never had any reason to doubt his own courage, his brew of feelings might have made him proud or cruel. If only to ease the baffling pains of them. But they have not. Instead all the debatable feelings seething nameless within him work in a curious way to make him seem to his hearers, these others, to be humble among them. They take him to be a truly simple man. The very idea of which charms them all. Which likewise fulfills their hopes and expectations of him even as it eases any envy for him they might feel. Who can envy the gifts of a simple man? Who can wish for the good fortune of one who has no notion that he is any way lucky?

The result is they admire him. They wish him well.

Besides which, though they do not take his reports from the world of real kisses and wounds to be more truthful than any other tales (not doubting what he has witnessed, but knowing that what is true is always more secret and subtle than what is witnessed and that there may well be as much or as little of truth in a tale of talking ravens as in a messenger's report of victory or defeat in battle), still they feel, deeply, the need for news from that world, too. He was there. Saw this and heard that. Without the tales of witnesses we should have to imagine a world too strange to bear.

Besides which, one and all, they love to hear the tale of Kinmont Willie for the sake of the grief and shame it brought to the English. Which was plenty. . . .

Well now.

There are many tales told about it these days. The English have theirs and tell it their own way. And the Scotsmen have as many versions of it as there are tellers. And it keeps changing with the passing of time. It has got so that nowadays you cannot go to a horse race or a market fair without hearing the ballad makers singing about it. And except for the names (and sometimes even they are strange and new) I would not know that it is the same tale.

Well now. Mine is plain enough, like it or not. I cannot change it for better or worse. All I can claim is that I was there in the midst of it. And I know what I saw and heard.

These troubles began at the middle of March in '96. A wet one as I remember it. Wet and windy all across the Marches. Cold spells coming and going. Cold lingering longer than anyone cared for.

But then, like a taste and a promise of summer, the weather turned warm on the day of March 19. Which, as it happens, was a day of truce. With deputies there—Thomas Salkeld for the English and Scott of Haining for our own—and many riders from both sides. Among them Kinmont Willie himself, as ever involved in some dispute.

I sometimes think to myself that it was the weather as much as anything else that waked up trouble. For when those first days come along it is easy for a man to deceive himself and begin to believe that maybe he shall live forever. And once a man believes that, even ever so briefly, why it seems to follow that any kind of mischief is allowed and likely to succeed.

I have seen it happen before.

Never mind the reasons for it. Mischief it surely was. A breaking of the faith. For the English plainly broke the truce to take Willie that day. . . .

The parley and meeting ends, a long day's doings of grievances stated and heard and (sometimes) amends and redress made. At the end of it all they ride off. Safe from enemies, by the Law and by the ancient and honored customs, until sunrise of the next day.

Happened that Willie with only a few of his men was riding home on one side of Liddel Water. A crowd of Engishmen, more than a hundred, were on the other side, heading westward for Carlisle.

Well now. It remains a matter of dispute what happened to cause the English to cross over the water and chase after Willie. They claim it was Willie that broke the truce and that they had every right to pursue him and take him. They would have to say that, and stick to it too, wouldn't they? But they cannot or will not name anything that he did, at the meeting or on the way home, that would justify the breaking of the truce day.

There may have been some words. I do not doubt that there were words between them. And if there were words, then Willie got the best of it. For he has a terrible tongue and loves to use it on the English. No doubt at all in my mind that Willie hooted them and gave them grief.

If insults were weapons every man on the Borders would be a cold corpse by now.

How it was, as I believe, was this way. There they were, many of them; and there was Willie with only a few of his men. There was Willie hooting and hollering at them for being lily-livered whoresons and pox-riddled, bowlegged, womanly English bastards. Willie, who for so many years with fire and sword had caused them such woe. Taking their cattle to enjoy a better home in Scotland. Burning their houses and barns and fields to improve the look of the landscape. Taking hostages to prove if their kin-folk loved them enough to pay ransom for their safe return. Disproving, with many a lusty demonstration, that old wives' tale that there's no pleasure so dry and tedious as rutting with an Englishwoman. Teaching them the art of warfare with many a cunning ambush. And instructing them in the benefits of prompt justice by hanging a few here and there as he went. And doing all of his service without getting caught and with none of it, so far, lawfully proved against him.

Well now.

Nobody, none of us, would go so far as to claim that Kinmont Willie was a blessed saint. But neither would we take him, as the English did, to be the worst and bloodiest malefactor from the Solway to the mouth of the Tweed. No, sirs. Not even Willie would claim that for himself. For there are others (and we know who they are) who would dispute it.

Anyway there he was and there they were. In open country without a soul for miles around to be a witness. So all of a sudden over the water they came with a rush. And Willie made a run for it, riding for a few miles before they caught him and took him back to the great red Castle at Carlisle. Where they turned him over to Lord Scrope and kept him there. Trying to find a way to hold him for good in spite of the Law.

Now if the English have lied in their story, the Scots have painted the truth in colors to please themselves. To your ballad makers it is wonderful and pitiful to picture old Willie all chained in irons and deep in the dungeons of the Castle Keep. Where, it is sadly true enough, many a fine reiver has been chained and left to consider his sins. It might be expected they would treat him that way. Or worse. And Willie has said nothing at all to discourage misunderstanding. For Willie, as much as anyone else, would like to think his story was as wonderful and pitiful as any other you've ever heard of. He may even believe the ballads by this time. Who knows? What I do know is young Scrope had him put, in decent comfort, in a house on the Castle yard. And even allowed him liberty within the walls.

If Willie had been in irons in the Keep, I can promise you he would be safely there to this day.

All pity and wonder aside, what Willie did was get himself caught. And what we did was to set him free.

One thing more to be said. As long as I am shoveling up plain truth.

Much has been made about how we got into the Castle. The English will have us, in much larger numbers than we were, breaking in by force and surprise by the sally port. But it is not clear how that was done. And most Scots picture us cleverly taking and opening the postern gate. And just the same—ask and see the sheep looks, the yawns and shrugs you get in answer to your question—it is not one bit clearer how that trick was played.

Well now.

Truth is we were well prepared, with ropes and new ladders and plenty of tools, for what we might have to do. And, to be sure, we left them there behind us when we departed. Partly to confuse them, I'd guess. Hoping that they might take these things as evidence that we had used them. But the truth is also that the English, and most especially the Lord Scrope who was made to be the biggest fool on both sides of the Borders by what had happened, were looking diligently for any kind of excuse they could find that might serve to ease somewhat the blame of it. And no wonder. From all that I've heard, the words that poor

Scrope received from his Queen were written in blazing, raging fire. He was being cooked by rage and laughter on both sides and did not know whether to laugh or to cry for sake of himself.

Maybe it has done him some good. For Scrope was ever a most proud and scornful man. Even for an Englishman.

As for the Scots, well now, your ballad makers and such have an obligation to make this tale as full of wonder and mystery as they can.

And those of us who were there are sworn not to tell how it was accomplished. But look you. I need not break my oath and tell you any secrets, either. Use your own heads. And you'll arrive at the conclusion any thoughtful man would come to. That a way was opened for us. That we had aid and comfort from inside the Castle. How else could it have been done?

Yet the English will never admit to that. For that would be even more shameful than to be tricked and surprised. And the ballad makers would rather not ruin the shape of their songs by allowing any Englishmen to be a part of it. And we are saying no more than I have already allowed. For if what I'm saying is true, then we still have friends in that Castle and we'll want to keep them safely there until such time as we may need them again.

But pardon me. I am far ahead of myself and of my story. . . .

Which is true. What has happened so far is that a prominent Scotsman of the Borders, and specifically of the West March, one William Armstrong of Kinmont, called and widely known as Kinmont Willie, has been taken (unlawfully in the view of the Scots) near Liddel Water (in Scotland) by Englishmen at the end of a truce day. Taken from there to the walled city of Carlisle and directly to the Castle, perched squat and powerful on a bluff above the River Eden. It is an old castle much fought over between the English and the Scots. Often besieged, in those old days, sometimes taken. Here King Edward I held Court and even Parliament during the years when he earned himself the title of "Hammer of the Scots." Here the Queen of Scots came first as a fugitive and found herself, gradually and certainly, to be not a guest but a prisoner. Here now came Kinmont Willie, unlawfully a prisoner, to be unlawfully held there by Lord Scrope.

To which problem at once addressed himself Sir Walter Scott of Buccleuch, the Keeper of Liddesdale. First to Deputy Salkeld, then to Lord Scrope, himself. Demanding the immediate release of Willie.

Buccleuch was purely furious, Red Tom tells them. Because for once and without question, he was altogether in the right. A thing that happens almost never in the lifetime of a Border reiver. Of which, you'll have to admit, young Buccleuch's a powerful example. To be in the right, and his enemy Scrope wholly in the wrong, was a matter of importance and pleasure to him.

No doubt it was a matter of hateful embarrassment to Scrope. Except for one thing. He had the possession of Kinmont Willie. And so long as he did, just so long did right or wrong add up to nothing at all. He should have known better. Should have known that to refuse Buccleuch was not likely to end the matter. Known that the pleasure that that refusal gave him was bound to be paid for and many times over. But put yourself in Scrope's boots. Short of war—and the King of Scots would not so much as raise his voice against the Queen of England for the likes of Kinmont Willie and Buccleuch together, even if Scrope had hanged the both of them—what could happen that would set Willie at liberty again? Law or no law, only Scrope could do that. And he planned to take his sweet time doing it.

It would make an amusing tale to tell next time he traveled south to the Queen's Court.

Not dreaming that Buccleuch would go to the English Court to meet the Queen long before he would.

Not considering that Buccleuch would never take his refusal as final.

Not knowing that Buccleuch would look to find a way to bring Willie out and home.

And, even if he had known that much, never imagining that Bold Buccleuch *could* do just that. And do it soon.

First week in April Buccleuch began to bring us all together to prepare for it, quietly as can be, at Willie's place at Morton. With Willie locked up in the Castle there wouldn't be any use of spying on his tower. We would be as safe there as anywhere. And less than a dozen miles from the Castle.

Come the second week of April we had half a hundred of the best riders of these Borders there. And all of us ready to ride when he gave us the word.

Come Saturday morning and Buccleuch and a few of his best men, Auld Wat Scott of Harden and Gilbert Elliot for two, went to Langholm for the horse races. Where they could be seen, in a blithe, cheerful mood, by some of the English who had come across for the racing. Where they could cast wagers on this horse and that, as if they had no other purpose in the world.

Where, also, I'd reckon, they passed words with some of those English who were later to help us.

A long, loud, happy, easy day of horses. And drinking. And gathering together for a meal at the tavern there. Not one least sign that any mischief was afoot. Which, to anyone else but the English, would have been a sure indication that the time was come to ride flat out for home to put on armor, sharpen edges, post guards, and lock up all gates. But it is ever the weakness of the English that they cannot imagine that anyone else, and especially a Scotsman, could be quick-witted enough to deceive them. Therefore they are the easiest geese in Creation to deceive.

Came Sunday with rain and wind again. Perfect weather for a quiet ride over to Carlisle, and just before dark we mounted up and set out. . . .

Fifty and more picked riders. Each armed lightly and those arms tied down tight so as not to offer any betraying rattle. No firearms this time, not caliver or dag among them for fear that wet powder would fail them. A few with the lances the Border riders use so well. These few to act as forward scouts and screen and also to cover the withdrawal from England. The others for one purpose—to break into the castle, to snatch Kinmont Willie, and to bring him out and safe home. With everything, for once, well thought out, well planned. With only one persistent fear, something which could not be settled until they tried to do their work. Since it was essential to involve some disaffected Englishmen in the plan, there was always the possibility that any of these would turn and betray them. That therefore ambush might even now be laid for them at the Castle or somewhere on the way of their coming and going. Buccleuch has to worry over it. And they, his men, though they will ride wherever he tells them to, even into the burning gates of hell, worry less, but are not without a stifled unease. Red Tom will always remember that even in the rain and misty cold he managed to sweat as if it were high noon in July or August. They know that Buccleuch cannot be sure of these Englishmen no matter how much they may hate Scrope, no matter how many old scores they may have to settle, no matter how bound they may be to Buccleuch by old favors or new promises, by kinship or long friendship, and finally by fear (being in full knowledge of what will happen to them, to their families and kin and to everything they possess if they betray Buccleuch), still no matter what, any one of these men may decide to risk all for what would be his if Buccleuch were surprised and taken. Or may not wish to risk anything, but may nevertheless, in tavern drunkenness or pillow mumbling in some woman's ear, say one thing too much. Something which taken together with other clues may mean enough to Salkeld or Scrope to have half the English in Carlisle armed and waiting for them even now.

Besides the danger of betrayal there is the one unspoken truth. What they are doing has never been done before. It has been too outrageous to imagine doing. So absurd as never to have occurred to anyone on either side—except, perhaps, at some idle, half-dreaming moment, Buccleuch—until now.

Something to think about. To try not to think of. As they slip along across moss and turf. Going very carefully. With many halts while riders go forward to scout the route. Changing the route a little this way and that. To avoid ambush. Bent over in rain. Slumping low to their horses. Silent. No words. No whispering. The loudest noise the rain on steel bonnets.

And probably all of them, just like Red Tom, sweating as if it were midsummer. . . .

All the streams were running high and swift. And mist rose thicker as we came toward Carlisle. It was not long before the dawn when we got our horses (and, praise God and the Bold Buccleuch for it), without losing man or beast, across the Eden. And came by Stanwix Bank on the north up close under the walls of the Castle. Huddled close underneath. Listening to rainfall and the noise of a couple of guards or so up there above us. The clink and clank of their gear might as well have been bells.

Some of ours had ladders with them. To go up and over the walls if we had to. If we could not enter by the postern gate. And others had tools to break down the gate if they had to. Buccleuch gave a signal (whatever it was, I never heard it) and all of a sudden that gate was open for us and in we went.

Shouts from the guards as some stood to fight and others ran crying alarm. One rattling shape (a big man he seemed but in the dark all enemies on foot seem huge) came at me. Making a sound like a low-snarling dog. I took him with my sword. Coming so close in that thrust that I could smell the sweat of him and the odor of ale on his lips. He tumbled, like a groaning of pots and pans, on the stone. And died there I reckon.

I ran on following the others to the house where Willie was. And he came running out to greet us, dressed to ride.

Much hollering all around and torches lighting in the towers. Someone ringing a bell. A cannon went off loud and to no good purpose, except maybe to wake up the town; and that scared me the most of anything all night.

Now our men were yelling too, as we ran back toward the gate. Bringing Willie with us. Willie was yelling and Buccleuch was yelling. And so were we. It was like we were all drunk. Some of our men blew hunting horns as loud as they could. Some began to talk of taking the Castle or, anyway, at the least, of seizing Scrope out of his bed and bringing him back home with us. Let the Queen ransom him.

For a moment we were giants and invincible. Which, when I think of it now, was the greatest danger of the night. Buccleuch knew it. Ran about trying to beat sense into heads with his fist and the flat side of his sword.

And we ran back out the gate and mounted up. Buccleuch took his own trumpet and blew a blast. And away we went, back the way we had come. Covered by our own people. And not losing a single man or beast.

A quarter of a mile due north from the walls toward the River Eden and then both town and Castle vanish from sight. Likewise Buccleuch's band of men, riding hard now and dangerously over the soggy, rain-soaked turf, pass out of sight also. Disappearing into rain even before they have sought to cross over the swollen Eden and then to ride on through the land of the Grahams and the Debateable Land, crossing the Lyne and the Esk and many a lesser stream, heading not for homes but beyond into the fastness and safety of deep Liddesdale. For they can believe that the English will follow them in a hot trot with as many horsemen as they can quickly raise in town and nearby country. Will follow more swiftly than they ought to over the dangerous ground, their leaders, Scrope himself and Salkeld too, in a fury as with the coming of the gray-wet dawn it dawns on them what has happened. As they realize what has been done and what it may mean. In their haste and fury the English will lose both men and horses to the rivers and by sudden tumbles in marshy ground. And finally, soon enough, the English will lose the Scots also. Losing track of them as they scatter into the wild, narrow, rocky dales. Where no one, not even a whole army, can safely follow them.

They are gone, and the English have to turn back, headed for home all empty-handed. Sorely bedraggled and purely furious.

So that band of Scots vanishes from sight in a few minutes. Gone first from sight but not from sound. For there is a loud blowing and tooting of horns. Cheerful rattle of weapons and gear. They vanish from view, leaving a brief cloud of noise behind. As if to prove they have been there.

And just so they vanish from fact. Becoming, themselves, no more and no less than figures of a myth. As if they were made wholly and forever out of mist and air. Belonging now and ever after to the tale tellers and the ballad makers. . . .

Red Tom, therefore, chooses to end his telling of it with their safe escape from the castle and that hard, heady ride. Laughing and hollering, wet with rain and sweat. Laughing and shouting in this chamber, this tower to celebrate the scene. And it is meet that he should choose to let it end there. After laughter comes near-silence. Hiss of the fire. Someone, too far from the fire's glow to be seen, is coughing. The jug is passed around. Beginning with Red Tom, who is driest from talking most.

Right that he should end it there. Stopping well before the end of it. Which, in truth, has not yet come to pass. And which, so far, he has not been witness to (other than by universal hearsay) any more than any other man here.

Anyway they all believe that they know what happened afterward. How Scrope and Salkeld, who had been feared and hated by so many, became for the Borders (on both sides) no more than a pair of clumsy clowns. Laughed out of all real power. Ruined in their own kingdom even more than here. How the Queen of England, in highest dudgeon, roared and raged and demanded that the King of the Scots should turn over Buccleuch to face her justice, the offense having been, after all, committed against her Castle, her people, and in her country. How (think what you will of him) King James managed for a time, by one means and another, to resist her wishes. But how, finally, and only within the past year or two, his resolve dwindled. For hers did not, and he has ever had one eye cocked toward the English crown. Hungers for it more than for anything else. Even honor. And so it was arranged, they understand, for Buccleuch to agree to go south on his own. Freely to travel to England, there to turn himself over to the English to be judged by the Queen. With the clear understanding that he had come for the sake of his honor and the honor of Scotland to receive pardon and that she would be entitled, if she chose to, to indulge herself in public anger and a public reprimand. And not much else.

But so much happens between the cup and the lip. Neither James, King of Scots, nor the Bold Buccleuch could trust her altogether. Her history of changes of mind and plans, her chronicle of broken promises and of tricks and betrayals was too formidable to be ignored. Thus Buccleuch, presenting himself to the English Queen and her Court in the Presence Chamber, proud and courageous as he was, must nevertheless have been troubled with doubts.

How they picture that event:

Which they do now in the quiet of the tower, a quiet not so much broken as reinforced by the sound of rain falling. For even while tales were being told the wind turned around and the sky clouded over. Moon vanished, stars winked out, and then the rain began to fall. And now they hear it on the tower and spitting into the smoky fire. One of the lads coming in from the barmkin is soaked and glistening.

(It is well that moon and stars have vanished and that the night is thickened by heavy rain. For out there, coming this way, is the master and his band, riding for their lives. Victims of an English ambush and fleeing for home. Some have been killed. Others badly wounded. They will bring home no loot this time, having earned nothing but wounds for their labors. They will bring no comfort either except that, all things considered, their luck held. For if the wind and weather had not turned they might all have been killed or caught by now. As it is, more will endure—and even recover—than ought to. Not their master and leader, though. He will ride into the barmkin an hour or so from now, hanging on to his horse. Bleeding and groaning from terrible wounds. Will ride in, slumped and holding on, to let go and fall into the trampled mud of the yard. Then there will be much shouting. Men will carry him, and one or two others who arrive at the same time, up the steep twisty stairs to the highest story of the tower. Where it will be up to women to nurse them. To grieve over them. For some will die there, bloody on the bloody floor. Will die while the men in the tower hurry to defend the tower against the English. Who this time will not arrive. Having already turned back. All this will happen in the next hour or so. The time which is too near and soon for prophecy. All this will come to pass and will sorely grieve them. Yet will not truly surprise them. For there are only a few surprises in their hard world, and sudden death is not one of them. Nor is the sure and certain knowledge that all fair things fall to ruin, that all joy and rejoicing this side of the grave is destined to end in sorrow and tears, that in this world it is the tears of things which ever prevail. In honor of which truth—and paradoxically with the deepest wordless joy—it is their wild pipes which play out the shrill and beautiful lament.)

Now in the quiet they are imagining how it was for Buccleuch on that day. When he came before the Queen.

As they like to see it, it takes place in a huge Hall. Large as the nave of St. Giles Kirk in Edinburgh. At one end, on a raised throne, sits England's lean and terrible Queen. Bejeweled. Her crown shining. So much color! Color of the hangings on the walls. Color of her foppish courtiers (each one another version of Scrope or Salkeld), each a creature in outlandish clothing and glittering jewels. Candlelight brightening the halberds of her guards whom they picture to be at least a thousand or more. And the women. As many fair women as guards. Wonderfully cream-skinned Englishwomen. Ladies. A field of them. How these reivers would like to run naked through a field of naked English ladies. Pleasuring themselves like bees among the flowers.

Before they can think anymore upon that supreme temptation there is a great toot of trumpets. A beating of drums. And here, surrounded by knights and guards, comes our Bold Buccleuch.

How is he dressed? As one of them. Wool and canvas and leather. Ready to ride. But clean and brushed. For it is a Queen he is meeting. And one who (they say) prefers things to be sweet and clean.

Sweet and clean, then, perhaps for the first time in his life, but dressed out like every reiver there is, here comes Buccleuch. At a motion from the Queen, some jeweled and subtle signal of her hands, the others, guards and knights, step aside. Leaving Buccleuch to make the long walk toward her, through the parted crowd, alone.

If he has noticed that or anything else—and, of course, he has, for this is Buccleuch, he does not show it. His head is high, his eyes fixed directly upon her as he advances with a slow and steady pace. Spurs of his boots make a little *chink-chink-chink* sound. . . .

Advances slow and steady and almost too near, close enough so that the guards beside her begin to shift their weight to move quickly if they have to. Close enough so that there is a gasp behind him as many in the Court believe he will not stop and kneel. Close enough so that he can see that she, the Queen, must be uncertain of him; for though her fixed and regal expression has not altered, might as well be stone, her hands reveal her inner mood, gripping the throne like talons.

And then suddenly he stops in midstride, drops on both knees and bows his head. Then, as if in response to her laughter at the surprise of it, he raises his head to look into her eyes. They both smile at each other. And something, a flicker of the Queen's eyelid, is almost a wink. He resists the impulse to wink back at her.

"Well," she says.

"Ma'am," he answers.

"You may stand and be easy."

And so he does.

"Ladies and gentlemen," she surely told them all. "Look well upon this man. For he and only a few of his fellows took possession of the strongest castle on the Borders. And took their comrade safely out of our keeping. And made fools out of the Lord Scrope and his band of lily-livered loons!"

Then directly to him.

"You, sir! What on earth do you have to say for yourself?"

"Why nothing, ma'am. You have said it all perfectly yourself."

"God's wounds!" she cries. "Your silly King is a lucky man. With ten thousand men like you he, even he, could shake every throne in Europe. Go home now. And tell your King I envy him."

"Ma'am."

Buccleuch, the Bold Buccleuch, bows deeply, backs away some steps, then turns and swaggers out of the palace. While the whole English Court applauds him on his way.

Did it happen that way? No man here in this tower knows. It is how they have heard it, how they prefer to believe it. It gladdens their hearts, for a little while, to think so.

Well now.

KING

MARCH 1602–1603

Whilst we, in tunes to Arthurs Chayre
    Beare Oberons desire;
      Then which there nothing can be higher
Save James to whom it flyes:
But he is the wonder of tongues, of eares, of eyes.

BEN JONSON—"Oberon"

Look not to find the softness of a down pillow in a crown, but remember that it is a thorny piece of stuff and full of continual cares.

King JAMES—Meditations on St. Matthew

Cold is now a clenched fist. Gripping all this island, both kingdoms. Days of driving rain, winds brawling out of north and northeast, blowing high whining gusts to torment the trees. To rattle the leaded panes of window glass, to swirl damp thick snorts and puffs of smoke down the chimneys and coughing into the chambers.

Better, though, to stand close by the fire. Even at the risk of ending up as well smoked as a ham or a salmon. (Ham which he hates, salmon which is a joy to his taste.) Than to be outside, facing foul weather.

Here in the north, uneasy in Scotland, restless in Holyroodhouse, this splendid palace set just beyond the walls of Edinburgh, the King is standing with his back to the huge fireplace in the Hall. A crowd of companions, courtiers, and officers is gathered around him. This Court of his is free and easy, not stiff with ancient ceremonies as is (he hears) the English Court. And considering the condition of King and courtiers at this very moment, it is just as well. Formality and pomp would be only a comedy. All are soaked to skin, cold to bones. Fugitive scarecrows in odd scraps of finery. Their clothes, limp and dripping, are beginning to steam. No doubt but some will shrink to fit as tight as buttoned gloves. All except the King have removed their hats. The feathers on his high-crowned, broad-brimmed hunting hat droop like wilting flowers. Servants hurry to heap up logs. Others are bringing bowls of strong malt spirits. Soon enough, clothing dried, skin rosy with warmth, relaxing to enjoy the spiritual fires of the drink, they will all be cheerful again, these Scots noblemen. Who are easy to please. Who are able to laugh at their folly of trying to ride out to hunt on a day like this.

Or yesterday or the day before that. . . .

Now two sturdy servants come, huffing and puffing, lugging a heavy oak chair for the King's comfort. But he waves them away. Preferring still to stand there and to be toasted, head to toe, by the blazing fire.

Early this morning wind and rain had slackened, seemed at last to be dying away. Mild raindrops splashing the shiny cobbles of the forecourt; gutters and rainspouts dripping. A thin wink of daylight, followed by bits and patches of clear blue, like the torn pieces of a rich cloth, set among the beggarly rags and tatters of sky. A word from the King and here came grooms running with the saddled horses. And these men hurried to mount up and follow the King and his huntsmen and the loud choir of the hounds. Riding out of the courtyard and up and into the park behind the palace. A park well stocked with deer, both red and fallow. It's a good hunting ground, though it is somewhat too tame for the King's taste. Easy or no, though, that is where he would prefer to spend his time. Sitting tall and straight on his padded French saddle. Riding well ahead of other riders, far ahead of all but the best, across rough open country. Running to the oldest, wildest tunes of hunting horns and the immemorial belling of hounds. Rain or shine no matter. This King's a hardened horseman, a tireless hunter. Will hunt in a daze of joy, in any season, in any weather, fair or foul. Will go forth all smiles when the ground is stony with frost, when horses and dogs and men (also the fleet-footed, smoke-colored fleeing deer) make a chorus of white ghosts with their sharp breathing. And in the heat of midsummer when horses and riders are dust-covered, sweat-soaked. Nothing dismays him when he's at hunting. And nothing dissuades him when he is of a mind to hunt. Not urgent state business. As probably (God willing, this should not ever be tested) war or rebellion would have to wait for the finish of a hunt. Gladly, blithely, and also to the teeth-gritting pain (grit that the King will take to be a grin) of his servants and companions, he'll taste his truest pleasure in the art of hunting. From the first hints of the light of day to the last flash of it.

There are some among this Court who would tell you that the King seems very like to undo the labors of Noah. To rid this world of beasts, if he lives and rules long enough. First will van-

ish all the wild beasts, then next the tame. And after the last of
the cows are gone, and the pigs and sheep, the dogs and cats and
mice, why, what shall be left except the horses that we ride?
Nothing but . . . us! Devil take hindmost and all but the swiftest
among us. And where there are antlers on the walls of the Hall
now, there will be many a hoary, grizzled head. Fewer of them
with horns . . .

You are to understand that this wit among Scots nobles and
gentry has its ragged shadow in high seriousness. As do most
jokes in Scotland. For the King, you see, young as he is still, has
already managed to separate many heads from the bodies of his
enemies. Even from friends who have, one way or another, opposed his will. And, like many another jest in this Court, this one
means more. Reminds the hearer what he should already know—
that the King is a creature of paradox. That though he has no
qualms concerning blood and guts of hunting, and no reluctance
either in sending his enemies to a bloody end, he does not in
truth enjoy other bloody matters. Hates war with an almost
saintly passion. Cannot bear to hear the details of cruelties of
men to other men, in this cruel age of a cruel world, spoken of in
his presence. And will not usually (the torture of witches is an
odd exception) choose to witness the terrors of justice when justice must be done.

Finally, then, in repeating this little jest, some whispering gentleman of the Court has shared with you, there is a comment on
the weather. If it does not cease raining soon, why we might be
better off to return home and busy ourselves with building an
Ark. Instead of wasting time at Holyrood.

And so today—as yesterday and the day before that—when the
sky was beginning to clear and weather seemed to be about to
break and change for the better, they had not managed to get
far, not beyond half a mile, to a place just past the little tower
and chapel of St. Anthony of the Crag, when all of a sudden bits
and scraps of blue sky and shards of sunlight disappeared. Sky
was crowded with low, fat, ragged clouds. Wind rose up and
those clouds ran like frightened cattle. Without waiting for
proper warning of thunder and lightning, a swarming rain filled
the air. Bent, half blind in the sheets and pellets of rain, the
hunters had to turn back.

From now on no more hunting until the weather truly turns. He must resign himself to it. To staying indoors, to keeping close to the fireplaces. He will rub his heavy-lidded eyes, trying to keep awake. He will send for his clerks and secretaries. Busy himself with affairs of state, with all the work that must be done within an hour or two. And then what? Cards and dice, household gods and chief delights of Scotland, are soon tedious. Even though he seems to win each time he plays. He could retire to the relative privacy of his chambers in the northwest tower. Perhaps to read and study. Perhaps to play chess with his old tutor, Peter Young. Peter . . . who loves the game and still believes it can teach the King something. The King who loves and honors Peter Young, but hates this game with its confusion of little pieces, each depending upon the others. Kingdom of chessboard, though it may be close to the image of life, is not the kind of kingdom he would cultivate. He would have that piece called the King empowered to clear the board of any other piece whenever it pleased him.

During this time of waiting it is no comfort to be too private. No, he needs familiar faces and known voices nearby. The Queen and all her Court are over at Linlithgow, as custom demands. She awaits the birth of his new child. He could ride there to visit her and indulge himself in a change of scene. But the ladies and gentlemen of her household whose deepest loyalty seems to lie with her, make him uneasy. More than that now. For now he knows, on best authority, that there are Roman priests among them, well disguised. Which does not disturb him much. For he has some he knows to be priests who are playing at being gentlemen of his Court. So be it. He knows who they are. He finds it flattering that the Papists would seek to be close to him, eager to effect his conversion. Finds it flattering that in nearly forty years, and all but one of them as a crowned King, he has been important in the affairs of Christendom, so that it is necessary to keep a close watch on his doings. Further, he delights in the doubts that the presence of these secret priests creates in his Protestant subjects. Especially their arrogant preachers. If it were not for the Papists, why these Church of Scotland preachers would seek to make him, the King!, their servant. Which will not happen. Not so long as he can play off one against the other.

But he is uncertain about his Queen's Court. Whether there is truth in rumors that the balance has been tipped in favor of the Papists. When there, he feels he is among strangers. No, he will keep close to familiar faces and voices. And if companionship should become too tedious to endure, why he can always summon musicians and shut up conversations with sweet sound. Or, should that go stale for him, he can always drink. Can drink as deeply as he wishes and stand (*more likely sit*) by the fire and appear at ease and untroubled. Smiling vaguely and evidently indifferent to the bells and chiming of clocks.

Another time, at almost any other, it would not be a demanding task to cultivate patience by feigning that virtue. For as long as he can remember he has been required to be a kind of player, playing the part of a King of Scotland. Thanks be to God, and to His special and manifest mercy and providence (*Thy will be done*), he has lived through many perils to become at last truly a King and no question of it. Has learned to rule and, so, has ruled this kingdom longer and better than any Scots King in memory. Others may have been loved and admired more. But few were able to accomplish as much and to do so with so little. He has been tested and has endured. No, more than that. He and this kingdom have *prospered*. It can be proved. Against all odds and expectations. Others, richer rulers, may laugh at the poverty of Scotland. But if they allow themselves some truth, face to pillow and no one to read the expression on their royal faces for clues to the secret motions of their royal minds, if they allow themselves any truthful, solitary reflection . . . he is thinking here mostly of the King of France, Henri IV, powerful, popular, arrogant, who has made his Court laugh at a vulgar joke concerning James . . . then they must imagine how it would have been for themselves to begin so weak and frail, with so little means. Surrounded by so many enemies. And out of that weakness and danger, like the phoenix in flames, to rise renewed. Even Henri of France, with all his joking about barbarous Scotland and its King, must thank God he was not chosen to be so tested.

And yet, in his secret heart, James sometimes permits himself to wonder why God chose him to rule *here* . . . *in Scotland*. Which is, no doubt, every bit as rude as the King of France takes it to be. Perhaps God had intended to teach a lesson, perhaps as a pedagogical chastisement. By the logic of the faith of Rome, as he understands it, his life from day of his birth until now might be viewed as a sacrifice, an offering up made in hope of something new and different. Hope—that is the master key. For as long as he can remember, he has possessed (thus been possessed by) one great hope. His deepest wish for the future has been to find himself set free from the ragged coasts and borders of this country. To become, translated and gloriously transformed, King of England. He would, then, be the single ruler of this whole island. And would also at least be styled as King of Ireland and of France. He has lived chiefly upon that hope.

And, in doing so, he has been tormented by a multitude of doubts. Any man alive can be taught, can even teach himself how to live undaunted in the unremitting presence of doubts. Can do so if hope is strong and well founded. Just so, for example, a man may learn . . . no, *must* learn to live in peace with his weaknesses. Hope need not ever die on account of doubting.

It is through hoping that James believes that he has been able to endure so much, unbroken by vicissitudes, by whimsical wheels of Fortune. Bearing, enduring all things, he has learned how to be humble in weakness. In times of triumph (and he has known these joyous times also, else he would not be here) he has been able to be as ruthless and unswerving as any of the kings out of the Old Testament. And yet, he tells himself, his justice has always been tempered with mercy, where mercy was appropriate. More than enduring, he has, through the terrible times of gut-melting fear as well as the joyous, winy, heart-pounding moments of triumph, grown in wisdom and stature.

Surely he is entitled to think of himself, without stiff-necked arrogance, as chosen for this purpose. By his whole life, well prepared for the future.

Surely he has earned the right to wear hopes as openly as jewels.

And yet this restless, awkward present time, this siege of waiting for his future to be somehow settled, if not directly by others, then by the fates and fortunes of other men, many of them strangers, by them *and by one old woman*. . . . This waiting, confined by the worst kind of weather, has taxed his patience to the quick.

Well, it is not easy for these others either. They share something of his mood. And even if all of his hopes should come to
pass, it remains to be seen what will become of them—his Scotsmen. He cannot take them all with him. Would not, if he could.
Truth is, secret though it must be, he would as lief take none
with him. If he dared to, he would leave them all here. To
preserve a Court in his memory. His desire is that in changing
from one place to another, from one throne to the other, he, too,
will be changed. Which is to say (even as his skeptical mind must
reject the idea) that something profoundly childlike in his spirit
would be more satisfied than surprised if suddenly, upon the
happy consummation of his hopes, he were to turn toward a tall
mirror, there to behold himself as new made, newly clad in fresh
skin and bones, having discarded his own as he might cast aside
a muddy cloak. His quick mind laughs at the thought and quickly
suppresses it. Yet not to deny it outright. For even so suppressed,
the idea persists and brings comfort. Concealed lest somehow it
might be perceived by others. Who are always close to him like a
congregation of hostile shadows. Even so, the child at the heart
of the man is not to be completely silenced. Not easily to be sent
away. Something much like his own voice whispers to him that
since he so wishes it to come true, then a complete reformation
of himself, a new birth (as it were) at middle age may also come
to pass. It will not come in any way that the world can see and
measure. Alas, he will still seem to be the same man. At least in
the indifferent eyes of others. But by the inexorable powers of inward changing he will feel freed of himself. Perhaps not different
from himself. Instead becoming most fully himself for the first
time. Past sufferings overcome, present fears disappearing, hopes
expanding, he will feel the ineffable yet palpable awareness of
himself as God's chosen viceroy. He will be humble in the light
of that mysterious certainty. Will be beautiful because of it.
Beauty, like a lantern's light, will shine outward from within
him. He will be whole at last.

Yet even if the lawful Succession to the throne of England
should come unambiguously and unchallenged to him, he will
still have need of most of these men. There are many Scotsmen,
some among these here and now with him and others elsewhere
in the kingdom, who will succeed to profit in the greener fields of

England. And there are plenty who will not. Who will be left here to preserve this kingdom. Some who will be left behind because he is weary of their faces and their actions and their histories.

Ah, see how they study each other, behind masks of smiles and manners, the nosegays of inconsequential talk. To whom (each is wondering) has the King made promises? How can it be determined which are sheep and which are goats? They are like exegetical pedants, each one seeking to gloss every wrinkling of the King's forehead, the least rising or knitting of the King's eyebrows. They aim to translate the language of light in his eyes, to read fortunes in his laughter.

And he would laugh out loud at this comedy if he were not, in his own estimation, the chief clown of it.

So it is, he thinks, that we are all shackled. Like galley slaves at their oars. So goes this world on its long voyage. . . .

Late in January he was told that the Queen had left her Palace of Whitehall in Westminster somewhat suddenly. Had moved the Court to Richmond Palace. Not long after came reports that she was now suffering from failing health. Not for the first time in these years, to be sure. And at her age any illness or indisposition could easily become her last. He had been advised by allies, here as well as in England, to move his own Court to Holyroodhouse, so as to be close by the walls and the powerful castle of his chief city and so as to be near to the end of the long road north from London. Here he should be in case the news does come. At first post riders seemed to be arriving in troops, and within this fortnight a special messenger from the Queen's cousin, Sir Robert Carey, came with news that the end is near and that the King should stand in readiness. But now, most likely because of the wild cold weather, there has been no news from Richmond Palace. Perhaps there is no news to report. Perhaps there will be none. Perhaps even those first reports were not wholly to be credited. For all in England who send reports to him know the words he wants most to hear. Or perhaps even now there is urgently important news for him. Which the weather is withholding. Or perhaps the bearers of the news have been prevented (by English enemies?) from coming to him.

Who can know?

Who is to be trusted?

If wishes come true, some of these men, his tried and true hunting companions, will ride south beside him for the longest and best hunt of all. If all his hopes are now to be dashed, then he and all these men (and many more besides) will make the journey south in armor. May God forbid that! For the idea of the battlefield weakens and sickens him. Yet it has become necessary that his nobles and gentlemen should be sworn. As long ago as late '99, the earls and barons and lords of Scotland wrote and signed "A General Bond Made by the Good Subjects of the King's Majesty for the Preservation of His Highness' Person and the Pursuit of his Undoubted Right of the Crown of England and Ireland." In which they pledge "bodies, lives, lands, goods, and gear" to the King's cause. Did so, to the King's amusement, in language and phrases which arrogantly parody the Bond made by the English Court and Council many years before, against his mother, the Queen of Scots. By now, more privately (for he was told that the Bond of '99 outraged the English Queen), all have sworn, if it should come to that, to go forth to kill or to be killed for the sake of his claim. That prospect stuns him. For, all private scruples aside, if it should come to open war, then win or lose, in victory or in defeat, many of these men will never gain more than at most six feet of English earth to call their estates there. That has happened before, to their grandfathers and time and again before that to generations beyond counting. Still, some of these hot-blooded men seem to be eager to tempt God and to test His providence. There is talk of the scouring of armor and of the grinding of edges of swords and axes. No talking of it in his presence. He will not tolerate such talk. And they know the rumor how even the sight of a drawn and naked blade offends him. They do not speak of weapons when the King is in earshot. But he hears what he hears and knows what he knows.

In one sense it is well for the English to know that oaths have been taken and that preparations are being made in Scotland. But the King shudders to think on it. Because in war and in defeat (which all men know can come to pass from a loose nail in a single horseshoe) he might find himself King of no kingdom, north or south, ruler of nothing.

Yet and still, despite all these doubts, he does not fear the future. It is sufficient to have endured the past and to spend his fear on the present. How much will wind and rain, these long nights, muddy roads, swollen streams, and flooding rivers delay a messenger who is bringing him news? A day or two, perhaps even a few hours, could make the difference between success and failure, war and peace, crown or no crown.

Wind rattles the windowpanes at Holyroodhouse. Cold rain spurts from spouts and splashes in the courtyards. Smoke coughs in the fireplace. The King's legs, though warm at last, have commenced to ache from too much standing. He calls out for a chair and a footstool for his feet. And he calls for another cup of spirits. Settling on the cushions of the chair, raising his feet on the soft stool, sipping from a tall, ample cup, he can close his eyes and picture a horseman riding north. Can see a horseman shrouded by a long cloak and bent low to his horse. Moving slowly, ever so slowly, against wind and rain, toward Scotland. Can picture the image of that horseman clearly, perfectly. But not the rider's face. Try as he will, he cannot imagine whether the news coming toward him will be good or ill.

MESSENGER
1566

Who judgeth well, well God him send;
Who judgeth evil, God them amend;
To judge the best therefore I intend,
For I am as I am and so will I end.

Sir THOMAS WYATT

. . . into the valley of Skerne and crossing the Tees on a stone bridge of three arches into Yorkshire.

"Shake a bridle over a Yorkshireman's grave and he'll rise from the dead and steal your horse. But, never mind, you can drown your sorrow if they do. For there's no place in England to match it for the strength of its ale."

Lonely riding through marshy ground broken only by fording the River Wiske. Till he comes to Codbek, spanned by a single stone arch, and leading into Northallerton. Village of solid limestone houses facing a single length of street. A prosperous place on account of the cattle-and-horse fair, but its castle's no more than ruins and the name of Castle Hill. Then seven miles and a way bit to Topcliffe, sitting on a low hill and marked by the embattled tower of the parish church of St. Columba. Crosses an old timber bridge above the dark swift water of the Swale. Near to the road are vines of black grapes like none others grown in England. . . .

Now through open country with trees few and not much sign of plowing and planting. Country riddled by brooks and streams. Good grass for grazing. Mobs of sheep. At sixteen miles from Topcliffe to pass through the ancient Forest of Galtres. So cut and thinned of timber that only the name is left to bear witness to the oaks that grew there. To the wolves and bear and red deer. To hunters and hunted who ran in the shade, then vanished forever with it.

Soon to arrive at York, second city of England, set on both banks of the River Ouse and safely contained within a three-mile circuit of white stone walls. All overlooked by the towers of the largest cathedral in this country—York Minster, Church of St. Peter. Made of the same stone as the town walls, still splendid with stained-glass windows as fine as any in this world.

Here where Ouse—itself an assembly of rivers having taken away both names and waters of the Ure and the Nidd and the Swale (themselves having swallowed countless rills and becks and creeks and streams) and then soon after this city stealing the Wharfe and the Derwent and the Aire and finally the Don before mingling with and melting into the equally avaricious Trent to form the wide full Humber—is joined by the little River Foss with its dams and string of watermills, there has been a town since before all chronicle, long before the Romans built their fortress town called Eboracum. Oh in the high and golden days there were forty churches here and four monasteries and four friaries and sixteen hospitals and nine guildhalls and two castles and five strong towers! Now since Dissolution and the disastrous Pilgrimage of Grace there has been steady decline. Though it remains the seat of the Archbishop of York. And a seat of government. For the old Abbot's House of St. Mary's Abbey (now called King's Manor) is palace for the Council of the North.

Entering near the Manor through the north gate called Bootham Bar. Going perhaps to the *Blue Boar* or maybe the *Bridge Inn* near to the river to change horse and then across the six-arched bridge built upon the very piles of the ancient Roman one.

Ten miles across fertile country of growing grain. With patches of woodland. Planted with oak and ash and elm for standard. Tall lime trees, their yellow flowers besieged by clouds of bees.

Next a fine bridge of eight arches, crossing the Wharfe into the village of Tadcaster. Best known for brewing and truly famous for horseshoes. Fording the little Cock Beck beyond the southern end of the village he now has a dozen miles before Wentbridge. Fording the Aire at Ferrybridge he has only four miles remaining he'll come down a hill to a stone bridge of five arches set over the Went. Then uphill again and gone across open country. Aiming for the innyard of the *Angel* in brick-walled Doncaster. Where the River Don runs wide and cloudy. Busy town with watermills by the river and brick kilns within the walls. With markets for

wool and leather. And with a celebrated cattle fair. Solid timber
houses with slate roofs and well shaded by elms. Here in Doncaster they have taken the Scots fashion of horse racing for wagers on the wide Town Moor.

If only he still had his little Scots mare and time to spend.
Then he would linger long enough to relieve some Yorkshiremen
of their prosperity. But he must be gone. First through sandy
country to the village of Bawtry. A poor place with a few shabby
half-timbered houses set close to a little pond. Lying low and
swampy next to River Idle. Then farewell to Yorkshire and welcome to Nottingham. Road running through flat red-clay fields.
To Scrooby (a mere hamlet only) with its large moated manor
house for the Archbishop of York.

Crossing Barnby Moor to the tile-making place of Petford, set
on both banks of the Idle. Thence over Markham Moor to the
hills around Tuxford, with apple trees planted. Then down into
the town, houses of brick and tile and limestone barns for the
crops of wheat and beans. With two large inns—the old *Crown*
(where they tell you Princess Margaret Tudor rested on her way
to become Queen of Scotland) and the larger and newer *Black
Lion.*

Road running flat and straight for ten miles among the
branches of River Trent. Seeing the narrow, shallow-draft boats
of that river. And at deeper places seeing barges with sails.
Keeping watch for the spire (one of the tallest in England) of
the Church of St. Mary Magdalen. From miles away marking the
center of Newark.

Now crossing the river there on a wooden bridge. Passing close
by walls and gatehouse of the Castle that Edward the Confessor
first built. And where (as story goes) King John died from eating
peaches given to him by the monks of Swineherd. Through
streets toward Beast Market Hill, and into the cobblestoned marketplace. It's a brewing and malting town (for the cool, calm,
amber-colored water of the Trent is most excellent for brewing)
and a famous cattle market too. And Newark's a town of many
inns all close by the market—the *Saracen's Head* and the *Angel*
and *Maiden's Head* and *Cardinal's Hat* and *Trip to Jerusalem*
and the *Lion* and *Bell* and the *Swan* and the *Salmon* and the

elegant timber-and-plaster *White Hart* with a gallery overlooking the market.

Then out by South Gate and into the flat fen country. . . .

Sometime, while he was still a child, this man now calling himself Scarecrow or Beanstalk for the fun of it, must have come to the attention of William Cecil. And soon after would have come under his patronage. Sir William Cecil to whom he therefore owes everything he is and is not, all he has done or had to leave undone. For whom his deepest feelings will always be deeply mixed.

His picture of pleasure comes directly from the hospitality of the Cecils. He's almost certain to base it upon the recollection of dinnertime with Cecil and his family. Dinner as served in the Hall at Stamford Baron or at the Canon Row house or, later, with Queen Mary dead and Elizabeth crowned, when he had returned from exile to rejoin the Cecil household, at the old Rectory at Wimbledon. Anywhere they were, where, now as then, all things will be soberly ceremonious, always dignified without partaking of either stiff-necked, self-righteous rigidity or of haughty ostentation. Table linens, cloths and napkins, always snowy. Spoons of silver gleaming and knives sharp and the plate and tall salt shining in candlelight. The bread, only the best manchet or wheaten bread, is well baked with never least stain of burned crust that must be scraped off. The fish or meats, the fowls and salads, the cheeses and fruits, will all be fresh and abundant. Never crudely disguised in sauces or hidden in a cloud of spices. Beer will be new brewed; cider will be the best pressing, never musty and sour; wines will never be cloudy, but clear and crisp and only lightly sweet, without any cloying aftertaste. Servants will be neatly dressed, with clean hands and faces, moving to and from the kitchen and pantry, or to and from the sideboard with cups and glasses, as quick and as quiet as shadows. And there will not be talk of affairs of state or of business, no matter how pressing and urgent. Not even (he fancies) if the Spaniard or the Turk or the Moor were busy bombarding the walls and battering the gates of London. It may be there will be a consort of music coming from the minstrels' gallery or from behind the carved screen of the hall, but most often there will be a topic for conversation. Cecil will lead the talk, his fine handsome face, composed of delicate features, lively and animated; his dark eyes beneath a high smooth forehead, capturing the candlelight. Leading and directing, like a musician himself, as if talk were music, engaging all who are seated at table by his continual curiosity and, especially, by his attention for each person present. During those dinner conversations at the Cecils' it seemed possible to have his thoughts taken seriously, to take himself seriously. . . .

After rising from table, unless there happened to be some truly extraordinary and unavoidable business, there was always a leisurely time spent in the garden or, if the weather were poor, then in the parlor or solar or within the cleared Hall, with dinner's colloquy not tossed aside, but continued, expanding its boundaries.

William Cecil will labor as long as any farmhand at harvest (and often, also, far into the night), wearing his clerks and servants into early old age with him. Yet there will be no sense of that—weariness of labor done, tedium of work to follow—imposing upon the pleasure of the dinner hour.

"And there will never be any unseemly hurry, either, at the times set aside for prayer and worship. I can imagine that one day there may well be rabble and soldiery—bands of inimical Frenchmen, of Spaniards, Flemings, Germans and Italians, every Lord have mercy on us!, of rowdy Scots—directly at Cecil's gatehouse. And yet I believe that the entire office of *The Book of Common Prayer*, from opening sentences and General Confession down to last words of the Collect for Grace, would be offered up. And as calmly and sedately as ever."

From the example of Sir William Cecil he has learned that it is possible to live well, even richly, in this world and yet without pride and vanity. Learned, too, that a man can fare deliciously (in all things) without waste. That he can cultivate sober elegance without relinquishing the refinements of simplicity.

Yet this simplicity can be deceptive.

Take, for instance, the newly acquired and newly refurbished house Cecil has established for himself in Westminster, an imposing brick building with four tall embattled towers and wide, paved courtyards, standing on the north side of the Strand, across

from Russell House. The messenger will see it for the first time
at the end of this journey and will see so much of his master in
the choice of that place for his city establishment. A house which
is strong and plain, then, proud without ostentation. And he will
find it (as he might expect) well equipped and appointed inside.
Where the guest or visitor may be startled by the contrast between outward simplicity and inward beauty. Cardinal Wolsey
would never have understood it—except as some kind of curious
jest. But any rich city merchant would. More than that, the merchant will appreciate it, seeing Cecil as more like himself than
the nobility. Those who do not know him well will consider the
simplicity of his residence, and its location on the north side, facing road and not river, to be proper for Mr. Secretary. Appropriately undistinguished. Appropriately unenviable, indicating
the man's awareness of the limits of his ambition.

Others, friends and allies, take delight from this slight duplicity (a plain cloth glove disguising jeweled fingers) which Cecil
wisely practices against the unimaginative. Who must be protected against envy and malice. Indeed, they must be protected
from knowledge that they lack power which is commensurate
with their image of themselves. Friends and allies will appreciate
this. Seeing that, in truth, Cecil does not wish to aspire to climb
too high too quickly. They will see how (in the most serious
sense) discreet Cecil is.

The messenger understands this well; for, in a different way,
he has had to play at the same game. He has long ago learned
(else he would not be here to prove it) that those who are weak
must be encouraged to feel as strong as they would like to be.
And the powerful must be generously unchallenged lest their
deepest fears—that strength will fail them, will vanish like a sunbeam—should be exposed.

Child of his times, William Cecil has to be fearful also. And in
some ways which this messenger, his servant, does not imagine.
For, Cecil, with good reasons, has come to doubt not only the
Queen's continuing favor toward him (is not the Earl of Leicester, an enemy when all's said and done, closest to her of any
man alive?), but also her ability to defend this kingdom from
fractious elements within and from the tightening ring of implacable foreign enemies which surrounds even as the sea does this

island. Elizabeth has already ruled longer than her brother or her sister. All odds are against a long life. Twice already she has been sick enough to die.

Cecil fears more than a change in his own fortune. What he fears is the ruin of all the world as he knows it.

Nor can the messenger imagine how much Cecil, overburdened and overworked, driven by his many duties, has aged beyond his years. His joints ache from more than common English ague. His bowels trouble him. His feet swell and wince from gout. Too often precious energy fails him. He is an old man (disguised) in middle years. Occasionally a journey to Bath, or to the blue warm bubbling springs in high Buxton, seems to restore him somewhat. But not for long. Cecil has come to believe that chances are he cannot serve for many more years.

Not many, even among those closest to him, can have guessed this. For Cecil has, since youth, affected a grave dignity, an old man's careful self-possession. And his discipline is such that he could probably maintain a soft voice and a smiling mask even if his feet were on fire.

And so it is that there has come to be something urgent about Sir William Cecil's rush to regain the old and to build up the new. On the one hand there is the haste to finish as much as he can before it is too late. Hoping, against the odds, that he will be able to leave an estate, something of real value, for his sons and daughters, his old mother and his widow. Especially for the two sons, the bearers of his name. What sadness (and irony) there! Thomas, a wild youth, ne'er-do-well and, it seems, lazy and ill educated and self-indulgent, but still the eldest and first born, child of Mary Cheke, Cecil's first wife, dead more than twenty years ago. And now a new half brother Robert, three years old, quick of mind but small and sickly. Robert who, even if he lives to become a man, cannot be expected to come to much. If only there were a way to graft some of little Robert's intelligence upon Thomas's good health.

It may be that the prospects of his sons have worn Cecil more than his body's pains.

Still, it is his Christian duty to have faith in the future and to provide for it. And if in the end he should fail, and if this estate, these houses with their extraordinary accumulation of rich and

beautiful and worthy things, should come not into the hands
of lawful heirs, but into the possession of others, unimagined
strangers or perhaps even known enemies, still there will be some
undeniable harvest of honor there. If these things of this world
are truly worthwhile, then chances are that they will be well
cared for by whoever takes possession of them. Even deadly enemies. True, his coat of arms may be painted or plastered over. Indeed his very name may be erased, struck, blotted, cut from
every paper and all records and documents. His tomb and monument can be defaced or destroyed. And yet, even if only in stub-
born memory, it will be known that once upon a time William
Cecil was creator and owner of these things. And when that is
forgotten, too, then the things themselves, being preserved precisely because they are beautiful and worthy, will carry some
sense of being, to perfect strangers. Who will be compelled to
wonder at what they cannot imagine—*who owned these splendid
things?*
Whatever else, gigantic footprints will have been left by him.

Yet there is another motive, a better and wiser one, which
even Sir William Cecil may be unable to define clearly. At the
same time that he is seeking to preserve something against the
ruins of time, his desire is also to perform an act of good faith for
his sovereign. Against the promptings of reason; against the
weight of the odds; against the examples of history as he knows
them; surely against the strong tide of events, as he perceives
that tide to be running; it is an act of faith in (still young at
thirty-two years) Elizabeth the Queen. Faith that she will rule
long enough and in peace and prosperity and safety, for all of his
monuments to have any meaning. Faith, also, that by Providence
he will be permitted to continue in her service, and that she will
continue to reward him for it.
A sad and witty way of thanking the Queen for her bounty
even as he is asking her for more.
His courtly way of telling her that he understands and ap-
proves of her weakness for brave and extravagant gestures.
His counselor's way of reminding her that there is a future
which must be prepared for. . . .

. . . and soon—broad and wet beneath pale skies—in Lincolnshire. Called land of yellow bellies, for there are more frogs and eels than men there. The rider suddenly there, startling a flapping and whistling of waterbirds from the reeds, shivering aspen and willow as he's gone again leaving dust clouds and mud clods behind.

Up and down Gonerby Hill (highest between Edinburgh and London) and into Grantham on the Witham, town of red-roofed, half-timber and brick houses. Changing horse at the *Angel*, then up steep Spitalgate Hill. To run through rolling pasture land thick with grazing animals. To arrive at last at the ancient town of Stamford. . . .

"Where at the age of seven, armed with a new satchel to carry books and papers, with a sharp penknife and some candles, I was sent to Stamford School in St. Paul's Street."

Never to forget the hard benches where they sat, two boys sharing each of the slanted oak desks set in rows in a heavy-beamed, high-ceilinged room.

"Cold as a key in a door it was in wintertime, and my nose always sniffing and running and my fingers as stiff as twigs. In summer afternoons it was as sweaty as a chimney corner. Laboring winter and summer under the unblinking gaze of the tall, thin, weary Master, perched up there on a stool in front of the schoolroom, with a supple birch rod in his hands like a wand of high office. Behind us, unseen and always felt, was the Usher spying on us. I tell you it was a long, heavy-lidded, fart-rich day, from first light until first stars. And every day, too, except for Sunday."

Learning Latin by heart through ceaseless exercises of recitation. Never to forget the weight and feel of William Lily's grammar and Nicholas Udall's *Flowers of Latin Speaking*. Trained to read and write, in prose and verse, in the slowly dying tongue of Caesar and Cicero and Terence, of Horace and Virgil and Ovid. . . .

"And all things taught, enforced upon memory as it were, to the sharp tune of a ferule laid smartly across an open palm or swollen knuckles. And often enhanced by the swish and smack of the Master's birch rod as it made acquaintance with the wincing bare flesh of my backside.

"Though let me say, as I learned later, it was better at Stamford than elsewhere. For, bless him and thanks be, Mr. Cecil has always disapproved of too much use of the rod on young students. Except for necessary matters of discipline."

He will pass along Stamford's High Street, going by churches and small squares and gateways and finally a whole row of inns, one of which, the *Tabard*, is partly owned by Cecil. But will not change horses there, but will continue to the bank of the Welland and go into Northamptonshire on narrow Packhorse Bridge. Past Cecil's parish church of St. Martin and then in less than a mile to enter the outer gateway leading to Sir William Cecil's country estate. Where he'll have a strong fresh horse and a better saddle. Where he'll receive a replenished purse and some food and drink in the huge high-vaulted kitchen (all that is left of the monastery that was here) with its hundreds of burnished copper pots and fireplace large enough to roast an ox whole.

No time for more than snatches of news in kitchen and stables. But time enough to marvel at the confusion as a swarm of masons and carpenters and joiners and glaziers and craftsmen of all kinds (Englishmen and strangers too from Flanders and France) hurry to ready the place for the Queen next month. And what a place they have made. All built of the warm yellow-gray stone called Barnack Rag. And set around a large courtyard with a tall four-story turreted gatehouse and large angle towers at the corners. The walls of the house are a wonder of mullioned glass windows. And a roofscape like a wild forest with turrets and pinnacles and vanes and balustrades and decorative miniature castles. With chimneys grouped and pillared as in the Tuscan fashion. All of this set amid thirty acres (not counting the six miles of park and woods and ponds) of orchards and gardens. For the growing of every kind of herb and flower needed for health and for contentment. Every kind of bush and shrub and tree for berries and nuts and fruit.

On this subject the messenger will hear of lemon trees and orange trees and even a pomegranate tree recently planted. To be maintained by continual and exquisite care.

"Better to be an orange tree than a poor man."

He will see women busy with yards of cloth being cut and sewn to make new livery for servants. Old servants drilling many newly hired ones in the artful details of service and good manners.

Thanks to the Lord he has no part to play in all of this.

And must be gone. To carry more letters and papers and reports from here to Cecil in Westminster, given into his hands by the new Steward—Mr. Thomas Bellot. Who does not know him from any other dusty horseman passing through.

Just as well.

Finishes food and drink and leaves the kitchen to keep on riding. For London. Which is now some ninety miles away.

Having done well enough at Stamford School, he was packed off, across the stream-stitched miles east of Stamford to study at Cecil's own College of St. John the Evangelist in Cambridge. And, thanks to Cecil's generosity as a full-fledged pensioner, beholden to no man. Except to his patron.

Required to wear, outside his chambers, a plain and sober academic gown. Not like the few sons of the nobility allowed to affect gaudy colors or to wear satins or velvets or silks. Nor permitted to wear a sword.

Required also to obey many and various rules. Though always free as old Adam to disregard. To risk the consequences, fines, and loss of privileges. And, for certain offenses, to risk the humiliation of a public whipping in the Hall. Which rules and consequences never served wholly to inhibit him (or most of his fellow students) from their full share of japes and pasquils. Times of drunken bell pulling. Times of panting flight from proctors and porters. Times of (strictly forbidden) swimming in the Cam.

Meantime he studied at logic and rhetoric, trivium and quadrivium. Attended lectures and disputations. Was exposed to the excellent instruction in Greek to be had at St. John's. Acted in Latin plays in the college Hall.

And followed the advice of Cecil, paying a fee to the college bell ringer to come and wake him at four o'clock in the morning. So that he might have an extra hour for his studies.

Mostly his memories now are of weather.

Often, and especially if he is possessed by a melancholy humor, this remembered weather will be composed out of many shades and nuances of gray. Cold mists rising up, ghostlike from gray earth and gray water, partly concealing the twisted shapes of gray leafless trees. All the while a light rain is falling out of a low sky whose clouds are the texture of muddy wool.

Sees himself there, too, small and shivering, thorn-jointed from damp and cold, his hidden flesh a landscape of goosebumps. Can see, as if from a bird's-eye view, this figure of himself with one or two others—for the rule is they must always go at least in pairs— leaving chambers on the south side of the court at St. John's. Floating across the courtyard in their gowns like a little squadron of black-sailed ships. Coming outside through the gate onto the cobbles of the street. All of them ignoring what fog anyway mostly disguises—not merely the towered, three-storied grandeur of brickwork and stone that is the college gatehouse, but, over and above the arch of the gate, a wonder of rose and blue and gold set there in honor of the benefactress of the college, Lady Margaret Beaufort, Countess of Richmond and mother of King Henry VII. Showing, beneath the brightly painted statue of St. John, the arms of England and of the Tudors and the Beauforts. Crowned rose and portcullis. Daisies and borage. And even a pair of spotted yales—proud beasts so seldom to be found outside of books, sporting tail of an elephant, body of an antelope, and head of a goat. . . .

"I am not yet old enough or forgetful enough to cherish the illusion that my youth was a springtime."

And yet, nonetheless, unquenchable and irrepressible, like flame catching kindling, sometimes an image of the Cambridge springtime will overwhelm him. Trees in flower, their leaves as delicate as if beaten into shape and brightness by goldsmiths. Rinsed air trembling with the wings of butterflies. Sky embroidered with birdsongs. And not only the gardens, but also the grass of yards and fields, the banks of the swollen river, surging with crowds of flowers. Such opulence and excess that you can easily imagine these are tattered pieces of Joseph's coat of many colors; how certain rebellious (reforming) angels have just now broken one of heaven's windows and these, then, are joyous fragments which have fallen in a silent storm to gravel the reawakening earth with all the colors and shades of hoping.

But most often he will find himself recalling the weeks of September before Michaelmas and before the beginning of term. The harvest is in. The reapers have swept across the fields, stooping and kneeling with their sickles. Corn has been cut and stacked, left afield a brief time to dry, then carted home to the barns. Stubble has been mowed for gathering straw and for stover. Harvest supper has been held in halls and churchyards. And now the sky goes blue and gold and the light changes, casting long shadows.

Time for the Stourbridge Fair, set in the fields between Newmarket Road and the river. With people coming there from all the shires and from Scotland and the Continent. To buy and to sell and to pleasure themselves. Strange odors cast into the air in the smoke of the cookfires, mingling with the scents of the enormous market of spices and herbs. Hearing the languages of other places and the dialects twisted out of his own tongue, falling on his ears as if these words were being sung. Taste of foreign foods, tingling the mouth. Sight of strange faces, with different cuts and lengths of beard and hair. Sporting so many different kinds of clothing. Moving among the crowds and touching, say, soft furs worn by a Dane or a Hanse merchant, perfumed leather of a French wine dealer, or sleek Italian silk of a Venetian here to sell the spices of the East. To feel and to heft the sweatslick weight of foreign coins in his palms.

Moving amid the profusion of sounds and broken music of voices, he could hear an inner voice telling him, with the sad solemnity which only youth can manage, that never, ever again beyond the limits of Stourbridge Fair would he experience any of these things again. He was not able to imagine days to come (soon enough) when he would make his life among strangers in other countries. Times when it would be a matter of life and death to comprehend the languages and dialects of others. Times when it would be necessary to speak and even to act like a native. Mercifully he was unable to envision days to come when the least common sights, sounds, and odors of England would seem as strange to him as anything in distant lands. Times when, dreaming himself back, would find himself hungry for the simplest things of England.

Only now, years later, can he perceive how those careless, ale-warmed September days, spent in wandering the Stourbridge Fair, were more practical apprenticeship for the life he would have to live than all of his other courses of study at the college taken together.

Soon after the Fair comes fall and the beginning of the new term. The light is now like wine in a clear Venetian glass. And the days end with sunsets like the coals of a dying fire. The moon too rises slow and huge and fat, a ruddy face among the glitter of crowded stars.

Nights belong to the owls. As days become the property of rooks and crows and gulls gleaning the fields. Which now must be turned and plowed and well spread with dung. And the firewood for winter cut and hauled and stacked close at hand. The year's last fruits must be brought in and carefully stored.

And one final skywide fountaining of swifts and swallows before they vanish from the bleak air.

Then the rains begin again.

"Well, let rain patter on the roof and run down the spouts. No matter to us. For we shall sit by a fire and enjoy the end of the season. With new cider. With hazelnuts and roasted chestnuts. We shall darken our teeth and our tongues with the sticky sweetness of new-picked blackberries."

And so, resurrecting autumn, he recollects the place more clearly. The colleges, built around their courts behind walls and gates and thin turreted, battlemented gatehouses; the halls and hostels, the inns with their huge signs and the vivid colors of their painted plaster. He knows the way by heart from the old castle facing the Fens at the north edge of town, down past St. Giles and Magdalen College, then crossing the river on that old five-arched bridge of stone and timber. Following Bridge Street for a couple of hundred yards, past the church of St. Clement's to the corner of the High Street. . . .

"Where was I?

"Oh yes, with my companions, I had just left the gatehouse of

St. John's. Turned right to walk briskly past elegant Trinity, shabby Glonville, and next King's. . . ."

Just beyond that still-abuilding college, standing gray and white, alone and wetly shining on a wide field of sparse grass and tree-lined paths, is the newly completed Chapel, a line of slim pinnacled buttresses which somehow magically hold not merely the weight of an enormous roof of timber and lead, but also the long walls so pierced with tall windows as to seem to be made mostly of stained glass. And these windows are still whole and shining, though Reformers have whitewashed many a painted church wall and have broken as many windows in and around Cambridge as elsewhere in England. These are still all of a piece even though King's is a powerful center for the reform of religion.

And so it is that on rare, sunkindled days, a certain slanting light will transform this Chapel. Making it seem not to have been made of timbers and cut stones set on the solid earth, but instead mysteriously composed of something else, something insubstantial like woodsmoke or ground fog.

Sometimes the light of a still and windless dawn, silhouetting this Chapel, will cast its reflection, wavering but whole, upon the surface of the Cam. Sometimes, seeking to follow that floating image to its source, he has entered the Chapel to walk the length of the Antechapel and the choir. Inwardly rejoicing as he saw those windows broadcast many-colored lights. Which (he imagined) are the coinage of heaven. Looking up, above that spindrift color, above the carved-oak screen, above all monuments and heraldic emblems and ciphers, higher than the Gospel stories told by the stained glass of the windows, looking all the way up to where the delicate, intricate vaulted ceiling, defying rules of weight and burden, soars as if to prove the theorems of a new geometry, demonstrating the airy architecture of God's (loyal) angels, he, becoming in that timeless instant as light as a puffball of seed, a dandelion, say, boneless and bodiless, created no longer of clay and dust, but as if now made only out of light and breath, felt able to rise and float and soar into empty air with graceful ease.

If only he had possessed full faith (*as much as a mustard*

seed) to do so. If only he had known the prayer, the words which, like some spell, would free him from the shackles of his doubts.

In self-defense now, when doubts seem more an armor than a burden, he will recall his own age in years and the age of the world. To justify such feelings. To explain the times. Times when a boy was swept over by feelings as if by sudden gusts of wind. Maybe he was then (as he would insist) as stuffed with idle hopes and false illusions as any Whitsun goose is crammed with bread and spices. Yet if so, he was not alone. So, likewise, were all the others all around him. The whole world was on fire, burning with change and revision and reform. And Cambridge became a center for it in those (*ah, lost now*) days of the reign of the young King Edward. Who would surely (no one doubted it) follow the pattern of his family, his grandfather and father, and live and rule long. Those were days, too, while the King was still young, of rule by the Lord Protector. So they were days not without profit for the Protector's Secretary—Mr. William Cecil. And so not without reasonable hope of future preferment for himself.

In fairness to himself, this man can now point to that small, black-gowned figure moving along the High Street of Cambridge with his companions. Not only, after all, the child of one age and time. But also the child (and victim) of the timeless condition of youth. A very young man full of the sap and juice of life. Though, of course, hoping then that he might be waking soon, as from a long sleep full of dreams, to find himself a full-grown man. Taking the whole world, past, present, and future, precisely as he found it on a damp early evening, made just as it was and made so just for him, as he and his friends hurried along past the field and the ghostly white shape of the Chapel at King's without any special thought or feeling beyond the recognition of something standing, as it should, beautifully in its appointed place.

They are on their way to the old *White Horse Tavern* across from the walls of St. Bene't's, close to the clutter of shops and houses and the buildings of St. Catherine's. To find a seat or a bench or at least someplace to lean against the wall. Of that Tavern which had the ambiguous nickname of Little Germany.

Where a man can learn all the latest Protestant songs and dances from the Continent—including the pure Geneva Jig.

By custom, even from times before he was born, debates on religion took place at the *White Horse*. Here men from the Cambridge colleges talked freely and openly and passionately. There he listened to subtle, sometimes dangerous discussion of delicate subjects—transubstantiation, predestination, the true and proper nature and number of the holy sacraments; the virtues and faults, strengths and weaknesses, of the newly published *Book of Common Prayer* and also the best ways and means for translation of the Scripture into the common tongue; and thorny questions such as the place of good works if we are justified by faith alone; and whether or not the Pope in Rome may be taken literally to be the Anti-Christ; and the place and purpose (if any) for altars and images and vestments and candles and incense and all such things and whether these were things adiaphoric and indifferent or merely tolerable and foolish things; and whether there was any place for these things in a reformed and purified service of worship; and if there should be, by name and title, any Bishops; and if priests should marry and whether married people may ever lawfully divorce; and which stands foremost (when and if they must come to stand opposed to one another), private conscience or civil and public ordinances.

All of it left him speechless and perplexed, yet somehow joyous in his confusion, as he and his friends headed back for the college in the foggy night, broken only here and there by a wall lantern.

He can still see himself, a rumple-gowned figure, stumbling along, as they all do, up Mill Street. Going past the high Dutch-brick walls and the gatehouse of Queens and then coming to the fields just beyond, which are open clear down to the riverside. There's some talk, then, about a run to the river by the group of them and of a swim there. But that is all swashing braggadocio. For not a one of them has courage to test the chill water or heart to risk punishment for it. So, instead, turning up a path, they walk to rejoin the High Street. Their voices are raised louder than they may realize in unending discussion as they begin to hurry to reach the college before the gates are locked. Then stopping. All gathering around and laughing out loud as one of them, unable to control himself, stands in the narrow lane with his gown hiked up high so that he can piss long and hard, an arching stream hissing and splattering against a wall. And he laughs, too, when he's able to see that his pissing foolish student is none other than himself. Next, all the others must join in. And there is a kind of pissing contest.

Cut off by bell sounds in the air. Clock striking. Soft bells ringing, muffled by fog, as now they go racing up the pavement, their gowns flying out behind them, each like the tail feathers of a crow.

Running through the sound of the bells. For a quarter mile to the gate of St. John's.

Just in time. As the porter pulls the gate to and bolts and locks up.

They are staggering across the courtyard. Panting too deeply to laugh anymore.

And now someone, not himself this time, groans and begins to heave and vomit.

And another, someone else (it must be the Fellow charged with governing them and their chambers), has lit a candle and peers down from an open window. He begins to curse them. Promises punishment. . . .

He cannot remember if there was punishment or not. Cannot care much, either. For what may have been serious, even fearful for him then is only foolish to him now.

"And that's a blessing, after all. Let us suppose that instead of shedding old fears in forgetfulness, from crib to coffin, we were to accumulate more and more, keeping them as we grow and change from one age to the next. Suppose that we were destined never to be free of fears, but doomed to acquire our own unique treasury of wounds and scars, each one vividly memorable. Well, sir, if that were so, then to live would be chiefly to wince and to cringe. Past would be insupportable, present unbearable, and the unknown future would be more terrible than both together."

So much has happened to him, to the world as well, in the dozen or so years since he and his friends ran panting and giddy in the night, their young hearts fisting and pounding. Their heads as full as any angler's creel, crammed with the writhing of large ideas of every kind, the shabby hopelessly intermingled with the inestimably precious.

"Well, sir, no matter now; for ideas, trivial or treasured, are not much use to me now."

He is not what he seemed sure to become. Not a lawyer. Not a minister. Not teacher or scholar nor clerk to an important master.

"No, and not even a soldier, for God's sake! I am not much more than a dog on a short leash. Fit to spy on other men. Fit to keep secrets and carry urgent news."

His trade is crafty, tedious, and sometimes dangerous. Likely he will die of it. Likely a squalid and a violent death.

He shrugs at that, even as he prays that it will be sudden if it comes. When it comes, it will not astonish him much.

Now he is thinking that not all the lectures he heard and the books he read, but running in the dark was the best education he was given.

So much has changed. So has he. And yet—he will not deny this truth—the memory of pain, even the most painful disappointment, finally vanishes. But memory of pleasure, and even of the hope that humbly attended it, is always near enough to be called forth like a benign, obedient spirit. For as long as memory will last.

"Since this is so, I would as lief follow the good advice of St. Paul and seek to think on only those things which are true and beautiful and of good report. If only I could do that. . . ."

Does he fear sleep? It is not sleeping but dreaming he is afraid of. The time of dreams when any kind of ghost can rise. When ghosts are savage and unruly. Where Time is the fearful teacher whose punishments are endless.

COURTIER

1626

Thus after I passed my best time in court, and got little, I betook myself to the country, after I was past one and thirty years old, where I lived with great content: for we had a stirring world, and few days passed over my head but I was on horseback, either to prevent mischief, or to take malefactors, and to bring the Border in better quiet than it had been in times past.

Memoirs of the Life of Robert Carey

Excerpt from a letter written by Robert Carey, Earl of Monmouth, to Sir Ferdinando Gorges

. . . and, all in all, the lad is working out well. Much as I trust your good judgment, Ferdinando, I could scarcely have expected you to find the right man for this techy problem of mine.

In my memoir, which I plan to write down before the last coals of my mind have burned out, I shall be speaking to my own posterity. I am writing to my family—children and grandchildren, to be sure. And also, God be willing, to their children and grandchildren and so on for as long as the Lord wills our line to continue.

Now I know, sir, that all your thoughts are set on a course for the future, that your dreams are of the New World now. It may be what keeps your heart and mind younger than your years. You must find my course, tacking slowly and awkwardly against the wind and into my past, a puzzling choice. Maybe a foolish one. And yet I believe we are prompted by something of the same spirit. My destination, though roundabout, is the future also.

Be that as it may, I must seek to waken a weak and sleepy memory. And this young fellow is excellent for my purposes. For he listens well. Pays deferential, mannerable attention to an old man. Yet being young and lacking (as yet) the fine polish of duplicity, he cannot disguise it when his attention wanders away or when the tedium of my recollections begins to be a yoke on his shoulders.

By the way, Ferdinando, this fellow would be well advised not to gamble, until his face and eyes have learned to keep secrets more closely.

What might have been annoyance, even outrage to me, coming from my own servants or (especially) from my own kinfolk, is a benefit coming to me from this young scholar. I find myself suing for his attention. Which, though an exercise in humility, is better than losing it without knowing so. Secondly, however, and far more valuable I think, is this—that much that I rehearse for him is, clearly, altogether strange to him. From his puzzlement I discover much that we took for granted has either vanished or else become baffling to these young folk.

Take, for instance, the wars . . . our wars.

These fellows, like this lad here, who grew up in the slack time of peace have no memory of war. None other than our own—the recollections of old veterans. Which memories, as we both know, are faulty, more sham than truth, and all the more so as time passes. When you speak to them of soldiers, they can call up only the image of what they have seen. Poor shabby wretches plucked out of the prisons or pressed into service by brute gangs. Ill fed and ill equipped, poorly trained by fellows who know no more than they do, they are shipped off to die of fever or ague (if not starvation) if they are lucky. They have seen the leftover scum of these late disasters, sitting on their stumps of legs at the gates of manor houses, leaning on crutches in marketplaces, begging. . . .

Having seen these things, what can they believe except that we were madmen to go to the wars? They cannot imagine the wild glories of it. Foolish it may have been, but, Ferdinando, there were times when heart pounded and the blood sang like a choir, when breath was short and sweet and we seemed to carry our very souls like water in our hands. There were times of exaltation worth all the pain and danger. Times when the cries of the wounded, even the groans of the dying, were like music. For we who heard them were marvelously alive and whole. God forgive me (God forgive us all). But there were bloody times more joyous than anything else I have known.

I tell you, Ferdinando, all those years I served as a Warden on the Borders (always chafing to return to Court) were the happiest years of my life. And if the Wars were not so pleasing, still they were the best schooling I ever had.

Only yesterday I was telling him about the siege of Rouen in '91. When we served under Essex and the King of France. Remember that winter? I was seeking to explain to him the folly of that night *scalado* we attempted against the walls of St. Catherine's Castle. How my Lord Essex ordered us to wear shirts over our armor. And how, as a result, I lost most of my shirts that night, which I loaned out to others who proved not so lucky as I. How we crouched in trenches with our scaling ladders. Waiting upon the signal from my Lord. Trumpet and drums and then forward we ran toward the walls, welcomed by plenty of shot. For they were well prepared for us, though we were somewhat aided by the dark. Running forward with ladders into shot and fire. Then suddenly in retreat, running back the way we had come, still peppered and falling, tripping and staggering over the bodies of poor wretches who had fallen. Back to the trenches to hide our heads. And then, soon after while we panted like hounds, catching our breath, there came a sudden quiet. And into that quiet came the laughter of the Earl of Essex.

"Jesus, Jesus, oh sweet Jesus!" He was calling out even as he laughed. "Sweet wounds of Jesus, we have done it again. The damned ladders are short by two yards or more!"

How, all of a sudden, after that bloody charge, the stupidity and failure of it, this seemed the greatest jest in all the world. And all of us in those muddy trenches began to laugh, too; and the French Papists on the wall began to laugh, unable to contain themselves against the noise of several hundred men laughing as if to empty themselves of laughter forever.

Ferdinando, I began to laugh aloud again even as I told of it. He managed a smile, out of his best manners, but he looked at me as he might have looked at a Bedlamite.

I sought to explain to him the sense of it. How time and again, in the reign of the Queen, the English scaling ladders had somehow proved to be made too short for walls to be taken. How we did well enough in open field of battle against all manner of enemies, even the Spaniards. We were best of all when besieged ourselves, and we could hold a place as well and as dearly as any soldiers he has ever heard of, ancient or modern. But how, time and time again, in attack to scale the enemy's walls we failed. How it was the damned ladders that failed us and left the field littered with dead and crippled Englishmen.

"Ah," he told me. "That is a terrible pity, and I cannot understand how you could crouch in the trenches and laugh because of it."

"Nor can I, lad. Nor can I. I shall never understand it. But we did so. Laughed until we were spent and gasping for breath, some staggering like drunkards, some rolling on the muddy ground."

"Still, it is strange."

"Well, lad, the best I can tell you is that we laughed with all our hearts and perhaps because we had no tears left by that time. It was laugh or turn to stone."

Since we were talking of the siege of Rouen, I could not let the subject pass without some mention of your valor there. How you saved the lives of my Lord and his best friends (myself also). How we had ridden close to the walls on a fine morning and, as Essex always enjoyed, were busy exchanging insults and challenges with the Froggies on the walls.

How while they had us thus engaged, they aimed to cut us off from our own people by sending a half a hundred men out of a sallyport. And they would have done so, too, except for you, Ferdinando. You were in command of the trenches that day. And seeing the Froggies come out the sallyport, you led a band of your best men out of the trenches to attack them first. Yourself—and indeed half of your men also—all unready for combat. In doublet and hose only, no armor. Armed only with a rapier. Outnumbered and poorly armed for it, you and your men came shouting out of the trench. So startled the French that some of them dropped their halberds on the spot. And they ran like a flock of sheep for the safety of the sallyport.

There was a great volley of shot from the ramparts. And I think (do I remember it right?) you were sore shot then and there. I know you earned a wound at Rouen, but cannot remember when it was.

Well, you are much with us still, Ferdinando, with only a limp to show for your French wound. And you were never such a

prancer or dancer, if I may say so, that the wound has anyway
hindered you.

Saved all our lives, you did on that occasion. If I have failed to
thank you for it, then I do so now. And if I may have thanked
you often, well, sir, here's another.

To continue.

The innocence of my listening scholar has made me look again
at the old world (somewhat) through his own eyes. Which is
like seeing myself, ourselves, in a peculiar looking glass, one of
those which can make us seem fat or thin, short or tall, deformed
or beautiful, as the case may be. It is as if he were such a glass
and I were making faces in front of it. Which can lead me astray
from the truth if I am not careful. But which can also be, I
confess, more than a little entertaining. Good Ferdinando, the
labor (and sometimes pain) of raking my memory must finally
please me if it is to succeed.

Even the unfortunate fact that he is somewhat of a Puritan in
matters of religion has proved a help to me. That he seems to
feel himself to be, by birth and education both, my moral
superior, is an aid to memory. It is far more gratifying to be able
to shock the fellow than it would be to find that my worst
excesses could not raise an eyebrow.

The other day I told him a tale of you and me, Ferdinando.
Since it all happened so many faded years ago, I trust you do not
mind my retelling it. But if you do mind, it is too late now. The
mischief is done, and all that remains is to smile and to bear it
with patience. Good digestion is more important than justice to
men of our age.

Seeing that I was losing his attention, I told him the story of
the hundred-crown wager. About that time when we both had
come home to Court from the wars in The Netherlands. How we
looked to be rewarded. And how we were not.

I told him how, before time frosted and fattened us, you were
a handsome fellow and as handsomely dressed, too, as anyone at
the Court. How you allowed yourself a certain vanity about your
appearance. And why not? After all, there you were, alive and
not much the worse for wear after hard campaigns in the
Lowlands. Where many a good man had found a home beneath

six feet of wet sod. Those of us who were fortunate enough to be
alive had reason to swagger a little. And you more than most.

So l proceeded to tell the lad how one evening after supper
you and I and some others (whose names are lost to me now
forever) were playing at cards in my father's old chambers at
Blackfriars. How you happened to make the brag that at a
certain brothel in Southwark, an elegant fishpond frequented by
the finest gentlemen of the Court, you were so highly regarded,
on account of your good looks and the excellence of your
amorous performance, that you were not asked to pay any fee for
their favors.

This claim resulted in an harmonious motet of hoots and jeers.
One thing led to another until you announced that you were
willing to hazard a wager, odds of ten to one, against any of us.
If we were to go there together, that, offered a choice, these
fancy strumpets would choose you first among all the rest of us.

How the others were willing to concede the laurels of the
brothel to you. But how I accepted your wager. And I put up ten
crowns, against your one hundred, that they would choose me.

Up we jumped from the table and brushed and combed and
polished ourselves. Put on our swords and called for torches.
Then rushed out into the night and directly down to Puddle
Wharf. Where it required a little whoremongers' armada to carry
us all across to Bankside. Torches burning brightly and all of us
singing cheerful bawdy ballads we had learned (if nothing else)
in the wars.

It's a wonder we did not wake the Queen in her bedchamber
in Whitehall.

Landed and made a great show and confusion of paying (and
cheating) the watermen. Then off we went, all in a drunken
pack, following behind you, Ferdinando, who knew the way so
well you could have found it blindfolded. Directly to the right
door. Much knocking and pounding till the porter came. Then
much talking and pleading (and the payment of a coin or two)
before we could be admitted. At last to stand in the chamber like
a rank of soldiers while they were to study us and pick the best
men. How they carefully looked us over, one at a time, as we
stood there solemn in our best Court finery. And how when they
came to look at me, I doffed my cap and made a deep, most

courteous bow. Not for the sake of satirical good manners, as you and the others may have thought. But because, unknown to you, I had pinned a shiny gold Angel at the center of my head and hair. So when I took off my cap and bowed to the whores, that coin caught the candlelight like a little sun. And, just so, it caught their eyes and hearts.

Which was why they chose me for their very own, ignoring you. Carried me away to the upper chambers for a night of pleasure. Whilst the rest of you were left to feed your vanity on astonishment and empty air.

Yes, it cost me the price of a gold Angel. Much too much for a night with any whore in London. But balanced against your extravagant wager of one hundred crowns, it provided me with a tidy profit for my pleasure.

The moral of which tale—as I told you at the time, Ferdinando—is never make a wager against a man who has had to gamble for his living. For he will find some way to win the safest wager and take your money for his own.

Well, sir.

When I told this boy the story, he blushed like a girl. Which led me to the inference that he is not completely unfamiliar with such places.

Did he believe the story? You are wondering. I doubt it. For to believe it he would have to stifle his doubts, good Ferdinando, that the likes of you and I were ever as young and foolish as he is.

Mr Secretary
AND THE LETTERS

1603

Certainly the politic and artificial nourishing and entertaining of hopes and carrying men from hopes to hopes is one of the best antidotes against the poison of discontentments. And it is a certain sign of a wise government and proceeding, when it can hold men's hearts by hopes, when it cannot by satisfaction, and when it can handle things in such manner as no evil shall appear so peremptory but that it hath some outlet of hope, which is less hard to do, because both particular persons and factions are apt enough to flatter themselves, or at least to brave that they believe not.

FRANCIS BACON—*Essays or Counsels, Civil and Moral*

A Monsieur Mon Bon Frère et Cousin le Roy d'Escose

I hope, my dear brother, that my weighty affairs at present
may make my lawful excuse for the retardance of the answer to
your ambassador, but I doubt not but you shall be honorable
satisfied with all the points of his commission. And next, after my
own errand done, I must render you my innumerable thanks for
such amicable offers as it hath pleased you to make, making you
assured that, with God's grace, you shall never have cause to
regret your good thoughts of my meaning to deserve as much
goodwill and affection as ever one prince owed another, wishing
all means that may maintain your faithful trust in me, that never
will seek aught but the increase of your honor and safety. I was
in mind to have sent you such accidents as this late month
brought forth. But the sufficiency of master Archibald Douglas
made me retain him. And I do render you many loving thanks
for the joy you take from my narrow escape from the jaws of
death. To which I might easily have fallen but that the Hand of
the Highest saved me from that snare.

And because the curse of that design rose up from the wicked
suggestion of the Jesuits, which make it an acceptable sacrifice to
God, and meritorious to themselves, that a King not of their
profession should be murdered; therefore I could keep my pen
no longer from discharging my care of your person, that you may
not suffer such vipers to inhabit your land. They say you gave
leave under your hand that they might come and go. For God's
love regard your surety above all your persuasions. And account
him no subject who entertains them. Make not edicts for scorn,

but to be observed. Let them be rebels, and so pronounced, that preserve them.

For my part, I am sorrier that they cast away so many goodly gentlemen than that they sought my ruin. I thank God I have taken more sadness for some that are guilty of this murder than bearing them malice that sought my death. I protest before God. But such iniquity will not be hid, be it never so craftily handled. And yet when you shall hear all, you will wonder that one accounted so wise will use such matter foolishly. But no wonder. For then they are given over to depraved feeling, they often make such slip.

I have been so tedious that I take pity of your pain, and so will end this scribbling, praying you believe that you could never have chosen a more sure truth, that will never beguile than myself, who daily prays for your long prosperity.

Your most assured loving
sister and cousin,

Elizabeth R.

The letter is dated the fourth of October, 1586. Written in her own hand. Quick, easy, and, as always in those days, legible. But not with such care to suggest any more than an expense of spontaneous thought at the moment of composition. As if she were thinking out loud on the page.

Therefore intended to be taken as the truth.

It was clear and as straightforward a letter as any she would ever write to him. Yet, even so, it is thick with the shadows of her own inimitable and often times impenetrable style. Crabbed, many have called it. And others say obscure. He thinks now— years having past and vanished since then—that it is a matter of adroit ambiguities. Devious is the word he would use, thinking it but not speaking it. Subtle is what he would choose to say.

It is easy for him to summon up the King of Scots, poet and scholar, poring over the letter. Studying it so carefully. Wide brow wrinkled. His full lips (if paintings and drawings and the descriptions of others are to be taken as true) pouting with annoyance he is seldom able to disguise.

What in the world is this woman trying to tell him? What is it that she is really saying?

Alone as he is, except for the gentle and regular snores of a servant sleeping on a pallet just inside the door of this chamber, Sir Robert Cecil cannot help smiling at the King's puzzlement of long ago. Alone in the late quiet night and, for the moment, feeling secure in the company of papers. Where he is, after all, most content. Where, even if his eyes are heavy and he nods with sleepiness, he is most completely alert and alive.

As it is with the world of clerks, like himself, so it is with kings. They sit still somewhere at the heart and center of the busy hive. Ambassadors, messengers, agents, and adventurers (yes, even spies and sometimes murderers) come and go from the Presence. Bringing the world with them in bits and pieces. Returning it to itself in shards and coins (sometimes jewels). The Prince sits enthroned at the center. Caged by custom and ceremony. Urgently vulnerable to deceits of flattery and the blunted, softened truths which, so misshapen, are indistinguishable from outright lies. Yet somehow the best Princes, those who survive and succeed, can translate false into true. Can, from some broken pieces, imagine and re-create the world anew.

Stunning, dazzling power and freedom of hobbled imagination to consume and to create.

He thinks of your wily London merchant. Those merchants who, from their houses in this city on this island, buy and sell daily from all the world—wood and timber from the Baltic, fur from Muscovy, spices and silks from the East, fine glass from Venice, wines and oil from the sun-struck Mediterranean, ivory from Africa. Their daily trade. The Merchant (as Cecil knows and imagines him, with a mixture of awe and contempt, the proper mixture for a debtor to maintain) sits at a large, carpet-covered table with scales and coins, pens and ink and papers, maps and charts. From all these, He constructs the world. Then he sends out for sale to these imaginary places his real English wool or cloth or corn or tin or brass. His ships follow the winds to and from all the raw edges of that world. Cargoes come and go, are lost and saved. Factors and agents arrive and depart. While he (together with his little brood of clerks), wise or foolish, sits at the center and succeeds or fails. Sits still and yet is forever changing.

So it is, in this new age, with Kings.

Busyness is all. Except at the quiet still center. Where Kings (merchants of kingdoms) keep watch upon each other. Most often compelled to piece together friends and enemies out of words and numbers. Each invisible to the other. Yet each joined and linked to the other. Sometimes like lovers. Often like Jacob and his Angel. Urgently wrestling to gain a blessing and to learn a name. . . .

From his patient father William Cecil, Lord Burghley, he has learned to love the secrets of papers. The same love and same secrets which made it possible for Philip II of Spain to govern this world's widest empire from an austere chamber not much larger than a monk's cell. The first secret (he tells himself) is this: that it is not so much the words or numbers, though none can be ignored and all of them must be embraced, as it is the invisible fire within them. The thing which from one imagination kindles another. Or put it another way. Call it the unseen power which serves to set imagination free to adventure as much as any soldier, sailor, or adventurer. As much and more than any common merchant.

Oh, many a good man, a King or clerk to Kings, has been buried beneath cold papers as by a great settlement of snow. Weight becoming intolerable. Yet those same papers can be indescribably light. Lighter than feathers blown in wind.

Which is how he takes these letters to be. His own feathers. From which wings are to be made which will permit him to fly free out of the maze and over the tops of the walls and soaring high into blue astonished sky.

He is too educated, too ironical and skeptical, to allow himself such thoughts for long. Must wake from them. But, still, he cannot deny he warms body and soul by the white fires of these letters. Cannot imagine living without them.

These letters of Kings and clerks are—if truth be told; which it will not be; for he must, by custom, sigh and complain at the tedious, heavy-lidded burdens of his vocation, else too many would envy him too much—are all the wine and poetry and music, all the joy he can wish for. Now that all love is lost. . . .

Tonight he is studying the letters he has at hand which passed between the Queen of England and the King of the Scots. And likewise, in light of them, he is considering his own yearlong correspondence with King James. Which began almost at once, following the execution of the Earl of Essex. And which will continue until the matter of this Succession is finally settled. One way or the other.

He considers this letter from the Queen to James in the fall of '86.

James was twenty years old at that time.

He, Cecil, was twenty-three, already working with his father and for the Queen. Though without rank or office yet. Merely a clerk to the Queen's great Clerk. Observing everything. Learning what he could know and, as well, learning to know what he could not know. Looking over his father's shoulder.

And King James in the fall of '86?

Most surprising, he had managed to survive. On which no good gambler would have risked a wager. Friends and enemies, favorites and rivals, had come and gone. He had suffered dangers (often) and many humiliations. But he had come this far.

Most important for the King was that his mother was still very much alive. And still possessed of some power in those days. Still styled and recognized as Queen of the Scots by most of the world. In which sense he was her son and a Prince, but no King. She was Queen whether she remained a captive in England or no. And there was the possibility that she might marry again. If not to some English nobleman, then perhaps to some foreigner. At one time it seemed she might marry the hero Don Juan of Austria. To rule jointly. And there had been talk of Philip of Spain. And what if she were to have children by another husband? And the Queen of Scots still had the allegiance of a powerful faction of Catholic lords in Scotland. Whose strength was more dangerous than ever before. For it was now uncertain, since they had ceased an open rebellion against the rights of James. Truth is, by '86 any number of these Catholic lords had become his allies in his effort to maintain some power to balance against that of the Kirk, which had never feared to preach and to speak against him whenever his actions were disapproved of. Nor had been abashed by his outrage against them. "I care not a turd

for thy preaching!" he had yelled. But neither that nor (more serious) the Black Acts passed by Parliament against the Kirk deterred or much discouraged their zeal. And there were the Protestant lords. Some who favored the Kirk, more who, for one
reason and another (and always chiefly for private greed and
personal ambition) were at odds with each other and with everyone else. And who had proved, many times, to be a threat against
the King.

Once, not long before, from August of '82 until June of '83,
James had been held captive by a group of these—the Lords Enterprisers. With the encouragement and connivance of the English. He had managed to revenge himself upon the leader of the
Enterprisers, the Earl of Gowrie. But the others had fled to England and remained until they were needed. Now they were
close around him again. The Lion of Scotland surrounded and
supported by enemies. Who, fortunately, hated and envied each
other more than they hated or envied him.

So there he was, a paradoxical creature. On the one hand
confident, even perhaps too confident of his abilities, because he
had come through so much. Alone in the center of this ring of
enemies and indifferent, often double-dealing friends, he had
learned to keep his own counsel. And had learned, too, that he
had a better mind, both by natural gifts and through rigorous
training, than anyone he had ever known. More than anyone he
had ever favored. For already, by '86, there had been favorites
whom the King had loved and honored—with extraordinary gifts
of titles and offices and with the riches to go with them: Esmé
Stuart, James Stewart, and Patrick, Master of Gray. But his mind
had always proved more than a match for these.

As far as James could tell, he had no equals except for other
Kings.

On the other hand, body and spirit were not so proud or
kingly. At the same time that he rejoiced in his intelligence, flesh
shrank, winced, quailed. He had lived all his life in constant fear
of death by violence. (With every good reason in Scotland.) And
he wore a padded doublet always to protect himself from the
thrust of a knife. Which, so far, had not come.

Cecil, frail and himself almost wholly dependent upon the
power and agility of mind, can understand the contradictions of

the King. Cecil has a deep sympathy for the Scotsman, albeit a sympathy gently but firmly modified by the necessary sense of his own superior abilities.

False humility being, in Cecil's view, as crippling an illusion as rash, intemperate pride.

No question the King has great intelligence, but Cecil's sense of superiority derives from years of experience with the Queen. Her particular ways and means. There is neither question nor doubt in Cecil's mind that the Queen is far more intelligent than James of Scotland. Or, for that matter, than any other Prince, living or dead, that he has known of. And even this is not a matter of natural gifts; though hers are undeniable. Nor of her education; though John Cheke and Roger Ascham were surely equal to George Buchanan and were, in all ways, kinder and more generous pedagogues. Nor could it be defined as the difference in the experience of the two. For, if anything, Elizabeth's life had been as anxious and as dangerous as James's. It is something else. Comprehensive understanding. Fire of imagination lifting her thoughts and her spirit above themselves.

If the figure for it is fire, then he, Cecil, has been well-warmed by standing close. It is this warmth, this sharing of the fire of the Queen, which gives him a sense of superiority over the King of the Scots.

He could tell the King a thing or two, if he should ever choose to do so, about this Queen whom he and his father have served. In fact, he has already told the King a few things. Beginning from the first of the careful, secret letters which he has been exchanging with the King. Letters which are lightly disguised, nicely decorated with little ciphers and mildly enigmatic allusions. Such things as the King takes delight in. But nothing so gnarled or obscure that anyone else except a fool could be fooled for long. Does he imagine the King to be a kind of fool? Even, as he has been called by some, *the wisest fool in Christendom?* The simplicity of the codes and allusions reflects on Cecil and not on the King. Flatters the King by confirming his own superiority. Besides which it gratifies his restless spirit. Allowing him to dispose of these matters with deliberate speed and to be off and about his pleasures. Which he much prefers to the business of state.

Aside from these tropes of conspiracy, Cecil's less obvious message is delivered more like the Queen's. Is more a matter of inference, of implication, of insinuation. That is: it is his aim to say one thing, with clarity and emphasis, while meaning not something else, but something more. So that the meaning of any letter is more than the sum of all its parts. The whole is intended to play directly upon the King's hopes and fears. No hope without fear. No fearing without hoping also. Playing on these as a skilled musician will pick out music from the strings of a lute.

For, as the proverb has it: *There is no music without frets.*

Take this particular letter for instance. The letter he has only just read and tossed aside. Its purpose seems plain enough. To offer a brief, polite excuse for a delay she has taken in responding to his last letter. Which was, evidently, delivered to her by an ambassador. Also to thank him for his concern and apparent joy at her recent escape from the latest plot against her life, the Babington Plot. So named after its young, rich, and altogether foolish leader, Anthony Babington. The letter is dated only days after Babington and more than a dozen others paid for their treason. Undergoing the death on a specially built high gallows at St. Giles' Fields. A few days after that, and only a week before a Queen's Commission, newly created, will assemble at Fotheringhay Castle to try the Queen of Scots.

There is no direct mention of her. It seems to Cecil now, though he cannot be any more certain than was the King then, that there is an obvious allusion to Queen Mary—"And yet when you shall hear all, you will wonder that one accounted wise will use such matter foolishly."

This must have aroused the King's curiosity. Absence of any mention of the Queen of Scots or of the extraordinary Commission and the extraordinary trial—things which James would have heard of from his own sources—served to force him to bring up the subject himself. If that subject were now to be raised between them, it would have to be his doing. It was as if Elizabeth did not consider her plans for the Queen of Scots to be news worth reporting to him. More important to James, it seemed that she was assuming that these things lay beyond the limits of his power.

Whatever her motives might be, the King was left in an awkward position. And *that* (Cecil believes) would have been precisely the Queen's chief motive. To leave him doubtful, puzzling at her motives and all the while feeling an awkward dependency. Finding himself having to wait upon Elizabeth to say or do something before he could do either. What the King could not have imagined then was that the Queen must have already made up her mind not only to see to the trial of the Queen of Scots, but also to entertain seriously the possibility of killing her. Either by murder or execution. The Queen also allowed herself freedom from the first inception to the irrevocable execution, *not* to follow through with her own plan. Permitted herself to be able to change her mind. In any stratagem she sought not to arrive too soon at definitive endings. For she did not imagine that she could understand the future. All that she was sure of was the ineffable strangeness of it. The future was always wilderness. *Terra Incognita* by definition.

She employed gardeners (Burghley, Walsingham, the preeminent examples) to manage her present affairs and to make plans and contingencies for an imaginable future. But it is not the imaginable future which concerns her. It is the wilderness of the unimaginable.

It has ever been the characteristic quality of the Queen's designs that when and if they come to pass, they must seem largely accidental, the results of impulse. That is to say, it should seem that she had never had any plan or design. And insofar as she has, in any given instance, been able to defer firm choices, there is a truth in that misperception.

All of which has added value for her. For whenever an enemy does perceive the direction of one of her stratagems, he can never be sure that she will follow the logic of her own design.

A true dissembler will honor (or fear) her as possibly the greatest dissembler of them all. For whatever happens will seem to have been achieved by her duplicity.

And so by placing the fate of the Queen of Scots in a shadowy future, she could choose to avoid any mention of that future to James.

She used the occasion to play upon the deep-rooted fears of the King whose life had always been in danger since birth. She chose the seasoned hero's easy shrug (knowing that he would be offended by this) and the unarguable statement that only the hand of God had saved her life. Ignoring, for the moment, the busy hands of Walsingham. And then stressing future danger, *the dangers for him,* likely to come from the Jesuits. That warning being one of the practical purposes of this letter. To see if she might frighten James into closing his kingdom to these priests. Or at the very least perhaps she could encourage the King's suspicions of his Catholic subjects and of France and Spain. Anything which might inhibit their influence on him at just this time. Anything which might increase his sense of standing alone in the world. Anything that would increase his sense of dependency on the English Queen.

Only that summer, in June of '86, had she finally awarded him a pension. Something which had been the subject of negotiations between them for years. Something which, in spite of the persuasions of her Council, she had always managed to find reasons not to do. Looking back years later, Cecil can see that concerning payments to James (or to other Scots) there was a strong case either way. The Queen believed that Scots were not to be trusted at any price; therefore that if they had to be bribed, it should always be at the least possible expense. Walsingham and Burghley, and most of the others of the Council, believed that a few thousand pounds, properly distributed, might allow them to control affairs in Scotland. The Queen considered that an unnecessary extravagance. For the most part she did not want to control the affairs of Scotland. Rather, she was content to encourage them to continue in their feuds and factions. So long as they were fighting among themselves there was no need for her to spend much to seek their goodwill. But now she had at last settled a reasonably generous pension on King James. Less than he asked for, but more than he must have expected. This in return for what amounted to a defensive alliance. All that he had received concerning Succession was her (private) assurance that she would not prejudice any lawful claims he might have.

As for the Succession nothing much has changed since then. Except that the Queen is older. And the King is no longer to be called young either. He is, however, a more attractive prospect to many Englishmen these days. Having maintained his government well in that almost ungovernable country. And, favorites or no favorites, he has married a royal princess of Denmark and has produced heirs. If he should come to the English throne there need never be such an urgently confusing time as this again. He brings his own Succession with him.

As recently as March of 1601, soon after Essex ended his days on the scaffold on Tower Green, some prominent Scotsmen came calling upon Sir Robert Cecil in his offices of the Duchy of Lancaster on the Strand. Chief of these were the Earl of Mar, Governor of Edinburgh Castle and Master of the Household for James, Edward Bruce, and David Foulis. With Essex gone and his faction broken and dispersed, they had nowhere else to turn but to Cecil. So he agreed to begin a secret correspondence with King James.

Taking the Queen's letters as a model he wrote a lengthy letter to the King in which he suggested that though his service to his Queen was, as it should be, completely loyal, nevertheless "I perceive when that natural day shall come, wherein your feast may be lawfully proclaimed (which I do wish may be long deferred) such shall not be rejected, as lacking their wedding garment, who have not falsely or untimely wrought for future fortunes."

James was being reminded that even though the end of the Queen's days is certain, his own accession to the throne of England, his "feast," is much less so. It may be lawfully proclaimed. That word *lawfully* is coiled like a snake on the garden path. For there are certain quite serious legal problems, matters which might prohibit James from ruling in England. For, so long as the Queen lives, they cannot be discussed or dealt with.

Moreover, he continued, there was the matter that the Queen's wishes must always be paramount. That if her mind were ever somehow to be set against her cousin, she might be "inclined (if not resolved) to cut off the natural branch and graft upon some wild stock." A prospect which could not have pleased James.

Finally, at the end of his letter, Cecil chose to offer some counsel:

Your Majesty know that jealousy stirreth passion, even between father and son, that passions beget injuries between Princes, and that injuries either given or taken, in your case, breed alienation. To the first weakness in Her Majesty's mind I have already briefly said—That what was possible for art and industry to effect, against the person of a successor in the mind of a possessor, hath been in the highest proportion labored by many against you. Out of this conclusion, that the eyes of Her Majesty's suspicion could not be diverted from other practices, unless it were engraved in her heart that you were impatient of any further attention. It being well known, that as love is of all things subject to the greatest blindness, so fear once multiplied, neither trusteth profession nor heareth reason. To resort therefore to my just grounds, your best approach toward your greatest end, is by Your Majesty's clear and temperate courses, to secure the heart of the Highest, to whose sex and quality nothing is so improper as needless expostulations, or overmuch curiosity in her own actions. The first, showing unquietness in your self, the second challenging some untimely interest in hers.

All of which was sound advice. For as the Scots King had sent many agents to treat with influential men of Court and Council to make his case for him, so in his impatience to settle the issue, he had overlooked the Queen's sensitivity concerning this subject. She would not (and will not) permit it to be discussed. Unless she herself should choose to discuss it. It is a felony to write about the Succession or, for that matter, to be found in possession of any books or pamphlets dealing with it. There is no question but that she could be alienated from her cousin if he should prove to be too demanding.

So Cecil had done the King a good service to caution him. Yet with his emphasis upon dangers, upon the doubtfulness of his cause, Cecil had heightened the King's anxiety. For, from much study of the King's words, his books and literary works and especially his letters, Cecil took him to be a man made easily anxious about things yet to come.

Because the King is hopeful he is also anxious.

Like his father, Cecil believes that when all else may be in doubt, still papers can be trusted. For words, not spoken, but frozen on paper (*even when those words have been intended as a lie*) cannot lie. There is a golden essence of truth in them which cannot be refined away to nothing. And (he imagines) this gold becomes purer with the passing of time.

Take the Queen's letter of the fourth October of '86 again. Something she tells him. After shrugging off danger and casting blame upon the Jesuits, she presents herself as altogether unlike the King in wise magnanimity toward her own guilty, misled subjects: "For my part, I am sorrier that they cast away so many goodly gentlemen than that they sought my ruin. I thank God I have taken more sadness for some that are guilty of this murder than bearing them malice that sought my death. I protest it before God." It was well she did not also protest it before Walsingham or Burghley. From whom she had demanded, in rage against these conspirators, that new and special torments be devised to dispatch them all as painfully as possible. Burghley had patiently explained to her that, under the Law, such a thing was not possible. But that if the full rigor of the sentence for treason were skillfully applied by the executioner the results would be at once sufficiently painful to the victims and terrifying to beholders. And, indeed, upon that high gallows, built so that a huge crowd could witness it well, when the first three conspirators were executed it was done that way. With all the agony the executioner could pluck from their bodies. The crowd was not pleased. Cried out against the cruelty of it. And so the prisoners killed on the next day were, by the Queen's own command, more kindly treated. Allowed to hang and die before being drawn and quartered.

James would have known this. Would have known her to be dissembling when she swore she had borne no malice against the conspirators who had planned to kill her. Do we not read our own faults directly into motives and actions of others? Whatever she might say for herself, he was sure to assume the worst. Therefore why not say whatever it pleased her to say?

But there was more. Well before the fall of '86 she knew him well enough. And had spoken aloud (where it could be heard and was reported) on the subject of his character. The occasion was the execution, in June of '81, of the Earl of Morton, the former Regent. Who had been a friend to England and Elizabeth and an enemy to the Queen of Scots. James, then only a lad of fourteen, had connived with his favorites, Esmé Stuart and James Stewart, to arrest Morton at Council on the last day of December in 1580. The very day before James had spent in the company of old Morton hunting together. And at the end of that day the King declared to him—"Father, only you have reared me. And I will therefore defend you from all your enemies."

When the news was brought to Elizabeth that Morton had been executed in Edinburgh, she was outraged.

"That false Scotch urchin!" she cried out. "He could say he had no friend like Morton and that he would protect him. And then the next day he had him seized and cut off his head. What must I look for from such a double-tongued scoundrel as this?"

Double-tongued scoundrel! False Scotch urchin!

Had she changed her mind? Not so much so that she was embarrassed to lie to him. And then to challenge him, if he dared, to disbelieve her.

But (Cecil wonders) did she really find his duplicity reprehensible? Only when it surprised her. As in the case of Morton. Whose life she might have had the power to save if she had known how threatened he was. But the Queen herself never doubted the efficacy of a lie to protect her crown or her kingdom. Therefore there was (he thinks now) a certain admiration in her anger: "What must I look for from such a double-tongued scoundrel as this?"

Cecil accepts the idea that the essential nature of a man is best revealed by his actions at times of danger. For the King of the Scots the time of greatest trouble, in a lifetime ridden with fears and disappointments, must have been during those months of '86. When the Queen first arranged the trial and condemnation of his mother, then contrived her execution in the Hall at Fotheringhay Castle. No question that the Queen outplayed him. If it can be taken as a kind of game between them.

Once the Queen of Scots had been condemned to die, the Scots (even those many who had opposed Mary) came together against England and Elizabeth. James, waiting upon Elizabeth to act next, but seeming certain she would not dare to take the life of the Queen of Scots, found himself unpopular in his own kingdom. In November he sent one ambassador, Sir William Keith, to intercede for the Queen of Scots. Again in January he sent Sir Robert Melville and the Master of Gray. The latter, as Cecil knows, served Elizabeth as well as the King. As did many another Scotsman. James was willing that his mother should be imprisoned for life. Or banished, perhaps, to some safe country. But she must not be executed.

Cecil knows that the Queen did not take his arguments seriously or consider his pleas for long. For by two clear signs it was plain she could kill the Queen of Scots without much worry: first, that he did not threaten to break off the newly made alliance with England or offer to do without his pension. Secondly, he coupled all his arguments for sparing the Queen of Scots with questions and proposals concerning the Succession. Elizabeth and her Council concluded that his pension and his hopes for the English throne outweighed everything else.

.Cecil nevertheless wonders how the Queen may have judged this. Whether James gained or lost value in her eyes. Certainly he lost some respect. But, even so, he can imagine a certain admiration by her for the young man who, ruthlessly tested, proved to be so ruthless himself. Willingness to sacrifice anything in his lust to be King of Britain was contemptible. Yet on the other hand . . . The notion that he so deeply desired to wear her crown and sit on her throne must have been a flattering one. But to this day Cecil does not know which judgment, contempt or admiration, is paramount in the Queen's estimate. This should not surprise him, for he, too, is full of mixed feelings about the King.

In the last week of January James wrote to Elizabeth once more to try to make a case for sparing the life of the Queen of Scots:

A Madame ma tres chère Soeur & Cousine la Reigne d'Angleterre Madame and Dearest Sister,

If ye could have known what divers thoughts have agitated my mind, since my directing of William Keith unto you, for the soliciting of this matter, to which nature and honor so greatly and unfeignedly bind and oblige me; if, I say, you knew what divers thoughts I have been in, and what just grief I had, weighing deeply the thing itself, if it should so proceed, as God forbid, what events might follow thereupon, what straits I would be driven unto, and amongst the rest how it might peril my reputation amongst my subjects: If these things, I yet say again, were known to you, then I doubt not but you would so far pity my case, as it would easily make you at the first to resolve your own best into it. I doubt greatly in what fashion to write in this purpose, for you have already taken so evil of my plainness, as I fear, if I shall persist in that course, you shall rather be exasperated to passions in reading the words, than by the plainness thereof be persuaded to consider rightly the simple truth. Yet justly preferring the duty of an honest friend to the sudden passions of one who, as soon as they be past, can usually weigh the reasons, then I can set them down. I have resolved in a few words and plain to give you my friendly and best advice, appealing to your ripest judgment to discern thereupon.

Well. Was ever a reader more humbly warned? This letter seems to begin not with the bowing of courtesy, but with the crawling which, they say, is the fashion in the Court of the Great Turk.

All of which acts to blunt sharp words in the letter that follows.

What thing, Madame, can greatlier touch me in honor, that both is a King and a Son, than my nearest neighbor, being in straightest friendship with me, shall put to death a free Sovereign Prince, and my natural Mother, alike in estate and sex to her that so uses her, albeit subject, I grant, to a harder fortune, and touching her nearly in proximity of blood. What law of God can permit, that justice shall strike upon them whom He's appointed supreme dispensors of the same under Him; whom He hath called Gods, and therefore subjected to the censure of none in earth; whose anointing by God cannot be defiled by man unrevenged by the Author thereof; who being supreme and immediate lieutenants of God in heaven, cannot therefore be judged by their equals on earth. What monstrous thing is it that Sovereign Princes themselves should be example-givers of the profaning of their own sacred diadems? Then what should move you to this form of proceeding (supposing the worst, which in good faith I look not for at your hands) honor or profit? Honor were it to you to spare, when it is least looked for? Honor were it to you (which is not only my friendly advice, but earnest suit) to make me and all other Princes in Europe eternally beholden unto you, in granting this my so reasonable request, and not (appardon, I pray you, my free speaking) to put Princes to straits of honor, where through your general reputation and universal (almost) misliking of you may dangerously peril both in honor and utility your person and estate. . . .

And now, Madame, to conclude, I pray you to weigh these few arguments, that as ever I presumed of your nature, so the whole world may praise your subjects for their dutiful care for your preservation, and yourself for your princely pity; the doing whereof only belongs unto you. Respect then, good Sister, this my first so long continued and so earnest request, dispatching my ambassadors with such a comfortable answer, as may become your person to give, and as my loving and honest heart unto you merits to receive. But in case any do vaunt themselves to know further of my mind in this matter than my ambassadors do, who indeed are fully acquainted therewith, I pray you not to take me to be a chameleon, but by the contrary take them to be malicious imposters, as surely they are.

And thus praying you heartily to excuse my rude and longsome letter, I commit you, Madame and dearest Sister, to the blessed protection of the Most High. Who can give you grace so to resolve in this matter, as may be most honorable for you and most acceptable to Him.

From my palace of Holyroodhouse, the twenty-sixth day of January, 1586–87.

Your most loving and affectionate Brother and Cousin,

JAMES R.

What interests Cecil now is not the arguments James mounted in hope of saving his mother's life. If indeed he really feared for her life. Cecil thinks that James misunderstood the Queen, misconstrued her delay. Cecil conceives it is that profound misunderstanding which gives his pleading letters now such a perfunctory character. As if they were matters of form only. Some have thought so. The Queen herself may have thought so, may think so still. She has implied as much. But, as Cecil begins to understand the man, James simply never imagined that his mother would be put to death. Therefore his letters were written, and his arguments, such as they were, were made *so that he might be entitled to feel that he had helped the Queen to make up her*

own mind. Laughable? Hardly; for it was the stock-in-trade of
Burghley (and others) for all those many years. And it remains
the tactic of Sir Robert Cecil. With a difference. That difference
is that more and more she does not appreciate *any* kind of explicit persuasion. Rather, in the same sense that she insists more
upon the rituals of flattery than ever she did as a younger woman,
so she prefers to imagine that she has arrived at all decisions by
herself. That it is she who persuades Council, counseling them,
rather than the reverse. Perhaps it was always so. If so, then
James erred badly if he hoped to gain favor by a demonstration
of his powers of persuasion. Even if he had succeeded, he would
have been recognized by her not as an equal Prince, but rather
as a young man with the makings of an excellent clerk.

No matter.

Whatever his motives, the case failed. And that was that.
Words could not save the Queen of Scots.

More to the point for Cecil and for England are his views of
kingship. The most he could have gained from presenting his
philosophy of kingship, in the letter was her weary annoyance
at his presumption to seek to teach her what it means to be a
Prince.

No one, except a rebel or a fool, would deny that Kings are indeed God's viceroys on earth. Beyond that claim, however, are
many subjects for debate. Our Queen might well agree with
James in theory that Kings are subject to no law on earth and,
likewise, are not subject to any kind of judgment. Even by their
equals. She might think that a pretty theory. But she knows better. She will vigorously defend her prerogative and privileges.
But she prefers the limits of her power to be more cloudy than
clear. With Parliament, indeed with her own Council, it has been
a business of give and take. And she has taken care not to challenge the Laws of her own kingdom.

Since that time there is more evidence to go by. Poet and
scholar, James has written two books on this subject—*The Trew
Law of Free Monarchies* (1598) and *Basilikon Doron* (1599).

When Cecil first read these books, Essex was still alive and the
chief supporter of the claims of King James. Therefore Cecil
studied them for clues to the character of a man who might be
an enemy to him. Recently he has examined them with more

sympathy. Seeking to know the man through his theories. Yet also bearing in mind that these were written to be understood in Scotland. By arrogant and almost ungovernable lords and by a Kirk which has strenuously resisted his view that the King's authority is inherently ecclesiastical as well as secular. They were also written *against* other works. Especially the celebrated *De Juri Regni apud Scotos* of '79. Written by George Buchanan, his old teacher whom he had feared and hated to Buchanan's dying day. What troubled James most about Buchanan's book was the argument that it is the right of a people to resist tyranny. As, indeed, the Scots had done with both his grandmother the Regent and his mother the Queen. And as some had tried to do with him.

By the time he came to write his own books on the subject, Buchanan was dead and he had had the old man's work banned and burned. Yet it had been popular in Europe and in Scotland. It needed to be answered. And so he did so. Basing his argument upon the special divinity which is conferred upon Kings. "Kings are called Gods by the prophetical King David," he wrote in *Trew Law*, "because they sit upon God His throne in the earth, and have the court of their administration to give unto Him."

And in *Basilikon Doron*, addressed to his son and heir Prince Henry as a guide to kingship, he says the same thing with more emphasis.

"Therefore (my Son) first of all things learn to know and love God, to whom ye have a double obligation; first for that he made you a man; and next, for that he made you a little God to sit on his Throne, and to rule over other men. Remember that this glistering worldly glory of Kings is given them by God to teach them . . . so to glister and shine before their people, in all works of sanctification and righteousness, that their persons as bright lamps of godliness and virtue, may, going in and out before their people, give light to all their steps."

These books are King James's letters to the world. A portrait of himself intended to be more attractive than revealing.

For the time being, it is sufficient to know that James has assumed that a literal divinity is conferred with a crown. Which may make his studies of Scripture and of history, and especially of the intricately snarled chronicles of Scotland, more than a little baffling to him. But which may also serve to make the laws and customs of the English difficult for him to fathom. If and when that should be a practical matter.

The last chance for James to act on his mother's behalf came in that January. While his ambassadors were there in London yet another (timely) conspiracy against the English Queen was uncovered by Burghley and Walsingham. She wrote to James about this. Briefly, but with a clear warning of what was to come.

You may see whether I keep the serpent that poisons me, when they confess to have reward. By saving of her life they would have had mine. Do I not make myself a goodly prey for every wretch to devour? Transfigure yourself into my state, and suppose what you ought to do, and thereafter weigh my life and reject the care of murder, and shun all baits that may untie our amities. And let all men know that Princes know best their own laws. . . .

To my very good brother and cousin, the King of Scots.

Transfigure yourself into my state. Ah. Exactly his hope, his dream, his intention. And yet exactly what he was incapable of doing. Still, that invitation may have inspired him. For it allowed him, if he were foolish enough, to misinterpret it as doubt and weakness on her part.

Her next letter to him came in February within days of the death of the Queen of Scots. It is a letter which seems, still, to be weighing and sifting choices she must make. Nothing in it could have seemed final. Which was just as well. Seeing as Elizabeth would claim that the death of the Queen of Scots had never been intended by her.

Your commissioners tell me that I may trust her in the hand of some indifferent Prince, and have all her cousins and allies promise she will no more seek my ruin. . . . Suppose you I am so mad to trust my life in another's hand and send it out of my own? . . . Let your Councilors, for your honor, discharge their duty so much to you as to declare the absurdity of such an offer. And, for my part, I do assure myself too much of your wisdom, as, though like a most natural good son you charge them to seek all means they could devise with wit or judgment to save her life.

Yet I cannot, nor do not, allege any fault to you of these persuasions. For I take it that you will remember, that advice or desires ought ever to agree with the surety of the party sent to honor of the sender. Which, when both you weigh, I doubt not but that your wisdom will excuse my need, and wait my necessity, and not accuse me either of malice or of hate.

How typical of her. To term his idea of sending the Queen of Scots to the care of a neutral Prince as an absurdity concocted by his ambassadors on their own. Nothing seems certain here. Except that she will not consider letting the Queen of Scots leave England.

By the time James received this letter the Queen of Scots was dead.

And here beginneth a kind of stage play. World for the stage.

The value of which performance, to the Queen and to all England, depended on ambiguity. The question was not one of truth but of belief. Queen must act as if she truly believed her own accounting. As if she expected others to believe it as well.

Her first public reaction to the news of Mary's death was of astonishment and grief. The Court was at Greenwich in that second week of February when the news from Fotheringhay arrived. It was Burghley himself who concluded that it should be kept from the Queen. And so he ordered it to be. . . .

Cecil knows his father would not have dared to do such a thing if it had not been understood between him and the Queen. So that she could have an adequate occasion to be surprised. And then to react to the news in such a way as to confirm and strengthen her story. There was no other reason to try to hide the news. And there could be no hiding of it. On the ninth of February the Queen, in the company of her Maids of Honor, came back to the Palace from an afternoon of riding in the Park to hear on the breeze from upriver the bells of London.

"Why are the bells ringing out so merrily?" she asked.

"Because of the death of the Queen of Scots."

First astonishment, then grief. Finally rage at her Council. Burghley banished from Court. Walsingham sick. Her secretary, Mr. William Davison, clapped into the Tower. For handing on the warrant for the Queen of Scots' execution. Which, indeed,

Queen Elizabeth had signed. But which, she insisted, she had no intention of acting upon.

She promptly wrote to James.

My Dear Brother,

I would you knew (though not felt) the extreme dolor that overwhelms my mind for that miserable accident which (far contrary to my meaning) has befallen. I have now sent Sir Robert Carey, this kinsman of mine, whom, ere now, it has pleased you to favor, to instruct you truly of that which is too irksome for my pen to tell you. I beseech you, that as God and many more know how innocent I am in this case, so you will believe me, that if I had bid aught, I would have bid by it. I am not so base-minded that fear of any living creature or Prince should make me afraid to do that which were just; or done so to deny the same. I am not of so base a lineage, nor carry so vile a mind. But as not to disguise fits most a King, so will I never dissemble my actions, but cause them to show even as I meant them. Thus assuring yourself of me, that as I know this was deserved; yet, if I meant it, I would never lay it upon others' shoulders, no more will I damnify myself that thought it not. The circumstances it may please you to learn from this bearer. And, for my part, think you have not in the world a more loving kinswoman, nor a more dear friend, than myself, nor any that will watch more carefully to preserve you and your estate. And who shall seek otherwise to persuade you, judge them to be more partial to others than to you. And thus in haste, I leave off troubling you, beseeching God to send you a long reign.

Your most assured loving Sister and Cousin,

Elizabeth R.

The audacity dazzles Cecil. Anything less would have implied some sense of guilt. She accepts none. It was all, simply, a *miserable accident.* . . .

After an appropriate delay, in early March, back came reply of King James:

Madame and dearest sister,

By your letter and bearer, Robert Carey, your servant and ambassador, you purge yourself of yon unhappy fact. As, on the one part, considering your rank and sex, consanguinity and long-professed goodwill to the defunct, together with your many and solemn attestations of your innocency, I dare not wrong you so far as not to judge honorable your unspotted part therein; so, on the other side, I wish your honorable behavior in all times hereafter may fully persuade the whole world of the same. And, as for my part, I look that you will give me at this time such a full satisfaction, in all respects, as shall be a means to strengthen and unite this isle, establish and maintain the true religion, and oblige me to be, as I was before, your most loving

JAMES R.

How easy it proved to be! He allowed himself only one sly little moment—the hope that the rest of the world (depending, of course, upon her good behavior) might come to believe her as much as he did. Otherwise it is a bill for payment due. A request to be named her Successor in order "to strengthen and unite this isle, establish and maintain the true religion," and to win back his love and goodwill.

The success of this request may be judged by the plain truth that it is still unresolved these sixteen years later.

There was no dancing in Scotland when the Queen of Scots was put to death. How James received the news was in question. Some said he took it with a strict, impassive face. Others reported that he became ill and took to his bed. Still others said that he could scarcely contain his joy.

"Now I am sole King!" he cried out.

He put on purple for mourning, but declined to respond to the challenge of his nobility. Who said that armor was the only proper mourning dress for the dead Queen.

There was much talk of revenge and punishment. And nothing came of it.

The Queen and everyone else of importance were all too busy preparing against the enormous power of Spain to trouble themselves much about Scotland or its unhappy King. In '87, in his raid on Cádiz, Sir Francis Drake caused the delay of the Armada. But by late spring of '88, it was certain that the Armada would soon sail and that at last the great Enterprise Against England would begin.

It was necessary, then, to secure herself against danger from

Scotland. And for the Queen to counteract Spanish influence and any offers which they had made to win over James. The occasion of this letter was twofold: to acknowledge the return of her most recent ambassador to him (she had sent her close kinsman, Henry Carey, Lord Hunsdon) and the news that, with some English aid from the castle at Carlisle, King James had been able to capture and destroy the castle of Lochmaben in Dumfriesshire. Which had been in the hands of Catholic rebels for a long time.

To our good brother and cousin the King of Scotland:

My pen, dear brother, hath remained so long dry that I suppose it would hardly have taken ink again, but, mollified by the good justice that with your own person you have been pleased to execute at Lochmaben, together with the large assurance that your words have given to some of my ministers, which all doth make me ready to drink most willingly a draft of the River Lethe. . . .

She announces *herself* as ready to forgive and forget. And emphatically (again) insists upon her innocence in the death of the Queen of Scots.

God, the cherisher of all hearts ever so have misericord of my soul as my innocency in that matter deserveth, and no otherwise; which invocation were too dangerous for a guilty conscience; as I have commanded the bearer more at large to tell you. And for your part, my dear brother, think, and that with most truth, that, if I find you willing to embrace it, you shall find me the carefulest Prince of your quiet government, ready to assist you with force, with treasure, counsel, or any thing you shall have need of, as in honor you can require, or upon cause you shall need. You may the more soundly trust my vows, for never yet were they stained, neither will I make you the first on whom I shall bestow untruth, which God will not suffer me live unto.

I have millions of thanks to render you, that so frankly told Carey such offers as were made you, which I doubt not but you shall ever have cause to rejoice that you refuse. For where they mean to weaken your surest friend, so be you assured they intended to subject you and yours. For you see how they deal even with their own in all countries lesser than their one; and therefore God, for your best, I assure myself, will not let you fall into such a danger, under the cloak, for all that, of harming other and advancing you. But I hope you will take Ulysses' wax to save you from such sirens. It were most honorable for you, if it so please you, to let them know that you never sent for their horse, though some of your lords (too bold with you in many of their notions and too saucy in this) made believe you consented to their message, which they themselves desired your pardon for. This will make them fear you more hereafter, and make them afraid to attempt you to weaken your assured friend. If I deserve not your amity, persecute me as your foe; but, being yours, use me like a Prince who feareth none but God.

Your most assured loving sister and cousin,

Elizabeth R.

So long as the Spanish threat continued that summer, so did the letters. Professing friendship and goodwill. And all based upon serious doubts about James. Cecil is familiar with Lord Hunsdon's memorandum on the King. Which the Queen took to heart.

"Look not for amity or kind dealing at his hand," Hunsdon wrote. "If there were any good inclination in him toward Your Highness, which I neither find nor believe to be, yet he hath such bad company about him, and so maliciously bent against Your Highness, they will not suffer him to remain in it two days together."

And so it continued until the Armada came and went, defeated and dispersed. Immediately after she had the news she wrote to James. In part to triumph, to be sure. But more to be sure that he would not come to the aid of any Spanish vessels blown to his coasts. And that he should keep a leash on his own Catholic lords who had been dealing with Spain and hoping for the Armada's success.

To my very good brother the King of the Scots.

Now may appear, my dear brother, how malice conjoined with might strivest to make a shameful end to a villainous beginning; for, by God's singular favor, having their fleet well beaten in our narrow seas, and pressing, with all violence, to achieve some watering place, to continue their intended invasion, the winds have carried them to your coasts. Where I doubt not they shall receive small success and less welcome. Unless those lords, so traitorlike, would belie their own Prince and promise another King relief in your name, be suffered to live at liberty, to dishonor you, peril you, and advance some other (which God forbid you suffer them live to do). Therefore I send you this gentleman, Sir Robert Sidney, a rare young man and wise, to declare unto you my full opinion in this great cause, as one that will never abuse you to serve my own turn; nor will you do ought that I myself would not perform if I were in your place. You may assure yourself that, for my part, I doubt no whit but that all this tyrannical proud and brainsick attempt will be the beginning, though not the end, of the ruin of that King that, most unkingly, even in the midst of talking peace, begins this wrongful war. He hath procured my greatest glory that meant my sorest wrack, and hath so dimmed the light of his sunshine, that who hath a will to obtain shame let them keep his forces company. But all this, for yourself's sake, let not the friends of Spain be suffered to yield them force. For though I fear not the end of the sequel, yet if, by leaving them unhelped, you may increase the English hearts unto you, you shall not do the worst deed for your behalf. . . . Look well into it, I beseech you.

The necessity of this matter makes my scribbling the more speedy hoping that you will measure my good affection with the right balance of my actions, which to you shall be ever such as I have professed, not doubting the reciprocal of your behalf, according as my last messenger to you hath at large signified, for which I render you a million grateful thanks together, for the last general prohibition to your subjects not to foster or aid our general foe, of which I doubt not the observation of the ringleaders be safe in your hands; as knoweth God, Who ever have you in His blessed keeping, with many happy years of reign.

Your most assured loving sister and cousin

ELIZABETH R.

Again it was the Succession, dangled as bait before his eyes, which the Queen used to persuade him to do what she wanted.—

"For though I fear not the end of the sequel, yet if, by leaving them unhelped, you may increase the English hearts unto you, you shall not do the worst deed for your behalf."

In truth, weather and winds saved James as they had saved England. For the Spanish ships were blown clear around Scotland, except for a few shipwrecked along the coast. To the King, as to many, even in England, the fate of the Armada must have seemed to be a greater disaster to Spain than it truly was. But Elizabeth knew Philip of Spain well enough to be sure that so long as he had any resources he would not hesitate spending them to conquer England. And that now that he had suffered a disastrous humiliation, there could be no negotiations for peace. That he possessed the power to continue to make war for as long as he chose to.

Thus, even as bonfires roared and bells rang and rang, as crowds cheered and as the men of her Court were suddenly warriors, all scoured armor and grandiose plans, even as she smiled and smiled, acknowledging the praise and prayers of her people, her inmost heart must have been as heavy and cold as a stone.

Even his father imagined (at first) that a victory or, anyway, a successful conclusion to this war was now possible. God had puffed His great cheeks and made the wind and blown away the Papist Armada. Surely God would continue to bless and favor His people.

The Queen believed only what had happened. But knew what was sure to happen next. Knowing, as if the truth of it had been suddenly lit as lightning can fill a night with a daylight brightness, that only her death could change anything. Knowing that even the death of Philip could not bring peace. Far from it. His heirs would be compelled, out of Spanish honor, to honor his vision. Knowing, then, in the sad wisdom of the heart, that this great victory settled nothing and that the war would go on and on. That more English blood would be spilled than all the wine flowing in celebration from the conduits of London and Westminster. That, sooner and later, more bodies by far than all these shouting crowds would die or be crippled by it. Knowing that they would come to hate her. That all this energy would turn against her, and, indeed, against themselves, as war continued. With its little rosary of victories and defeats. With its unimaginable cost in blood and treasure. Knowing that the next time they will ring the bells and fire the bonfires and dance in the streets with this much clamor and joy will be precisely then—at the death of her.

So, even as she smiled and smiled, she was, in a true sense, celebrating her own death. Was witness to what it would be like here after she died.

Smiling and smiling and smiling.

Like a skull.

And it is all there in her letter to James. Though it is put in the terms of a future for Philip: . . . that all this tyrannical proud and brainsick attempt *will be the beginning, though not the end, of the ruin of that King.* . . .

James may have ascribed the tone of her letter to weariness and doubt. Even to fear. But never mind his misapprehension. More to the point: he, who seems to have spent most of his energy for most of his days in dreaming of the future and waiting for it to arrive, seems not to have been able to imagine what that future would be.

One of the things it meant was that the exchange of letters between them continued. Regularly or irregularly according to events.

Sometimes warmly. As on the occasion of the King's marriage to young Anne of Denmark, a marriage of which the Queen was most approving.

And in the meanwhile, let it content you to give me so much right as to assure yourself that no witness there of so princely a pact shall wish it more success, nor greater lasting joy than myself. . . .

Letters of congratulation and joy upon the birth of his children. Letters of thanksgiving at one and another of his remarkable escapes from (real and contrived) dangers.

It amuses Cecil that even in her official letters she could not resist a chance to apply her usual pressure. Urging him to act more vigorously against his Catholic subjects. Forever pushing him toward the exercise of justice. And thereby, as Cecil sees it, committing himself more openly to the Protestant cause. Or, more aptly, to her cause. Making himself ever more dependent on her.

Nor could she ever seem to relax her pedagogical manner. She would somehow (to what end?) teach him how to be a King. And so her letters, whether of approval or disapproval, almost always contain instruction of one kind or another.

Slacking of due correction engenders bold minds for new crimes. And if my counsels had all as well been followed as they were truly meant, your subjects had now better known their King, and you had no more need of further justice.

Advance not such as hang their hopes on other strings than you may tune. Them that gold can corrupt, think not your gifts can assure. Who once have made shipwreck of their country, let them enjoy it. Weed out the weeds lest the best corn fester. . . .

You have had many treasons which too tenderly you have wrapped up. I pray God the cinders of such a fire breed not one day your ruin. God is witness that I malice none, but for your security is the only care of my writing. I desire no blood, but God save yours. Only this my long experience teacheth me: when a King neglects himself, who will make them enemies for him?

A long-rooted malady, falling to many relapses, argues, by reason, that the body is so corrupt that it may be patched but never sound. When great infections light on many, it almost poisoneth the whole country. It were better, therefore, that the greater part were kept solid though some infected perish. Preserve the better part and let example fear the follower.

I hope that you will remember, that who seeketh two strings to one bow, they may shoot strong, but never straight. And if you suppose that Princes' causes be veiled so covertly that no intelligence can betray them, deceive not yourself. We old foxes can find shifts to save ourselves from others' malice and can come by the knowledge of the greatest secret, especially if it touches our free hold.

Let not shades deceive you, which may take away best
substance from you, when they can turn but into dust or smoke.
An upright demeanor bears ever more poise than all disguised
shows of good can do. Remember that a bird of the air, if no other
instrument, to an honest King shall stand instead of many feigned
practices, to utter aught may any wise touch him.

Assure yourself that no greater peril can ever befall you, nor
any King else, than to take for payment evil account; for they
deride such, and make their prey of their neglect. There is no
Prince alive, but if he show fear or yielding, but he shall have
tutors enough, though he be out of minority.

I confess that divers be the affections of many men, some to
one, some to another; but my rule of trust shall never fail me,
when it is grounded, not on the sands of every man's humor, but
on the steady rock of approved fact.

Judgment of others was not necessary (after she had endured
some time as a Queen) to build her confidence. But the flattery
of others was and is demanded.

Even James had to be prepared to be a flatterer at the appropriate times.

And except for some flourishes of a high and weighty style,
James has found few occasions which have allowed him to address the Queen in a pedagogical fashion. A few aphorisms scattered here and there. Like wild flowers growing among weeds.
But for the most part the King has always been on the defensive.
Most often forced into that posture by the Queen. Who is not
only forever lecturing him upon the subject of kingship, but also
demanding explanations of his actions. He so often has had to
begin letters with apology. Apologizing not only for things done
and left undone, but also for his words. Words which he must
claim to have been well meant, but somehow misinterpreted.

Over the years the King has often found himself craving the
pardon of the Queen. In the epistolary quarrels between them
when, teeth gritted in fixed smiles of politeness, they have attempted to settle the issue of frays between their subjects, especially along the ragged Borders. Or have sought justice, asking

that some malefactor or other be returned to face trial. As if justice were a contest between them. When you gamble with the Queen (Cecil well knows), it is not necessary that she should win every hand to be happy, but when she does win a hand she must be paid in full then and there. There is no waiting for the end of the game to reckon up winnings.

It may have been greatly satisfactory to the Queen to know, even before the execution of the Queen of Scots, that nothing in the world (beyond preservation of his own flesh and bones) seemed to be more important to James than his pension and his hopes for the Succession. The latter impinges upon the former. To this extent. Very often, so frequently as to belie any other explanation than as a pattern of deliberate forgetfulness, payment of James's annuity has been late. Treaty or no treaty, he has been kept waiting and often required to remind her of the promised payment. And then, upon the receipt of it, must thank her profusely. Which manages to multiply his expense of gratitude for the original promise by precisely the number of payments that must be made.

In short, it is as if he must renegotiate his treaty for each payment.

She knows that he cannot do without his pension. He would be absurdly destitute without it. It is reported that he has not one full set of plate to his name and must borrow from his nobility for any large feasts or banquets. Moreover, he cannot accept, openly at least, gifts from other sovereigns without losing this one.

And he must tolerate this, *like the poor cousin that he is*, without anger. At the least sign of impatience he has been chastised. At each (rare) display of anger he has been treated to a taste of *her* anger and to the nearest thing to a box on the ears or a slap in the face that can be conveyed by words on paper.

For a loving friend anxious to reassure the King and to assist him to shore up the power of his sovereignty, the Queen has displayed a remarkable capacity for discovering all kinds of enemies in his own kingdom—the Catholic lords, the preachers of the Kirk, his very Councilors. If he has truly believed her, he must have imagined himself to be ringed on all sides by hostile enemies. But whether or not he believed her, nevertheless doubts were planted and continually cultivated. She fed fuel to his fears. Not the least of those fears was (and is still) the fear of *her*, of her habitual ambiguity, of her evidently passionate and impulsive temperament, of her undeniable duplicity. And, finally, of her rage. Which, from time to time, exploded. As if to justify his worst apprehensions.

I doubt whether shame or sorrow have had the upper hand when I read your last lines to me. Who, of judgment deemed me not simple, could suppose that any answers you have writ me should satisfy, nay, enter into the opinion of anyone not void of four senses, leaving out the first.

When the first blast of a strange unused and seldom-heard-of sound had pierced my ears, I supposed that flying fame, who with swift quills often passes with the worst, had brought report of some untruth; but when too many records in your open parliament were witnesses of such pronounced words, not more to my disgrace than to your dishonor, who did forget that (above all other regard) a Prince's word ought utter naught of any, much less of a King, than such as to which truth might say "Amen." Besides your neglecting all care of yourself (what danger of reproach, besides somewhat else might light upon you) you have chosen so unseemly a theme to charge your only careful friend withal, of such matter (were you not amazed of all senses) could not have been expected at your hands; of such imagined untruths as never were once thought of in our time. I do wonder what evil spirits have possessed you, to set forth such infamous devices, void of any show of truth. I am sorry that you have so willfully fallen from your best stay, and will needs throw yourself into the whirlpool of bottomless discredit. Was the haste so great to hye to such oprobry, as that you would pronounce a never-thought-of action afore you had but asked the question of her that best could tell it? I see well that we two be of very different natures, for I vow to God I would not corrupt my tongue with an unverified, uncertain report of the greatest foe I have, much less could I distract my best-deserving friend with a spot so foul as scarcely may ever be removed. Could you root the desire for gifts from your subjects upon no better ground than this quagmire, which to pass you scarcely may, without the slip

of your own disgrace? Shall embassies be sent to foreign Princes
laden with instructions of your rashly advised charge? I assure
you the travail of your words shall pass the boundaries of many
lands, with an imputation of such levity, as when the true
sunshine of my sincere dealing and extraordinary care ever for
your safety and honor shall overshade too far the dim and misty
clouds of false invectives. I never yet loved you so little as not to
moan your infamous dealings which you are in mind. . . .
Bethink you of such dealings and set your labor upon such
mends as best may. Though not right, yet salve some piece of
this overslip. And be assured, that you deal with such a King as
will bear no wrongs and endure no infamy. The examples have
been so lately seen as they can hardly be forgotten, of a far
mightier and potenter Prince than many that Europe hath. Look
you not therefore that without large amends I may or will ignore
such indignities. We have sent this bearer, Bowes, whom you
may safely credit, to signify such particularities as fits not a
letter's talk. And so I recommend you to a better mind and more
advised conclusions. Praying God to guide you for your best and
to deliver you from sinister advice. . . .

Your more readier sister than your
self hath done, for that is fit,

ELIZABETH R.

Poor James. Forever having to make "large amends." Apologizing, explaining, defending words and actions. And at those
rare times when the shoe was on the other foot, when it was *he*
who was in the right and (it seemed) *she* who must find a way
to explain or apologize, he was treated to yet other forms of her
indefatigable guile. Silence was one kind of reply. A month or
two or more, followed by a letter which made apology merely for
silence and delay, explaining these away as the result of too
much necessary busyness. Without any reference to the subject
of his earlier complaint. Leaving it for him to try to return to
the subject of it. If he dared to.

Another tack of hers: to answer him with perfect innocence, as
if confused by any complaints that he might possibly have.

It is very welcome to us, and at all times shall be, that you, invited as you write by our example and by the obligations of true kindness, do use plainness in opening unto us any thing that lies in your heart. But why at this time the same is used as a means to obtain the curing of some wound (as your letter doth insinuate) we do not well understand. For in the examination of all our actions toward you, we do not find that any thing hath passed from us that may be construed for a wound, except the same language of plainness, which yourself do well affirm to be an undisseverable companion of true friendship, but do change habit when it cometh from us and not from others; with which contradiction if we may know your mind to be possessed, and that our frank and real dealing hath (out of your own apprehension) strucken deeper than we intended, or bred any other conceipt in your mind than in his own nature the sincere and mutual expressing of each other's thoughts should do between friends, we will from henceforth be more reserved; as being one who, neither in deed nor in word, either have or mean to violate our former just and affectionate profession.

Leaving the King regretting that he complained to her about anything in the first place.

It could be a subject fit for laughter. How a wonderfully clever Queen was able to control her young cousin (and all his neighboring northern kingdom) without the use of force of arms. And without fulfilling the usual requirements of large bribes and pensions. Indeed without spending more than the most frugal sums. And how? Chiefly by and through words. Her letters. No small victory in that mastery over a King who is poet and scholar. Defeating him, then, on his own ground and with his own favorite weapons.

But there is the much larger matter of the Succession. Which was the chief, if not the only, reason that her crafty game with him had so long succeeded. For, first to last, he would sacrifice almost anything to achieve that ambition. The more it had been dangled and deferred, the more his hunger for it increased. So that, as he grew into maturity and wisdom in other things, the dream of the Succession grew stronger also, from desire to lust to (by now) obsession. Meaning that if he were willing to offer up his mother's life for the sake of his dream, then by now his willingness to sacrifice had increased that much more. In a sense Elizabeth's letters, her often arrogant pedagogy, her long-winded and emphatic advice upon any and all subjects that interested her, whether or not these in any way truly concerned her, the ice of her sarcasm and the fury of her unbaited temper, all these things tested and proved to her that his dream had in no way diminished.

It must have proved something to him also. That if a man can learn to swallow pride and to live with shame, then he is possessed of greater power to realize his hopes than many another who values the world's estimate. That is, James had learned from the Queen the truth that every good servant (even Cecil himself) must come to know—the heady, liberating power of outward and visible humility. Learned that shame and humiliation, which James had known since childhood, can not only be borne, but also can sometimes lead to more profit than honor and pride. Many a proud man, among those who dazzle the world into admiration, has died shamefully to preserve and defend . . . *what?* The very pride and honor he lost with his life. King James is a student of Scripture and much taken with the Sermon on the Mount. It may be that he has learned how (literally) the meek may inherit a goodly portion of the earth.

If this is true, then the Queen has done right. Has been just and fair with him. For she has taught him what he must know to be a King of England. Others were willing, like the Queen's grandfather, to fight to possess the crown; that is, to wager their own lives, and the lives of many others, to seize it if they could. But who among them, if any, could wait for it humbly? Who would be willing to live for it, upon the hope of it only?

Cecil doubts that she would, even in anger or out of perversity, name any other successor than James. Provided that James continues to play the role she assigned to him. The moment of final decision for the Queen, as Cecil sees it, came after the Essex rebellion. It was then that she could have denied him his hopes. And with justice, too.

In April of 1601 she sent a lengthy letter to James. To be carried by special ambassadors, who had come to England evidently to plead for Essex's life. While seeking to determine how much might be known concerning the King's friendship with

Essex. And to learn what they could about the King's right at the Succession. In particular they came to propose that James might be awarded some lands in England which had once belonged to his grandmother, Margaret, Countess of Lennox. Thinking thereby to circumvent the English law which forbade the throne to anyone not in possession of land in England and (at the same time) forbade a foreigner to own estates in England. Thinking that if he were awarded his grandmother's estates, he could claim to be *de facto* an Englishman. But thinking (truly) that the Queen's response to this request would give a strong clue concerning the Succession.

Of the Essex rebellion she said little and, as usual, was both casual and indirect. Yet also pedagogical.

> And where your ambassadors have congratulated us from you
> on the occasion of our happy prevention of the late treasonable
> attempts, the suppression whereof, praised be God, fell out to be
> only the work of one day, we do accept in very good part that
> office from you, and requite you with this good wish, that the
> like may never befall you or at least be as easily passed over; that
> being utterly extinguished in twelve hours which was in hatching
> divers years.

Surely, Cecil thinks, there is an implication which will not be lost on the King, that she knows more about this plot than she will choose to say. Surely there is a message in the ease with which the plot fell to pieces.

Much of the rest of the letter, all but the final paragraph, is concerned with matters of business between them. Finally she comes to treat the problem of the Countess of Lennox's lands:

> Lastly, touching your desire to have some lands where the title
> remains yet undecided, we will speak shortly to you, that we
> found of all things most strange, considering how well ye have
> discerned our disposition therein heretofore that such demand
> should be renewed, since yourself cannot be ignorant that some
> consequences which depend thereupon hath made us forbear to
> dispose of it one way or the other. All which considered, seeing
> you profess so clear a desire to remove all scruples, we hope to
> hear no more of any of these matters, which are so unworthy of

our dispute, who have and do resolve to nourish and perform all
princely correspondency, which can be by nothing more
disgraced than when our common adversaries shall see, that
when new causes rise not, old and bypassed scruples are revived.

. . . we hope to hear no more of any of these matters . . .
So much for the King of Scotland and his latest stratagem to
assure himself of the Succession. Her letter must have chilled
him well. As if written in ice.

And yet. . . .

His ambassadors returned to Scotland with other news and letters. Among them the first letter to the King from Sir Robert
Cecil.

It was the King who initiated the correspondence between
them, once he had some sense of certainty about Cecil. He wrote
to Cecil as soon as his special ambassadors, Mr. Edward Bruce
and John Erskine, Earl of Mar, had returned to Scotland and reported to the King what had been understood between them in
Cecil's offices of the Duchy of Lancaster in the old Savoy. The
King (Cecil knew this as soon as they did) had sent them with
instructions to warn Cecil to support the claims of the King or be
prepared to suffer the consequences. The King was not dreaming
that his ambassadors would arrive to find Essex executed and all
his faction scattered. Finding no one stronger than Mr. Secretary.
They saw that threats and bluster would not do. Cecil might not
promise the Succession to James. Clearly no one in England
could do that and be believed. But just as clearly (it seemed to
them) no one could now succeed to the throne in the face of
Cecil's opposition. The King could never *peacefully* come to the
throne if Cecil were prepared to oppose him. With Essex gone—
and who could know, for certain, how much Cecil knew of the
dealings between Essex and the King of Scots?—they must now
deal directly with Cecil.

Thus the first letter from James, with its quaint little code—30
for the King, 10 for Cecil, 3 for Lord Henry Howard.

I am most heartily glad that 10 hath now at last made choice
of two so fit and confident ministers with whom he has been
honorably plain in the affairs of 30, assuring 10 that 30 puts more
confidence in them, according to the large and long proof that he

hath had of them than in any other that follows him, like as 10 is most beholden unto them for the honorable report that they have made of him to 30, to whom they have, upon the peril of their credit, given full assurance of the sincerity of 10. . . .

Something more than the end of Essex's power was required before Cecil could seriously begin to support James. Convenient that Cecil's cousin, spymaster Anthony Bacon, had died at the same time. Bacon, long in correspondence with James, could have caused difficulty. Would have made any kind of correspondence with James much too dangerous to pursue. And, as the King's first words serve to stress, it was essential to have trustworthy messengers. There had been earlier opportunities for Cecil to begin to treat with the King. But he could never trust those who suggested it. Cecil has not managed to prevail by trusting other men with his fate. It is rather because he feels sure that the King trusts his ambassadors.

And because 30 cannot have the occasion to speak face to face with 10, that, out of his own mouth, he may give him full assurance of his thankful acceptance of his plain and honorable dealing, he therefore prays 10 to accept of his long approved and trusty 3, both as a surety of his thankfulness and his constant love to him in all times hereafter, as also to be a sure and secret interpreter betwixt 30 and 10 in the opening of their minds to one another; whom 10 hath the better cause to like and to trust, since, long before this time, 3 dealt very earnestly with 30 to take a good conceipt of 10, offering himself to be a dealer betwixt them. Whereupon 30 was contented that 3 should deal between Essex and 10, for a conformity betwixt them, as well as for 30 in his own time, but that 10 mistrusted and aspiring mind of Essex, 30 cannot but commend, taking it for a sure sign that 10 would never allow a subject should climb to so high a place, and that he should ever be in thrall to a subject that hath been from childhood trained up in the service of a free Prince. . . .

That they should likewise make use of Lord Henry Howard (3) suited Cecil well. Lord Henry has been corresponding with the King for years now. And before that he was in correspondence with the Queen of Scots. And it was once the rumor that he had hopes to marry her. Brother to the Duke of Norfolk (who was executed for treason) Lord Henry has been continually in and out of difficulties. Mostly he has been out of favor with the Queen. His nephew, Philip Howard, Earl of Arundel (who, like Sir Philip Sidney was a godson of King Philip II of Spain) was implicated in the Throckmorton Plot. Finally was convicted of treason and sentenced to death. Lord Henry himself is Catholic, but with the understanding, if not the approval, of the Queen. He is obliged to Cecil who managed his release from Fleet Prison so that he could travel to Italy. The Queen has long given evidence of disliking and distrusting him.

And James?

Well. Here is a member of the great and ancient Howard family. A family which has been for generations close to the crown, kin to the crown, and mostly out of favor. Except, of course, for the Lord Admiral, the aging Earl of Nottingham, who is much favored by the Queen. The King has something to offer to Lord Henry and to all the Howards—hope of restoration to former glory. Thus Lord Henry's support has some value to the King, and Henry may be trusted. He has nowhere else to offer himself. Besides, there is a natural affinity between the two men. Lord Henry is a scholar, also. Indeed he has lectured at Cambridge and might have embraced the life of a scholar if it were not so much beneath him.

There are advantages for Cecil, too.

Lord Henry is beholden to him. On several counts. And will continue to be so. Lacking the Queen's ear and her trust, he is one of the least likely men alive to betray Cecil. And whatever the future may bring, come James of Scotland or some other, Cecil will need allies. The Howards are allies at this time. And it pleases Cecil to be in a position of simple, unequivocal superiority over this man. That kind of satisfaction is wonderfully satisfying. Lifts flagging spirits like nothing else. Except perhaps a just reward for good and honorable service rendered. But justice is so rare in this bruised and bitter world as to be discounted altogether. Revenge is not so rare. Can even be arranged. But much care must be exercised. It is not worth great risks. But when the satisfactory occasion presents itself, only a saint or a fool would deny himself the pleasure of it. Moreover Cecil would argue, since the other kind of justice—freely granted appreciation for work done well—is quite as rare in this world as any unicorn free of the threads of tapestry, then, good sir or madame, the rough and ready repayment of wounds and repair of injuries by acts of revenge is the only form of justice most of us will experience on this side of heaven.

Or hell, as the case may be.

That Lord Henry Howard is a vengeful man is another source of comfort to Cecil. He can depend upon him for more than if hunger for virtue and zeal for righteousness were the whips that drove him.

And yet 30 doth protest, upon his conscience and honor, that Essex never had any dealing with him which was not most honorable. As for his misbehavior there, it belongs not to 30 to judge of it, for although 30 loved him for his virtues, he was in no ways obliged to embrace his quarrels, but to accept of every man according to his deserts. . . .

As to the Earl of Essex.

Lord Henry had been his friend and had supported him. Though he was not directly involved in the rising. One cannot question the word of a King. Therefore, this King stands firmly on the strength of his word ("And yet 30 doth protest, upon his conscience and honor, that Essex never had any dealing with him which was not most honorable . . .") in places which are the most ambiguous. Cecil knows what went on between Essex and the King. And the King must know that he knows. Else he is a fool. Nevertheless insists upon the royal lie. Why? To give Cecil occasion to say something concerning Essex. The King, introducing Essex by name into his letter, is challenging Cecil to make his views known. Allowing Cecil the opportunity to defend himself against the story that he destroyed Essex. And, having lied himself, the King has obviously invited him to do likewise.

Cecil knew he must be very careful. With Essex gone, the faction fell to pieces, and only the dispensable parties were executed. Cecil saved Southampton. Who remains in the Tower, waiting for the Queen to die. If James comes to the throne, it will be his privilege to pardon Southampton. Cecil has saved Southampton for him—and as insurance for himself.

In the vulgar and popular world, ballads and satires and libels still appear. Cecil is blamed, together with Ralegh and Cobham, for the downfall of Essex. And the King knows that.

Would Cecil, lawyerlike, argue a case in his own behalf? Would he denounce Essex as unworthy of the favor of the King?

When he wrote his reply to James, he gave a single paragraph to answer the challenge.

And now I must leave the quick and resort to the dead, of whom I would to God I could speak the best, seeing by yourself his name was remembered, which is shortly this: —that if I could have contracted such a friendship with him, as could have given me security that his thoughts and mine should have been no further distant than the disproportion of our fortunes, I should condemn my judgment to have willingly intruded myself into such an opposition. For who know not that have lived in Israel, that such were the mutual affections of our tender years, and so many reciprocal benefits interchanged in our growing fortunes, as besides the rules of my own poor discretion, which taught me how perilous it was for Secretary Cecil to have a bitter feud with an Earl Marshal of England, a Favorite, a Nobleman of eminent parts, and a Councilor, all things else in the composition of my mind did still concur on my part to make me desirous of his favor.

The tone is sad and wise. Regret for what came to pass, but no regrets for his own part in it. Indeed, no admission (or denial) that he played any part except that of a dutiful, obedient servant to the Queen.

The subject was closed. Until such time as James might wish to open it again. Kings cannot, finally, love a rebel. Even one who acts in their behalf. Best that Essex should be dead, to be honored or despised at the King's pleasure, than to be alive and well to be feared and forever mistrusted. . . .

His servant's snores, like the snores of an old dog, from the trundle bed, these are the nearest things in Cecil's life. And the fitful swaying of candle flames, scent of melting wax. Shadows— his humpbacked body cast huge on the wall by these flames. As if the wall were aflame. As if he were dancing in those huge flames. Silently screaming there. Or as if the flames were like light in moving water. Light and water, light and flame. Dizzying. A feeling of the instant before falling. Feeling of what it must be like to drown. In the sea slowly sinking, end over end, a rag doll, while far above light and water join together to dance silently, to a music he cannot hear, cannot imagine. As if a moment before sleeping and dreaming. . . .

Rises abruptly to move to pitcher and ewer. Pour water, clear and cold. Drawn from one of the nine springs that feed the water, by lead pipes, to this palace. Nine clear springs. And in the larger chambers there are rows of pipes and casks. From which the water may be drawn, according to the separate springs, or blended together. Sometimes he thinks it is not warmth of this brick palace that brings the Queen here, as she claims, but the water. Which is good. Which is cool. Which is very sweet.

Splashes his face with cold water. Chill wakening him from the edge of a vision he could not bear. Himself in a nest of flames, screaming and screaming without making a sound.

Pauses a moment, as he dries his face with a linen napkin, hearing dimly, beyond his servant's snoring, the rise and fall of the wind. Rain beating on the roof. Imagines how it will be in an hour or two. When wrapped and muffled against it, his servant holding a covered lantern, he moves across cobbled courtyards and finds the way to his own comfortable chambers. Where there will be his great, curtained, four-posted bed waiting warmly. Where there will be fire in the fireplace. Where he can lie in the comfort of clean sheets and the warmth of heavy blankets. And stare at the watery shapes of the fire beyond the curtains. Ready to sleep. Heavy-lidded, but unwilling to let go for fear there will be no returning.

Never mind. He now returns to his table and papers.

The King must be encouraged (if and when he shall come to power) to understand he is deeply beholden to those who have worked to make it possible. And chief among those must be, when and if that time arrives, Sir Robert Cecil.

Cecil has warned him of the folly of seeking any kind of *popularity* in England.

Further I must presume (under the former pardon to do so) to say this much to Your Majesty: that although it be a common rule with many rising Princes to refuse no address or request, yet you will find it in your case, that a choice election of a few in the present will be of more use than the general acclamation of many. . . . Whosoever therefore persuades Your Majesty that it is necessary for you to be busy to prepare the vulgar beforehand, little understands the state of this question. Neither shall Your Majesty find my words untrue in this one thing more—that if the extraordinary persons (though small in number) whom neither base nor haughty humors draw to love you, should find themselves to be used as a motive to increase the public party (it being ordinary for the vulgar to follow better example, without any such precedent insinuation), surely the minds of men of spirit and value are so compounded, the addition that is sought of the greater part will be the privation of the other.

To which, with qualification, the King announced himself to be in agreement:

No. Ye need not think that I am so evil acquainted with the histories of all ages and nations that I am ignorant of what a rotten reed popularity is to lean upon, as some in your country have very dearly bought the experience thereof of late. I am no usurper. It is for them to play the Absalom. Yea, God is my witness that I shall ever eschew to give the Queen any just cause of jealousy through my behavior. And, besides that, I ever did hold this maxim, that a few great spirits were the ordinary instruments and second causes that made the world to be ruled according to their temperature. . . . But yet it is true that the hearts of the people are not to be rejected, but not to be compassed by any particular insinuation with every one of them, which would breed greater jealousy in the Queen than good success with them. But good government at home, firm amity with the Queen, and a loving care in all things that may concern the good of that state, these are the only three steps whereby I think to mount upon the hearts of the people. . . .

It is Cecil's belief that Englishmen have concluded that whatever comes to pass following the death of the Queen must be accomplished as peacefully as possible. Where a generation or so ago they might have been willing to fight to prove any claim to the crown believing, perhaps, that blood *must be* spilled to consecrate the wearing of a crown, they would now prefer a peaceful solution more than the rights of any claimant. All the more reason for the choice of James, outspoken defender of peace and concord.

Cecil, too, wants peace. And not only because, as a pensioner of Spain, he is charged to find a way to a peace. But he has learned that James would prefer to establish peace himself. For, when asked for his views concerning peace with Spain now, before it was in his authority to do more than offer advice, the King was strongly against it. All the more so in view of the claims of the Infanta to the English crown:

When I have advisedly considered and deeply looked into this matter, I cannot surely but think that the time being weighed, and the present state of things, such a peace at this time must be greatly prejudicial, first to the state of religion in general, secondly to the state, both in religion and policy of this isle in special, and lastly most perilous for my just claim in particular. Amongst many, three principal gates for procuring these forenamed mischiefs by this peace would apparently be opened. First, free trade betwixt these nations would so soundly conciliate and extinguish all former rancors as it would so more be thought odious for an Englishman to dispute upon a Spanish title; secondly, the King of Spain would thereby have occasion, by his agents of all sorts, laden with golden arguments, who would have free access to corrupt the minds of all corruptible men for the advancement of his ambitious and most unjust pretenses, besides the settling of sure means for intelligence at all occasion. And, lastly, Jesuits, Seminary priests, and all that rabble wherewith England is already too much infected, would then resort there in such swarms as the caterpillars or flies did in Egypt, no man anymore abhorring them, since the Spanish practices was the greatest crime that ever they were attainted of, which now by this peace will utterly be forgotten.

Not content to warn Cecil of the dangers of peace with Spain, the King felt free to offer criticism of the English treatment of the Catholics. As, of all things, too lenient . . . !

And now, since I am upon this subject, let the proofs you have had of my loving confidence in you plead for an excuse for my plainness, if I freely show you that I greatly wonder from whence it can proceed that not only great flocks of Jesuits and priests dare both to resort and remain in England, but so proudly do use their functions through all parts of England without any controlment or punishment these many years past. It is true that for the remedy thereof there is a proclamation lately set forth, but blame not me for longing to hear of the exemplary enforcement thereof. I know it may be thought that I have the like beam in my own eye, but alas it is a far more barbarous and stiff-necked people that I rule over. St. George surely rides upon a forwardly riding horse, where I am daily burst in daunting a wild unruly colt. And I protest in God's presence the daily increase that I hear of Papery in England and the proud vauntery that the Papists make daily there of their power, their increase, and their combined faction, that none shall enter to be King there but by their permission, this, their bragging, I say, is the cause that moves me, in the zeal of my religion, and in the natural love that I owe to England, to break forth in this digression, and to forewarn you of these apparent evils. . . .

The King's apparent zeal was intended to test Cecil. There was no way to avoid the issue. But perhaps it could be turned to advantage.

That Your Majesty vouchsafeth to acquaint me with the inward temper of your mind, in matter of religion, I take for an unspeakable favor, for what can give more rest to an honest man than to foresee the continued blessing of living under a religious Prince. . . . For the matter of priests, I will also clearly deliver Your Majesty my mind. I condemn their doctrine, I detest their conversation, and I foresee the peril which the exercise of their function may bring to this island, only I confess that I shrink to see them die by dozens when (at the last gasp) they come so near loyalty, only because I remember that mine own voice, amongst others, to the law (for their death) in Parliament, was led by no other principle than that they were absolute seducers of the people from temporal obedience, and confident persuaders to rebellion, and, which is more, because that law had a retrospective to all priests made twenty years before. But contrariwise for that generation of vipers (the Jesuits), who make no more ordinary merchandise of any thing than of the blood and crowns of Princes, I am so far from any compassion, as I rather look to receive commandment from you to abstain than prosecute. But of this matter there is enough said, for, though I confess that neither your commandment, nor the greatest power on earth, could make me alter my pace, for private consideration, in the matter of blood, against my conscience (if it were otherwise than I tell you), yet being, as I have showed it to be, as well against the priest as the Jesuit, I will presume only for Your Majesty's satisfaction (against the prejudice of rumor) to let you know particularly how Her Majesty resolves to proceed in this matter. . . .

It has been Cecil's policy to play upon the factions among the Catholics, working to increase division between the seminary priests and the Jesuits. He knows that the King's policy is similar. If Cecil were ignorant of the King's true feelings and if Cecil had been more flatterer than Councilor, he might have answered the King in kind.

Cecil has now concluded that the King's promises to Catholics, offering toleration in return for support of his claims to the throne, are very thin. That he may need an excuse to break them. But given the excuse, he will not be bound long by any previous understandings.

Cecil has been determined to be assured, even as he has been seeking to reassure the King, that the Succession of James can be peaceful. It can be done, he believes, provided that the King understands the role that he must play. The Queen has spent years in educating and preparing him. Now it falls to her Principal Secretary to bring that schooling to completion. Thus in a sense he has been making negotiations on behalf of the Queen. Though forced to do so in secrecy and without her knowledge or approval. An arrangement whereby he will be able to preside over the transfer of the sovereignty of this kingdom to the King of Scotland. While gaining and keeping the most favorable terms for England.

And for himself.

He has no intention of laboring long and hard, and at risk, without excellent prospects of earning favor. If the King has hopes of improving his rank and power in the world, well, so does Cecil.

This King has proved himself to be generous to a fault. Especially generous to those whom he favors. Yet often generous to anyone in need. Even among his enemies. As if he somehow innocently believed that ill will can be converted to goodwill by generosity. He has done this with only the most limited of means. And no doubt one of the strongest appeals of the Succession is the prospect that he will have at last the means to be more generous than ever before. But the King has nevertheless seldom favored those to whom he has owed much. Especially those to whom his debts have been greatest. It is for certain that the King does not like to feel beholden to others.

Cecil hopes to be well rewarded. If he brings the King to the throne. But he hopes to be rewarded from necessity. King must need Cecil even more to be King of England than he does to become so.

Meantime the Scotsman must be constantly encouraged. It is best that he should be allowed to maintain some burning coals of doubt until the moment when the crown is placed upon his head. Fortunately the Queen has long since planted doubts in him that will never wholly disappear.

And as it is true that your constant advised and uninfected flock, greater I assure Your Majesty, now than my pen shall need to express, in power and place, are so devoted to the present, as all the earth cannot change their duty or divide their affections from her person, to whom their only allegiance is due (until God Almighty shall otherwise dispose of her), so vouchsafe me in this to be your oracle, that when that day (so grievous to us) shall happen which is the tribute of all mortal creatures, your ship shall be steered into the right harbor, without cross of wave or tide that shall be able to turn over a cockboat. . . .

All of James's experiences at sea have been unfortunate. Going and coming, to fetch his bride from Denmark, he encountered the most terrible weather. It has been learned by careful investigation, including judicious torture, that a coven of Scots witches was responsible for the winds and waves that nearly took his life and treated his innards so roughly that he cared very little, at the time, whether he lost his life or not. Cecil could not have selected a more meaningful comparison to impress upon the King the need for a skilled pilot.

No question, either, but that he must offer appropriate flattery. Flattery being the most expeditious form of encouragement. And it must be taken as such by the King. But nevertheless it must be satisfactory. Only fools permit themselves to depend on the compliments of others to ease the heavy burden of awareness of their faults. Only a fool could seriously desire to have weaknesses named strength, deformities called beauty, folly identified as wisdom.

Deformity has taught Cecil many lessons. Some of them, he is willing to concede, have been beneficial. And one of these is a point concerning flattery. Point is that every man has need of it, even himself. Needs it like food and water, love and righteousness. Every man hungers and thirsts for the recognition which flattery confers. And all the more so as we feel the less worthy of it.

It is a ritual due to superiors. Like doffing and holding your hat in the presence of betters. Like bowing. Like kneeling. Its grudging absence connotes either ignorant misunderstanding of rank and degree or persistence of a proud and unruly spirit.

The King of Scotland is known to be a kind of coward. He greatly fears the possibility of tumult and violence anywhere around him. Would the King, then, be pleased to be called courageous? Flattery coming from a fool and addressed to another fool is what it would be to proclaim King James of Scotland to be a creature of heroic resolution. Lies might be sweet to hear. But . . . to seek to flatter away a man's flaws is, finally, insulting. Insolent. And tends to confirm the truth of the weakness that it seeks to disguise. There's nothing to be done to change the King of Scotland from a coward to a hero.

What has been done has been to name his firstborn son Prince

Henry as the new Hercules of the age, as the Isaac of Scotland and the militant Kirk, as, likewise, heir to the ancient King Arthur of Britain. As heir to James he is, therefore, heir also to his claims to England's throne.

The King has offered the magical possibility that all of his flaws would become virtues, that his weakness would be transformed into strength in the next generation. He may hope and believe this himself. Like any father with his child.

Meantime, Cecil judges the King has lived with his weaknesses long enough to prove that he can bear them.

The art of flattering that man who's not a fool is to speak not to his weakness, nor, for that matter, to his true strength. The trick is to address yourself to his . . . *vanity*. For in a true sense every man's vanity is his greatest weakness. It is the one weakness he has not learned to live with or to do without.

Cecil will never stoop to salute the King for his regal courage or bearing. He will honor him for spirit, for the enviable power and admirable quickness of his mind. And this succeeds precisely because the King's mind is just good enough to justify vanity.

When I beheld this latest letter of yours, so full of wisdom, greatness, and moderation it gave my mind a double consolation. . . .

For what could be more absurd for men of common sense than still to pester a Prince (whose time is precious) with so many petty particulars, if we had not tried your habit of patience; and what ought men of any understanding to be more afraid of than to offer so much counsel to a Prince of so much understanding, if it were not true that we have found in your mind a plentiful spring of favor and gratitude. . . .

Cecil found that an exchange of compliments was not unlike a game of tennis. For James could be superlative in his praise also:

My dearest 10,
I am ashamed that I can yet by no other means witness my thankfulness for your daily so honorable, judicious, and painful labors for the furtherance of my greatest hopes than by bare ink and paper, and that your travails of so great worth and inestimable value should be repaid with so poor recompense. But

the best excuse is that these papers are but witnesses of that
treasure of gratitude which by your good deserts is daily
nourished in my heart. . . .

All of which is encouraging to Cecil. Even though all promises
glitter like morning dew at first light, they all too often vanish,
like the dew, into empty air.

And as the proverb has it: *Great men are giants in their problems and pigmies in performance.*

To be indispensable he needs to appeal directly to the King's
fears. Fear can become such an habitual part of a man's being
that he would be confused without it. Cecil believes that James
would be suspicious if there were nothing to be afraid of. It is
part of Cecil's function to offer the King some dangers which, together, by superior intelligence and cunning, they can overcome.

The King takes pleasure in the untying and unraveling of plots
and conspiracies. Well trained by his father and by Walsingham
also, Cecil has proved himself expert at the discovery of plots.
The King knows this well. Knows, too, that there are at all times
plots against the state and the person of the sovereign. That is,
plots are always there to be found by looking for them. Most can
be safely ignored until such time as exposure may have value. As,
for example, to remind the populace of the Prince's mortality and
to bring them in unity to surround the sovereign with their love.
Or the exposure of a plot can silence or break apart some faction
which has become dangerous. As Throckmorton's Plot and Babington's scattered the Papists. As Essex's foolish rising removed
some dangerous malcontents. A plot can be uncovered which
serves to remove an enemy within the state, as Sir Henry Howard's brother, the Duke, was hopelessly entangled in the Ridolfi
Plot of '72 and died for it. Plots can be found which serve the
purpose of cautioning the Prince. Such was Essex's discovery of
the plot of Dr. Lopez to kill the Queen. Unfortunately for Essex,
the Queen was unimpressed, believing the plot was fabricated by
the Earl. Guilty or innocent, Lopez died the traitor's death (perhaps because the Queen was more concerned then to teach Essex
a lesson than to save the life of a foreigner), and the Earl gained
almost nothing by it.

In the absence of wars, which can be won or lost, or open rebellion, which can succeed or fail, it will be necessary, if and when the King shall succeed, that he has occasions to demonstrate his wise capacity for awarding justice and for tempering justice with mercy. There will be no difficulty in finding these occasions for him. There being no lack of serious crimes in England. Except perhaps that the practice of witchcraft is not so prevalent here as in Scotland. Though many gentlemen and ladies of the Court will have their stars cast by some doctor skilled in astrology, it has been a long time since there has been much concern about witchcraft.

Perhaps the coming of James will serve to revive some interest in the craft of witches.

If he should come in peace, and if there are ample occasions for him to demonstrate his judicial wisdom, nevertheless he will also need to show ability to overcome enemies. Even in peace . . . perhaps especially in conditions of peace where enemies are disguised if not unknown, there must be a triumph over some opposition. And at the very least places must be made for the King's men. Both Englishmen and the Scots he will have to bring with him. Some new places can be created, to be sure. And places and offices will multiply, also, in the lesser courts to be formed around the Queen and around Prince Henry. But at the beginning places will have to be made for new men. Surely men holding office now under the Queen will have to be promptly removed. This King will want to have such changes appear to be more a matter of justice than of royal whimsy.

Cecil's task has been made easier for him. That there are enemies in places of power has long been a theme of the correspondence of Lord Henry Howard with the King. It is his nature to suspect, to seek, and to find enemies. His misfortunes have confirmed the continual whispering (of himself to himself) that it is more the malice of others than bad luck that has shaped his fortune.

At this time it is fortunate to be joined in alliance with Lord Henry. Not only because King James trusts him; not only because Lord Henry's correspondence with the King antedates his own by years; and not only because friendship with Lord Henry helps ease away the difficulties of Cecil's having once been in opposition to Essex; but, beyond all these things, it is better to have joined forces with Lord Henry than to have to contend against his malice.

Lord Henry has enemies he has cited (again and again) as enemies to the King and to his Succession. Chief are Sir Walter Ralegh; Henry Brooke, eleventh Lord Cobham; Lord Grey of Wilton; and Henry Percy, thirteenth Earl of Northumberland.

Considering these.

Ralegh has been a partner to Cecil in business ventures, and a friend. But no matter how he might bestir himself on Ralegh's behalf, should he wish to do so, there is nothing much Cecil can do to save Ralegh's place. Lord Henry will insist on that. It will be part of the King's reward to Lord Henry, then. Moreover, quite aside from any slanders and libels spread against him, Ralegh is an offense to King James. He's strong for war and the King for peace. Ralegh has ridiculed witchcraft and the power of witches; and he has been named as a skeptic in religion. Even an atheist. The King loathes the custom of smoking tobacco and has written an angry pamphlet against it; Ralegh has dealt in tobacco at great profit. The rumor was that at the execution of Essex, Ralegh smoked his pipe and insultingly blew smoke on Essex as he passed on his way to the scaffold. It was widely repeated that gentlemen there asked Ralegh to withdraw from the scene. That he went to the White Tower (still puffing his pipe) and watched the execution (looking triumphantly pleased) from a window there. That afterward he scorned Essex's death, saying he died like a calf and a coward.

Cecil knows how rumors are spread and what can be cultivated from them. Surely the King's mind is firmly made up against him.

What's to say?

Ralegh has been blessed with good fortune under the Queen. Most of those who matter believe his good fortune to be undeserved. Of all the great men at Court he is now the most unpopular. In honesty, Cecil would have to advise the King that dismissal of Ralegh from his offices will win approval. Ralegh has become perfectly dispensable. Well? He can retire from Court, like many a man before him, and live quietly in the country. There are worse things.

As for friendship. When choice arrives between friendship and survival, then farewell friendship.

Ralegh knows that. Has written about it. Would sell Cecil's hide if he had to.

Something troubles Cecil, however. Though Ralegh is arrogant enough to deceive himself in many things, he is neither stupid nor foolish. Cecil cannot permit himself the luxury of imagining that Ralegh understands his own precarious position less clearly than Cecil does. He may know less than Cecil. But Cecil does not know how much Ralegh understands. Or what he plans to do. He does know that Ralegh dismissed overtures made to him by the Duke of Lennox, acting for the King, to reach an arrangement with James. Ralegh's rejection of Lennox has been construed by Lord Henry and taken by King James as strong evidence that he is committed to some other claimant.

More fool he, if that is true.

As for Cobham. . . .

Richest man in England. Whose house, Cobham Hall, has parks and gardens said to be the equal of any in all England except for Nonsuch and Hampton Court and for Cecil's own Theobalds.

Ah, easy for Cobham Hall to be fine to behold when all of Kent is one great garden. Where England's finest apples are. And pears and plums and cherries. Where the strawberries are fattest and the raspberries are sweeter than you can believe. Where the best hob nuts are gathered. And where the hops for making our beer are grown.

Cobham's father was his father's friend. Was Lord Chamberlain and Privy Councilor. And this his son is Lord Warden of the Cinque Ports and Knight of the Garter. Laden with honors. Yet, like the Howards and the Percys, the Brookes have had their share of traitors. Have been luckier in keeping heads and bodies together. Cobham's father (like Cecil's) once supported the Lady Jane Grey, then turned to Mary Tudor just in time. In Wyatt's Rebellion he was shifty and ambiguous. Now supporting his kinsman, Sir Thomas Wyatt, now betraying him and for Queen Mary. Queen Mary pardoned him on Good Friday. At the time of the Ridolfi Plot he was clapped in the Tower but soon released. Most said he was spared on account of his friendship with Burghley. Others took him to be a secret agent, albeit a noble one, for Cecil. Used to entrap Lord Henry Howard's brother.

Treason and double dealing are in the blood of the Brookes.

Now the son, since '97 Lord Cobham of Kent. Overbearing, proud, vain, violent, stupid, and dangerous. Elizabeth was his sister (*bless her, pray for her soul*) and he hated her marriage to Cecil. Now that she is gone, Cecil is free to hate him and all that family.

Well. Thanks to the malice of Lord Henry Howard and the follies of Lord Cobham, Cecil need not do anything to guarantee Cobham's future fall.

Lord Grey?

A man of the war party, a zealot of reformed religion. He will not have favor from James. Also he is Southampton's mortal enemy. When James frees Southampton, as he surely will, then Lord Grey is finished.

The inveterate hatred of Lord Henry for these men, together with the disposition of the King to fear and distrust them, makes it awkward. In many things Cecil has worked inwardly with Cobham and Ralegh. The three have been sometimes taken to be a faction, an unholy trinity in the eyes of their enemies. It was against them particularly that Essex claimed his rising was directed. If that cause did not bring crowds out into the streets to support it, never mind. The charge remains.

So it has become essential for Cecil to disassociate himself from the other two—in the King's mind at least; never you mind about the sweaty rabble who shift with the slightest turning of the wind. Lord Henry's adamant hatred for the two is good help. And it is comforting to know that he can convince the King that there is no other sure way to come into this kingdom save by the labors of Sir Robert Cecil. The King can hardly be expected to allow himself to be enthralled by a swarm of doubts about Cecil even as he must trust his future to him. No, what he will do, as all men must do, is exercise his freedom obliquely (like a man dancing in chains), choosing to suspend some doubts and to transfer others upon the shoulders of other candidates.

All of which simply means this: that the King wants to believe in Cecil and wants to believe Cecil has disassociated himself from all pernicious influences.

But Cecil must meet the King halfway. To do this, however, calls for sleight of hand. For he cannot arouse any suspicions in Ralegh or Cobham. If anything, he has to ease whatever inclination they might have to suspect Cecil. Can do so by binding himself more firmly in outward and visible signs of friendship and goodwill. Which he has done. And yet he has to be careful not to rouse doubts in the King.

His answer to this difficulty has been to admit it. To announce his duplicity to the King and to invite him to share in it.

For this I do profess in the presence of Him that knoweth and searcheth all men's hearts, that if I did not sometimes cast a stone into the mouths of these gaping crabs, when they are in their prodigal humor of discourses, they would not stick to confess daily how contrary it is to their nature to resolve to be under your sovereignty; though they confess (Ralegh especially) that natural policy forces them to keep on foot such a trade against the great day of mart. In all which light and sudden humors of his, though I do no way check him, because he shall not think I reject his freedom or affection, but always use contestation with him, that I neither had nor ever would contemplate future idea, nor ever hoped for more than justice in time of change, yet, under pretext of extraordinary care of his well-doing, I have seemed to dissuade him from engaging himself too far, even for himself, much more therefore to forbear to assume for me or my present intentions.

Let me therefore presume thus far upon Your Majesty's favor—that whatsoever he shall take upon himself to say for me, upon any new humor of kindness, whereof sometimes he will be replete (upon the receipt of private benefits), you will no more believe it (if it come in other shape) be it ever so much in my commendation, than that his own conscience thought it needful for him to undertake. . . .

In a sense this is most flattering to the King. Whether he believes it or not is less important than that he should conclude that Cecil is truly a duplicitous man. Which will confirm the

King in his own feeling that he is quicker and more clever than even Cecil. Therefore need not fear him too much.

As for Cecil, is he troubled in conscience by this? Not much. For a man's first obligation is to himself and to his estate. As his father once put it in writing for Robert and his brother Thomas— "Trust not any man too far with thy credit or estate, for it is mere folly for a man to enthrall himself to his friend further than, if just cause be offered, he would not dare to become otherwise his enemy." Be free to be a just enemy, then. Especially when that friend insists upon the same freedom. For Cecil has seen what Ralegh wrote to his own son on the same subject: "Take especial care that thou never trust any friend or servant with any matter that may endanger thine estate; for so shalt thou make thyself a bondslave to him that thou trustest and leave thyself always to his mercy."

Northumberland represents another problem. . . .

He is one of the ancient nobility—indeed, by the intricacies of blood kinship, he happens to stand eighth in line to the Succession. Not so close as to be feared, but near enough to the throne to be listened to. A leader among loyal Papists, he is not known to be a Papist himself. He is a man of intellectual brilliance who has spent much of his life living not in the Percys' North Country, but in the mansion at St. Andrew's Hill, Blackfriars. His studies and experiments have earned him the nickname of the Wizard Earl.

Reasons for the antagonism of Lord Henry toward Northumberland are clear to Cecil. Both come from Catholic families of ancient nobility. Both families have suffered at the hands of the Queen's justice. Northumberland's uncle, Thomas Percy, was beheaded in '71 for his part in the Northern Rising. His father, the twelfth Earl, was three times in the Tower, and the third time died (mysteriously) by his own hand. It could be said that Lord Henry and Northumberland had equal disadvantages. But Northumberland has fared better. At the time of the Armada he was trusted with a command. Lord Henry was not. He has enjoyed enough of the Queen's favor to maintain his family's wealth. For years Lord Henry had to depend on a modest pension. Lord Henry's enemies are Northumberland's friends. More Papists look to him for leadership than trust Lord Henry.

Northumberland also has been carrying on a correspondence with James. Which James has passed on, together with copies of his replies, to Cecil. This to demonstrate to Cecil that he will keep no secrets from him. Cecil knows better. But takes the King's gesture to mean that the problem of Northumberland will fall to Cecil.

There are sundry reasons the King fears Northumberland. The Percys have been foes of Scotland for as long as memory allows. Wealth and pride of the Percys must be an offense to the penurious King. For Northumberland can endure comfortably without the favor of the King. He cannot rightly be ignored, but he cannot be rewarded as easily as others, either. Then there is the matter of his marriage. For a time it was truly believed that Northumberland might marry the Lady Arabella Stuart. If he had, then James's chances for Succession would have been greatly diminished. As it happens, he married the sister of the Earl of Essex instead. But James must surely blame him for the anxiety he caused. And finally, not least of their differences, the directions their scholarly minds have taken—the King dedicated to theology and poetry; the Earl toward the new philosophy—have made it a certainty that they could never be friends.

And yet Cecil believes it is the letters of Northumberland which have troubled the King most. True, the King has professed irritation with Lord Henry's letters, calling them "Asiatic and endless volumes." But he relishes them. Enjoys the richly decorative flattery, as if words were gilded plasterwork. Delights in the malice, the embroidered malevolence of gossip. Is pleased by the pedantry and learning, which are much like his own. Northumberland's letters are different. In both style and substance. While dutiful, their tone is nevertheless more nearly that of an equal than that of any of the other letters the King has received from England.

Direct, plain, and straightforward.

The two main points that are most in question among us, and that I think I may give Your Majesty best satisfaction to understand are these: the one, whether after Her Majesty's life your right will be yielded to you peaceably, without blows or not? the other, whether it be likely Your Majesty before your time will attempt to hasten it by force.

As for the matter of your claim after Her Majesty, I hear almost none that call it in question. . . .

Surely James must have (inwardly) started, as if reaching for fruit in a basket, he had taken hold of a snake.

In such plain words must rise up from the dead his tutor, Buchanan and the stern Regents of his childhood, the great Lords who made him weep for fear and shame and laughed to do so.

Failure of imagination on both sides.

For surely poor Northumberland must believe this King, close to his own age and eager to be the King of England, would prefer plain speaking from the nobility.

Cecil sees at once that Northumberland's counsel, blunt as it is, is truthful in premises and wise in conclusions. Moreover, it has this much more value to Cecil—that it spares himself the awkwardness of having to say certain things to the King. Take, for instance, Northumberland's judicious reassurance to the King that the ancient nobility of England can be relied on not to stand against his Succession. Northumberland arrives at his assessment of the English nobility as a part of his persuasion against any idea of the King's to seize the crown by force.

If the weary time of Her Majesty cannot be long in the course of life—for it is certain that young bodies may die, but old bodies must die out of necessity—would the hazards of war then countervale the time that may be (but perhaps) gained? For the dividing of our forces into so many different businesses, soon they would be recalled together when it should come to the question of so essential a point. It is true that of the nobility, some are not satisfied, the gentility displeased, the men of war muttering, and the popularity is grieved. Yet let it be considered from whence these discontents do result, and they will be found weak pillars to adventure so great an action on.

In theory the King should be reassured to know that he need

not consider the choice of war. It should give him strength to resist the persuasions of those Scots who believe otherwise. Essentially, it is the same advice which Cecil has offered—be calm and be patient and the kingdom can be yours. And the King, with his picture of himself as one among the (blessed) few peacemakers in this fallen world, should be pleased to understand that peace is the most reasonable, most expeditious policy. And yet, much as he hates and fears war, the King does not wish to be denied the choice of it. Wishes peace to be considered his gift to England. Peace-loving or not, he does not wish to be told that it would not be possible for him to win the crown by force. Besides which Northumberland has already, in this same letter, carried truth too far for his own good. Reminding the King that if things should come to the edge of war, it need not be settled on the field of battle.

Besides, Your Majesty is not ignorant that if any of these courses be discovered afoot, that your own subjects, being so prone in their disposition to lay violent hands upon their Prince, how easy it would be to find instruments to take you away, which all of your servants could not hinder nor help; and if taken away, either by fortune of war or otherwise, in the minority of your son, he being but a child would hardly be invested ever with his right in this kingdom, others having once taken possession over his head. . . .

Good Lord deliver us!

If the thing which Northumberland desired most was to frighten the King out of his wits, he could not have chosen a more efficient means. Rekindling the memories of his past, reminding him of the ever-dangerous present and awakening fear for the future. A fear not only for himself but for his heirs.

Woe unto the messenger who bears harsh tidings. Northumberland cannot have conceived that his common sense might be taken as a threat. Being a man without much fear himself, Northumberland cannot conceive of the tactics of the truly fearful. Cannot know how fearfulness engenders in the spirit so much self-contempt, self-disgust, as to be unbearable.

Insofar as truth threatens his hopes, the King cannot bear to hear of it. Thus, ironically, his ears sealed, as if to the music of the sirens, the King missed much of the practical wisdom Northumberland had to offer.

The nobility are unsatisfied that place of honor are not given them, so soon as they become judges of their own desert; that offices of trust are not laid in their hands to manage as they are wont; that Her Majesty is parsimonious and slow to relieve their wants, which from their own prodigalities they burdened themselves withal. They repine that the state value them not at that rate they prize themselves worthy of; neither is there many in this rank, for some are pleased, and others are not capable; so Your Majesty may discern these things to spring from the heat of youth, impatiency, want, and self-conceipt, hot discontents soon born and soon dying in themselves, stings not bitter enough to lead them on to so great a hazard, when their considerations of blood shall tell them, that that Prince which shall follow cannot but conclude them in his heart to embrace the same disloyalties upon like apprehensions: discontents rising from the ingratitude of human nature, which for the most part forgets former benefits if unsatisfied in his last wishes.

Thus Northumberland's paradoxical view that the only nobility to fear would be those who would rise up to act in his behalf.

As for the people. The Earl expressed their discontents and warned the King against depending on popular support if he should try to take the crown by force.

The popular griefs are subsidies, taxes for the wars, grants of monopolies, and delays of justice, in all of which they rather condemn Her Majesty's instruments with the burden of it than conceive any hatred of her person; this observation being almost infallible, that a commonality may sooner be drawn to rebellions under color of setting justice straight than in advancing any man's title. I am of the opinion that it is much easier for a great man, popular in his own country, to move them to commotion, than for Your Majesty, if you were so disposed.

(And if Essex could not move them to commotion, how shall you?)

In his reply to his "right trusty cousin," James thanked him for his "wise, plain, and honest letter." He agreed wholeheartedly that war and rebellion would be as foolish as they would be dangerous:

It were very small wisdom, by climbing of ditches and hedges for the pulling of unripe fruit to hazard the breaking of my neck when, with a little patience and abiding the season, I may with far more ease and safety enter at the gate and enjoy the fruits at my pleasure, in the time of their greatest maturity. . . . And what confidence could I ever have in those that for pleasure of me had betrayed their present Sovereign? No, since the old proverb is most true that, though Princes sometimes make use of treason, yet they ever hate the traitor, with what security could I think to make my residence in a kingdom so full of traitors?

Soon James wrote to ask him about Cobham and Ralegh. And (again) Northumberland spoke to him more plainly than he should have.

As for Cobham and Ralegh and how they bend toward your right . . . Although they be in faction contrary to some that hold with your title, yet in that point I cannot deny but they be of the same mind and to run the same course. The first of these two I know not how his heart is affected. But by the latter, whom sixteen years of acquaintance hath confirmed to me, I must needs affirm Ralegh's ever allowance of your right. And although I know him to be insolent, extremely heated, a man that desires to seem to be able to sway all men's fancies, all men's courses, and a man that out of himself, when your time shall come, will never be able to do you much good nor harm, yet must I needs confess what I know, that there is excellent good parts of nature in him, a man whose love is disadvantageous to me in some sort, which I cherish rather out of constancy than policy, and one whom I wish Your Majesty not to lose, because I would not that one hair of a man's head should be against you that might be for you.

Whether or not the King could ever accept his judgment of Essex, Northumberland's account surely contained disturbing news for the King. That he was well rid of him: "I must say, justly, that although Essex was a man endowed with good gifts, yet was his loss the happiest chance for Your Majesty and England that could befall us; for either I do fail in my judgment, or he would have been a bloody scourge to our nation." But most surprising to the King was the statement that Essex had never had any intention of supporting the rights of James, but merely using James to bring himself to power.

Did he not decree it that it was scandalous to our nation that a stranger should be our King? . . . How often have I heard him inveigh against you among such as he conceived to be birds of his own fortune? Did his soldiers and followers dream or speak of anything but of his being King of England? . . . Well, to conclude, he wore the crown of England in his heart these many years, and therefore far from setting it upon your head if it had been in his power.

James could only hope that it was not the truth. But, true or false, until then he had never had reason to imagine Essex had been betraying him as well as the Queen. The King was left wondering how much Northumberland knew of what had passed between him and Essex.

These doubts are greatly to Cecil's advantage. He is grateful to Northumberland for planting them.

Finally, and perhaps more in private jest than for any other purpose, the King had asked Northumberland for his best judgment of an unnamed person. (Who appears to be none other than Cecil!) Thus Cecil has the pleasure of seeing himself presented favorably and defended against criticism. Saying first that Cecil supports his title, "that after Her Majesty upon whom he layeth the foundations of his fortune, that the secret of his conscience doth conclude your title to be the next right, that his heart will then wish that it may have approbation with all men and that for the present he will not be the man to wrong you. . . ."

Northumberland goes on to deny that Cecil could ever support the claims of the Infanta. Stakes his honor on it. Points to the clemency following the Essex rising as positive proof of this.

If he should affect to bring in the Infanta, as has been laid to his charge, which way would he work it, when all his friends be contrary with whom he converseth? By himself I know he cannot do it. And there is nothing more odious in his nature than such a thought, upon which I will pawn my honor, a thing that should not slide under my pen but upon assured grounds. This may be further induced for a confirmation that I hold—was not the clemency that hath been used to all the nobility that offended in the last rebellion and many others that were conceived to lean toward Your Majesty? Was it anybody else that saved Southampton? Has he not mitigated the extremities against Mountjoy? And should not Essex have gone near to have lived if an assured combustion in our state must not of necessity have followed by his life? If these are not sufficient warrants for my judgment, to conclude that his heart is not Spanish, I refer it to Your Majesty's wisdom and submit myself to your further knowledge. Nevertheless out of the trust it hath pleased you to repose in me, I must give you notice that I cannot believe he will ever open himself unto Your Majesty, upon any condition, so long as Her Majesty lives. For he is very wise and is not ignorant how harsh a thing it is to her disposition that any should think or look toward a new sun. . . .

For he is very wise. . . .

It is clear to Cecil that the King will not ever trust Northumberland. And that if the transformation of the King of Scotland comes to pass and he is settled securely on the English throne, Northumberland will be wonderfully dispensable. But Cecil can see that he will be of some value to the King at the beginning. And there is one important way that he will be of value to Cecil, though he cannot so much as hint at this. No doubt Lord Henry will be rewarded promptly enough. Will surely be sworn onto the Privy Council. The blending together of Lord Henry's general ineptitude and his malice toward many could make him dangerous. He will be better off with a rival on the Council. What better rival than Northumberland? Who will attract his malice and will leave Cecil free to consolidate and strengthen his own position.

Finding place for Northumberland on the new Council will ease Cecil's conscience. For, in a sense, he is beholden to the man.

Well, many in England now are writing letters to King James. Some from every faction. And some whose sole faction is self-interest. Thanks to the King's goodwill, but more than that to Cecil's own intelligencers, he knows who they are and what they are telling the King.

As far as he can tell there are few among the Court and Council who seriously support the claims of any other than the King. The Lady Arabella, far from London at her grandmother's Hardwick Hall (one of the few houses in England which Cecil truly envies) is being closely guarded. Thanks to her latest attempt to marry her way to the throne. No one can even come near without Cecil's permission. Which can serve a double purpose. Certainly she is prevented from plotting to seize the throne before James can be proclaimed. And yet, if something should change, if something should happen—*and who knows? who knows?*—to deny James the throne, she is, thus, protected so as not to be denied her rights.

Why does Cecil deceive himself? As if the wager were still to be made. As if he himself, studying these papers, even his own letters, like a scholar from another era, had not long since committed himself. Slowly, to be sure. As in love and seduction. But by now he stands or falls with James.

The Queen could change everything with one public word. But the Queen keeps her silence on the subject. She could die in the night, any night. Or she could live and rule for another decade. She has been melancholy since the return here to Richmond. The death of her old friend and cousin, wife to the Lord Admiral, the Lady Nottingham, here at Richmond has grieved her. She may not endure her grief. Or she may.

Tomorrow she may be dancing to pipe and tabor with her Maids of Honor. Tomorrow may send for Mr. Secretary and, aiming to lift a burden off his hunched back, may name her Successor at last. Who may be James of Scotland. Or may be not. . . .

Tomorrow she may.

But it is already tomorrow.

He rubs weary eyes. Carefully places his papers in the chest and locks its several locks. He splashes more cool water in his face. Pauses as he counts the bells of a chiming clock. He must now hurry back to his chambers and be snug in his bed when the time comes for his servants to wake him. He must shake one old snoring fellow just outside the door, wake him like a dog. To help him into his cloak. To light the lantern and, muttering softly to himself, lead the way.

As for himself, what's his hope and assurance? Why, promises and good wishes like everyone else.

The King has written:

I cannot also omit to display unto you the great contentment I receive by your so inward and united concurrence in all the paths that lead to my future happiness, most heartily wishing you to continue in that happy course as ye may be sure of my thankfulness toward you, whom I know to be only moved for the respect of conscience and honor, to deserve well at the hands of a lawful, natural, and loving successor to your Queen and country.

Your most assured loving friend—

Pray it may be true.

True or false, it is too late now to do anything more than hope and pray.

So be it.

MESSENGER

1566

London, thou art of townes *A per se*.
  Soveraign of cities, someliest in sight,
Of high renoun, riches, and royaltie:
  Of lordis, barons, and many goodly knyght;
  Of most delectable lusty ladies bright;
Of famous prelatis in habitis clericall;
  Of merchauntis full of substaunce and myght;
London, thou art the flour of Cities all. . . .

WILLIAM DUNBAR

Down the wide highway called Ermine Street & running across pasture & fields of grain & large clumps of timber. Road plunging steep down to bank of River Neve at Wansford. Where old bridge is in poor repair & work has begun on new one to be thirteen small & close-set arches.

Now into Huntingdonshire.

Crossing willow fringed meadows of Neve to dry little island, Water Newton . . . at edge of Fens & three miles beyond that where Ermine Street is joined by old road from north & east, from Peterborough & Lincoln & Hull. Then downhill & over into Stilton; fine place for craft of smithing; for here cattle are shod with horseshoes for their final pilgrimage to Smithfield. Going on quickly past Monk's Wood & Stangate Hole & then up Stangate Hill & soon long slow climb to top of Alconbury Hill where the two north roads from London meet & at that fork he'll keep to left. Shorter by a few miles. . . .

Passing lazy windmills & into Huntingdon on bank of Great Ouse & proud stone bridge left from olden times before Plague, over river & across common green & through village of Godmanchester.

Now fifteen miles of Cambridgeshire leaving watery country behind for fields with crops of barley & oats & wheat & rye.

Coming on to malting town of Ware. To change at *Old Bull's Head*, then eight miles close by the bank of the Lea, busy with barges from London. Down long easy hill into Waltham to change horse (he hopes) for last time before London. A dozen miles only remaining (out of nearly four hundred) to Bishopsgate. Will make honest oblation to vanity & hire there hand-somest, costliest horse he can find.

From here on cannot forget his first look at London.

Those years before . . .

"During the last of forty-nine and first months of the new year —when Edward Seymour, Duke of Somerset, fell from eminence and it looked like William Cecil was sure to stumble also, I spent much time in Cambridge listening to sermons. I began to imagine I might have a calling. In those shortest days of the year, I began to believe I might become a preacher of the Gospel.

"Now you will laugh out loud at the idea. And so will I.

"Time and more daylight and better weather soon relieved me of most of my religious fervor. By Christmastime of fifty Cecil had managed to separate his fortunes from the Duke's and soon climbed higher—to be Secretary to King Edward. This fallen world began to look shinier then. . . ."

Cecil sent word for him to come down following the present term. And so it was that early in the week after Easter, light-headed less from the spirit of the risen Christ than from the prospect of leaving people and neglected studies behind, he hefted the wooden chest containing his worldly goods out of the gate of St. John's and up along High Street, to the *Black Bear Inn* on Market Hill. Placed chest among the goods and baggage of a four-wheeled, six-horse wagon. Then climbed up to sit on it among a few other passengers bound for London.

"I remember next to nothing of that journey now. I recall inconstant spring weather. Sunshine, then rain, then mud, next sun, and soon again dust rising from the road. Clusters of clouds and then clearing. Myself soaking wet. Then steaming dry in my cloak."

And on the last day of it, rainy winds vanished. Sun burned warm in a cloudless sky. And earth, and everything that was now suddenly sprouting, growing, and blooming on it, was as sweet as can be after a rain and everything was invested with shining clarity as if seen through fine glass. He felt as if he gulped down a glassful of strong wine, every bit, taking the last few drops on the tip of his tongue. He was no longer stiff and sore from cramped traveling. Had already forgotten the miles behind him.

Forgetting finally even himself. Becoming only part of the day he was witnessing. Possessed by the skywide splendor of it.

It is just so, in that spirit, that he first sees the city.

As the wagon continues to crawl—feeling as if it might be a barge floating on calm water—along Bishopsgate Road, he sees off to his left the squat church towers and spires of the villages of Hackney and Stepney. And to his right, to the west, on somewhat higher ground, the windmill and the slender spire and the cluster of trees marking Islington. Now straight ahead, directly down the road, across fields with scattered houses and buildings and churches, rising to fill the wide horizon like a vast painted cloth, there stand the battlemented wall, the gates and gatehouses, towers and tourelles, of London. Many more than a hundred spires and steeples of the churches there. Wild forest of them jumbled all together. Harbor where spires and towers are like the masts of ships. All of it stretching between, to his left, the White Tower, at the heart of the Tower of London, weathervanes glinting from four corners, to the tower and tallest of all spires of Paul's Church atop its hill.

And then farther to the west, a distance beyond the city walls and earth and green of some open spaces, the towers and long roof of St. Peter's Church at Westminster Abbey and, too, the roofs of the Hall, the Old Palace and Whitehall Palace and of the great houses lining the banks of the Thames.

And all of it shining for him then and now, this city built between and among low hills and marshy ground by a river. This ancient city, newly baptized by this day's skyful extravagance of afternoon sunlight.

Within him as the wagon rolls on, routine and unhurried, a paradoxical spirit prevails. It is as if he were made of canvas, a sail filled by a fair wind. He's at once tense and lighthearted. Feeling from his first sight that whatever has altered himself has done so for as long as he may live to remember it. Feeling—as much with his skin now as inwardly—smitten, blinded. Like some foolish knight in one of those old tales of courtly love.

Schoolboy that he still was, he turned away from the intensity of experience, like someone stumbling, and reached out to catch hold of something that he had by heart:

Urbem quam dicunt Romam, Meliboee, putavi
Stultus ego huic nostrae similem . . .

Tityrus speaking out, in the first *Eclogue* of Virgil. Telling
Meliboeus how it had been for him to come to the city of Rome
from his little market town in the hills. Confessing how nothing
in all of his life till then had prepared him for what would happen there and for what he would see and feel. *Like a poor fool,
my friend, I imagined that the city called Rome was like
ours. . . .*

But it was not. Was not a larger, grander version of his provin-
cial market town. It was altogether different. It emptied the in-
sides of the purse of Tityrus like a gutted fish. Sent him home
with a broken heart.

So London also would prove not to be another market town.
Not like any other English town. He knew this at first sight,
thanks to the advantage of Virgil to guide him. To guard him.
For there was, at his heart, just as there is in lust, a palpable
sense of danger. Which served to heighten joy and excitement.
To make them all the more precious for being threatened.

But that was once upon a time. It will not be so again. Never
the same (as he knew even then) though a hundred or a thousand times in memory, he will see himself as a youth on a baggage cart. Coming toward this magic destination as once, say,
pilgrims and crusaders came toward the walls and gates of
Jerusalem.

The man remembering knows this and knows also that even
the look of the city would change soon and continue changing.
That in less time than it takes to tell its fields and suburbs would
be filling up, crowded with new houses and buildings. That
much that was old and fine in the city would come down for the
sake of what could be called (for its brief time) new. That even
the most proud and permanent shapes could be altered forever in
one wink of time. A crack of thunder and a flashing tine of light
in the sky. And the spire of Paul's Church was all on fire and
soon all gone.

He can still picture that young man coming along with the
baggage cart. Bouncing on Bishopsgate Road. He can picture

that, and even now his spirit will dance. But will dance to a different tune.

Sometimes he wishes he could cry out a warning to the boy with his name and face. That he could enter into his own memory, as a dreamer can sometimes enter his own dream, as if it were a stage and the dream a play, with full knowledge that the dream is only a dream. That he could leave the pitiless present and step into his past. Could speak to the young man he was.

But if he could, what would he say?

What could be said that the boy would be able to believe?

And, belief or not, what could he say that might serve to change anything?

There's another question that he would prefer not to ask himself. And that is—whether a change, any change at all, good fortune or bad, better times in exchange for worse, would be worth the weakening and diminishment of the once-realized feeling of precious and precarious joy?

He would not wish to lose that to gain anything.

Instead, in this memory which is so close to a dream, he stands by the roadside watching the cumbersome wagon pass.

PLAYER

1602

But besides these gross absurdities, how all their plays be neither right tragedies, nor right comedies, mingling kings and clowns, not because the matter so carrieth it, but thrust in clowns by head and shoulders, to play a part in majestical matters, with neither decency nor discretion, so as neither the admiration and commiseration, nor the right sportfulness, is by their mongrel tragi-comedy obtained.

> Sir PHILIP SIDNEY—"An Apology for Poetry"

Gallows and knock are too powerful in the highway: beating and hanging are terrors to me: for the life to come, I sleep out the thought of it.

> *The Winter's Tale:* **IV, ii**

You have yourself an excellent seat, most comfortable bench with a back and a soft, fat embroidered cushion you'd be happy to own.

You have a view of all the stage (as well it ought to offer at the price) and of the crowd of groundlings in the yard, gathered around the stage platform. You can see the people in the ring of penny seats in the lower galleries. You sit highest, beneath the thatched roof.

There are the young courtiers, too, gaudy flock, with their chairs and stools set upon the stage at the edge of it. A few in the Lords' boxes directly over the tiring-house. Who must see the action backward and from above, but who can be well seen and appreciated. Curried and curled and shined and barbered and groomed, they are here for all to see in all their Court clothing. The clothes worn by any one of them, it's said, would buy and sell any theater several times over. Even such a grand one as this. Is that surprising? Hardly so anymore. Many of these fellows are sowing more debts than wild oats, and will live at the mercy of any sort of pawn-taker or Dutch moneylender to die on hay among the company of debtors and felons. Yet meanwhile how they do glow and shine! Truly they are fantastical! They are players from a more encompassing play. Who have come here to witness this one especially because it's new, but also because they have heard that its subject and performance will suit them well.

It was played first, less than a fortnight ago, across the river as a part of the revels in the handsome Hall of Middle Temple. It is something that must be seen. Better be seen now, since it's not likely to be played often. Well, it did well with those lawyers and judges, to be sure, and few of the courtiers have left during performance. Those who did so made no great show of departure, but tiptoed away like embarrassed shadows. Meaning they had appointments that must be kept. Those who have remained have remained quiet and still.

This play would seem to be somewhat too sharp, somewhat too satirical, even, in a curiously comic sense, somewhat too sad to show for the Queen this year. Perhaps such a thing might have diverted her once upon a time. A good while ago. But there was no play like this one, then.

Now she needs cheering. And since this company is the Lord Chamberlain's, it will be called upon to make some of that cheer at Court. But with something more suitable for her mood.

It's not a play for merchants and the men of the Guilds, either. But, then, few plays are. Anyway, they will hear all about it from their servants and apprentices who've come here today; who are better off spending three hours in the playhouse than in a tavern, drinking and gambling.

It is not a play—oh, no, not by any means!—for your sober Puritans. Who would not laugh and who would be confirmed and strengthened in their opinions of the Devil's playground. Yet they might be surprised, if they looked and listened, at how close the world of this play is to the real one they worry and pray over. Truth is, this play might confirm certain beliefs they must sometimes question; since the rest of the world goes always about its blithe and doomed way as if perceptions of the pious were Bedlam lunacy. Yet they do not need this, or any other play, to assist them. They have lectures and sermons. God bless them, they can sing their psalms together and be content.

This is not even a play intended to be diverting to the general crowd. It's never likely, for instance, to empty the Southwark alehouses or the Bear Garden. Or to trouble the rival playhouses —the little Rose, the Swan in Paris Garden—if it ever opens up again. Or the Fortune, across the river and the other side of London's wall near Cripplegate. Or handsome Blackfriars, all indoors under roof, where some of these same gentlemen of Court will go by coach this same evening.

This play's not likely to be played here (or anywhere) often.

But still, all in all, there's a good-sized crowd for it. More than a thousand and less than two. They have turned a profit by their labors today.

Labors which are almost over now. . . .

Poor Hector is dead at last, as we all knew he would be. Killed here, however, in this version, by a trick. Achilles has had the body dragged offstage to be tied at the tail of his horse. To ride in his triumph. No one, on either side, seems to be greatly pleased. Ajax says it for the Greeks when he gets the news:

> If it be so, yet bragless let it be,
> Great Hector was as good a man as he.

Agamemnon is skeptical, but hopeful that, finally, "our sharp wars have ended."

The surviving Trojans—Aeneas, Paris, Antenor, Deiphobus—believe they have won a battle. But, of course, have lost the war. Troilus is allowed to say some last troubled words. Ending with an unlikely strong resolve. Which, even if honored, will amount to nothing. As we know. As all the world knows.

> Strike a free march. To Troy with comfort go:
> Hope of revenge shall hide our inward woe.

And, ceremoniously, sadly, they leave by means of two of the curtained tiring-house doors at the rear of the stage. From the third door, old Uncle Pandarus wanders in. Just in time to be cursed and beaten by Troilus. Who has, at least, learned something from his brief, unfortunate experiences in love and war.

Thus Pandarus (here played by a fellow who calls himself William Smyght), though somewhat the worse for wear, is left onstage to have the last words in an epilogue. A sort of parodic benediction. The task before him of pleading for sympathy. When only laughter is forthcoming, he pulls himself together, French pox and all, to win their applause with witty insults:

> . . . weep out at Pandar's fall;
> Or if you cannot weep, yet give some groans
> Though not for me, yet for your aching bones.
> Brethren and sisters of the hold-door trade,
> Some two months hence my will shall here be made.

It should be now, but that my fear is this,
Some galled goose of Winchester would hiss.
Till then I'll sweat and seek about for eases,
And at that time bequeath you my diseases.

Rude laughter and applause. Comic bow, clownish, and he exits quickly as if he expected oranges to be thrown at him. A curtain concealing one of the Lords' boxes above is snatched open. And there are the musicians beginning to play. The chief players now reenter for the dance around the stage. That wonderful fool, who seemed in performance a moment ago so clownish and little and deformed (it's Robert Armin who's chief clown now that Will Kempe's gone) as scurrilous-tongued Thersites, is back to lead the jig. He's not half the dancer that Kempe was, but they love him for the parts he plays so well. Now courtiers are up and strolling away, leaving empty chairs behind. One of them steps forward to seize the pretty boy who played Helen of Troy and leads him/her (wigless now, but still dressed as Helen) in a lively dance. Cheers from the ground. Players dance away. Music plays the audience to the doors.

And now a boy has come to fetch you to the tiring-house to meet the player you have come here to see.

. . . Come now, he says.

He, like the other actors in this noisy cheerful room—there's wine, there's laughter and much crowding about of friends and admirers—is dressing, with the assistance of an apprentice for the tricky lacing of things, for the world. Half locked in study of his looking glass as he removes paint, he is talking like a man who has not spoken to anyone for a while. Like someone who has been shipwrecked and only just now saved.

. . . Come now, he's saying. You must admit that there is in our bestial nature the very twitch and shudder of contrarities—so many of such that a stranger to this earth, a man, say, from the far Bermudas, or a proud Court lady descended from the shining moon, observing our sundry mundane chores and pleasures, watching us as we seek to go on living till we die, would swear in good faith that that is all we are, namely, no more than bundles of contradictions, like bundles of kindling wood in search of a fireplace to call home; this contradiction, then, this wince of paradox; which, like a rotten tooth that shortly plans to bid mouth and jaw farewell; this tooth which is beginning to reveal its secret intentions by a shivery and shooting pain; and then, mind you, only when the tip of the tongue may choose to explore it; only when tongue touches it, will that forlorn, rebellious, alienated, soon-to-be-excommunicated wretch of a tooth, so white and shiny and sound on outside and all poison and corruption at heart (like certain fine gents of Court who shall never be named this side of Tyburn's gallows by these lips of mine); only then will this wretched and dissembling tooth send forth an unmistakable message of pain; like yet another one of Job's howling messengers running eagerly toward you to bring you a generous invitation to join in the world's close harmony with some loud howling of your own; and, sir, I ask you, does the sure and certain knowledge that this consort of pain, this petty concert of inner and outer howling, will follow as swiftly behind the touching of the aforesaid tooth as, shall we say, the swiftest greyhound coursing half a step and one snap of jaw behind the puff of white fluff at the arse of a running hare, does knowledge of what will happen serve to prevent your educated tongue from doing its worst (?); I'll answer it does not; not so, for the tongue, though lord and master of many pleasures, until that same tongue finds himself too old and tired to care what's the difference between white salt and sugar; the tongue of man, I say to you, by its very nature is forever an adventurous explorer—a Drake or Hawkins, a Cavendish or Frobisher, proud Ralegh or a hopeful Humphrey Gilbert; tongue would explore every inch of this world, bitter and sweet, smooth and rough, hot and cold; tongue would touch and taste it all; but can only go where head is; and this side of Tyburn or the Tower, head is most likely to be found where feet will take it; which—that is, where head and feet go—is too often, between meals and the sweet and sweaty sessions of love, likely to be nowhere that tongue would choose to be; tongue then, comfortably imprisoned and idle, yet curious as any house cat, will explore the pains and pleasures of where it is; will therefore touch that tender tooth and will start with an innocent surprise each time the pain makes you howl like a krummhorn or a hautbois; and so tongue will continue until that poor tooth be yanked out and discarded; and even then, sir, it will continue to find content, in exploration of the empty space where tooth was, remembering the poor old fellow fondly; as you might sometimes fondly remember a halfwit cousin you once pushed into the well. . . .

. . . I began with the notion that there is contradiction within us, division in one and all. One of a bundle of many of the same. Which, taken together, make us whoever we are. I began there and then, like a spider on a summer morning, I spun out of myself—and, I might as well confess, out of the rags and tatters of many others, my betters, from whom I must beg, borrow, and steal as best I can—I spun out a figure for my thought. An odd figure of speech, made all the more so by both the style and the digressions, by all the *decoration*, as it were; making strange that which is common. That is, I could have said, couldn't I?: *There is a paradox in our nature. Though we love pleasure, we play with pain like a tongue toying with a bad tooth.* What could be simpler than that? We could have nodded in acquiescence, like Papist priests bowing around an altar. As we might nod and agree to such wisdom as: *The wolf eats the sheep and the great fish eat the small.* Ah, yes! Yes, indeed! *If fools were wearing white caps, then we should all of us seem no more than a flock of geese.* Can you quarrel with that? *He that leaves certainty and sticks to chance, when fools play the pipes, he must dance.* No? All gems from the treasury of the accumulated country wisdom of England. I could say such things and you would nod agreement, thinking safely to yourself: *I will get common sense and wisdom from this fellow as soon as I shall get a fart from a dead horse.*

. . . There now. As soon as this lazy, turnip-fingered boy can finish my tags and points correctly, I shall be ready to call myself dressed. And then we may go. Where was I?

Paradox. Tooth and tongue. Something or other about contradictions which define the nature of man.

. . . Oh, well. Nothing so monumental was intended, I assure you. Merely a figure of speech in anticipation to what I assume your first question will have to be.

And what would that be?

. . . I am assuming, sir, that having bravely sat for more than two hours and witnessed our play—and I trust in good comfort and hope with some pleasure, having sat there and seen this afternoon's performance, which, on the whole, went well, I do believe. . . .

Very well. From first to last.

. . . Why, I thank you, sir. For myself and all these others. To resume, you will no doubt have wondered why our poet and these players should trouble themselves with the matter of Troy. Why a crowd of people should have come here to spend their afternoon transported to an antique, imaginary Troy. A Troy that never was, nor ever will be, beyond the edges of our stage. Why they should spend their money for the privilege of seeing this company strut and swagger, rant and rave, pretending to be Greeks and Trojans. You are wondering, what with all the strutting and swaggering, ranting and raving, out there all around us in every which direction, with London and her suburbs offering up more comedies and tragedies, more wonderful jests for ninnies and more miserable tales of woe than company of players could ever hope to imitate, why we are here. For a penny they could climb the tower of Paul's Church. For a penny they could see the Tower of London and the wondrous zoo there. For a penny they could be guided through Westminster Abbey and touch the graves of kings. Why have all of these people come here to be transported to an antique and imaginary Troy?

. . . Come now, he says. Surely you have been wondering about that.

I might have wondered about that if I had had a chance to do so. But I never left Troy and the tents of the Greeks.

. . . God's wounds! You sound very much like one of us. More than could be expected, I think.

Lowers the looking glass to stare in your face, frowning, his eyes narrowing. Someone else, someone who has not been where you have been and done what you have had to do, might even be intimidated by his expression of controlled ferocity. For you the problem is not to laugh. Lest like a flushed bird this fellow shall flee away before he can be snared. So be it. You hasten to reassure him.

Perish the thought. Pray continue if you please.

Now his laughter bubbles at the lips, then bursts out loud.

Fills the room. The others, startled, pause in the midst of their changing from Greeks and Trojans into Englishmen. Pause to watch as he pulls away from the lad who's lacing his right sleeve at the shoulder. Pulls away and, without a glance to see if it is still there, falls back upon a joint stool, shakes his head, and laughs and laughs.

. . . Please forgive me, sir, he says when he can. I always seem to be acting whether I want to or no. Forever playing the fool. It seems to be my nature.

"And you are more convincing off the boards than on them," one of the actors (the youth who played Troilus) calls out.

. . . Surely someone was convinced this afternoon. You heard the applause.

"They were happy to know it was over and done with," says another, the boy who played Helen, cause of all trouble and tragedy.

"Oh, it is true that you were excellent today," Ulysses tells your player. "As Pandarus you have no rival. You could play the part without rehearsal, without troubling to learn by heart a single speech."

. . . Don't tell that to the poet or he will punish you by cutting some of your interminable speeches. Chances are he'll make you the arse end of a horse in his next comedy.

"We shall hire you for that part, knowing how you need employment."

Turning back to you. Rising and standing again. The apprentice patiently lacing his sleeve.

. . . I am not, as you see, a member of this company. They wish you to know that. Yet to whom do they turn in haste and with many pleas and promises, at the very last minute, mind you, when their own worthy Pandarus overeats or overdrinks or overdoes whatever it may be (aside from acting) that he truly does well? To whom do they come when they must have someone or have no play at all? Why, for certain, they come pounding on my door like petty constables. Coming to find me, because, coarse threads though they are, they know where quality goods may be found.

. . . It's true I am not one of this proud company and never will be.

. . . But by far heaven and the Pope's red, rosy ass, I was already a player and performing every kind of part you can imagine when most of these scurvy fellows were still trying to learn the trade of turning a roast on a spit or shoveling horseshit in a barn.

. . . Listen, your honest English player has got as many scars on his back as any old Winchester whore. To prove thereby his longevity among the fraternity of rogues and vagabonds, of minstrels and fiddlers and jugglers and suchlike masterless men. I'll wager gold I am the only man here in this tiring-house who has been whipped down the street at the cart's arse and can prove it, too.

"I do not doubt you at all," says Achilles, who has been brooding most handsomely until now, and who now stands, dressed and looking more like a courtier than those who sat on the stage today. "No doubt, however, it was not so much a matter of law as it was their unanimous judgment of the quality of your acting."

Before Pandarus, stung, it seems (who knows?), can rise from his stool to reach for his sword on its hook, it is Helen of Troy who speaks out and, inadvertently, sets them all, even Achilles and Pandarus, to laughing again.

"There was a fellow that was with this same company last year —or maybe it was the year before—who had lost one ear in the pillory. Whether it was the left ear or the right one, I can't remember. But no doubt at all that one ear was gone."

. . . See that ye despise not one of these little ones, for I say unto you that in heaven their Angels behold the face of my Father which is in heaven.

"Where is that speech to be found?" poor Helen asks.

. . . Why, 'tis a part I am struggling diligently to memorize and later to play.

More laughter. Dressed, putting on cloak and buckling sword, he's ready to leave. He leads you with him, passing close by Achilles.

. . . If it seems that I have been appropriately cast as Pandarus in this play, consider young Achilles here. Who would sooner creep into his scabbard, if he could, than draw a sword.

"Pandarus?"

. . . Yes?

"Were you really whipped at cart's tail?"

. . . Yes, by God, I truly was. And it was in Bristol—of all forsaken places, a town where half the population could be whipped on one day and the other half on the next without doing injustice to any innocent person. And, do you know?, they hired a fiddler, a fellow I knew well, as it happens, and so pickled from many years in many taverns that he'd lost the knack of it and played the fiddle about as well as a Barbary ape. Hired this poor fellow to walk along and play in front of the cart while I was whipped through the streets. And the whole time, in all that pain and shame, I was thinking that the worst punishment was having to listen to his fiddling.

. . . Ah, but that, my friends, is another tale for another time and place. It has been my pleasure to be in Troy with you. If one of your fools falls ill again, pray remember me.

And out into brisk air, waning afternoon light. Shouts rising up from the Bear Garden. Where, no doubt, some English mastiff has just now had his head crunched like a ripe apple.

And so the world's bloody afternoon continues. As it was and ever shall be.

So begins your part in it. Well, you can kill this fellow here, this common player, if you have to. Can leave him dead in alley or ditch, if it comes to that, not losing sleep over it. Oh, sweet Lord Jesus, no! Too late for that, for regrets or bad dreams. Yet you find yourself hoping that all will go well. Except for a hearty thirst, you are feeling fine. The play was a pleasure, and this odd bird may yet amuse you.

. . . Sir, he is saying. May I recommend that we walk to the Bridge and cross over there? It's a custom of mine whenever I perform in a play at Bankside. Something for luck. Besides, if you save the money you would spend on the hire of a boat, let me tell you there are two excellent taverns, one at each end of the Bridge. And it would be a shame to pass them by without pausing long enough to wish each other good health and good fortune and a safe crossing of London Bridge.

. . . And what could be more pleasant than a walk on such a fine day as today?

Yes, it is more than tolerable for the time of year.

. . . Indeed, sir, it is so. Well, then, let us walk back through the Clink to the Bridge.

. . . You are not a Puritan, are you? I mean, sir, you do not look like one. But in this duplicitous age all the world seems to be populated with players. Listen, I have seen whoremasters who could pass for Scots preachers. And just the other day I saw a Bishop of the Church of England—I must admit he was at a distance—who looked every inch an Italian fop.

Since you were open enough to ask a question to settle your doubts, may I ask you one?

. . . At your pleasure.

You are not Irish, are you?

. . . Oh, my God, sir! You ask a question like a cudgel to the side of the head. Irish? My God, not hardly! Not hardly at all. Why, that is like asking if my mother was a whore and my grandmother a better one.

I am sorry if I have offended you.

. . . Your question showed nothing of impercipience. The truth is, I have spent some time, and too much of it, in Ireland. After that unfortunate business in Bristol, I was impressed and shipped over to serve as a soldier in the bogs. Where they must have believed I would be buried with many another Englishman, not to mention the Irish, who've kept the grass green with their rotten bones. But here I am. I have lived to tell the tale of it. And in a sense you may not be so far from the mark, after all. For if I have not one drop of cloudy Irish blood in my veins, I confess there must be a crew of Irish bastards who may have more than a drop of my own. There's no waste in nature. I've left more new ones behind me than ever I killed.

. . . In the name of good old double-dealing Nicodemus, let us talk no more of Ireland. Let us look to the present and try not to dwell too much upon the cloudy past.

. . . Here we are in fair Southwark. Home for most of the watermen and half the whores of London. Home for the Bishop of Winchester's Palace and for five different jails. Three of which have, at one time and another, sheltered my poor, and always innocent, skin and bones. Home also, sir, of many fine inns and taverns. Of which I have the honor of recommending we enter that one yonder with the sign of the *White Bear*. Which we call the *Bear at Bridgefoot*.

✦ ✦ ✦ ✦ ✦

Now, you begin to spend time visiting a number of taverns. The two of you are keeping track of neither how much time is passing nor at how many of these cheerful places the time goes by. As to the former, you depend upon London law which says that no drink may be sold after eight o'clock in the evening at this season. You count on this, allowing always for the possibility that any such fellow as this will know of a place or two, within his ward and neighborhood, where he and his friend may circumvent the letter of the law. And as for the latter, why, it's true that these taverns are as different in a little of this and that as one man is from another, but as afternoon blends into evening, they begin to seem as much alike as a row of trees.

They are crowded and noisy with some music being played and many voices raised to the very edge of a shout in order to be heard at all. There are thick gray clouds, a patch of fog if you will, of the aromatic tobacco smoke from many pipes. Which, no matter how expensive tobacco is, hold the fashion in London nowdays. You can hire a pipe in any of these taverns if you feel inclined to smoke. The Player has his own which he carries with him in a fat wallet on his belt. It's a short-stemmed pipe with a large silver bowl, upon which bowl is graved somebody's proud heraldic arms.

. . . It came to me fairly and honestly, he says, and by a single roll of the dice.

He keeps puffing like a blacksmith's chimney. He has mastered the art of making circles and other odd shapes with the smoke. Which allows him to call himself a Professor of smoking, prepared to teach these tricks to anyone foolish enough to pay him to learn.

No one in these taverns is so foolish. For they all seem to know him well. There's an uproar of greeting at each place you enter. Goodwill grows warmer when they discover the Player is accompanied by a gentleman with a purse who can pay the reckoning. They gather in groups around the table to exchange jests and quips. To watch him, free for nothing, blow his marvelous shapes with tobacco smoke. And a few to cadge themselves a free cup of wine or a bottle of ale.

You and he are not drinking ale. Nor beer, the son of ale, nor hard Devon cider. Nor any of the lighter wines—claret or cute. None of your muscadine or malmsey, no old Rhenish or new Rhenish, not Italian Vernage, Malvesin Greek, not Rhine wines nor either your full-bodied Romeney from far off Romania. No, sir, nothing will do for today (and tonight) but something restorative, a medicinal drink for healthy men—shining Sack from Canary (he'll have it from no place else, not even Andalusia) with just a mite of white sugar stirred in as an aid to good digestion. And to begin things properly, a proper prologue to a session of Sack drinking—for our Player has been a full three hours now without a drop of anything stronger than some double beer for the sake of his throat and voice and must now make haste to recover lost time, you commenced at the *Bear at Bridgefoot* with a full cup of what they call (schoolmasters of taverns) *spiritus dulcis*, and he translated on the spot as "the spirit that giveth life when flesh is ready to hang itself and be damned." Which, whatever it is called, is alchemical creation composed of Sack distilled twice over and flavored with spirit of roses and with candy. It clears nose and throat, cleans the eyes with fresh tears, tingles the toes and fingernails and does cause the stomach to leap and rejoice like a young lamb.

. . . And now, says he, you are baptized for serious drinking of good Canary Sack.

By the time you have done both ends of the Bridge and then turned away, west, from Fish Street, with the vague goal of the *Mitre*—"not, mind you, the one by that name in Cheap, up by Mercer's Hall close to the Conduit and St. Mary Colechurch, but rather the other one toward the south end of Bread Street, close by the river," or else to the *Mermaid* found on Old Fish Street, between Bread and Friday's; or probably both, both places where you stand a good chance to meet with players and poets and the self-anointed quickest tavern wits in London; by that time you will be feeling careless as a wide-winged Angel soaring along the edges of an April breeze; feeling much too cheerful to permit yourself to worry much over the knowledge which you cannot dismiss with a shrug and a quip—namely that when you

awake in the morning (if you live that long), you will feel nothing like any Angel and like nothing so much as a shabby black-
bird baked alive in a piecrust. Your best hope for the future is
the silent, solemn promise to yourself that before the starry sky
begins to turn like a wagon wheel and the cobblestones of London begin rolling beneath you like the deck of a ship, you shall
begin to care for yourself like a well-paid physician. That you
shall begin, very soon now, to measure and count your doses of
this medicine. That you shall decline some refreshment or, failing
that, you will, sly fox, pour out some of this very drink in lieu of
any attempt to match this fellow. For it's clear as can be there
shall be no keeping up with him. Not since London Bridge has
there been any serious rivalry between you. He has already
swallowed enough to drown a warhorse; yet still his eyes are
open and alert. His tongue has yet to turn into a woolen blanket
to wrap around words. And his words, they run like hounds
finding and following one scent after another. More (it seems)
for the joy of running, for the sake of barking and belling, than
for anything else.

All this while names of taverns begin to flash by like the cards
in a shuffled deck—the *Horn* and the *Cock* and the *Dagger*, the
Swan and the *Star* and the *Phoenix*, *Windmill* and *Tripoly*, the
King's Head and the *Saracen's Head*, and not to forget the *Wool-*
sack or the *Three Cranes in Vintry*. Where, at the last, and grateful for the large mercy of it, you are introduced to Oysters in
Bastard Gravy, oysters cooked with ale and bread crumbs and
seasoned with ginger and pepper and sugar and saffron. Which is
enough to send you on, without tripping or toppling, to the *Mer-*
maid. Where a winter salad of boiled turnips and beets and car-
rots, followed by sturgeon cooked in claret, some chicken and
fruit in a pie, and ending with a sweet pie of apples and oranges,
leaves you if not as sober as a Tyburn hangman, then more sober
than any Justice of the Peace in England. And thus both of you
able to find your way to his house, with the aid and comfort of a
pair of link boys from the *Mermaid*, bearing torches to guide
you. Able to walk upright, singing and whistling a little, it's true,
but not loud enough to wake any sleeping citizens or to cause the
Watch to arrest you for a pair of common Rousers and Night-
walkers.

. . . Don't worry and fret, he assures you, clutching a brace of two-quart pottles of Sack, bought just before eight o'clock. They know me well, the Watch, for what I am—a gentleman and scholar.

Gent and scholar seems to have lost his hat. Perhaps at the *Mermaid*.

But you have yours on, squarely, and you can manage to walk with shoulders back and a certain loose swagger at the hips.

As you follow the player and the shadow and dancing of the torchlight, you pass the time between here and there by the reinvention of your conversation with this fellow. Most of the time it was more like soliloquy than exchange. But no matter. Soliloquy is his craft. And none of it was truly pertinent until it came time at last to tell him why you are here. Why you have come to find him. All the time before that was only preparation for you. Meantime you had him to listen to.

Story of his life. Which telling you have been resigned to since you entered the tiring-house at the Globe and shook his hand. Has there ever been a player who did not love the story of his life better than any other? Has there ever been a player whom you could take as an honest witness? Not that all actors are liars, but that actors lie as much as anyone else and are more gifted at it. Well, true or false it can sometimes be entertaining. Which is some consolation since you are going to hear it, like it or not.

. . . From my speech you probably take me to be a Londoner. And I think I can never be so truly at home or at ease anywhere else; and I have been to many places in my travels. But like nearly every other Londoner I was born elsewhere and came here later to find my home, if never (yet) my fortune. Someone has described London as the seed-plot for the shires of England. A place from which new plants come. The opposite is true. Raw country stock comes to London and takes root here. It's those who have flourished and come into wealth here that go forth to spend it by buying lands and building houses.

Begins a tale that's familiar, but no less true for being so. Story of a poor child in a parish far from London. He is vague, but by the sound of it and the harshness of the life he summons up, it must be the north. Though likely no farther north than Yorkshire. His father was a laborer for the manor farm. Working for wages and those wages small. Often hungry (as he remembers it) often cold and raggedy as Lazarus, the children, his brother and sisters and some other kin who were orphans. His father, a vague tall memory, died young. His mother became an alewife and used the cottage for a village alehouse. Then she married again, a younger man, a worker no richer than his father had been—"which is to say, sir, penniless." One who had lost his own wife and had some young children to look after.

This boy had early proved himself quick to learn. The Schoolmaster took care with him, and there was talk of sending him away to the grammar school in the nearest market town. But then it was that his mother married again, and soon he was sent off to be an apprentice to some kinfolk of his mother. Who lived, as it happened, in London.

. . . I sometimes think, he says, I might have been a scholar. Gone on to the university or the Inns of Court. But what then? There's many a university wit I've known here in London who has been forced to borrow from me to pay his reckoning.

To London to learn a skill, and he not quite twelve years old at the time. Not that his learning ceased, for he must go to school and study also, under the Queen's law, her dream that all of England shall read and write in her time.

. . . You mentioned mixed feelings, often opposed to one another. As in a mock combat. A tilt or a joust in the Tiltyard upon Accession Day. Myself in a suit of silver armor, in two suits of silver armor. Each suit worth the price of London Bridge with all the shops and houses on it and all the goods therein. Myself against myself, layered with the favors of half the ladies of Westminster, on a huge English warhorse, ready to break a lance on the shield of myself.

. . . Oh I never miss it when I am here in London in November and can acquire a ticket, preferably without paying for it. I can strut and jet with the best of them. And doff my borrowed hat and cry *Vivat Regina* when the Queen and her ladies appear in the Gallery and the games begin.

. . . You may smile, sir, but I have been there. And once was among the knights and lords in the yard. Albeit not as one of them, but as one of a flock of Centaurs—players we were, set cunningly upon hairy little ponies from the isles of Scotland. Part of a pageant—the cost of which could send a fleet to the Indies or, anyway, the Azores—created by My Lord of Essex to surprise and please the Queen. May he rest in peace. As well as, alas, in two pieces. . . .

. . . But there are other times. Bleaker. Darker. When the emblem of my feelings is not so grand. When I close my eyes and picture no palace and tiltyard, but rather a stinking prison, cold and dirty. Wherein a pair of half-naked wretches are wrestling with one another, groaning and gasping as they roll and slither in filthy straw. For what? For a loaf of stale bread tossed to them. Which they will not share. Bloody and sweaty and as tricked out with straw as any scarecrow, they wrestle until one is defeated. Lies spent and limp, heaving to breathe. While the other scuttles away to the corner like a rat—indeed, most likely kicking aside the rats to act like a rat himself—to gulp and choke down his tasteless bread. Yet with a sense of joyous triumph and with contempt for the other fellow on the floor, my wretched, meager, distressed, and disgusting companion. Who now is weeping like a woman or a child. Who now rolls over so that the thin light from the window falls briefly on his face. And then, of course, I see that he is cursed with my face also. That my enemy is only myself!

. . . You see, then, the layers of it. Truth must be a woman, for it is so covered and disguised with so many layers of clothing. What I mean to say is that it seems even my mixed feelings are an odd alloy and often counterfeit. False coins. Even my memories change. And what do you make of that, sir?

Perhaps it is the source of your craft as a player.

. . . Could you believe and accept my Pandarus?

I cannot imagine him other than as you made him out to be.

. . . Bless you, then! Let us drink to the stage.

. . . Let me return to the solid earth. If I can. It's Sack and sugar that has taken away my tongue with a writ of *habeas corpus*. Maybe I should change my drink. I hear of a doctor in Bishopsgate who sells a most wonderful medicine made of distilled spirits and the essence of the poppy flower, cleverly blended together. A good draft of which is said to put the drinker into a nodding, speechless, happy, dreaming trance. I must remember to try some one day. It might improve my dispostion.

I know the stuff and don't advise it. Pray continue with your story, if you will.

. . . Less than twelve years old I came to London to be apprenticed to a kinsman who was a cordwainer. And like everyone else who comes to London, I was ambushed by it. Had never imagined anything like it. How could I? Though, for sure, I was no fool then. I had listened, all ears and hopes, many times to travelers speak of the city. I had formed an impression— Jerusalem and Babylon, together with some words from Nineveh and Tyre and some bits and pieces of poor old Sodom and Gomorrah. But was not prepared for this city.

. . . Now one of the first things London does to anyone who comes here is to force him to reconsider his whole life up to that time. Saying to himself: "Where on earth have I been before coming here?"

. . . As to life with my kinsman, let me dispose of that simply. My story is not like the one you would hear, for the price of a tankard of beer, in this tavern or a hundred others. Malcontent tavern wits will tell you tales of harsh masters and hard work. Of beatings and running away. Of being cheated and deceived. *Et cetera, et cetera.* While if you were sitting down to supper even now, at the high table of some merchant's house, some fellow from one of the Guilds; who, if he has not already been so, has every good chance of being chosen as a Sheriff of Middlesex and maybe one day as Lord Mayor of London, such a fellow would tell you tales of industry and frugality, of skill learned well, of virtue rewarded. "It's these ne'er-do-well, scurvy, and idle sturdy rogues, whose very souls are as lazy as old cats; who will not work a day unless they have to; who are perfectly content, and so have no other purpose in life, to enjoy a full belly and shoes that fit well enough, warm clothes in the wintertime, and the frequent companionship of a poxy drab, some wench whose ministrations can transform oak into willow, make hempen rope from a soup bone, if you follow my meaning; antic, bird-eyed fellows, jolly robins who sleep through morning, lose the afternoon at the playhouse, and then haunt the taverns and alehouses as if they were graveyards and every night were All Hallows Eve; ill-

educated cynics who'll tell you there's no purpose in industry
and diligence, in honest deference to one's betters, because (to
them) the world is all a besmeared painted cloth, no more, and
what's to be had is all leasings and orts and rotten reversion.

"Look about you, sir, and consider that thirty years ago I did
not own more than my wits and a pewter spoon. Let them scoff
as may. Their betters will live in almshouses endowed by me.
And as for themselves, a lucky few will end their days in a spital
house. And their bones will rest in unmarked graves!"

You do the merchant vehemently well.

. . . Why, thank you, sir. Do you imagine they really speak
like that at the supper table?

Who knows or cares? Let us agree that they do.

. . . Done! But I shall tell you neither of these lies. I was never
ill treated or overworked. I was taught and I learned the skills of
leatherwork well. I can still make you a fine leather belt and an
excellent pair of riding boots. I delighted in learning the craft
and in working at it. Likewise delighted to put on my blue coat
and my flat statute cap to go forth (whenever I was free to,
which was often) to explore the wonders of this city, stem to
stern, root to highest branch. I cannot claim to have been cor-
rupted by it.

. . . Yet, nevertheless, I often thought of home.

With mixed feelings.

. . . Exactly so.

What he now tells is one of the oldest stories of England. True,
as he says, the labor was almost unceasing. True there were bad
times for all of them; and these latter recollections strike at surprising times, when least expected, often times of good cheer and
contentment. And as player he finds these memories useful to
summon up and settle in the spirit of some character created by
a poet.

Child of this Queen's reign, he has known no other sovereign,
save by reading and by the tales of elders. Child of this Queen's
times, he knew (at least until he was a grown man and was
pressed to serve in war himself) nothing but peace. Oh, as a lad
he heard stories of the Earls' Rebellion of '69. When the northern
Earls rose up for . . . whatever it may have been. Was shown the
very tree where some men from this same village, who had

marched with the Earls and were too poor to be either fined or ransomed, were hanged in the Queen's name to set an example.

. . . I never pictured myself—certainly not in those days—as being among the ragged wretches standing at the back of a cart with a rope around my neck, waiting to be hanged from a tree limb for the edification of my kinfolk and friends. No, sir, I would be the Queen's own man, the gentleman on a horse, looking much like the statue of St. George (which no one had the Puritan malice or piety to deface) in the parish church. A handsome fellow in armor, a knight myself no doubt. No pity in my eyes. A sneer on my lips as I told those rustic rebels to hurry up with their prayers so we could drive the cart out from under them and be off to the alehouse to wash down the dust.

. . . Ah, I was a pitiless child! At least in the stories I imagined for myself. I learned to read early, and our goodly minister would let me read in the copy of *Foxe's Book of Martyrs* which was kept in the church. Sometimes I would read aloud for the benefit of some of the older folk who could not read a word. I would read to them in a loud, clear, somewhat pompous voice, in imitation of our parson reading the service. They would be amazed that a little child, one of their own from the village, could read so well. And I would be amazed that these old folks, the oldest and wisest in the village, though they could not read a word, would sit there and weep for the suffering and deaths of people they had never even met, much less known of, without I had read the book to them.

. . . Soon enough I knew what would move them most and soonest. And therefore I would blend and interpolate Foxe's stories to that effect. It pleased me greatly to see them weep. Or to save them from weeping. Once or twice I took the liberty of saving a martyr from rack or fire either by a miracle (which they liked best) or by the timely arrival of a band of good Christian men, who were rather like Robin Hood's band, though led by a fine handsome fellow who looked much like the St. George in our church.

. . . Those versions got back to the parson. And I earned a whipping for it.

So you were an apprentice actor before you were ever a cordwainer. It was your first craft.

. . . I reckon that's so. Not that I ever imagined myself as a player or any such thing. Though sometimes, I remember, I would be taken in a wagon with other children of the village to a market fair. Where we could see jugglers and tricksters and sometimes a few fellows performing a play. Most likely some story from the Scripture. Which everyone could be expected to know something of. Or else, perhaps, some old piece from the legends of old England—tales of King Arthur and his knights. Perhaps a jolly comic tale stolen out of Chaucer or Gower.

. . . I have done it myself in lean times. Played to the bumpkins on a platform at market fair. I have been hooted as Herod and cheered as King Arthur. I would often see boys no older than I was. Some lad with a straw in his mouth and a sneer on his face. And I would wonder how different my life might have been, better or worse, except for a turn or two.

You see how memory softens the past. No news to you there. But there is some sweet truth at the heart of changing. For, to begin, he knew no other way of living. Except what he read of in books. Which he took to be mostly false. He could conceive that his life was hard and was poor. But he never imagined, till he left home for London and for good, that his life was in any way seriously different from anyone else's. Excepting, of course, the beautiful Queen with a jeweled crown on her head, sitting in glory on her throne in what might have been Fairyland or Heaven.

And then there was the Knight who possessed the manor there, which included their village. Who was seldom there, except to keep Christmas hospitality, being a gentleman of the Queen's Court. In his case there must have been (as the child thought then) either some great mystery or some great mistake. For this gentleman was as unlike St. George as a glove is to a shoe. Perhaps, he thought, it is a disguise that he wears—his huge swag belly made from a cushion, his frounced gray hair and his scraggly beard being both wigs. No doubt if he and his lady, who, though somewhat more comely, seemed to be dressed in disguise also, came in their true glory, they would turn poor villagers to stone.

The boy took no chances whenever, during Christmastide, this knight came riding up the village lane, aiming generally for the inn, looking, for all the world, like a loosely packed, two-handed grain sack, with a hat set on top of it, and the whole thing set on a saddle on a scrawny and unwilling nag. Boy would see him, quick doff whatever rag of a hat he was wearing, with a bow and a flourish, all of this with his eyes closed. For safety's sake. Once when Knight was coming from the inn, after his daylong adventure of wine and cards, the boy did not see horse or rider until the last moment. Startled, he leaped to pull off his hat and close his eyes. Saw only that the horse jumped, startled also. With his head bowed and his eyes closed he heard a sound, like a sack of grain (indeed) falling onto the muddy lane. Followed by a groan. Followed by the drumming of hooves running off into distance and silence. Followed by a snort and then a snore and then a sequence of snores as steady as breathing.

Keeping his eyes closed he backed away to where he knew there was a tree he could slip behind, then peer around. Did so and saw that Knight on his back like a beetle. Sound asleep and the rain beginning to fall.

Ran to the inn and told the keeper that the Knight had gone to sleep in the lane.

"Which is where he rightly belongs," the innkeeper said. "We should leave him there to drown in his own juices. But never let it be said that we are not good Christian men in this village. Come, lads, let's drag the lord out of the mud."

So off he went with a brace of drunken fellows to see if they could save the Knight without falling down themselves.

Once in those days, the parson arranged for the boy to read aloud the gospel for Epiphany from St. Matthew. It was on the occasion of Twelfth Night at the manor house. When all the village, young and old, came to the Hall for cakes and ale and singing and games of chance. ("Even as little children we knew better than to play at any game of chance with the Knight; for it was understood that manners and Christian charity required we should let him win whatever game it might be. Though this was somewhat difficult to understand. Since the parson and the innkeeper and the others cheerfully took every coin in his purse when he played at cards or dice at the inn.") It was the hope of the parson that the Knight would be pleased by this intelligent child and might take an interest in his education. They had rehearsed this in Church until the parson was fully satisfied.

And now the time comes and the boy is brought forward to stand before the Knight and all of the company, *The Book of Common Prayer* in his hands, and to read:

"When Jesus was born in Bethlehem, a city of Jewry, in the time of Herod the King, behold there came Wise Men from the east to Jerusalem, saying, where is he that is born King of the Jews? For we have seen his star in the east, and are come to worship him. . . . Then Herod, when he had privily called the Wise Men, he inquired of them diligently what time the star appeared, and he bade them go to Bethlehem and said, Go your way thither, and search diligently for the child. And when ye have found him, bring me word again, that I may come and worship him also. . . . When they saw the star they were exceeding glad, and went into the house, and found the child with Mary his mother, and fell down flat, and worshipped him, and opened their treasures, and offered unto him gifts: gold, frankincense, and myrrh. And after they were warned of God in sleep that they should not go again to Herod, they returned into their own country in another way."

The old Knight, full to brim, to the edge of lips and the fringe of beard with the fumes of spirits if not with the good spirit of Christmastide, rocking back and forth on the heels of his boots . . . ("For he was always booted and spurred both indoors and out; and likely, it was guessed, he slept in his boots either to save the effort of bending over to put them on or because no one had found a way to pull them off his feet with ease.") . . . before the blazing logs on the fire, was simply furious.

"Priest!" he cried out. . . .

("Whenever he was displeased by anything the parson said or did, which was not infrequently, he would call him 'priest' to remind him of his Papist days and, also, as the Knight imagined, to shame him for the unhesitant ease with which he had retained his parish by taking oaths and becoming a clerk of the Church of England without any struggle of conscience. The Knight was overlooking how he himself had undergone the same transition from one faith to another, from one order of worship to another, with no more response than his outspoken annoyance at having to learn anew when it is proper to stand and to kneel etc.")

"Priest!" he cried out. "You mock me in my own house!"

"Not at all, sir," says the parson. "I thought it might please you to see a village lad who has learned so quickly and so well."

"Oh, indeed it does, Priest. Indeed it does. . . ."

Turning to the boy he pats him lightly on the head, as you might pat a waggy-tail dog who has just done an unusual trick. Hands him a shilling. Which is more money than he has ever held in his hands before. One hand closes over the coin like a claw. It would take torture to cause him to open that fist. And the boy decides that this Knight may now say and do whatever he pleases. Because the payment of a shilling buys that privilege. Indeed for a penny he would sing and dance and turn a cartwheel. For a shilling he'll read through the Bible forward and backward without stumbling over any words. Even the tongue-twisting names of the Jews.

"Indeed he's a gifted little pup. No question," the Knight continued. "A most amazing little country crow able to read those words from the book without hesitation or embarrassment. And, Priest. . . ." (Back to the parson, his voice full of gravel again.) "You have prepared him well for this world. There is neither place nor office at Court no more for an honest man of the sword. 'Tis an age, with a Queen on the throne and ne'er any husband to guide and direct her, 'tis an age for sweet fellows who can dance and sing. And most of all these times are ripe for clerks who are quick with words. They thrive and prosper and take precedence while those of us whose service is to protect and defend the hearthsides of England, are passed by, left high and dry, our services belittled by perfumed, lacy scroyles who are more at home with a feathered pen than ever with sword and buckler, dagger and rapier, black bills and brown. . . ."

("The satiric beauty of all this, you understand," the Player tells you, "is that our Knight had never come nearer to war than attendance at the county muster. He safely rode out the Rising of '69 in his bed, suffering from an ague, brought on, no doubt, by his inability to determine which side was worthy of his assistance. In truth, no one in our parish, indeed the whole country, could recall his ever drawing sword from its scabbard. Not even to cut a pie or a piece of cheese. None had ever seen the fellow's blade out of the scabbard. Though he often, in moments of brief fury, such as after losing at roll of the dice or a hand of cards, swore a mighty oath and clapped hand on the hilt, as if his next move would be to yank it free and to carve up everyone in sight. Hand on hilt was as far as he went. Which divided our village into two factions. There were those who believed there was nothing more to his sword than the hilt, that hilt and scabbard were all. Others, more admiring, said that there was, indeed, a real sword there, but it had rusted tight in the scabbard through times of peace. And whoever could pull it free and draw it would be the next King Arthur.")

"Whilst men of the sword are ignored, sneaking, sniveling, dungstraw scarecrows, whose fathers might be any one of a dozen scabby ditchdiggers and jakesmen who found their mothers willing behind a haystack in harvest time, rascals, then, without blood or breeding or reputation, fresh from their Oxford and Cambridge and their quibbling Inns of Court, coming out of those academic laystalls where idle, cowardly, parasitical snots learn Latin words and numbers, and songs and dances and witty jests which will serve to advance them in Caesar's world and at the expense and discomfort of their inherent betters! There is no justice at Court in this age. And there never will be, neither, until Frenchman or Spaniard shall land in England or the Scot shall cross the borders again. Then, by God!, these dainty fellows will be as scarce as wolves are in the city of London. Then the call will go out for swordsmen! Pray it shall not be too late!"

With which exhortation he clangs hand on hilt and, tugging (in vain, as ever) steps backward into the fireplace and damned near falls into the flames to become the first burned martyr this village has produced. But two husky fellows jump to seize him and pull him safely forth with no more damage to him than some scorching and smoke at the arse end of his galligaskins.

"All too true, I fear, sir," the parson says, matter-of-fact and quietly. As if nothing had happened. As if he'd made a remark about the weather and the Knight had grunted agreement. "But now, as for the lad. . . ."

"Aye, the little bit of a horse turd reads as well as any Bishop. And he shall have his reward."

Another pat on the doggy head. Another shilling. Having, no doubt, forgotten the first one. Thus making the boy (with both fists turned to claws now and the Prayerbook clamped tight underarm) the richest person beside the Knight and his lady (who seems to have vanished) in the Hall.

"Priest," he says. "We shall dress this mouse up in silk and satin, and I shall take him with me to read for the Queen. And I'll wager he'll not leave the Presence Chamber without acquiring at least the reversion of an office or a lease of some crown lands. Then, perhaps, we can go to serve him. If he can find a place for a simple old swordsman who can only claim to have done his duty, always, as he saw it to do. . . ."

At which point, just as the first large, clear tears began rolling down his cheeks, a great blast of a ram's horn came from the far end of the Hall like a giant breaking wind. And here came servants bearing tankards of nappy ale and wonderful cakes and cream. A fiddler began to play for the country dancing. Which our fat gray knight was good at. For though he was no doubt as clumsy as a calf at Court with all their galliards, pavanes and allemandes, their basse dances and haute dances, when it came down to your true country dance or hornpipe, your Shake-a-Trot or Bishop of Chester's Jig and suchlike, he was as lightfoot and quick as a fox moving across the crust of the snow.

. . . But can you believe he truly spoke like that?

I believe you. Which is much more to the point.

. . . Two shillings! That's the most I've ever earned for a performance in all of my life.

May it happen sometime again.

. . . To continue.

(And so he does.)

You want to be just. The man saves himself from the squalor of self-pity by his unquenched humor. Which allows him to see some of the riddles of remembering as adding up to something like that sign you'll find in certain alehouses, called the Sign of Three Fools, depicting two obviously foolish men. And where's the third? Why that must be you; sir, who is looking at the sign.

. . Look, sir, he's saying to you. Look what happens when your London merchant or your gentleman of the Court comes into money. That money goes into land. Land in the country and a house there. It is the dream of every ambitious man who comes here. Even native-born Londoners sing the same tune. They long as much as any of us, born and half raised in the country, to return to the land. Returning in triumph, to be sure. No one would slink back and pick up his old shovel and hoe again. A man would rather die here than go home again, admitting to folly and failure.

Which evidence—that no one returns saving in prosperity—might cause countrymen to misconstrue to draw inference that all who go to London prosper there.

. . . Ah, sir, they know better than that. But just as I cling to illusions about country life, so the countryman keeps his illusions about the city. It makes him feel better to believe there is a place he could go, where all men prosper. Where there's money to come by as easy as picking apples off a tree. Without illusions we would be at each other's throats like dogs, cut and long-tail, barking and snarling over a red bone.

. . . And you would not have to be here long, sir, to notice how the Court, following the fashion of the Queen, affects country dances and such things. To observe how all the City and the Court do contrive to keep a country calendar of holidays. As if both Court and City would prove to be pure cloudy illusions while the country and the old customs of England were as hard and true as baked Flanders brick.

I have heard that Queen and Council are troubled that hospitality is not kept in the country as it once was.

. . . Yes, that's the paradox of it. Your Court gentleman cannot afford to be absent from the Court for long.

Except when the Queen goes on Progress.

. . . True, then they are scarce enough. Because these Progresses are tedious and troublesome for everyone but the Queen. They are uncomfortable, and there is small gain to be had on a Progress for lesser gentlemen. Unless it's his pleasure to steal silver spoons and such.

. . . And behind all this, sir, is the great unspoken thing. What must not be said aloud, but must surely be understood as the secret cause behind so many actions of these days.

And what would that be, in your opinion?

. . . Well, sir, it is the Queen's age and health. May she live and reign long. But it does not seem likely. It is given out that she is healthy as a horse. But there are other stories, too. Those who saw her at the latest Parliament reported she looked not well at all. That crown and robes seemed all too heavy for her. That she stumbled and had to be helped.

Well, no question the Queen is old.

. . . What's on the mind of the others is the Succession. Who shall follow after her?

Who do you suppose?

. . . Oh, sir, I have neither opinion nor favor. What good would it do? I shall do honor and be loyal to whoever shall lawfully succeed the Queen.

Well said.

. . . Carefully said. Allow me that. . . . But, to dispose of your question. As I take it, the younger gentlemen of Court (who will honor and serve whoever sits next on the throne) tend to favor the claims of King James of Scotland. Because he is a man and a practicing King who must have learned some lessons in Scotland. And because he is a stranger. One who can offer England a new beginning. Of course, every new reign is a new beginning, but a new reign by a foreigner is fresh enough so it can be every man for himself. And unlucky he who gets the hind tit of the sow.

But surely he will bring many Scotsmen with him.

. . . I have heard that. And have heard an answer to it, too— that he has in Scotland a small and shabby Court. And, sir, I can attest to that, having been there to perform at his Court.

Oh?

. . . Another story. For another time.

Pray continue.

. . . The first reason, then, is that he has such a meager, shabby Court. Which, even if he brought them all and gave away Scotland to the Danes or the Irish or, perish the thought, to the Wild Scots of the North, still would be lost here among us. But the men of Court are willing to wager he would want to be rid of many of both old dogs and old fleas. They wager that he, too, is desirous of a new and clean beginning.

. . . And the second good reason is this. It has been a long time in England since there has been a second Court. Not since our grandparents. But this King of Scotland and his Queen keep separate Courts. And soon the eldest son, the young Prince Henry, upon whom much hope is laid, will be old enough for a Court of his own. In England he will be Prince of Wales. Which means that if James succeeds, there will be three different Courts to absorb ambition. And to offer offices and rewards. A miraculous multiplication like the loaves and the fishes.

. . . Moreover, a third reason that he seems to be favored is that his own Succession is clear. With children, with two sons of his own, we would find ourselves spared the worry that has troubled so many.

Are there doubts about the Scot?

. . . They wonder at his nature. Whether, from what they have ascertained, he may prove to be a vengeful ruler.

You are thinking of his mother—the Queen of Scots?

. . . Yes, and other matters.

The Earl of Essex. Was he not a favorite of the King's, in a fashion?

. . . Perhaps.

Here he eyes you closely. He's not drunk yet. Nor so at ease as to be free of suspicion.

There seems to be a measure of doubt concerning the King's religion.

. . . Protestant, sir, though of what shade no one is sure. They say that Prince Henry has been raised an exemplary Protestant. Yet it is also told by Scots as well as Englishmen, that the King is tolerant of all Papists. Except for seditious Jesuits.

Too good to be true?

. . . Where were we before we became so uncautious as to talk of things which are none of our affair?

Country and city, I believe.

He continues with a catalogue of country holidays as they are practiced in London, relishing (as well he might on a chilly evening) the warmth of May Day and Midsummer Eve. Which leads him surely to recollections of happy village days.

. . . Lord, we had times then! On holidays you forgot all troubles and were glad to be alive.

You set your face attentively. Put your head at an angle for easy and timely nodding. Keeping your eyes fixed on his. Which change according to the light and how he now widens them, now narrows them with the words. They are light blue and alive and yet, you surmise, they are sad eyes. In opposition to the quick-smiling, expressive mouth. Very good, very white teeth. High-boned cheeks. Face as smooth and stiff as a mask, though the sad eyes and laughing, cynical lips give that mask a constant move-ment. Hair gold as ripe barley in sunlight. Hands, large and long-fingered, sturdy, countryman's working hands. Nails of fingers clipped and clean. The hands and fingers deft in gesture, some-times twins of simultaneity, at others, as a gesture may require, a couple of fractious brothers, a quarreling man and wife. He wears some good rings—borrowed? stolen?—on each. In a while you will interrupt him, fascinated by those hands—now wings, now country tools, now courtly dancers—to ask if he plays the lute. And he will answer that he plays not well enough to make it his trade, but that he sings well enough to disguise his flaws.

Meantime this player continues in his celebration of a country childhood. Like many another fugitive, one who long since fled to embrace the pleasures (and pains) of city life, he has forgot-ten much of it. Permits memory to paint it falsely. Like the face of some old whore who would wish to be taken as young and in-nocent.

Well, at least, you think, he has not (yet) tried to conjure up a tapestry scene of nymphs and shepherds. Like those languid fellows of the Court who write poems of a world that never was nor will be. Still, scholar of scars, pedagogue of honest callouses, you find you must speak.

You have forgotten the hard labor. Perhaps you went to the forest to find wild flowers on May Day. But you brought back firewood or else your hearth and supper were cold.

. . . I fear it's true, he says with a laugh. I can remember only the best times. Mostly we lived on white meats and windy beans. But when I think of eating as a child, what do I recall? Shrove-tide pancakes with meat of a boiled hen served with them. Black pudding when we killed the pig in the fall. A fat goose for Michaelmas; cream and the tarts of fresh-picked berries on May Day; frumenty—the red wheat perfectly boiled in cream and then cooked with sugar and eggs and saffron and cinnamon upon

Twelfth Night, and every year for that feast our Knight would send venison to all of us. . . .

The only way to eat it.

. . . Agreed! Fresh pears in August for Bartholomewtide, when they come ripe. And the new cider in the fall. And so on and so on.

But what do you picture when you remember true belly cheer? Tell the truth.

. . . Ah, well. A black iron pot simmering on the hearth, a steam of rich odors rising from it. Thicker than porridge it was. Why, you could float a pewter spoon on it. And I would walk clear across London tonight, if I could be sure a bowl was waiting for me.

The fellow is incorrigible. Best take another tack.

Tell me, how did you happen to become a player?

Tells how he did well as an apprentice at leatherworking. Might have gone far, might be a man of importance in the Guild, if he had not delivered a pair of boots to a player at an Inn in Southwark. If that player had not taken a liking to him at sight. And if that traveling company had not just lost one of their boys to the sweating sickness.

How he did not run away, however. But asked permission of his master. Who followed him back to the Inn and talked with the player.

. . . Some money changed hands. Some promises were made and exchanged over my ignorant head. And I changed hands. Went off on the high road, walking behind a gaudy cart, together with this little band. To learn a new craft. Which was soon exercised in innyards and guildhalls, in drafty castles and the high Halls of great houses. In fields and markets and market fairs. And once on the deck of a ship.

. . . In the country we were well received. For the folk were grateful for any spectacle. We could have been the immaculate angels descending to astonish shepherds on Christmas Eve. But in London it was different for us. In London you must prove yourself beyond a shadow of a doubt. Which, sir, can be a true satisfaction when you are with an excellent company, performing a play written by a poet of great reputation.

. . . London is your town for plays and players, believe me. I have been all over this kingdom and in much of Scotland, too. I have been in Flanders and Germany. Never in Paris. Never in Italy, either. Where I hear they do right well. Oh, I have seen some of their players—their Pantalone, Gratiano, the doctor, Spavento, the Spanish Captain and one or another zany. Indeed this year there was a company of the Italians here and one Flaminio Curtesse, said to be among the finest of them all. I have seen them.

. . . I have played before the crowds in the Bankside theaters and the suburbs. Have performed at the Inns of Court. More than one time have played in the presence of the Queen of England and her Court. And once, as I said, I played my part in Edinburgh before the King of the Scots.

. . . And yet, sir, there is a true sense in which none of it can satisfy as it once did, performing some simple part—a foolish lovesick lad, a foppish courtier, a country slut who longs to be a lady or vice versa, an Abraham man or a ˊcup-shotten knight, Herod the Jew or old Mack the shepherd, Friar Tuck and Little John, and the like—before a crowd of wide-eyed country folk at a fair. Sometimes I believe I would rather find myself as a moth-eaten St. George (though more often, I confess, in those days I was to be found playing the hind end of the dragon) on the village green at a parish wake than to be Tamburlaine the Great in London.

. . . Do you believe that?

If you say so.

. . . Sometimes there was plenty of money knocking together in our purses. Other times we were so poor that we were reduced to unlawful tricks to remain alive. I know a thing or two about cutting a purse with nimble fingers or catching a conny with a nimble tongue. Sometimes we were feasted and full. And other times we were so hungry we would leap and jump and play any trick for the sake of a dry crust. Would fight each other for it, too. So hungry that hard bones tasted like sweet beans.

. . . I learned many things at my trade. To speak clearly and to be heard by all without effort or strain. To dance the dances and even to sing a little without needing to be ashamed of myself. To handle a sword as well as any man except a true fencing master. To walk like a lady and to talk like a gentleman. And, yes, to live like a gentleman, too, whenever circumstance permits.

. . . But, sir, I do not think you have come to hear me tell my tale.

He spins a coin on the table. Lets it go. To spin and die, as he rests both hands, palms down, on the table. And looks at you with cold steady eyes.

Now it is for you to perform. Not taking your eyes from his, you reach beneath the table into a little leather wallet chained to your belt. For two coins. You have been paying reckonings with silver coins. He has seen that. But not this. Each coin appropriately has (for inadvertently he has given you a cue) the winged St. George on one side, busily slaying the dragon with a short spear. On the other a ship and the arms of England. These coins are eighty grains of old gold. They do not glitter in the light like silver. They bask in it.

You ease them forward on the tabletop. Then you smile, releasing the coins to stay there and letting your hands return.

The old Knight gave you a shilling to hold in each hand. Mine begins by offering you a pair of angels.

For a moment he says nothing. You have to credit him with his skill. Nothing about that angular face, sharp as the face of the Knave in a deck of cards, has changed. Except there are a few, small, clear beads of sweat forming in a line along his brow.

. . . My knight was a drunkard and somewhat forgetful.

Mine is neither. He lives in good health and gives promise to live for many a year.

Until now he has not allowed his eyes to glance away from yours to look at the coins. Has not so much as blinked. But now blink he does as all at once he licks his lips and clenches and unclenches his hands (rings winking in light as he does), and his eyes, quick as the blink, no more, assure him he's not deceived.

The saint of your parish church. You see how everything fits.

Which may be excessive. For the player, sensitive as a wild hare, sets his jaw.

. . . I was not asking for anything.

Nevertheless it is the way of the world and we are all in it. You have money and he has need for it. And it's all as simple as kisses under the mistletoe.

I know that (you say quietly, politely, feeling your smile firmly in place). *And you never would, either, for you have your pride. You have rings on your fingers and, as you say, a net of scars across your back. You are a man to be reckoned with, no question.*

His face clenching like a fist. He cannot be sure how much you are mocking him. Nor can he know if his pride will permit him to decline two gold angels on the table under any circumstances. And there's fear in his eyes. They blink nervously, not quite obedient to his will. Those beads of sweat on his forehead are large drops now.

It is proper that he should be afraid of you. Because it is true you would kill him, though not unless it were necessary. Likely it will not happen, but he should understand that it could. Fine-tuned as he is, he understands it well. And when you move one hand quickly out of sight again, he winces and has to grit his teeth from cringing away from whatever it is you are bringing up into sight.

Well, what you have put on the table deserves reaction. A wince will have to do. This coin is old gold also, more than double the size of the angel and three times its weight. On one side the Queen herself, full-face, crowned, seated on a throne and holding her mystical orb and scepter. On the other the arms of England at the center of a decorative design. This is the largest coin that's made in the Tower mint—the Sovereign. Five of these makes a year's wages for a skilled blacksmith in this year of Our Lord.

The difficulty of living like a gentleman in this day and age is the continual rising of prices. It becomes more expensive every day.

. . . I have nothing that's worth this money. I know nothing. . . .

We believe otherwise.

Let him sweat. Let him wipe at his brow with a handkerchief. While you look away from him to signal to the drawer to send a waiter with a fresh supply of Sack.

. . . Sir, I believe that you may be mistaken about my abilities to offer anything which might be of value to your master.

He is speaking hesitantly. Monotone. As if he has lost most of his purse of words. Now he's picking and choosing as if these were the last words he will ever own. His face seems to be slackening. As if it were melting wax.

It is not pleasant to cause a man's confidence to crumble. There are some fools who enjoy nothing better than to smash the illusions of the weak. You do not take pleasure in it. But it must be done now. And can be done quickly.

God's wounds, man! No need to play the hangdog, tail-between-the-legs, with me. We know about you, more than you can guess. I have better things to do than haunting Bankside playhouses and taverns along the river. I have more pleasant duties than following the track of some rogue of a player through half the gaming houses in Lambeth marsh and, I hope, all the houses of good fellowship—those places which unmannerly folk do persist in calling bawdy houses—of Cowcross and Clerkenwell, of Saffron Hill and Charterhouse Lane. . . .

He manages a slight, slightly twisted grin.

. . . Pray do not overlook the "French Library" of Paris Garden.

You have to laugh and credit him with that.

Two things astonish. One is where you find the money you manage to lose at gambling. The other is where you find the strength to keep so many London whores content. Is there any man better known in the brothels than you?

. . . There once was a tall Blackamoor who sold Spanish needles on London Bridge. An amazing fellow, equipped like a plow horse.

Never mind. Your sins are not of significance to us.

. . . I never felt called to be a saint.

You have, from time to time, been called to be a spy.

. . . What do you mean?

For Sir Robert Cecil.

. . . *Robertus Diabolus.* Ah, well, sir, that was many years ago. Before he was given the great signet and was named to be Secretary. It's true I did some small service for him. For his old father, too. A little looking and listening was all. And that, sir, not involving matters of estate, but concerning some felonious crimes in this city.

Did you not perform some service for the Earl of Essex?

. . . Well now, the Earl was a patron of poets and players. It's true I did sometimes perform for him, with others, in the Tiltyard (as I said) for holiday masques and such.

I was thinking of something more than that.

Here he flushes briefly. Sips his Sack, as if thoughtfully, and leans closer to you, lowering his voice.

. . . Only during the last year. When he was home from Ireland in disgrace and was forbidden the Court. I did him some modest service. But I was only one among many.

You were never a servant of the Earl's?

He starts, as if you had slapped his face.

He may have thought so. But is it not true that you spied on Essex? For someone else. Who was that?

He sighs. . . . Not spying. No, sir, I merely observed what happened and made some report of what I observed.

. . . There were two men. Gentlemen I presume. Scotsmen they were, at least by accent and dress. But who can tell what is true and what's in disguise in this age of players?

. . . Next they prevailed upon me—by threats and promises—to, yes, spy somewhat upon the Earl of Essex. On behalf of someone else whom they did not choose to name.

Ah, it is ever so. And who do you suppose was that unnamed person?

. . . I imagined it might be the King of Scots. Or perhaps someone close to him. I had no reason to be sure.

What did they ask of you?

. . . That I should find a means to be of service to the Earl. And in doing so, I should spy on him. That I should prepare some memoranda which would be delivered, all in due time, to this person on whose behalf they were acting. That I should begin, even before I had done or accomplished anything, by accepting from them a large sum of money.

Which you accepted.

. . . Which, you may be sure, I did accept. They told me there would be more money for me later.

And?

. . . I did what I had been asked to do. I found employment with the Earl.

In what capacity?

Here he giggles and has to use his hand to stop himself.

. . . As a kind of an agent. I served Mr. Anthony Bacon directly. As an agent and jack-of-all-trades.

Mr. Anthony Bacon was a spymaster, is that not so?

. . . It is true he was the chief intelligencer for the Earl—his own Walsingham or Cecil, if you will. Mr. Bacon lived in chambers at Essex House, often sick and seldom beyond the gate of it, except sometimes to go to the country for refreshment. He lay there, as it were, like a thin spider at the center of a sticky net. And the world came to him. I suppose I was one of his many flies.

Did you furnish reports for your new friends?

. . . I did so. In the form of letters which I left for them at an inn on Bishopsgate Road. Where also they were to leave any instructions they wished to convey.

And did they?

. . . Never a word. I left my letters and received none. Then, after a while, there was the whole affair of the Earl's rebellion. After which I never heard anything more from these men. And after which, since there was nothing left for me to report, I took a position with a traveling company for some months.

You were wise to do so.

. . . Except for the undeniable money, I think that I must have dreamed it.

And now the money's undeniably gone. Perhaps you dreamed it, too.

He shrugs.

The person or persons whom I represent would like me to look at any papers you may have.

. . . How are you sure that I still have any papers for you to see?

Because I am, by now, well enough acquainted with you to believe that you would not destroy anything which might have some value. I am reasonably sure your thinking was—what a couple of Scotsmen paid for once might be paid for again, sooner or later, by someone else. And, you can see, you were right.

. . . It can be arranged. When would it please you?

Tonight.

. . . Then it will have to be at my humble lodgings.

He palms the coins on the table and stuffs them safely in his purse. He looks you in the eye again, and with a sly little smile, almost shy. A look that conveys apology.

. . . There is a woman at that place . . . and some small children.

Your wife?

. . . Unfortunately. She is a good woman, a pious woman, a shoemaker's widow, too. Who brought with her a little money, soon spent alas, and the house we live in.

He shrugs heavily. As he must have when he played Herod, King of the Jews.

. . . Every man needs a roof overhead and a worthy woman to come home to.

You are laughing again. He looks puzzled.

. . . She may not be greatly pleased to see me at this late hour. She has a sharp tongue, sir, my wife, and is sometimes given to contumelious speaking.

I have no doubt that you can find a way to soften her anger.

He offers you his hand upon it. A firm handshake. A merchant's handshake.

. . . Shall we have some supper first? I fear that our cupboard may be somewhat bare.

By all means.

A four-story house, tall and narrow. Somewhat decayed, it seems. You can judge better when daylight comes. A house set on a twisting unpaved lane. House and lane lost in this ancient liberty, Whitefriars, set between Fleet Street and the River, bounded on the east by Whitefriars Street and on the west by the walls and grounds of the Temple. Bearing the nickname Alsatia (for that disputed territory between France and the Germans), it is still a lawful sanctuary.

There are some fine houses, ones which have not been converted into tenements for the sake of rents, belonging to gentlemen of the Court and owned, as well, by some men of the Guilds, especially among the Cordwainers. But mostly it has become a place of some ill repute.

You sit at an ordinary trestle table set up close by the fireplace, where a bed of sea coals broods and glows. A horn lantern, holding a thick cheap tallow candle, offers a dull pool of yellowish light to read by.

It is quiet now except for the steady snoring of the Player and his wife in their old curtained bed across the room. And the occasional rustling of children bundled together for warmth on little pallets in a far corner.

The chamber is on the ground floor. What was once the shoemaker's shop and workshop. Now they have chosen to rent out the chambers of the upper floors. The Player was right to warn you. The lean woman was in a fury when you arrived, the Player burdened by his two large, straw-wrapped bottles of Sack, and the tavern linkboys holding their torches to light the scene. There they stood, giggling and snickering, while that woman cursed and reviled and berated the Player, yourself, the linkboys and everyone within hearing distance, with the language of a boatswain making his feelings known to a crew of completely inept seamen. If she had produced a whistle and blown it, you would not have been surprised. Indeed, without a second thought you and the Player and the linkboys would probably have climbed up the side of the house like monkeys, ready to set or furl any sails you could find there.

There was no whistle, but instead a loud rough voice coming from a window across the lane. You had to dance out of the way as the contents of a full chamberpot splashed in the already stinking lane. Followed by a shredded heap of threats of worse things to follow unless quiet were restored.

Inside the house, the children swarmed all around you. You found a halfpenny for each. And the Player fed them some sweet cakes he had brought along from the taverns. And all the while her amazing voice was playing its raucous simple melody of one or two notes. Like a peddler's horn. Until she was calmed by the Player's announcement that this gentleman whom she had been describing to all the world in most rude, unmannerly and opprobrious terms, was in fact a benefactor to this family at a time—namely now—of distinct need. Her face brightened and her body gracefully straightened. As if years and troubles could be cast aside with no more than a shrug. Her eyes held light from somewhere. She proved she could smile and even speak softly if she had a mind to.

Still, suspicion was not so easily discarded. She was more than mildly curious as to what might be expected of them in return.

The Player had taken a lantern and a shovel and gone out into the garden. And so it fell to you to assuage her doubts. To reassure her (even as she began to shoo the children into their beds) with the explanation that her husband happened to be in possession of some papers which might be of value to the person or persons in whose behalf you had the honor of acting. That only by examining these papers yourself could you determine the value of them. That, therefore, you had been authorized to purchase those papers. And not for the purpose of holding or keeping or copying or carrying away. But simply to examine them here and now, this night in this place.

"After which?"

After which, you tell her, you intend to burn them to ashes in the fireplace.

"Why?"

There are reasons. Let it be understood as a protection for your husband.

"Have you thought . . . ?" she says softly, standing close to you now and showing a shrewd smile. (*You can begin to sense what it was that attracted the Player to this woman, above and beyond this house and whatever money she had.*) "Have you stopped to think that if these papers are so precious, my husband might be wise not to give up all of them just now? That he might hold some back from you?"

To sell a second time—to me or to someone else?

"Such things have been done."

You are suspicious because I seem to be so willing to trust you, I take it.

She stands close enough so that by a slight shifting of your weight you would be touching her body. There is a vague sweetness (perfume?) about her.

"If I were standing in your shoes, all in all, I should not find either of us, my husband or myself, to be entirely trustworthy."

It does not touch upon trusting you, you reply, looking deeply into her eyes. Which, as you can feel clearly now, convey a kind of predatory lust. Which could, under some circumstances, waken a corresponding lust in a man.

In this matter there are only two things to be believed in. First, there is gold. Old gold is the key to much in the world that is locked up tight from those who are without it. You can, and should, trust that money. And, second, there is this. If your husband tries to cheat me, then not all the money in London could shield your husband or yourself from the consequences which would be sure to follow.

She seemed to weigh that for a moment.

"You say it gently," she said. "But it is a wicked thing to say."

Ah, lady, it is a very wicked world we are all living in. Take my word for it.

"Don't you fear the fires of hell?"

If hell proves to have fires, I fear you and I shall both be cooked to a turn.

She laughed out loud. Just as the Player returned from the garden, windblown, muddy almost to his knees, and bearing a small somewhat rusty, locked casket. He put it on the table.

. . . How on earth have you managed to make that woman laugh?

"Hellfire," she said. "This gentleman is of the opinion that I am destined to enjoy the fires of hell."

. . . Then that makes the two of us in perfect agreement. For if you escape hell, woman, there is no justice under the sun.

He opened the casket.

. . . There now! he said, lifting out papers which were all wrapped in a woollen cloth. Let us have one more cup of Sack for health and sweet dreams. And then leave our guest to his . . . scholarship.

Now they are snoring. The children are deeply asleep, though one says words aloud from the depths of a dream. Fire is dying, and in a while you will have to shovel another portion of sea coal onto it. But for now it is warm enough, and you sit there, in the best chair and with a soft cushion, too.

What you are looking for you will not find. Which will please your patrons. About whom only this much can be said without violating your sense of discretion. Men of the world, they found quiet ways to be of modest support to the Earl of Essex. Especially during the last year or so when he was deprived of most of his income and hopelessly in debt. Thus, though in a fairly remote sense, they were supporters of the rebellion. If rebellion is what it truly was.

Their thinking was this: that they recognized there was a chance that Essex might succeed in his strategies. Which were? Ah . . . surely to remove his enemies—Cecil, Ralegh, Cobham etc.—from power and to return to power himself. Perhaps (though never openly charged by anyone) to expedite the Succession of the King of Scots to the throne of England. Certainly to put himself into a position to guarantee Succession to the Scot. Perhaps to play false with everyone and to make himself King. Whatever his aims truly were, your patrons, men of the world, wished to offer him a measure of support. Not so that he might succeed. You imagine that they were not displeased with the way things came to pass. Not so that he *could* succeed, but in case he should. They could not afford not to be of aid and comfort to the Earl. But, by the same token, they could not, either, afford to be found out by the Earl's enemies. Of these enemies, the chief three present no great problem. Cobham is the richest Lord in England and could not care less what some inconsequential lesser gentry, remote from the center of affairs, may have done with little driblets of money. Cobham, half cracked anyway, could have hedged his bet by offering support to the Earl, himself. It is a family, the Brookes, who have, in our history, played closely with treason and rebellion more than once. And this Baron, Henry Brooke, eleventh Lord Cobham, is a bully and a coward. A blending that often goes together. It would be not beyond his character to offer support to a man who professed to be after Cobham's death. Figuring, perhaps with wisdom, that a little money might mitigate the Earl's designs against him. Figuring, as any coward might, that it is better to buy the goodwill of one's enemies than to reward the investment of goodwill by one's friends. Who will be of little or no use if your enemy succeeds. Though a coward and bully loves himself as much as any man since Adam, he (forever Judas to himself) hates and condemns himself also for lacking courage to find a tree limb and a length of rope and be done with himself. Therefore, to such a man, friends are contemptible also. If they can be friends with such a one as he is, then they must be seriously flawed, deficient in understanding. Thus readily expendable.

If you could find in these papers some evidence of Cobham's involvement, well, *that* would be of interest.

Of the other two. Ralegh is proud and rich enough and almost utterly indifferent. No trouble for your patrons there. Sir Robert Cecil, with all his power and with an inherited network of spies and agents, and with his hands upon half the papers of the kingdom and fair copies of the rest, and with his mountains of debts, might well be a problem. Except that he is not. For your patrons have wisely, and for some time, given comfort to Cecil. And with such regularity that their support could be called a pension. Cecil has no good reason to trouble them.

Still there is always the Queen. Who, while she still lives and breathes, still rules. Who would be outraged to learn that some whom she had trusted had given any support at all to an enemy. The Queen, though supple about many things, is absolute in matters of treason and rebellion.

And then there is whoever it is that shall succeed her.

You have therefore come to London to tie up loose ends in this business of Essex. With some dead and others in prison and silent (these days) as moles, with Anthony Bacon dead and gone, from natural causes, and with him, evidently, most of his own papers and records, then the last pieces left to be gathered are small. Like this Player. Whom your patrons hired through the subterfuge of a pair of Scotsmen. Hired why? Mainly so that Anthony Bacon would know that your patrons had a genuine interest in the Earl's strategems. Bacon, master of the art, would know at once that the Player was a spy and would have credited your patrons for it. And proof of that is the ease with which the Player was admitted to employment.

As for the Player, he would not have been surprised. Because the self-love of actors, bless their hearts, does not allow them to know they are as easy to read as a hornbook. Still, this fellow may have somehow stumbled on more pieces of knowledge than he ought to.

Early you discover he has not. Which is well. For if he had known too much, it might have been necessary to have him killed. Or kill him yourself. Which, either way, by hired hacker or with your own piece of steel, is always troublesome. And which would be a loss, for you took much pleasure from his performance on the stage.

So you are relieved that nothing among these papers speaks to the fears of your patrons. That now you may relax and read through them with an easy disinterest, looking only for what they may tell you about that fellow over there in bed, snoring in a duet with his wife. And for what they may tell you about the affairs of the Earl of Essex. There is much you would like to know; there is a deep curiosity in you about the man. Though perhaps it is not the same kind or degree of curiosity that used to bring out London crowds (*always . . . but once*) to cheer him. Which public seems, even now, to remain undiminished. For they still sing ballads about him and broadsides are still secretly printed. For them, he is no man at all, but rather a kind of statue or painting. Some colorful tiltyard figure, player in his own right, who moved awhile and acted his role. Then left the stage. Perhaps they imagine he will return, resurrected and whole, to dance in the final jig.

If he does, it will be the final jig of this world.

You yourself have seen Essex at close hand; though never in England, only in the wars. But you have never known him. Did not wish to, then, in those lost days, not so long ago, though they might as well have been a century ago. For all that anyone safe at home in England cares. In those days wars were all your life. Whatever first led you to soldiering—desire for glory? hope for reward? simple necessity?—you had lost the reason for it by the time you first saw Essex. Close to the same age, give or take a year or two, you were older than he and his companions by far. Contemptuous of him and of his kind and envious also. For you brought nothing home from the wars, in the end, except yourself. In truth you could not even manage that. You were brought home to England; sent home by your wounds.

Now you spread out papers on a plain table. You look about the room to be certain that no one is still awake and looking at you. And only then do you put on the little pair of spectacles. Which, mind you, you do not *need*. But which do make reading somewhat easier. Especially when your eyes are tired.

You shuffle the papers. You bend to read.

Even half amused at your own inexpressible vanity, you remain (always) close to despair. But despair may serve you well, making you better able to contend against these times than if you still could believe the world might be saved from the insatiable greed and overmastering savagery of its inhabitants. Is not all the world only one step or two removed from an irrevocable despair? Is it not better and wiser for you to believe that justice will never be done in this world while we are in it?

Your outward wounds have healed as well as wounds can. But this world (in its old age) is very tired. And so are you.

One reason it is possible for you to keep awake tonight, searching among these papers, is that you would not be sleeping much in any other place. In the inn out along Holborn Street, you would be pacing the floor of your chamber. You might fall asleep, finally, in spite of yourself. Chances are you would fall asleep at the edge of dawn. And chances are then to wake yourself (perhaps others) with shouting. Sitting up suddenly, wide-eyed, breathing like a half-drowned man.

Like many another old soldier afflicted with nightmares.

So, though very little can surprise you any more, nevertheless you are puzzled that this Player can fall asleep so easily and sleep so well. Snoring, contented and echoing in the chamber, as if from the bottom of a well.

You are surprised at the skill of the Player's penmanship and the varieties of it that he displays. Not many are as fluent and easy, as expertly graceful in the skilled professional hands—Secretary, Chancery, Court, and Text. Has he labored to perfect the craft of writing in the hope of somehow gaining a position as clerk or secretary in some important office or household? Perhaps. Yet in his jottings to himself he affects the Roman hand. As if that were his natural habit. Well, among certain of the younger gentry and nobility (of just the sort with which Essex surrounded himself) it is the fashion to write, always with a studied negligence, in the Roman hand. Slight negligence—with blotting and scratching out here and there; with the lines often uneven and sometimes unruly—gives the sense not of tedious sincerity, never of the dusty, sweaty, ink-stained urgency of some creature of ambition (ever eager to please betters and hoping to be rewarded), but rather the impression of the spontaneity of an influential personage, far too busy to trouble himself with false gestures. Someone whose accomplishments are so various that he would never insult you by pretending to be expert at any of them.

Yet why would a sane man wish to create such an impression for . . . himself? Unless self-deception could bring him some comfort. Unless, as Player, he were rehearsing, imagining, even by means of penmanship, how it must be to be a member of the younger gentry.

Unless (also) at the heart of the Player there remains an unchanging, unreformed, unreconstructed child, a child who, given a steel glass, will not discover himself, but instead will be content to make faces, becoming anything that may please him—saint or hero, great lord or lousy beggar. Meaning then (perhaps) that the child at the heart of this man truly believes that this world is made more out of the stuff of cloudy fables than out of hard facts.

Meaning (therefore) that this child-man will freely and easily render unto this world, Caesar's world, almost anything—except belief.

In the morning (coming soon) when you breakfast with the Player, you will compliment him on the skill of his penmanship. Hoping to learn what his reasoning, if any, may have been. But having taken your compliment as literal and pleased by it, too, he will produce a writing box. A very fine one. Surely that of a gentleman. Taken at pawn, you will surmise. Well equipped with pens, with ink and sand and wax for sealing and with a plenty of good paper. Directly then he will offer you an exhibition of the mastery he possesses at all of the usual hands. All of which will look to you like the work of a trained scrivener. While doing so, he will justify himself. Telling you how he has often earned some money, while traveling in the country, by writing letters and preparing documents for poor country people. And also has done so even here in Whitefriars.

He will end his demonstration by revealing to you yet another skill. One which will delight you because it is the next obvious step in the craft, appropriate, but nevertheless the last thing you expected.

He will ask you to jot down a few lines on paper and to sign it. You will oblige, producing something in your own legible but somewhat careless version of a Secretary hand. Ending with the flourish of your signature.

He will be watching over your shoulder while you write. When you have finished and signed it, he will turn away. Turn his back to you. Taking a piece of fresh paper, and without looking at yours again, will produce the same words in the same hand and end it all with a very fine copy of your signature. A nearly flawless forgery.

Essex. Robert Devereux. 33 years of age. Earl of Essex, 3rd Viscount Hereford. 6th Lord Ferrers. 9th Lord Bourchier. Ancient & honorable of titles. Yet taken by many as the exemplar of the new age. Celebrant of new ways. If there is any fashion—cut of clothing, colors of, size & width of ruff, length of hair & beard —he is so nearly first to affect it as to be credited with the invention. Yet with his tilts & jousts, his challenges & single combats, love of honor & ceremonies, he might better have thrived in olden chivalric times.

Sir Philip Sidney left to E— his sword. E— wears it. E— also has married Sidney's widow (daughter of Walsingham). Distinction without wealth. Chivalric gesture? Superstition? Does E— dream of becoming Sidney redux?

See him then as new/old man. Much divided. Riddle of contradictions.

Proud & ostentatious. Yet generous to a fault.

Arrogant & quick-tempered. Yet humble in repentance when persuaded he has done wrong.

Extravagant to extreme. Item. Essex House reputed to require 200 servants. Easy to believe that. In their white & tangerine livery they are everywhere. And they in turn maintain their own servants. Surely E—'s is largest household in England. Except for the Court. And is a rival to the Court.

Richly rewarded by the Queen with many offices & grants & hands & loans & monopolies (is there any other in all the Court now, indeed for all her reign, upon whom so much has been lavished?), he is widely known to be nevertheless the same as the youth who first came to Court. Poorest Earl in England. Managed to spend far more than all his gains.

At the age of 23 (!) he was sworn to the Privy Council and

*made Knight of the Garter. Among the offices he has held—
Master of Horse, Master of Ordnance, Earl Marshal of England.
Yet he has always wanted more. Sought to be Master of the
Court of Wards after Burghley died. Battled Cobham for the
post of Lord Warden of the Cinque Ports. Was furious when he
failed to gain these posts. And the same whenever he failed to
gain a particular post for a friend.*

Who has been so public in this age as he has?

*So often seen by crowds coming & going in barge or coach.
Both of which rival the Queen's own. Performing at the Accession Day ceremonies & jousts. Yet some of his gestures have gone
poorly for him. Item: In '98, learning that Ralegh planned to pay
to equip the Guard with special livery and plumes for the occasion, Essex's merry jest was to equip some 2000 men with identi-
cal finery. Which impressed the crowds and surely produced the
desired laughter at Ralegh's expense. But Queen was not pleased.
For his gesture did more than bite a thumb at Ralegh. It
belittled Her Majesty. All the world knows how much the Queen
is displeased by large groups of liveried retainers, as in the old
days, when some among nobility were richer & more powerful
than kings. The Queen was greatly offended. The more so since
the wealth by which the Earl could afford to make such a gesture
came from her. She called off the tourney & departed.*

*Parades . . . Has London, except for Coronation, ever seen
any parade to equal E—'s departure, with the largest English
army of our times, for Ireland? Has any other among the councilors & nobility, spent so many hours in the Bankside theaters?
Plenty of players have spent less time there. E— known at sight
by the multitude like a king or a prince of old times. Talked
about endlessly. And not merely in taverns, either. Often from
the pulpit as a hero of the faith. Is subject of pamphlets & broadsides & ballads. For the sake of everything he's done. And whatever has been done is always called a triumph. . . .*

Amen to that, you say. Of all his adventures none save the ex-
pedition to Cádiz in '96 can be called a true success. And even
that venture was much flawed. Queen and Council thought so.
He was never a cruel leader. Nor in any way cowardly. Which
separates him clearly from so many English commanders. Young,

fiery in audacity, he was admired by officers and soldiers alike. He lifted their spirits. Nevertheless they died in large numbers. He could lead a charge or lay an ambush anytime. But never could manage to feed and clothe and to save his men for the one right time on the right piece of ground.

What astonished you is how his reputation grew and was believed—*even by veteran soldiers*—when so much of it was false. How many blithely left guts and bones in fields of France and Flanders and Portugal so that he would be honored and admired at home? What possessed them? Was it that in the Earl's youth and courage (even his folly) they felt something utterly untrue, but something which they would like to believe? The Earl seemed as magically blessed as any knight of the fables of the Round Table. Musket balls passed through his hat brim and his cloak, but never broke bones or left him screaming and wallowing in mud. In his case the calls of the trumpets, the sound of fife and drum, the flapping of flags and banners in the breeze, all seemed real and true. If only for the briefest time.

You are not contemptuous of your comrades' illusions. You tell yourself that just as many a soldier would rather risk death with a full stomach than an empty one, so, given a choice, many might prefer to die in the highest spirits they can reach. If the Earl led many to death (and from their deaths gained much repute), perhaps they died better than they might have under the guidance of a wiser commander.

To be here understood. That in no way does E— seek to discourage adulation, gossip, rumor & speculation. Quite the opposite.

None other among the public men is seen by so many, so easily accessible, so much discussed. So popular. Yet also it is difficult to imagine any other public man of whom so little truth is known.

Here the Player is fascinated by the paradox that the more Essex was seen the less he was known. The more open he became in his actions, the more secret was the truth of him.

Perhaps, you think, by a steady progression of self-revelation (like the whore who adroitly undresses herself by candlelight for

your pleasure and excitement), the more he revealed, the more
he became a creature of fantasy. Which was how the world
would have him. Whore to the world, then. It is truth that the
world turns away from in its lust to cling to the fantastical.

Thus he was able to be many different things to many different
men. Except, perhaps, his enemies. No. Especially to enemies.
For what they feared and hated most had no more substance,
was every inch as shadowy as what others admired.

And neither was the truth.

As for himself.

Most likely he was, to himself, a mysterious, fantastical creature
also. Wasn't he, too, turning away from the truth of the world to
live, if he could, in the center of some fable? Living only in the
eyes of others, he became more completely an actor than any of
those who practice that art upon the stage.

And at the last, in Tower Yard, even the executioner must have
been stunned to see him bleed like any slaughtered beast.

Easter Sunday
23rd March—

Gentle Sirs—

*I am pleased to report to you that the Earl of Essex has been
released from the custody of the Lord Keeper Egerton at York
House. On the night of Good Friday, shortly after eight o'clock
he was returned to Essex House in the custody of Sir Richard
Berkeley. Who will hereafter serve as his guardian. All of the
Earl's family and friends, together with Mr. Anthony Bacon and
most of the Earl's servants have been sent away from Essex
House.*

*He is to be very strictly kept there. He will not be accessible
without the Queen's leave. It appears he will be so kept until
such time as there can be a hearing concerning his offenses and
disobedience in the matter of Ireland.*

*Early in February it seemed likely that there would be such a
hearing at Star Chamber. On the 6th it was given out that the
hearing would take place on the next day. Preparations for it
were being made and large crowds gathered there. Then it was*

announced that the trial had been postponed. No official reasons
for the postponement were offered.

Thus (whether by design or by accident) rumor and
speculation flourished.

From the Court the bruit was that the postponement came as a
kindness from Sir Robert Cecil, who had prevailed upon the
Council to spare the Earl embarrassment. It was implied that
Mr. Secretary was working in behalf of the Earl, hoping that the
passage of time might soften the anger of the Queen. And that,
in due time, a reconciliation between the Earl and Her Majesty
might be effected. Needless to say, the Earl's supporters viewed
the postponement in a contrary manner. It was their surmise that
the Council and Essex's enemies feared any public hearing.

Lacking evidence of any offenses except what malice could
produce, his enemies are aware that the occasion would turn
against them. The longer they can prevent the Earl from
defending himself, from speaking in his own behalf, the safer
they will be. They can hope he may die in captivity.

It is true, sirs, that the Earl was, briefly, thought to be dead in
December. Church bells were rung all over London in his
memorial before it was learned that the rumors were false. Who
began those rumors, I cannot say. Some say it was done by his
supporters to prove his popularity in the City. Others say—noting
that the Queen was very angry at all this ringing of death knells
for the living Earl—that the thing was instigated by the Earl's
enemies for the purpose of causing the Queen's anger.

There have been other conjectures.

It was suggested that the hearing at Star Chamber was
announced, and public preparations were made, so that there
would be an assembly of the Earl's allies. So that Cecil's spies
could determine precisely who these might be.

As you can see, nothing is clear at this time. All things seem to
be shifting and changing. Much waits upon the Earl's recovery
of his health and of some measure of liberty.

Even the seasons seem to be confused. It is bitter cold this
Easter Day. Snow on the ground and thick flakes in the air. I can
recall no other Easter like it, at least here in London. . . .

It is understood that, lacking unmortgaged land, the Earl

derives the largest part of his income from the Farm for Sweet Wines. Which was awarded to him almost ten years ago by the Queen. Whereby, as I am sure you understand, sirs, he receives a certain amount for each and every tun of sweet wine brought into England.

Of his offices and income there is something more which, with all due respect, ought to be observed. It is well known that the Earl of Essex has sued for offices for his friends and servants as well as for himself. And that the Queen has sometimes gratified him in these matters and sometimes not. It has likewise been noticed that each office he fixes his mind on becomes, as it were, a battleground rather than a disputation.

Whether this may prove to be a weakness or no, it would seem that the Earl of Essex does not always clearly distinguish between what is a pastime and what are matters of the most profound concern. If I may be allowed an observation, sirs, this would seem to me to offer the Earl of Essex a certain advantage in all that he does. As, for example, on the tiltyard while others, no matter how eager or ambitious, conceive of the display as a diversion (and, indeed, more a matter of diversion for Her Majesty than for themselves), he rides out with the same kind of dedication he would muster up against a Spanish invasion. Given the skill at arms that he possesses, that dedication could likely make the difference between victory and defeat. Just so, his demeanor on the fields of battle seems to have been, always, cheerful and lighthearted. As if it were all a play or a game from which, at the conclusion, the dead and wounded will rise up whole and dance a jig to universal applause.

Although I have never myself been a soldier except, of course, in parts upon the stage, I can . . .

Why would he lie to them? Or is it myself he was lying to?

Although I have never myself served as a soldier, except, of course, in plays on the stage, I can understand how it would be pleasing to follow such a leader. One of those who seem, by Fortune, to bear a charmed life. Faced with the prospect of a fearful death or crippling wounds, any soldier could hope that some of the Earl's good Fortune might serve him, also.

It is known by all how, as not much more than a boy, he fought at Zutphen, side by side with Sir Philip Sidney. There is something there like the laying on of hands from one Bishop to the next. Going back to the Apostles. In war to Achilles and Hector, Ajax and Aeneas. And this is confirmed by the marriage of the Earl to the Lady Frances Walsingham, widow to Sir Philip Sidney.

In addition to a large establishment and many servants, the Earl is reputed to have acquired, upon the death of his father-in-law, Sir Francis Walsingham, a large part of that gentleman's band of intelligencers, both foreign and domestic. They are believed to be the equal to, if not superior to, the agents serving Mr. Secretary Cecil. Thus, upon one occasion and another, the Queen has been furnished with intelligence by the Earl of Essex. And so it was, until the Earl's most recent disgrace, that messengers and agents and even ambassadors from foreign countries came to call upon the Earl at Essex House (and sometimes at Barn Elms or Wanstead when he was in the country). As if his household were a Court.

While the Queen may have been pleased to receive useful information from the Earl, it is not thought that she has been pleased either by the appearance of a lesser Court at Essex House (as if the Earl were Prince of Wales) or by the appearance of the Earl conducting state business or scheming even to make policy on his own.

It has to be assumed, sirs, that Mr. Secretary has planted watchmen within the Earl's household.

Sirs, in our conversations, you asked me what, if anything, I could determine of the Earl's thoughts concerning the Succession. Rumor has it that the Earl is a strong champion for the claims of the King of Scots. Because the Court is so split into factions these days, this means that others may well (and wisely) support other claimants. Wisely? As things go here, it would surely mean a fall from power by his rivals if the next ruler should be beholden to the Earl of Essex.

Strange to be reading this now. Strange after so many things—excepting always the vexed question of the Succession—have been resolved.

You credit the Player with understanding. You cannot fault him for what he did not perceive. He was not hired to play the role of a prophet. Even the astrologers were divided in their prognostications.

The Player's letters continue, at intervals, not adding much information to the first one. For nothing changed until the Queen was at last willing to allow the Earl to have some liberty again.

In early June there was (at last) a formal hearing held in York House. It was a privy proceeding, but not intended to be strictly secret. How could it be so? Eighteen of the most prominent men in this kingdom for judges, including the Lord Keeper, the Lord Admiral and the Lord Treasurer and Archbishop Whitgift, Councilors and Judges, in their robes and collars etc., gathered at York House early in the morning of the fifth of June. And the Earl was brought over by water from Essex House—thus to be seen, yet to avoid the throngs along the Strand. Now then. With all of these important men, together with their various clerks and servants, with their guards and coachmen and watermen, with all of Lord Keeper Egerton's household at York House, from the high steward down to the sweaty turnspits, and with some hundred or so invited witnesses, these from the City as well as the Court, there was no way to prevent some rumors concerning the proceedings from rising up out of York House like a flock of frightened birds. Perhaps a report would be published and perhaps not. Meantime rumor would serve.

What a good scene for a play could be made out of this!

Coming in coaches & by boat & barge on the river, the arrival of the graybeards & togati at York House. Fine June morning. Gardens at York House in bursting bloom. Bees humming like tuning viols among the flowers.

Enter men of the commission. Likewise lawyers: the Queen's Sergeant at Law, Sir Henry Yelverton in his particolored, green and black gown; Sir Thomas Fleming, Solicitor General; Edward Coke, Attorney General, fully robed in black silk. And also Mr. Francis Bacon. As Queen's Counsel Extraordinary.

Presence of this one, this last, must have set people to buzzing like the bees in the garden. Well known that Bacon served Essex, sought the office of Attorney General for him & failed to win it.

Next to office of Solicitor General. Which went to Mr. Fleming.
Known, too, that Bacon had once sought to marry the Lady
Elizabeth Hatton (great Burghley's granddaughter, Cecil's
niece) & that Essex acted in his behalf. But the Lady
married—Edward Coke.

All these & then too the invited guests. Taking places in the
Hall there. Commissioners seated at a long table.

Then, the last one, enters briskly, as if out for morning
exercise, the Earl. He has not been seen by anyone for many
months. All turn to stare at him. Eager & even apprehensive. For
Essex might do anything. He whips off his hat. A wide gesture.
(Do some, surely they do, remember the account of how at the
great victory at Cádiz in '96, Essex whipped off his hat & hurled
it into the sea for joy when the order came to attack the
Spaniard?) Papers in one hand & hat in the other. Impeccably,
fashionably dressed. But soberly, too, so soberly. Could be a
preacher. Or could be the parody of one. Yet also every inch the
swordsman & commander. Advancing across the Hall toward the
table where the commissioners are seated. As if—who knows?—he
plans to sit down there among them.

Then suddenly, when he's no more than a step or two from the
table, he is falling down to the floor. On his knees before them.
Tears in his eyes—& soon in almost every other eye—when he
speaks up, announcing his sorrow & repentance even before the
hearing can begin.

Archbishop Whitgift orders a cushion for him to kneel with
more comfort. Soon he'll be invited to stand & finally to sit.

Lawyers now rise, one at a time, to make charges against him.
There seem to be mostly matters of disobedience & of contempt
to Queen & Council. Nothing is mentioned of any treasons or
even hint of same. No one speaks of truce he made (against all
orders) with the O'Neil.

Mr. Bacon raises up a problem from the past. Something that's
said to have puzzled the Queen. That Book by Dr. John
Hayward, the History of Henry IIII. *Which had been dedicated*
to the Earl. And dealt with the dangerous subject of the
deposition of King Richard II.

At one point only does the Earl cast aside humility & defend
himself. Edward Coke used the word "disloyalty." Essex rises to

deny that. Lord Keeper Egerton must then deny that there is any such charge intended.

At the last, after a day of it, the Earl is censured, one by one, by each of the commissioners. Each speaking a little less harshly than the last. (Progression by rote?) Each recommending a somewhat more lenient punishment.

At the very last, then, agreeing to recommend no other punishment than that he will have to remain honorably confined to his house at the Queen's pleasure.

It is night by the time the Earl is returned to Essex House.

Is he smiling in the darkness?

If it were I . . . if I were to play that role, I would turn away from the commissioners & lawyers, judges & persecutors, with a small smile. So to tell the audience how I have just now won another triumph. A victory through humiliation. Who could have lost so much. Having lost nothing else but a little pride and the liberty which I did not have when I came here.

And which, I'll wager (who, among you, will bet against me?) I shall have soon enough.

Likely before the Queen goes on Progress.

How can it be otherwise?

I have shown how I can be humble & contrite. Now I shall prove that I can be patient.

This hearing was my punishment. And mark well, friends, dear friends, it is now over. Oh, it will live again. Be reported & repeated by these witnesses.

It will be reported to the Queen. But no one can argue that I was proud or disdainful or insolent or impudent or in any way unrepentant. It will be well described to her & I'll wager that that old woman will weep.

And (think on it) even if they intend to publish all the words of it, that will be greatly to my advantage. My words & silences will plead for me better than lawyers could.

As per the others. All report will be to the disadvantage of those who spoke against me here today.

Worthy & dutiful gentlemen, some among you shall be paid back in full & with good interest for this.

Oh yes, oh yes, oh yes. Yes. . . .

All in due time, gentlemen.

All in due & proper time.

My enemies would have taken my life this morning. If they could have. If not, then would have taken my fortune & my honor & all my liberty.

Would have humbled & punished me.

Would have transformed me from lord to beggar.

But—look how it is!—I have endured humiliation & punishment. I have turned these into triumph. I have proved how I can be humble. Now I shall be the perfect model of patience.

Queen will soon call me back to be at her side. Who else? All her warriors are dead & gone. These fat & gray Togati are no use to her or England now.

She may need swords before she's done. Knows it, too.

And after that?

Well, he shall need swords whoever it is who succeeds her.

And who shall that be?

It will be no man without my approval.

Wait for the next scene to see what I shall do next. . . .

That, all of that, is what my brief, tight, little smile (seen by the audience for only a moment, but not seen by the commissioners whose final view of me was a very picture of stunned & humble resignation) would say to them.

Seeming to be downcast, I would turn away from the table. Would grin my eloquent little grin & exit quickly.

No.

At the very last, just as I am about to pass through the curtain at the Tiring-House door, I would hesitate. One brief moment only. As if in second thought.

Grin gone, I wrinkle my brow. Hunch shoulders & lower my head slightly. Just as E— himself does when thinking. Conveying a mind that's as busy with hammering as a forge.

Thinking.

Plotting.

What?

My revenge! Revenge!

Then quickly exit. . . .

But this is all foolishness. What am I thinking of?

There's no such play.
I am not Essex!

No, you were not.

But you came close there. Closer than many could have done. You could never become a noble Earl. But he was always a player.

More than most public men he invites that kind of response.

Invites the beholder, even at a great distance and at second hand, to share his thoughts as if there were no others.

Among these papers it is still the summer of 1600. The Queen has gone on Progress. Essex remains at Essex House waiting for word. He writes letters in the old high courtly style to the Queen. Receives no answers. People at Court, given occasion, speak in his behalf. She is silent. But does not, at least, deny their suits.

There is another question that interests you. The Player. Let us assume the Player was not lying when he told his tale of service in Ireland. And being lucky enough to live to come home and tell of it, years later, to a stranger in a tavern.

Then he will have felt to bone marrow the fearful sorrows of that misty, savage, bog-ridden, mysterious land. What Essex himself once named as "a moist, rotten country." The player will have been there, suffered and endured. Not as a gentleman volunteer on horseback. But as a sick and frightened common soldier, frequently unpaid, hungry, ragged, ill equipped. Will understand how Essex's army that had marched away so proudly, with half of London to cheer them on their way, melted to a rabble in less than six months.

Does it not anger him?

You understand the rage of the Queen. At a time when much of this kingdom is suffering from the wars and from bad harvests and high prices and sickness—she trusted Essex to do his duty. She took a great risk with precious blood and treasure. He went forth in triumph. Promptly failed in every detail. Disobeyed her every order. Including, finally, the order not to leave Ireland. No, he deserted his post and army in Ireland to come home.

With what result?

His popularity continues. The Queen's diminishes. For now

she is blamed for his failure. And yet the people who must be taxed to pay for his follies wish him well. The rogues who will be soon pressed into service and sent over to Ireland on account of his failure will stand at his gate and cheer him. You understand the Queen's anger and can only wonder at her restraint.

If he had been a captain in any of the wars you know about, he would have been left hanging from a tree for it.

But here is this Player, an old soldier (of sorts) himself, ready, it seems, to follow the Earl in whatever he may do next.

On August 26 the Earl was given his liberty. With the proviso that he must not come to Court without leave. He promptly asked permission to come to see the Queen, to kiss her hands just once more before retiring to the country for the rest of his life.

From that first week in June until the last week of August the Player remained diligent in writing his reports. Which must have required some skill at seeming to be saying much when there was next to nothing to say. For in truth nothing happened concerning my lord of Essex.

Over the summer months the Player was reduced to sharing idle gossip as if it were news and to use common news as if it were acquired intelligence. This his unknown and unseen patrons (*and what if they happened to be, O Lord!, a couple of gents from right here in London who would know that what they had paid for & were now receiving was information which the youngest apprentice could & would furnish to them for a halfpenny?*) were told:

Of news from Ireland and Flanders. Which was, for a change, of victories. A great victory in the Dunes of Flanders. Small events in Ireland, but favorable. Together with the negotiations at Boulogne, which could well lead to peace with Spain—and there's an end to the employment of swordsmen in our time.

Of such news coming from Court as might have some effect on the Earl and his hopes. That the Queen still seemed bent on annulling all the knighthoods Essex had awarded in Ireland—fifty-nine they say—against her explicit orders. That a proclamation to that end was already prepared. But that she was persuaded that the annulment was unwise. Even so, the drawing up of the proclamation served a number of purposes for the Queen. *Item:* That the Earl, still hoping for his liberty, could take it as a signal that the Queen's anger was unabated. *Item:* That all those who had received knighthood at the Earl's hands must now be beholden to her. She became their benefactor and not the Earl.

The great news of August was the report of how the King of Scots was almost murdered by Mr. Alexander Ruthven and his brother the Earl of Gowrie under most curious circumstances. Wherein the King was miraculously, at the last moment, saved. And where (conveniently for the King) the Earl of Gowrie and his brother were killed. Much doubt concerning the details of this conspiracy. Because the family of Ruthven has long been closely allied to England. It is also said by some who may know of these things that there was jealousy of the King of Scots; for the young and handsome Earl of Gowrie was often in close company to the Queen of Scotland. While the King went his own way. . . .

Shortly after Essex received his liberty and took himself off to the country, the Player was busy doing errands and performing services of one kind and another, both in the country (at Wanstead and Barn Elms, and at Twickenham where Mr. Anthony Bacon remained) and in London and Westminster. All things were moving quickly. Even with the Earl in the country, Essex House was as busy as it once had been. It was as if Ireland and the long confinement had been only brief interruptions. The shadow court again had formed. All sorts of enterprises seemed to be afoot. Furtive, yes, but none of them secret.

You will understand my doubts when I tell you that in the absence of Mr. Bacon (who is very sickly at his place in the country and is unable even to hold a pen), there is no authority here among the Earl's servants. That is to say, Mr. Henry Cuffe remains the Earl's secretary and counselor and Sir Gilly Meyrick is his steward as before. And these gentlemen are obeyed in all things. But much that should be known only to a few is known by too many. It has been altogether too simple for me to learn things which could be damaging to the Earl. This may seem to be a curious complaint, coming from an intelligencer. But it makes me exceedingly anxious to be careful for myself. And, sirs, for your interests as well. It is certain that everything that happens either at Essex House or in the country is well watched.

Both from within and without. There can be no secrets here. I cannot imagine that anything which is said or happens is a long time before being repeated to Mr. Secretary.

The single great concern of the Earl is a very simple one. And is known to anyone who cares to know from here to the bridge at Berwick. That, sirs, is the matter of the Earl's chief source of income—the Farm of Sweet Wines.

Debts of the Earl are growing enormous. All income from his offices is pitifully inadequate even to make the requisite payments on these debts. Without the duty on sweet wines it seems certain that the Earl's establishment is finished. The Farm of Sweet Wines ceases to be in the Earl's hands on this coming quarter day—Michaelmas.

The Earl continues to write submissive letters to the Queen. Some speak for him at Court, but though the Queen is willing to listen to them, she has said nothing. Time is passing. His creditors are many and are bold. This past summer saw the Earl of Lincoln clapped into Fleet Prison for failure to pay a judgment much smaller than anything owed by Essex.

In short, sirs, he stands to be ruined. Others of the young nobility, especially among that group known at Court as the Fantasticals, will be ruined with him. All their servants and dependants likewise.

It is believed that the Queen is not aware of the consequences of a refusal to renew the Farm. If that is so, then someone, some ones, are keeping truth from her. Here the blame is seen as pointing directly at Mr. Secretary. At Ralegh and Cobham and Lord Grey (who is the Earl of Southampton's greatest enemy) and at all the family of the Howards. It is believed that these enemies are working together against him.

Meantime there is much exercise of religion here. The Earl listens to sermons every day. And those of us who cannot escape or busy ourselves with other duties are herded together to listen too. So that these various gospelers and hedge preachers can perform their ministry before an adequate crowd.

He continues, describing courses of action which the Earl's friends are urging on him. One group has urged that he should flee to France. Where the King of France, his friend from the wars, will surely find some employment for him.

More serious (and dangerous), for there has been correspondence between them for more than ten years, is the idea that the Earl should join with the King of Scots to make some kind of demonstration, to make the Queen name King James as her assured Successor.

Sirs, I do not know the contents of the letters which are coming and going (as regular as royal post and somewhat more swiftly) to and from Scotland. It is possible that none of what is openly talked of in Essex House is mentioned in these letters. There is no way, save by stealing the letters, to determine that. But there can be no doubt that Mr. Secretary and others know all that is to be known about the letters and, as well, about the words spoken here.

He must know, too, who is coming and who is going. One and all. Even myself. Inconsequential as I may be amid all this bustle. . . .

This letter, the last addressed to his patrons, ends with a plea (bargain if you prefer) for some money. After mentioning dangers, he respectfully points out that he himself is also in debt. To be of any use to the Earl's household it has been necessary for him to incur certain expenses including a horse and saddle, new clothing, good boots, sword and scabbard ("There's no man here that would walk across the courtyard without putting on his sword.") etc. He has, likewise, been forced to give up several excellent opportunities for this coming season of stage plays etc. etc. etc.

He looks forward to some communication at the earliest possible leisure & convenience.

You also know what he could not know. That this letter was the end for your masters. Too dangerous by far. That though they had been helpful to Essex in the past, it was clear enough, from the way the wind was blowing, that the Earl must now fend for himself.

Now you wonder if others also chose that same time to cease their support. It cannot have made things easier for Essex.

Never mind. What concerns you is the Player. How even though he could see that nothing for him could come of it, he continued as a kind of servant to the Earl. There was nothing in it for him but peril.

Unless he was thinking to sell his services to someone else.

If so, there is no sign of that in his notes. Rather he seems as surprised as you are by his own actions:

Why do I pull on boots & buckle on sword & mount my too costly horse & ride like a gent to Essex House to swagger about the courtyard? To swap lies with the others who have no more good purpose here than myself.

And who are these others gathering to wait & watch? Impecunious gentlemen from all over England. Leftover captains from Ireland. Welsh swordsmen. Papists & Puritans alike. As ragged a band as Robin Hood must have had. A rabble of England's malcontents.

Some of distinction. There are earls & barons & knights who come & go. And some who ought in a just world to be taken to Tyburn & danced at the end of a rope for the sake of multitudinous sins & felonies & misdemeanors.

Folly! It's folly to be here. And so why am I?

I cannot answer my own question.

Would have to answer other questions first.

Why do I go at dawn & stay all day at Essex House waiting for some errand or other to be assigned to me? Any service. Happy to be noticed at all by the Earl's servants.

Happiest to be noticed by the Earl himself.

A few days ago, just before dinner, he saw me & spoke to me. He & some of his knot of fellows came clattering into the courtyard. Coming back from somewhere in the City. Jumped from their horses & started walking toward the entrance of the house. When he saw me.

"I know you," he said. "You are an actor."

Turning to include his companions. While all in the courtyard are watching us, listening to hear what's being said.

"Look here, I have often times seen this fellow on the stage. He is a most excellent player. He has performed here in this house. Is it not so?"

"Indeed, sir. And once or twice at the Tiltyard."

"He can play any part that's written," Essex says. "King and fool alike."

"Why, that's no trick, my lord," says one of them, "since the two are so often so much the same."

"Ah," says Essex with a slight smile; then to me: "And could you play the part of a lord who, like some figure from a child's tale, was changed into a beggarman by a wicked Queen?"

"My lord," I reply, "I will play any part. But, as I live and breathe, I pray that that part will never be written down."

"The Queen!" one of them says. "He could put on a wig and play the Queen."

"Nay, he's much too pretty to play the Queen," another says.

He ignores them. Looks directly at me. Noon sunlight sparkling in his eyes.

"Player," he says, "what part are you playing now?"

"Your true and faithful servant, sir. If you will allow it."

"I shall insist upon it," he says.

Giving me a coin & moving on.

Why did I then feel weak in knees, light-headed with delight? Why have I kept that coin with me as if it were a jewel? Why would I rather go hungry or thirsty than to spend it?

Michaelmas Day come and gone. No renewal of the Farm for Sweet Wines. And yet no refusal either.

Clearly the Earl had not yet given up all hope. He took silence as promising. Thinking that the Queen would soon be returning to Whitehall for the Accession Day and the Christmastide, believing that surely he would be returned to Court, believing that she would not let him return to Court and then deny his suit.

Meantime there are wagers in taverns as to whether or not Essex will be ruined. The player notes that the odds are against the Earl.

On the thirtieth of October the Queen settles the issue. She will hereafter keep the income for herself.

It was reported that she said this of Essex: "When horses become unmanageable, it is necessary to tame them by stinting them in the quantity of their food."

Now the gate is kept closed day and night. There are passwords. Whispered conferences. Sudden arrival & departure of messengers. Little flocks of boats moored by the water gate. Crowds of faces. New faces mingling with familiar.

It looks that Mr. Secretary has poured honey to catch himself some flies. Here we are buzzing & humming for all the world to see.

Essex House has become the new Bethlehem Hospital.

Well, there was a game between the Earl and the Queen. Had not gambling with cards been one of their pleasures for years? In those high times, they played at cards all night. Essex was one of the few who won at cards with her. And, like her, he had demanded payment on the spot.

Queen and Earl had last seen each other, face to face, on that morning in September when, dusty and muddy from his wild ride from the coast, returning from Ireland, he brushed past guards and all protestation to burst into the Queen's bedchamber. To kneel and to kiss her hands. She greeted him with smiles and loving goodwill. How else? And so she would again if only he could again have access to her presence. He had tried all the usual gestures of repentance. Given time, they would work for him again. But with his money gone, his creditors ready to gnaw him to bits (by Law, oh yes always by means of the Law, Mr. Double-face, Doubledealing Francis Bacon and his Law!) like maggots at work on a carcass. No time. And with mortal enemies ascendant, surrounding the Queen, there could be no sure advocate for him. In the excitement and pleasures of the coming Christmastide there would be small time to remember Essex and his troubles.

It is possible that he had determined to frighten her. Meaning that he believed she could be frightened. So his actions must be known to be efficacious. The broils and excitement day and night at Essex House continued into Christmastide. Outrageous sermons preached there. Offensive words said there. The Earl acting strangely. Like a man possessed. He who had always been the model of elegance is now indifferent to dress and appearance. Often slovenly and unkempt.

Is it a part he has seen on the stage?

Faced with these questions which you cannot answer, you try to look at it as it was seen from Court. One mile west of Essex House.

Thinking, first of all, that in his youthfulness (and that is one of the secrets of it, is it not?, that he preserved the mind and spirit of a boy), the Earl was correct in assuming the Queen saw through him as if he were made out of clear glass. Correct in assumption, also, that if the Queen looked into the man of glass, she would see his loyal, loving heart.

But just as his inner youth gave him the enchantment which could please her, it was, also, a grave weakness. For he could not comprehend that the differences between them were more than a sum of years and wrinkles. He could not perceive that experience of mind and spirit, which are ageless until they cease to be, gave her a wisdom which he did not possess. The wisdom of this world is a sad wisdom. Of which disappointment is only one teacher and an early one at that.

Because he had been as close to the woman as any man, he saw her more as woman than as Queen. His enemies had the advantage of him there. They saw her only as the Queen and never so much as imagined her to be a woman also.

Fatally, the Earl misconceived himself as (in mind and spirit) her equal.

For the Queen that was an intolerable disappointment.

That she could still be disappointed must have been a surprise to her. And frightening, too. For when the hard wisdom of experience is all your armor in Caesar's world, it is frightening to acknowledge that you can still become a victim of your own wishful illusions.

How bitter it must have been for her to see the younger generation of nobility drawn to him. There were four other young Earls in his band—Southampton and Bedford, Rutland and Sussex. And others (she knew some, suspected others) who were more or less sympathetic but too shrewd and, finally, too comfortable to involve themselves. Once upon a time, a generation and more ago, in '69, the rising of two Earls almost succeeded in turning England upside down and tumbling her off the throne.

Now came five Earls and many more of the gentry who, at their finest, fiercest moment could not manage to fight their way past a little group of the Bishop of London's guards at Ludgate. Knowing the end of it, you allow yourself to leap to it. Perhaps the final lash of disappointment for her was that these young men, the flower of the nation, did so poorly as rebels also. Their fathers might have made her run for her life. What would become of them without her? It was much too sad to consider for very long.

Better for you to consider the hard-edged facts. And so you return to the Player and his firsthand view of the things.

So wonderfully crowded & such cheerful carousing & good fun that I cannot but believe the Queen's Court must be thinly peopled this year. All the youth & manhood, all the swordsmen, are here. Let the graybeards of Court hang close to the fires to keep their blood warm. . . .

Already he sounds like a young courtier himself. A swordsman, home from wars and far adventures. Still this Player could not have been any more deluded than most of these foolish men.

It's true the Puritans are here with a vengeance. You must listen to a great deal of theology before your dinner is served. But it is well worth it. Each dinner's a feast & everyone (saving the Puritan preachers who pretend not to notice) drunk as can be. At dinner & supper there are toasts & oaths & speeches. Much courage. Last evening two Welshmen at our table settled a point of honor with rapiers on top of the table. Bread & salt & a side of beef & heaped plates went flying. There was much applause & cheering even from the high table where, led by example of the Earl, they began to throw little loaves of manchet bread at the Welshmen. For (all being more or less drunk) all supposed that it was part of the evening's entertainment. Until one stuck the other with his sword. Not dangerously but with copious bleeding.

Then the Earl would have made a speech in favor of good
fellowship. But he commenced weeping & could not speak &
was led away by his friends.

There are many here who cross the river by boat after dinner
to see the plays. On several occasions I have been brought along
also, as friend & companion to men of high station.

In my new clothes have sat upon the edge of the stage with
the other gentry. Something I never dreamed to do.

Ah, the expression on the players' faces when they strut &
stride out on the stage to find . . . me! Sitting there among the
gentry.

Maybe folly and madness are carried like infection from one
man to the other. Like the sweating sickness. It may be he
believed he had somehow changed his life. That he was at last a
new man, new made. So must they all have believed that.

It seems appropriate that he began to recover his senses at the
theater. . . .

This day with a crowd from Essex House. To the Globe to see
the Chamberlain's Men perform an old play—The Tragedy of
King Richard the Second.

Had no notion that was the play we would see. Was half-hazy
drunk from a surfeit of wines at dinner. Did not know until the
play began what it would be. Did not know, for certain, why this
play was done. Until afterward when I spoke to friends in the
tiring-house. Sobered me quick enough when the play began. My
God, I had a part in it once in '95. Played the Bishop of Carlisle.
One & only time I have played a Bishop. Moment King Richard
& old John of Gaunt & the others entered I was sober as a
clock. The players were troubled to remember their speeches. I
could tell the play had not been well rehearsed. But more than
half of the audience were from Essex House. Who cheered &
laughed & applauded. All knowing how Essex has been called the
new Bullingbrook & the Queen herself called (privately)
"Richard the Second." And when came the celebrated (& now
forbidden) scene, where Richard is deposed & gives up his
crown, you would have thought it was some clownish comedy.
Such roars of laughter & catcalls! The poor players, frightened,

sweating drops like pearls, tried to continue as if nothing were wrong.

I was ashamed to be among such rude company.

Yet it is a long scene & they grew quiet before the end. When Richard, King no more, takes up a looking glass to see himself:

> Was this the face
> That every day under his household roof
> Did keep ten thousand men?
> Was this the face
> That like the sun, did make beholders wink?
> Is this the face which fac'd so many follies,
> That was at last out-fac'd by Bullingbrook?

When he dashes the glass into "an hundred shivers," you could have heard hearts beating in the shivering audience.

Afterward the players told me that they had not wished to scour up the play. But that yesterday they were told to do so by the Lord Monteagle & other of the Earl's followers. And being given forty shillings for their pains, they did so.

Next morning, Sunday morning, he was beginning to have second thoughts about the whole affair. Slept late and thus arrived at Essex House at midmorning. To find a great crowd and great excitement. All arming. Preparing themselves for battle. Council had sent for the Earl. Fearing for his life he had refused to go.

Much stirring & yelling by the wicket gate. Entered in their robes the Lord Chief Justice Popham & the Lord Keeper, he with a servant bearing the Great Seal of England. And two others whom I did not recognize, but later learned to be the Earl of Worcester & Sir William Knollys. They came in, amid shouting, & from the house came the Earl to greet & deal with them. The men stood all in a knot & we could hear nothing of what they were saying to each other. Some of the swordsmen began to shout to the Earl—"Away, my lord!" & "They betray you!" & such.

Soon many were calling together, "Kill them! Kill them! Kill them!"

The Lord Keeper tried to speak for the Queen, but no man could hear him. At least where I was standing.

Then the lords all went inside the house together.

Leaving the crowd to shout & to wait.

I found a fellow who had been close enough to hear some of what was said.

"What did the Lord Keeper say?" I asked.

"He commanded us, on allegiance, to lay down our weapons and to depart."

Ah, Sweet Jesus, I thought to myself, not daring to say anything more. Now it will be treason if we do not obey. Lords may always parley among each other & save their noble skins. But I am only a poor player & have come to the wrong place for certain. . . .

There was no way to escape. Not until, a little after ten o'clock, the Earls, our Earls, returned & prepared to lead their army forth. I drew sword & shouted blood & thunder as loud as any other. We ran out the gate. Turned right & east (thank God for that!) toward the City. Myself figuring to slip away down the first footway I could take.

Did so, too, on the swiftest pair of feet in London.

Found an old man, half drunk from the night before, who was pleased (no questions asked, no answers offered) to trade his leather jerkin & rough wool clothes for my courtier's garb, my hat & sword. We stood in a frozen garden just off Fetter Lane & stripped ourselves & traded clothes.

Off he went to the City, every inch a courtier's swordsman. I slipped to Whitefriars & lay as quiet as fox in his den.

Wife less than pleased by my changed appearance. She had found my role as gentleman somewhat to her liking. But I charged her to forget it forever.

As to the fellow in my clothes?

Well, he somehow fell in with the others. And when they all came to the Sheriff's house on Fenchurch Street & the Sheriff excused himself etc., he & a goodly number of others began drinking the ale there. Fellow became drunk again & fell asleep in the Sheriff's cellar. Was thus arrested & taken to the Tower. Strictly held & straitly questioned. Until it was clear the old man had not the slightest idea what had happened. They took away his fine clothes & his sword and set him free.

Is he any the worse for it?

No, sir, not as this world goes.

He haunts taverns & will tell you his story for a penny. How he was taken to be one of the Earl of Essex's most ferocious rebels. Was taken to the Flint Tower of the Tower of London. How he saw them bring in (just before dawn on Monday) the Earl of Essex & the Earl of Southampton together. Though he's not sure which was which.

How one of those foolish Earls greeted him at the window as if he were an old friend. And how that took him a week to explain away.

Many in the taverns he frequents have slept on straw in one (or more) of London's prisons. But few have had the privilege of accommodation in the Tower of London (even by mistake) upon suspicion of high treason.

An old soldier (among other things), you cannot picture any military action without picturing yourself there in the thick of it. You have sought to cultivate the soldier's habit of tightly leashing your imagination, training fancy not to follow the strong impulse to place you, as if in flesh and blood, in imaginary battles. Every soldier who lives long enough to tell of it believes that it is best to suffer only from real wounds. Better to be prepared for one death only.

What do you know of the Earl? Truly. . . .

Your guess that the very breath of his life came from others. That without the eyes of others he possessed no more life than clothing folded in a press, than his armor perched empty on a wooden frame. Now. All men imagine others (is it not so?) to be compounded of the same elements, a like mixture of breath and dust, of virtues and vices as themselves. Essex must have believed that others had no more life than he granted them. By beholding them. Thus that he, and all the great men of this world, were scattered in many pieces like figures seen in the shards of a broken mirror. Of no more substance than light, they move like swimmers in clear water. Thus it was his folly to believe that the Queen had no more substance than the crown and robes she wore. That without his eyes to give her life she was diminished to the edge of nothingness.

Once you had exchanged words with Essex. At the time of the siege of Rouen in '91.

On that morning, a day in late September with trees beginning to be touched by the coming of fall, you were on horseback, with some other officers, on a hill at a distance from the walls of Rouen. Observing a party of enemy cavalry which was making a sally among the besiegers. A crusty group you were. In your stinking old wool and rotting leather, your battered morion set on your head and your light pieces of armor flecked with rust.

Abruptly appeared on the crest of the hill a fantastic band all wearing the orange-and-white livery of the Earl of Essex. As if dressed for a parade. And amidst them Essex, himself, with his orange velvet clothing and his cloak glittering with jewels. Bareheaded. His hair red and gold in the light. A hooded hawk on his arm. The others, you noticed, had hawks with them also.

So that was what they were doing this morning—hawking. Had come up here to see a little killing of men. In the distance below. They, his people, chattered with excitement like a flock of birds in a dead tree. He, taller than the others, sat silent and smiling. Looking.

They seemed to be arguing with each other. The Earl was appealed to. He shrugged first, then noticed your group for the first time.

"Are any of you English?" he asked.

You alone in that group were an Englishman; for you were serving the French in those days. You removed your helmet from your head.

"Sir," you said.

"Who are they?"

"Sir?"

"Those horsemen. Are they ours or theirs?"

"They are the enemy, sir."

"Ah, too bad," he said.

And in a moment, just like a flight of birds taking flight on a gust of breeze or impulse, the whole gaudy crew galloped away in another direction. Looking to continue their hawking, you guessed, until dinnertime.

You spat on the ground in response to the laughter of your French comrades.

Who was this foolish overgrown boy of an Englishman, the leader of the English forces no less, who could not tell which ones were the enemy?

Ah, well, It is late now. Much later in this world's age and weariness since then.

Bone and muscle of you, you know how it was to have been there among them, among Essex's mob of followers on the day of the rising. Not exactly as yourself. For you would never have been there. Not now. Not ten years ago. You were never young enough, were you?, but you can imagine yourself as someone else who might have. Perhaps one of his Welsh captains, full of rage and poetry.

How it would have been, finally!, when the Earl and the others were ready, to rush out of the gate of Essex House. All shouting "To the Court!" But not going there. Turning right and east to go along the Strand and then Fleet Street. Into the City at Ludgate and on to Paul's Churchyard. Where by then the morning sermons at the Cross were over and done with. Going along Cheapside, Poultry and Lombard. Some along the way cheering. Others coming to windows to look out and see you. No man joining. Long wait at Fenchurch Street. While the Earl and the leaders had their dinner. And the rest of you drank ale and waited on his pleasure. Next comes the herald, indeed the Garter King at Arms, Mr. William Dethick, to read the proclamation against them. Then a rapid thinning of your ranks. And at last, in late afternoon light, smaller in number now and somewhat bedraggled, back you go the way you had come. To find Ludgate guarded by some soldiers and a captain. A brief fighting. One small ragged volley fired by both sides. Four killed, two of them simply citizens of London standing nearby. One other was Henry Tracy, the Earl's page, standing directly next to the Earl. His page shot dead and holes shot through his own hat, but the Earl unscathed.

Is it any wonder Essex believed he bore a charmed life still?

("His truth shall compass thee with a shield: thou shalt not be afraid of the terror of the night. Of the arrow that flieth in the day, of the business that walketh about in the dark: of invasion or of the noonday devil. A thousand shall fall at thy side, and ten thousand at thy right hand: but it shall not come nigh thee.")

There is a saying of old soldiers, which the Earl may have been spared in all of the wars he went to, on account of his exalted rank. When one among the company is somehow miraculously spared and is congratulated for his good fortune, it is meet and right for him to put on a long face and to reply: "The Lord must be saving me for something worse."

Racing down Friday Street, every man for himself, to Queenhithe. Where you jostle to board boats. Some falling and nearly drowning. Now rowing upriver past old Baynard's Castle and Blackfriars and Bridewell. Past Whitefriars and the Temple. Leaping ashore and running up through the gardens (where there were already soldiers of the Crown) to prepare to defend Essex House. Soon surrounded. Night falling. Skirmishing. Some killed and wounded. Threats and parleys. Defiance of the Earl. You are as ready to die as you have been all day. And, like the others of the faithful few, would rather die here and now than in the hands of the common hangman. But that is not to be. At ten o'clock, by torchlight, with some ceremony, the nobles came forth from the house and knelt before the Lord Admiral surrendering their swords. The rest of you to be more roughly treated. Cuffed and pushed about. Tied up and marched off to prisons, through the streets.

Where you will wait with the others, lesser fry, expecting the worst. Which will not come to pass. Besides the Earl, only four men will die for this day—Henry Cuffe and Sir Gilly Meyrick at Tyburn, Sir Christopher Blount and Sir Charles Danvers on Tower Hill. Southampton will remain in the Tower. The rest will be fined and released.

You have to laugh about it. How it will remain in the memory of the best of them—being those few whose courage and loyalty did not falter—as an act of folly. Nothing else. Have to laugh at the Queen's worldly wisdom in acting with unexpected mercy and allowing most of these to live and go free. Unexpected? Well, after the rising of the northern Earls she peopled the gallows of the North Country with hanging bodies. And that has not been forgotten and will not be forgotten for a long time to come. The last great rising in London was a winter rebellion also— Wyatt's Rebellion of '54. Against Queen Mary. After which rebellion there were so many hangings in London that new gallows had to be built all over the city. There are still old people who remember the sight and the stink of it. It was to be expected that Elizabeth would do much the same thing. And though the citizens of London, who failed him, may now be writing their broadsides and ballads to lament the death of Essex, those who offered their lives for his cause (and received them back from his foes) will not mourn him much. Owing him nothing, not even regret, now. He squandered their love and faith. And though they may not hate him for that, there will still be a sadness in their thoughts of him. There will always be sadness that at the last, all pretense cast aside, he proved himself to be . . . unworthy.

Well, not quite.

In the morning you will hear the Player tell of the trial of the Earls of Essex and Southampton. Which he had witnessed at Westminster Hall. On Wednesday, the eighteenth of February:

"Well, I had failed him on that Sunday, fortunately for me and thank God for it," he will say. "Came time for the trial and I felt it to be seemly to be there, for him and his sake, as it were. As if I owed him at least that much."

The Player having evidently (conveniently) forgotten that he was spying upon the Earl, and for pay, in the first place.

"Felt that I should be there. Even at the risk that someone might recognize me as one of his people. The risk was real enough. For, ever since the rebellion, London and Westminster were thick with soldiers brought in from the shires. Crawling with agents. Daily people were taken up—mostly knights and gentlemen to be sure—and placed in London's prisons or the Tower to be examined.

"I confess that I turned to my craft, changing the color and the cut of my hair and my beard. And finding a means to have the use of a gown belonging to a careless and impecunious member of the Middle Temple. So that I appeared to be properly there as a gentleman and a scholar of the Law, together with others of my kind. I should also add that there was a further benefit in that we scholars of the Inns of Court were given good places from which to see the trial."

So he saw it all, from the ceremonial beginning in the middle of the morning until its ending by torchlight.

"Some of my fellow scholars had brought pomanders and nosegays with them, fearing the old winter stink of the place. Especially since we were almost come to the end of Hilary Term. And before going in, I could have pinched myself for forgetting. Thinking that I would have to hold my nose to endure it. But that was not to be. When Earls are to be tried for treason, they can make the old Hall seem as fresh as an April garden. All the stink of misery and the sweat of greed, which are the blossoms of the Law, being banished for a day at least. Even the wooden angels flying at the ends of the beams of the roof looked, to me, as happy as they had ever been.

"Not long before the clocks of Westminster could be heard tolling nine," he'll tell you, "the Guard formed up and marched outside. And then in the near distance we could hear the noise of the crowd lining the way between the Water Gate and the Hall, past Star Chamber and across New Palace Yard, to see the Earls of Essex and Southampton brought in by boat from the Tower. Then the crowd in the Hall began to grow quiet—nothing more than stifled coughs and sneezes—as a processional began."

First of all the Lord Treasurer, gown and collar and his white wand of office, acting as the Lord High Steward for this trial. Then the seven Sergeants at Arms, solemnly, each bearing a mace. Eight judges in scarlet gowns, led by Judge John Popham, Chief Justice of King's Bench. Then came Counsel in appropriate garb—Coke, the Attorney General; Fleming, Solicitor General; Henry Yelverton, Sergeant at Law; the Recorder and others including (again) Francis Bacon, attorney.

All took seats. Next a Sergeant at Arms arose and ordered, in a loud clear voice, that the prisoners should be now produced.

Everyone turned to see Lord Thomas Howard, the Constable of the Tower, and Sir John Peyton, Lieutenant of the Tower, come down the length of the Hall. Followed by the Gentleman Porter, bearing the great axe and leading Essex and Southampton to take their places. Essex all in black, Southampton as if clad in silk flowers, his long blond hair falling to his shoulders, resting lightly on a snowy white falling collar—no ruff for him that day.

"You know, curious things flash through the mind, like birds coming in one window, darting about a moment or two in the light, then out another window to be lost in the large world. The bird that flashed across my thoughts as I saw the Earl of Southampton walking the Hall, every eye fixed on the two of them, first thing that truly caught my eye was that wonderful filmy lace collar he wore. Whiteness and elegance of it. And I wondered where, in what shop, from what lacemaker, he had bought it. And I wondered that men coming from prison, albeit not without comforts for men of exalted rank, could look so handsomely dressed and barbered. Wondered, for an instant, how the laundering and ironing and starching and shining and such was arranged from chambers in the Tower. Knowing, of course, that money can work all things. Suddenly possessed, as a player will be (for every player, like a woman, will not be content till he tries himself out in every role he can imagine), by a picture of myself as the third prisoner in the group—shabby, dirty, beard and hair tangled, straw and dirt sticking to my clothing.

"Then that bird was gone to roost. And I found myself studying the faces—the Earl of Essex seeming to be troubled, Southampton looking calm and composed as a choirboy."

Those first impressions were false. For once the trial began, Essex was at ease, composed, in charge of himself if not of events. While Southampton slowly, steadily (as if he were inwardly melting) weakened until at the end he begged for his life.

"Even that was somehow . . . satisfactory. His fear gave Essex's pride more meaning than it might have had. His dishonor served Essex well. By the same token, I suppose, Southampton's cringing would have been without value to him except in contrast to Essex. That is, Southampton owes his life not alone to his own demeanor, but just as much to the refusal of Essex to humble himself."

Now came the jury to sit in place, each one rising as his name was called. Twenty-five barons and Earls. Some of these friends and kinsmen. Many of them old enemies. A few mortal enemies.

"And now burst forth, like a covey of started quail, as if flushed to life by laughter, the first points of Law."

Maybe on account of his costume as a scholar the Player will make much of points of Law, but to no good purpose or avail. For, all protestation to the contrary, it is the stage play of the trial, a show of characters, betrayals, discoveries, entrances and exits that interests him most.

At least he will show the good manners to defend his actor's inclinations.

"Now, sir, I do not know anything of your acquaintance with the Law. I can, however, safely assume that anyone alive in this most litigious kingdom of the world has enjoyed some experience of our courts. You are a gentleman, clearly. So it may well be that you have sat as Justice of the Peace. Served on juries, too. Been called upon as a witness. *Et cetera.*

"And, sir, you have the manner of a trueborn country gentleman. Not used to the city ways. I mean no offense, you can be sure. It takes a thief to catch one, as they say. And someone like myself, raised in the country, though eager to forget it, can feel the country in another countryman as surely as if you had straws in your hair and pig shit on the soles of your boots.

"Now. In the country it is the points of Law and not the spectacle (which in my experience, is most often a meager little show) which are of the greatest interest to folks. When you are dealing with a matter concerning collection of rents or the ownership of some sheep, enclosures and boundaries and so forth and so on, there is nothing of more importance than the points of the Law that may apply to the case. I think that there may be many an old countryman, one who can neither read nor write, who will prove to be as well versed in relevant points of the Law as Mr. Coke or Mr. Bacon or Judge Popham himself. But here in Westminster, sir, it is usually the spectacle that interests them most."

Soon the Earls were sworn and the Clerk read out the indictment. Which charged that they had conspired "to deprive and depose the Queen's Majesty from her royal state and dignity, and to procure her death and destruction; and also to cause a cruel slaughter of Her Majesty's subjects, to alter the religion established and to change the government of the Realm. . . ."

It was wondered at, that the first charge which had been made by the Queen in her proclamation had been dropped from this indictment. In the Queen's proclamation, published the day after the rebellion, it had been charged that the conspirators began this plot in Ireland and with the knowledge and collusion of the rebellious Earl of Tyrone:

> Whereas the Earl of Essex, accompanied by the Earls of Rutland and Southampton, and divers other their complices, Gentlemen of birth and quality, knowing themselves to be discovered in divers treasonable actions, into which they have heretofore entered, as well in our Realm of Ireland, where some of them had laid plots with the traitor Tyrone, as in this our Realm of England. . . .

Nor was there even a whiff of a suggestion of any possible part, active or passive, played in the conspiracy by the King of Scots.

"Thus, sir, the Earl was somewhat reassured. If the government chose to keep the King free of any blame, then they must also depend upon Essex to do so, too. At any moment he could confess that he had conspired with King James concerning the Succession. And that would bring great trouble and difficulty to everyone. Himself? The sentence of death was inevitable. But, sir, the execution of it was not. As witness that the Earl of Southampton remains alive to this day in the Tower.

"It was not unreasonable for Essex to assume that if he chose to keep silent, he might be rewarded with his life. And, all in due time, should the King come to the throne of England, he might hope to regain his freedom and to be restored. By the same reasoning it must have seemed that if he acted with discretion and yet was executed, it would go poorly for those who had done this to him. And after all, sir, if the King should succeed our Queen, it may go poorly for those who were the Earl's enemies. Especially Mr. Secretary.

"I do not wish to build a case of my own. Only to say that a man who is fighting for his life will cling to the least hope. Unless he shall be content to shrug his life away. Thus the Earl must have seized hope when he saw that they were very careful not to mention the King.

"It was this, sir, that I believe explains the sudden moment when Mr. Secretary Cecil came bursting out of his hiding behind the arras and rushed forward to kneel before the Court and demand the right to defend himself and his reputation.

"Ah, you are smiling, sir. Laughing inwardly. Thinking for a player like myself that was the highest moment of spectacle. A little scene much more in place on the stage of the Globe or the Fortune than beneath the high-flying angels of Westminster Hall. Well, true enough. It was, indeed, a scene worthy of our poets. One in which any player would relish to play either of the principal roles—the small and crippled Secretary; the tall, handsome, imperious and doomed Earl.

"You are right to smile at it. For at that moment both of these men were players. And I . . . I could perceive how it would be to be the Queen's Secretary or the great Earl. It was indeed the highest point of the trial for me.

"Others sensed this, too, but took it differently. The lawyers whom I have heard speaking of it think that this was a very bad turn for the Earl. Especially coming late in the day—for it was between five and six o'clock in the evening, and they were setting more torches to light the Court. And until then the Earl had done himself no great harm with his quips and arguments."

But: the Earl interrupted Mr. Bacon to claim that Sir Robert Cecil favored the title of the Infanta of Spain. That Cecil had said her claim was "as good as any others."

It was this that brought Cecil out of his hiding place in a hurry. To prove, as he was able to, that the Earl had lied.

Now, these lawyers were correct in perceiving that to be disproved by Cecil—and Sir William Knollys, Queen's Comptroller, who was sent for to testify directly to the issue—did the Earl no good. But there was nothing whatever which could have done good for the Earl. He knew that. As did everyone there, though some judges and lawyers may have pretended otherwise for the honor of their profession. Nothing could do him any good. And nothing could harm him either. But he might still save his life.

Cecil would be the key to that. And Cecil was not present. Which must have puzzled Essex. Nearly everyone else who mattered, of Court and Council, was present in the Hall. Except for

Cecil. Well. No need for him to be there. He could learn all that he needed to know from the records and from the reports of others. Yet, the Earl would be thinking, someone must report this trial to the Queen. Who would do so? Appropriately Mr. Secretary.

And so the Earl must have guessed that Cecil was hidden there somewhere, bearing witness to his ruin.

"See how often, sir, the Earl had guessed right in his lifetime. He could not be faulted for trusting the promptings of his spirit. Oh, there are many who profess to believe he was crazed, that he proved it, too, by believing in fantasies and illusions. Yet he had reason to trust his fantasies. For over and over they had proved true. Only at the end did he deceive himself. Like the hero of a tragedy. Which is how I came to imagine him. Which is how I imagine I would play his part."

Very well, the Earl thought, let us bring this little Cecil into the light. Let him bear some public witness to himself.

The Earl thinking also that it could possibly serve to test the truth of his idea concerning King James of Scotland. That is, true enough that if Sir Robert Cecil had indeed said that the Infanta of Spain, or anyone else for that matter, had as good a title to the Succession as any other, and said so to another who would so swear, why it would have been a criminal act. But if he denied it (as he would in any case), the Queen would most likely have believed him. What choice would she have to do otherwise? He had proved faithful to her during the rising. She could not allow herself to imagine that he, too, was against her, could she?

The Earl seems to have concluded that if Cecil responded to this unexpected charge, it would be for the sake of his reputation with . . . the King.

"And there is something else about this encounter. Something I knew. Thus all in Westminster Hall certainly knew. How since the Earl's father had died when Essex was a child and since he was thereafter a ward of Lord Burghley, these two men had known each other from childhood. How in a sense they were like brothers. Each so different from the other. Each lacking what the other possessed. Both desiring the love and praise of the father, Lord Burghley. And both, like all sons, desiring freedom from the father. And Lord Burghley himself desiring that each serve the Queen. Wishing for each the satisfactions of ambition. Never imagining, in the midst of his hopes, that each would hate the other. With the special hatred a man reserves for that part of himself which disgusts him most. Old Burghley could not conceive of the depths of their hatred for each other."

(There remains a story which made the rounds. Story of how at a Council meeting, in the last months of his life, old Lord Burghley wearied of Essex's blood-and-thunder debates for war. From which even deafness could not spare him. Burghley abruptly produced his Psalter. Began to read, looking for something, fumbling pages. His lips moving silently, his fingers trembling a little. Talking ceased as all at the table looked at the white-haired, lean-faced old man. Who was muttering to himself. When he had all their attention, he found what it was he had been looking for. Stabbed at it with his finger. Marked it deeply with his fingernail. And in an equally emphatic, sudden gesture, hurled the book along the table toward Essex. Who dutifully raised it, looked at the page, and read aloud the last verse of the fifty-fifth psalm: "The blood-thirsty and deceitful men shall not live out half their days: nevertheless, my trust shall be in thee, O Lord." Read it aloud to the Council, like a pupil called upon to make recitation. Then looked at old Burghley and smiled a little ambiguous smile. As if in expectation of some kind of approval. . . .)

"Mr. Secretary Cecil came rushing out before the Court in a passion. Crying his innocence and anger at the top of his voice.

"Out he came shouting. As if violently pushed from behind. Kneeling to the Court to beg permission to speak. Then rising to denounce the Earl. Indeed, sir, for the sake of contrast he could not have selected a more disadvantageous grouping. For, standing mind you, there were the forty Guards, each taller than six feet, and Ralegh, their Captain, at six and a half feet standing taller than even the Earl. And Coke, huge as well as tall, the equal or taller than Ralegh. Oh, Mr. Secretary was like a small dog yipping among the legs of horses.

"Out of your malice toward me, Your Lordship desires to make me odious. Having no other sure ground than the breach between us about the peace with Spain. Which I labored for, for the profit and quiet of my country. But with you it has ever been the maxim to prefer war before peace. . . . I confess that I have said that the King of Spain is a competitor of the crown of England. And that the King of Scots is a competitor. And my Lord of Essex is a competitor. For he would depose the Queen and call a Parliament and so be King himself. . . ."

"Ah, Mr. Secretary," the Earl of Essex told him. "I thank God for my humiliation—that you, in the ruff of all your bravery, have come hither to make your oration against me this day."

The ruff of all your bravery. . . .

That would hurt like the stroke of a whip.

"Mr. Secretary's speech was more for the ears of King James than anyone else. His profession of being a lover of peace, 'for the profit and quiet of my country,' was designed for this Scots King who desires to be known chiefly as a Peacemaker. Likewise naming the Earl as a competitor for the crown—something that had been hinted at by Coke and others, but never openly charged and not a matter of the indictment against him, was aimed at turning the King against Essex.

"And so, even as he humiliated the Secretary by forcing him to come forth and to show himself in public, why, sir, Essex gave to him a small victory with which to salvage his dignity.

"Thus when Mr. Comptroller confirmed Cecil's testimony over against the Earl's hearsay, it was bound to end in reconciliation.

"It must have seemed to Essex that the reconciliation with Cecil meant that they would join together in the future, in the next reign. It must have seemed to Essex that he had here demonstrated how much the one needed the other."

"I forgive you from the bottom of my heart," Cecil said.

"And I, Mr. Secretary, do clearly and freely forgive you with all my soul. Because I mean to die in charity with all men."

His last words addressed to Sir Robert Cecil were of his death. Reminding Mr. Secretary that when the time for his execution came, Essex would have the last words. Like any other man about to die. To die in charity with all men might possibly require some open speaking about some secret things.

The Player, rinsing his mouth with beer, will continue to recount this celebrated trial. Seeing it as forming a row of little scenes. Each scene a kind of duel. Between the two Earls—and chiefly Essex, for Southampton did not have as much to say until nearly the end of things—and a sequence of adversaries. Somewhat like the order of old tales of knightly quest. In which the knight must overcome or escape one danger after another.

First, then, Henry Yelverton, the Sergeant at Law. Who spoke generally and not directly to the indictment. Compared Essex to a crocodile in ambition and appetite. Chided him for ingratitude to the Queen. Then compared him to the Roman traitor Catiline.

"As Catiline did entertain all of the most seditious persons in Rome to join with him in his conspiracy, so the Earl of Essex entertained none but Papists and recusants and atheists for his abettors in this his capital rebellion against the whole estate of England."

To his speech the Earls made no reply except to furnish a loud, mutual amen when the attorney ended with the prayer for the Queen and that "God long preserve her from the hands of her enemies."

Next Edward Coke to make the chief case for the Crown. Larger and richer than Essex and, indeed, richer than most of the nobility, ancient or new, in the Hall. But except for the awesome power of his office as the Queen's Attorney General, he was without any title. Pointing out that under Law the very thought or imagining of the death of the Prince is treason. But these thoughts and imaginings may not be known or "be so adjudged until they appear by discovery either by word or writing or some outward act." The case of the Earl of Essex was elegantly simple. "He that raises a rebellion or insurrection in a settled Government does, in the construction of the Law, thereby imagine the death and destruction of the Prince and is therefore guilty of treason." He cited precedents from many cases. He recited the events of that Sunday. Acknowledging that not many had died and that no great harm had been done. But arguing that none of these things should be considered by the jury.

"At the end of his arguments of Law, Mr. Coke turned directly on the Earl of Essex, denounced his life and ingratitude. And ended with a picture of what might have happened if the rising had succeeded:

"This was not all. For the Earl would then call a Parliament and himself decide all matters which did not make for his purpose. A bloody Parliament that would have been where my lord

of Essex, who now stands all in black, would have worn a bloody
robe. But now in God's judgment he of his earldom shall be Robert the Last. Who of a kingdom thought to be Robert the First.
Why should I stand upon further proof? This treason is so evident that my lord himself will not deny it."

Essex turned this last, which went far beyond the indictment,
to his own advantage.

"Mr. Attorney playeth the orator and abuseth Your Lordships'
ears with slanders against us. These are the fashions of orators in
corrupt states. And such rhetoric is the trade and talent of those
who value themselves upon their skill in pleading innocent men
out of their lives. . . ."

Next came the testimony of witnesses. A deposition by one
named Henry Widdington. Who had been present at Essex
House upon that Sunday morning. Then Judge Popham. Sworn
now as a witness himself.

Next one who had once been called a friend, now the Earl's
mortal enemy. One of those whom the Earl had named as laying
a plot against his life. Sir Walter Ralegh. Captain of the Guard.
Here to tell of his meeting on the river with his kinsman—Sir
Ferdinando Gorges.

If this had been a playhouse, they would have hissed at him,
like a flock of geese, at sight.

He seems to invite that.

Even Essex could not let it pass without acknowledgment.
Waited until Ralegh put his hand upon a Bible to take the oath.

"What booteth it to swear the Fox?" he asked in a whispery
voice which carried throughout the Hall.

"Ralegh's evident indifference, as if he had heard neither the
Earl's words nor the soft laughter in the Hall (not a wince or
flinch from him; I must remember that calm indifference and
save it for some villainous role), was so right as to confirm the
Earl's contempt.

"Which leads me, sir, to this observation. God alone knows the
depth of the Earl's duplicity. But men tended to trust him. Partly
because they believed they could read him like a book. His face,
alive, showed all his anger and admiration, his passions and contempt, his delights and even (it seemed) his fears. His face, lit
by his inmost feelings, would never permit him to conceal him-

self from others even if he had wished to. Ralegh, on the other hand, shares little of what he may be feeling. Therefore he is said to be coldly without them. Merely a guardian of secrets, a man whose only passion is ruthless, implacable ambition.

"But, as a player, whose bread and beer comes from duplicity, whose art begins with the making of faces, the revelation of inward humors and passions which are none of them true, I cannot say that the Earl was any of the things he was thought to be by others. There were times when, captured by his words and actions, I believed him wholly and doubted every witness and all of his enemies. Then, at other times the player in me took command. Reminded me that if I were to study him long enough and with a proper attention, why then, sir, if we had changed places, I should have been able to play the Earl of Essex almost as well as he. Meaning that everything about him—not only the outward and visible postures and habits and attitudes, but also the inmost promptings of his spirit—was imitable. Meaning, then, that either he was of no more true substance than a scarecrow in a field or that he was ever as secret and disguised as Ralegh or any other duplicitous man.

"It is my guess, sir, that what I perceived was what others, friends and enemies alike, came to. That with the Earl of Essex there was neither answer nor explanation, but only doubt. Those who loved him best were those who could bear with the weight of doubt for the longest time. Those who were, then, truly . . . skeptical. But, sir, when he found himself forced into a small place, from which he must prove himself beyond all doubt and establish the unimpeachable foundation of his loyalty for the Queen and this her kingdom, try as he would, he could not do so. It was his property to create doubts, not to settle them.

"Ralegh spoke only to his interview with Gorges and to the warnings they had exchanged with each other. When Ralegh finished, Essex allowed that Ralegh's testimony was in conflict with what Sir Ferdinando Gorges had reported to him."

This, the Player believes, may have been a trap for Essex. For, unbeknownst to him, Gorges had submitted a full confession concerning the conspiracy. To settle the issue the Clerk then read this confession.

Essex demanded to have Sir Ferdinando Gorges brought there before him face to face.

"Now that I think on it, I conclude that all this had been arranged for by the attorneys. Or someone else (Mr. Secretary?) who knew Essex well enough to wager on his responses. Ralegh testifies at the bar. The Earl then challenges that. Thus giving them the perfect time and place to read out the confession of Gorges. Which was, surely, news to the Earl. He then demands the privilege of a confrontation. Guessing, I would surmise, that this would be denied. Or that it would be unwieldy. For the delay in bringing Sir Ferdinando from the Tower, or any other prison—except perhaps the Westminster Gatehouse, and why would he be kept *there?*—would be too great.

"And the Earl knew Sir Ferdinando for a timorous sort. A man whom he could influence by a look and the habit of command. If he could face Gorges and force him to change his story, that might greatly strengthen his case and weaken theirs.

"Therefore he must have been astonished when his request was granted.

"Even more so when very shortly (as if he had been waiting just outside the Hall for this reason) Sir Ferdinando Gorges was brought in. Somewhat dirty and disheveled. Obviously uneasy. And who would not be so? Who would not be sorely distressed to face a friend whom he followed as servant to master? A friend and master whom you admired and feared. . . . Feared enough so that your greater fear would be that in some way, by persuasion or threat or by some trick, the Earl would make you change your testimony to his own advantage. Which, if done, would be sure to cost you the life you may have saved by betraying him.

"I tell you, sir, if they had dragged me into the Hall in Gorges' place, my bony knees would have been knocking together and I would have been as white as goat's milk, too."

Meantime consider the Earl. Knowing that he had been tricked. How then to gain something from it? How also to retain his own composure and dignity.

"Good Sir Ferdinando," the Earl told him. With authority. Gorges must imagine that Essex is almost in command here. That the trial has gone well for him. That maybe—the worst possibility for a betrayer—it will end with the Earl going free. "Good Sir Ferdinando, with all my heart I do desire thee to speak freely. I see that you desire to live. And yet I pray thee—speak like a man!"

Gorges, however, would not be so easily persuaded or shaken.

"I pray you to answer me," Essex said. "Did you truly advise me to leave my enterprise?"

"My Lord, I do think that I did."

"Think?" Essex said. "Nay, this is no time now to answer upon thinking. These are not things to be forgotten."

When he saw that he could not in any way move Gorges, Essex turned to the jury.

"My Lords, look here upon Sir Ferdinando. See if he looks like himself."

To no avail.

Next Attorney General Coke rose up again and had the Clerk to read some other declarations. One after the other he read the confessions of the Earl of Rutland, Lord Cromwell, Lord Monteagle, Lord Sandys, Sir Charles Danvers, Sir John Davis, Sir Christopher Blount (his own stepfather), and some others. All blaming Essex for misleading them. All having turned against him in the hope of saving their own skins.

Here the Earl had no alternative save to imitate Ralegh and wear a face of stone. Except the effort of it was too much for him. Though his face said nothing, his body talked plainly for him. As these confessions were read it was as if he had been yoked like a beast and then weighted down with a heavy burden. His proud shoulders curled and slumped. His knees bent and his back sagged.

By then the Earl must have been numbed by the impact of so many betrayals. Had not been fool enough to believe he could *vindicate* himself by this trial. No. But not unreasonable to hope that through his conduct he might yet save himself. A gamble, to be sure. But always the Queen had responded to his enchantment. A large part of which, at least, was his undaunted pride and honor. So much so that humility could not serve him well. As it might serve some other person, needing her favor or her mercy. Humility would seem to her as inappropriate. Therefore he must emerge from this humiliation with something of pride and honor (the last of his magic with her and the world) intact.

He had steeled himself for this. Was prepared for almost anything. Prepared for the confessions of his companions. How could they do otherwise?

But. . . .

Confession of guilt is one thing. Betrayal and the casting of blame is quite another. This, in his view, was the utmost humiliation. For it meant that he had terribly misjudged the men closest to him. Meant he had been a greater fool than he had allowed himself to imagine.

He could have laughed if he had not been fighting against tears. For these false friends, each a poor Judas, had forfeited their best chance of saving themselves. He might have been able to save them. By betraying him, they injured themselves as much as they hurt him.

Here, even before the finish of the reading of the confessions, he must have vowed to ruin them for it.

Finishing (for the time being) the case against Essex, they turned to Southampton. Who crumbled. Who played the coward well enough to satisfy their worst enemies.

Then came the betrayal by Francis Bacon.

"For all this long day people had been waiting to see what it was the Mr. Francis Bacon might do. It was thought by his friends that he was there at the command of the Queen. It was thought by his friends that his betrayal of Essex was required to save his brother Anthony. True, as I said, Anthony Bacon had withdrawn himself from Essex House when the Earl had been allowed to return there to live. And true, also, that at the time of the rising Anthony Bacon was very ill and like to die. Indeed he was dead and gone not long after. Within only a few weeks of it. But since for a good many years, ever since '92 I do believe, he had been the Earl's confidential secretary and chief agent in all matters that involved spying and in the conduct of his correspondence and business with prominent men in other countries, it seemed certain that it would be necessary to arrest and question him closely about many things. Any number of things.

"The arrest and questioning of Anthony Bacon did not take place.

"Which I find passing strange.

"Perhaps it was the influence of his cousin, Cecil, which caused him to be spared.

"Perhaps Anthony Bacon had already given testimony. In this sense—that far from being a rival to Cecil, he was, in truth, a spy for Cecil all along.

"Perhaps Cecil wanted others to arrive at that inference whether it was true or not.

"Or perhaps Cecil, knowing how desperately sick his cousin was, took pity on him. Knowing that he already had more than enough evidence against Essex and the others whom he was determined to destroy.

"Perhaps it was a sum of all these things.

"And perhaps it was the dutiful public betrayal of Essex by Francis Bacon that turned the trick and saved his elder brother.

"On the other hand, sir, Bacon's enemies do profess that none of these considerations so inspired Francis Bacon as much as his own unsatisfied ambitions. They maintain he betrayed his old master willingly. They say that he hoped to gain some favor from the Queen. They called him a Judas, then, selling his honor outright for whatever he could gain. They laughed at him (behind their hands) for his failure to realize that the Queen would despise him for such a betrayal. For she has always scorned those who betray their friends and masters. Even when those friends and masters have been her enemies. His enemies like to imagine that Francis Bacon betrayed Essex and ruined his own repute for no good purpose. Gaining nothing for his pains.

"If his goal was to save his brother, they feel entitled to laugh at his waste of effort. On two counts. First that the brother died soon anyway. And second that the death of Anthony Bacon brought Francis very little beyond a multitude of debts. Including, to be sure, debts acquired by doing work on behalf of the Earl of Essex."

Perhaps Francis Bacon was aware of all of these things and betrayed Essex out of pure malice.

Bacon stood up and approached the bar. Bowed to judges and jury. Then turned to face the Earl directly. Spoke directly to him as if not to the Court at all. A middle-sized man, with hazel eyes, looking into the eyes of the Earl.

He compared the Earl's tactics to those of one Pisistratus of Athens "who, coming into the city with the purpose of procuring the subversion of the Kingdom, and lacking aid for the accomplishing of his desires, and as the surest means to win the hearts of the citizens unto him, he entered the city after having cut himself with a knife, to the end that they might all conjecture he had been truly in danger of his life." He compared him to the hated Duke of Guise in France. He compared him to Cain, the first murderer. He was the first to attack the Earl's assertion that he had acted out of sudden fear for his life. "You, my Lord, allege this matter to have been resolved of a sudden. No! You were three months in deliberation."

Malice and long premeditation were, then, added to the case.

Bacon turned back to the judges and the jury.

"I have never yet seen in any case such favor shown to any prisoner," he told them. "So many digressions. Such delivering of the evidence by fractions. And so silly a defense of such great notorious treasons."

All that the Earl could do was to remind the Court that Bacon had once pretended to be his good and trusted friend.

"I call forth Mr. Bacon against Mr. Bacon," he said.

And there was some coughing and stifled laughter at that.

Bacon defended himself. "I have spent more time in vain studying how to make the Earl a good servant to the Queen and the State than I have done anything else. . . ."

"It was at about this time, sir, that the matter of Mr. Cecil and the Infanta's claim to the English throne came up. Brought up, as I recall, by Essex. And then out from behind the arras tripped little Sir Robert. And we had all the pleasure of that strange scene."

By the time Cecil had made his appearance and then, after summoning the Comptroller from Whitehall to testify in his behalf, had refuted the allegations Essex had raised against him, by the time that Essex and Cecil had managed a public reconciliation it was past six o'clock.

Coke summed up the evidence. In response to his questions the judges affirmed that it was treason under the Law to raise and use force for the purpose of removing anyone from the Privy Council. As had been attempted, by admission of the Earl. And also that it was clearly treason to use force to gain the presence of the Queen.

Then both the Earls spoke to the Court. Essex demanded to be believed. If he had lied, he asked God to punish him for it here and now.

"O Lord! Show Thou some mark upon me in this place as a testimony to all the world of Thy just vengeance! And Thou, O God, who knowest the secrets of all hearts, knowest that I never sought the crown of England, nor ever wished to be of higher degree than a subject."

Lord Buckhurst, acting as Lord High Steward, then ordered the prisoners removed from the bar. And they were led away to wait upon the verdict outside the Hall. When they had been taken out, he ordered the jury of peers to withdraw to consider a verdict. They were led into privacy, going behind the same arras from which Cecil had appeared.

"The rest of us remained there waiting for the ending of it. Not imagining it would require much time. All of us hungry as can be, having missed our dinner. All, from such whispering around me as I could gather, planning to head out for cookshops and taverns the moment verdict had been rendered and sentences delivered.

"But they took more than an hour. Though I believe they might not have spent so much time if food and drink and tobacco and pipes had not been provided for them. We could smell the food and soon could see the tobacco smoke rising above the arras to cloud around the angels of the ceiling.

"When they returned, they were asked, one at a time, what verdict they had reached concerning each of the Earls separately. Twice then, and one at a time, all twenty-five peers rose and answered the Lord High Steward, hand on heart.

"'Guilty, my lord, of high treason upon my honor.'

"When that was done, the two Earls were brought back, solemnly, to the bar and asked if they had any words to say before the sentence was passed.

"Essex made the best impression. Southampton made a humble plea for mercy—some thought it was too humble to do him good. And indeed, sir, the Earl of Essex (who spoke first, as I recall it) also asked for the Queen's mercy for Southampton. He asked none such for himself."

"My lords," he said. "I am not at all dismayed to receive this sentence. For death is far more welcome to me than life. And I shall die as cheerful a death as ever man did. And I think it fitting that the poor quarters of my body, which have done Her Majesty true service in divers parts of this world, should now at the last be sacrificed and disposed of at Her Majesty's pleasure. Whereunto, with all the willingness of my heart, I do submit myself."

Southampton asked for pity and received some. Essex would not stoop to do so and so gained admiration.

You wonder how much he was a player and how much speaking the plain and honest truth. A curious question to ask of a player.

"At the time he spoke, amid the sputtering torchlight and looking into the shadowy faces of his friends and enemies, I could see only the back of him. Which was straight and soldierly at the shoulders, yet somehow indolent, loosely relaxed at the legs. I studied that pose, thinking to use it some day for the posture of a confident man. For it is possible to be courageous and even to show the signs of courage without any confidence at all. For many of us, as I'm sure, sir, you'll agree with me, courage is not needed until confidence has gone.

"His posture struck me as being as unusual as it was admirable. And I found myself asking—whence came that confidence? At the time I attributed it to his encounter with Sir Robert Cecil. To his certainty that the King of the Scots could do something for him. To his unshakable belief that the Queen loved him, favored him too much to allow him to be executed.

"No, I do not believe he seriously thought that his life was in danger. I must confess, sir, that at the moment he was speaking, I shared the Earl's confidence. I did not imagine that he would die. And when I heard the news of it I must have been as doubtful and astonished as Essex himself when the ax fell. . . ."

Whatever his confidence on behalf of Essex, the Player's own was, as he will be first to admit, less than assured by the sentence of the traitors—to be hanged, drawn, and quartered. Of course, it was likely that the Earls would find that sentence altered to a more honorable beheading.

"But the words. The words struck me with a chill to my bone and joints. And pray remember that it was by no means clear at that time how many of the Earl's supporters would find themselves being drawn to Tyburn on a hurdle at the tail of a horse. Captain Lee had already been put to death even before the trial of the Earls began. And it was the middle of March before Henry Cuffe and Sir Gilly Meyrick were executed. With all the full rigor of the Law. And shortly after, only a day or so later, Sir Charles Danvers and Sir Christopher Blount were beheaded on Tower Hill. But then, sir, that was the end of it. The rest were fined and imprisoned. Most were released. Even before summer I felt free of any danger to myself."

The rest is hearsay. How the Earl, in a fit of religion, made a full confession in the Tower. Blamed all who had made depositions against him. How less than a week after the trial the warrant for the Earl's death was signed by the Queen and sealed. How upon Ash Wednesday he was brought onto Tower Green and beheaded.

"I can only imagine, sir, that the Queen chose the time and circumstances of his execution. For if, as he had said at the trial, he was willing, even eager to die, why then let him have his way. And if he had become so sincere in his Protestant religious beliefs, why, then, let him die on the first day of the Lenten Season. Let his life be an Ash Wednesday offering.

"I mean to say, sir, that our Queen has been known for dillying and dallying, her procrastination and second thoughts concerning these executions. The Earl must have been counting on more time to pass. Depending on delay to save him. Must not have believed she would choose Ash Wednesday for his death. So when they told him the night before that the Queen had signed the warrant, he could hardly be faulted for allowing himself the comfort of a little doubt.

"Moreover it was upon that very day, Shrove Tuesday, that ambassadors from Scotland and the King of the Scots arrived in London. Late, but not too late. He would know that. Wouldn't she impress them, and their master, the King, with her mercy?

Wouldn't it be profoundly insulting to them, and to their King, her kinsman, to hear them out on Tuesday and then kill the man on Wednesday? Unseemly haste. The arrival of the warrant and the preparations must have given him cause for hope. She would delay the execution while she duly considered the plea of the King of Scots.

"Now, sir, you may know as well as I—excepting that you are from the country and may not be as abreast of our customs as you might be—Shrove Tuesday has become a great occasion at the Queen's Court. These latter days it's Shrove Tuesday, and not Candlemas, that marks the end of the Christmas Revels at Court. (I believe that sooner or later they will find a way to do away with Lent, too.) It's a day for feasting and dancing and for the performing of plays before the Queen. Often times Queen will celebrate Shrove Tuesday up river at Richmond.

"Essex must have taken it as a good sign that the Queen had chosen to remain here at Whitehall for Shrove Tuesday. Taken it that, warrant or no warrant, he would be spared for the time being. So long as she was still at Whitehall, and celebrating Shrove Tuesday there, why that could be evidence that a reprieve had already been decided upon.

"He could not in his wildest fantasies imagine the Queen would wish to be nearby when he died.

"And surely, sir, he took it for a confirmation of hope when he learned that the Lord Chamberlain's Men were to perform for the Court on the night of Shrove Tuesday. They were well-known to have been associated with Essex and Southampton for some time. And it was that same Company which had given the performance of *Richard II* on the Saturday afternoon before the rising. Clearly, then, they must be held in good repute to be asked to perform the last play of the season.

"Strange, is it not? I do not remember what play was performed. Most likely it would be something new. For the Queen and her Court never sit still for an old play. Yet there are exceptions. I would think it would have to be something lighthearted—a comedy. For with the fasting and abstinence of Lent staring them in the face, it seems to me that the mood would require diversion. I do imagine it must have been a comedy. But what it could have been I am not sure."

You have to admit to yourself that you have enjoyed the company of this odd bird. More than you imagined you would. Young, and you were rigid. Closed with contempt against such parasites and butterflies. World was sweat and cold, swords and fists then. And you had hard thoughts for all the soft ones who were safe. Now, paradoxically, older and poorer and well wounded by the world, you are weary of who you were. Not ashamed, mind you. For you need not be. Have earned through your blood the right not to feel shame. But you are tired. You could doze off in this tedious world if it were not for surprises which waken you to the wish to live. It is pleasure to know that there are continual discoveries left to make while many your age are already shrugging and yawning. This Player here has been just such a discovery for you.

And now the thought of coming back again to London is pleasing. You picture meeting him again. You picture a leisurely dinner at an excellent tavern. And then you will hire a boat to cross the Thames to see the very latest play. Perhaps even to meet and to talk with the poet who wrote it. You feel you could be easy with the man who wrote *Troilus and Cressida*. A man who must, somehow, have learned some of the things of this world that you have.

Well. It is all a pleasant prospect.

Something to cheer you on the long, slow, lonely ride north to your home parish on the muddy, rain-riddled, wind-troubled wintry roads.

But it will not come to pass that way.

For, as it happens, it will be some time, several years, before you have occasion to return to London. By then there will be many changes. Some for better and some for worse. World and this kingdom will be different.

Within less than a year this Player will be dead. Player, his witchy wife, their brood of children, all will be dead from the Plague which will soon ravage the City and suburbs. Plague which is coming to this city even as you finish your breakfast and wipe your mouth and beard with his best linen napkin. Even as you take your leave. He will walk you out of the tangle of White-friars and point you along Fleet Street. You'll walk briskly into the early morning until you come to the great cistern, with its tower of stone and its images of St. Christopher and of angels and sounding bells, marking Shoe Lane. Will turn north going all the way up Shoe Lane to where it runs into Holborn at old St. Andrew's Church. Then turning left and west to your inn.

Going up Shoe Lane you will hear the church bells beginning to ring all over London and Westminster. You will be weary, heavy-eyed from a long, sleepless night. But pleased that you have accomplished your task. And lifted in body and spirit by cold air and by the sudden sound of all those bells.

Plague will take him and many, many more in this city besides.

When you learn that years later, next time in London, you will go to a tavern and order a cup of Sack and sugar. Not your favorite drink, but you'll drink it in honor of him. Who probably loved it all too well.

But none of that will trouble you yet. Or for a time to come.

A Sunday of rest at the inn. And Monday morning early you'll begin the journey home. Wrapped in bulky wool as you ride at a walk on muddy or frozen pathways. Pleased that you will be able to report to your masters that they have nothing to fear from the player of his vague knowledge of them.

A night or two later, after a dismal day of not much more than a dozen miles gained against wind and rain, you will have given up early, well before dark, and settled on the first good inn you can find.

You sit in your chamber, eating supper and watching rain lash and splatter against the windows. There is a fire in the fireplace and your cloak and clothing are steaming dry on a rack set close to it. Fire in the fireplace and food and wine in your belly. Your eyes are heavy with weary comfort. Large clean bed inviting. And, who knows?, it may rain all tomorrow too, forcing you to stay here for another day.

You sip wine and stare at the flames. And now you are on the shores of sleep. Can let go and sleep at any moment Any moment you want to. There, dreaming, lax on the edge of sleep, you can picture how it was for him, for Essex, that Ash Wednesday morning.

Gray February morning. Cold wind blowing in gusts. Damp in the air from the river. See how he comes now lightly guarded from the Develin Tower and out onto the Green. All in black. Black-velvet cloak, black-satin suit. Black as the glossy ravens there. Tall man with preachers on each side of him, praying. Walking on cobblestones and the grass yard of the Green, moving toward the low squat scaffold. Smelling the river in the gusty air. Then the odor of tobacco smoke. Seeing next the small group gathered at the scaffold, some of them smoking pipes.

It must have been as he imagined it would be. Which would be a comfort. So long as it was not beyond imagining, then he was not without hope. He might live.

He was not afraid, had not been afraid of death and did not fear death, either, as he walked to the scaffold and mounted it, not out of logic or false hopes, but purely and simply because, until this moment, he had borne a charmed life. He had been in the midst of death and nothing had touched him. Oh, a very slight wound or two. Like the little wound he earned in his brief duel with Mountjoy years ago. Nothing more than scratches. Men had died or been smashed into crippled shapes and forms all around him. But he bore a charmed life. Nothing had touched him. Fortune had always smiled on him, even in adversity. And so he trusted her. As he trusted the Queen.

He trusted his charm, his fortune, the Queen.

What else could he do?

He had never known anything but good luck.

Well.

You have been in darker places. Your luck has been thin. That you are alive and well enough to be sitting here even as you think of him then and there in the Tower a full year ago, you take as a gift and a blessing. Not since youth have you doubted you would die.

The Earl of Essex has never had any reason to practice death or prepare for it.

So that the first part of it, when he stood, tall and black before them, to speak, was not so difficult as a stranger to these things might conceive. He says the words he has by heart loud and clear. So that they can be heard and reported. Acknowledging both sin and guilt and asking pardon. Though not asking for mercy.

"I confess that I have received an honorable trial and am justly condemned. And I desire all the world to forgive me, even as I do freely and from my heart forgive all the world."

Finishing his words, he began to remove his cloak and ruff. With difficulty. Awkwardly. For he had need of a servant to help him and there was none.

There, you think.

There is the turning point for Essex. The moment as, awkward and alone, he struggled with his own clothing. Clothing made to be removed by another pair of hands. That was his Gethsemane. Ungracefulness of it. Trembling fingers. Knowing then, for the first time in the last minutes of his life, that his lifelong charms had failed him. All his luck and magic had vanished.

Knowing what other, lesser men learn early and always know: knowing suddenly that he would die. That nothing would save him. That all his life had been a stage play and this alone, himself on a cold morning in a windy place, set with chaplain and headsman on the rude scaffold, this only was real. All the rest had been a dream.

Knowing too, without the words for it, indeed knowing more swiftly than words can tell, that other men, lesser men, had always known this truth. Knowing that his magic, his fortune, his charms were rooted in ignorance.

Many a man would have broken at that moment.

Many a man in England might have rejoiced to see Essex broken and trembling before he died. There would have been a certain justice in that.

Yet in this sense his good fortune held. Startled, and indeed in dread and terror of the certainty of death for the first time in his life, he still had the power to summon courage and save his honor even as he lost his life.

Now his fingers were surer, even as he was pretending to be sure. He removed his black doublet to reveal, theatrical to the last, a brilliant, blood-red waistcoat.

Then without any binding or blindfold he lay down, placing

his head on the chopping block and repeated softly, together with the minister and some of the others, words of the fifty-first psalm.

Thou shalt purge me with hyssop, and I shall be clean; thou shalt wash me, and I shall be whiter than snow.

Thou shalt make me hear of joy and gladness, that the bones which thou hast broken may rejoice . . .

"Come, Lord Jesus! Come, Lord Jesus and receive my soul!"

At last even the executioner bungled. It took him three strokes before he managed one right and severed the Earl's head from his body.

Well.

Well, it was harder for him to die, heavy with the wound of sudden knowledge and the loss of a lifetime's illusions, than it would be for you or for me or for many another who has never had any reason to imagine himself to be a god.

COURTIER

1626
(1603)

Tell men of high condition,
That manage the estate,
Their purpose is ambition,
Their practice only hate:
And if they once reply,
Then give them all the lie.

Sir WALTER RALEGH—"The Lie"

—Well now, he says, even while they are still laughing at the merry tale he has told them, something or other concerning the ghosts (himself among them) he summons up out of that other age, the times of Queen Elizabeth, gone before some of these young people were born, more than half forgotten by everyone before they sat down at this table.

—Well, now, let us blame it all, my folly and your laughter, on the wine. Let us say it is the wine talking and not myself.

True, it is a most satisfying Greek wine, sweetened and spiced to perfection and arriving at the end of an altogether excellent dinner, a wine which has eased everyone present away from stiffness of manner, a wine which will not allow long faces. And most of all it has set free the Earl's memory. To wander happily and graze like an old horse put out to pasture. Freed memory, and simultaneously loosened his tongue.

—Mind you, he continues, as a servant, knowing his cue, brings the Earl a fresh glass of wine. Mind you, after my nap, I doubt that I shall remember saying any of these things. And so I can deny everything in all honesty.

—Ah, but it's no matter. No one cares what a clown says. And when you have acquired reputation as an . . . eccentric fellow, then you are forgiven much.

He sips for a moment, then continues. Somewhat more seriously.

—It is very strange how reputation will ignore the larger part of a man's life, choosing some particular event as an emblem for all of it. When you have lived as long as I have, you shall see how time turns great men into fools and vice versa. How men

who were highly honored are now recalled, if at all, with a raucous fanfare of the black trumpet of Ill Fame.

—Well, now. In my lifetime I have done many things. Perhaps
too many. Too much doing without pausing to reflect on the
sense of any of it. I served as a soldier with Leicester and later
with Essex. I was Deputy Warden and Warden of all three
Marches on the Scots Border. Crossed swords and tested wits
with some very great rogues. Went to sea against the Spanish Armada in '88 aboard the good ship *Elizabeth Bonaventure*. And,
by God, if you look close enough, you'll find my face on the Armada tapestry at Whitehall.

—And yet, my friends, none of this mattered a whit. For in the
Queen's time I was known for two things only. First, that I married for love only and endured the Queen's wrath for doing so.
And, second, that I maintained myself at Court by the wagers I
made and won. Between my father and the Queen I had next to
nothing. I had to depend upon good luck and quick wits.

—Now the plain truth is that the single thing I was well known
for in the Queen's lifetime was a wager I made in '89 that I could
go from the Court to Berwick in twelve summer days, going on
foot the whole way. And by God I did it, too! Won myself a
small fortune and lived well enough on it for a long time thereafter. Of course, I wake up late at night now in a cold sweat thinking what might have happened if I had lost that gamble. But at
the time it never crossed my mind that I could fail. And for some
time after it looked certain that that walk up the North Road
would be my one claim to any fame, that it would be chiseled on
stone as my epitaph.

—But then, when the Queen died, it was another kind of journey up that same road which became the emblem of my Fortune.

—When the Queen fell ill in March of 1603 I had been away
from Court for five years. Up there on the Borders. Hanging
reivers when I could catch them. Laying ambushes for them,
going hot trods after them. Doing a bit of raiding myself. All for
the purpose of keeping some order, if not the peace, there. I
mean, there was no peace and no chance for it. But order could
be kept, sometimes by bluff and persuasion and sometimes by
fire and sword. The world was powerfully simple then.

—When word reached me that the Queen's good health was failing, I thought it high time to make a pilgrimage to Court.

—To tell it briefly, I found Her Majesty poorly. Unable to eat or sleep well. And not merely ill disposed, but deeply melancholy. I guessed the end was coming soon, even though, at first, her physicians thought otherwise. So I wrote a letter to the King of Scots to prepare himself. And next I arranged for horses to be stabled along the North Road from London to Alnwick. With servants of my own to care for them. For it was my stratagem that if the Queen should die, and if she should name James as her rightful heir (both of these things uncertain and, believe me, the latter far less sure than anyone now cares to remember), then I would race off along the North Road, first and swiftest, ahead of all the King's men and of any of Council's messengers. To be the first person from whom the King should hear the news.

—I assumed that he would be pleased to hear it. And that was my wager with the future. For, in justice, he could hardly fail to feel warmly toward the man who brought him the good news. All the more so if this man, myself, were someone kin to the Queen. Someone he himself had known for years. Someone who brought him the news he had been waiting for, hoping and praying for, for most of his life.

—Naturally there were others with other things in mind. Beginning with the Council and little Mr. Cecil. But with my dear sister, Lady Scrope, at the Queen's bedside, I knew as soon as the Queen had died in the hours of the early morning of that Lady Day. And knew for certain from my brother, the Lord Chamberlain (thanks to him also I was able to pass through the gates of Richmond Palace which had been closed to coming and going) that the Council and the nobility had agreed to proclaim James. I took a fine blue ring from my sister to the King of Scots as a token of the truth of it. For, of course, I could not wait upon a copy of the proclamation or any other documents from Council.

—So much was unknown. Mr. Cecil and his Council were uncertain, to the last, what, if anything, the other heirs to the throne might do. Were uncertain how the Papists would respond. And I think Mr. Cecil did fear what was unknown and uncertain more than anything else. And he was far from certain what promises James may have made to the Papists in England in return for their promises to support his rights.

—I am sure he feared also that the Queen would reject James in those last hours. Would name another in the presence of witnesses. He must later, later (at the time he sweated pearls) have thanked his stars that the Queen had lost the power of speech. Or, anyway, did not choose to speak again. Yet anytime, until heart stopped and breath ceased, she might have spoken. Indeed she might have rallied and recovered.

—It was given out, afterward, that in the presence of the Archbishop and a few others, she was asked by Cecil to affirm that James of Scotland was her right worthy, chosen successor. And she was able to nod her head in affirmation. You can believe that if you want to. My own sister, who was in the chamber, doubts the truth of it.

—But, as it turned out (though who could have known it then) the people of England preferred to believe it also.

—So many odd uncertainties. . . . None knew what the others were going to do. None fully trusted each other. When Cecil and Council and the Heralds set out from Whitehall to make the proclamation for King James within the City, they found the gates locked and chained and the watch and trained bands in arms. The Lord Mayor, himself, refused them entry until he received assurance that it was their purpose to proclaim King James.

—Ha! he says. Cecil must have pissed himself with relief when he heard that.

—I was off at midmorning the moment James had been proclaimed in Westminster. Uncertain myself if I were, indeed, the first rider. Uncertain how far I might get. For they had forbidden permission and I had to steal away like a fugitive. Uncertain what lay ahead on the road, what might be stirring in the country.

—Made Doncaster the first day, over muddy road. Up before dawn was more than a hint in the sky. And rode like the wind that second day. Was clear into Northumberland in time to sup and sleep in my own house in Widdrington. Next day feeling safe now in my own country (for I was still Warden there), I

paused to proclaim the King of Scots, myself, in Morpeth and
Alnwick. Then set off riding hard into Scotland by way of
Norham with plenty of time to spare.

—Or so I thought. Not far and my horse took a tumble at a
shallow ford and tumbled me, too, arsie-versie and headfirst onto
the rocks. Sky flashed around me once and I even saw the rocks
that I struck, and with time to think to myself, *My God I am
dead!*, before I plunged into blackness. Woke up—rain and the
stream waked me—bloody as a butcher, feeling my head had
been cleft with an ax. Vomiting, sick, bleeding, muddy, and torn.
Not a soul to help me. But at least I had not lost my wits and I
had not lost my horse either. He was serenely grazing nearby.

—Well, now. I managed to make a bandage of my shirt. To
wrap around my head and stem the bleeding somewhat. And
then I put my hurt body back upon the saddle of my horse (I
felt as though every bone, large and small, had been snapped like
a twig in a bundle of twigs). Rode on. Though not so swiftly
now. For fear that in my weakness I might fall again. Sun was
past noon. I must have lain there like a corpse for at least an
hour or so. Surely someone had passed the ford during that time.
And I was in a fury against whoever that might be. Until I
thought what a Scotsman might think when he saw the bloody
body of an English gent. Not naked as your poor Samaritan but
dressed out for Court in silks and velvets, lying half dead in the
mud. Better to leave his fate in the hands of God.

—Why, instead of being angry I had every cause to be grateful. 'Tis a wonder one of them did not slit my throat for my purse
and the rings on my fingers. And there were certain rogues who,
if they had recognized who it was, would have cut my heart out
in payment for old scores.

—I arrived at the gate to Holyrood a little before midnight. I
was taken at once—half carried, in truth, for I might not have
been able to walk on my own if a couple of stout lads hadn't
taken me under the arms—in a crowd of men across the court and
directly into the northeast tower. Up the stairs to the King's bedchamber.

—They let go of me, as we entered, pushing me forward so I
staggered and almost fell. There we were, a crowd of men with
torches for outdoors (oh, there were many candles burning too,

for the King was not happy to sleep in the dark) rushing into his chamber. This had happened before and never with any good news. He sat upright in the bed, clutching sheets and blankets to his chin and his nightcap dangling loose and limp. His eyes were as wide as the eyes of a frightened child. What else could he feel but fear? My God, I must have been a sight to behold, a ragged, half-naked man covered with mud and blood.

—Ah, it was not as either of us had planned it. But there we were and the time had come. So, as if it were high noon in the Presence Chamber and I were as neat and shiny as a new knitting needle, I fell to my knee and found my voice. Hailed him not only as the King of the Scots, but as King of England, Ireland, France, Defender of the Faith *et cetera*.

—And then he leapt straight up out of the bed, barefoot, in his nightshirt, half dancing, half singing for joy. Until one of his men said aloud—"What proof. What proof have we of this?"

—And then to me: "Have you a letter from the Council?"

—"No, sir," I told him. And I thought the King would crumple to the floor and cry. But then I gave him the sapphire ring from my sister. He examined it close by a candle for a moment. Then he burst out into loud laughter.

—"Proof! Proof!" he cried. "We have here proof enough and all that we shall ever need!"

—By the time messengers from Council arrived to proclaim the news, it was old news all over Scotland. And I was up and about to greet them. Already sworn to be a Gentleman of the King's Bedchamber. And surely set in place for the rest of my life.

—But even before His Majesty arrived in Westminster all that was sadly changed. Cecil and the Council were furious, and to please them the King had to rescind my rewards and all but cut me off at the roots. Those fellows sought the ruin of me.

—I had a sad heart at how it had gone and how foolish I had become. But I tried not to show it. Being always merry before the King and the others. For I was taught that the King feared discontented minds.

—Well, now. I began to tell you of the eccentricities of Fortune. How I was known then and am known yet, if known at all, as the wildly foolish man who rode with the news to King James in less than three days. And then received nothing but trouble for his reward.

—I had only the living of Norham Castle left to me and Sir George Home, he that was Lord Treasurer of Scotland, wanted to buy it off me. Cecil was made umpire between us. And I was greatly afraid I would lose even more. But Cecil arranged it as beneficial for me as could be. To my surprise.

—When I was at Norham packing my stuff to leave, something —it must have been God Himself—put it in my mind to go north to Dunfermline and see if I could find some place in the service of the King's second son, the little Prince Charles. Now, the Prince was a weak child and looked likely to die. No one wished to be fastened in service to his fate. Besides there were places enough to be had, for those with ambition, at the King's Court or the Queen's. Or, best of all in the new Court of the elder son, Prince Henry, who was sturdy as a young Achilles.

—Ah, the men who wagered their futures upon the future of Prince Henry!

—What happened next will prove my point—that God's providence is mysterious beyond all understanding. My wife, that woman who had brought nothing but her love to our marriage, was given the keeping of Prince Charles. Raised him up in good health while poor Prince Henry died in youth. Now Charles is King and I am Earl of Monmouth. I suppose it could be called a long-deferred payment for my ride to Holyroodhouse all those years ago.

—And now (draining his glass and rising from his chair) I must have my nap or else fall asleep here at table. And you have better things to do with a summer afternoon than to sit and listen to an old man's snores.

MESSENGER
1566

What would men have? Do they think those they employ and deal with are saints? Do they not think they will have their own ends, and be truer to themselves than them?

FRANCIS BACON—"Of Suspicion"

Then will ride down through Shoreditch with houses lining both sides of the road & behind them gardens & orchards & green of fields & Spittle Fields off to left with close by brick walls of Artillery Gardens where gunners from the Tower try their weapons.

And Finsbury Fields at right hand with windmills & archery butts & kennels and

Next Moor Field with little streams & crisscrossing paths & space for spreading of laundry for drying in fair weather and

Through Bishop's gate just beyond St. Botolph's Church & keeping to Bishopsgate Street until Three Needle forks to right & runs down into Cheapside.

(And there, wholly new to him since last in London, adding to the clamor of City, will be the noises of building. For in that space between Three Needle and Cornhill all the buildings have been torn down and are being replaced by Flemish craftsmen with Sir Thomas Gresham's Exchange—piazza and colonnade and three stories and hundreds of shops of all kinds. Standing in the shadow of a tall column with a bell. Everything presided over by Gresham's emblem of the golden grasshopper.)

And easing his way through crowds of Cheapside with tall houses of many windows & fine woodcarving & painted plaster work & with more than half a hundred goldsmiths' shops & especially among these the line of ten houses & fourteen shops built between Bread Street & the Cross and alike as brothers & named Goldsmith's Row.

Passing Conduit with its quiver of lead pipes for fresh Tyburn water & crowd of water carriers & next the pump called the Standard & near to Wood Street the Eleanor Cross and . . .

Then to lead his horse on foot through Little Gate of Paul's Churchyard where booksellers' signs are bright as banners & out of the wide yard at Great Gates & mounting again to go downhill & out of City again at Ludgate and . . .

West on Fleet Street to Temple Bar and . . .

Then only short way along Strand (not far as St. Martin's Lane or Charing Cross) to gate of Cecil House close by & across from Ivy Lane & Russell House and . . .

To hand over horse to first pair of hands & brush past Usher or Butler and any house servants to go directly & only to Sir William Cecil and . . .

Cecil will hear his news & nod & ask one or two questions & then rise to give orders for a boat for himself to be rowed to the Queen at Greenwich & for the messenger some refreshment & comfort at once.

Which begins with a bath in a wooden tub in the high-ceilinged kitchen. Steamy water scented with powdered herbs and oils of flowers. And himself, modestly screened from view, feeling the pain and stiffness beginning to leave his limbs, hearing the voices of the kitchen servants at their chores, breathing in the odors of cooking in the smoky air, tasting a cool wine from a silver cup, easing slowly into a daydream.

Ahead of any other messengers, a full day and more ahead of the official Scots ambassador sent for the purpose, it is he who has brought the first word that the Queen of Scots, after a long and difficult labor, has given birth to a son and heir. And a cousin (perhaps an heir also) to our Queen.

And thus has brought word that all of the world that matters to them has been altered. Changed because of this and will not be the same again. Come what may. . . .

He cannot imagine if this is good news or no. Only that the world has changed. As if a star had fallen away in flames. Better: as if a new and unknown star had risen to shine in the Firmament.

Later (soon enough) Cecil and his chief clerk will take time to question him closely concerning the things he has witnessed, overheard, inferred while spying in Scotland. He will, as ever, discover that he is able to tell them more than he thinks he knows. Then there will be payment for his services and the pleasures of this City for the taking again.

And then?

And then he thinks he would, if he could, prefer to change his situation. Change the nature of his services to his master. He, like Cecil's other spies and secret agents, is generously rewarded. No one pays more for information and service. No complaint there. He can be sure he will receive a sum of money amounting to more by far than the yearly income of several of Cecil's most senior servants taken together. Indeed he will be (not for the first time) almost a rich man. If wealth can be measured in ready money. Paid, then, in silver and gold and not in those things— land, office, opportunity—which last and can grow, however slowly, in value. Sometimes he thinks he would gladly settle for some minor indoor office or clerkship in Cecil's household, to be rewarded perhaps with an office in the government, a wardship, the rents from the lease of a piece of land. This last being best; for land is true wealth. Would gladly accept anything with a future.

But . . .

He will not seek to change his life even should a propitious occasion to do so arise. He knows he will once again have sold himself for the brief pleasures of silver and gold in hand. For a time will dress well, eat and drink well, will enjoy the City, and (again) take solace in the illusion of love, meaning that love which can be bought and paid for just as his loyalty has been.

Just as his loyalty will be. For he will be generously paid and will spend it all and soon enough will be empty of purse and ready to begin again whatever tasks his master may assign to him. Going wherever his master sends him.

Here and now, though, he will allow himself no unhappy thoughts. Will think no more of the past than that it is leaving him like the dirt and pains of his journey clouding the warm, scented water where he soaks. Thinking no farther into the future than that he will be here in the City (only a day or two from now, depending . . .) for the celebration of Midsummer Eve. Will have seen the preparations for it—cressets to hold lights at doorways and gateways; bonfires prepared and tubs of water set out against the dangers of fire; fresh birch boughs gathered for decoration; and come the Eve there will be the five, fat, yellow fingers of St. John's Wort and the blue feathery flowers of larkspur set over the doorways. A night of much dancing and singing, eating and drinking. A fine time to be free with money in his purse.

He's half asleep in the tub by the time they bring him warm towels and clean clothes. . . .

Cecil, meanwhile, sits beneath the little shelter on a tilt boat and considers the effect of this news. Certainly an interruption of this evening's festivities (for the Court does celebrate Midsummer for several days both before and after) will not please the Queen. But beyond that annoyance? Some might suppose the Queen will take the news badly. Someone also might imagine that Cecil will find bringing this news to be a bitter chore. For if angry, then surely she must turn her anger upon him.

And yet . . . there is much that is disguised. Hidden beyond the power of easy imagining. For even as the Queen's enemies may be cheered by new hope, many of her closest supporters will be disturbed. Will be moved to think, if not yet to act, toward a gradual disengagement from her. The question of the Succession is pressing and serious. She has not only avoided making any clarification of the complex matter of the rights of a possible Successor, but has also refused to allow it to be discussed. In this short reign she has already been so sick as to be no more than a breath or two away from death. Closeness to death. Closeness to the bloodshed and chaos which are certain to ravage the kingdom if she should die at any time without a settled Succession, has not, it seems, served as either a warning or a chastisement to her. She seems more adamant than before. Simply refuses to permit her subjects to consider any future without her.

So it might seem that the news from Scotland can be only trouble to the Queen, leaving her more isolated, lonely, and weaker than before. Even more than those times when as Princess, as the Lady Elizabeth, she had only the shadowy power of popularity, the fickle acclaim of the people, to guard her.

Out on the river, perhaps already having eased carefully under the Bridge and passing now, on the north bank, the familiar landing and walls of the Tower of London, Cecil cannot help picturing Elizabeth's first trip to the Tower. No, not in triumph, to bells and trumpets and cannon salutes, at the time of her accession. But that time on the morning of Palm Sunday in '54. By barge from Whitehall to the Tower under guard and accompanied by old Winchester and young Sussex. A rainy morning and a cold one. Much suspected of her for complicity in Wyatt's Rebellion. Which had been put down so recently that the rotten bodies of rebels were still hanging from gibbets all over London. She without cap or cloak, dressed as if to go dancing, standing on the barge to be seen by half the citizens of London. Her face white beneath red hair. Her demeanor proud, haughty even. Fat raindrops falling on the river. And the people with their branches of pussywillow, pausing on the way to the churches, to see her. Perhaps (they must have thought so) for the last time.

So she must be thinking it.

Something is there, in the story of it. Something beyond the image of the slender young woman standing in full view in the rain. And in quiet except for the pull and drip of oars and the sound of heavy raindrops At that moment all her future was in doubt. And she knew that beyond doubting. In her actions, then, and in her demeanor lie some clues (Cecil thinks) to her inmost character. Some are already clear: her pride, courage, style, her capacity, then and now, to court popularity successfully. But much remains obscure. . . .

She has always been, as Princess and Queen alike, alone and weak and gravely threatened, with only wit and luck for true friends. Hope is foreign to her. Doubt is her proper element. She is not, therefore, likely to be frightened at having to experience more of what she takes to be the very essence of her condition.

No man alive knows with certainty what her motives may be, or her full purposes, in any given business. Delay and procrastination seem to be a kind of pattern. Yet she will act upon impulse often enough to cast doubt on that. Truth is that no one can ever be sure of her.

Many men, wise in the world, attribute their constant uncertainty to her inconstant womanhood.

True, all the world knows, an honest woman is worth a crown of gold.

But likewise the whole world believes: *A woman is as wavering as any weathercock & A woman's mind and the winter wind change as often & Women can weep and lie at will & Many a woman sad in countenance has a merry heart & Women and wine make men out of their wits & Women in state affairs are like monkeys in glass shops etc. etc. etc.*

And he is mad who quarrels with women and wild beasts!

But Cecil supposes that because she is a woman and alone she has learned to be a spy in her own kingdom. Moving often, as a spy must, with the truth masked and disguised. To the good spy, all news must be ambiguous. Only to be named as good or ill according to results. When and if results can ever be discerned. Thus a spy's future is whatever may come to pass. And the future may not be felt until it is happening. Nor can be judged until it has ended, becoming the past.

Therefore the future is never to be feared.

From all this it may be imagined that the Queen may even welcome the birth of her new cousin in Scotland.

Should the infant live, he can be a great security for her. Mary of Scots may now become more friendly and more patient, if only so as not to prejudice her son's claims, stronger even than her own, to the Succession in England. Likewise, now the Queen Elizabeth's Catholic subjects may be more content to be patient, having been given the comfort of hope for the future. They may now protect her from pressure by friends and allies to marry in haste (and repent at leisure?) for the sake of bearing heirs of her own. And now, by the same token, her Suffolk kin will have to behave better. Will have to give up, at least for the time being, their plots against her. For their best hope will lie now in maintaining loyal kinship with the Queen. That is, Catholic Stuart cousins may now be set against Protestant Suffolk cousins. And each may now be forced, for the sake of their own desires and hopes, to protect her from the other.

And now her health and welfare may be more precious to her contumacious Protestant gentry. Even if reluctantly and grudgingly so. However disappointed they may be that she has turned away from the hopes of the exiles from Zurich and Geneva, refusing to become the image of their prophetess Deborah, they will band together in her behalf now. Forming as much a bodyguard as her Yeomen in scarlet and gold. For her sake, they will be forced to suppress their own extremists. They will, of course, continue to seek to persuade her to purify her English Church. But that will take time.

Seen in this light, the Queen may be entitled to rejoice. In a sense, through no doing of her own, she has been freed from a kind of captivity. And this royal infant (born after long and unenviable pain to her much-envied cousin) now becomes a hostage in her place.

As to how the Queen will choose to *greet* this news (which will hardly be surprising since she has had some months to weigh the possibility). . , . . Oh that is another story. Quite beyond the power of guessing.

Cecil is roused from his silent meditation by the sounds of his young clerks talking to each other. They are pleased, it seems, to be going to the Palace at this time of celebration.

"There will be no sleeping at the Palace on Midsummer Eve," one is saying.

Except for the old and sick and the very young. It is a vigil time much like All Hallow's Eve. For it is English country wisdom—and country wisdom is all the courtly fashion these days— that upon Midsummer Eve a soul can easily escape from its sleeping body. And, from those who are supposed to die in the year to come, the soul will go forth to inspect its final resting place. Which can be prevented by the simple expedient of staying awake all night in the company of others. If you will go out and wait close by the churchyard, you can sometimes see lost souls flying by.

"They are usually white and look something like a patch of mist or a puff of smoke."

Well, Cecil thinks, you won't find the souls of many of these courtiers flying near any churchyards. And as to the color of them, it's their one and only virtue. Think of the flutter of a butterfly, the flash of a kingfisher. Fading into the everlasting dark. . . .

Th n one of the clerks, thinking out loud, allows as how they may arrive at Greenwich just in time for something to eat.

Which thought leads his clerks into a dispute about what dishes will be served to them this evening.

I say a swan's-neck pudding.

Oysters stewed in white wine and spices.

Then a roast of pigeons with a lemon and claret sauce.

Fresh lampreys cooked in a pie?

Better pickled eel and onions.

No, I doubt that. For there will be much kissing after midnight.

Then capon in orange sauce and rabbit boiled in claret.

Venison roasted and beef carbonado.

A summer sallit of greens and flowers.

And fine cheat bread.

And to end it all fresh fruits and nuts and almond cakes and cold Italian cream.

And what shall we drink to wash it all down?

Well, sir, there'll be Sack and sugar and hot Madeira to begin.

Then Gascon red and Rhenish white. And cordials after.

But none of your strong double beers.

None of your Mad Dog.

Or Whoreson.

Or Dragon's Milk.

Of which the Queen is so disapproving.

"Hush now, you gluttons," Sir William Cecil tells them. "And you may hear something."

They listen and look. The Palace landing is in sight ahead. They can feel that the tide has turned around on them, is running out now. The oarsmen are pulling smooth and swift. And, for a moment, all they hear is the creak of the locks and the breathing of the rowers and the drops of water splashing softly from their blades.

Somewhere, as near as the reedy bank, a gull cries like a hurt child.

And then faintly, but growing slowly louder and clearer as they begin to skim forward, the sound of music being played in the Palace. Music for dancing. Music coming toward them across the water. . . .

But none of this has happened yet.

For, in truth, it is much too early, only an hour or so past noon judging by the slant of sunlight between patches of blown clouds.

A few gulls glide or hover up there, high and lazy. Something, a spicy scent, lightly perfumes the air. And there is the horseman sitting astride a shaggy little Scots mare. A rider who might be anyone going nowhere urgent. Who could be almost anything except a messenger, since he is obviously in no kind of hurry. He's moving south toward the Borders, following the threads of trails along the eastern edges of the Lammermuir Hills. Taking his time about it. Seeming half asleep on his horse.

And it may be that he truly is dozing in a kind of long daydream. Seeking not to waste himself in regret for a lost past. Hoping never to allow himself to fear the future.

"To imagine too much beforehand," he would tell you, "can only double the pain of disappointments when they come along. (As they will come.) And, so far as I can judge, imagination can add nothing at all to life's pleasures. Therefore, let be what will be."

After which you'd be sorely tempted to challenge him. For what has he been doing in all this time (though it's brisk as the passing shadow of a cloud) but rehearsing the past and imagining the future? No use arguing. Confront him with that contradiction, with the paradox at the center of his being, and he'll shrug that away, too.

"Ah, well, now," he'll say. "Did I not already say that we are all of us like leashed dogs? Thanks be to God that most of us lack the gift of prophecy. It would be too much to bear. No, we only sniff and follow our noses as we go along. And that's the long and the short of it."

CHRISTMASTIDE

1602–1603

Leaves fal, grasse dies, beasts of the wood hang head,
Birds cease to sing, and everie creature wailes,
To see the season alter with this change:
For how can Somer stay, when Sunne departs?

From "The Queen's Entertainment at the Earl of Hertford's,
1591: The Fourth Daies Entertainment"

O Lord, thou hast set me on high. My flesh is frail and weak. If I
therefore at any time forget thee, touch my heart, O Lord, that I
may again remember thee. And if I swell against thee, pluck me
down in my own conceipt.

From Queen ELIZABETH's "Second English Prayer"

After these many years of our Queen's reign, there are habits which, though they may have begun as nothing more than whim are now so enhanced by repetition as to have become as fixed as any of the feasts and holidays we hold in memory. And so it is that about the middle of November, no later than that, while Westminster and much of London are still crowded because of the business of Michaelmas term, the Queen will return to take up residence there. Coming home to her father's palace of Whitehall. Coming most often from her grandfather's towered brick palace at Richmond.

Queen, Court, and all her household to come by the river or by land. If by water, then, Lord save us!, what an assembly of barges and tilt boats and wherries bobbing on the tide! And if by land—and even so they must cross over the river from the Surrey side at Richmond Ferry even to begin the journey—then they must gather up half of the carts and wagons of London and all the villages around. No coaches permitted in this processional. Unless Her Majesty shall choose to sit in hers rather than riding a palfrey with Edward Somerset, Earl of Worcester and new Master of Horse, walking beside her. Must also requisition hundreds of horses to carry not only this army of people, but also, very much like an army burdened with loot, bringing beds and mattresses, blankets and bedclothes, tables and chairs, tapestries and hangings, paintings and clocks and books, clothing and candles, and all the necessities of life at Court. Carrying these things safely intact for those few miles. This procession moving at its stately measured pace of perhaps three miles in an hour.

Either way they come, land or water, daylight or torchlight, as the Queen chooses—and everyone in Court silently praying that she will not change her royal mind too often—there will be much ceremony. Drums and trumpets. Bells ringing from towers and steeples all along the way. Salutes by cannon and musket. Fireworks fountaining overhead. Waits and minstrels standing to play at roadside or perched, uneasy and unsteady, upon rafts and barges.

Now, if they come by daylight, then they will pause while the Queen has dinner at the house of Mr. John Lacy in Putney. Then mounting up and going on. To halt again at the outskirts for the formal greeting by the Lord Mayor and the Aldermen, all dressed in scarlet robes and wearing chains of gold. Huge crowds will come into the fields—or in boats on the river and along the banks—to witness these things.

Queen and Court coming home to the sprawl and pleasures of Whitehall. Arriving in time for the celebration of the Queen's Accession on November 17. When there will be the usual chivalric tournaments, shows and spectacles and allegories in the Tiltyard.

Next comes Advent Season as the Christian year begins. Four Sundays of purple and penance. A little Lent looking forward to the coming of Christ and the Last Judgment. And looking forward, also, to the feasts and celebrations of Christmas. Which once ended at Epiphany on Twelfth Day. But have now grown to longer life: for most folk in England not coming to an end until Plow Monday. At Court the Christmas season has grown to be twin to Lent. Continuing for a full forty days until Candlemas.

Time again, then. . . .

Time again in spite of strange weathers. Spring, summer, and fall too wet or too dry. Winters too cold. Ice and a red sun brooding in gray sky. Lean poor harvests leading to scarcity of grain and meat. Prices never so high. Hard times for the poor and, truly, for all the common folk. Aggravated by rumors of private hoarding. And never mind the truth; for rumor has the same power to create fear that truth does. Already we hear of good country people, rivals now of fatter pigs, going to gather acorns to make their bread. And there are some people who foresee the time when not a few in this kingdom will have to go down on their knees. And not chiefly to pray but to graze like and among the immeasurably more valuable sheep. People will feed themselves on leaves and nettles and grass and bark and roots. And soon they will take on themselves the latest fashion of bloated belly and green-stained lips and teeth and tongue. Like the Irish. Poor, benighted savage Irish dying in their sad bogs.

Time for celebration again, also, in spite of wars. War on the high seas and the war of sieges, endless skirmish and ambush in the Lowlands. Of which no wise man can see any ending. Not in victory or defeat. Not until there can be peace with Spain. And war in Ireland, as always; though some see hope of victory there.

Wars taking place elsewhere. Far from Court. From wherever the Court may light in its restless, immemorial progress to no place in particular. If far from Court, then far from London, too, with all its swollen rage of busyness and idleness, ebbing and flowing tides of buying and selling, unceasing search for new pleasures.

Wars often forgotten in city and country alike. Except for the late, slow-traveling news of deaths and wounds. A village gained, a castle lost. Ignored or forgotten except for sudden musters. Which can send large numbers of grown and able-bodied men into hiding or disguises (O England now has many sturdy, hairy, poxy milkmaids whenever there's a muster!) until enough poor fish are caught. These being chiefly the slow and the stupid and the purely unlucky. Who will be marched away to the tunes of jeering from safe windows and from behind walls and hedges.

Wars ignored at the Court and in the City until sometimes report arrives to tell of some worthy enemy captured and held for ransom. Or perhaps a prize taken at sea, crew and cargo. Now that is news that can quicken and kindle imagination!

Wars, then, far from the palaces and mansion houses where a healthy man can prove his courage and spend his sweat at the bowling alley or the tennis court. Or at dancing, late into night, in a pair of jeweled, satin dancing slippers. Places where the greatest risks are only wagers. Not wagers of life and limb or even honor, but of money and land. Betting on anything, everything that may or may not happen. Betting on fighting cocks in the cockpit. Or the baiting of bears and bulls by the dogs. . . .

Wars whose straggling marches and forlorn retreats are forever at enormous distance from the long, slow, lazy, solemn summer Progress of the Queen. And likewise from the long, slow, lazy time of autumn when the Queen and her gentlemen and ladies do ride out not to do battle, but for sake of hawking and hunting and horseback riding amid the sweet-wine glories of the season's red and gold. . . .

Time come around again for the festive celebration of Christmastide in spite of crowds of lean, hard faces, blank-eyed, rigid with apathy (when they are not frantic with rage). Hurt faces of vagabonds and other masterless persons. Who can be seen in forests and wastelands, on shoulders of high roads, and sometimes even moving among decent folk in remote villages. Among these you can find enough survivors of war to encourage rogues to counterfeit themselves as discharged soldiers of the Queen. Forgotten by the Queen and their fellow countrymen, crippled by wounds and by the inexorable grip of poverty.

We shall enjoy the revels of this Christmastime and shall never mind, if we can, the decay of hospitality in so many country manor houses, seats of stingy housekeeping in this hardhearted age of rusty iron.

Pray against danger of the sweating sickness and infection of Plague in the new year to come. Plague has already traveled here from the Lowlands and other places abroad. To work its black spells. To waste and kill man, woman and child. Plague has come close to the City, prowling among the back alleys and muddy lanes of Southwark this summer past.

Some say that worse than plague and sweating sickness are coming. Some are reading the signs and saying the end of the world is near at hand.

End of the world or no—and will anyone care to hazard a wager on that?—so many things are going so badly in this time of the Queen's old age. Consider the subjects, if not the long-winded and rolling rhetoric of lawyers' words, of the Proclamations lately published:

Enforcing All Former Statutes Against The Forestalling Of Grain . . . Ordering Hospitality To Be Kept In The Country . . . Enforcing All Statutes And Orders Against Poaching And Hunting . . . Enforcing Martial Law Against Army Deserters, Mari-

ners, Vagrants And London Vagabonds . . . Enforcing All Statutes Against Rogues And Vagabonds . . . Enforcing Martial Law Against All Unlawful Assemblies . . . Enforcing Statutes Against Handguns . . . Banishing All Jesuits And Secular Priests . . . Ordering Punishment Of All Persons With Forged Credentials . . . Offering Rewards For Information On Libels Against The Queen. . . .

More dangers than libel against Her Majesty are being feared. The Queen has ordered her guard to be doubled. And, for the first time that anyone can recall, the Queen goes armed. She keeps a sword within reach. Sometimes, struck by flashing rage or a gust of sudden, unappeasable fear, she will thrust her sword through an arras. In case there were spy or assassin hiding there.

True, these are sorry and dangerous days.

Yet it is Christmastime again. Time for the great houses to open their gates to welcome neighbors and strangers. Time again to bring out all the best lamps and candlesticks. Time now to put away torches and plain tallow candles and sputtering rushes that have been dipped in fat. Time to use only best candles of berry and beeswax, scented with herbs and perfumes. Lit to be left burning night and day so that all the chambers of a house will seem to be choirs of candle flames.

Time to bring in the Yule Log. Rolling it (*all together many hands at once*) into the hearth of the Hall. Time to kindle it, this Christmas's fire, with a brand preserved from last year's log. And time for Christmas cakes and ale.

Time has come round, city or country, village and town, to bring out very best clothing. To don the most gaudy, light-colored, lighthearted costumes. Time to put on jewels, both true and paste, all that you own, any you can beg and borrow. Time for hobby horses. For dancing while wearing strings and ropes of little bells twisted around each leg. Time for mumming and masking and disguising. Time for tuning of instruments to make music. And time for singing (*all together many voices*) the ancient and ageless carols.

And late, late on the vigil of Christmas Eve, leaving the parish church, to go and stand still in the cold, star-dazzled night to hear the last echoes of the midnight bells fade into silence. Then all of nature holds its breath. Comes again that hushed time for one and all to picture the scene. Crude manger sharply cold in winter weather. Yet sweet, too, from the light dry scent of hay and a few strewn, simple herbs. And rich with the warm odors of living beasts and of their fresh droppings. And, as legends have it, you are to imagine that this one time in all our history those animals will be kneeling also. Just as living souls do kneel in prayer and adoration.

And it is said that on the eve of our Savior's birth we could hear and understand the speech of the birds and the beasts. If only our hearts were pure enough. . . .

Who would not choose to believe it? That all created beings honor the birth of Our Lord and Savior, our only Mediator and Advocate, Who came down from heaven to take on flesh and to live and die for us and for our sins. Then to rise in triumph and glory to sit at the right hand of the throne of God the Father Almighty.

Time for cock to crow. To sound dawn's cockadoodle all the night long. Time for poor ghosts to leave off shadowy wandering. To return to their narrow graves in peace.

Time, outside of time and history, for shepherds—and weren't they a crew of lusty guts, as rough and ready as any you'll find in a country parish?—stunned into adoration by the arrival of a blazing host of angels and archangels, now to come so quietly, as if walking on tiptoes, into the sweetness and light of the holy manger. Breathing ghosts of frosty breath, hats off, crooks in hand, heads bowed. To come around the crib and there to kneel down in straw next to the Virgin Mother, near to the Holy Child.

Ah, who would not wish to be there among them and kneeling too?

It may be that some of the high and mighty of this world, busy with Caesar's business, would not choose to be so simplified. To be common shepherds. Not even in return for a vision of the birthday of the Son of God.

Well, this wicked world is hard to shed and lose.

Perhaps, too, some of those who make their livings at Court, at the Court of our good Queen, would not wish to change places with shepherds. Unless, perhaps, in the acting out of some old play or in a masque. Why seek to follow example of these poor men who, as Gospel tells, were merely keeping watch over flocks in frozen fields, beneath a spangle of glittering stars which none of them could name? Instead, you think those who try to live in the light of Court must fancy themselves to be more in similitude to the heavenly host who, sudden and brilliant, appeared in and out of the windy night, singing and praising and rejoicing.

Each day gentlemen of the Court and their ladies will come to Whitehall (those not already lodging in chambers there), bulky as bears in layers of cloaks and furs and boots. Peeling off these things, discarding them into the hands of servants. Emerging like butterflies from wet sleep into sparkling light and air of a daylong dream of the sun. Ushers will lead them into the Hall or Presence Chamber, all now looking to be clad in the material rainbows are made of. Seeming to be flowers made of silk and velvet and satin, of jewels and lace. A field of wild flowers swaying in the breeze, keeping time, half dancing while half a hundred of the Queen's musicians play welcome and while tables and cupboards are burdened with a wealth of fine food and drink. Surely they must imagine themselves to be players chosen to act the role of the Gentiles—those three tall, enigmatic Kings, Melchior, Caspar, and Balthazar, who did follow the star across the world to bring gifts, to worship the Holy Child upon the Twelfth Day.

In whose honor the Queen herself will come into the Chapel Royal upon Epiphany to leave upon the altar her gift of gold and frankincense and myrrh.

Oh, no, no, no! These hardhearted, featherbrained people are much more like the Court of King Herod, stiff-necked Reformers tell each other. Taking the wisdom of John Calvin to be the whole truth, these do profess to scorn the custom of a season of feast days, half Papist and half pagan. Which festivals, with all their wasteful extravagance, loud clamor and proud folly, idleness and licentiousness, have more to do with the works of the Devil than with matters of faith and salvation. And (speaking softly, softly and only to each other) it could therefore be justly said that these things are blasphemous forms of dishonoring the blessed memory of the birth of the Lord Jesus!

Those at the Court believe otherwise. The more the Puritans rail and complain, the more they shower blizzards of seditious pamphlets and broadsides, then the more elaborate and ostentatious the Court celebrations become.

Serving, therefore, to entice common people to follow wicked fashion wherever it may lead them. Thus if he feels he can trust you, though speaking in whispers and behind cupped palms, this Puritan may argue that the old woman, our Queen, is plainly squandering fine candles and heaps of sound, dry hardwood. . . . *Mind you, sir or madame, that good firewood has come to be far too dear for poor and honest folk to use it any more for their cooking and warmth.* . . . Squandering these things. And not as any kind of offering, not out of any pious sense of devotion to be made manifest in works of joy. No, it derives, you see, from her own fear and trembling aroused by the inescapable, irremediable ravages of cruel time. True, to be sure, her heart has always been somewhat set in the ways of the old religion. That she has been attracted to certain observances which are matters of error and superstition. Consider that these feasts and triumphs, these jewels and fantasies of clothing . . . *with one gown worn by a lady worth more than the fruits of ten years' hard labor by an honest workman. Doublet and hose of some fawning fop of a courtier being of more value than a fair-sized farm with all of its houses and tools and stock* . . . being contrived in vainglorious hope of concealing the ruin that time has already wrought upon her and this land.

This land of England now in the new century becoming as old and as tired and frail as she is. These shows being contrived in the (foolish) hope of denying that the Queen's natural lifetime. . . . *Her time, therefore also their brief sweet time for pomp and vainglory; I mean her silly and vicious courtiers, the apes of her Privy Council, her goatish Bishops and arrogant, ignorant priests, and her wily and subtle Archbishop Whitgift, cruel as a serpent* . . . has almost ended. Praise the Lord. Soon over and done with. And no amount of music, marching, lighthearted singing and dancing. . . . *It is published that the old woman has taken to dancing late at night to fife and tabor. As if to prove her eternal youth.* . . . No, no praying and fasting, weeping and wailing and gnashing of teeth, can retard by so much as half an hour the triumph of time. . . . *No and not any more so than, upon learning from the Prophet Daniel the mean-*

ing of the words scrawled across his palace wall, could that old and wicked King Nebuchadnezzar manage to save his skin. So be it ever and always. . . .

Not words now, but the thoughts of a disenchanted Reformer. Who would not dare, in peril of his life, to utter them aloud, not even to his own face in a looking glass.

To all of which a thoughtful gentleman of the Court might answer that surely it is true, much of the brightness and gaiety of this Christmas revels is kindled, like beacon fires burning, against the power and dominion of time. But not alone against the fading light of the Queen's lifetime. If this were all, then the expense of flesh and spirit, money and time, would be unworthy. But these lights and fires are yearly lit against the darkness of the world. Contrived in faith and hope and (one may faithfully hope) in loving charity, our Christmas revels are set like candles against the coldest, shortest days of the year. Days of early nightfall. Days when the old absent sun, if he can be flushed from thickets of clouds to be glimpsed at all, will offer up less heat and shining than a sad, daylight moon. Days of iron frost. Of snaggly grinning icicles on roof edges and bare branches. Days whipped into raw tatters by the wind and rain. Sometimes thick with snowflakes in the air. Followed by days and skies of icy blue. Days with small birds brooding black on fallen snow. Or else, abrupt and whimsical in scattering (like the smoke of exploding gunpowder) see a flock of rooks rising, cawing in the wind. Or perhaps starlings, the flock clenching and unclenching like a huge gloved fist high over the tossing, wind-tormented heads of imploring, leaf-shorn trees. . . .

True, sir and madame, there is a waste of firewood. Not much of stinking sea coal will be burned. In these days you can hear the hard-hollow sound of axes, the rasping hum and whining singsong of long saw and short saw. To be carried by carts and then by the wood bearers to feed greedy crowds of fireplaces and stoves and braziers. From flames of which rise up the insubstantial dancing of woodsmoke. And true enough that we must make light from our largest, fattest candles, scented with the distilled essences of flowers, to flame with the captured spirits of springtime and summer. And there are perfumes in oil for the lamps.

Or made into cakes like soap. Musk and the leaves of flowers are burned. And in the Hall and all public chambers—*this for the sake of remembrance of green times gone and also in unquenchable faith and hope of their everlasting return*—wreaths and branches of evergreen are hung everywhere. Slender, brittle branches of potted rosemary, whose narrow, shiny leaves will serve to comfort the brain and preserve your good memory. (*And if you will place some leaves of rosemary beneath your pillow or under the bed, they will drive away nightmares before they can even begin.*) Blue-green juniper, with its stiff, bristling little leaves, which did once shelter and conceal the Holy Family from Herod's murderous soldiery. Strong-scented myrtle in honor of true and unfeigned love. Glossy, fragrant leaves of bay. (*Cast them in fire and they crackle wonderfully.*) Ivy with clusters of black berries and thin, smooth, shiny, sharp-pointed, sharp-edged, sharp-cornered leaves, each looking snipped and cut out of tin and then painted with rich green. Mistletoe, its twin leaves like a pair of slender, delicate wings, its berries like tiny pearls And, always abundant, the smooth, prickled green of holly. Which is brightened by round, blood-colored remembrance of the most precious blood of Our Lord and Savior. (*Whose true Cross, as all the world knows, was cut and made from a holly tree.*)

All these evergreens will remain in place until Candlemas. When down they will come for good luck, to be fed to fires. Then replaced, through Lent until Easter Day, by the deep green leaves of the box tree.

Fire and light and evergreens. . . .

Likewise at Whitehall, in the mansions of London and Westminster, at the Inns of Court, the best tapestries and painted cloths will be hung. Woodwork and wainscoting and furniture are scoured and polished with lemon balm. Where there are no turkey carpets, floors of chambers are cleaned and strewn with fresh rushes. And made more pleasant to walk upon by scattered herbs and flowers. Some carefully dried and powdered in their seasons; some made into distillations in the still rooms; some fresh from the hothouse. Clean spearmint for the sake of fragrance and wisdom. Pennyroyal whose scent is strong medicine against all attacks of giddiness. Marjoram for happiness and also to do its good work against cold in the nose, ague in the joints, and wambling in the stomach. Lemony leaves of flag; aromatic roots of angelica, the Holy Ghost's plant; hyssop and wormwood for the thick smell of licorice. Violets and johnny jump-up, wonders for sound and deep sleeping, for beds and bedchambers. Rose petals and lavenders, both purple and rare white, for the cushions and linens, for leather and gloves. (For virtue also and well known to be most helpful against headaches and grief.) That old judge's plant, rue, with its sweet spicy blue-green leaves for nosegays and pomanders. Rosemary (again) all blue and gingery, equally welcome at weddings and funerals and here for strewing so that when walked upon there is set free a marvelous perfume. And best of all for strewing and favorite of the Queen (itself called queen of the meadow), that ghost of the midsummer—meadowsweet. Which can always make a weary heart to be merry and glad.

And because it is Christmas we shall scatter among the rushes the three herbs which were strewn in the manger in Bethlehem: wild thyme and groundsel and sweet woodruff which can make the oldest hay smell newly mown.

Now chests and coffers are picked clean of their precious possessions. Closets opened wide for all to see. Best tables and chests, made of polished and inlaid woods, decorated with damask cloths and fine carpets, are placed in Hall and Gallery. There to hold and to show treasures.

Gold and silver plate. Knives with enamelled and inlaid handles. Long, slender-handled silver spoons—those handles long enough to be safely used by a lady who's eating while wearing a great starched ruff. Silver gilt bowls enriched by chased, enamelled ornamentation. Engraved cups of silver and gold. Standing cups and fashionable steeple cups, brightened with jewels. Cups made of such odd things as coconut shells and ostrich eggs which have been silvered over. Tall gilt standing salts for the high tables. Musical clocks and watches. Bronze and silver belt pistols from Germany, engraved and ofttimes with inlays of mother of pearl. Small Italian bronze sculptures showing scenes out of ancient myths. Carved ivory and ebony from Africa. Shining gold containers in the form of a sailing vessel, shaped by goldsmiths. Feathers of rare birds from the Indies and China. And jewels and stones and coins acquired from across the world and from out of all its history. Paintings in miniature and medals and jeweled fans. Silver handbells, dotted and speckled with jewels. Trophies and majolica dishes. Rare instruments of mathematics, of navigation and of astronomy. Manuscripts and printed books, bound in leather or velvet or silk, clasped and hinged with silver and gold.

In Hall the scoured weapons of war will be set on the walls. Together with shields and banners and devices of heraldry. In gallery the portraits are uncovered. Maps and genealogies are on display. And many kinds of musical instruments, with books of music for playing and singing, are everywhere handy. Chairs have been set out, and some of these are the broad and comfortable newfangled chairs, wide enough for a lady wearing a stiff farthingale, and also have soft, stuffed, embroidered cushions for comfort.

Such glowing and glittering!

Such shine and dazzle!

O easy enough to imagine an heavenly host would feel at home here!

Though many of the Court are prodded to go home, to look to their lands and their people, most will find good reasons to remain. Just as in summer most can find pressing reasons not to accompany the Queen on her Progress. (*World is upside down and inside out these days. All things changing for the worse and no help for it.*) And there will be feasting and entertainment during all the time. At Court each dinner and supper will be a feast. Even the ordinary Bouche of Court—the commons of bread and ale, together with candles and fuel, for all who are lodged in the Palace—will now include cakes and wines, too.

Each night from after supper until midnight and after there will be revels. Entertainments and music and dancing. Masques where gentlemen and ladies, common musicians and singers and actors will mingle together, tricked out in costumes. New plays (with sometimes an old favorite by request) performed by the players of the most popular companies. For this season it is already said that upon the feast of St. Stephen the Deacon, the day after Christmas, the celebrated company of the Lord Chamberlain's Men will cross the river to perform for the Queen. Next night after, upon the feast of St. John the Evangelist, it will be the turn of their rivals, the Lord Admiral's Men, to try to equal or even surpass them in surprise and delight. Then next, on the Day of the Circumcision of Our Lord Jesus Christ, will arrive the Children of Paul's. To perform in some special masque—witty and more subtle than any of the children can know. And on occasion of Epiphany, the Earl of Worcester's Men, who have been playing at the *Boar's Head* for more than a year now, will come to Whitehall.

And so the Office of Works is busy with the building of the stages and settings and the seats for spectators.

By now the Queen's cousin, George Carey, second Lord Hunsdon, the Lord Chamberlain, will have examined the texts of the plays that are to be performed. Looking for those things which will please the Queen and lift her spirits. Likewise searching diligently for hidden slanders or satires against Her Majesty, her Court, and her Government. Or any other words or actions which may cause offense.

As the Lord Chamberlain is her close kin and as he and his whole family are beholden to her for all their eminence, he would like for her to be truly diverted. He would be happy to bring the light of pleasure to her eyes again. Content if he could oversee the dispelling of melancholy, the easing of the aches and pains that old flesh is home to. And so to be witness to the sunshine of her countenance, to the irrepressible overflowing of her laughter. Her applause and laughter leading the laughter and applause of the Court. Why, that would be the best service he can imagine rendering this Christmastide.

Easier said than done.

For he will have heard what she has said so recently to Sir John Harrington, her favorite godson whose poetry was once such amusement for her. At Richmond she interrupted his reading of some witty verses:

"When thou dost feel Time creeping at thy gate, Boy Jack," she told him, "then these fooleries will please thee less. I am past my relish for such matters."

Meantime in the suburb of Clerkenwell, within the embattled gate and walls of (*what is left standing of what was fair in its time*) the Hospital of St. John of Jerusalem, the shows for the

Court are in rehearsal. For here is located the Revels Office, under the charge of the Master of Revels—Mr. Edmund Tilney. His tailors and embroiderers and haberdashers are busy with preparations of the costumes which have long since, in good weather, been sunned and aired. His painters and plasterers and property makers are hard at work, day and night, to finish the settings and properties. Proud Mr. Tilney may wring his hands in secret, fearing that nothing will be finished in time. But surrounded by his servants (*when he comes to lodge at Court he even brings his own Doorkeeper like a great Lord*), he will confess nothing except that this season is likely to be more splendid than the last. Which was, as everyone must know, the finest arrangement of Christmas revels in memory. Just so, year by year, the revels are better and better. Ever since Mr. Tilney was chosen for this office.

No disrespect to Mr. Tilney (oh no, sir, by no means), but it is not so. So Thomas Clatterbocke, newly appointed to the new office of Groom of the Revels, will tell you. There are some very old (but very clear, sir, and unfailing) memories, his own for instance, which must honestly report otherwise. True enough, last year's spectacles were memorable, and one may be allowed to hope that this year's will be even more brilliant to behold. And yet . . . consider a moment that Clatterbocke has been working at the Revels Office for longer than our Queen has reigned. Who knows (does he?) when he first began working there. He was already the Foreman of Tailors in '48. And thus will know, from many who witnessed them if not from firsthand, all about the revels held in the days of Great Harry—King Henry VIII. How fortunes were spent by the crown on tournaments and pageants, on fantastic scenery and on elaborate machines and costumes. In those days there was still a Lord of Misrule for the Court. Dancing and disguising and deep drinking lasted until sunrise. When the King and his favorite companions—all who could still sit on horse and keep eyes open—rode forth in wintry pale sunlight for hours of hawking and hunting.

Will the old man express opinion as to what will serve England best in the future—whether he thinks the time has come to be governed again by a King? He did not live so long and hold office by offering indiscreet opinions on matters beyond his concern. But what he will say, comparing these times with the days of Great Harry, is that our age, for all of its pride, is poorly diminished. All things grow old and gray together.

To which, if he heard of this, Mr. Tilney would snort and laugh. In the old days they spent more time and money because they managed both badly. But now, by example of our frugal Queen and out of necessity, we have learned to nurse a little money well. Let old men nod in fireside dreams. No harm in them, but not much truth, either. The truth is England was never before so merry as now.

Here is how it is on these long candlelit evenings of Christmastide.

Ceremony of supper. First—just as at dinner—the Queen's table will be set in public. All with much kneeling and flourishing. Next kettledrums and trumpets. And barehead a line of scarlet guardsmen enters, bearing the various dishes prepared to be served to the Queen. The Guards are assisted by Maids of Honor; for each dish must be tasted and then symbolically served before the Queen's empty chair. For the Queen, always abstemious and not wishing to impose her habits upon others at a feast, will dine most privately in the presence of her Maids and of a trusted few. Who may not share her desire for privacy, but will smile and smile and not show the least sign of discontent.

After all this the formal feasting of the Court begins. With a score of dishes or more, served in two courses, by servants wearing her livery of black and white. And everyone at Court, each at an appointed place at an appointed table, eating and drinking cheerfully while the musicians play from the high minstrels' gallery at the end of the Hall.

After dining we shall gather in the Presence to wait for the arrival of the Queen. Again the fanfare of drums and trumpets and sackbuts. Again her guards, now armed with gilt halberds and partizans. And now the ranking noblemen and men of office, bearing the Sword of State and the various seals upon velvet cushions. Then comes the Queen herself, alone. And all kneel now, bending to their knees as she passes by. She is wearing a red wig and her face painted into an almost youthful beauty, her clothing a wild garden in which jewels and pearls and precious stones are flowers. Six Maids of Honor chastely clad (beyond their reputation) in virginal white. And her ladies, old companions, shining like the Queen, but none so brightly.

To be followed by Nobility and Council, each according to office and degree, and the chief officers of the Household—Lord Steward, Master of Horse, Treasurer, and Comptroller, etc.—bearing the white staffs which signify authority. Then the whole crowd of the Court trooping after. All directed by the Lord Chamberlain and his corps of Ushers.

They enter the Hall (or another chamber large enough to hold them) which is as brilliant as if bathed in the light of a rising harvest moon. Into this light the Queen and her Court, these figures move as if made of the moonlight. As if only just now, moment before last, they had stepped out of a framed painting or from a tapestry, a procession of shades, boneless, bodiless, made wholly out of breath and moonlight, moving slow and solemn toward some marvelous destination. Moving, in fact, to take their proper places. Queen on her throne. Ladies and favorites on cushions close around her. Guards on all sides. Court finding chairs and benches. Music fading and dying. Voices hushing. As a lone player, one, who though nervous enough, can walk more like a born Prince than anyone here except for the Queen, struts out upon the raised stage. Begins to speak the prologue of the play. . . .

Come January 1, Feast of the Circumcision (and, in the olden days in England, Feast of Fools), and it is time for the giving of gifts. No place is the getting and giving more important than at Court. Where the Queen's clerks make a receipt of every gift that is made to the Queen. And likewise prepare a counterlist for the gilt plate which the Queen gives in return. Noting the exact weight of the plate in ounces and its market value, too, to the nearest halfpenny.

Then at last, after dinner on this day, all the presents which have been given to the Queen are set out in exhibition on long trestle tables.

Queen and ladies and Maids will then pass along the tables admiring gifts while a clerk reads aloud from the roll. A reputation can be built upon a smile. Ruined by the clouds of a royal frown. Something or other she takes in her hands, bends and holds closer to the light to examine. Perhaps an exclamation of pleasure. Maybe a request for the clerk to read again the name of the giver. Someone, by name, has been magically singled out. Which brief attention may prove to be of enormous value. Here promise and prospect are all. For the Queen's favor is immeasurable in value and remains so until it is withdrawn or until it is set within fixed limits of fact like a field surveyed and then set and marked by fences and hedgerows. Her exclamation of pleasure. Her request to the clerk to speak up more loudly. (*Nowdays you must raise your voice, but without seeming to, when you speak to the Queen.*) And so someone begins a new year with good fortune.

It is not New Year's gifts which can move her most deeply. In her private chambers, with a cup of watered wine and a sweet cake only to sustain her while elsewhere her Court is gorging at the feast, she will have sent a messenger hurrying to bring rolls of former New Year's gifts. And sometimes she will sit and read silently, bending close to the parchment, peering through spectacles. (*Which glasses she will never wear in public for any reason.*) Sometimes she will have one of the Maids read aloud to her. A young woman reading slowly in a clear young voice while the Queen—her lean, pinched, lined face entirely impassive, but her quick, dark eyes vaguely damp—listens as if she were hearing lute music. Moves only her long-fingered hand (*beauty of her hands so often praised by so many*) to signal the woman to cease or to begin again. Lists neatly divided into a linked chain of ranks and degrees: Earls and Viscounts, Duchesses, Marquesses, and Countesses, Bishops, Lords, Baronesses, Ladies and Knights and Gentlewomen, Chaplains and Gentlemen and so forth. . . .

Not for more than thirty years—so much time? has it really been so swiftly gone?—has there been an English Duke upon the list.

Well, he was the last.

Item: By the Duke of Norfolk. A purse of purple silk and gold filled with sundry coins of gold.

Her Howard cousin. The only Duke in England and the richest man in this kingdom. Lived at his palace of Kenninghall in Norfolk more grandly than any Prince. Earl Marshal of England. Commander of the Queen's forces in Scotland in the War of the Insignia in '60. Thomas Howard, ninth Duke of Norfolk, fifteenth

Earl of Surrey, thirteenth Lord Mowbray, tall, thin, proud, and handsome. Proved also soft and weak. Proved, finally, to be faithless. Once dreamed, indeed aimed to rule this kingdom as husband to the Queen of Scots. Thus, by his own doing and before his thirty-fifth year, felt the cold edge of a heading ax. And all his pride and honor forfeited.

Dead. . . .

Item: By the Earl of Northumberland. A purse of black silk and silver knit. Filled with gold Angels.

On one side of the coin St. George slays the Dragon. On the other are stamped a sailing ship and a cross and the lions and lilies of her arms. Coins of good weight and purity. But Thomas Percy, eleventh Earl of Northumberland, first Lord Percy, had the counterfeit blood of a traitor in his veins. Led the Rising against her in '69. His rebel army marching south beneath a Papist banner (said banner carried by one old Captain Norton of Norham Castle) of the five wounds of Christ. Which rebellion bloomed so dangerously before it came to grief and harvested a huge crop of hangings in the northern counties. And likewise led this Earl to meet his master—the common executioner.

Dead. . . .

And his traitorous brother, Henry Percy, twelfth Earl. Who took his own life (so they say) in the Tower in '85.

Item: By the Earl of Westmoreland. A red-silk purse filled with Sovereigns.

Together with Northumberland, he dared to offer the gift of treason and open rebellion in '69. Charles Neville, sixth Earl of Westmoreland and Lord Neville. Coward also. Fled first to Scotland and then into exile at the age of twenty-six. To live a long life in exile. Waiting. Waiting for what? Waiting too long, it seems. For within this very year the word has come of his end.

Dead. . . .

So year after year the lists of the gifts of purses filled with coins. Nearly always her Bishops and Archbishops had given gold. Also her nobility and great men of state.

Item: By the Lord Keeper of the Great Seal—Sir Nicholas Bacon. A purse of silver knit filled with gold coins in Angels.

Gray's Inn lawyer and Privy Councilor. Silver tongue and wise and honest spirit. Did he not sometimes dare to argue openly against her when he believed she was wrong? And wholly faithful. Wit and spirit and fidelity condemned by fortune to lodge within a prison of fat flesh. At sickly last he was too fat even to mount and ride on a horse. Had to depend upon servants to lift and heave him into and out of his chair. Yet, never mind that, he lodged body and soul very well indeed, and there graciously entertained the Queen and Court, at York House here and at his estate—Gorhambury. Those places still stand proud. But he is long gone, since '79, and often regretted.

Dead. . . .

Item: By Sir Thomas Gresham. A purse of black knit. Filled with gold coins in Angels.

Ah, well. Speaking of regret. Here is one who is very much regretted.

Dead also. . . .

Gone, alas, in the same year as Nicholas Bacon. Has it been so long ago? She can count the years (she thinks) in the lines etched and printed on her face. Alas for him to be gone so long. She could urgently now use his cunning and craft and skill and subterfuge. Gresham the Mercer and Merchant Adventurer and Moneylender. And sometime the Spymaster. Better at that game while he played it, than Burghley or Walsingham. Royal Agent in Antwerp and The Netherlands. Servant and adviser to her here in London. Quick of worldly wit as a Jew. As clever and duplicitous as any suave Venetian. Served first her father, the King, as his own father had done before him. And also served her brother and her sister Mary. But served Elizabeth best. Perhaps because her need was greatest challenged him to most art. And maybe because, unlike all except her grandfather, she has some understanding of the magic of money. Knows how to raise it and how to keep it. How to spread it (*like sweet butter?*) so as to make a little cover much. How to spread it freely (*like steaming fresh manure?*) so as to reap rich harvests. Perhaps because, like himself, she delighted not so much in the possession of money as in the use of it. Even when the Emperor and the Kings of France and Spain could not find a banker in all Europe to lend them more money, Thomas Gresham managed to find the sums she needed. And by his unflagging attention and patient negotiation at bargaining times, he was also able to save her huge sums of interest, too. Yes, many times. And at his instruction she always found ways to pay off interest and to repay the loans in time. Even though this meant, too many times, selling off of crown lands and estates, the gradual disposal of her jewels and treasures. So, as the credit of Kings and their kingdoms declined, that of a frail woman alone with a small island kingdom, ringed by enemies and beset with difficulties, steadily rose.

And now his golden grasshopper marks the turning of the fickle winds atop the roof, and the tall bell column, of his Exchange. That wonder for merchants and shopkeepers of every kind together, set in the center of London. He built it. And she named it Royal, the Royal Exchange, with a proclamation and trumpets and a herald, when she came to see it. While trumpets sounded, Gresham drank to her health with a cup of wine in which a jewel had been ground to powder in her honor, for her sake. . . .

In her most private chambers the Queen will sit, half reclining, on large soft cushions laid on the floor. Coals glowing, winking red and orange in a brazier close beside her. And a fire blazing in the fireplace. Warm here though a chill wind blows a ragged flock of crows across barren sky beyond window glass. While one of the women reads to her from an old roll of New Year's Gifts. Other women are scattered about the chamber, wherever light falls best, working silently at their sewing and embroidery. And one of her musicians, a lutenist, plays softly for them.

Maids struggling to stifle the impulse to yawn. So much to do everywhere else in the palace. Except here. In these privy chambers. Well, they should be thankful to her. Because it is for them that she has come to Whitehall for Christmas this year. She would much prefer to be in Richmond. And not only because it is so much warmer. It is also that her astrologer, old Dr. John Dee, he with his hair and beard as long and white as Father Time's, came over to Richmond from his place at Mortlake to warn her against Whitehall. They must surely have wondered at him—this extraordinary old man who, in his black cap and long black gown, looked like Merlin come to life again. Perhaps they overheard some of the words he spoke to her. He was heard but not listened to. Not believed. For all of their thoughts are set upon their own futures. Not upon hers. Hers which is unbearably imaginable. Their thoughts, those which go beyond the borders of themselves, are devoted to one great uncertainty. Who will wear the crown of England next? And what on earth will become of them? She could give them some certainty if she wished to. The Queen knows what is happening. Knows that all of them are thinking forward to a time without her. And doing more than thinking about it. Are forming new factions and alliances. Trying to make friends of strangers. Plotting, scheming, conniving. Planning how to thrive in the new light of a rising sun. She knows the roads of England are crowded with messengers.

What is the business of England these days? someone will ask.

Why, sir, it is the sending and receiving of letters on the subject of the Succession.

She could give them some certainty about it. If she chose to. But why? Let them learn to live with the uncertain future. Even as she must now—because at last her future is becoming plain enough—summon up a past.

Sad folly of it, her own as much as theirs, would allow her to laugh out loud. If she did not cleave to the wisdom of her own chosen motto: *Video et faceo. I see and say nothing.* . . .

What she prefers to see now is in the past. And this cannot claim the attention of those whose hearts are invested elsewhere. Besides she has said it all now, made her own valedictory in her speech to Parliament that afternoon in November of 1601 when she accepted their thanks and bade them farewell.

"There is no jewel," she told them, "be it of never so rich a price, which I set before this jewel—I mean your love. For I do esteem it more than treasure and riches, for that we know how to prize, but love and thanks, I count invaluable. And though God hath raised me high, yet this I count the glory of my crown—that I have reigned with your loves. . . ."

Much trouble this Parliament caused her. Cost her, too. For she has had to begin to give up ancient prerogative of patents and monopolies. With which she has been able to reward so many of her servants in the past. Well, they will have to do without and so will she. From this time on. Bought goodwill of the Parliament, then, by promises and prospects and with these golden words (which, as promptly as they were published, were named Her *Golden Speech*). At the opening of this Parliament her ushers had difficulty to make way for her. But at this ending, once she had spoken, they waited, one at a time, to step forward and kiss her hand.

Were they ashamed? She thinks not. Even though, having won over their hearts, she did not hesitate to remind them of her generosity.

"Of myself, I must say this. I never was any greedy, scraping grasper. Nor a strait, fast-holding Prince. Nor yet a waster. My heart was never set on any worldly goods, but only for my subjects' good. What you bestow on me, I will not hoard it up, but receive it to bestow on you again. Yea, my own properties I account yours. To be expended for your good. . . ."

It was a shame to her to have to say these things in her own behalf. But if she did not, who else would? No one nowdays. And it was an easy shame to bear. For she has never put pride ahead of policy.

Thinking how these givers of purses and gold coins, faithful and faithless, wise or weak-witted, all of them are dust now. At last having been transformed, by God's alchemy, to the perfect equality of dust. Without rank or distinction, privilege or prerogative. Except that sometime or other a little dust may begin to dance in motes and flecks within a shaft of sunlight pouring through a window or suddenly finding a clear downward path among the murmuring thick leaves of the summer. How dust will begin to dance and then be gone again with the coming or going of a shadow! Dust dancing, like the wine of sunlight. One moment dancing and the next instant gone for good. All the same. Whether it may be dust of some honored lord or lady. Or of some rogue or common whore without a name that anyone will ever remember.

Just so it will be with her own. With the brief dancing dust of all the Kings and Queens. . . .

Many of the names on these rolls are forgotten too. Even by

those who may have loved them. Would be forgotten forever except for these lists that record them. And now the lists, themselves, are dusty.

All that wealth of gold has vanished, too. And yet (she is thinking), even so, even though the coins are spent, that gold is not yet dust. Though the angelic wings of England's avenging saint have grown smooth, though the face of the Queen on those coins may have become worn down slick as a skull, beyond any distinction from anyone else, cursed or blessed with a crown, having been altogether altered by the constant tight pinching of thumbs and fingertips, by the clutching of countless fists, by the passing back and forth from sweaty palm to palm, from concealment in one wallet and purse after the other, and all for gain and loss, still. . . . Still that selfsame gold, however much used, worn smooth as pebbles in a stream, remains *alive* somewhere. Somewhere or other, in a locked chest or a knotted purse that same gold still burns with ever-brimming, overflowing excess of ghostly heat and light. And, for proof of that, see how it will leap and writhe as if in flames when it is exposed stark naked to the light. That gold burns most fiercely in the desires of the living. For it has the power to refine hopes and wishes into nothing but ashes. Truly, more martyrs burn alive, daily in doing and nightly in dreaming, in the cold flames of gold, than the sum total of all who have been burned at the stake in this world's age of the burning of men and women for the sake of true religion.

And so, too, this Queen has been compelled to burn and to freeze with the fever of gold.

Thinking often how those coins, given and dutifully listed so long ago, will last longer by far than the silk of the beautiful purses which once contained them. Thinking that those purses will be—no, have long since become so—worthless scraps and rags. And worms will own the wood and rust will break the locks of every chest which imprisoned it before that same gold has lost the first shine and glow of youth. And so it will continue to endure, calm and cool and fat, beyond the price of the blood and the tears and the sweat which have been offered up as if in unholy sacrifice to its name.

Each and every one of these coins, most common and least valuable among them, will outlast the pith and marrow of her royal bones.

And not to forget that later on the same gold will be transformed to enjoy new life. Some other, another King or Queen, will cause old coins to be melted down and new minted. Marked and stamped with new faces, new flags, new signs and devices. Thus gold, no matter how ancient and weary, can be renewed as nothing human can be. And thus is perennially able in any of its shapes and forms, old or new, to stir men to action, to arouse desire and surely to command more firmly and guilefully than any Prince or Pope or Emperor.

And always to lead to the same sure and certain ending.

Which is to dance briefly in a shaft of sunlight among other flecks and motes of nameless dust.

Now that she has lived long enough to arrive in the cold harbor of old age, this truth causes her no sorrow. Instead there is a kind of inner smiling, to consider that the true spirit, the soul of this world, Caesar's world, may be manifest not in any treasury of golden words and golden deeds (which, though they may be counted and numbered like the hairs of the head and accounted for in the infinite, ineffaceable records of heaven's exchequer, are nevertheless destined to remain mostly unreported, unrecognized, and therefore unremembered here below sun and moon) but instead is to be found in a measurable hoard of golden coins. Which hoard will not, itself, ever vanish, though it be spent and scattered and though all who schemed for and desired and perhaps possessed it, who loved or lost, who hid and husbanded it will (themselves) vanish like white soft crowns of dandelions in the wind.

Since that gold was given to her and then was spent, the selfsame coins passing in and out of her coffers many times in her lifetime; and since that gold will last beyond the time of her life and breath, beyond memory or recollection of her, let it stand as a kind of consolation to her to think how much of her treasure has been spent in these recent years. Oh, often she has been outraged that the expenses of the wars and the steadily rising prices have so swiftly drained away what she has been able to save through years of scrupulous frugality. Yet now . . . now that she knows and feels her age in all her bones, then it is solace in imagining that whoever comes to rule after her will have to ponder these same records (among others) of getting and giving.

That they must all follow after.

How they must seek to follow these same threads in the laby-rinth, maze without any monster in it, but also without any ending.

Sometimes ladies and gentlemen of the Court gave her not purses filled with coins, but clothing, just as much needed, perhaps more valued, and equally precious. Made of finest materials and in many colors. Clothing like sunlit fields and meadows in the month of May.

Often the ladies of the Court—her ladies of the Bedchamber, Ladies of the Privy Chamber, Ladies of the Presence Chamber, and the Maids of Honor, not to mention all the long list of wives (in or out of favor with her no matter) of the Nobility, the courtiers, the officers of Court and government—presented her with gloves, doublets, sleeves and gowns, petticoats and smocks, cushions and fans etc.

Item: A petticoat of cloth of gold. Stained with black and white. With bone lace of gold and with spangles of gold laid to look like waves of the sea.

Item: A waistcoat of taffeta embroidered all over with flowers of Venice gold, silver, and some black silk.

Item: A doublet of satin, all garnished with goldsmith's work. Set with eighteen very fair clasps of gold, enamelled, and every pair of them set with five diamonds and eight rubies, one diamond in each pair being bigger than the rest. With a fair lace damask gold and damask silver.

Item: A fair scarf of green sarcenet embroidered with birds and flowers in gold and silk of sundry colors. Fringed with Venice gold and lined with silk.

Item: Four pairs of gloves, perfumed, and set with twenty-four buttons of gold for each and every one of them with a small diamond.

Item: A girdle of velvet with buckles and studs of gold. This same girdle set within fifteen emeralds and three pearls. All these set in gold.

Item: A cap of black velvet. Garnished with eighteen diamonds and a band about it with fourteen large buttons of gold, each of them garnished with diamonds.

Item: Three score buttons of gold. Set with one fine pearl in each button.

Well then.

All these diamonds and rubies and emeralds and pearls, all these gold buttons and beautiful things, are gone now to pay her debts. Thinking now (she often does) of all that cloth—taffeta, cloth of gold, silk and sarcenet and satin—rotted to pieces. Not enough left to clothe a wooden doll or two with the remnants. Gone. As Holy Scripture warns and promises. World without end. Thus these beautifully made, inordinately expensive articles of apparel, though they were dutifully recorded upon receipt thereof and thereafter constantly cared for, are nevertheless already given over to feed the insatiable hungers of the moths of God.

But beyond all this there are gifts which can still give her a painful pleasure of heart to hear of, to think of, to remember.

Some for the sake of the giver:

Item: One long cushion of tawny cloth of gold, backed with taffeta. From Mrs. Blanche Parry.

Blanche Parry who knew her, cared for her, since the Queen was a child. One, among the very few, who could be trusted for remedies and with secrets. Blind for her last years and now dead.

Ah, Blanche, sometimes I think I would gladly kneel on your cushion and pray until you are restored to life. . . .

Item: One round kirtle of white china damask bound about with lace. From Mistress Mary Radcliffe.

Merry Mistress Radcliffe who gave up the idea of marriage in honor of the Queen's royal virginity. And served her from the earliest years. First as a Maid of Honor, then as a mother over them. Never too old to frisk and hey about the room with the youngest of them. . . .

There are names which are not to be mentioned in her presence if they should happen to appear on any list or document.

Some are her peers and rivals—Kings and Queens, Princes and Popes, living and dead. Some are those who have failed her or have proved faithless. And among these latter are the names of any number (too many) of the former Maids of Honor. Who, for instance, having married without the Queen's permission, or not married though they were swollen ripe with child, have been banished from Court and from memory—Bridget Manners and Frances Vavasour, also Ann Vavasour and Elizabeth Vernon and Elizabeth Throckmorton. Not to ignore the most recent, poor Mary Fitton, whom the Earl of Pembroke flatly refused to marry.

Then there are those who may be mentioned; for, whatever their deeds or schemes, the Queen has chosen to take them in recollection as appropriate for laughter.

Item: A casting bottle of agate, garnished with gold and sparks of rubies, and a woman holding in her hand a scroll on which is written this word—ABUNDANCIA. By Lady Margaret Lennox.

Well, Lady Margaret, you never ceased scheming until the end.

Once, in the reign of Queen Mary, she held precedence over the Princess Elizabeth and enjoyed it too. Mother of Henry Stuart, Lord Darnley, she was grandmother to James, King of the Scots. Likewise of his rival for the crown of England now—the young Arabella Stuart. All her life she plotted to beget a royal dynasty. Now that she is dead, it could happen after all. Which (some suppose) the Queen finds amusing.

Now that she is dead, the Queen forgives her everything.

Not so her own dead cousins Mary Grey and Katherine Grey (sisters to Lady Jane Grey). Whom the Queen found ridiculous in life and finds hateful in death.

And there are others. Those who, one time or another, were favored and trusted, but who in the end proved themselves without loyalty. Pity the young woman who, yawning and thoughtless or thinking of other things should read this from the list:

Item: A very fair jewel of gold, like a rainbow. Having therein two pillars, the one broken and garnished on one side with diamonds and opals. Under them three table diamonds and one ruby and four pendants of sparks of diamonds and a pearl pendant.

    Given by the Earl of Essex.

And likewise there are names almost certain to bring tears from the Queen if they are mentioned. But, it is understood, these are not to be avoided. Chiefly these are her closest, dearest friends among women. Not only Blanche Parry, but Lady Catherine Ashley, who was her governess and a companion since childhood; Lady Mary Sidney (mother to Sir Philip Sidney) who nursed her through the smallpox only to catch the disease herself and to be terribly disfigured by it.

"She took away my scars and wore them for me for the rest of her life," the Queen has said. "And that was more precious than all my jewels."

There are names from the living, from those still close to her.

Item: Two knots of gold garnished with sparks and pearls pendant. Given by the Marchioness of Northampton.

This is Helena Snakenborg. Who came to England in '65 as one of the Maids of Honor of Cecilia, Princess of Sweden. And has remained to serve the Queen as Maid of Honor and Lady in Waiting. The Queen has seen to it that Helena has enjoyed two husbands: first, old William Parr, Marquis of Northampton, who died quickly and left her a wealthy widow; the other, young Thomas Gorges, groom of the Privy Chamber and a secret confidential messenger for the Queen. The Marchioness of Northampton who is held up as example for the Maids of Honor. Where patience, obedience, good service, and cleanliness (for Helena, like most Swedes is addicted to frequent bathing) can lead. The Queen has promised that Helena shall be Principal Mourner at her funeral. Which means that Lords and Countesses will assist her and carry her train. . . .

So it is that the Queen can be moved to delight or anger or sorrow by names being read to her by young women to whom none of these names is likely to mean anything.

If any of these names should waken a memory, like the winter moon seen through small leaded panes, it will be a vaguely irritated recollection of some face from among the portraits hanging on a gallery wall. Calling up (to a young mind) a weather too wet or cold for walking or riding outside. An inner weather of te- dium. Names which, then, cannot mean more than letters of the alphabet which spell them. No matter. These fading letters on old parchment finally spell out only one true word. And that word is *dust*. . . .

If they can still ring and shine for the Queen, she knows that these names, together with deeds they stand for, are not imper- ishable. Indeed they will perish long before either documents or portraits. Like a waning moon, each name will vanish, diminish- ing to the thinnest edge and shadow of itself as her own memory ceases. And even now she needs promptings for memory. She must listen to names and lists of gifts being read aloud to her, so that she may recollect these ghosts from out of the cloud of spirits, truly remembered and purely imagined, who haunt her waking hours. Who once had dared no more than to intrude upon her dreams. When she is taken into the last cold silence, when silence and cold assume command, who else will recall their deeds and misdeeds, vices and virtues, songs and sorrows?

Item: A very fair jewel of gold. Being a bird. In the breast thereof is a fair diamond and a large ruby. Above it are three em- eralds and all the rest of the jewel wings is garnished with dia- monds and rubies.

These things she specially delights in—altogether frivolous and fantastic gifts. Coming from her most favored servants. Who chose to be extravagantly frivolous in outward expression of an inner fidelity.

Given by Sir Christopher Hatton.

Someone who loved her.

Tall, handsome, always handsomely, fashionably dressed. A most graceful dancer, he caught her eyes at a Christmas masque at the Inner Temple. Came to favor first, then more and more into trust. As Gentleman Pensioner, Captain of the Guard, Knight, Vice Chamberlain and sworn to the Privy Council, Knight of the Garter, Chancellor of Oxford, High Steward of Cambridge, and, for the last few years of his life, the Lord Chan- cellor of England. He was given a nickname by her—"Sheep."

Sometimes, more comically, her "Mutton" and "Bellwether." Other times, because she called Leicester "Eyes," she allowed him to be "Lids." He acquired and renovated the Bishop of Ely's Palace at Holborn. Built, chiefly to entertain her and the Court, the prodigy house of Holdenby in Northamptonshire. Chivalric and pleasing to a fault, he never married. And every year presented to her a gift so original as to tax the skill of the clerks who tried to describe it.

Dead. . . .

Died owing half of England huge sums. Owing the Queen enough to manage the whole business of this kingdom for at least half a year.

Well, even if she had, in the end and in fact, paid the price of the gifts he made to her, it may have been worthwhile, if only for her pleasure in the style of his imagination.

His mind and spirit danced, too, ever agile and handsome.

Item: A purse of gold, enamelled, garnished with diamonds, rubies, and opals of sundry bigness, and with a blue sapphire in the top. With two strings having pendants of pearls of sundry bigness hanging at a small chain of gold. And also one Croulet of gold, containing six pieces. Four of them pieces like crosses. Two like half crosses. All fully furnished with diamonds, rubies and pearls of sundry bigness on one side. With a row of pearls and rubies on each side of said bracelet.

Someone whom she had loved.

Given by the Earl of Leicester.

What to think or say of him? Whom she might have married as a woman, but never could as Queen. Say what is known. That to this day, years after, she keeps his portrait in miniature, locked in a chest, together with certain letters which are wrapped and tied with a ribbon. Say also that more than one time she risked much, perhaps too much, for sake of his love and friendship.

Handsome when he was young, unquestionable courageous, and often foolish (though more like a king than a clown in his folly), he was at once fascinating and frightening to her. Never allowed himself to be second to any other in the lavish and fanciful abundance of the gestures he made for her, the gifts he gave to her. And, like Hatton, he left behind an army of outraged creditors. Not least of whom was the Queen.

Dead. . . .

Item: One plate of gold, graven on one side with a ship. With a string and tassels of Venice gold, silver, and silk.

Someone who served her best.

Given by William Cecil, first Baron Burghley.

In so many ways closer and nearer (and dearer) to her than any favorite or even lover could ever be. A name more likely to bring tears than any of the others.

Dead. . . .

Item: A pair of bracelets of gold, containing twenty-two pieces; in 10 of them are agate heads, and twelve of them garnet, and two small pearls in each piece . . .

His wife, Burghley's. Not by any means envied on that account. Or for any reasons, really, but two. Her compassionate charity for the poor. Which will be awhile remembered. But more than that she is among the very few whom the Queen could envy for intellect and education.

Dead. . . .

Item: A collar of gold. Being two serpents, their heads being of opal and sparked with diamonds. In the top thereof a strawberry represented by a large ruby.

Two serpents from her own best one.

Given by Sir Francis Walsingham.

Diplomat, Principal Secretary, and, in the end, the greatest spymaster of this age in any country of the world. Whose knowledge proved to be of more value than armies and armadas.

Shy, stern, guarded. She called him her "Moor" on account of his complexion. He was said to be able to see in the dark like a cat.

May it be true. For it is in darkness that he must do all of his spying now.

He, too, like most of her strutting courtiers, swaggering soldiers, proud judges and Councilors, left more debts than anything else as an inheritance.

Dead. . . .

Not only the names of the rich and powerful are to be found here. There are many others recorded from among those who, for one reason and another, have enjoyed a moment in the light of favor and good fortune.

Item: One salt of gold. Being like a globe standing upon two naked men. Being the history of Jupiter and Pallas. With a naked woman holding a trumpet in her hands. The foot being all enamelled with flowers.

Given by Sir Francis Drake.

Dead. . . .

Item: A jewel of gold. Being a whip garnished with small diamonds in four rows. The words of the whip being of seed pearls.

Given by Mr. Philip Sidney.

Dead. . . .

Most of the famous names of these times are to be found somewhere among the rolls. Though there have also always been some who gave to her privately. Even secretly. Trusting themselves wholly to the mercy of her memory.

If the great and the powerful are gone from light, and if their gifts are gone, then this also is the case for the less expensive (and usually more useful) gifts from lesser servants of the Court.

Item: Two pots of orange flowers and candy ginger. By Mr. Doctor Hewicke.

Item: A pair of knives with a sheath covered with purple velvet. By Richard Matthews.

Item: Eighteen larks in a cage. By Morris Watkins.

Item: A picture of Judith and Holofernes. By Putrino (an Italian).

Item: A sugar loaf, a box of ginger, a box of nutmegs, and a pound of cinnamon. By Lawrence Shref, Grocer.

Item: Two greyhounds, a fallow and a black pied. By Sir

James Strumpe. Delivered over to John Coxe, Yeoman of the Leash.

And also:

By Dudley, Sergeant of the Pastry. A great pie of quinces.
By George Webster, Master Cook. A Marchpane. Being made like a chessboard.
By Thomas Ducke, Servant of the Cellar. Two bottles of Hypocras.
By Twyst, the Laundress. Three fine handkerchiefs.
By Smith, the Dustman. Two bolts of good cloth.
By Mrs. Thomason, the Queen's Dwarf. One handkerchief of Cambrick wrought with black silk.
By Ambrose Lupo, Musician. A box of lute strings.

Sweets and spices have been consumed and the wine drunk; music played and lute strings broken; the hunting has ended, and that pair of hounds is only bones.

Laundress and Cook, Doctor and Dustman and Dwarf, Grocer and Court Musician, are dead and gone. Each replaced by some other. Who in turn will make offering on New Year's Day.

Item: One comfit box of silver. Fashioned like a tortoise. With little folding spoon therein.
No report who gave it.
Well then. Most likely dead also. With or without credit.

Item: A flower of gold garnished with diamonds, rubies, opals, and an agate. With a pearl pendant and sundry devices painted on it.
Given by the Eight Maskers of Christmas Week.
Who were you?
Where did you come from? Where did you go?
You spoke your verses and sang your songs and danced your dances.
Is there anyone who can remember a line of verse, one tune, one turn of your dance?
Does anyone alive remember the name of one of you?

At which point in her remembering the Queen will motion for the young woman to cease reading. She will rise up from her cushions and demand some service or other. More music or more silence. More light or shade. More flame or put out the fire.

These days the Queen sleeps little. And when she does, she does not sleep well. The Ladies and Maids must be prepared for late nights. To read to her. To sing and to play on the virginal or the lute. To dance and be lively at it, too. To play at dice with dice of gold or silver or ivory. To play into the early morning with cards—Primero (her favorite), Sleek and Noddy and Post and Pair. Wagering and losing on each hand.

All to keep her from sleeping and dreaming. For when she dreams, she cries out and then they must wake her and seek to lullaby her to sleep again.

They have heard what she has told Dr. Dee—that she often dreams of figures in flame. And especially of one figure, thin and wasted, who seems to be turning into a flame.

Herself . . . !

These women cannot imagine themselves as old and therefore cannot believe that the Queen could ever have been young. Tales of royal suitors from many lands are fairy tales for little children.

Item: A jewel. Being a ship of gold. Garnished with six fair diamonds and rubies. With the sails spread abroad and a word enamelled on them.

Given by Monsieur.

Monsieur being none other than François, Duke of Alencon. Son of Catherine de Medici, younger brother to the Valois Kings of France. And the Queen of England's "Frog."

Came to England more than once, apparently seeking to woo and win her. Spent in England the Christmastide of '81. Before, swearing he would soon return, within six weeks, he left her for good that February. Left her to seek, with her money and support, military glory for himself in the Lowlands.

Could the Queen ever have believed in any of this?

She was nearly fifty then, a full twenty years older than the

Frog. And he . . . he was short and awkward and well marked by smallpox.

The Maids have seen portraits of the Frog and snickered among themselves. Have giggled and been corrected for it by the Ladies. Corrected by homely (and tedious) truth. That the Duke was royal and bright and witty as can be. And thus a delight to the Queen. That there is more to a man than handsome face and stature. That though ours was spared that, Queens must wed for policy. No other reason. That it served the policy of France for a time for Alençon to court the Queen of England. That it served the policy of England for our Queen to permit herself to be courted. That the Queen wept copiously in public, in the presence of foreign ambassadors and of her Court, when the Frog bade her farewell. That a few minutes later she retired with her women to her chambers. Where she danced for joy.

They listen to the Ladies and nod. In one pretty ear and out the other.

Someone wise in the ways of the world, someone who knows the history of the times, perhaps someone like Sir Robert Cecil (who enjoys the company of young women, younger the better) could patiently instruct them how the foolish courtship conducted between the old Queen and the Frog may very well have held off the fury of Spain, and the war that was coming, for some years. How if that is so, then that courtship was of inestimable value to all of us.

They can care little or nothing for the lost names and old portraits of her forgotten suitors.

None of the Englishmen. Not (most scandalous) Thomas Seymour, Lord Sudeley and Lord High Admiral of England. Who, well before she came to the throne, was adjudged of high treason and beheaded. And of whom, in her ruthless youth, she said: "This day died a man of much wit and very little judgment." And said nothing more about him ever again.

There was Edward Courtenay, Earl of Devon, last sprig of the White Rose of York. Whose part in Wyatt's Rebellion came close to causing Elizabeth to lose her head. He died in exile in Italy. Murdered, some say. . . .

Leicester can be believed in. His passions and deceptions, nordinate ambition and fortune of sad follies make him, for the young, for these young women, more real than any Prince in a fairy tale. Oh yes, the Maids can sigh over Leicester.

But not for poor Henry Fitzalan, Earl of Arundel. Who was, early in her reign, proposed a most appropriate noble husband for her. His scraggly beard, his fat nose, his ears like twin sails full of wind. They can chuckle at his brief pretensions, if, indeed, he ever truly entertained any hope. Yet must do so with a cold sense of awareness that for themselves, and in the absence of fairy-tale knights and princes, their best hopes may lie in the arms and lusts of just some such rich, gray nobleman. Who will, if there is any justice, repay them for the gift of their youth and beauty by not living to enjoy it for too long.

None of these Englishmen for the Queen. Nor any of the strangers who, out of policy and necessity and sometimes simple greed, sought to gain this kingdom by marrying her. Not Philip of Spain nor the other Valois brothers of France. Nor the Archdukes of Austria. Nor Eric of Sweden or the Earl of Arran from Scotland.

She wore a ring, a wedding band, as the wife to this kingdom. Until this very year. When it became necessary to remove that ring by filing it off her finger. There is a white scar where the ring was set for so long. She will touch the scar. And then she may begin to weep. Or curse like a drunken tinker. Heap coals of scorn and sarcasm on those whose misfortune it is to be close to her.

She will slap a face. She will box the ears of anyone who is near enough.

These Maids, her young women of gentle birth and of so much hope and ambition, will endure this without flinching. Secure in their certainty that no one, suitor or favorite, Englishman or stranger, could ever have truly loved or desired this wrinkled, stiff-jointed, shrill and rough-tongued, terrible-tempered old woman.

They can afford to humor her. If they are called witches ("who can do hurt but no good for anyone") by the skeptical, the thwarted, the everlastingly unlucky, the Maids of Honor are not much troubled.

Their comfort against her worst excesses of bad temper, and

against all other humiliations and indignities, is that soon enough they will have the duty of walking in her funeral procession. Soon enough, like the things which she once owned, she, too, will be only a dream. Another dancer in the darkness, her share of borrowed brightness being (even as she has surmised) no more than a glitter of dust in a shaft of light.

And *her* comfort—for while she lives, she is not comfortless—is that they are too young and ignorant, too foolish and foolishly hopeful to comprehend how soon, how swiftly and shortly, as the music of time is played, they must follow after her.

That truth gives her comfort. Allows her to enjoy the pleasing spectacle of their natural, youthful beauty and animal pride.

Her anger, if fiery, is brief.

See, few moments later, the Queen will be all sunshine and smiles again.

Beyond these chambers where it might be called continual April if it were not for the misted windowpanes and the rain-swept, fog-haunted precincts of courtyard and garden. . . . Beyond these chambers where the Queen can snuff out some of the unceasing troubles of the present, even as she orders the doors to be shut to the Privy Chamber and closely guarded by her Yeoman Ushers following the ceremony of All Night. . . . Privy Chamber where the Captain of the Guard and a few trusted gentlemen will pass the night playing cards. . . . As, beyond them, Esquires of the Body will be sleeping in the Presence Chamber. . . .

Beyond these chambers from which, if only briefly, the Queen is able to banish the clamor of the present and to deny admittance to the future. So that she may then feel free to shuffle and deal the greater and lesser cards of memory. Arranging and rearranging them in different patterns. . . .

(*Is that how God creates the future? In the same way that we, who can create nothing out of nothing on our own, constantly seek to recover, repair, and redesign our past?*)

Beyond these chambers, this bedchamber where one old woman, Queen of England, deeply fears dying, yet inwardly smiles at the thought that all these, her servants, must be fearful of her death, too. Even though they may wish for it. That all in this Court are now hostages of the future. They have only a little faith, but many are filled with hopes. They are facing, if not yet kneeling to, the rising sun.

And yet all their hopes and schemes (like all of her memories and faith), in these damp, cold, December times, are not of more substance than the woodsmoke rising out of the tall chimneys of Whitehall. Their thoughtful words and unspoken thoughts, all their dear or dread concerns may be taken to be smoke rising up to float over the river and above the glistening roofs of Westminster.

Rising to follow the wind and to blend with the smoke of winter fires burning to warm the city of London.

Where there must be much thinking on the future, also.

Although at this season the signs hanging from inns and taverns and innumerable alehouses are wreathed with Christmas greenery; and though within these warm, noisy, crowded places, good beer and ale and all the best wines are pouring (and O for a cup of claret with a roasted apple in it!); though beggars will have their fill each day at the gates of great houses and even the baskets of prisoners are full of good things to eat and drink; though by daylight there are plays at the theaters and crowds, too, at the Bear Garden, if blood is your pleasure; though by night the streets are lit with lanterns and torches, and there are waits and minstrels to make music and young men ringing church bells until it seems that the spires and steeples will tumble down in a heap like the walls of Jericho; yet, even so, the great men of this City are as rapt in their dreams of the future as any gentlemen of the Court. They, too, are thinking of what the rule of a new sovereign may bring for them. As to the Succession they are chiefly concerned that it shall not be challenged, that it shall be smooth and peaceful. Wars and rebellions may bring glory to the gentry . . . at least to those on the winning side . . . may even, for a time, bring profit to the City. For the nobles will need ready money if they plan to pay the price of marching soldiers back and forth across England. And the readiest money is to be found in London, to be borrowed at high interest. Yet in their larger, longer view, these London merchants have concluded that peace is best for all their affairs. So they hope for a peaceful Succession. And also hope, next after that, for peace with England's enemies. As soon as can be. And as cheaply as possible.

War or peace, good times and bad, whoever hopes to rule England must come to them and strike a bargain. These merchants know enough of the shadowy chronicle of England's history to perceive that if there are truly any barons of this new age, it is they, themselves, who are so. For the nobility, lost in the pride of history, looking backward to prove themselves, cannot yet see how the world is changing all around them. Any new ruler must now make a new kind of Magna Carta (though unspoken and unwritten) with the merchants before he can safely rule. And thus they can afford to act humbly with and be generous to their betters.

Which is to say that this Christmas, while Queen and Court entertain themselves; while the largest part of London, including their own apprentices, servants, wives, and children, is lost in happy diversions; these men are weighing other matters. Prices of wool and grain and the market for both. Cost of timber and furs from the Baltic, spices from the Levant, wines from Greece and France and the islands. Risk of a ship to carry a cargo of black slaves to New Spain. Or to bring home silk from the farthest East Indies. Ventures for digging sea coal in Durham, tin in Cornwall, iron in Wales. Hopes for buying more land in the years ahead.

Change is the music these merchants sing and dance to. Change is the fire where they warm hands and hearts. Their fathers feared change—and thus now seem foolish and diminished in the eyes of the living. The living who believe that a man need only be prudent to be safely a pilgrim into the unknown. Believing that there are no more dragons on the roads of England. Now St. George and his Dragon are figures on certain coins and nowhere else. Figures for a Christmas play to be performed for little children. The sort of a tale which cannot attract a crowd in London these days. Not even at Christmastime. . . .

And there is more by far to this season than the Court or the City may remember. Beyond London's spires and towers and gates and walls, beyond the river and the fields and suburbs all around, beyond the long memories of the Queen (and all the ghosts she recollects); beyond the divers hopes and fears of her Courtiers and Councilors, of judges and lawyers and merchants, of her Archbishop and Lord Admiral and all the rest; the hopes and fears of London's beggars and vagabonds and sturdy rogues; beyond plotting Puritans and scheming Jesuits; beyond all of this fretting and fuming, hemming and hawing, Christmas is being kept in England as it has always been. According to the old traditions and customs, which, since they solve no riddles from the past nor answer any questions put to the future, must be wholly of the here and now. Each time recovered and renewed. Each time—you only have to look into the faces and eyes of the children to see it—partaking of the spirit of the first time. When, shepherds or wise men, cruel King Herod and the callous innkeeper, we were all witnesses and actors together.

Here and now in this holy, happy time there will be no more fear of war or the Plague, droughts or floods or famine. Trouble, pain, sorrow and suffering will surely arrive. If not sooner, then later. According to Scripture. Which is the one true story of this fallen world. But, if you please, there is no time to be wasted on fear now.

No, it is time to celebrate the birth of Our Lord and Savior. Next day to pray and to feast in honor of the martyrdom of St. Stephen. And next after that to rejoice on the day of St. John the Evangelist. Then many will pause to fast and pray upon the following day. Which is Childermas when we are to think upon the bloody slaughter of the Holy Innocents by King Herod. And some of us, and more than the Papists too, for there are many who simply refuse to relinquish old ways for sake of the new, some will not fail upon the twenty-ninth day of December still to recall (if only in a private, silent prayer) our English saint, Blessed Thomas à Becket of Canterbury. For whose death an English King once bared his body and knelt to be whipped in penance. And for the sake of whose blessing so many generations of pilgrims took the Pilgrims' Way to go and pray at the shrine. To partake of the miraculous waters of St. Thomas and to be healed of afflictions of body and soul. That shrine is closed tight since King Henry VIII ordered an end to such superstitions. Yet it is not an easy thing for Englishmen, no matter what they may profess nor whatever may be their religious persuasion, to forget their own communion of English saints and martyrs.

Come January and still the feasts and holy days continue. Circumcision the first day and the feast of the Holy Name of Jesus on the second. Epiphany on the sixth. Which will be the end of holiday and idleness in the country. For on that day the plows will be blessed so that come Monday morning, Plow Monday, there can be a race at plowing beginning at sunrise.

And then there will be no more holidays until Candlemas comes around.

Well, after two weeks of eating and drinking and living like a Lord, a man had better come to his senses and to see to his tools and his stock and his work again. Had better sweat if he plans to endure the rigors of Lent and be ready for feasting again at Easter.

So much has been done in winter season, from Michaelmas to Christmastime, with threshing of harvest and cleaning of chimneys, with the slaughter and butchering, salting and smoking of all but a few of the best of the beasts. And with haste to sow the first wheat and rye. Now between Plow Monday and Easter they must sow beans and barley, oats and peas. Must dung the fields when the weather's good. Must look to the labor of ditching and woodcutting. Must eat lightly of the leanest diet of the year. Waiting for spring. Living on the memory of the good belly cheer of Christmastime.

For feasting is the best of it, after all. For one and all, man and wife and child. Most of whom, for most of the rest of the year, have to be content with roast meat on two days a week and otherwise fish or the white meat of peas and bacon.

But few, if any, go empty at Christmas when all of the houses, from Lord's to lowly Ratcatcher's, are open for hospitality, and all of the tables are burdened with the best that they have to offer.

And when the tables have finally been cleared of the feast, you watch the children playing their games and perhaps you join in late singing and dancing. Until you feel cheerfully inclined to be (briefly) alone, to go outside and to breathe fresh air. So out you go, then, likely stumbling a little, moving away from the blaze of lights and the sounds of music until the only sound remaining is of your own irrepressible laughter. And that, too, fades into blessed silence. . . .

Now still reeling a little and staring up into a sky lit with cold starlight. Fearful of nothing, not past or the future. Except for the certain knowledge that your head will be heavy and aching by daylight. And your laughter will have turned into such groaning as will arouse the laughter of others. But for now you are full of food and drink and gratitude.

You believe you are full of love and charity also. And you can wish all the world, your friends and your enemies, nothing but well. Nothing but good fortune. Wishing the dead, from Adam and Eve until now, their rest in peace. And wishing the living, one and all, from the beggar in his hedge to the Queen in her soft bed. . . .

And what is it she can be dreaming of now, as he, half dreaming, imagines her, that lady minted on his hard-earned coins, lady of ballads and of prayers in the parish church? Is there a place in her dream for this happy drunken plowman, mud of good English earth thick on his boots, out under the stars, who is wishing for her and the rest of the world, for the sake of our own sweet Jesus, a good night?